A PARANORMAL ANTHOLOGY

Copyright © 2023 by JL Casten, EP Bali, Nikita Rogers, Dartanyan Johnson, Isabelle Olmo, Sj Stewart, and Britton Brinkley

Published by EldriaPress

All rights reserved. No part of this publication may be reproduced, stored or transmitted in any form by any means, electronic, mechanical, photocopying, recording, scanning, or otherwise without written permission from the publisher. It is illegal to copy this book, post it to a website, or distribute it by any other means without permission.

This novel is entirely a work of fiction. The names, characters, and incidents portrayed in it are the work of the author's imagination. Any resemblance to actual persons, living or dead, events or localities is entirely coincidental.

Authors assert the moral right to be identified as the author of this work.

Cover design by Shay Stewart.

First edition

Contents

Dedication	IX
1. Chapter 1	1
The Impastusae Witch	2
2. About the Book	3
3. Savisberry Pie	4
4. Story's Ingredients	5
5. Chapter 5	6
6. Jhaeros	7
7. Obscura	14
8. Jhaeros	19
9. Obscura	23
10. Jhaeros	28
11. Obscura	32
12. Jhaeros	37
13. Jhaeros	44
14. Obscura	47
15. Jhaeros	52
16. Jhaeros	58
17. Obscura	64
18. Jhaeros	68
19. About SJ Stewart	73
A Song of Steel and Shadow	75

20.	About the Book	77
21.	Advisory	78
22.	Chapter 22	79
23.	Aurelia	80
24.	Aurelia	83
25.	Aurelia	88
26.	Aurelia	94
27.	Aurelia	98
28.	Aurelia	102
29.	Savage	106
30.	Aurelia	108
31.	Aurelia	112
32.	Aurelia	116
33.	Aurelia	120
34.	Savage	125
35.	Aurelia	127
36.	Aurelia	130
37.	Aurelia	135
38.	Aurelia	141
39.	Aurelia	142
40.	Aurelia	145
41.	Aurelia	149
42.	Xander	152
43.	Aurelia	155
44.	Aurelia	159
45.	Aurelia	163
46.	About EP Bali	166
47.	Chapter 47	167

	The Devil You Seek	169
48.	About the Book	170
49.	Chapter 49	171
50.	Chapter One	172
51.	Chapter Two	179
52.	Chapter Three	185
53.	Chapter Four	189
54.	Chapter Five	193
55.	Chapter Six	201
56.	Chapter Seven	206
57.	Chapter Eight	210
58.	Chapter Nine	214
59.	Chapter Ten	218
60.	Chapter Eleven	223
61.	Chapter Twelve	227
62.	Chapter Thirteen	234
63.	Chapter Fourteen	240
64.	Chapter Fifteen	244
65.	Chapter Sixteen	250
66.	About Isabelle Olmo	259
67.	Chapter 67	260
	Feathers Of Truth	261
68.	About the Book	262
69.	Advisory	263
70.	Chapter 70	264
71.	Chapter One	265
72.	Chapter Two	269
73.	Chapter Three	272

74.	Chapter Four	276
75.	Chapter Five	280
76.	Chapter Six	283
77.	Chapter Seven	287
78.	Chapter Eight	290
79.	Chapter Nine	294
80.	Chapter Ten	297
81.	Chapter Eleven	302
82.	Chapter Twelve	306
83.	Chapter Thirteen	310
84.	Chapter Fourteen	314
85.	Chapter Fifteen	318
86.	Chapter Sixteen	321
87.	Chapter Seventeen	325
88.	Chapter Eighteen	329
89.	Chapter Nineteen	333
90.	Chapter Twenty	336
91.	Chapter Twenty-One	339
92.	Chapter Twenty-Two	343
93.	Chapter Twenty-Three	347
94.	Chapter Twenty-Four	351
95.	Chapter Twenty-Five	355
96.	Chapter Twenty-Six	361
97.	Chapter Twenty-Seven	366
98.	Adrian	371
	About Britton Brinkley	376
99.	Chapter 99	377
	Grown From Tainted Seeds	379

100.	About the Book	380
101.	Advisory	381
102.	Chapter 102	382
103.	Chapter 1	383
104.	Chapter 2	390
105.	Chapter 3	402
106.	Chapter 4	407
107.	Chapter 5	412
108.	Chapter 6	418
109.	Chapter 7	422
110.	Note from the Author	427
111.	Also By Dartanyan Johnson	428
112.	About Dartanyan Johnson	430
113.	Chapter 113	431

Beautiful Untamed Things		433
114.	Advisory	434
115.	About the Book	435
116.	Chapter 116	436
117.	Gubbins	437
118.	Untamed, stupid magic	452
119.	Rise and Shine, Motherfuckers	458
120.	Beautiful, Untamed Thing	466
121.	Melting Memories	474
122.	Bleed	486
123.	This Won't Be Pretty	494
124.	We Will Not Be Silenced. Not Anymore	508
125.	About Nikita Rogers	514
126.	Chapter 126	515

	SpellBound	517
127.	About the Book	518
128.	Advisory	519
129.	Chapter 129	520
130.	Starfall	521
131.	Flee	524
132.	Night Ride	527
133.	Distractions	530
134.	Shaky Ground	535
135.	Plots and Plans	540
136.	Homage	545
137.	Fever Dreams	548
138.	Musings	550
139.	Waylaid	552
140.	Unending Night	557
141.	Found	561
142.	Misdirection	565
143.	Aftermath	570
144.	Misinformed	574
145.	Tales and Wonders	577
146.	Denial	581
147.	Mistbriar	585
148.	Bitter Truths	588
149.	Destiny	593
150.	Meant	596
151.	About JL Casten	599
	Acknowledgments	600

For those who made their own families, who found their people, and for those still searching.
The Blood of the Covenant is Thicker than the Water of the Womb

The Impastulsae Witch

SJ STEWART

About the Book

Deep in the centre of the woods is a cabin where all beings befall a feast. Many eat and leave, but a trial must be survived by all who eat the pie. Jhaeros was thrown into the dungeon with a belly full of pie. The magic of the impastusae witch assaulted him as he realized he was a prisoner. If he wants answers, he is going to have to do something he'd never been good at. Jhaeros was going to have to play nice.

Obscura had survived more of the witch's trials than she cared to keep count of, with each being plucked up for the cauldron, another was thrown down to join them. Jhaeros was no different than any other being, though his arrogance caused anger to burn in her belly. He wanted to escape, and he didn't care just who he had to step over to do it.

With their numbers dwindling, beings usually at odds need to work together to avoid the cauldron of the wicked witch.

Savisberry Pie

SAVISBERRY PIE

1 1/2 TBSP of temptation
1 TBSP of glutton
2 1/2 cups of wholewheat flower
1 TSP salt from the sea of sorrow
1 cup of butter from a bleeding maiden's hands
4 TBSP ice water
6 cups of savisberries
3 tears of joy
2 pinches of daydreams
2 pinches of foolhardy
1 TBSP of the sandman's sand

- Preheat oven to 500 degrees.
- Line a 9-inch pan with prepared pie crust (flour, butter, salt, and ice water, see recipe for pie crust)
- Combine temptation, glutton, tears of joy, foolhardy and sandman's sand in a bowl. Add more daydreams if berries are tart.
- Layer savisberries in prepared pie dish, sprinkling each layer with mixture. Dot top layer with small pieces of butter. Cover with top crust.
- Bake pie on the lowest rack of the preheated over for 10 minutes.
- Reduce oven temperature to 450 degrees and continue baking until golden brown and filling bubbles (30-35 minutes more).
- Serve to the confused and lost.

Story's Ingredients

This story is a dark reimagining. It contains scenes of violence that may include blood and gore. It has scenes of torture and cannibalism and kidnapping.

Though it's not my intention to willfully admit a trigger, it is possible I may have overlooked something that may trigger some readers. Please be advised.

Jhaeros

Each sharp and jagged step cut into him as he somersaulted down through the trapdoor. Pain was an explosion through every inch of him, fireworks that lit him up from the inside. Stones hit him harder than blasts of magic as he was pummelled. His hands lifted in a poor attempt to shield his head, but he felt a sharp stone slice against his brow. His world rocked. Stars danced over his eyes and he lost his breath.

He landed in a breathless heap, a wheeze forced from his lungs as the door creaked closed and slammed shut. The cold stones at his back provided him a semblance of relief as they tried to bite past his skin to where the aches hid. He lifted his hand with great effort and pressed it to his already swollen brow before he bent his knee and rested his foot on the stone floor by his ass.

Fucking pie!

That witch was going to know the heavy hand of his wrath once his wounds were healed and he collected himself. He would make sure of it. Vapid, feral beast of a woman! Jhaeros reached for his magic. Called to it to soothe all the pain and fix the damage. Nothing happened.

What the fuck?

He tried again.

Nothing.

Blasted witch!

All this because of a slice of pie. How embarrassing!

He'd fought in wars. Shed blood battling the mightiest of warriors. If this was his end, and it had been brought on by a slice of savisberry pie, he would never live it down. His soul would never find rest. He would be forever haunted by the dishonour.

It had been simple magic cleverly placed. A tired he couldn't think through swallowed up all his logic and made the woods — treacherous and weaving — feel *right*. His feet moved of their own accord, bringing him further and further into her illusion, his magic separate from a mind too tired to remember it was there. Those feet brought him to the feast, to the caring woman with the soft face and fiery red hair and her offering of pie.

Fucking pie!

A groan left him as his eyes fell closed and he tried to think through his predicament. Strategize.

He could get out of this. This was just another puzzle to solve. Another war to win. He was nothing if not formidable. All he had to do was find her weakness, burrow into it and stretch it until she cracked. And he would. He would break her. Of that, he was sure.

"You ate the pie, didn't you?"

Despite the way his body screamed in protest, he was on his feet and across the room in a blur. The blade he kept in his boot pressed against the throat of a woman slumped against a wall. Dirt and grime covered her face, but the corner of her plump pale blue lips curved up in a grin as she regarded him with eyes as dark as his thoughts. Intricate thin braids were piled haphazardly on her head, while some trailed down the side of her face and down her back.

He felt a prick against his belly and looked down to see the end of a broken bone, filed and sharp, pointed at his groin. Her long brown fingers wrapped around its thickness, though she made no move to run him through. To prove just how prepared she'd been for his attack.

Thank the celestial mother!

At her silent threat, he pulled the dagger away from her neck and settle back on his ass on the floor, his arms folded across his knees as he stared at the mysterious woman.

"Yes," he admitted miserably. "I ate that cursed pie."

Lips pursed, she tilted her head slightly and mimicked his pose. She was slow to lift her legs, like her very bones were weary. "It's good pie."

Mouth watering at the memory, he knew denying that would get him nowhere. "Yes. It was." He'd always been a sucker for pie, it never occurred to him that the tasty dessert would be his downfall.

Bone held in hand, she pointed it around the space. "It would have to be to catch so many of us."

Jhaeros looked around the dungeon at the beings that littered the space. The dim lighting showed him stone walls and floors. There were shackles attached to the walls in some places, chains wrapped around pillars, though no one was bound. Everyone slumped against the walls in the small space, looking just as weary as the woman before him. He counted four others besides the woman.

He observed the woman who inspected him in turn, brow cocked, a slight grin on her lips. She looked battle worn. Her brow was split as was the centre of her lip. Her obsidian eyes were dull and hollow beneath. Something in his chest made him gravitate toward her. His hand lifted of its own volition, hovering in the space beside her slightly swollen cheek. Something visceral moved through him, vengeful at the battered sight of the woman he barely knew.

Odd.

"Are you alright?"

She didn't flinch away from his hand, though her eyes narrowed. There was no fear, not even caution, more like a curious question in her gaze. He understood because his brow furrowed in turn.

It wasn't like him. He wasn't nurturing. His hand curled into a fist and he let it slowly fall away.

"We're all bruised and battered here." Her hand lifted, but the movement was slow as she pointed to his brow to make her point.

Jhaeros lifted his hand and winced as his fingers prodded the gash. "This will be gone in a few moments."

Her chuckle was a slow purr that made goosebumps assault his skin. It burrowed under his flesh and he had to work hard to suppress the shudder that wanted to move through him. "It won't."

"My healing is accelerated," he argued.

"As is the case with most of us, but no one heals here. Not unless she wants it." Her eyes lifted to the ceiling to gesture up to the woman who threw them down into the cellar.

The witch with the pie.

A million questions surged through his mind, but they got tangled before they reached his lips. The air was cold, yet thick. Each breath coated his lungs and made them feel heavy.

Why was he so sleepy?

"She likes to keep us tired," she answered the question he never asked.

Jhaeros fought against the heaviness of his head as fatigue rendered his neck almost useless. "Why?"

"Because she's old and weak," she replied easily before her eyes closed and her head fell back to rest on the wall. "And though her magic is fierce, it's draining. She can't even use it for youth anymore. She only uses it for the trials."

A knot creased the space between his brows. "Trials?"

"Mhmm."

"What trials?"

Chaos filled the silence as chains rattled and debris rained down on them. The dim lights flickered as a bellow vibrated through the space. No one moved, no one flinched away from the sound. They all remained propped up against the walls wrapped in the sands of the sandman, so close to their descent into slumber.

"He never tires," she supplied.

"He?"

"The minotaur." She swallowed hard as her tongue, a deeper blue than her lips, dragged across her bottom lip. "Not even her magic can quiet him."

Heaviness held a hand over his lids as they drooped before he forced them open. His head dropped in his hand, palm pressed to his brow. "A minotaur?" he slurred.

"Dante."

Fingers pressed to his temple, he tried to use his magic to rid him of whatever spell currently fogged his mind and tried to steal his faculties.

"It won't work. You can't exactly capture magical beings and allow them to keep their magic."

Jhaeros forced his eyes open to look at her. "What does she want with us?"

Her chuckle was a sad thing. It was the kind of slow chuckle one gave when despondency had leached down into their bones and settled. "What else would an impastusae witch want?"

It pained him to admit he didn't have an extensive knowledge of witches. They were just a step above mortal, and he seldom had a need to bother himself with either. Their blood was a watered-down thing, and he could often find a fae to accomplish anything a caster could. "An impastusae witch?"

She sucked in a sharp breath. "You know... the ones from the tales. Hansel and Gretel."

He'd never heard of such a tale.

"Antin and Boola. Ret and Wrenchil..." she paused to peek through her slit lids to look at him. "What are you?"

"Fae."

If his species meant anything to her, she was too tired to show it. "Mhmm... what kind?"

"Elf," he replied, though he didn't have the strength to summon the pride that usually went along with the declaration.

Her brow dipped in thought. "Trevan and Sorrell."

His heart seized in his chest. It had been forever since he heard the old tale. The one where two siblings were left alone in the woods as a sacrifice to the cannibalistic witch who could grant their families riches in both magic and possessions. His mother often told him the tale when he misbehaved. She'd admonish how much easier it would be to be childless if he was going to be the pest he often was. Threatened there would be no pixie dust to lead him back home, not if he wasn't a good boy. His rebellion didn't last long after she reminded him of the tale with a pinch to the cheek, always a tad too tight.

'She'd like the taste of you too... still plump from infancy.'

Jhaeros always thought it was nothing more than a tale. Something his mother said when she had reached the end of her patience. A reminder of all the things she shielded him from — bad as she claimed he was.

Recognition moved across her face as she watched him, saw the moment the old tale took root in his mind. "Well, that would be an impastusae witch. Their cottages usually sit in the most barren part of the forest, too far from any other option when your stomach is rumbling and your bones are weary. The smell of the feast draws you, reminds you just how long it's been since you've had food and how long it will likely be... since it's been an eternity since you lost your way. Their woods have a way of doing that... making you lose your way." She sighed, summoning strength to finish the story. "It's part of their powers, making the woods they build their cottages in feel like mazes you can't find your way through. It's funny to think we could have gorged ourselves on all she had to offer, and it was the pie alone that did us in."

Jhaeros watched the slow smile curve her lip, as though that thought was humorous. "Never eat the pie."

If only there had been a sign, he would have left that stupid pie alone.

"Every species has a tale of the cannibalistic witches... nasty things. They're usually weak... unless they're full."

Just what he needed. To somehow be in the clutches of the witch that his mother used to threaten him with. The very one that had been the focus of his nightmares for so long.

Fuck!

"So, elf, do you have a name?"

"Jhaeros. And you? What are you?" His heart hammered through the fatigue as he awaited her answer. She had a draw to her. Something enticing that made him desperate to know.

"My name is Obscura and I'm a tenebrae."

He hissed and shuffled away, teeth bared. "You're a leech. A vile thing that thrives on misfortune!"

A slow sigh left her lips as her eyes once again fell closed. "Stop flirting with me, I'm too tired to sleep with you."

"I would never stoop so low."

A roll of her eyes was all she offered in response. "Seeing as we're both likely to meet our end in her cauldron, I think you can swallow those bitter feelings, elf."

Elves were a proud lot, and beings from the shadow realm had always been seen as scavengers so far beneath them, it was like talking to vermin. He couldn't completely forget the lessons seared into his mind over centuries. Not even if he *was* as close to Death's door as she tried to make him believe.

When he said nothing, she chuckled again. "You'll change your tune after your first trial. We're all just meat for her stew. Nothing more, nothing less. And as we battle for survival... we all bleed. Tenebrae and elves alike."

More debris rained down on him as he scooted away and rested his back against a stone pillar. His arm wrapped around his middle, cradling his sore flesh and bones as he scowled at the woman who remained where she was, unperturbed by his presence. She kept the bone in hand as her eyes fell closed.

A shiver moved through him as flurries of snow blew past his face and made his teeth chatter.

Sleepy eyes looked around the dungeon. Someone with pale pink hair in a bush around their head slumped over against the wall. Dirty goggles with copper rims covered their eyes as they hugged their knees against their chest. A slim man sat with his legs bent and open, his long blue limbs lifeless as his chin rested on his chest, his white hair a curtain over his face. A pink woman with deep purple hair singed on one side rested her brow on her folded arms, her knees propping her up.

Another flurry made him wrap his arms around himself as his eyes landed on the woman who lay on the floor a few metres away. Her arm was thrown over her eyes, the tips of her fingers blue until they turned white at the nails. Curly hair was a white flurry of coiled curls that cushioned her head from the floor as her mouth hung open and she snored. The snow was carried on her breath.

Jhaeros frowned. It didn't take a genius to see the frost was her magic.

How?

If the witch cast a spell around this place to strip them of their powers, what the hell was that woman and how could he convince her to help him escape?

The question was loud in his mind, until the witch's magic pulled it away, made it fade to a whisper. He couldn't focus on it long enough to decide on an answer, and before he knew it, the sandman's sands weighed him down, and he was pulled into the arms of sleep.

Obscura

She couldn't help but grin as the elf wrapped his arms around himself to stave off the cold. If she wasn't so petty, she would tell him everyone stayed against the wall to avoid the path of Lumi's frigid snores, but she wasn't about to extend him any kindnesses while he still had his head buried in his pompous ass.

His thick hair was spiral curls braided back from his temples and around the crown of his head. Gems and carved stones embedded in the intricate weaves. The tips of his brown ears poked up from within the braids, the colour of his skin warm brown and glistening like he brushed it over with pixie dust. He was a wiry thing. Tall. Though he was a few metres away, when he stretched his legs out, they quickly bridged the space between them.

Elves were prideful things. She knew that long before she landed herself in this witch's cottage. Pride would be surrendered quickly. It would do nothing to help them survive.

Though the fatigue magic held him under the sands of sleep, his was restless. Shivers wracked through his body and his brow creased, lines of pain etched around the edges of his mouth as his teeth ground and clenched. When Dante's calm hinted morning, she felt a twinge of guilt for not giving in and telling him how to avoid the frosty gales.

Altie rolled on her side and inched closer. Her hand stretched out to wrap around Obscura's waist. Her fingers were long, her pointed nails only made them that much longer. She made a noise deep in her chest, one that could almost be a sound of contentment were they anywhere else. Her tight, kinky pink coils cushioned the space between Altie's head and Obscura's lap. Often, when the dungeon fell quiet and sleep dragged most of them away from consciousness, she would run her fingertips against the baby soft tendrils of the hair along Altie's temples. Hum to her if she seemed uneasy. Obscura reached out and cupped the side of Altie's face. Her thumb traced a slow circle against her rounded cheek, dirt falling away with each brush.

A surge of magic moved through the room.

Obscura could almost see it. The faintest shimmer of green coated everything for an instant before it was gone.

"It's almost time, Altie," she whispered.

The room swayed, and Dante's chains rattled to the floor.

It *was* time.

The fatigue that went down to her bones lifted and Obscura gently sat Altie up and got to her feet in time to watch the dungeon transform from stone and torchlight into a canyon. The wounds that burdened her since the last trials slowly stitched, her aches dissolved, and her magic awoke. She looked up at the massive rock formations that closed them in on both sides of the river that ran through it.

Rane stood next to her, his white hair billowing behind him. He lifted his face and inhaled, a fresh change from the thick dungeon air. He turned to look down at Obscura, the blue of his body constantly shifting — gentle clear waters in the sun — without the spell restricting his magic. His shoulders set and the muscles of his jaw flexed as he took it all in.

Deinn walked toward the river's edge. She dipped her pink hand beneath the surface and cupped the water. Wet hands wiped the back of her neck, washing away some of the filth they'd collected over the past few days. The selkie had been there for the least amount of time aside from Jhaeros. This would be her third trial.

Teeraw — the being who had been the last taken before Jhaeros — was lost in the last trial. So soon after his arrival, she didn't even have the chance to learn what he was. He spent all his time between being tossed in the dungeon alongside them and his first and only trial weeping.

Helplessness did that to some.

"What's happening?" Jhaeros asked.

Obscura flicked her dark eyes toward him before she followed Deinn's lead and set to wash herself. She couldn't be sure if the next trial would afford her the luxury and she'd answered all the questions she would for him, especially knowing how he felt about tenebraes — how he likely felt about them all.

Asshole.

The water was cool on her neck. She ran her hands over her face and scrubbed at her skin while she could. Cautious eyes kept watch on Altie as she slowly explored, the back of her hands dragged over her eyes as she tried to shake off the last vestiges of sleep.

Deinn went further, walking past Obscura to dive into the rushing water.

"It's a trial," Rane answered flatly. His voice was a soothing cadence, like water flowing over rocks in a shallow brook.

"For what?" Jhaeros asked.

"To determine who will feed the witch."

That answer brought a sombre mood to the group. A bellow sounded as Dante joined them. Unlike everyone else, he was in his true form. His hooves plodded along the ground as he walked to the river's edge and tilted his massive bull head up to look at the rock formations. Smoke blew from his nostrils, lifting the heavy gold hoop. He looked pensive, as he always did at the start of a trial.

Jhaeros kept a wide berth. Suspicion was clear on his face as he perused the scene. He lifted his hand, magic gold wisps danced around his fingertips. "It's an illusion."

"Always a different one," Rane offered.

"With different adversaries," Altie added as she tucked her thumbs in the front of her dirty dark overalls.

Shoulders squared, Obscura prepared herself. She may not have been in the witch's clutches as long as Dante, but she had been there long enough to know the quiet didn't last. The witch was mulling them into a false sense of calm, watching as they took everything in and revelled at the change of scene, before she fixed herself to pull their strings.

The beginning of the trials always came with a swell of peace. That was the real illusion. A sense of calm. A rightness so similar to the woods that lured them.

The ground shook beneath her feet.

Splashes sounded as pink arms shot out of the water. Deinn's head broke the surface as she gasped. "Get away from the water!"

Rane's eyes narrowed.

The water swallowed her whole. Devoured her and erased any sign Deinn had ever been there.

Obscura took a step toward the water, eyes searching. "Rane?" If there was something treacherous beneath the water, he would see it.

A massive head broke the surface. It stretched up, towering well above everyone. Serrated teeth gleamed from its pointed muzzle, sharp fins lined the back of its head as its yellow eyes looked down at the group on shore. A clicking noise sounded as a forked tongue escaped its mouth. Its body was smooth and a purple so deep it almost looked black. Its long tail wrapped around Deinn as she squirmed. The massive eel ignored her once it held her in its grasp.

Magic came off the beast in waves. It rattled against her flesh and filled the air with unfiltered terror meant to stall them in their tracks. Confuse them. Break them.

Rane ran forward, his body dissipating as it hit the water. He became the water as he disappeared. There was nothing she could do to help them, not in the water. She would have to trust Rane would know what to do. The adversary was one he knew.

She knew where her attention needed to be. Who she needed to protect. Obscura wrapped a hand around Altie's arm and pulled her away from the river. She turned Altie to look at her as her heart pounded against her chest. She brushed soft knuckles gently against Altie's cheek, stealing a moment while she could. Fearful she may not get another.

Hissing sounded as the ground under their feet continued to shake.

"Altie," she whispered. "Save yourself."

Whatever shook the ground beneath their feet, it wasn't the eel that had Deinn in its grasp. There was something else. Something big.

There was always a desperation in these moments when she waited to see if Altie would listen. She felt a bond with the woman she couldn't explain. One that made her bleed from a place she couldn't see every moment she was in danger. Her focus was always a fragile thing when Altie was around and danger made its way toward them.

Anxious as she was, Altie quickly shifted. Pink magic surrounded her before she transformed into a large mole, as tall as Obscura's hips. Her clawed hands dug into the ground at their feet and she was gone, tunnelled deep within the ground of the illusion and safe from the Inkanyamba and whatever else was coming.

Jhaeros's eyes widened as Altie disappeared.

The first trial was always confusing. She could only imagine what went through his mind.

Relief filled her as soil fell into the hole Altie left behind.

Dante stepped up behind her. He twirled the heavy double-headed axe in his hand before he held it out to her with another blow of smoke from his nostrils.

Obscura shook her head before she held her hands out before her. She needed no weapon, she had plenty of her own. Shadows danced between her hands before a black longbow appeared. It shone like obsidian; the string covered in dark shadows. She held it before her, pulled the string back, and watched as a phantom arrow appeared in its nook. With a deep breath, she readied herself.

A chuckle-like grunt came from Dante as he widened his stance and held his axe at the ready.

'You'll not die here today, Obscura. Death is an admirer not yet ready to claim you,' he spoke into her mind.

The words made her smile. "How very romantic of you, Dante."

He chuckled again. *'Ready?'*

Excitement pulsed through her. She had been under the witch's thumb for so long, she craved the heady scent of fear that had once been her daily sustenance. The dark perfume of the unknown. Tenebrae's fed off fear, sorrow, rejection, and helplessness. These trials should fill her to bursting — or they would, if most of those emotions weren't her own, and if the witch didn't strip it all away along with the illusion when the trials were through.

At the end of the canyon, their foe appeared. Eight hairy legs held up its massive body as a dozen red eyes stared them down.

Obscura grinned.

Spiders were a cherished thing to her. She rather enjoyed their lonely existence. The way they caused hearts to speed up and terror to become a rampant thing. It was a magnificent beast, massive and terrifying. It paused with four legs on each side of the river. A high screech sounded before those legs moved in quick succession, carrying their adversary toward them.

In the witch's illusions, no beast could live. Not when it meant one of them would die in its place. Cherished or not, this spider would taste her shadows.

Poor beasty.

"Ready." And she was.

Jhaeros baulked when Dante roared and ran straight toward the beast.

As much as it pained her, Obscura released the string and let the arrow fly.

Jhaeros

The tenebrae released an arrow. As it flew through the air, a shrill high-pitched scream accompanied it, as though the phantom thing cut through the air itself and the illusion couldn't swallow back the sound of its suffering. No sooner had she released the arrow, another flew behind it, and another.

Her bare arms flexed with effort as she grinned. Her pale blue lips pulled back to show sharp fangs set in purple gums as she took sure steps toward the beast like it wasn't set in their path to hand them over to the cannibalistic witch that would be their undoing.

She was a fierce thing.

Fear was a stranger to her as she followed behind the minotaur who ran toward the massive spider. Her arrows flew true, sinking into the eyes of the beast. It released another shriek that shook the illusion. Rocks slid down the sides of the formation to tumble into the river, where two of the other prisoners battled a foe of their own.

This witch was a clever one.

Dropped to a squat, Jhaeros grabbed a fist full of dirt and let it fall from his hand. If he didn't know any better, he would think he actually stood in a canyon. That all this happened around him — this was as real as it felt.

Interesting.

Lips pursed, he huffed a thoughtful breath.

If these trials determined who lived and who died, the best thing for him to do was shatter the very illusion they tried to survive. Inhaling sharply, he held his breath trapped in his chest as he summoned his magic and pressed his palm to the ground.

Another bellow left the minotaur as he launched himself through the air and sunk his axe into the beast. He scaled up a leg, the screech doing nothing to dissuade him. Obscura stood beneath the spider, her bow aimed up as she fired arrow after arrow. Black blood rained down on her, slick like tar. It painted her face and made her look like this macabre image of madness, with a grin stretched over her face.

The blue man flew over Jhaeros's head. He landed hard on the ground a few metres away. He coughed up blood as he snarled before he dragged his arm over his mouth and stared back at the river. The pink woman was nowhere to be seen, the giant eel sunk beneath the surface. He slammed an aggravated fist against the ground before he got to his feet and ran back toward the water.

This illusion was pure chaos.

Jhaeros felt the splash of the water on his face as the blue man dove back into the river. Felt the heat make the back of his neck sweat and frizz the curls at his temples. The air was warm, and the breeze did nothing to soothe his hot skin.

This was borrowed magic. Stolen magic. *Devoured* magic.

A shriek so loud shook the ground, it disrupted his process. His hand left the dirt as he clamped his palms over his ears, the sound so sharp it made his ears ring and his teeth hurt. His eyes whipped to where the minotaur battled the spider alongside the tenebrae. The minotaur straddled the beast's back as he raised his axe and buried the blade into its body, only to pull it free and repeat the process.

The tenebrae was missing.

A fleeting wave of anxiety moved through him as he got to his feet. His eyes were wide as they scanned the space but still couldn't find her.

Break the illusion.

The tenebrae was not his concern.

On his knees, he pressed both his palms to the ground and closed his eyes. He felt the warmth of his magic coat his hands. The comforting tingle moved through him and set all his nerves on fire before the familiar comfort swathed him. He focused on that comfort. The comfort only his power could bring.

It sought the magic. The spell that coated the dungeon in the surrounding illusion.

There.

A crack.

He pushed his magic into it. He was no mere babe. His magic was extensive. His bloodline was strong. Jhaeros's magic pushed deeper, and he felt it. The dirt under his hand turned into stone, and he knew he triumphed over the foul witch.

The head of the spider toppled off as Obscura emerged from the wound covered in black blood. Its legs gave out, the minotaur still hacking away. The stream of the river slowed and the blue man once again was thrown onto the shores. Blood clouded his watery flesh, a massive bite mark covered the whole of his abdomen, and the blood dripped inward to sully his watery flesh. The pink woman screamed as she was lifted from the river, the sound tapered away as she slumped unconscious in its hold. Panic widened the blue man's eyes as he squared his shoulders and prepared himself to once again go against the beast.

Jhaeros forced his magic into the crack. A glitch cut the scene, made it pause, made parts of the illusion blur, before it all shattered and they all sat on the stone floor of the dungeon.

Black sludge still covered Obscura, while the minotaur huffed and fought against the chains that pulled him back across the dungeon. His hooves dug in, but to no avail. He flew back out of sight and, once again, debris rained down from the ceiling.

The blue man growled in agony as he rolled onto his stomach and pounded his fists against the floor. "What did you do?" Sorrow was a weight that cracked his words.

"I saved us," Jhaeros quipped.

"I could have saved her." His eyes glassed over as he shot a furious look at Jhaeros. "I could have saved her!"

Jhaeros looked around and found the pink woman absent. Tension filled the air, more treacherous than the witch's illusion.

"I could have—" a sob robbed him of his words.

"Rane." Obscura's eyes glistened.

"She... was right there. Right within my grasp. I could have saved her. I know I could have."

Obscura dropped to her knees beside him. The grin she wore as she battled the spider from the inside was gone and replaced by despondency. She swallowed hard and swiped at some of the sludge on her face as she clasped her bottom lip behind her sharp teeth. Long fingers reached out, her nails as sharp as her teeth, as she hesitated before she touched him.

"Rane." His name was a sad thing leaving her lips. Somehow, the uttering of the single word was filled with grief and regret. With apology that wasn't hers to offer, yet she did just the same.

He shoved up to his knees and curled against the floor. "I can't do this anymore, Obscura. I can't keep watching them disappear." He rested his forehead on his fist as a whimper left his quivering lips.

She rested her hand on his back and rubbed her hand along his spine. Her mouth opened but shut before she said anything.

The mole woman stepped up behind them. Her entire face was covered in dirt aside from the circles around her eyes as she rubbed her goggles on her shirt to clean the lenses. Her chin wrinkled and her bottom lip quivered as her eyes glassed over. Accusation shot his way, a fleeting thing, before she dropped her eyes to the floor.

An icy breeze made his shoulders bunch up around his ears as a flurry took over the room again.

Jhaeros turned to see the woman sleeping right where she'd been before the illusion took hold.

She hadn't been with them in the canyon.

Confusion warred through him, but he swallowed his questions, knowing now wasn't the time. His eyes turned up to the ceiling as Rane continued to quietly sob.

He'd survived the first trial, but that survival came with nothing more than questions.

The impastusae witch had to get something out of the trials besides weeding out her next meal. She could easily just reach down and scoop one of them up, tear them from their sleeping place on the dungeon floor and throw them into a pot before they could shake the sands of sleep from their eyes.

Why didn't she?

The minotaur's raging fell silent to the sound of the water elemental's grief.

He needed to figure it out before the next trial. Before he ended up being the one who didn't return.

Obscura

Deinn's loss ate away at Rane. It was understandable. Under different circumstances, a water elemental and a selkie would be a love story worthy of tales. Their bond was one that forged quickly, and they often stuck together during the trials. Usually, that was enough to ensure they both made it out alive.

His sobs were a heartbreaking thing she didn't want to take part in. Normally, the sad sound would fuel her, but instead, she felt a sadness she'd never known. She ached for the poor water elemental and for the loss of the selkie, who had been fierce, at times funny, and sweet when she thought no one could see her whisper to Rane in the dark.

They had lost six since the witch captured Obscura.

Since she'd foolishly eaten the pie.

A wolf shifter, a mage, a witch, a nightmare, a demon and now Deinn. Seven... if she included the one she never got to know.

It was hard not to get attached. Normally a lone creature, the thought of losing Altie or even Dante made her chest ache uncomfortably. She cleared her throat and slumped back against the wall as the fatigue set in, and listened for Rane's breathing to level out, hinting sleep had taken him.

"How often are the trials?" Jhaeros's voice cut through the silence.

Obscura looked at Altie slumped against the wall, asleep. She stayed close. She often did. The sound of Dante raging still filled the room as she let her dark eyes settle on the elf across from her. He'd taken up refuge against the same pillar, one leg bent as he rested his forearm on his knee and toyed with his dagger.

"Are you sure you want answers from me, your highness? A lowly tenebrae?" Pettiness was something she wore effortlessly, and while the witch has stripped away so much of who she was, this was something Obscura just wouldn't surrender.

His dark brow cocked as his gold eyes looked her over. "My options to gain answers are few."

Her dark eyes took him in, but she said nothing.

Jhaeros met her gaze. There was a challenge there, one that told her he wouldn't let her disrespect him and that her snark wouldn't go unanswered.

Good. She wanted a reason to lash out at him. To show him how true the stories of her likely were. How dark she could become when she stopped trying to shove the cage where she kept the vicious parts of her closed.

"I wonder what tales monsters could tell one another of this witch. What could you possibly say to scare beings who thrive on fear?" Accusation filled his icy tone.

He thought she was just as evil as the witch. As though being a being of shadow automatically made her bloodthirsty and vile. How jaded he was. Existence was so vast to have thoughts so limited.

Obscura met his gaze, a challenge of her own in her dark eyes. "We don't have a tale, we just keep everyone else's and we wait. Wait for a moment when the quiet is so loud it gives birth to peace... and then we whisper into that quiet. Fill it with stories moulded to fit the little spaces in your mind. Puzzle pieces of misery created just for you... by you."

Her words made his face twist. "You're as wicked as she is."

"I am dark. I'm twisted and macabre and there are parts of me where agony would be better received than joy, but if we are comparing wickedness to the witch upstairs, I would say she would be better company for *you*. For the man who finds enemies in the captives because they weren't born to his realm or don't bow to his queen. A man who measures power in these frivolous ways and tries to decide who is worthy to hold it."

Anger made the muscles in his jaw tick. "Outside of this place, you would torment me."

And how she would enjoy it. "Yes... but I wouldn't kill you. Could you say the same?"

Teeth bared, he rolled his eyes and looked away.

She knew the answer. Obscura found herself at the end of a blade more than once. A hand wrapped around her throat and the threat clear on their face as they let her soak in the moment. Tried to make her feel the same fear she spread so effortlessly before they sunk that blade in deep.

Many would kill her if given the chance. Many just like Jhaeros.

And yet... she harboured no ill will toward him when he first arrived. Despite knowing better and having him force her poor decision down her throat. Made her taste the bitterness of it.

Altie slumped toward her. Her head settled in Obscura's lap, and she busied herself sinking her fingers in the heavy bush of tight coils. A smile lifted her lips as Altie's lips parted and a sigh escaped her. As sinister as it was to keep them tired, Obscura loved the way sleep stole away Altie's troubles.

Jhaeros chortled under his breath. He was a man who didn't like to lose. Her words made him sit with himself. Play through their conversation over and over and try to find a way to set her in the place he thought she ought to be. She could see his discontent.

And she enjoyed it.

He huffed again, eyes narrowed.

Big baby.

The thought of rolling her eyes took so much effort, she decided against it.

"You were impressive," he said, his words jilted.

"Ah. Wonderful. I was worried in the thralls of chaos and survival, I would miss my chance to impress you. With your acknowledgment, I can fall into the witch's spell of fatigue a happy woman." Her nails scraped lightly against Altie's scalp, making her preen.

The corner of his mouth quirked up, and it lacked the distaste it had the last time he sneered at her. "Are you going to answer my questions?"

"You mean like I was willing to when you first arrived before you became abhorred by my very existence?" She huffed a tired breath and let her eyes fall closed. "Before I found out you were nothing more than a vile, treacherous, pompous elf?" Sarcasm dripped from her every word with excruciating effort.

She was so tired.

Tired was how the witch captured and kept them.

"If I'm to get out of this cursed place, I'll need a little information."

"You plan to escape alone? And what of the rest of us?" She tried not to judge him too harshly. Perhaps it was just a slip of the tongue.

"The lot of you seem content going through the trials over and over. It doesn't look like any of you plan to escape this place. You've all just laid down and accepted your fate. If you don't care about your freedom, why should I?"

Anger was a small ember in the pit of her stomach, unable to become the flame or fire she knew it would be outside of this cottage and away from the impastusae witch. "You think we don't care?"

"It doesn't seem like you do."

"And everything is always just as it seems here…" her words trailed away. "Perhaps our complacency is an illusion… brought on by your ignorance."

"Ignorance?" He kept his voice low, but she could tell she struck a nerve by the rasp as the word left his lips. "I'm far from ignorant."

A chuckle left her, slow and draining. "If that were true, you'd have no questions." Her eyes fell closed as exhaustion worked its way through her. She didn't bother using the voids inside her — where her shadows lived — to swallow some of the magic pushed into her to keep her awake. There was nothing to stay awake for.

She could do without the prideful elf and his questions.

"Why does she not partake in the illusions?" Jhaeros asked.

It seemed he wouldn't take the hint. He had questions, and he was going to ask them whether or not she wanted to give answers.

"The sleeping one that breathes snow," he clarified.

He didn't need to. She knew who he meant. That woman had intrigued her from the moment she arrived. Trapped alongside them, but unaffected by the magic that held them prisoner. Uninvolved in the trials. She was there, much like the stones in the walls or the chains that held Dante. Exempt from the sick game of elimination.

"I didn't see her in the illusion," he continued.

"Because she wasn't there," she said on a sigh.

Obscura didn't need to look at him to know he wore a look of confusion. It was the same look they all wore after their first trial when they returned to their prison covered in blood, only to see she still slept, unaffected by it all.

"Sleep. You'll need your rest. The next trial will be here soon enough."

"But I have questions," he argued.

"And the answers to those questions will do nothing to help you escape. This isn't the tale. In reality, the children in those stories, if they befell the witch and ate the pie, likely died just like so many others. Pixie dust did not lead them home. They didn't outsmart the witch. She devours us to gain power… a power than ensures she doesn't need smarts to keep us locked up here. In this world, just like so many others, power is the crown worn by the victorious… and your answers will do nothing to dethrone her."

"Pie," he hissed under his breath. "Fucking pie."

His frustration made her smile lightly. Fucking pie indeed.

Obscura slid lower against the wall. She let her knees drop as she turned slightly toward Altie and let sleep take her.

She would need her rest too.

Another trial would be coming.

Jhaeros

Stupid fucking pie!

He jumped back as fire bit into the fabric of his pants. It devoured them with ease. The deep green fabric disappeared from his thigh down to his knee before he could rip away the bottom of the leg to keep it from searing into his skin.

This illusion was powerful.

The mole woman disappeared at the beginning of the trial, though Jhaeros couldn't be sure where she could have gone. To burrow in this ground would have brought her down into the lake of fire.

His feet planted on the floating mass, the heat from the lake lifted through the ground as it floated down the lake. It bumped against another mass and he stumbled. Magic shot out of his hand, creating a pillar in the centre he could hold on to as it teetered and one side dipped below the surface of the fire.

Magic seeped out of hands wrapped around the pillar as he searched for a crack to free them from this wretched place.

Stalactites hung from the ceiling, veins of fire moved through them and some dripped hot magma. The surrounding cave had jagged ceilings and walls. There was no way out. All they could do was stand on their little islands and wait to see where the river of fire brought them.

It was so damned hot!

Sweat slicked his brow as he looked over at the remaining beings. There were only six of them now — five if he didn't count the sleeping woman who was immune to the witch and her sorcery. Rane, the water elemental, still wore the distressed signs of grief. He used his water to put out any fires that got too close to Obscura or Dante but made no move to be on the offensive. All his movements were lethargic, even without the witch's enchantment. Dante was much the same as he was in the last illusion. He leapt from small island to island, advancing further down the river. Obscura followed. Whatever foe they faced, they seemed sure it wouldn't come from behind them.

A growl pierce his ears as the cave shook.

Jhaeros's arms shot out as the island he stood on lifted from the river and shot through the air. He flipped back as a gold cloud appeared beneath his feet, keeping him from his fiery death. His eyes locked on the beast who emerged from the lake. A giant made of stone and magma. Its massive hand swiped through the lake, knocking all the floating shelves from its surface.

Find the crack.

Shatter the illusion.

Flutters and shrieks sounded above him. Bats flocked around them, their claws shone in the glow of the fiery light as they swooped around him, trying to grab hold.

They lifted the minotaur from his little island. Bat's claws sunk into his arms as he flew over Jhaeros's head. He dropped as he grabbed one and ripped its wings off, but another quickly took its place. Blood matted his brown fur as one sunk its fangs into his thick neck. The minotaur bellowed as he tried to free himself.

Arrows sunk into the bats before a massive hand of woven shadows grabbed him to keep him from falling into the lava. They placed him down with care before he took off again. The wounds that littered his body did nothing to slow him as he scooped his axe up from the ground at his feet, let off an earth-shattering bellow, and took off toward the giant.

Obscura dodged a sweep of its arm, disappearing in a cloud of smoke to appear on another floating platform. Her hands lifted, bow in her grasp, to shoot more bats from the sky above their heads.

He ignored them. He had no intention of participating in the trial against the beast. His only intention was to shatter the illusion, only this time, he wanted to slip into the cracks he created, see the magic, and gauge the power. Peek in at the witch to see where her defences fell weak.

Water rained over him.

He lifted a hand over his head and waved his magic above him to prevent distraction. He could do this. His magic was strong.

Concentration knit his brow as he rubbed his hands together and held them parallel to the little island at his feet. A deep inhale filled his chest before he pressed.

Jhaeros fell.

His hands pushed through a wall of magic, and he somersaulted through it. Fire from a hearth licked across his skin, surrounding him with the familiar scent of ash and wood. It heated his skin but didn't burn. It ripped away the illusion and left him standing in a pit. The stone walls were black. Nail marks carved into them, like some unlucky soul stood in this very pit and tried to escape. Jhaeros walked toward the walls and traced his finger along the carved marks.

It was a small pit. Five steps from the centre took him to the walls.

Palm against the wall, he walked the perimeter.

"Why am I here?" his voice echoed around him.

Interesting.

Hands clasped together, he rubbed and rubbed before he shot them away from him. His magic moved through the pit.

There.

A shimmer caught his eye. A tapestry pressed tight against the side of the pit. The intricate weave towered up above his head to where he imagined an escape hidden out of sight.

"I've got you, witch," he whispered as he brushed a hand over it and searched. All he needed was a single thread to unravel her. A single pull to reduce the tapestry of her magic — stolen and devoured — to nothing more than thread at his feet. Bent at the waist, he found it.

Small, almost unnoticeable.

"A weakness."

"You'll fail here, boy," she taunted. Her voice was terrifying. As much around him as it was in his mind, burrowing into his thoughts. It was a high screech, nails on a chalkboard that made his teeth clatter together as pain assaulted his ears.

"I won't."

"You will... they all do."

That the voice echoed around him at all, dark and haunted — the sound of a creak in the night off in the distance that tightened his muscles and urged him to run — told him he was very close to defeating her. Why else would the elusive witch speak to him? Taunt him? Try to dissuade him?

He'd almost won.

He pinched the thread between his finger and thumb and grinned.

This was it.

The pit disappeared.

The air ripped out of his lungs as he landed hard. Water doused him, but the frigid feeling was quickly replaced by agony brushed over his skin as it seared, pressed against something too hot.

"What the hell are you doing?" Obscura yanked him away from the river and back onto his island. Her hand wrapped around her middle, the fabric of her shirt melted into her flesh as she heaved laboured breaths into her chest. Pain etched across her face, but it was no match for her ire. "Are you *trying* to lose the trial?" Her dark eyes were hard as she snarled through her teeth. Her scornful look was short-lived as she turned on her heel, raised her bow, and fired.

She'd been hurt. That shocked him. From the way she moved through the previous trial with ease, he thought she was as untouchable — or unmoved by the damage she received there — as Dante.

"I'm trying to escape these blasted trials," Jhaeros hissed through his teeth as he opened his palms, ready to dive in again. "Just stay out of my way!"

"I just saved your sorry ass!"

"Two things you need to know about me; one, I am rarely sorry and this isn't one of the instances when I am, and two, I had everything well underway. I would have succeeded too... if you hadn't intervened." Blasted tenebrae. He needed nothing from her. No one told her to intervene. Any injuries she got were her own damned fault. Hers and this blasted witch.

And that fucking pie!

"In dying!"

"Perhaps that's just what I wanted to succeed at," Jhaeros retorted, annoyed at being chastised like a babe. "Just leave me be, woman. I have this well in hand!"

"Could have fooled me," she rebutted, her hands a blur as she loosed arrow after arrow.

Stupid tenebrae. What could she know about the complicated nature of unravelling an illusion?

"Get up!" she barked. "I don't want to have to save you again."

Any attention she offered him disappeared when Rane screamed.

Obscura

Anger, the likes of which she'd never felt before heated her usually cold skin. It burned and boiled in a way that shouldn't be possible here as she looked around at the dungeon that had quickly become a breath of relief between the trials. Steam rose from her flesh and her forearms sported blistered burns.

Dante's bellows filled the room as the chains took their place and pulled him out of sight.

She gave a weak smile to Altie, who fought against the fatigue best she could to look at the burnt flesh of Obscura's abdomen. "It's fine, Altie," she tried to assure her, but she saw a glint in her eye foreign to the little shifter.

"This is all his fault." Though Altie blamed him, she didn't look back at Jhaeros.

He scoffed. "Don't blame me for the actions of your foolish tenebrae."

"I'm a mole shifter." She turned and pointed her long, black fingernail at him. "Which means I can dig a hole so deep, no one will ever find you!"

"Whoa, I like it when you go dark." Obscura started to laugh, but winced when it brought pain to her tender flesh.

"Why don't you just go to sleep?" He waved a lazy hand, dismissing her. "Relax into the magic that hides you from this dungeon just as you hide away in the trials and let the grownups talk." He had the audacity to lift a hand and inspect his nails. "Worthless shifter," he muttered. "Just as worthless as that elemental with his wallowing."

Obscura lurched to her feet. She ignored the burning pain that stung and throbbed as she towered over Jhaeros. He could sit there with that pompous look on his face and act like he was above it all, but he wouldn't insult Altie. Not on her fucking watch. And Rane —

She saw red.

Altie coughed up smoke as she reached hesitant hands up to try to calm Obscura. "It had to be one of us," she said lightly, though the sadness was there. It always was. Quiet as she was, it tore at Altie just as much as it did Obscura to lose someone else.

The fatigue did nothing as the dark voids inside her sucked at the witch's magic. "What the fuck were you doing anyway?" She pointed an accusing finger at Jhaeros. "If you weren't just looking out for yourself, I wouldn't have had to... Rane wouldn't have had to protect you, and he would still be here."

The stupid elf had the gall to cock his brow at her. "And who would you sacrifice to the witch in his place? Your precious mole, who you're sure to send off before the fight even begins? Perhaps your raging bull?" His blasé reaction to yet another loss made her feral.

Obscura wrapped her fist in the front of his shirt and lifted him from his seated place on the floor. She knew her eyes darkened, her shadows barely caged inside her as grief waged war against the witch's magic.

As much as she hated to admit it, he was right. She wouldn't have sacrificed Altie or Dante. That didn't make the loss cut any less deep.

"You think you're getting out of here?" Her whisper was low. Dangerous. Threatening. "You? Who just arrived here, thinks he knows this place better than us? Better than the *lowly beings* who have resigned themselves to this torturous existence. Who used magic to get into the head of the witch, gaze at her tapestry of magic and try to unravel it like it was some feat to be proud of? Something that, of course, could only be accomplished by you?" Her chuckle was the sound of madness barely contained. The collar slipped from around the beast she was as it pulled at its lead and tried to get at him. "You think you're so special? That what you are puts you above us and any attempt we've made thus far, when the sad truth is anything you think you've accomplished, we've done ten times over. You're nothing special, *elf*," she spat the word at him with the same derision he used when he identified her. "The sooner you learn that the better your chance of survival will be."

Wide eyes stared back at her, iced over in a glaze of guilty surprise.

"Obscura." Altie stepped forward. "Obscura, please, she'll feel you." Fear rattled her words.

She couldn't help it. Couldn't contain herself, even though she knew the consequences.

"You're going to get us all killed!" Obscura pulled him closer, and watched his eyes move back and forth between hers as a billow of her shadows clouded around them.

"Obscura!" Altie's protests were cut short as she fell to an unconscious heap on the floor.

The ferocity in Dante's pulls at his chains increased when the trap door creaked open and a sinister hiss filled the air.

Heavy lids struggled to remain open as Jhaeros fell deeper and deeper under the spell.

She should loosen her hold on him, should slump back against her place on the wall and pull back the shadows that devoured most magic. She should be complacent. A good little prisoner so that she didn't have to suffer the wrath of the witch when she learned she could be defied.

"Obscura!" Dante screamed.

A dark-robed figure appeared behind her, the face hidden in the darkness of the hood, as arms covered in stitches reached out from the heavy sleeves and sunk black claws into the sides of Obscura's neck. Her tongue clicked as her hold tightened. It was a sound that summoned fear and held it captive. Shoved it into her chest — or it would if she wasn't so damned angry. The putrid scent of brimstone and decay assaulted her nostrils as her feet came up off the floor, and Jhaeros fell from her hold.

* * *

The creak was shrill as she swung from the ceiling like a pendulum. Blood dripped from her brow into her eye, forcing her to blink it away as it collected on her lashes. The iron shackles dug into the sensitive flesh of her wrists as she lifted her head and looked across the cottage at the witch.

She moved in a blur. Something stuck that couldn't keep time with the world around her. She was too slow. Her movements jolted as the tattered train of her robe trailed behind her. Carved wood decor filled the room. Intricate patterns and scenes were whittled into the dark wood of the walls, almost black. The candlelight from the sconces and iron candle holders as tall as the witch scattered around the room flickered, making the scene look eerie.

In the centre of the room was a black cauldron. The fire crackled beneath it and let off a greenish light. A blue arm bent over the rim of the cauldron as the contents bubbled.

Her stomach churned as her eyes glassed over. The scent in the air was malodorous. It thinned her saliva and made bile rise from her belly. The feeling of sickness made her feel dizzy, and she found herself missing the fatigue that normally plagued her. Maybe it would battle against the pain.

Feet bare, they throbbed where the witch had struck the soles of her feet until the skin swelled and split. The back of her shirt was ripped open, her flesh a tapestry of wounds the witch inflicted to tire her. It was only tired that her voids became less ravenous. That they'd cease the feast on the witch's magic.

Another shrill creak filled the air, accompanied by the witch's clicking.

Hot, rancid air blew up toward her face as the witch appeared before her. Her long, filthy fingers clutched a piece of blue flesh in her hands. She brought it to the darkness in her hood and the sickening sound of teeth in flesh filled the air. Her free hand reached out and pressed blackened fingers into the burns and blisters on Obscura's belly.

She saw white. Her vision wavered as her head fell back, and a scream tore through her throat. Every inch of her body scream alongside her as ragged breath tried to fill her lungs but failed. The scream filled too much of the space in the hollow of her chest. Her body heaved, her wrists alight with fresh agony as she tried to steady herself. Tried to power through the pain. Swallow it down. Become it.

The void inside her grew. Devoured the misery.

'Defiant little thing,' the witch spoke into her mind.

Her ears rang, but all she could do was flinch and pinch her eyes closed.

'Your power will sustain me in a way none of those before you ever could.' She held a dark goblet up to Obscura's face and collected some of her blood. Her hood slipped as she brought the goblet to her mouth, revealing a tapestry of multicoloured skin covered in black stitches. Her teeth were serrated, her gums as black as Obscura's shadows. *'Your time will come, tenebrae.'*

Obscura gritted her teeth and jolted toward the witch. "I will kill you," she promised. "If I have to completely surrender myself to my shadows so I can rip the flesh off your bones, I will make it happen!"

The witch lifted a hand, and another piece of blue meat appeared in her clutches. Her cackle was sharp in Obscura's ear as she gnawed at the flesh. *'Such fight. The strong always taste better.'*

She kicked out, but the witch dropped the empty goblet and caught her foot. She pressed a jagged black fingernail into an open wound, making Obscura huff out an agonized breath.

'That's right, tenebrae. Fight. You'll taste all the more savoury for it.'

She couldn't eat her, not now. She could only torture her. Try to break her so she didn't fight against her magic enough to cause problems before the next trial. This wasn't Obscura's first time hanging from these chains. This wasn't her first faceoff with the impastusae witch. She'd keep her up there, rip into her flesh until a natural exhaustion became more powerful than the one blanketed over those in the dungeon below.

The witch couldn't eat her now, but one day soon, she would. Obscura couldn't go on like this forever.

"I hope you choke on me, you bitch!"

Jhaeros

Time moved differently in captivity. Every second stretched to blanket the span of a day, while a day felt miniscule. He didn't know how long Obscura was gone, only that the longer she was, the more unease swallowed him.

He forced himself to stand. The dungeon swayed under his feet. The high arched stone ceilings came down to meet him, before it all balance out and set itself right. He blinked hard, teeth clenched in frustration.

"What is she doing to her up there?"

"The same thing she always does," the minotaur huffed. He'd fallen silent. He rampaged as best he could for what felt like an eternity when Obscura was dragged up the steps, the sickening sound of her flesh battered off the harsh corners echoed toward them, a warning from the witch, he was sure. All too soon, he fell silent. Nothing but the sound of his laboured breath filled the space.

Jhaeros wished he could hear her up there. Even if it was only her screams. He needed to know when it started — when it ended. If she lived.

Desperation made him growl low in his throat. "And what is it she does up there?"

Silence filled the space and Jhaeros took a shaky step around the pillar toward where the minotaur was chained. Surprise flickered through him as he looked down at a man. He had short, brown hair. It was shorn on the sides, his scalp on both sides visible, and tight curls covered the top of his head. His broad shoulders shimmered in sweat, setting his warm brown skin aglow. A heavy iron cuff wrapped around his neck, the chain pooled on the floor between his legs as he rested his forearms on his bent knees. His feet were bare, though brown suede pants covered his legs. The only part of him that looked the same as the beast Jhaeros knew, was the large gold hoop in his septum.

Jhaeros leaned back on the wall and slid down to the floor, mirroring Dante's pose.

"What does the witch do to Obscura up there?" It was one of the rare times he used her name. He needed to say it out loud, remind himself who she was in case he didn't see her again.

It was odd and made him feel anxious.

Brown eyes looked over at Jhaeros. They were... warm. Human. So unlike the red eyes of the beast who wanted nothing but bloodshed in the trials. "To break her."

A fist reached into his stomach and held it tight. "Why?"

Dante looked down the hall that kept him sequestered from the rest of the group. Jhaeros followed his gaze and watched as snow flusters blew by on an unseen gale.

"She wants them most. The ones whose magic can't be so easily stifled. They'll change her. Transform her. Make her into whatever sick and twisted thing she wants to become." He picked at the flesh around his thumbnail, a sign of his anxiousness. "But she can't take them unless they lose the trial."

A knot formed between Jhaeros's brows. "Why?" He thought the trials were just another way to break them. To give them a semblance of hope before she ripped it all away and thrust them once more into the prison she created. Like seasoning for the meat she was to prepare, the hope was a taste she couldn't deny herself. Much like their fear.

It didn't make sense that she could *only* take those who lost. What bound her to rules in her own twisted game?

Massive shoulders rose. "We don't know."

Jhaeros's thoughts were wild as he tried to figure it out.

"She hasn't stolen another," the minotaur interrupted his thoughts. "She is growing tired of waiting. She'll no longer settle for the ones she doesn't want. She'll pick us all off. Altie next, then you, then me..." his words trailed away. "Then it will just be her."

"And the sleeping woman."

He chuckled low, but there was no humour in the sound. "Lumi doesn't participate in the trials. The witch could keep her until the end of existence and never claim her or her magic."

Jhaeros shook his head. "How? How does she avoid the trials?"

He shrugged again. "None of us know, and she doesn't rouse long enough to give us answers. If this bothers her, she hasn't let on."

As fascinating as he found the woman deep in slumber, the list Dante laid out echoed in his head. "You think you will outlast me, minotaur?"

"Dante," he corrected, though his tone made him seem like he could care less what Jhaeros called him. "You've not been the first elf, and as high as you hold yourselves, you're all the same. Tunnel vision keeps you from seeing you can't escape this place alone. As powerful as you are, she's devoured many just like you. Houses the power under her knitted flesh. Are you stronger than a dozen of your kin? How about a dozen elves, just as many shifters, demons, and whatever else she's gotten her hands on? That wicked thing is an army of power, and you're just one elf." Dante sighed. "Your head is big, but your power will never match its size."

As much as he hated to admit it, Obscura was right. He was ignorant of the ways of the impastusae witch. If she held on to the power of each of her victims, Dante was right. He would never escape on his own.

"Tenebraes are rare out in this world. We see them in our nightmares... feel them in the dark. She punishes Obscura because she knows she likely can't win against her. Not even with her army. The same could likely be said about Lumi."

"Lumi?"

"The sleeping woman."

Jhaeros's attention once again went to the end of the hall. "What is she?"

Dante lifted his nose and inhaled deeply. Beasts had a way of scenting one another. Identifying a being by smell alone. It was something that often made Jhaeros envious. "A yeti."

Once again, he was surprised. "You're joking."

The shake of his head was slow. "She's the first I've encountered, but her smell is unmistakable."

A yeti.

Dante might as well have told him the woman in there was Santa Claus. Yetis were a thing of stories. In all his travels, he never imagined he'd stumble onto one.

"How the hell did she end up here?"

"Just like we all do, I guess," Dante groaned. "That witch and her fucking pie."

"Fucking pie!" he cursed.

Pie. He still couldn't believe he may meet his end because of pie. The whole thing was utterly ridiculous.

Something Dante said struck a chord. "If she's an army, then we'll need an army to defeat her."

He scoffed. "You can likely tell by the fit of my pants, these pockets aren't large enough to hold an army."

Jhaeros thought back to Obscura and her rage. The way her smoke left her flesh. Black devoured the colour of her eyes until they leaked shadow. Teeth bared, she looked like the thing of nightmares he knew she was. "She was unaffected by the magic."

Dante cocked a brow. "Obscura? Yeah. She's got a temper. When it gets out of hand, it's like something inside her opens and devours."

"Devours the witch's magic?"

"Yup."

Interesting.

"She gets under your skin. Warms the places in your chest no shadow being should be able to." Dante's eyes were warm even through their fatigue.

"Because of her magic..." He was quickly learning Obscura's power wasn't something to scoff at.

"No." Dante's chuckle was a deep sound so similar to his beast's bellow. "Because she's Obscura. I see you, Jhaeros. See the way she's already wormed her way into your chest but you fight against it because of things people told you. People who hold hands over your eyes and prevent you from truly seeing us for who we are."

Dante's chastisement hit hard.

"You like her."

No. Maybe...

"Despite her darkness."

A darkness that defies the witch.

"I think the only way to beat her is here. If she can only claim whoever loses the trial, then if we fight her here, even if we lose, she can't take us." Jhaeros thought about it. "Obscura may be army enough."

His head tilted, considering. "If she's mad enough." A quiet conversation moved between them when their eyes met and Dante shook his head. "I don't know if that's a good idea."

"Probably not, but it may be our only chance to get out of here."

Smoke billowed from his nostrils, and it looked weird coming from his wide nose covered in flesh. "Alright, elf. Tell me what thoughts rattle in that big head of yours."

* * *

Obscura landed on the bottom of the stairs and the trapdoor slammed closed. The scent of blood assaulted his nostrils and turned his stomach. Her normally pale brown skin was almost grey, covered in dark purple bumps and bruises. The back of her shirt hung open at her sides, the flesh burst open in dozens of angry slashes.

"Fuck," Jhaeros hissed under his breath as he stumbled over to her. His hands hovered over the brutality of her flesh. His hands shook under his barely kept emotions. He craved to have the witch within his grasp to show him the flavour of his wrath. Summoning his strength, he gently lifted her into his arms.

She was eerily still as he slumped back against the wall, Obscura cradled in his lap. He brushed the hair off her brow and looked down at her face. She looked almost peaceful. A macabre sight covered in blood as her thick lashes fell against her high cheekbones. Her long braids were loose from the binding atop her head, they curtained over his arm, heavy and dark.

It felt overtly intimate, looking down at her face when she couldn't observe him in turn. His eyes followed the line of her nose to her wide nostrils. His hand lifted to brush at the baby hair matted to her hairline.

Chains rattled as Dante pulled against them. "How is she?" he called.

A sad sigh left Jhaeros. She looked battered. All the flesh he saw was either slashed open, swollen, or bruised. Her wide, full lips parted, and he heard the battle her lungs waged as she inhaled disturbed breath. Wet and uneven. Her wounds went past her flesh. He could hear them with each breath.

Yet, in his arms, she felt perfect.

Jhaeros frowned at the thought.

"Jhaeros!" Dante yelled, anxiety made his words desperate.

"She's..."

"What?"

He wasn't sure. "Breathing."

Debris rained down on them as Dante pulled at his chains.

"Would you stop that?" Jhaeros shielded her face from the dust.

Dante calmed under his chastisement.

A cold breeze brushed against his skin and he scowled over at the sleeping yeti Dante called Lumi. He knew her, which meant she didn't always sleep. There was a time when she likely sat with them. Conversed with them. Maybe.

"Lumi," Jhaeros called. "Will you stop that?"

Silence was his answer.

"I know you can hear me, don't ignore me."

Words came from her stillness. "I would ignore Death himself for a nap... on many occasions, I've done just that."

"A nap?" he hissed, careful to keep his voice quiet enough not to rouse Obscura. He wanted her to stay in the relief sleep could afford her. Nothing but pain waited in wakefulness.

"I'm hibernating."

His lips quivered with kept rage. "While we die... you're fucking *hibernating*?"

"Yes." Another gust of wind left her mouth on the tired sigh.

"Stop that!" he scowled as he tried to use his body to shield Obscura from the snowflakes.

She rolled, her hand thrown lazily over her brow. Lumi cracked open a single eye and peeked at him. "She will enjoy the cold better than the rancid humidity down here." Her voice was heavy with sleep and disinterest.

There was no point arguing. She looked like she would dismiss him before she found the energy for a battle of words. "Did you hear what we discussed earlier?"

Lumi yawned and stretched out before returning to her comfortable position. "Yes."

"And?"

"And..."

Jhaeros tried to calm his irritation. If they were going to escape, they needed her. She was the key to the door that slammed shut above them.

Obscura adjusted in his arms, the pressure on her back made her whimper. The sound tore at him. It sliced open his chest and punched at his heart. His stomach felt too low, his chest hollow as his heart rang like a gong. His brow furrowed at the physical reaction. The way he instantly adjusted her to ease her pain. So unlike him.

Lumi's brow cocked, her eyes open and more alert than he'd seen them at the sound. She stayed where she was, relaxed on the floor, but he could see the tension in her.

"The trial will be pushed back," she said with another yawn.

He pulled his attention away from Obscura and gave it back to Lumi.

Her face was propped on her hand as she lay on the stone floor, her ice piled beneath her in a snowstorm of blues and whites. "The witch will want her to suffer before she heals her."

"The witch?"

A nod was all she offered before she laid down, rolled on her back, and folded her hands on her stomach. "Everyone has to be in tip-top shape for the trials. As broken as beings return, she makes sure they're at one hundred percent come a new trial."

Sadistic bitch.

"And Obscura is one she enjoys to torment. She'll want her to sit in the pain she caused. Feel the throb of her aches like surges of power she commands."

His thumb traced slow circles on her upper arm as he held onto her. "Why?"

"Those who want power hate those who have it."

"Will you help us?"

A slow sigh left her lips as they vibrated together. "I suppose."

Relief made him almost giddy. It may not be breadcrumbs or pixie dust but with a yeti on their side, they may just free themselves from the hungry clutches of the impastusae witch.

Jhaeros

"How long have I been out?" Obscura's voice cracked.

"Shh," Jhaeros cooed. He gently adjusted his hold on her and tried his best to hide the joy he felt at seeing her eyes open. Her face was more swollen than it had been, dried blood caked her hairline and blue and purple bruises covered her dull brown skin.

"How long?" she repeated, her dark eyes lifted to focus on him.

It pained him to be unable to give her a clear answer. "Time avoids us here."

"Mm," she moaned. "Right."

A smile teased at his lips, but he pressed them thin to hide it. His thumb gently traced the line of her jaw as he leaned over her, his fatigue forgotten.

"Don't look at me like that." Her voice was tired, but that was nothing new. He revelled in the normalcy of it. Happy there was no signs of the witch's brutality in her voice.

"Like what?" His hand trailed up to rub the flesh behind her ear.

"Like you no longer see me as a monster. I'm still what I was yesterday... or whenever it was she took me." She wiggled slightly, putting the barest amount of distance between them before she hissed, her pain remembered, and resigned herself to remain in his hold.

She looked nothing like she did when she was taken, as odd as that seemed. He once again felt that pull in his chest he did when they first met, before he'd been so foolish as to judge her by the things he didn't know. By his ignorance, she would say. His eyes bore into her and he felt none of the disdain a part of him said he should, while the man who held her told him he'd be a fool to feel anything remotely close to aversion to the woman he was quickly beginning to see was wonderful.

She was fierce. Strong. Loyal. Smart. Funny... that was who she was. A tenebrae was just what moulded her flesh, not *who* she was. She was better than him, that realization hit him when he listened to the endless silence in her absence and knew he wouldn't put himself under the unforgiving hand of the witch for anybody. Wouldn't sacrifice the way she did without question.

There was a different kind of magic in that. A dignity few could obtain.

"Maybe..." his words fell away as he looked at her.

Obscura was beautiful even like this. Her eyes were fierce even as fatigue took hold of her. "Maybe I'm the one who's changed."

"Hmm," she hummed low as her eyes fell closed.

Silence built between them, and he was sure she'd fallen asleep.

For the first time since he ate the witch's pie, he felt content. The warmth of her in his eyes made him feel like they would survive whatever came next. He *wanted* her to survive whatever came next.

He really had changed.

"It's funny to think about the ways we change... adapt even." Her eyes remained closed as she spoke, her face turned into him so each exhale of her breath warmed his stomach through his thin shirt. "Not too long ago, I could taste the bitterness of your vitriol in the air. Now, I'm almost certain you like me."

"Perhaps before... I didn't know any better." He was ashamed that was true. That he could have lived such a long life and never stopped to stare long and hard at himself. At who he was and how his beliefs shaped him. At the monster he became while calling other beings the same thing.

"Before the pie..."

"Fucking pie."

Her exhale of breath was slightly humorous. "Help me up."

Jhaeros hesitated, unsure if getting her up was the best idea. He leaned down, his hand cupped lightly against the side of her face. "You should sleep."

"I'm not tired," she argued lightly.

He chuckled, the heat from her breath on his face something he was hard-pressed to admit he enjoyed. "Everyone is tired here."

"True enough." She looked up at Jhaeros. Her eyes widened as she took in how close his face was to hers.

A better man would have pulled away, but Obscura hadn't ever hesitated to tell him he wasn't a better man.

"If I didn't know any better, I would say you want to kiss me."

"You always do, Obscura." His tongue ran across his bottom lip.

"Know better? Than you? Always."

A sigh left him as he willed himself to pull back. "I do want to kiss you, Obscura. Somewhere between the moment I hit the bottom of the stairs and now, you've burrowed inside the depths of me and changed me from the inside. Shrouded my innards in your shadows, filled my brain with a darkness that keeps me from thinking about anything else but you. So yes, I want to kiss you, but as you said, I've changed."

"Have you now?" she murmured. Fatigue made her words turn to a whisper.

"Yes. Enough to know right now I don't deserve one. Not from you." As much as he wished he did.

Lips pursed, she tilted her head as much as his hold would allow. "A kiss from me is something I'm not sure if you'll ever deserve."

Jhaeros laughed lightly. "You're likely right." He dropped his brow to hers and inhaled her dark scent. "Sleep."

Obscura obliged him. Her eyes fell closed and her breathing levelled out. Sleep would be her friend now — as much as it would be theirs. They needed her asleep until their plan was ready to be set in motion.

He adjusted his hold on her, his eyes on her blue lips.

A kiss was something he didn't deserve from her, but maybe when all this was said and done, it was something he could earn.

Obscura

The pain was a welcomed escape. It reminded her of what she was and where she came from. A deep dark pit she could fall into, pressed in on all sides, tight enough to squeeze. The kind of endless pitch that caused anxiety to creep up in the core of most, accompanied by a tightness that brought helplessness.

It was blissful comfort as familiar to her as her own face.

As sad as it might seem to some, it was home.

She'd taken her existence for granted. Existed in the dark without feeling the delight hidden at the core of others' darkest miseries. Now the pain was bitter in a way that turned her stomach. Accompanied by a slow tracing of her arm, light enough to make her skin pebble.

The scent of hot filth slightly covered in a dusting of snow met her nose. Obscura inhaled deeply and let the scent assault her before she slowly opened her eyes.

Gold eyes bore down at her. Intensity made them swirl, like a storm of gilt flurries his pupils barely fought back.

Obscura cleared her throat and pressed a light hand to his chest as she felt the heat of his legs beneath her. She shoved lightly, forcing herself to sit. A low hiss left her as she put space between them, the cold that enveloped her a comfort that kissed at the pain. Vulnerability moved through her, the last conversation they had one that made her feel there was a shift in their dynamic. One she wasn't sure she could fully trust just yet.

Jhaeros kept his eyes on her. His lips pressed thin as he reached out a hand to steady her before he folded it into a fist. There were words trapped in his gaze, but even when he opened his mouth, he didn't set them free. His mouth clamped shut before he pressed the pads of his finger and thumb to his eyes and let out a long sigh.

The surrounding quiet made her heart stutter. It was never quiet down there, at least not like it was now. There was always a battle of rage as Dante fought against his chains, the slow snore of Lumi and the gust of winds that came with it, the whistle of snow flurries through tight spaces. Altie constantly moved, even in sleep. Restless. All of that was gone now.

Eyes wide, she shoved against the wall. Her balance was off, parts of her so bruised and broken, her body wouldn't move the way she wanted it to. Cold stone met her knees a split second before her hands did. Heat gripped her waist as Jhaeros tried to help her, but she swatted him away.

"Altie?"

"Obscura," Jhaeros whispered.

Her arms shook under her weight as she tried to crawl forward. "Altie," she moaned the mole shifter's name.

"Obscura. You were up there a while..."

Eyes closed, she shook her head and tried to think. The witch devoured all of Rane. Nothing but what was left in the broth of her cauldron remained of him. She'd watched her sit at that table, a banquet laid out for her alone, night after night.

How long, she didn't know. It felt like an eternity as much as it only felt like a day or two.

"Altie... she didn't come back from the last trial."

Panic stole her breath as she whipped around and looked at him. "No."

"She just..." Jhaeros stood next to her and reached out a hand like she was a feral thing he was desperate to calm. "She wasn't as strong as Dante or I, and with only the three of us within the illusion..." his words tapered away.

Anger forced her to her feet. "No. She never does a trial while I'm up there. She would have waited. She wouldn't have—" Her throat tightened. The truth of the matter was the witch was a wretched thing, and there was no way for Obscura to know what that witch would do. For a long time, new beings came in as often as one was stolen, but she'd changed. Decided she only wanted those left there. Picked them off like petals of the corpse of a flower.

"Obscura." There was a sadness in Jhaeros's voice she didn't know. It made her anxious.

With her feet finally beneath her, she stumbled down the hall.

Dante sat at the end. Heavy chains bound him, but they had no use. Not as he sat there with one arm lazily resting on his knee and his head hung in defeat. His dark eyes glistened. Shone.

"Dante." A fresh ache bloomed in her chest.

His eyes flicked up and met hers before they dropped back down to his feet. He picked up the iron chains, his thumb ran along the links, busying himself with a task so he wouldn't have to look at her again.

"Dante."

A single tear left his eye and trailed down his cheek. It settled in the nook by his nostril as he sniffled before he wiped it away with the back of his arm. His head cocked slightly to the side before it fell again. "I'm not you, Obscura. I couldn't protect her from the trials the way you did."

Her legs gave out. She slumped to the floor, legs folded under her as she stared at Dante. Her bottom lip quivered as her chest inflated. Sorrow was a balloon that filled her in a way her shadows never could. Her fingers clutched at the ground, but it did nothing to steady her as her shoulders heaved with the short breaths that found their way past the tightness in her throat.

Altie. Obscura's sweet girl. With her wide, doe eyes and her dirt-smeared face.

No. No!

"It all happened so quickly. I was so honed in on the tasks of the trial, I didn't think to keep an eye on her. She always burrows until the end, but the quakes kept uprooting the ground. Kept turning everything over. It was as if the witch knew and tried to keep her from the plan that always kept her safe. We couldn't... I didn't..." His face fell in his hands.

Her mind shuffled through the faces of all the beings she tried to help since she arrived in the den of an impastusae witch. All the weakened smiles, the whispered words, the tarnished hope they kept trying to shine after a trial was survived. Hands held, wounds tended to, tears wiped away. She lived a lifetime surrounded by illusion and bound by a witch. This dungeon had been all she was — all *they* were for so long, it was like time began there.

Altie's face stayed in her mind.

Sweet. Innocent. Humorous in the face of their woe. She was like a younger sister Obscura saw and immediately pulled into her bosom. She was hers in a way that wouldn't have made sense anywhere else but in captivity.

And she was gone.

The void opened.

Her darkness was a rolling fog that moved through her, swallowing up everything she couldn't use. It devoured the parts of her that knew better. The places where she tried to harbour tiny pieces of light she knew didn't belong to her, but she wanted to keep just the same. Obscura's anger had always been a ravenous thing, which was why she locked it away. Starved it.

Until now.

The latch on the cage inside her flipped open. It didn't happen in an explosion but in a slow roll of darkness. A black cloud that gradually covered the sun and stifled away every bit of light.

"Step back, Jhaeros," Dante warned.

Arms thrown out at her side, her head fell back. Her shadows were cold as they embraced her. A chill that tickled against her flesh like tiny cuts trying to get beneath it.

She was just so angry.

A plume of darkness swallowed her whole as the dungeon flickered. Threads of a new illusion wove at the edges. A sinister thing that would pull them away to their doom. She welcomed it, wanted the chaos so that she would have somewhere to direct her ire. So that she could take aim at something and revel in its destruction.

Vibrant colour cut into the darkness, a lure meant to make them feel a sliver of relief before it all went to shit. Before the witch attacked and cut them down.

Cold air cut down to the bone as a meadow was laid over the grim dungeon. Ice frosted the edges of the room. It quickly devoured the threads of illusion and kept the tapestry from being completed around them.

A shrill scream sounded as the ceiling above their heads vibrated.

"Loose my chains, Obscura," Dante growled.

She extended a hand and watched her hungry shadows feast. They wrapped around the thick chains and coated them in obsidian clouds before they fell away. Dante rotated his head on his shoulders. A hand rubbed at his throat where the heavy cuff once weighed down before he widened his stance. His own smoke billowed around him as he transformed from man to beast.

Excitement vibrated through her knowing what would come next. Free or dead, she would leave the clutches of the witch.

Thick snowflakes filled the air. It flurried down on them, coating the floor at their feet. Each step released a crunch under her weight as she walked down the hall to look at the empty place where Lumi often slept. The space was barren, nothing but a snow pile.

The threads of illusion pushed in again. Green wisps of magic licked at the frosted edges that froze its path. Another shrill scream shook the foundations.

"Are you ready to be rid of this place?" Obscura's voice was an echo of voices that didn't belong to her. It was an eerie thing, a worm in the ear of anyone who heard it that would burrow deep and pick away at their sanity.

Dante's hooves tapped against the stone as he moved to stand beside her. His bull head towered over hers, her head barely at his chest. A strong hand clasped her shoulder and squeezed a breath too tight.

Lumi stepped out of the shadows, surprising her, even through her fury. Careless expression covered Lumi's face as she waved a hand and a flurry of flakes was carried by a sharp wind up toward the trap door. "Shall we?"

Obscura stood at the bottom of the steps responsible for some of her aches. The sharp edges taunted her as she looked up at the door that would lead her to what she wanted now more than anything.

The witch.

Her nostrils flared as the stairs filled with darkness before the trap door exploded into kindling. She was going to make her pay. Was going to tear into her flesh until she was nothing more than aching wounds. She was going to strip her of all her magic, bathe her in a darkness the likes of which she had never dreamed, even in her darkest nightmares. Then… when all was said and done, she was going to watch her cook.

A wild smile stretched across her face, one that hinted the madness she'd hidden from her fellow captors. "We shall."

Jhaeros

Not for the first time since he ate that cursed pie and was thrown into the sick games the impastusae witch lorded over them, he was enraptured by Obscura.

Her power seemed immeasurable. Her ferocity impossible to contain. Dante had been right about her, she was a force Jhaeros would be foolish to keep at his back. She would only end up blowing him over trying to get to her goal. It was better to stand at her side, to marvel in all she could do.

Obscura was magnificent.

That thought made him still at the bottom of the steps as he watched Dante and Lumi follow her up. So quickly she had transformed from the hissed whispers of his people to something awe-inspiring. She was more than the tenebrae he'd often thought to be scavengers who fed off the toxic runoff of emotions burnt and destructive. She was — *Obscura.*

And he was about to bear witness to how magnificent she actually was.

Jhaeros willed his feet to move. He took the steps two at a time and burst up into the witch's dwelling.

It was... not what he was expecting.

The room was one of finery. Deep green brocade wallpaper decorated the walls with wood sconces alit with torches. Large wood framed windows made up the far wall, evenly spaced. They framed an expansive view of a forest so unlike the one he had wandered through before he befell this cursed place. It was paradise. With golden rays that kissed through the leaves of the trees and set the forest below aglow. Deer picked at berry bushes, while foxes scurried, and other creatures moved through the forest they called home, unburdened by the fear he felt like an oppressive punch to his chest when he took that first bite of pie.

Fear so effortlessly swallowed by an endless tired.

Warm light filtered into the room where chaises and other furniture were strategically placed. This was so like the homes of the aristocrats his parents would visit when he was a child. Proper, elegant, welcoming. A home worthy of their patronage.

A fire crackled in the hearth as the sound of laughter echoed through the room. *Children.*

Little feet tapped away at the hardwood, just out of sight. Jhaeros turned on his heel, looking around. He took a quick step toward the archway he knew led to a hall.

"There are no children here," Lumi drawled. Her shoulder leaned on the wall as she peered out the window. "Just another illusion."

"How can you be sure?" His heart skipped a beat at the thought of them leaving children behind in a house with a cannibalistic witch.

She pressed a palm to the wall. Frost coated her fingers before it spread, ate away at the scene like fire through paper, and showed the thick wood logs beneath. "For someone who seemed so content to be held in a higher regard than the likes of us, you're not very bright, are you?" Her mouth quirked, though her words were as stoic and removed as everything she said, there was humour on her face. "Just what would keep us from burning this place to the ground with that witch inside? Harming innocents, perhaps?"

Jhaeros turned to see they stood alone in the room, Obscura and Dante nowhere to be found.

"Just another illusion, Jhaeros. Clever enough to fool the likes of you, it seems." Shoved off the wall, she took heavy steps, her feet weighted down by something unseen as she disappeared through the archway.

A tickling urge to follow filled him for the span of a breath before he heard something clatter to the ground and another shrill scream.

Magic warred in the air. It left behind a sickly sweet smell strong enough to turn his stomach. The glamour of the witch's devoured magic shone at the edges. Worn paint she carefully applied, but that didn't hold to the wall as strongly in the places where shadows lurked. It was something so clear to him now as he paid attention, struck by Lumi's words of foolishness.

The yeti had long disappeared, bored by their new predicament. Dante's bellows ceased — swallowed up by the glamour, perhaps.

As much as Obscura swayed him to care about the odd combination of beings, he couldn't summon the energy required to seek them out. The only person on his mind was the very shadow beast that freed them.

Wisps of darkness settled in the places shadows lived. Too large and too deep. They were like a living thing that breathed as they ebbed and flowed. Millions of moving legs of insects scurried in place — waiting.

They smelt of sweet despair. A scent Jhaeros was quickly beginning to crave. A scent so *Obscura*.

A dusting of snow moved through the room. It made a shiver dance up his spine and reminded him of his task. They may have escaped the dungeon below and been spared the chaos of another trial, but they were not free of the witch yet.

His bare feet plodded along the floor, reminding him of just how he faired in the witch's tests. A wave of his hand gifted him fresh pants and boots. The change of attire such a small thing that brought back so much of the confidence of who he was. Reminded him of the fight he'd been forced to abandon below. His soiled and dishevelled cotton shirt tucked into the black of his pants. The ties at his neck opened as he rolled the sleeves up to the arms. He wasn't fully who he'd been before, and keeping the minor flaw in his usually well-kept look made him feel a reckless abandon he knew would serve him well. One that made him a part of the team absent now.

The house quaked.

The question of who was responsible was stolen from his mind as the glamour shifted. Gone were the rich furnishings, the thick and welcoming wallpaper, and the brilliant view of an ethereal forest. Everything shifted. Flipped. Was swallowed by a void of darkness and destitution.

Rotted floorboards took place of the polished hardwood. Cobwebs stretched over the corners of the room against walls decayed and greying. The black paint brushed over everything chipped at the corners, revealing more darkness beneath. Rancid stench filled the air, so potent he curled his nose at the sudden change. Outside the window was a dreary scene as rain pattered against the panes.

Gilt dust billowed around his open hand and his trusty dagger pressed into his palm.

The house cried under each step he took. The sound eerie as it echoed through the corridors, an alarm that let everything in the house know he was on the move. He didn't pause to adjust, determination fuelling each step that took him further away from the trap door in the floor and into the rest of the witch's dwelling.

Blackness climbed up, it covered his feet, hungry and desperate as it ascended up his legs to his knees. He felt the scratch of fingernails against the fine leathers of his boots. Hands that clamoured to hold on to him.

With each step, the glamour slipped further. A sign Obscura — wherever she was — was successful at her task.

Laughter lilted around him.

He turned on his heel to see the pink woman. Deinn. The bright pink of her flesh was dimmed, it peeled much like the pain of the walls around her jaw exposing her teeth beneath. The flesh of her body was in a similar state as she hummed to herself, arms stretched above her head as though she hung from chains unseen. Her wrists cocked uncomfortably as she swayed, her feet just off the ground.

"*In the seas where the waves are tumultuous, she called to the man on the ship...*" the haunted sound of her voice echoed around him, quiet, though it pushed painfully into his ears. "*Enraptured by the song that vibrated the waves, his hand beneath the surface did dip.*"

A haunting sea shanty came from her lips.

"*Her heart was an aching but desperate thing, it wanted for all she did see,*" a deep baritone joined her as Rane stepped out from one of the rooms and into the hall. His white long hair fell against his back, though his ocean blue skin was a grey now. A patch of bare skull peaked through the thinned hair. His left eye was gone as he turned to look at Jhaeros before he smiled up at Deinn. He limped with each step, his right foot turned at the wrong angle.

She returned his smile, a sad version of joy on her face. It was a macabre scene. Happiness wrapped in death, painted up pretty with rays of joy and music. It made his chest ache.

"*Her love she would drown him in if he wasn't careful, and she wished for a moment he'd flee,*" Deinn continued.

Jhaeros felt the creep of unease move up his spine. "You're not real."

A giggle left her, as she turned. A bone pressed up against the flesh of her neck as she did, her head tilted unnaturally, though the smile remained. "Are we not?"

"No."

"Though the trials were nothing more than illusions, were the consequences not real?" she asked.

Muscles flexed against his jaw.

"Am I not real, Jhaeros?"

His brow furrowed. She hadn't known his name, there hadn't been enough time to give it to her. "No, you're not."

"Hmm," she hummed in her throat. "And yet, my consequences will be real enough to tear the flesh from your bones."

"Real enough," Rane echoed. His eerie smile stretched too wide and made the flesh from his cheek rip and peel.

Fucking hell, he was going to have to kill these two all over again.

The thought perturbed him. It felt like a betrayal even though he owed them nothing. That in itself was curious. It was something that would have never crossed his mind before — *her.*

Damn tenebrae. The curse lacked the vitriol he usually had when addressing different species. This was playful. Different. He grinned at just how much he'd changed.

A wave of magic moved through the hall. It coated everything and transformed the remnants of Rane and Deinn into the versions he knew from the dungeon and the illusions. They were bright and alive before they weren't. Back to the rotting flesh they were.

The rattling of chains sounded, whispers too far away to hear as Deinn moved closer to him. The piece of flesh from her face fell to the floor as she grinned.

Dark water rose. It surged around his feet and covered his boots to the ankles as Rane reached out a hand and brushed his knuckles against her cheeks. "Are you hungry, pet?"

"Ravished." Her teeth chattered.

"Tell me what you want?" He leaned into her, his rotted brow pressed against hers.

Her intake of breath was a sharp moan. "I want him to swim."

Jhaeros coughed. Water spurted from his mouth as it filled his lungs. His eyes widened as he pressed an open palm to his chest and tried to undo whatever magic the water elemental trapped him in.

An exasperated sigh sounded as he dropped to a knee. Lumi's arms crossed over her chest as she looked down at him. Her lips vibrated together, eyes lazy. "His magic isn't even at full strength," she drawled. "Weren't you going on about how much better you were than everyone else because of your breeding or some such nonsense?"

His mouth opened and water poured out. "Help," the word bubbled from his throat.

An annoyed sigh left her as she rolled her eyes dramatically. A mere flick of her wrist turned both Rane and Deinn to ice. Frost held them suspended as air whooshed into his lungs.

Jhaeros dropped to his knees, hands braced on the floor as he coughed up whatever water was left in his lungs. "What's your problem?" he huffed, voice ragged.

"My problem?"

"You sleep through the trials, ignoring everyone and now you just stand there and watch me almost drown. Are you psychotic?" His voice lacked the vehemence he wanted to shoot at her.

Her shoulders lifted. "I'm supposed to be hibernating."

"What?"

"This whole *cannibal witch and desperate to survive prisoners* thing has really harshed my sleep pattern. This has been a huge inconvenience."

His eyes widened as he forced himself to his feet. "Are you telling me you weren't sleeping because of the witch?"

"No."

Jhaeros swallowed his anger. "You could have left any time you wanted?"

"Yes."

His teeth ground together with an intensity that threatened to grind them to dust. His left eye twitched as he wrapped his hands into fists he reminded himself he shouldn't throw at the yeti. He had yet to fully comprehend her power and the last thing he wanted was to be knocked on his ass by a woman who wasn't even fully awake.

"Are you fucking with me?" he hissed.

Lumi cocked a brow before she rubbed at her eye. She blinked her bleary eyes to clear them and frowned. "No. You're not my type."

"Fucking yeti!" he cursed. "Fucking *pie*!"

She waved a hand before her as she turned away from him, her dismissal further rattling his faculties. "Follow the darkness to Obscura."

Right. The sooner he found Obscura the sooner he would be rid of this cottage and the irksome situation. He could yell at Lumi later — not that she'd care she earned his ire.

He followed Lumi through the doorway but was met with nothing but a flurry of snow, a hallway in the same state of decay, and an ominous howl.

"Fuck."

Jhaeros

The chaos was a trail he followed easily. He took the steps up to the second level of the house, where Dante's bellowing could be heard. Shadows moved like black smoke up the railings and along the walls. Plumes that ebbed and flowed into themselves over and over.

"Dante," Obscura's voice was a warning.

A thud sounded before the floor vibrated beneath his feet.

"Move!" she urged.

A roar shook all the doors on their hinges. Jhaeros followed the sound to the door at the end of the hall and slammed it open. The knob shattered as it hit the wall and littered bone fragments on the ground at his feet.

The ceilings were angled like the roof of the house. The single window against the back wall was a circle covered in grunge and grime. Black, thick candles lined the outside of the large room. Green flames flickered from the wicks, the smoke that rose the same sickly green. It made the room look ominous.

Chains crept up from the cracks in the floor. Massive irons that lashed at Dante, tried to bind him to keep him from the thrall of action in the room. He fought against them, weight leaned forward as his hooves scraped against the floor.

He scanned the room, but Lumi was nowhere to be found.

"Damn yeti," he murmured under his breath.

Obscura had no weapon. She held her hands outstretched beside her, palms parallel to the floor as streams of shadows poured from them. Her braids lifted around her head, only her toes touched the floor as shadows seeped out of her eyes and made her look like a vision of barely contained darkness. The shadows circled the witch as she tried to battle back.

Stitched hands poked out from her open sleeves, the tips of her fingers black as the scent of fae, elemental, caster, and even demonic magic enveloped her. It was a whirl of colour slowly being devoured by shadows.

A hiss left the witch. An odd click came from her mouth as her sleeves slipped down to her elbows and revealed a tapestry of flesh. Blue, purple, orange, browns and pinks all stitched together.

The sight made his stomach churn.

Dante bellowed.

Jhaeros whipped out a hand. His magic surrounded the chains and kept them from pulling the minotaur to his knees. The dark irons were alit with Jhaeros's gold magic before they burst into dust that lit the room in an ethereal glow that didn't fit the haunting scene.

A shrill scream left the witch as Obscura's shadows became too much for her to bear.

"Leave us!" Obscura warned again.

Dante snorted his stubbornness. "No."

"Dante."

As the shadows bore down on the witch, she lunged.

Jhaeros leapt into the room. The breath left his lungs as he slammed hard into a wall of shadows. He could see through them like a dense fog as Obscura fell back, toppling a candle. Green flames bit into the rotted hardwood as their positions switched and Obscura wrapped her hands around the witch's throat.

"You killed her!" she yelled. "You killed them all!"

Dante stood desperate beside him. His hands came up to press into the shadows, but it was no use. Jhaeros beat his fists against the shadows as he watched the flames devour the room like kindling.

"Obscura!"

His heart hammered in his chest as he pushed his magic against hers and felt its easy resistance. He couldn't get through, not while she burned with anger.

'We have to get her out of there!' Dante spoke into his mind.

Helplessness held him by the throat.

Obscura's fists wrapped around the front of the witch's robe. The anger on her face was something that would have made him sneer at her before, that would have further labelled her the monster he believed her to be, but all it did now was make him want to save her from it. To find a way to douse it so she didn't look so thoroughly gutted.

'Jhaeros!'

"Okay." He paused his pummelling of the shadows to think. "Okay, I have an idea but you have to listen to me."

The minotaur paused, glowing red eyes taking him in as he considered. *'Okay,'* he agreed.

He dropped his voice low, unsure of whether Obscura could hear him as she lifted the witch and slammed her against the floor again and again. "Bring her," he whispered.

Dante paused.

"Trust me." It was a hard thing to ask, until recently, he knew he wasn't exactly trustworthy. He'd been out for himself, content to let them all die if it meant he would escape. How quickly that changed. He wasn't even sure when it happened.

Dante hesitated a moment before he disappeared down the hall.

Jhaeros could do nothing but watch until he returned. Each second held an eternity in it. Despite knowing it wouldn't work, he pressed his palms against the erected shadows and willed his magic to muddle through. His teeth ground together at the resistance. At the way his magic bounced off hers, no match for its depths.

Pride bloomed in his chest. She was magnificent. Not because she seemed powerful beyond what he felt she could be, but because she was fearless. Because she was loyal and loving, and reached for the people she cared about, even if she didn't realize she did it. So ready to sacrifice for them. Die for them. Kill for them.

Fuck. His eyes widened.

Jhaeros was already lost to her. His heart was erratic as it banged against his ribs, just as desperate to be free as he was to get past her protective shadows.

She had grown on him.

Fuck.

Hooves interrupted his inner musing. Dante stood beside him, his presence as powerful as the wall before them. He rested a hand on the wall, as though it would have changed from the time he left. A grunt left him as he stepped slightly to the side.

"Obscura?"

The small voice was like an axe that sliced through the chaos. Everything froze as tension filled him to bursting.

A brown hand with dainty fingers and long, pointed nails pressed against the wall of shadows. "Obscura."

Obscura's grip remained tight in the front of the witch's robe, but her head snapped to look at them. Her mouth dropped open, surprise wiped some of the darkness from her face, pulled it back, tucked some of it away. "Altie?"

Altie shoved a shaky hand into her bush of pink hair. "Yes." Her head tilted, nerves clear as she struggled to meet Obscura's gaze through the shadows. "Obscura, I—"

"You're—"

"Alive," Jhaeros interrupted as a part of the roof crumbled behind Obscura and the witch. "She's alive, but you have to get out of there!"

She blinked, the action slow with a slight shake of her head like she was trying to clear her mind of the shadows that spread there as easily as they'd taken over the room. Her head whipped around, eyes wide as she realized just how much of the space the witch's flames had devoured.

He turned to Dante, the vision of Altie alive and well enough to pull Obscura from her fury. "Take her, Dante," Jhaeros commanded. "Keep her safe."

"With my life." The minotaur huffed, his eyes on Obscura, though his arm wrapped around Altie's waist and lifted her. She squealed, surprised as he took a step back in retreat.

"Wait," she protested.

Altie's pleas were ignored as she was carried away from the flames and out of the house to safety.

Jhaeros turned to look at Obscura. Her eyes were wide as she stared at the empty place where Altie stood before being scooped away. Her dark eyes glassed over as her chin wrinkled. Emotions waged through her, and she battled to keep her faculties as the witch squirmed beneath her. Her attention dropped, but some of her wrath dripped away.

"They'll not leave," the witch hissed.

Dante's chaotic bellows sounded below as the ground shook beneath them. Whatever illusions she put in place to try to keep them within her cottage, Jhaeros was sure Dante just plowed through, likely taking out a wall on his exit.

Heat pressed through the shadows against his face. The small space where Obscura straddled the witch was one of the few places in the room not engulfed in flames.

"Obscura." He tried to keep his hand from shaking as he rested it on the wall between them. "Listen to me, this place is coming down. We need to get out of here."

"Out." Her eyes were distant as she repeated the word, her voice hollow.

Teeth bared, he kept his voice steady and calm. "Obscura."

Her gaze flicked down to the witch. "We'll get out."

The hood covering her head slipped back. The face he'd only seen cast in complete shadows was finally brought to light, the sight one that wrinkled his nose. She was a tapestry of stolen flesh. One of her eyes was milky white. No iris or pupil. The flesh beneath was sunken, it left a black void, its depths one he couldn't measure. The other eye was a vibrant green that matched her flames. Her nose was teal, slight, with the nostrils narrow and vertical like a siren's or a finfolk. Her mouth was too wide. It stretched the entire length of her face and almost met ears that were pale and pointed. The teeth in her mouth were jagged and blackened by the gums. Thick stitchings wove over her face. Her blackened fingertips pressed against Obscura's chest as she tried to will her magic into her.

Panic flared in his chest. He still didn't know the extent of the witch's power.

Obscura hissed and her wall wavered, but she held on and leaned in. "And I'll make sure everything in these woods hears your screams as you're trapped here in flames of your own making."

A final explosion of magic separated them. Obscura flew back through the flames and slammed against the wall.

The barrier between Jhaeros and the room disappeared as her hand whipped out, the other braced against the floor. Shadows wrapped around the witch's wrists and pulled her back against the opposite wall. It bound her hands above her head and hung her suspended much like Deinn appeared to be.

A shrill scream left her mutilated lips as she kicked her bare and blackened heels against the fiery wall behind her, flames licking at her stolen flesh.

Jhaeros dove into the room. He waved a hand and doused the flames that ate at Obscura's clothes, though it did nothing for the rest of the room. He reached out and wrapped an arm around her waist. The feel of her in his arms sent a wave of relief through him, even as she squirmed and pointed an angry finger at the bound witch.

Her shadows coaxed the flames, fed them.

"You'll burn, witch! Cook like everyone you've trapped here." It was a promise as it left her lips.

Jhaeros hissed as the flames licked at him, hot enough to burn without even touching his flesh.

"And the sound of your screams will be..." She sucked in a shaky breath that transformed into a manic laugh. "A lullaby that soothes my soul on nights when nothing else can." Her eyes fell closed as her head rested on his chest. "Burn."

Jhaeros carried her out of the room, the sounds of the witch's screams music to his ears.

Obscura

Her breath heaved as she watched the flames devour the witch's cottage. The illusion she held over the woods burned to ash alongside it. Embers lifted from the green, lush grass at their feet. They devoured the trunks of the trees until the glamour was stripped away and all that was left behind was a sickly, eerie wood. The magic there leached from the very soil and made it a diseased thing.

A scream rang through the air. Constant and tormented.

"I just saved your sorry ass," Jhaeros grinned.

All the negative feelings that had thrown her into the darkest depths of her shadows pulled back to the place where she kept them when she met his gaze. Playfulness danced in his gold eyes as she returned his grin. "Two things you need to know about me; one, I am rarely sorry and this isn't one of the instances when I am, and two, I had everything well underway. I would have succeeded too... if you hadn't intervened," she repeated the words he'd said to her once. Back when he still had his head shoved up his rear.

"In dying," he retorted with a smile.

"Perhaps that's just what I wanted to succeed at."

Something weighted moved between them that stole her breath. She watched as wisps of darkness were sucked from the world, settled in her skin, and found home wherever it was she kept them. His gilt eyes glistened, sparkling and beautiful as she tilted her face up and smiled at him. Gone were the wounds the witch made her endure. Dull, blemish-free brown flesh stretched over her firm jaw, her high cheekbones, and the expanse of bare flesh of her belly seen through the burnt tatters of her shirt.

He inhaled sharply and took a hesitant step toward her. "I think you..."

"Yes?"

"I think you've infected me with your shadows," he rasped, humour in his accusation.

"Is that right?" She tilted her head, her long braids falling over her bare shoulder.

"Yes. That's right."

Lips pursed, she took a step toward him. "Whatever will we do about that?" It was odd, to be flirting with a man she'd thought about running through with a broken bone. The same man she wanted to torment, to watch squirm, if only to wipe that cocky grin off his face. He was insufferable — or he had been before the witch threw her back in the dungeon. Before she lay in his arms and listened to him whisper to her in the dark, never fully asleep.

Before he confessed to seeing himself as she'd seen him, and knowing he needed to change. Admitted how easily she'd changed him. Declared he would do whatever it took to keep her safe, to free her from the confines of the witch so she wouldn't have to suffer under her hands any longer.

It was a promise he kept.

"In time, I hope to live as well amongst the shadows as you do." Jhaeros grinned. His last step closed the space between them.

Her brow rose as she swallowed hard. The heat of his chest brushed against hers. "You wouldn't survive me."

"I'm not foolish enough to think I could, but maybe in time I can earn you letting me live."

"Maybe..."

"Obscura."

Everything in her tensed as her eyes widened.

Timid hands pulled at her fingers as the toe of her shoe dug into the ground at her feet. Wide eyes glistened with the threat of tears as her throat bobbed when a hard swallow dragged through it. "I knew it was wrong..." Altie started. "To deceive you."

Obscura's mouth gaped open as she took a jolted step forward. Her hand grabbed at Altie's hand, wanting to make sure she was not just another illusion meant to crack at her already splintered soul. Not another way meant to break her. When she felt the warmth she knew covered in a layer of grime, a shaky breath left her.

"You and Lumi were the only ones who could escape, but you had to get angry enough to let your magic do what it does best." The corner of Altie's bottom lip pulled between her teeth as she looked everywhere but at Obscura. Her nostrils quivered before she sniffled. "It may have been a little selfish of me, but I couldn't listen to her tear into you again. I wouldn't have survived it."

A possessive hand clasped behind Altie's neck. Their eyes met, and she stared into pools of kept misery. A chill filled her chest before it slowly warmed. Her head dropped, and she pressed her brow to Altie's.

How could she be angry with them? They were right. Had she not unleashed the darkest parts of her to free them from the witch's clutches, Altie would have been the next one gone. She could only hide away from the trials for so long, and without Obscura there to ensure her survival, she would have been another body boiled in the witch's cauldron.

Her stomach turned at the thought.

"You live." The words felt silly as she shut her eyes and breathed her in.

"Yes." Altie held Obscura's wrist as it held her close. "Thanks to Jhaeros and his plan."

Altie smelt of turned soil. Fresh and wonderful. Obscura felt the remnants of it on her brow as she held onto her, so afraid that the moment she released her, she would fade away to nothing but her memories. Tears captured on her lids as she squeezed her eyes shut and forced herself to release a shuttered breath.

"I suppose I should thank him then. For helping us... despite our differences."

"Foolish notions implanted in a mind too young to see the err." Jhaeros stepped forward. She didn't open her eyes to look at him but felt the way his presence pushed against hers. The smell of him was clean and magical. Hyacinth carried on a breeze of pixie dust. "I have you to thank for my newfound clarity, Obscura."

"And what clarity have you found, Jhaeros?"

The deep rumble of his voice stirred her in a way she wished didn't, but she couldn't fight against. "I've realized you're something far more marvellous than anything I've come upon in all my years. That your splendour has everything to do with who you are and not *what* you are. That you've a heart as deep as the shadows that spared us. And that... I'm sorry."

Her eyes fluttered open, and she turned slightly, her brow still pressed against Altie's. "You? You're *sorry*?"

"Yes," he admitted as he took another step toward them.

His apology was something she didn't expect. Not out here, back in the world that divided them. Down in the dungeon, it was easy to forget who they were. What they were. Death breathed at the back of their necks, the goosebumps his breath brought reminded them how easily their lives could be stripped away. In the dark with the end in sight, it was easy to want things merely because they were there. Because there may not be another chance to want for something and actually get it.

With freedom all around them, an apology from Jhaeros was the last thing she expected.

"It pains me to look back on the person I was before... the pie."

A smile quirked up the corner of her lips. "It was good pie."

"Yeah, that's how they get you. Good pie," Altie agreed.

Obscura laughed and released her hold on Altie's neck so she could pull her under her arm and into her side. "Not really worth all this, but definitely the best pie I've had. Hands down."

Dante's head fell back as a laugh rumbled through him. "If I never have another slice of pie again, it would be too soon."

"Agreed." Jhaeros's eyes trapped hers.

They all looked worse for wear, like they'd crawled out of one of Altie's holes, alive after a trial.

Altie wandered toward Dante. She giggled lightly as he swooped her off her feet and into his arms.

Tension made her mind a useless thing as she stared at Jhaeros. He looked so unlike the man she barely began to know. Muscles flexed over his jaw as he adjusted his weight from foot to foot, his thumb hooked in the top of his pants. Something akin to bashfulness made his eyes look vulnerable as they whipped from Dante and Altie, to her and then down to the ground.

His hand rubbed at the back of his neck as he cleared his throat. "Deception is—"

"Usually how you get things done, I'm sure," Obscura interrupted.

"That used to be true," he admitted.

"It's not anymore?"

"Hopefully, that will change too."

The way he stood there, vulnerable in his confessions, she had a feeling it would.

Jhaeros

Flames as hungry as the impastusae witch lit up the night sky as they devoured the cottage, quaint and luring. The very cottage that snared them all. It was a beautiful sight, made sweeter still by the shrill shriek that came from inside. It would be a slow death for that wretched woman.

Evil died slow.

Obscura took his hand. She threw it casually over her shoulder before she burrowed under his arm and leaned into him, their fingers laced together. She tilted her face up, a smile beamed through the soot and grime as her dark eyes took him in.

Surprise rippled through him at her affection.

"That wasn't so hard," she joked.

Altie shook the dirt from her shoulders and adjusted her goggles before she pushed them off his face and onto her brow. Her nose twitched as she pulled her eyes from the flames and looked at them. "Piece of cake, really."

"Piece of pie," Dante snorted.

Jhaeros's eyes narrowed.

"What?" He lifted his massive shoulder and ran his hand under his nose, rattling the large gold ring there. "Too soon?"

Obscura's lips vibrated as she shook her head. A snort escaped her as she chuckled, low and deep. "Dante, you are something else."

He winked at her, a wide smile on his face as he threw the axe over his shoulder and pulled Altie into him. She yelped before she stumbled into his side. "I like you, Obscura. Your dark and twisted heart understands my humour. That's why I have every intention of keeping you."

The careless words and how easily Dante offered them made Jhaeros tense. It was hard for him not to be overcome with possessive jealousy. He wasn't sure he would stand there with this woman, the very woman who ripped open his chest and reached in to capture his heart in her hands. There had been instances where he wasn't sure they would make it out alive, as determined as he was. Where he wouldn't change enough to earn her acceptance.

Flakes of snow slowly flustered around them and it stole his attention before Dante smiled at him. "I'm keeping you too, you wet blanket." He tightened his hold on Altie as she batted a hand against his massive forearm.

"That's too tight, you big oaf!" she sputtered. "You're going to kill me."

"I would never kill you," he argued lightly as he pressed a kiss on the top of her head so hard she shrunk under the force. "How would I keep you if I killed you?"

"You're keeping me too, then?" she asked as she shoved at his arm. "Dante!"

He loosened his hold. "Of course I am. I can't very well let my family go off on their own, especially knowing how much we need one another."

Jhaeros's brows rose. "Do we?"

"Of course we do," Dante scoffed. "None of us would have escaped that hag alone."

"Speak for yourself." Lumi walked out of the shadows. Her eyes were still heavy with fatigue as she dragged a hand against her lids. She lifted her icy blue eyes, vibrant despite the haze of sleep, and looked at him. "I would have been out of there no problem."

There was no doubt in his mind that was true.

If it hadn't been for Lumi, they all might have still been beneath the witch's house, trapped in another illusion that would determine their fate. What surprised him was that she remained in the witch's clutches for so long.

Lumi was an enigma, one he wasn't sure he would ever figure out. "Why *did* you stay down there then?" he asked.

Her shoulder lifted. "It doesn't matter so much where I hibernate."

"It was a witch's dungeon. One who meant to eat you," he argued.

"Meant to... but never would have." Lumi scrunched her face as though the very idea of the witch ever getting close to eating her was preposterous. "Her hospitality wasn't all bad. I got to fill my belly with a massive feast before my sleep."

"Lumi... you can't be serious," Altie gasped.

"Did you not like the food?" Lumi's brow furrowed in confusion. "It wasn't the *best*, but very close. That roasted lamb was divine."

They all stared at the yeti wide-eyed. She was mad. Completely out of her mind, of that, Jhaeros was sure. Complimenting the witch on her cooking...

His mouth gaped, but he decided it best to leave it alone.

Dante scooped a fighting Altie off the floor and held her under his arm as she beat his chest before he walked over and picked up Lumi. "You're unhinged... I love it. That's why I'm keeping you too!"

Ice covered his arm.

Dante yelped before he released his hold on her, a pout on his lips as he shook his arm, frozen from his elbow to his wrist. "Hey! Undo it, Lumi."

"Why don't you wander closer to the fire?" she suggested, then held up a hand to stop him. "Without Altie."

He hesitated before he gently placed Altie on the ground and stalked back to the witch's cottage, still engulfed in flames.

"Thanks." Altie grinned as she shoved the goggles that fell from her brow back up in place.

Lumi gave her a nod.

"So..." Altie toed the ground at her feet. "What now?"

He had a life before all this, one none of these people would fit into, and yet, none of that mattered. Not anymore. The thought of walking away from Obscura gutted him, and something told him she had no plan to abandon the ragtag team before him now. His eyes dropped to take her in, waiting.

Whatever answer she gave would be the one he followed.

Her arm wrapped around his middle, waking all the butterflies in his belly from their slumber. "I'm sure there's another adventure out there for us somewhere." Obscura grinned, her sharp teeth on display.

Lumi rolled her eyes. "Pass."

"No passing!" Dante wrapped his arm around her shoulders and pulled her back into his chest. His lips pressed to the top of her head, clearly not having learned his lesson. He shivered as snow flurried around him, but didn't release his hold.

A yawn stretched her mouth as she blinked slowly and leaned into him. "I could do with some rest."

Obscura laughed, the sound was a string that pulled at his heart. "More rest? Really?"

"Yes," she retorted. "It was impossible to get any sleep with all the constant shrieking and blubbering."

"Well, excuse us for fighting for our lives." Obscura's face was alight with humour. "I'm used to being the one making beings scream. This was a change of pace for me."

Jhaeros captured her chin between his knuckle and thumb and tilted her head up. He hovered his lips above hers and shuddered when she breathed shadows into his mouth. "I'm sure there will be time enough to wrestle screams from me."

Obscura planted her hand and smooshed his face before she pushed him away. "Don't be fooled by my affection. You haven't earned a kiss yet."

"I will," he promised.

"Ugh." Lumi groaned, even though her eyes were closed. "Gross."

The shrieking ceased, and they stood in a soft snowfall and silence. He had so many plans for this woman, plans he wanted to start immediately. "I have a place," he told them. "A place where we'll all be comfortable."

Altie's nervous demeanour shifted as she smiled. "Really? We're staying together?"

Obscura pulled Altie toward her. She stepped out of Jhaeros's hold and he immediately felt her absence, but didn't argue as she wrapped her arms around Altie's shoulders and held onto her. "Of course, because like Dante, I've decided I'm keeping you. All of you."

Altie's feet danced under her, jostling them both as Altie's hands wrapped around Obscura and she shrieked with excitement.

Unable to keep his distance, he stepped into them and wrapped his arms around them both.

Fine. They may not be worthless wastes of skin and magic like he first thought them to be. In all honesty, they'd all burrowed their way into his chest and found a home.

Dante lifted Lumi onto his back and held her wrists against his chest. Her sleepy cheek rested on his shoulder as her soft snoring began. Dante stepped toward him, his brawny arm encasing the group until Jhaeros thought the air would be squeezed from his lungs.

"Alright, alright, you big lug. Release us before you finish the job the witch started. Come on..."

Dante obliged, adjusting his hold on Lumi so he held her legs at his sides.

He snatched Obscura back into his hold as he turned and took his first steps away from what he thought was a nightmare, but may just have been a blessing in disguise. She held onto Altie, keeping her arm wrapped around her shoulders as they fell into step beside him. Dante took two steps and quickly fell in line next to them. Lumi's snores were a soothing soundtrack in the air, light snow coating the tops of their heads.

This may not have been what he had in mind when he had visions of a family, but he couldn't imagine starting one without them.

All of this... because of an impastusae witch's pie. The thought made him chuckle. It really was the thing of stories.

"Let's go home."

About SJ Stewart

S.J. Stewart is a Canadian author who lives in the bustling city of Toronto with her husband and toddler. She wrote her first novel when she was sixteen that now lays in a dust covered pile with most of her other manuscripts, and never stopped writing, though she didn't get around to publishing her first book until 2021. She is a genre jumper and dabbles in everything, but her published work is Adult Fantasy, Billionaire Romance, and Dark Romance.

Her goal is to get all the stories out of her head before they slowly drive her to madness.

A Song of Steel and Shadow

HER VICIOUS BEASTS
THE BEGINNING

E.P. BALI

About the Book

In a world of vicious beasts, if you are not a predator, you are prey.

Aurelia Aquinas is a discarded girl. Forced to live a life of isolation, she is forbidden to speak of her powers and forbidden to find her soul-bound mates.

She awaits the day she can escape to a human college and live a life free and away from her father and the beasts that might come after her.

But when she is called to heal and injured beast, locked away in a dungeon, the course of her life changes forever.

This is book 0.5 in Her Vicious Beasts, a contemporary fantasy spicy shifter MMMFM WhyChoose series with a lot of plot and a lot of heart. It is best suited to readers 18+.

Tropes: Found family, fated mates, shifters, prison/captivity

Advisory

Please be aware of the following triggers:

Profanity, abuse by a parent, assault, murder, explicit scenes, mention of torture, Misogynistic society

Aurelia

My vibrator is broken.

Pressing the on/off button aggressively over and over again does nothing. Neither does changing the batteries. I swear under my breath, tossing the cheap pink silicon towards the end of my bed where it bounces off my faded purple coverlet and onto the floor with a *thunk*, almost knocking over my huge stack of thrift store romance novels.

That tiny saviour of a device had been the cheapest I could find on my limited budget, and I can't afford to get a replacement. A heavy blow, to be sure.

Morning beams of sunlight stream through my tattered curtains and I fling an arm over my eyes for a single moment of mourning before I have to get up for the day.

An orgasm—fuelled by Draco and Hermione fanfiction—is the best way to recharge my powers, and the one highlight of my miserable days. I'll now have to settle for being a little lethargic and irritable until I can get back home tonight for a proper self-care session. My anima prowls under my skin, annoyed and demanding release, but the poor beast inside of me will just have to make do. She's been particularly jumpy lately, but I'm sure it's all to do with me leaving town soon.

Reaching for the phone on my bedside table, I open up my *Animalia Today* news app and check the latest:

A rabid wolf serial killer has finally been caught, many thanks to the Lioness Moms United Retrieval Team. His head is on display at the front of their headquarters for all to see.

Relations between the human population and Animalia are "better than ever" according to the Council's latest reports.

There's a missing dragon, heir to the Drakos line, who appears to have gotten caught up in some underground crime ring.

The Deputy Headmaster of Animus Academy is being praised for his feral youth rehab program.

Political nonsense, *yada yada*. Council of Beasts ass kissing, *yada yada*.
Nothing new.

I only have two weeks of summer holidays left before I leave for college. An actual *human* college. For the first time in seven years, I'm actually excited about something. After I finished high school, I did an online course on advancing my healing skills where I did super well, so that got me a scholarship at an interstate college. My bags are already packed. I'm making a life for myself, *by* myself and I couldn't be prouder.

When I turned twenty earlier this year, I was officially an animalia adult meaning that freedom from my father is on the horizon. After moving states, I'll join the local branch of the Court of Wings and get to live my life away from him forever.

I only have to survive fourteen days in my aunt's shop.

When I turned thirteen, my dad made an agreement—well, let's be real—had *ordered* my aunt that I was to work in her store every day after my schoolwork was done. Now that I no longer needed a guardian, I'm to work there until I leave for college. In exchange, I get a tiny allowance to cover food and am allowed to stay in this one-bedroom rustic affair, one huff and puff away from falling apart. The paint is peeling in every one of the three rooms and the living room ceiling leaks during even in the lightest of rain, but it is mine to do with as I please.

Which is just as well because I'm not allowed to leave it for anything other than work.

It's a way for my father to keep me in my place. To show me where I belonged after I hit puberty and it was revealed that I'd taken my mother's genes and my anima was *not* a serpent like everyone had hoped. Father moved me out of home, I got kicked out of the Serpent Court, removed as serpent heir and put here, out of sight but still under his thumb.

I'm forbidden from speaking about my mother and the genes I inherited from her. In fact, I'm forbidden to speak to any animalia at all unless it involves one of the occasional jobs I do for my father.

But nothing can stop me now, and I grin at the thought of finally making some friends at college as I haul myself out of bed and into the bathroom. I just manage to shower and get my work clothes on before a tingle of warning shoots through me.

Someone is walking through the shield I've set at the perimeter of the house. I stand to attention, heart pounding, simply listening to the dreaded panging of my heart.

There is only one person in the entire world who could get past one of my shields and simply walk onto this property.

Just one.

Aurelia

Panicking, I dart from my bathroom into my tiny living room just in time to see the front door slam open and two of my father's lackeys skulk in. I stiffen, frozen to the spot as the two women, wiry and hunched, dressed in black overcoats and black jeans, check my house for threats, looking anywhere but me. They both wear black lipstick and heavy black eyeliner, paired with glossy black lips. The snakes of my father's court prefer this style of fashion. In general, animalia always liked to dress to the style of their order, so there are always telltale signs of what beast they are:

Lions always wear their hair long, often braided; males and females both.

Eagles and other birds choose spikey hair styles, mohawks and so on.

Wolves love denim on a religious level, and their men always wear short beards.

Part of this is so other animalia can discern who they're dealing with quickly. We can usually tell via scent, but human perfumes and other conflicting smells in public make that difficult.

With their tongues darting out, tasting the air in the habit of half feral reptiles, my dad's servants come to stand on either side of my front door.

I stand facing them in a sort of lame disbelief as two tall males come in next—security guards by the guns they openly carry at their waists. They give me a droll look before bracketing the women to stand against the wall, their arms crossed, eyes staring over my head.

My heart threatens to leap right out of my ribcage.

This is *very* bad.

He's come himself with his full contingent—as if I'm some foreign court member and this is a formal meeting. The warning bells are loud in my head. Either he has one last big job for me, or something much worse.

I haven't always feared him. He had been a good dad when his hopes for me were grand. But the same day my anima was revealed, he'd gone from doting father to cruel taskmaster in the space of minutes.

With his presence announced, my father comes in next, striding through the door in military-grade black boots. He is a wraith of a man, far too tall and far too lean, his cheeks hollowed out, deep bags under his eyes—as if the King Cobra bore some great worldly burden on his shoulders. But I know better. That was the weight of black magic, and he used it like an addict. We look a little similar, I suppose; I get my olive skin and dark hair from his side of the family and I'm thin from my diet of two-minute noodles and the rare poptart.

I haven't seen him for an entire year—his assistants text me his orders—but he doesn't look any different from the last time.

Those black eyes fix upon me like a predator's hunting gaze and I want to sink inside the ground and never be seen again. I can't help but notice he's standing just inside the doorstep, as if he's too disgusted to come in any further. As if it's beneath him to enter properly. I only have two weeks left until I'm out of his life. He couldn't have just left me alone?

"Aurelia." His voice slithers up my spine and I suppress a cringe.

"Father." I nod, keeping both my voice and face blank.

Both female scouts hiss with displeasure at my lack of use of his honorific, 'Your Highness'. If I were any other person, that would warrant a death blow, or in serpent court style, a call for slow execution via poison. He doesn't like it when I call him *father* or *dad*, because I could be no daughter of his. But in a world where complete submission is expected of me, calling him 'father' is the single act of defiance I allow myself.

The only sign of his displeasure is a twitch at the side of his mouth as he raises his hand to placate his lackey scumbags; the picture of a fair and benevolent ruler.

"Are you well?" he asks flatly, his eyes clinically darting around my body to check for signs of disability or disease. His dark presence falls upon me like a heavy blanket, and I suppress the urge to shift uncomfortably. I want him gone, out of my space and out of my life. I'm a legal adult now and not a part of his court—that surely means I have some autonomy. *Some* leg to stand on now.

"I am well," I confirm, and in a sudden burst of uncharacteristic bravery I say, "What do you need, father? I need to get to work."

He takes a single step forward, and that movement has my heart skipping multiple beats. I can't help the fear rising in me and I am so ashamed of myself when I take a woeful step back in response.

His black eyes gleam at how much I'm acting like prey. "You will not be going to the shop today, Aurelia," he says.

I know he can feel my fear, taste it in the air, hear it in my heartbeat. But I can't control that right now. Not as they crowd my tiny house, not as my entire world narrows onto one realisation.

I *am* twenty now.

I am a woman in my father's eyes.

Perhaps going away to college was a fool's dream. The dream of a stupid, hopeful girl.

Is this it?

Is this my day of reckoning where my father reveals our secret for his own gain? Where he sells me like chattel to the highest bidder? The Old Laws permit it and there are many who still hold on to them.

"And why is that?" I hate the tremble in my voice.

"I have a colleague in need of your healing abilities."

Cool relief washes through me like a king tide and I know I visibly sag under the weight being released from the thought that I was being sold into marriage or a breeding pen. I let out a shaky breath, almost laughing out loud. He needs to let me go to college. I can't be doing his *tasks* anymore.

"You have access to better healers than—"

"You know that's not true." His voice interrupts me with a flash of his fangs. I shudder.

For a secondary power, I'm rather good at healing. While it's rare for a shifter to have a second power, I—like my mother—am a rare creature.

My father has kept me hidden so no one finds out exactly *how* rare I am. But all the same, it's taken years to become a good healer. To learn all the ins and outs of a shifter's body. Whenever my father wants me to help, it means the case is something unusual and dangerous no one else will touch. Something that will, no doubt, put me at risk.

"I'm twenty now," I blurt. "I'm not a part of your court. You can't order me anymore—"

His eyes flash in anger and he flings out his arm in a strike. The shadow of his huge serpent animus flies out of his palm head first. It hurtles through the air straight for me, its jaws dislocate, snap out, and find their place clamped around my neck. I choke on a scream, staggering backwards as sharp teeth pierce the delicate sides of my throat. My back thumps against the kitchen wall and I blink rapidly, trying to stay still as my father advances on me. His lackeys grin behind him.

This is why he is king of his court. It's easy for animalia to shift into our animal forms. To shift part of our body one at a time was rare. To remove the spirit of it and use it to attack someone else? Unheard of. It's unnatural. But *unnatural* is something serpents respect.

When my father speaks again, his voice is dangerously calm. "You will be given the name and address of the place I need you to go today. And you *will* go. Is that clear? I have already spoken to my sister."

I grind my teeth as the shadow-serpent squeezes its jaws around my cheek, choking my blood supply. Stars erupt in my vision, making my father's face twinkle with faint lights. He looms over me, grim-faced; no love, no light in those black eyes. My heart splits in two all over again, and I understand just how naïve I've been.

His voice drops even lower. "I *said*, Aurelia, is that clear?"

I let out a sorry grunt. My age means nothing to him. It's no more than a legality. He will always own me. "Yes, father."

He turns on his heel and the serpent is ripped from my throat, disappearing back into my father's hand, leaving me reeling. I gasp, my knees buckling, and I collapse onto my kitchen tiles.

They leave in a procession and I watch them, a hand over my burning neck. The last—a female viper—turns and gives me a black-lipped smirk before she slams my front door shut, making my windows quiver in their frame, just like me.

I can't help the hot tears that slide from my eyes as I feel them all depart through my shield outside.

Fuck. Fuck. Fuck. I bring my hand away from my neck, and it's smeared with red. I stand on shaking legs and hobble to my mirrored kitchen splashback, leaning down to check the damage. All seven of the personal shields I permanently keep around me are down—that's the effect my father has on me.

But it means I can see myself properly, and I'm forced to see my latent mating mark on the right side of my neck. It's a mark that only animalia from your mating group can see, marking you as soul-bound in all lifetimes. Animalia spend their entire lives looking for others with the same mark. Mine is a skull with five streams of light bursting from it.

And the five reasons I'm forced to live the hidden life that I do.

Oozing crimson dots line both sides of my neck. As angry tears burn the backs of my eyes, I heal them just enough to stop the bleeding.

I want those wounds to remain painful.

Because every time I feel that burn, I want to remember the type of man my father is. That one day, I *will* be free of him. Somehow. Some way.

My phone pings and I fish it out of my pocket to see that his assistant has texted me the address he wants me to go to. I sigh in resignation. Wherever this leads, it's not going to be good.

I fling all seven of my shields back up and watch my mating mark disappear along with my scent. Being hidden is how I will survive this life. What my father has left of it, anyway.

Aurelia

I've been working odd jobs for my father since I was a child, even before my anima was revealed. Back then, he tread carefully, using these *jobs*—as he'd called them—to train my shielding and healing abilities to make me a powerful addition to his court; someone he can use to strengthen his hold over other beasts.

But once I'd been exiled from said court, the jobs became a little riskier, a little more dangerous. My father, being the king of serpents, deals with the dangerous and wealthy. So they'd gone from simple healing tasks to life-threatening injuries after big fights, even *during* inter-court fights or underground fighting rings between valuable beasts. I'd often have to make myself invisible using my special eighth shield, so no one knew I was there. It made my father a sort of enigma, that he could promise powerful healing but no one knew by what means. I think they all assumed he used some type of black magic from a distance.

I'm sure he got paid well for my services.

Since my father forbade me from getting a proper job, I had thought about taking up human sex work for money to generate an income. A side-hustle. Stripping was too public, but I could possibly make money quickly selling my body. Any money I made I would have to hide from him, so cash payments were my best option, and in addition, I'd get a power boost. I never got the balls to follow through with that idea, though it would have really helped me recharge some days, I'm sure.

They'd messaged me the location of one 'Mr. G Halfeather', and an address of a property a little way from town I'm not familiar with. It can't be an illegal cage fight or a battle for territory. The former are in locations well known to me and the latter are always in Council-approved fields or warehouses.

Nervous, I grab my handbag and keys and jump into my beat-up old blue Beetle, my precious Maisy, and follow my phone's directions down the highway. I don't know what I'm expecting—perhaps a dark den full of shifters smoking pot and snorting cocaine—but I find myself pulling into the circular driveway of a palace-sized mansion with an actual boom gate at the front complete with a security booth.

It reminds me of the place I used to call home as a child. But I shove that thought away as fast as it came.

Having been frequenting cage fighting dens for years now, I'm no stranger to brawny males flinging their animus around. I usually eighth-shield myself in the car park, however, and don't have to have contact with them when they can't see me.

So, nervously, I roll down my window as a smartly dressed male in a grey and black security uniform and a gun at his hip strolls up to me.

"Aurelia Naga?"

"Aurealia Aquinas, actually."

It's animalia protocol that you take the surname of whichever parent you take after—so I naturally took my mother's name.

He nods as if this suddenly makes more sense, and waves me through the boom gate.

Okay, so this Halfeather is possibly more loaded than my father. I wonder if he is a dragon. They are rare—only a handful of families in our state—and they are always higher-up officials in the government or businessmen. I mean, who would say 'no' to a *dragon*? The threat there was permanent and assumed, so it only made sense they get whatever they want and are able generate extreme wealth.

I find out immediately what order of animalia I'm dealing with as I drive through the boom gate, though the name should have given it away. The fountain in the middle of the circular drive is of a massive stone eagle, its wings poised as if about to take off in flight.

I personally think that arrogance of the bird shifting population is warranted. There is no greater pleasure in this world than flying. Soaring high above everything and letting the wind carry you? Honestly, everyone else *should* be envious.

But I'm no more comfortable knowing what type of beast this Halfeather is. Each order of animalia has their own genetic powers, and it just so happened that birds are the healing beasts of our kind.

If he is a wealthy eagle, that means he is probably related to, or best friends with, the top healers in the country. Whatever he needs, the fact that *I* am being called to help makes my skin crawl with anxiety.

Another security male, tall and in all black, guides me to park in a designated space next to a shining red Ferrari. I inwardly cringe, knowing full well I haven't washed Maisy in months and her faded blue paint is practically peeling off the roof. But on sight of the young male guard, my anima begins purring and preening inside of me alongside a bubbling nervousness. I clamp down on it because I need my head clear to deal with this.

The tall security guard, also an eagle by his dark blond spiked up hair, gives me a handsome smile as I get out of my car. He gives me the usual, assessing once over unmated males give unmated females. Heat flares in my cheeks at his approving smile and I'm glad my shields hide the likely desire in my scent. I haven't had sex in over a year—a lone serpent who'd seen me at the shop, and *that* had ended badly. I really feel the absence of it in my life and an ache throbs deep within me.

Once animalia hit puberty, we are taken to the city's Oracle, who is a member of the ancient house of Phoenix. They have the ability to see a person's soul-bound mates by the touch of a hand. When I'd gone at thirteen for my reading, the news had not been good. Another strike against me.

I had five mates. And two of them were already in jail.

If I'd thought my father had been furious about my anima, it was nothing compared to his furore when he'd found out how many and what order my mates were. He'd gone back inside to the Oracle to blackmail the names out of her. He told me that he didn't end up getting any of them, as it was a difficult skill for an Oracle to perform.

It didn't matter because I had then been forbidden to speak of my mates to any living soul under any circumstances. To do so would lead me to disaster, father had said. If anyone knew who my mates were, everyone would know what *I* was right away. It would be a dead giveaway, and that information could not be out in the world. I would be stolen away by powerful beasts, chained up and used as career breeder.

No one can know what I am.

That means I have to stay away from my mates and do everything in my power to avoid them finding me.

I follow the security guy—Beak, he tells me his name is—as he leads me past the white Grecian pillars of the entrance into the mansion.

It's all gold and white marble inside, gilded portraits of birds on the walls and clinically clean. There's a small table off to the side where Beak puts on latex gloves and checks my battered black handbag. I shift with unease as he searches through it, pushing aside my case of tampons and compact mirror and opening my wallet to check my driver's license. Then he apologises as he confiscates the entire bag into a big safe behind his desk.

I raise my brows but say nothing as he leads me up the marble staircase, through a maze of red-carpeted corridors, and to a mahogany door. The entire time I stare at his ass and I let out a puff of air to try and let out some of the pressure building up in me. He glances back at me then, and I heat up like a wheatbag. Smirking, he smartly raps on the expensive wood, opens it, and leads me through.

"Aurelia Aquinas, Mr Halfeather," he announces formally.

I gulp as I enter, feeling underdressed in my jeans and t-shirt combo as the wealthy male's office is revealed, dripping with all the expensive trimmings. Wood-panelled walls fitted with expensive oil paintings, gilded wall sconces, and a heavy mahogany desk. The room is big enough to hold a full lounge set, and everything matches in maroon leather.

What is *not* matching is a weaselly man coming around the desk, a sly smile curving his face.

My skin crawls at the pale, narrow-faced male and the brown eyes eagerly focused on me. He wears a long black robe like a medieval sorcerer, though he can't be older than fifty. His hair is black and receding and he gives off an observant, scummy sort of energy.

"Aurelia." He purrs my name with the familiarity of a doting uncle. "Thank you for coming."

I suppress a cringe as I try to give him a small smile. My father's *colleague*. I wonder what dark business they do together. "It's no problem."

"Your father tells me you are a talented healer."

I'm surprised my father has revealed to someone that he has a daughter. It's not like it's a huge secret, but he hides it when he can with non-court members. "Some might say that, yes, Mr Halfeather."

His smile widens as I say his name. He's a man with an ego as big as his house, no doubt about it. But I'm kicking myself because *who* would say I'm a 'talented healer'? I've been so isolated, no one, except my assessor during my healing course, knew me well enough to say that.

"Do you have any other powers?"

"No, sir." I lie.

He nods as if this confirms what he already knew. "I have a rather difficult situation that none of my healers have had much success with. I'm afraid you are my last effort at recovering this certain individual."

Ice slides down my spine at his clinical manner of speaking, at the fact that experienced, qualified healers have already tried to heal this person. Halfeather himself had probably also tried.

Is this a trap? A way for my father to teach me a lesson about trying to leave for college? I try not to appear nervous, but I think it still shows because Halfeather leans forward and speaks as if to a child. "Can you keep a secret, my sweet?"

I clear my throat. "I guess I can, Mr Halfeather."

"Just for me?"

"S-Sure."

Every instinct I possess tells me to run from this eagle. To leave and never look back and ring my father and blast him for sending me here. But they have my bag, they have my phone, and there is a bloody boom gate at the front.

There is no escaping.

He leads me from the room and a second security guard joins us from nowhere—another eagle, bulky, with dark brown hair and blonde tips. It seems Halfeather only trusts his own kind. It makes sense if he's doing shady business with people like my father.

Instead of taking me up the stairs, where I imagine the living areas are, we go *down*. One set of stairs and then another, and another. The elevators don't go down to wherever we're going. I know that because we pass two on our way.

We reach the end of a final set of stairs and Halfeather beams at me as we emerge into a dark, room made of grey stone.

It's cold and barely lit with little lights on walls. I put my arms around myself, rubbing my gooseflesh and cursing my father's name. It looks more and more like the shady place I'd first expected. The entire thing is creepy, but I'm somehow drawn forward, wanting to know what the hell he's keeping down here. I've been privy to the secrets of many animalia, but no secret as grand as this one. Despite my rising panic, my feet move forward by some primal curiosity. Power is floating at the corners of my shields, but I do my best to ignore it.

We walk through one set of locked steel doors, and then a second set. Talk about secure.

"Here we are," Halfeather says brightly as the second set of doors swing open. "My pride and joy."

We stand before a cold, shadowy maw. There's stone set into the shape of a wide, low-ceilinged corridor that's long and dark enough that I can't see the end of it. Tiny lights are set at intervals along the walls, barely fighting away the shadowy gloom beyond. In between those intervals are steel bars. Cold realisation trickles down my spine.

Holy Mother...

Cells. This is a dungeon.

Aurelia

*S*hit.

I stare around at my icy cold, stone-walled surroundings. The steel bars of the cages are like the bare incisors of a greedy animal, ready to gobble me whole.

Ahead, in the dark, something *shifts*. My insides turn into slush.

He's keeping people down here. Gods help me.

"It's not exactly *legal*," Halfeather says conspiratorially, his dark eyes gleaming with excitement.

"I dare say It's not." I smile sheepishly, as if I'm being coy. "Is this where you keep your debtors?"

He tuts at me in a casual manner that suggests he's thought about it before. "Hardly, my dear. Just the feral beasts who do me wrong. Cross me, as it were."

I try to hold myself together, at the same wondering how I could have been so stupid not to think my father's type of colleagues kept prisoners. *Of course* they do. They are all monsters like him.

"If you do this for me, my dear," Halfeather drawls, "you can consider your father's debt repaid in full."

My father's debt.

Fucking asshole! Rage bubbles through my veins, heady and hot as I realise my father is using me as his lackey. That to him, I am a valuable *thing* he can use over and over. That the likelihood of him actually letting me go for good is not likely at all.

If this is what my life is going to be like until the end of time, I will *not* accept it.

I need a plan. I need to figure out how to get out of this. How to get out of my father's clutches. Merely crossing state lines to go to college isn't enough.

I have to maintain my composure here, with this powerful beast and his security. So, I act like I already know about the debt.

"Really?" I say, stopping our advance down the aisle to stare at him.

"Really," he replies with a wan smile.

I hesitate before saying, "I'd like that in writing, please."

His smile widens. "Clever girl, aren't you?" I bat my eyelashes in what I hope is a pretty manner, but I'm not sure because I haven't had much practice. It must work because he says, "I'll have my lawyer draw the papers up right this minute."

"You're so kind, Mr Halfeather."

He makes a contented sound and sweeps me deep into the dungeon. Our four pairs of footsteps echo off the stone walls and I see hulking shadows lying in the cells we pass. We're surrounded by darkness when Halfeather stops in front of another steel door set between two cells.

"Just here is my prized possession. But he is consumed by a deathly illness of some kind that won't heal. Can you fix him, my little healer?"

I try to ignore the condescension in his voice as I look at the shadows about us uncertainly. I can barely see through the gloom and am more than certain that the large cells just feet away are all occupied with animalia.

"It is virtually impenetrable, my love," Halfeather says breezily, noting my nervous look at the other cells. "They cannot harm you, and they know better than to talk to you."

Talk to me!

Geez, he is far too comfortable in this dungeon, and it makes me think he enjoys coming down here. I look back at the steel door he's indicated. Unlike the others secured with bars, it looks like this inmate is in confinement. There'd be no light in there at all.

My skin crawls at the thought of such mental torture. Asshole father or not, as a healer, I have the innate urge to help people, and that is something I won't fight my anima on. "How long has he been in there?" My voice is quiet, and I hope he finds it respectful. This is not a male I want to be on bad terms with.

Halfeather waves a dismissive hand. "You can do it, can you not? Your father assures me you are some... anomaly?"

"I suppose I am." I shrug. "I just think I have more patience than others." It's only half a lie.

"You can reach him through the door, yes?"

I close my eyes and send my awareness out towards the door, then through it. The thing is made of metal as thick as the length of my arm and I almost swear out loud. What kind of beast are they keeping in here that requires *this*? An animalia in human form lies on the floor, unmoving but breathing. I can't register the order he is, which is odd in of itself.

"I can get through," I confirm.

He turns on his heel. "Simply knock on the door when you are done." He strides away as if business is done, the two security males following him.

My heart sinks into my nether regions. "You're going to leave me here?"

His voice gets further and further away. "As I say, it's quite secure. Beak and Scuff will be down to check on you."

I swallow. What choice do I have here? "Right. Okay."

The boom of the steel door shutting echoes down the passageway like a prophecy of doom. Okay, so that's a bit dramatic, I know, but I'm in a real live, literal dungeon. I can't help but feel I'm being made a prisoner, too. Mr Halfeather's message is clear to me. I *have* to do this.

I stand in the gloom for a moment, my skin crawling, my heart pounding, feeling all the resentment in the world for my scum of a father. I really should just focus—

A masculine voice reaches out to me like midnight silk. "You can't help him."

I freeze like a deer, straining my ears, not daring to breathe. The voice comes from the cell next to the steel door and I'm close enough to look inside, but I can't make anything out. The voice says nothing further and heavy chains slide across the floor. Gulping, I slowly swivel my head to look into the other cells down the dungeon. I adjust my eyes by pulling my eagle form into them, and even with that, I can only just make out a man-shaped figure in the middle of the cell.

I squint into the cell on my right and see a shadow of a man sitting at the far wall. I look behind me, and with relief, I see a stone wall—I won't have my back to one of the prisoners. But on either side of that wall are two occupied cells.

Cloaked in darkness, the prisoners are nothing but menacing shadows, and that makes the whole thing worse.

But I know where the voice came from, so I look again to the cell to the left of the steel door.

I clear my throat. "Why do you say that?"

Chains clink as if he's moving closer to the bars. "None of the healers could do anything and they were all a lot more experienced than you."

I know two things from his voice. One, that he is *not* rabid because those beasts don't talk properly, and two, he's had some sort of education by the confident way his mouth moves around his words.

Animalia criminals deserving of a dungeon usually aren't the school-going sort.

That arrogant voice, that condescending tone cuts into me and I know then that I will fix the beast behind the steel door, even if it kills me. Do I have an ego? Maybe. I suppose this means I do. Perhaps a lifetime of being shunned by my own family has made me into someone who scrambles to achieve *something* with her life. And every healing I do is an achievement. A success.

And some arrogant male questioning my ability is the single most irritating thing to me right now.

I level a look in his general direction. "Interesting. I suppose we'll see."

The figure of the beast who'd spoken shifts, and he leans further forward, pushing himself between the bars and into the field of the meagre light.

My breath catches in my throat as a face of wolfish, masculine beauty comes into view. Oh, he's a wolf, no doubt about it. He has wavy black hair and scruff on his jaw, but neither of those things are what gives him away. No, it's the devilish, white-toothed smile and a rogue gleam in his eye that promises *trouble*. Metal glints and I know he wears a stud on his ear.

He licks his lips and I can't help but zone in on the movement. When he speaks again, his voice is heavy with flirtation, and he cocks his head playfully. "What is your name, princess?"

"You're not supposed to be talking to me," I say, forcing myself to look away.

A second voice, from the cell behind me and opposite the wolf's, drawls in a slow voice like molten fire made into sound. "There are no cameras." Then his voice takes on a deeper, colder cadence. "There's no one to see what goes on down here."

Aurelia

A chill trickles down my spine at the fiery menace in that voice, like the deep parts of a volcano. I have no idea what to say to a barely concealed threat like that, so I simply turn around and decide ignoring these beasts is best. I check my shields, knowing full well I can withstand any attack that is thrown at me. But if I'm correct, that heinous twang I feel in the air hovering around the cells is a magical dampener—and a very expensive one. So, without fear but a lot of alertness, I hone back onto the male behind the steel door.

What manner of illness does he have?

I feel gross for invading his body without consent, but with an unconscious patient, I don't have a choice. I quickly scan his insides, intending on sweeping my magic from his crown to his toes, but I stop short at his neck. My heart beats irregularly as I recognise what it is.

Why my father specifically sent me to heal this male.

A darkness clings to his spine, curling around his spinal cord as if it wants to choke the life out of him and his animus. It's an actual snake of shadow and malice, his jaws set around the base of the male's skull. Very similar to the way my father had me pinned by his snake's jaw just an hour ago, except I've never seen a shadow snake coiled *inside* a person's body.

It is dark magic, typical of serpents, and I have no doubt in my mind that this is a magical disease brought on by contact with dark magic.

I wonder if my father did this. He's capable of it, and I know in my heart that if anyone could figure out this illness, it's him.

Then why send me here to undo it? No, this has to be someone else's work. Someone just as dark and cold.

Being so entangled with his spine, I'm going to have to remove it one bloody inch at a time, prising it away slowly to ensure his spinal cord is left intact. No wonder the other healers left him for dead. *Any* mark on his spine and he will be left with permanent paralysis that no run-of-the-mill healer could fix.

It will require meticulous and painstaking work, hours of slow focus, and I'd be lying if the thought of such a task doesn't excite me just a little. Maybe I'm insane, but this is why my father considers me his best healer. This is real complex work, and it makes me feel like there's a reason for why I was born.

I take up a seat, cross-legged on the dungeon floor, the cold tile seeping into my ass uncomfortably. I pull my cardigan off as I'm going to generate heat from all the work.

A low whistle sounds behind me, from a different cell than the last prisoners who'd spoken before. I try not to let it bother me. I'm not here for them. They're not my patient and are therefore unimportant.

I work for an hour, beginning right at the male's tailbone, persuading the shadow snake to uncurl himself with tiny, precise manoeuvres of my power. I'm sweating within minutes, and it almost feels like no time at all when I hear the distant slam of the dungeon door and the heavy booted steps of the guards.

Disentangling myself from my patient, I open my eyes to see the two eagle males staring down at me.

I groan, cracking my neck as they frown at me sitting on the dungeon floor. My hormones must be raging because before I can even think about it, I raise my hand in a silent question for help. Beak is nice enough to offer his back. I grasp it and am silently shocked by the warmth of his large male hand. I don't know exactly long it's been since I've even *touched* a male with my skin. Even a female. Accepting and giving people change at work is the only way I get people contact, but even so, most people make EFT purchases these days.

Even without the power usage from the hour of healing, I'm more thirsty than any regular female anima, and am wet just from the touch of this fertile male.

I might not be able to hunt down my mates and bed them, but my anima *desperately* wants to do something.

Beak doesn't scent my desire, though. My shield is titanium and has been that way since the day at the Oracle. I cannot let any male scent me, because within seconds they'll know I'm no common eagle.

My fingers leave Beak's hand oh so reluctantly and I'm ashamed that he notices, a mildly hungry look flashing across his face. He seems to struggle with it for a moment as I follow the two of them down the corridor. He looks back at me once and his companion grunts something at him I don't hear. One downside to my seven shields is that my hearing can't be as good as other animalia. But I do see Beak shake himself and become a professional once again. I get a tiny bit of giddy satisfaction from this interaction just before a pang of sadness hits me.

I'm destined for a life of *this*. If I can't let males scent me, I will be a single anima for the rest of my life. I'll die with both my honour and my secret intact, but *god,* sometimes honor seems overrated.

I stare at both fine guards' asses all the way to Mr Halfeather's office, my eyes half lidded, my fingers twitching, telling myself it's just the healing exertion having me look for a boost and not desperation for real, skin-to-skin company.

The old eagle is sitting at his desk as I walk past the two guards towards him.

"I'll need to return daily," I say softly, "until It's all out. Shouldn't take more than a week."

"A full week?" he asks with raised brows. I feel his eagle's vision take in every one of my sweating pores.

I grimace, wondering when I last exfoliated. "It's a persistent...illness that requires tedious work. I don't think anyone else would have the patience for it, honestly."

Thinking he'd be annoyed by the delay, I'm surprised when a slow smile spreads across his face. "Well, I can't complain if I get to see you every day now, can I?"

I drive away from Halfeather's mansion, trying not to think about the way Beak pulled open my car door for me. It had been a feat of willpower not to let down a shield, stand on my tiptoes and sniff him properly.

How I wished he'd slipped his number into my handbag, but he hadn't—I'd checked twice. The desperation was probably written all over me and he'd likely been put off by it.

Pondering on what a not-desperate female looks like, I do something I usually avoid and stop to get drive-thru takeaway, wolfing down an entire burger, fries and shake meal. I feel a little better afterwards, so once I get home and shower again, I decide to get ready for work.

My eyelids droop a little from tiredness, but I don't want to mope around thinking about what happened with my father here at home and then spending my morning literally locked in a dungeon and then again lusting over Beak, fine as he'd been. I need to keep myself busy. Sometimes my aunt gives me a bonus if I work overtime. My goal is to make as much money as I can before college starts, when I'll have to purchase ridiculously expensive books and accommodation.

My meagre allowance isn't going to cut it and there is no way my father is going to pay for any of my college things. I am financially on my own.

My mother would not have wanted this for me. I'd never known her as she'd died when I was five, but in my head, she loved me more than anything else in the world. I held onto that thought like it was a life raft, and on my first nights living alone, that's exactly what it had been.

When I reach work, a moderately sized grocery and convenience store, Aunt Charlotte looks up from where she's filing her nails, fluffs up her bleached blonde curls and looks me up and down with a disapproving frown.

Some things never change.

Nothing is more important to my father than his family, and he's looked after his sister since they were young. Always giving her money for Louboutins and Prada handbags whenever she batted her overlong eyelash extensions at him.

"What are you doing here?" she says through shiny red lips. "Mace said—"

"I'll be working for him during the mornings this week, so I thought I might as well help out here until close. You'll be home to have dinner with the kids that way."

Charlotte made regina to two mates. Uncle Ben works in the mines, fly in fly out style, and Uncle Ron is a plumber. They are all sworn snakes to my father's court and hence avoid me like the plague. Ben is the nicer of the two, probably because he isn't here to see the political nightmare I am. When I first moved out to the bungalow at the back of their house, he would bring me leftover dinners, often sneaking a piece of chocolate or two wrapped in a napkin.

I'm pretty sure my father uses this store for money laundering or worse, but I'm not allowed in the back office, so I can't be sure.

Aunt Charlotte looks down her nose at me and nods stiffly. I thought that me leaving for college at summer's end would cheer her up, but she's as sub-nosed as ever. But I understand her because I'd *been* her once and you don't understand your privilege until it's taken away.

Aurelia

The next day, I roll out of bed, scull two mugs of coffee and head back out to Mr Halfeather's mansion.

So what that I wear my nice pair of skinny jeans and a blouse that shows a teensy bit of cleavage?

A girl can dream.

When you've lived by yourself, in isolation as long as I have, that's all you have. Your imagination and your dreams. And I'd say I'm pretty proficient at using both—perhaps it's the only reason I'm still sane.

I'm greeted in much the same manner as yesterday, except Halfeather snatches up my hand and kisses it delicately, as if I'm something precious.

My stomach clenches at the royal treatment, wondering if there's anything ulterior behind it. But I stick a smile on my face as if I enjoy it and he releases me to my guards. Beak and Scuff have easy smiles today and I don't fight the racing of my heart when I smile back.

It takes me two flights of steps to gather enough courage to ask Beak, "So, is this your permanent gig?"

"Sort of." He scratches the back of his head, one huge, tanned bicep flexing. My eyes follow the movement and he grins at me. I tear my gaze away, realising he's showing me his body on purpose. Bloody eagles and their peacocking, I swear he's going to be the end of me. "We go to college in the fall," he continues, leading me down to the dungeon. "This is just a summer job for us."

"Sweet." I nod. "Which college?"

But he's opened the final set of doors and ushers me in. I quickly ask, "Er, are there any lights there?" I rub my arms against the cold. "It's ridiculously dark and I practically can't see where I'm walking."

Beak and Scuff shift uncomfortably as they escort me past the first lot of cells. "Mr Halfeather likes it dark down here," Scuff says.

"Maybe just for the hour I'm here?" I bat my eyelashes at Beak, trying to channel my inner, sexy, helpless, Aunt Charlotte. They exchange a look. I whisper to appeal to their subconscious male animus. "Just a little bit?"

My cooing wins in the end. "Just a bit," Beak says kindly.

I grin at them before they head out and inevitably shut the massive steel door. It actually worked! I wondered what else I can get away with by channeling Aunt Charlotte.

Alone once again in the gloom, with nothing but predators shifting in the dark, chains clanking, I wait there until the lights come on, a gentle silver glow. It's hardly better, but I can actually make out the colours of the dull grey stone brick beside the steel door of my patient.

A low, rough chuckle skulks through the air, sending my hackles rising. It's not a laugh of amusement or joy, it's sheer nastiness.

"Scared of the dark, princess?" someone jeers from behind me.

Animalia males pounce on fear, some of them even enjoy provoking it, their animus wanting to hunt prey. The idea that I'm acting like prey has me gritting my teeth.

"I fear nothing," I say into the shadows. "Least of all some animalia stupid enough to get locked up in here."

The male in the cell to the right of my patient's door is sitting on a steel chair. It's pushed as far back into the cell as possible, so the light only reaches his bare, tattooed thighs so I know that he's naked. He's tall and no more than a shadow, his hands tied behind his back.

I wonder how he pees.

He doesn't speak, but the male in the cell opposite him and behind me says in a leering voice, "Show us your pussy, girly. I bet it's real sweet."

Okay, so I'm regretting my choice of nicer clothing as my nose wrinkles in disgust.

Before he can say any more, a voice growls from my other side. "Get away from him, princess. He's a dirty bastard."

I recognise the wolf's voice. Because I'm not entirely stupid, I do listen to him and position myself closer to my patient's door.

The wolf is there, in the cell directly to my left, and pushes his face through the bars to look at me.

Did I think Beak was handsome just before? Because by all the wild gods, every cell in my body rears their little molecular heads to register the sheer masculine beauty of the wolf's face.

A face that is currently hungrily fixed on me.

I'm glad I'm not the only desperate animalia around, but I doubt this male lacks women in his life when he's not chained up. Women probably fell on their knees begging and panting wherever he went.

I frown, more at myself than anything, and he shows me a row of straight white teeth. "So you'll flirt with the dicky birds, but not with me?" he asks coyly.

My heart skips a beat and I remind myself to keep my breathing even. He might not be able to scent me, but wolves are more socially aware of body language than the rest.

I eye him for a moment, getting a better look at him in the new light. There's dirt smeared on a bare muscular torso so ripped I know at once he's been bred for fighting. I've been to enough illegal fights to know the feral, bloodthirsty, I-eat-beasts-for-fun look. I wonder when he's last had a shower as I note the sheen of sweat glistening over the wolf tattoo spanning his muscular chest. I can clearly see now that his earring is a black stud, a gem of some sort. His smile widens as it becomes very obvious that I'm checking him out, so I turn my head away from him in arrogant dismissal.

Clearly my anima takes over because even without looking at him, I'm flirting back. "Beak's got big muscles," I say, pushing my ponytail over my shoulder. "What do you have?"

From my periphery, he scoffs, then pouts. "I have pretty eyes, though, don't you think?"

I don't look at him as I sit down in my cross-legged position. "Yeah, they're alright, I suppose."

He gasps in mock offense, and I have to refrain from grinning outright. This is all because of my dud of a vibrator from yesterday. I *knew* I should have broken into my savings to get a new one. My own fingers only did so much with an appetite like mine and I can't very well be flirting with the prisoners. I blink at the steel door, wondering what the wolf has done to displease Halfeather enough to land himself here.

"Give me ten seconds with Beak," comes that angry molten voice in the cell opposite the wolf's. "And I'll fuck him to high hell."

"You'll fuck him?" the wolf jeers. "With your big dragon dick? He'll be sore for days."

There's a bloody dragon in here too?! Why hasn't his rich daddy pulled him out?

But the dragon drawls, "Not with my dick, you idiot. With my claws. His pretty face won't be a face anymore."

"I'd take him out in two seconds," the wolf says, sighing as if thinking about a wonderful fantasy. "What I'd give for *two* seconds."

Animalia males measure dicks whenever they get together like this. Especially when females are about. I suppose they haven't been around females in a while if they're peacocking for *me* right now.

I can't help thinking that, whatever they've done, this whole thing is wrong. And leaving them without proper hygiene? Or clothes? It's inhumane. I've seen feral animalia treat their subordinates better in their forest communes.

I sigh and glance at the wolf still standing at the bars, staring down at me. Both males have quieted their bickering.

My anima is moving my mouth for me because I'm mad enough to ask in a low voice, "What's your name?"

He grins, his eyes brightening. They're hazel, I note, a swirl of delicious greens and browns that remind me of dangerous, ancient forests and they beckon to me with the call of a wild song. But he ruins it and says, "You show me yours and I'll show you mine."

I roll my eyes, scoffing at his choice of wording and turn away back to my charge behind the door. I have one hour and I need to get as much done as I can. I close my eyes.

"Savage," he blurts out. "My name is Savage."

Savage

The moment this woman stumbled into my dungeon like some angel floating through the gates of heaven, I'd thought I was hallucinating. Or dying.

Lightning had buzzed all around me, waking me up, and all at once I'd felt a hurricane of desire flood my veins. I had wanted to run my fingers through all that long silky raven hair, touch her cheek and see how soft it was. I had wanted to pull her into my cage and bury my nose between her legs.

I had also wanted to rip out Halfeather's throat for standing so close to her. And today, she'd come in with Beaky and Scuffy, all flirty and smiley, and I vowed to tear out their feathers and wear them as a coat.

I forget all of that right now as she glances at me again with those long, dark lashes fluttering over impossibly blue eyes and I feel something stir deep inside my cock.

Understandable, since I've not been in contact with a woman for a gods damned long time.

"Lia," she says quietly, as though she's wondering why she's telling me at all.

Ah, me and my charms loosened her tongue sure enough. It was only a matter of time.

"Lia." I taste her name, sounding out the letters and wondering how they would sound in a moan as I came inside of her. "What's it short for?"

She hesitates, but gives it to me because she can't resist. "Aurelia."

Perfect. Pretty. Angelic. A name I could get tattooed where everyone could see it.

It's also a unique name. I'd have no trouble finding her once I get out of here. She turns away from me once again and I lick my lips at her stunning side profile, wanting her to show me her blue ocean eyes again. I can't see him, but Scythe growls at me softly from the cell on Lia's other side—a warning.

My brother knows me, of course. Knows that it's dangerous for me to pursue a woman like this. He's probably trying to protect her—he's always trying to save the world from me and my dirty paws. So I settle down and watch Lia start up her healing magic on the bogeyman in confinement. He'd already been here when we'd arrived and I'd known that whoever he was, he was a part of our mating group right away. Even Halfeather's shields can't mask the ancient bond between us—a gold thread that links our animus' through space and eternity. But we'd not found our regina yet, our centre, and that was exactly what had gotten us into this fuck up of a situation.

I sit down on the stone, mirroring Aurelia—Lia, as she liked to be called. But I think I was going to stick with 'Princess'. It matches her delicate features, her haughty, sweet nose in the air, and her I'm-not-scared-of-the-big-bad-wolf personality. She walks a little like a princess too, and I can't take my eyes off her every time she walks up to me.

Every time? Dear Mother Wolf, I'm delusional. I've seen her walk all of *two* times. Who cares, though? I've known I want to take a bite out of those hips the moment I'd seen her. Not an actual bite, more of a mouthful, more of a "let me lick you all over and see if you taste as good as you look".

The magic dampener on my cell refrains me from feeling her out properly as she closes her eyes and broaches the bogeyman's steel door with her magic. It's such a shame because I'm fucking desperate to scent her and I just know it's going to be spectacular when I do.

I glance back at Xander, opposite me. He usually has his eyes closed, listening to whatever European rock music or Mongolian throat singing he has on his device. When we'd first arrived, he'd raged for a full week straight in his cell, almost tearing the place down, driving the rest of us mad until the guards had given in and let him have his music. The fucking old beaker didn't want to drive us rabid, which I took to mean he wanted us sane for *something*.

Xander is frowning at Aurelia through his old scars. He can't use his damaged eyes without his power and that's left him agitated—and creepy looking, because they're black hollows from where they'd dug them out with their bare claws when he was a kid. I turn back to look at Lia. It's pretty impressive that she can sit there for a full hour and fix the beast next door. I don't think I've ever seen anyone hold power for that long.

We sit and watch her—well, Xander listens—while Scythe remains still in his cage, which is the best anyone can ask of him. I lean my forehead against the bars of my cell, my stomach grumbling. They feed us whenever they feel like it, which is not often. Fair punishment, I suppose, for what we'd done. I don't care though, I'd do it all over again given the chance, and I know the others would say the same. Xander enjoys a good slaughter even more than Scythe and I, and that's saying something.

Aurelia

I'm quite happy about the progress I've made today with the shadow snake. I still can't tell what type of animus the male has, but it doesn't matter. I report back to Mr Halfeather when Beak and Scuff come to get me. He never asks me details about the illness or the manner of it, and I vaguely wonder if this is some weird thing my father is doing to test me. But none of that makes sense, given my father already knows what I'm capable of.

Whatever I did for the animalia behind that steel door, I was acutely aware of the three prisoners I'd seen a little more of today—and the fourth, a hyena, I think, who'd spoken so crassly to me. There were other creatures in that dungeon—I had seen them as I walked past their cages on the way back. They were all slumped on the cement floor with their backs turned towards me as if they were half alive. The only ones who seemed to be interested in what went on were the sleaze bag and the wolf, *Savage*.

The name given from a fighting family, if I've ever heard one. Wolves are notorious for underground fighting rings. It's a good way to make money if you're good at it. High risk, high reward, and with that expensive gem on his ear, I bet he did real well at his job.

I leave Halfeather's manor with Beak opening the door of my Beetle for me once again. Chivalry isn't dead, and it makes my beast of an anima preen and coo at him.

"Thanks." I only let myself smile at him as I get into my car.

"Will I see you at the Academy in two weeks?" he asks.

I choke. "You're going to *Animus* Academy?"

He runs a hand through his hair, smirking. "Yeah, I got the order a few weeks ago. My parents were so relieved."

Males seem to think it's a flex being ordered to attend the college we send our most volatile, promiscuous and errant new adults. The idea is to temper and civilise them before they hit the workforce and wider community, so they won't be such a menace to the fearful human population we try and live alongside. Naturally, once you receive the order to attend, you *have* to go, otherwise they hunt you down and take you kicking and screaming bound in tourmaline chains. Beak seems pretty controlled, but there must be a feral hunter under that pretty face.

Why he thinks *I'm* going there is beyond me.

"Do I look like I need to go there?" I ask in horror.

He smiles sheepishly. "Well, I thought because of your power, you'd be... no? Well, good for you then."

I leave the mansion, heading to my favourite fast-food drive-thru before I'm due at work. The entire way, Savage's face presses in on my mind's eye. Seeing these beasts behind bars in such conditions, slumped against the wall, dirty and one even without clothes, makes me cringe. There is no humanity in it at all. When I head into work, a discounted stack of sweatpants catches my eye and the whisper of a wild thought runs through my mind.

It's the morning of the third day of my visits to Halfeather's dungeon and I feel the edges of fatigue creeping in. My power is sizeable, but the strain of both maintaining my seven shields and being around these males has me feeling some kind of way.

But I find that a bubble of eagerness engulfs me. I'm likely finally going mad, but I actually look forward to it. It's almost like going to a real job where I have regular faces grinning at me upon my entry. I'm wanted here. Beak and Scuff shoot me flirty smiles and Beak even hands me a few Hershey's Kisses when he takes my handbag.

"You deserve it," he says, grinning.

Be still my fluttering heart! I blush and keep my mouth shut in case I say something dumb like, 'What time do you get off?'

A part of me shakes its head in dismay, but a reasonable part of me googled it last night and I know it has a name: Touch deprivation.

Even in Aunt Charlotte's shop I'm usually relegated to stacking shelves and cleaning, my contact with clients is limited to the occasional cashier coverage when Charlotte goes to the bathroom to fix her makeup.

My father took me out of school once he moved me out of home. I've been home schooled since then, using an online system one of the high school teachers in his court had set up. It was lonely, so I ended up at the local Salvation Army store, picking up as many books as I could manage. If I couldn't be a part of the real world, my fictional book worlds were always waiting for me along with my fictional friends.

No one has given me chocolate or anything similar since I was a kid.

So I know I'm a complete loony as I'm heading down into a dungeon of darkness with a group of apex predators and my anima purrs with glee. My lips twitch with a faint smile as Beak opens the final steel door.

I waltz in, the Hershey's Kisses in my hand and even the cold doesn't affect my good mood. Beak shakes his head in amusement as I pass him. He probably thinks I'm mental, and I doubt he's all that wrong. They've put the lights on for me already, and it's slightly brighter than yesterday. Making a surprised noise at the back of my throat at Beak's further kindness, I stride down.

It's like my body knows Savage is waiting for me because I immediately forget about Beak's lingering gaze and clench in anticipation of those wolfish hazel eyes. I'm walking past the leering male's cage, stiffening in case I get another lewd comment, but when I glance inside his cell, I stop dead in my tracks.

Dear Wild Mother.

Lying on the stones of his cell is a hyena, clearly having shifted into his animus form before his head was separated from his body. There's a pool of blood between the two parts and my stomach gives a fell lurch. One of my hands finds my mouth, covering it as if I can also cover the scene of the murder from my mind.

"*Lee-ah.*" Savage sings my name in the cadence of a happy children's song.

Chains scrape, a body shifts, but I ignore him and turn, forcing my eyes to the cell opposite to the hyena's, where the naked male is still sitting on his metal chair. I can see a little more of him today. He's a big beast, a late-twenties animalia covered in black tattoos from his feet to his neck. But one tattoo stands out: five fine lines of ancient text on the left side of his neck. This and two other signs tell me what his animus is. Ice-blue eyes glint at me through the dark. Long, silver hair that brushes his shoulders stands out amidst the gloom. Five lines of text representing five gill slits. He's a shark.

He's still. So still as he looks at me, powerful chest taking slow, deep breaths, large biceps pushed out from where his arms are tied behind his back. In my woeful life healing all sorts of dark creatures, I'd yet to meet a shark—and for good reason. Most of them go psycho on land, the theory being that they were never meant to leave their marine home. Indeed, almost all marine animalia choose to live out their lives in deep parts of the ocean in converted form, never turning human ever again.

So what the hell is this one doing here?

Aurelia

"Princess, get away from my brother." Savage's deep voice cuts through the spell the shark has on me and I shake myself before moving away to the steel door my patient lies behind. Savage pushes his head through the steel bars of his cage. He's sitting down already, but there are bags under his eyes. It makes him look even more dangerous. He gives me a sort of deranged smile that makes my stomach flop.

"What happened to the hyena?" I ask quietly.

A low, dark laugh, like a rumbling volcano, comes from the dragon in the cell behind me. "It got what was coming to it."

I turn to look at the dragon, feeling Savage watch my every move. I can't see much of the male except to note that he, too, is chained, but not to a chair like the shark. Instead, both his arms are stretched out, chains binding him to the walls on either side. Barbaric; his arms must hurt so much.

I can't make out his face, where the light doesn't reach, but I can see he has black jeans on the bottom half of a typical dragon male's body.

Cut from stone, lean, shredded muscle that's puckered with scars, old and new. He has a piercing on one nipple and, in typical dragon style, long black hair cascading down his defined pecs. But the thing most interesting about him is the pair of white headphone cords leading up to his ears. A device is hooked into the waistband of his jeans.

"Checking me out, hatchling?" the dragon rumbles. His voice is cold and monotone.

I jump, pulling myself out of a thirsty haze and hope my face isn't sheepish. "Sorry. Don't your arms hurt?"

I get the impression he's glaring at me through the bars, but Savage snorts from behind me. "My brother is a little bloodthirsty shark. He took care of the hyena, princess. You don't have to worry about him talking shit to you anymore."

My heart leaps into my throat as I whirl back around. "What?" I exclaim. "How did he — when — What?!"

Savage smirks, looking me up and down, and I heat up immediately. Even slumped against the bars of his cell, he looks capable of jumping up at a minute's notice and tearing somebody's throat out. But the shark in the other cell couldn't have gotten to the hyena in the cell *opposite* him, surely.

I don't know what is more confusing. The fact that he'd managed it, or the fact that he'd done it out of some chivalry.

"Don't you worry your pretty little head about it," Savage says.

I scowl at the condescension in his voice and then stop short of a retort. "Wait, did you say *brother*?" I frown at Savage.

He doesn't take his eyes off me. "Mmm."

"But he's a—"

"Our father was rex of two females. One wolf, one shark."

While it isn't uncommon to have a mating group with different orders, a marine in a soul-bond with land animalia is, incredibly rare and unfortunate since they could never all be truly together for their whole lives. But this is also the very reason I can't reveal my mating group to anyone—*all* five of my mates are males of different animus orders. It's more than strange—it should be impossible.

I promptly decide that's enough interacting with the prisoners for today and sit down in my usual spot in front of the steel door. Before I start, I glance behind me at the dragon.

"Why does he have headphones in?" I ask Savage quietly.

"Do you know where the term "berserk" comes from, princess?" he asks, looking at his fingernails.

I shake my head, wondering where this is going.

"It comes from the people known as the Berserkers of old Northern Europe. They were sort of like Vikings, a fighting and pillaging sort of lifestyle. But these people would run into battle and go into a trance-like state where they'd kill anything and anyone in their path. Including each other. So, Xander is kinda like that. Without his music, he goes nuts and tries to kill everyone."

I raise my brows and glance over my shoulder again, where I'm sure the dragon, Xander, is listening. But he remains silent in his cell.

That explains why they'd allowed the music, but the thought of a beast *needing* such a thing to control himself speaks volumes about the kind of life he's had. Dragons are brutal beasts, but usually their youth are extremely well cared for.

Savage smiles at me as if he hasn't just told me two completely murderous things in the last five minutes[MM2] . I've never been on the receiving end of a smile like *this* before. Not since I was child. It's genuine, doting, almost honest, and it makes my heart do funny, unwelcome things.

I can't help but return it. His eyes flick down to my lips, and I take a deep breath to calm my raging anima.

"Oh." I remember, reaching into my jeans pocket. "Do you want some chocolate, Savage?"

"Mmm, say my name one more time."

I glance back at up at him in surprise, but he's got his eyes closed. I take the opportunity to stare at his perfect, rugged face. The apex of my thighs is *throbbing*.

Clearing my throat, I say, "It's um... a Hersey's Kiss."

His eyes fly open, his hazel eyes no more than blown out, dilated pupils. "Yes, Lia, I'll take a kiss from you."

I sincerely hope there really isn't any surveillance on his dungeon like Xander told me that first day because I lean forward, going on my knees, and pass him the small, foil-wrapped chocolate. I'm careful to give it to him without our fingers touching.

"Do they feed you?" I ask, glancing at Xander behind me.

"Sometimes." With is his big fingers, Savage unwraps the foil delicately, corner by corner, as if he's trying to stretch out the pleasure of opening it. I stare at him for a moment before I look back at the dragon.

I'm nervous to ask but, hell, you only live once, right? And these males seem like they could use a bit of kindness. "I can put this in your mouth if you like, um... Xander?"

The dragon is silent for a moment, before he says as if it's a challenge, "Go on then, hatchling, how good is your aim?"

Blushing at the term of endearment used for winged children, I don't tell him that my aim is not good at all. I get to my feet, unwrap the second chocolate from its foil and re-wrap it into one of my speciality shields.

I'm powerful at my secondary power, healing, but I'm even *better* at shields.

I make a show of tossing the chocolate towards Xander's mouth, but in reality, I just levitate it really fast towards him. He shifts a little to catch it, but it finds its mark. But once the chocolate is in his mouth, he goes still. Apex predator still.

And I know he's sensed bubble shield I had around the chocolate.

He thinks I'm an eagle because of my healing powers. This is the narrative we've been weaving my whole life. I shouldn't have this extra magic like I do. It's not a known power to *any* animalia order.

It was a stupid, stupid risk, but he *is* a prisoner. Who's he going to tell? And who would believe him?

Hastily, I shuffle away, and to my relief, he doesn't say anything. The third chocolate is in my hand and I glance back at Savage. The wolf is concentrating deeply on his chocolate and I see that he's only taken teeny bites from the corners.

My heart pangs in sadness a little.

"Will your brother take one, do you think?"

"Who, Scythe?" he says, eyes darting down the dungeon. "Nah, he only eats raw fish these days."

"Ah, right."

So the shark is a little more than feral. I sit down to start my work, goosebumps puckering my skin as I remember those ice-blue eyes sitting just feet from me.

When I leave with Beak and Scuff after my healing session, I'm surprised by the pang of sadness I feel at leaving the prisoners behind me. I vaguely wonder if this is how people feel when they part with their friends.

Aurelia

I *know* I'm delusional in thinking the prisoners in the dungeon are my friends. I'm a complete idiot for playing happy families with them—*sharing* things, s*miling* and getting a fluttery heart. Except I don't have anyone else in my life and is it so bad if I have an alright time chatting to them briefly? Is it so bad if Savage's and Beak's attention brightens my day just a little bit?

It's pathetic, I know. They're dangerous males. *And* they're prisoners.

So the next day, even if one part of me is screaming not to do it, that the risk is too great and I'll get into trouble, I'm going to do something stupid and I'm not even thinking about the consequences.

It's so unlike me that I can't even comprehend it.

I find myself walking into Halfeather's mansion with one of my strongest shields hiding a folded pair of discounted XL black track pants tucked under my arm. I hold my breath as Beak opens my car door, his usual flirty smile on his face as he takes my bag.

Suddenly, I'm not surprised he's been ordered to Animus Academy. His eyes are telling me that he wants to fuck. Promiscuity amongst our males is an issue. STDs for one thing, inter-court politics for another. It leads to more bloodshed than it's worth. Oddly, my anima isn't rearing up and wanting to grab at him like I expect. Am I getting used to the attention?

Of course, with my entire life being a study in shielding, I get the pants into the dungeons without a hitch. Getting the pants into Scythe's cell will be another thing entirely. It will also give away my power.

So it looks like I'm a risk taker now. But here I am faced something I've never come across before. The primitive female anima within me appreciates that Scythe has *killed* a male for me.

I'd like to think they'd already had some sort of beef. That I'm not the only reason Scythe wanted that hyena dead. Whatever my brain thought, my anima wanted to thank the shark for such a display of blatant protection.

Perhaps the ferality of the prisoners is rubbing off on me because it seems like I'm letting my anima take control more and more by the day. Maybe Beak is right about me needing to go to Animus Academy after all.

Beak and Scuff lead me down to the dungeons once again, slamming the door shut behind me, but that ominous sound can't make me flinch today.

"Lia?" Savage's voice is a beacon in the gloom and a balm for any nervousness I feel.

"Hi, it's me." My voice sounds tiny compared to his.

I stride quickly past the cells, trying not to let my eagerness show. When I pass the hyena's cell, the body and head have been removed, and the scent of bleach even passes through my shields. I wonder what Halfeather does with the bodies of his prisoners.

The scent of fresh blood is also coming out loud and strong from the shark's cell. Yesterday, Savage said his brother's name was Scythe—another fighting name. Nervously, I step before him.

Ice-cold eyes like the dark depths of the Mariana's Trench shine through the gloom. *Danger*, my anima warns. *This one is a killer.*

I swallow as I reach out with my power and assess his body for the injuries I can smell. The shark doesn't show any response to my magic brushing against him. He simply sits there leaning against the back of the chair, eyes on me like cold, cold pokers. I can tell that his shoulder's been dislocated and that he or someone else has relocated it back into the socket—the tendons are all inflamed and a little mangled. There is also a break in his humerus, already healing due to his natural animus magic. I speed up the healing process and seal the fracture shut.

He's silent throughout the whole thing. Usually, I get a grunt or something from a broken bone, but Scythe just sits there as if it doesn't bother him, watching me with the kind of precision I imagine only a shark can muster.

Healing is instinctual for me. It's hard for my power to see someone in pain and not do anything about it. It goes against literally everything that I am in my core, not to heal. But I suddenly realise that I never asked for his permission.

An icky feeling crawls through me and I mutter, "I'm sorry, I should have asked."

He says nothing.

I can't help but feel his injuries are a punishment to do with what he did to the hyena. What he did out of revenge for me. I wonder what he's thinking. What desire he had to kill the animalia. How the hell he'd done it.

The track pants at my side burn like contraband. I paid for them fair and square and now it seems even more imperative to give this male a gift.

Will he take it? There is no kindness coming off him, nothing close to human connection. I get the urge to turn away from the cell, but something is urging me forward. He must be cold in there. He must be feeling awful, even though he won't let any emotion show. The only thing I feel from him is an icy indifference bordering on menace. He is a dangerous, dangerous creature. The anima inside of me *knows* that.

Perhaps he killed because he liked to?

Nerves bubbling in me, I take the track pants out from under my arm and hold them out to show him.

"Lia?" Savage's voice sails over to me. The rest of the dungeon is quiet.

"Just a minute," I say, keeping my eyes on the cold shark before me.

His eyes flick down to the pants, and *ever* so slightly, he cocks his head.

I take this miniscule movement as a sign I'm doing the right thing, so I levitate the bubble shield with the pants inside of it just in front of me.

The shark shifts in his chair.

Of course, being more than feral, Savage has preternatural instincts and notices something is up straight away, sticking his head as far as he can out of his own cell bars. "What's that?" he asks, and I can hear the amusement in his voice.

I levitate my little sphere through the bars of Scythe's cell and then I realise that I've not thought this through.

Scythe's eyes move from the pants to me as they levitate awkwardly in front of him. Clearing my throat, I steel myself and use a skill I don't often have to resort to.

It's a fair bit of concentration, but I manage to make another shield in the shape of my hand and use that to manipulate the pants. Lowering them to the ground, my phantom hands hold them out by the elastic waistband by his feet.

I glance back up at him, holding my breath. But then he lifts his feet. I almost sigh in relief as I hoist the pants onto his feet and pull them up his calves and knees, noting the intricate tattoos there. I swear when I reach his thighs, though, not knowing how we're going to do this.

But the chains around his arms must not be super tight because Scythe lifts himself off the chair, and quickly, I pull the pants up and over his lap. I let go before I touch his skin... or dick with my phantom hands.

With the pants on, he looks back up at me with absolutely no change in his face. I suppose he likes them if he let me put them on?

Trying not to think about it, and satisfied by this small success, I turn away and go to sit down in my usual spot between Savage and Scythe's cells.

I look at my steel door, releasing a breath as I turn to towards Savage.

"What did you give my brother?" the wolf asks quietly, his handsome face serious.

Clearing my throat, I say softly, "A bit chilly in here, isn't it? I got him track pants."

A look I cannot interpret shoots across his face, but in a flash, it's gone.

Savage says in a voice quite unlike his usual flirty one, "A little bit less now though, princess."

I say nothing and close my eyes, suddenly struggling to concentrate on my patient.

Savage's voice regains its flirty attitude, and he says, "I think princess likes us, boys." I know he's grinning from ear to ear, and though it takes everything in me not to open my eyes and look at him, I can't help the smile that creeps upon my own lips. The anima in me is a wanton thing because a wild heat sweeps through my insides at the pleasure I hear in his voice.

I clamp that shit down for all I'm worth because there is no way I can let it show.

Aurelia

When the hour is done, I'm happy with the amount of progress I've made with my patient. I had to lower one of my inner, heavier shields at the end to get a boost of energy to push through, but it was worth it. With Savage and Scythe on either side of me, I don't feel like I'm in danger in this dungeon right now. I open my eyes and crack my neck with a groan.

I turn to find Savage watching me, his eyes half lidded. He seems to snap out of some reverie because his face comes alive. He gives me a slow, hot smile, and I can't help but notice how pretty his lips are.

He turns his head to scratch the left side of his neck with a dirty, bloodied hand and I still in shock as tsunami like force hits me in the gut. Everything in my universe narrows down to that single piece of Savage's skin.

Because sitting there is a golden, glowing symbol. A skull with five beams of light shooting out from it.

My mating symbol.

Savage pulls out a red foil from his pocket and I realise he's saved half the Hershey's Kiss from yesterday. He puts the rest of it in his mouth and savours it as I stare at him.

"What's wrong?" he asks around the chocolate.

It takes a monumental effort to move my head from side to side to shake it. "Nothing."

A cold, dark feeling consumes my heart, and something tells me to look at the cell behind me. Slowly, in a dazed trance, I get to my feet and turn to look at the dragon chained in his cell.

In the darkness, there is a golden glow, and it's on Xander's neck. My symbol is obvious through the gloom.

I don't breathe. I don't blink. I don't think.

Shit. Shit. Shit. Fuck. No. How?

My feet move of their own accord, something *more* than me guiding me towards Scythe's cell. He's sitting there as he always does, only this time It's not only his ice eyes that glow. It's the golden mark on the side of his neck, beckoning to the deepest parts of my being.

My anima lets out a roar of sheer, joyous release, and my knees buckle. I catch myself with my shield just in time and make myself go still.

With the pressure of containing my emotions, an involuntary tear trickles down my cheek and Scythe's alert eyes follow its trail.

It's a blow to the gut. My insides are going to explode.

I have to get out of here. I need to leave and never come back. How could I have been so stupid? How could I not have known?

But I know exactly why. I've had seven shields around me, and I'd dissipated my psychic one in order to get a better grasp on my patient today. I'd never let that shield down in front of the prisoners before and it was the one responsible for protecting me from external psychic forces—so it had also hidden their mating mark from me.

I want to be sick.

All three of these animalia are my mates. Three of the five I was promised to by fate.

I swallow through a sandpaper throat, knowing both Savage and Scythe are instinctually tracing my movements, pupils dilated. They do it because they are my mates and even if they can't see it, their animus is making them more responsive to me. To want to care for me. To want to kill for me.

Their beastly spirit knows who I am. I can see that plain as day.

But their minds don't.

I turn on my heel and all but run for the exit, but it feels like I'm walking through water, my limbs slow and wobbly.

Savage's rough voice chases after me in playful bound. "See you tomorrow, princess."

Thankfully, my time is up anyway, and Beak is smiling at me from the other side when he opens the door. The smile I give him is of genuine relief, and his face brightens with pleasure to see it. But my body does not respond to him in that desirous way it normally does.

Now that I've seen my mates, my body will never elicit that same response for anyone else.

I'm not prepared for the level of emotions I'm experiencing. For animalia, the mating bond is the strongest magic in existence and it is not in our nature to ignore it.

I stumble out of Halfeather's mansion in a dream-like haze. The world outside hits my retinas in a dazzling display of colour.

It's as if I'm seeing everything for the first time. My world had been black and white this morning. Now, I was seeing it in 4k surround sound. My soul has woken up and is crying out in a happy song. *We've found our bonds,* she sings, *we're finally home.*

Beak says something to me as I fall into my car, but I don't hear him.

I don't even know how I get home, but I'm drenched in sweat when I do. Functioning on auto-pilot, I somehow get ready for work, the faces of my three mates flashing in my mind like a slideshow on repeat. My stomach is swirling, my brain is tumbling. I feel like I've been lost at sea and now the port is within view on the horizon, but I cannot set anchor. It's relief and pain. Happiness and despair.

My mind rages for the rest of day, so much so that Aunt Charlotte asks me what's wrong multiple times. The third time I drop a can of tomato paste, she sends me outside for a time-out like I'm one of her naughty kids.

All I do when I go out to the loading dock is pace back and forth from the dumpster to the door. My mates are here. Does my father know? He can't know. Only the central mate, me, their regina, and the other males in the mating group can see the marking. They would've seen mine if I hadn't spent my entire life with a shield of magical titanium around my entire person. I'd had it drilled into me from the moment I'd returned from the Oracle and she'd declared my mating group numbering of five of the most dangerous animalia of our time. We should have known, being what I am.

With what I can do.

The anima in me wants me to get in my car and go back to them. It's demanding we go in there and jail-break my mates immediately. The desperate anima wants to mate with them and complete the bonding ritual—complete our union and make them mine. To join our power in a pool and share magic so intimately we all orgasm over it.

Fuck. Fuck. Fuck.

I can't do any of that. I'm sweating. I'm wet and aroused and wired to the extreme.

It's torture and I have no idea what to do. I pour water from my drink bottle into my cupped hand and splash it on my face. I slap my cheeks. I do star jumps to try and get rid of this insane energy I now have. Aunt Charlotte comes out to check on me, narrowing her eyes at my state. Then her eyes widen.

"What's happened?"

I scramble to save face. She can't know about this. No one can. If word gets back to my father, he'll have the three of them executed immediately.

In any other animalia, this would be cause for grand celebration. Finding your mating mark on a male was a success story, something to brag about. Something you tell your girlfriends and the women in your family, and you all jump up and down and scream in happiness together. Your aunts would tell you how to deal with protective alpha mates and cry, telling you how happy they are.

There were parties, engagements, drinks, dresses. A normal girl would hug and giggle with her aunt.

But I'm not normal animalia and I can't have them. I want to tear my hair out. I want to scream. Instead, I shake my head and grit out, "Too much coffee. Sorry."

She doesn't believe me, frowning and slamming the door shut behind her. She probably thinks I'm on drugs or something. In a way, I am.

I make it through the rest of the day, and eventually, I lie in bed that night. Sweating. Thinking. It is *madness* the level of lust I now have, pouring through me like bubbling champagne. There is no way I'm going to sleep this wet, this writhing for my mates. My mind is a haze of desire and all it does is think about those muscular bodies sitting there in that prison when they should be here with me.

Savage and those lips. Dear god, it's fodder for the biggest orgasm in the world. All this healing work has left me far more empty than any amount of burgers and thick shakes can refill, and an earth-shattering orgasm will fix me right up.

My mind is now fixed upon Savage standing behind the bars of his cell, with his low-slung jeans, covered in dirt, the sheen of his sweat highlighting the ridges of his muscled torso. My hands find my neck and trail their way down my body, caressing the mounds of my breasts. I imagine Savage's large hands stroking me down the swoop of my stomach and down the sheer fabric of my nightie. I hitch the hem up, dragging my fingers up the tops of my thighs and skimming my underwear.

I hiss, my back arching as I imagine Savage on top of me, his wolfish grin and hungry eyes waiting in anticipation. My right hand creeps into my panties while my left hand massages my breast. I circle my wet and throbbing clit, gasping at the feel of my own slick. I'm incredibly soaked and can't help but plunge my fingers inside myself, exploring my wet heat. Gods, what would it be like if he were really here? If any of my mating group were here, touching me, telling me I looked like a princess? I would simply die, I think; combust into a thousand flames of pleasure. My lips whisper their names into the dark of my bedroom. The names of my strong, dangerous mates emerge from my lips like prayer: *Savage, Xander, Scythe.*

Savage

Here I am, lying on my comfy dungeon floor, when the melody of a song runs down my spine in a warm caress.

I sit bolt upright.

Xander and Scythe shift too, except no chains are clanking with their movements. My heart pounds as every part of my being stands to attention.

I look over at Xander and realise that while his physical body is still chained to the wall, his astral body has woken up, blue-grey, transparent and frowning down at himself. I look down at my own body and see that I'm also blue-grey and see-though. My body still lies on the stone floor, eyes closed and asleep.

I barely have time to admire my own face before my attention is pulled by another, heady, quivering note.

Magic as old as time itself is in the air; delicious, strong, lusty.

Something has bypassed the magical shield around the dungeon and it can only be one thing:

The call of our regina. Our central mate.

I close my eyes and allow the song to take me, knowing the others will follow their instincts and do the same. It's too enticing to deny, and the animus in me roars in happiness.

Our mate is calling for us, and by all the fucking wild and beastly gods, I want to scream to her that I'm coming.

I float upwards on the melody, my cock twitching and excitement spinning through me. I get to see my regina. I get to see the woman I'm destined to spend the rest of my life with, to worship, to fuck, to make love to, to... fuck.

Passing through the levels of Halfeather"s mansion, the night sky meets me with a thousand twinkling lights. I grin like a madman to be in the outside world again after so many months. I can't see my bond-brothers, but I know they'll be carried in by the melody of her song too.

I'm pulled through the night, over the highway and through suburbia and I memorise the way there—it's imperative that I find her after we find a way to escape our imprisonment. The current lowers me towards a tiny, dilapidated unit, no more than a bungalow, set deep up a long drive behind another larger house. Excitement pounds through my ribs as it deposits me outside a bedroom window. I pass easily through the glass and into a small, darkened room where I feel Scythe, Xander, and two other shadowed presences with us. The fourth and fifth members of our mating group. To complete our merry band of nutcases. I've never met them, but I know they've been pulled here to satisfy our regina, same as me.

Speaking of our woman, she is, at present, writhing around on her bed in a tiny, thin pink nightie, her hand in her panties, her eyes closed. Holy fucking Mother of all...

It's Lia. Her black hair is spilling around her head, loose from her ponytail, her pale face a mask of pleasure, pillowy lips parted. Long, shapely legs squirm on the bed and I'm struck by the desire to jump on top of her. I can't believe fate brought her to us in our jail.

The mating mark on her neck glows in the night, as if it's happy to see us. The sight of it has me choked up because I've been looking for that mark my entire life. How the fuck didn't I see it before now? And her scent... by the gods, it's like a drug for me and all I can do is close my eyes and savour it.

I knew she'd smell delicious. Like cupcakes and vanilla and mint and strawberries. I really do want to devour her whole.

She must sense us because her eyes fly open and she blinks up with those blue eyes I want to drown in.

Her hand stays between her legs as she whispers in confusion. "What the..."

I look around and see the other males are motionless, probably dealing with their hard-ons or shock or whatever. But I'm ready for action, as always. I practically leap forward, half wanting to replace my hand with hers, half wanting to show her I'm not a pervert. But her scent is too strong for me to resist. With my heart pounding like a mad drum, I lean over her and whisper, "Lia? You've let out a siren call to your mates. That's why we're all here."

Aurelia

In my dream, my room is full of shadows, but I'm not scared at all. If anything, they are a comfort.

I'm so horny I could burst. It's come over me hard and strong, a sweeping desire tumbling through me like a tsunami, waves of lust making me want to spread my legs as wide as they will go.

And then one of the shadows steps forward and I recognise his wolfish face straight away. Savage. Looking down at me with such burning desire. I thank my lucky stars that my subconscious has given me exactly what I need right now. The mating mark on his neck glows bright and sharp. Eagerly, I reach for him.

"Come here, Savage," I say longingly. He hesitates and my voice takes on a sensual whisper. "Please?"

Thank all the gods he doesn't need any more encouragement, because he falls into my arms and captures my lips with his. His skin is hot through my nightie and I arch into his hard muscles. He groans, sweeping his tongue into my mouth, devouring me as if he's been waiting an entire lifetime to do this. He tastes me and I allow him access to everything he wants, curling my legs around him. He breaks our kiss, leaving my head spinning as he runs his tongue down my neck and over my own mating mark.

"Oh gods," I moan, and my voice makes his movements frantic. "I need you inside me."

"Lia," he groans against my neck, his hand finding my breast and squeezing gently.

What a fucking wonderful dream, but I'll have to thank myself later as I hiss again. Savage pulls down the top of my nightie to lick my nipple, sweeping his hand down the length of my body, leaving flames where his skin touches mine. He hooks his fingers into my panties and pulls them gently down. Drawing away from me, he quickly drags my underwear down my legs, and then he's back on top of me, grinding an impossibly hard erection into my center with his jeans still on.

I'm so fucking happy about this. I might not be able to have my mates in real life—but in dreamland? It's the next best thing.

I make a sound of dissatisfaction. This isn't fast enough. My anima wants him naked between my legs. I need all of him, all of *them* like my life depends on it.

The other shadows around us seem to darken, and I glance at our onlookers. I can just make out four broad shapes but no details—as if they don't want to step forward and be known just yet. I find that I don't mind being watched, though. If anything, it gives a kick to my desire.

They are my mates and I *want* them to be here and see me naked and in pleasure.

"Eyes on me, princess," Savage growls jealously. The raw hunger in his eyes is enough to set me tingling and I'm mesmerised by his desire for me. This pure, hungry predator who wants to devour me whole. He says darkly, "I want to be inside you while you squirm."

I gasp as he slips his hand between my legs and groans deep in his throat. He closes his eyes in pleasure, fingers exploring my wet core. I wriggle around him and he chuckles before plunging a finger inside of me.

I let out a strangled moan, arching my back and spreading my legs wider for him, a silent command to go deeper. I reach for his arm, enjoying the feel of his thick muscles flexing. He grins down at me, and then presses his lips against mine. I kiss him excitedly, holding his face, feeling his rough scruff under my fingers.

My anima keens for more and I must say it out loud because he whispers against my lips, "Greedy princess, wanting more. You want me to fill you up, don't you? You want all of us fucking you until you can't scream anymore, don't you?" His fingers plunge in and out of me to the beat of his words, and I can only writhe as tendrils of warm, dizzying pleasure ripple through me like the most delicious summer wind.

"Yes, Savage," I moan. "I want it all."

"Say please."

My eyes fly open and I find his eyes dark and serious. He reaches up and pulls my hair tie from my hair, already loose from my writhing, and puts it on his own wrist. "So beautiful," he breathes. "*Now say please.*"

I bite my lip as he makes slow strokes inside of me, his thumb brushing delicious circles over my clit. How I want this to be real. How much I want to please him. So I say it with lusty relish, "Please, Savage."

He plunges a second finger into me, and I whimper at the stretch. He increases his speed, the wet sounds of my own pussy winding me tighter and tighter, pushing me over the edge. I burst into a thousand pieces, screaming out his name as he buries his face in my neck and groans. I gush all over his fingers and he wrings every last moment of pleasure from me. He pulls away and I look up at him with a half-lidded gaze, his hazel eyes hungry, his beautiful lips parted. Even in my dreams, my mate made sure I got what I needed. It makes my anima flutter with happiness.

I sigh in satisfied pleasure, but then Savage is suddenly off me, standing next to my bed. Without taking his eyes off mine, he raises his fingers and puts them straight into his mouth, closing his eyes as if savouring the taste. I stare at his mouth in awe.

He frowns when he pulls his fingers out. "Fuck, princess. I can taste you even in this form."

But my eyes are fluttering shut, my body like butter, melting into my bed in the wake of the most mind-shattering orgasm I've ever had. I stretch out, a happy smile tugging at my lips. When was the last time I'd felt this... happy?

Dear gods, if only all dreams could feel this real.

Aurelia

The next morning, I wake up with the most heavenly afterglow still clinging to me like golden morning dew. I smile as I stretch out luxuriously on my bed and find the mess I'd made of my sheets. My underwear is on the floor and I chuckle as I bend to pick it up.

That was a bloody great dream and I'm *so* keen to do it all over again tonight. If I have that experience to come home to every day, perhaps... just perhaps, it will be enough to get me through the rest of my life without my mates.

I haven't slept so well in ages and my little fantasy even has me humming as I strip my bed of my sheets and shove them joyfully into my thousand-year-old washing machine. From my old laptop, I put some music on, bopping my head as I shower and get ready to head back to Halfeather's mansion.

The buzz I have is more than a post orgasm afterglow; my skin is practically luminescent with my power coursing through me in strong waves. I could very well get heaps of progress with my prisoner-patient today and be done with Halfeather's lecherous gaze sooner than planned. I flex my fingers and feel my power thrumming through me. Hell, I might even be done today.

As a dark pang shakes my heart, I tell myself that this will be good. Because then I can leave those males behind and move on with my life. The more time I spend with them, the harder the separation is going to be. My anima is writhing rebelliously within me today, hissing and flapping with excitement to see them again. I muzzle that sensation as quickly as possible.

So it's with great determination that I rock up to Halfeather's mansion with Maisy sparkly clean after a quick wash this morning.

"You're a in a good mood," Beak says as he opens my door. Then he drops his voice in what I think is jealousy. "Some beast treating you well?"

"Why does it have to be some guy, huh?" I say, playfully poking him in his oversized bicep. Yeah, at least I got to touch *someone* before I left this place. "Maybe it's all just me."

He grins and I smirk at the way his tawny eyes gleam, checking me out. If I can't have my mates, I could in theory, choose a human to spend my life with. A beast would figure out what I am as soon as I had intimate contact with them and that information would then be valuable and *very* sell-able. No, humans are my safest bet.

But as soon as that thought enters my mind, my stomach churns and I have to press my fingers over my mouth to stop the urge to vomit. I sigh at my anima growling angrily at the prospect of being with a beast other than one of my mates. I sour immediately as I follow Beak inside. Unexpectedly, he turns around to glance at me, his eyes swooping down my body.

All of a sudden, I'm cognisant of how I've dressed myself while my mind was busy re-living my dream this morning.

I'm in a *dress*. One of two that I own. It's maroon, tight, plunges a little low, and I remember putting lipstick on. I had been buzzing with power and lust and I'd had no fucking idea that I was preening myself like a bird in heat. I'm in way over my head and I realise I've not even packed a jacket. My anima is aware that my mates are down there and everything inside of me has been waiting and ready to see their faces again. It's a *blatant* attempt for male attention considering how I've been dressing the other days. It's practically a giant, sexy, green flag that announces, "Woohoo, female ready and available!"

I'm *not* available! I'm the least available anima in the universe right now.

A panic attack is building up in me by the time we get down to the dungeon. I don't know how I'm going to hide this from Savage. He's going to know something is different right away. He's too observant of me. Too interested in me.

As a mate should be.

I'm fighting embarrassed tears as Beak opens the last steel door for me and gives me a hot look that turns into confusion.

I force a smile on my face and the movement calms me a little. If I'm going to keep these males safe from my father, I need to keep up appearances. *That* is the most important thing right now, emotions be damned.

So I plaster an even wider smile on my face and all but strut past Beak and Scuff down into the dungeon corridor as if It's my personal runway. My step falters, but I pretend

I'm an actress on set, putting on the show of a lifetime. *No one can know. No one can know. I'm just a regular, horny animalia. No mates here.*

But the deeper I get into the gloom of cold stone, I can *feel* that something is different.

It's deathly quiet today. And something heavy vibrates between the cells. A whisper of something powerful.

I avoid looking at Scythe and stride right past his cell, though I can see the gleam of his eyes on me. Savage is standing by his bars as usual, and as I walk up to my patient's steel door, my shields are back up at full capacity so I can't see his mating mark.

"Morning," I say briskly. But I stand there for a moment, trying to figure out what's changed in my wolf.

Savage has a grin that could light up the whole world at midnight, and it takes my breath away.

His hazel eyes gleam as he says in a low voice, "Hello, princess." Both of his large, tattooed hands grip the bars so tightly it looks like he wants to rip them apart. My eyes are drawn to something new on his left wrist.

He's wearing a black hair tie.

Time stops as I breathe, "*No.*"

Male arrogance drips off him like oil. "I had a fun time last night, princess. We all did."

My hand flies to my chest as abject horror spins through me. "Oh gods, I can't breathe."

Xander scoffs behind me as Savage gives a deranged cackle. "Yeah, I know, I know."

I glare at him. "W-What the hell is going on?"

"I believe," Savage says with vicious mirth, "I astrally finger fucked your sweet pussy and you came all over my hand."

My knees go weak and I have to crouch down to make sure the floor is under me. This is a bad dream. This has to be nightmare. None of this can be real.

I can't look at him and his arrogant, beautiful face, so I cradle my head in my hands and squeeze my eyes shut. I can still feel his fingers in me as I think about my own body. My pussy does feel like It's been stretched by fingers bigger than my own.

It *had* been real. I'd actually called them all in with a mating siren song. Do they know I'm their mate, then?

I take a deep breath and look up to see Savage watching me obsessively as he normally does, just with an arrogant, very-happy-with-himself smirk.

"I think I'm gonna be sick."

"Weak stomach, hatchling?" drawls Xander. "Might want to check you didn't catch a canine virus or something."

My stomach is churning now, but not in disgust, in sheer, unadulterated embarrassment. They'd all been there—even glowering Scythe—and had seen me practically naked and lusty, spreading my legs for—

Dear Wild Mother, get a grip, Lia. You're a woman, they're your mates. You have nothing to be ashamed about. Nothing at all because it's normal and natural. They're the ones who should be embarrassed.

I collect my blabbering mind together with this thought and promptly stand up, crossing my arms and level both Savage and Xander a smirk. "I hope you enjoyed the show"—I raise my voice to make sure Scythe can hear— "Even if the others were too cowardly to come forward."

Xander is still in the shadows of his cell, as if he's imagining me from last night. I stand there and let him look at me with my dress, bare legs and all.

He flexes his wrists, and the chains around them rattle. "You're an arrogant little thing, aren't you? What's your animus and why can't we scent it?"

"I don't answer to you, dragon," I shoot back.

But then Scythe speaks from his cell behind me—a rasping voice that sounds like someone has sliced open his throat from the inside and let it scar over. "Why can't we see your mating mark today? What are you hiding?"

His voice, and the dark meaning behind his words is terrifying enough to give me goosebumps. But shit. They must've seen my mark last night.

I scoff to hide my rising terror and call back, "You're the ones in a dungeon, and you're asking *me* what I'm hiding? A bit rich, isn't it?"

This is bad. The three of them know. If they ever get out of here, they'll come for me. They won't be able to deny their own primitive instinct. My anima is calling out to their three animus' in a shrill mating call and I stomp on that immediately.

"I don't like you," says Xander.

Well, that is a good thing. I snap, "Yeah? Well, you're an asshole Xander, because I..."

Savage remained quietly attentive while I snapped at the other two, but he presses me now. "Because what?"

Because there is something in my dress pocket that I made this morning when I'd been happy and clearly insane—I'd brought Xander a USB with new music on it, alright?

But I can't very well say that out loud, can I? I inhale a calming breath, trying to ease my frazzled nerves. Then I create a shield-ball around the USB in my pocket, levitate it, invisible, through the cell bars and smack Xander on the head with it.

He flinches, but before it falls to the floor, I sweep it upwards and plug it into the device on his hip.

"Bunch of assholes, the lot of you," I scowl. "Now be good boys and stay quiet so I can concentrate on my patient."

My heart is pounding as I sit down on the floor and all I know is, that I have to get out of here and never come back. For some reason, the three beasts *do* remain quiet, but I hear Savage sit down and can practically feel him poking my side with his stare.

Whether it's my anger at the three of them, or the actual power boost from one of my mates giving me an orgasm last night, I finish healing my patient within the hour. I prise the jaws of the shadow snake's teeth one by one from around the nape of his neck. The entire thing dissolves in a mist of black magic.

Aurelia

The satisfaction at perhaps the best healing job I've ever done barely registers, because as I get to my feet, I know I won't be back tomorrow. I know this is the last time I will ever lay eyes on my mates. I shouldn't do it, but the wild, primitive anima part of me steps between Xander and Savage's cells to take one last look at them both.

Xander scowls at me and I wish, just for a moment, that I could see his face properly. But he'll just have to stay as a shadow in my imagination.

Savage's hazel gaze is searching as he stands half a foot away from me, and I can almost feel the heat of his animus. If my shields were down, I would have been able to scent him, too.

Alas, I will never know what he really smells like. That is the worst thing of all. But it is a safety thing, and it's smart for me to keep it that way.

I could, in theory, *touch* him. He must think this too because he pushes one large hand between the bars, palm up like a peace offering.

I stare at it for a long, long time, and he stares back at me in silence. Something inside of me breaks a little as I close my eyes and turn away from him. My anima whines in sorrow.

"Lia." Savage's voice is surprised, like he doesn't understand what's going on. I want to say that I'm sorry. That I wish things were different. That if I were a different beast, I would be running into his arms right now, kissing him, rescuing him from his prison, taking him home with me.

But for both his and my safety, I can't reveal anything. I'm passing Scythe's cell before I know it and against my will, my head turns to look at him.

He glares at me as I force my feet to keep moving, and it's the coldest thing I've ever seen. I can't read his expression because there's literally nothing there. His face has been hewn from ice and all I can feel from him is that he hates me. I didn't know my soul could feel so much pain until this moment.

When Beak opens the door for me, it's like I've surfaced from deep water. The heaviness around me suddenly dissipates, and I take a fresh breath.

"Are you alright?" Beak says, briefly putting his hand on the small of my back. I look up at him and smile at his kindness. I'll miss *that* too.

"I'm just happy because I'm done with the patient," I say. "I don't have to go down to that awful place ever again."

He nods as if he understands, but he doesn't smile back as I expected. "That's really great," he murmurs quietly.

Maybe he likes me after all and is thinking about how he'll miss me, too.

Back in Halfeather's office, the old eagle is dragging his eyes up my bare legs and I'm very grateful this is the last time I ever have to see him.

"I've done what I can for him, Mr Halfeather," I say quickly. "It's up to him and his power to have him wake up now."

"Indeed?" he says slowly, eyes stuck like glue on me. "Well, I must say it pleases me greatly that this is not the last time we will be seeing one another."

My brows shoot up as I register what he is insinuating.

"Mr Halfeather," I say, as if this is all a pleasant joke. "I'm the consummate professional. I take it my father's debt is paid?"

The corners of his mouth turn down. "Ah, that's the thing, Aurelia. Your father did not just sell me your services, my dear."

A chill consumes me as I suddenly realise there have been no signs that Mr Halfeather has a mate. That is unusual for a wealthy male such as him—usually they are rex for a harem of mates, bonded by fate or not.

My voice drops an octave as a deadly stillness falls over me. "What were the terms exactly, Mr Halfeather?"

A smile creeps over his mouth and he skulks towards me, his black robe swishing limply. "A bride contract. A princess of the serpent court. A worthy union, do you not think?"

I become stone. This whole thing is made worse by what had happened last night and the fact that three parts of my soul sit in a cell below me, so close my body can still feel them.

A distant whistling sounds outside and I frown, because who the hell is whistling in this place? Halfeather is not the type of employer who would allow that. But no one responds to it.

It's then that the ghost of Savage strolls into the room with his hands in his pockets, whistling that happy tune, closely followed by a see-through Scythe, wearing nothing but track pants and a murderous expression, and a transparent Xander looking curiously around with the strangest looking eyes I've ever seen.

I stare in horror at the three of them, this being the first time I can see Scythe and Xander properly.

Even in their ghostly apparition forms, I can tell that all of them are apex predators of the highest orders.

They're all tall, and the three of them dwarf the room. Scythe, with silvery hair that brushes his shoulders, a wide, square jaw and high cheekbones. Marine animalia all share an impossible, cold, out-of-this-world beauty, and Scythe is no exception.

Xander's arrogant posture has him looking like he owns the place, and knowing he's a dragon, I guess that his own house is probably even bigger than this one. But one thing is clear and confusing to me: he's blind. Both eyes are silver all the way around, telling me that his physical eyes don't work. They glow with preternatural force, meaning he's seeing with his power. I can tell he's looking at me, and even sneering, his dragon's features are stunning. His torso is bare and there's tribal dragon markings in a full sleeve down his left arm. He has a black nose ring and a matching dangling cross earring on his left ear.

I'm aroused immediately.

The ghosts look around the room, then come to stand next to Halfeather, crowding around him as if they want to kill him. Savage sticks a hand through Halfeather's head and it goes right through. Halfeather, nor Beak or Scuff, show any sign of seeing them.

Savage gives a dramatic sigh. "Looks like we can't murder him right now, princess."

"It's best if you don't react to this," Xander growls. "They'll think you're mad."

"I think I *am* mad," I blurt out.

Halfeather's brows shoot into his hairline as behind him Savage and Xander burst out laughing. But they're not nice laughs. Scythe simply glowers at me, probably taking offense, as most of his relatives probably *do* have the dreaded land-madness.

I swear inwardly, realising I need to ignore whatever is happening with these males in ghost form right now, because a very wealthy and powerful eagle is telling me something that is about to change the entire trajectory of my life.

It's also not lost on me that eagles and other birds of prey *eat* snakes.

I manage to unstick my lips and find my voice. "I *mean* to say, I'm afraid to disappoint you, Mr Halfeather, but I am not a serpent princess. I have never pledged to my father's court, nor has he graced me with any titles. Nor am I, actually, a snake. I take after my mother, an Aquinas."

My surname is another lie. And the biggest one of all.

Savage and Xander suddenly stop laughing.

"And that is why this union is an excellent idea," says Halfeather, not perturbed by my speech. "We are both of the same order!"

Savage growls and I shoot him a look, but he only has eyes for Halfeather.

I stare at the old eagle, then glance around, more than aware of Beak and Scuff at the door, likely listening closely. Will they try and keep me here? Will they stop me if I try to leave? The thought of Beak tackling me down and dragging me back in here gives me the shivers and not in the sexy way. My three ghosts won't be able to do a thing to help me, either.

"I'm afraid there's been a mistake, Mr Halfeather, I—" I am very aware that if I deny this powerful man, there will be consequences. I need to make nice as much as it irks me. "I... must talk to my father about the particulars."

"You're kidding!" Savage exclaims. "You can't marry this cunt!"

"Of course, of course," Halfeather says smoothly, stepping back and bowing. "We must abide by the Old Laws, naturally."

"Motherfucker!" Savage exclaims, aiming a kick to Halfeather's legs, but of course, it sails right through.

I stiffen as Halfeather frowns down at his legs as if he feels the whisper of something. The Old Laws say that females are to marry as they are told to by senior males of the family, if they have no mates of their own. I plaster a smile on my face. "Indeed. I will get back to you, Mr Halfeather."

"I would expect no less."

What an asshole. I turn on my heel and make for the door. Beak and Scuff hastily let me pass, their faces carefully blank, but I know that they are used to strange and unethical conversations in this office.

I all but storm back to the security desk, snatching my handbag when Beak holds it out. I stomp back to my car and gun the engine. I wonder why my three mates are suddenly able to move about in the mansion in their astral forms, and a dark feeling slides through me.

As soon as I'm past the boom gate and back on the road, I slap my steering wheel in anger.

Who the fuck does my father think he is, selling me like this? As the king of serpents, he can do as he pleases with me and no one will question it. No one will care. I am actually powerless here. I was so close to going to college, so close to freedom! Angry tears trickle down my cheeks and I aggressively swipe them away.

I've been terribly naïve thinking my father wouldn't sell me at the first chance. I need to get as far away from here; from my mates, from my father.

I'd fantasised about running away ever since he'd kicked me out of home. I'd planned the movements in my head, thought about the best places to go to hide from him. I'd just never had the gall to actually do it. But now? Now things are slipping out of my control so badly I'm thinking I have no other choice. If I want to take my life in my own—

"You're angry," comes a male voice.

I almost run my car off the road.

"Fucking genius, do you know that, Sav?" comes Xander's voice.

In my rear-view mirror are the ghosts of the three males, sitting there like we're going on a school field trip.

"Fuck!" I choke out, indicating, then carefully navigating onto the gravel shoulder on the side of the road.

I pull my up handbrake and swing around to glare at them.

"Just what the hell do you think you're doing?" I cry.

Savage gives me a sheepish smile. "Sorry, princess, but I think you only have yourself to blame for this one. I think it's because of last night that—"

"What?" I exclaim. "You think just because you had your fingers in me you can just follow me around now?"

All three men glower at me.

"Well," says Savage, running a hand through his choclate brown waves. "I *did* make you come."

"Just barely," I snap. "Get out of my car."

They all scowl at me.

"Leave!" I gesture to the doors.

"But this is too much fun, snake girl," Xander deadpans. "I'm not going anywhere until you tell us what you're hiding from your mates."

Oh, so I wasn't *'hatchling'* anymore. That stings more than it should. I turn back to face the front window and pinch my nose, sighing deeply. Things couldn't get any worse. How am I supposed to run away with these three following me around?

My phone pings and I pull it out of my handbag to see a message from my father's assistant.

Aurelia

Aurelia

I should have known Uncle Ben was trying to warn me with the meatball thing.

Not two hours later, I'm sending more messages to my father's assistant, demanding to speak with him, when Aunt Charlotte knocks on my perimeter shield. I let her in and skulk to the door.

She stands on my welcome mat with my four-year-old cousin, Trixie, who's jumping up and down with excitement, her blond curls swinging. I raise my brows at the black dress bag Charlotte's holding.

"What's this?" I say carefully.

Charlotte jerks her chin to tell me to allow her inside my house and I oblige, frowning at them both. She's dressed in a stylish red dress and her hair is freshly curled, as if she's going to an event. Her other five kids are at school. My father demanded the serpent population have as many children as possible to repopulate after the 70's purge.

"It's so exciting, Lia!" Trixie squeals. "I wish *I* was getting married!"

A dagger of white-hot horror pierces my core. "*What?*" I cry. At that moment, two snakes stroll up to the door, female scouts, both with unsheathed daggers angled at me. One of them runs her tongue over her bared teeth as she looks me up and down.

"We're to make sure you're dressed appropriately for Halfeather," she says through a smoker's throat. "Hurry up, you have twenty minutes."

Aunt Charlotte huffs and sweeps into my bedroom without another word. I wouldn't have followed, but Trixie grabs me with her little hand and hauls me after her mother, humming a wedding march under her breath.

Shit.

I mentally kick myself. I should have left immediately. I have a bag packed and everything in my closet—all the essentials, my entire stash of savings, passport, underwear, tampons, *everything*. This is happening too quickly. My father is a brilliant tactician.

He'd probably guessed about my plans and known that me running was a possibility. The smartest thing for him to do is to secure this marriage straight away.

If only I'd been more clever.

Trixie unceremoniously shoves me into the bathroom, tapping her bare wrist as if she has a watch on it.

I shower, rapidly trying to think of an escape route out of here. I could easily turn into a rat or mouse or possum and get out of my window. But how long would I last out in the world without my phone and money and clothes? I am well and truly screwed.

Trixie opens the bathroom door and shouts excitedly at me and I hastily get out and towel off. When I arrive back in my room, there's a dress hanging from my curtain rail. I stop dead, looking at the long length of thin black silk.

It's a traditional serpent *wedding* dress. Slinky so that it will cling to my body and thin so that it leaves nothing to the imagination. In the Old Way, everything needed to be on show for the groom and his family to see exactly what they were getting.

Dear Wild Mother, I'm going to faint. I grip the edge of my door, sagging a little while Charlotte *tsks* and rummages through my drawers, completely invading my private spaces. I thought this was a formal engagement or something, but they'd only dress me up like this for an actual wedding.

"Hurry up!" comes a gruff shout from behind me.

I flinch violently and turn to glare at the two serpent females of my father's court smirking at me. Scowling, I step inside my room and slam the door in their faces. Their cackles come through the door, grating and wild; a herald of my doom.

"Hurry, Lia!" Trixie said. "Look, I'll even turn around, see?"

Charlotte slides the dress off its hanger and brings it over to me. She sniffs as if this is all very beneath her. "No underwear. That's how we all did it. That's the proper way."

"I need a bra though," I say, trying to get around her to my underwear drawer.

"No," she says sharply.

I stare at her, mouth agape. "My nipples will show right through that!"

She gave me a droll look as if to say, *that's the point.*

The Old Laws can get fucked, honestly. I don't even have any pasties or tape of any kind.

I snatch the dress from her and drop the towel, ignoring her completely as her piercing brown eyes sweep comparingly down my naked body.

If only she knew that I'd had my five mates staring at my naked, writhing body just a few days ago. Her eyes are *nothing*.

A pang of sadness cleaves at my heart at the thought of my mates.

The silk of the dress is beautiful, with tiny, barely there straps and a swooping back that comes down low. In any other situation, I would have *loved* this dress. It somehow hugs my curves in the most perfect way. It's the nicest thing I've worn in seven years and makes me look like a real woman.

It's as if it came from a family who loves their daughter. He's probably trying to create the illusion of it—of my value. Just for a moment, I stand in front of my mirror, look at myself, and can see someone else. Someone who is going to marry her mates in a dress given to her by loving parents. There'd be black and red roses on my side of the family and every colour of flowers under the sun for my mates. Wolves, sharks and dragons would be at my imagined wedding. There'd be an extraordinary variety of foods; raw fish for Scythe's family and a spit roast for the wolves. Wealthy and respected members of the community would be excited to see the serpent bride and her five grooms.

Trixie makes *oohing* sounds, running her hand down the long train, and it snaps me back to reality.

Aunt Charlotte makes a noise in the back of her throat, her red lips twisting as she looks at me. My cheeks are wet and I hastily wipe at them. "Halfeather will be happy and that's all that matters," she says quietly, almost to herself. "Now, what should we do with this black hair of yours?"

Aurelia

We arrive at Halfeather's mansion in the serpents' Mercedes, with my hair in a fancy up-do and Trixie in a poofy flower girl's dress and slick ballerina bun. I hadn't been allowed to bring my phone, nor my wallet, or anything at all. Charlotte had merely put a diamond choker—a gift from Halfeather—on me, shoved flats on my feet—Halfeather is too short for heels to be a good look—and pushed me inside the waiting car where Uncle Ron and Uncle Ben avoided my gaze.

I get out carefully, my nipples fully peaked and visible in the chill breeze, and I have to suppress the urge to rub them flat. What a fucking mess. My heart pounds in my ears as Trixie takes my hand, batting her eyelashes at me, the *bride*. In a mild panic, I search the mansion as if I'll find friends here.

It's as if I'm seeing the place for the first time. This is to be my new residence. My new prison.

Beak and Scuff greet us at the door with grim faces. Beak won't look at me at all, and the tight leash I've been keeping on my fourth shield slips.

I might have done it on purpose, but I won't let myself think of why. Savage appears at my side, bursting with questions. Scythe and Xander stride out of the mansion a second later, trying not be obvious about their eyes taking me in from head to toe—or more likely, head to nipples. I work hard to ignore them all and focus on following Beak and my uncles inside.

"That's a pretty dress, princess," Savage drawls, but his voice is tight. "You were pretty rude shutting us out— Oh fucking hell."

Savage has noticed my father waiting in the entrance hall.

The serpent king stands, tall and menacing, an aura of dark power about his body, and barely looks at me. He kisses Charlotte on both cheeks and nods his satisfaction at her getting me here. Trixie skips up to him and he kisses her possessively on the head.

She is a princess of his court, of course she gets royal treatment. A spear of jealously hits me, and I'm immediately ashamed of being jealous of a child.

"Father," I say in what I hope is a cold, imperious voice. "We need to talk."

Savage and the males go quiet next to me and I can feel them there, almost flanking me like guards. But that was just my anima reaching—looking for people on my side when there aren't any.

"We do not need to talk, Aurelia," he replies coldly. His eyes flash in warning and a hint of shadow coils around his hand. "Your marriage to Halfeather happens now." He'll use his snake on me here, I know it. He won't care if anyone sees. Obedience is all that matters to him, and back-talk can get me in serious trouble.

I think about it for a moment, my eyes darting around to see if I have any exits.

"Not so strong now, snake girl?" Xander's snide voice comes in my ear and I want to cry. "You're going to be a plaything for this old eagle. I wonder if he'll let you out of your cage a few times a year?"

Biting the inside of my cheek before I completely lose it, I stalk forward. My arms are still crossed because I don't want Beak and every male beast in this room to see my nipples still taut from the chill that has nothing to do with the temperature of the room.

Silently, I follow the group, with Beak, Scuff, and my mates close behind me. My blood is pounding in my ears as we reach a new room, a sort of drawing room on the ground floor. We stop outside as my father strides in, followed by Charlotte, Uncle Ben, Uncle Ron, and Trixie, who skips through as if this is actually a wedding procession. My stomach churns, and I glance over my shoulder.

Savage, Xander, and Scythe are silently watching me, as if they hate me for what is happening. As if it's my fault. But Beak is giving me a look of warning—an order to get moving. I scowl at him and he has shame enough to look away.

I turn around and walk through the door as Savage says, "Want me to kill him for you, princess? I didn't know you were a *real* princess."

"Your father doesn't like you very much, does he, little snake?" Xander drawls. "I wonder what bad thing you did to make him hate you."

Being born. That's the bad thing I did.

I swallow my pride as I walk into the drawing room where everyone is waiting for me in position around a lacquered wooden table.

Halfeather stands there, his receding scalp extra shiny as if someone has polished it for him, just for today. His eyes greedily take in my body. I dully wonder if that'll be one of my jobs as his wife, scalp polishing.

An older male I don't know—a tiger, I think—wears a formal suit and holds a folder full of papers. Likely a Council member to witness us. Tigers are favoured for such things because they are usually impartial loners.

Halfeather rushes forward to take both my hands, eagerly kissing both, and I feel a hint of tongue. I shudder as he looks up at me with shining brown eyes.

"So beautiful, Aurelia. What a sight for an old *bone* like me."

I freeze in horror as I register the emphasis on that one particular word. An odd choice of wording made very purposefully in front of others.

He knows what I am.

My eyes slide to my father, who is smiling mildly, then Uncle Ron, who is staring at his feet. Holy Mother, they've told him, and that's why he's so ecstatic to marry me. This is no normal marriage.

Halfeather will get me pregnant immediately to produce more of me. He'll likely get others to do it too. The smartest thing to do would be to diversify the genes of my children to create the most powerful court since ancient times.

I wonder if I can turn into a mouse and scurry out the window, never to be seen again. But snakes eat mice. So do eagles, and my father is giving me a dark look that promises murder if I act out.

But I *could* turn into a tiger if I wanted.

Or a lion.

I've never tried it, but I could probably turn into a dragon, too.

I could destroy this house and everyone in it, if I wanted to. But then everyone would know that my mother was from the ancient house of Boneweaver. That we could turn into any beast we wanted as long as we'd been in physical contact with it.

But to do that would mean that everyone would find out and there would be a global manhunt for me. The valuable anima who could produce more of her kind. And a group of males and females who could turn into any beast? That court would be the most powerful group in known history. The Council wouldn't allow it, and every underground mob boss would be after me. Chain me up and use me to breed.

So as Halfeather leads me to the table in front of the tiger councilman, I let him, holding back the burning of my eyes with all my might.

I glance over my shoulder again to see my three astral prisoners watching everyone and everything closely. Scythe has disappeared and Savage stands by my elbow, peering over my shoulder to look at the papers. He lets out a breath that I swear I can feel and I shiver.

Halfeather brings out a tiny blue velvet box and my heart gives an unsteady beat.

"Perk up, little snake," comes Xander's voice on my other side now. "You're going to be living in a mansion instead of that old hovel of yours. You can come and visit us every day." And then closer to my ear. "He'll make you fat with little bird babies. How many do you want?"

I suppress a gag as Halfeather unceremoniously takes out the ring and grabs my hand. It's a huge diamond, round cut with a golden band. Halfeather gives me a haughty look as I stare at the massive rock, wondering how much I can trade it in for.

There has to be a way to get out of here, surely? Somehow, I can escape, I just know it. A piece of paper means nothing. Not to me, anyway.

"Sign here, please," the councilman slides forward a thick parchment and Halfeather picks up the pen and scribbles in an impatient but elegant cursive. Just as I go to take the pen, Halfeather hands it over to my father. My hand hangs lamely in mid-air for a single, disbelieving moment.

Xander chuckles softly behind me. "The snakes and eagles follow the Old Laws, eh? Nice little loophole for your filthy kind. They should have executed you all back in the old purge."

A chill creeps down my spine at the cold malice in my mate's words, but I have no time to ponder Xander's hate because I'm watching my father.

He signs the form in one brisk movement that tells me exactly what little importance I have to him.

And here I am officially, being given away as breeding stock.

Aurelia

Charlotte, Trixie, and my two uncles leave the room, my heart pounding faster and faster with every step they all take away from me. I glanced at Halfeather, who's looking at me greedily. How long will he wait to consummate the marriage? Because, honestly, he looks like he wants to do it right now.

I glance at Beak in alarm, and he shifts uncomfortably when he returns my look. There's be no help for me here. He can't step out of line with his boss, that's for sure. I don't want to get him in trouble, either.

"She'll spend one last night at her own house," my father says, "as we agreed, Charles."

My heart leaps into my throat. Is it possible? I look between the two males and the remaining councilman, who nods. "As per the Old Laws."

I had forgotten about that particular rule. After marriage, the bride went back to spend one last night with her female family members while the males of her family stayed at her husband's home to make sure it was up to scratch. The next morning, the bride would then return to her new house. It was a thing from a time long past, when the bride needed to be instructed on how to bed a man properly. Such a thing could only be spoken about to a married woman, of course, so the separation was necessary.

The whole thing is stupid, but I'm not complaining. The fire left Halfeather's eyes, but the look he gives me before I leave is a nasty promise of what's to come.

I cringe as I stride out of the mansion to the solitary waiting car, crossing my arms over my nipples again and almost cutting myself on the giant diamond I'm supposed to now wear. I glance behind me to see if my astral prisoners are still here, but it's only Beak and Scuff who stand next to my father, Uncle Ron, and Uncle Ben. I shove my fourth shield up again, completely unwilling to let my mates back into my life. My heart keens for them to return to me, but two of them hate me and the third just wants to fuck me.

What a mess that I had been born the way that I had.

When I get back to my house, five snakes—female guards from my father's court—greet me with a collective menacing *hiss*. They'll be guarding my house tonight, Charlotte tells me with a grimace, but I know she really means they're here to stop me from running.

It's midnight when I feel a familiar presence pounding on the outside of my shield.

"Aurelia? Aurelia!" Uncle Ben's panicked voiced sounds from outside. I lower my house shield and he lurches towards my front door.

There's real terror in his voice. Something is deathly wrong. I rush to the front door and throw it open. "I'm here, Uncle Ben! What's happened?"

Outside, my serpent parole officers are nowhere to be seen.

Uncle Ben rushes to me, still in his tartan summer pyjamas, his eyes wild, arms reaching out for me. He roughly shakes me by the arms. "Aurelia, you need to leave, right *now*."

That sense of dread I feel is suddenly in my throat. "Why?"

"Halfeather's mansion has just been burnt to the ground. Everyone is dead. Halfeather, the staff, all murdered. Just one security guard escaped. Ron and your father are fine. I've sent the guards there to retrieve him as a ruse." My blood pools into my feet as a sinister cold sweeps over my entire form. If anyone from my mating group had died, I would have known about it. Felt it. But I'd not felt—

"Aurelia, the prisoners in Halfeather's dungeon have all escaped somehow. And Beak, the security guard, said one of them kept repeating a name over and over again."

I already know whose name would be on the lips of the prisoners.

Uncle Ben is frantic. "Aurelia, Beak said it was one of the Slaughter Brothers, the wolf, who kept saying your name. He told me to secure you. Your father is telling everyone you caused the fire to get out of the marriage."

Shock at the injustice of this hits me like a blow to the head. But I don't need Uncle Ben to tell me to leave a second time. While I run to my room, Uncle Ben takes my keys and runs to get my car warmed up. I grab my duffle bag, shoving my wallet and the remainder of my hidden cash in it.

Once my father knows I've run, he will freeze my bank account or track my debit card, so I have to rely on cash from now on. I bolt out of my house, quickly checking the night sky for any sign of the sweep of a dragon's wings.

They know exactly where I live and having been pulled here once, they'll come to check here first... except they also know my car! I swear internally as I pull my house door shut and bolt to the driveway. I need to shield my car as well, then.

Uncle Ben gets out of the car and yanks his wallet out.

"Take this."

He is already taking great risk. "Uncle Ben, I—"

"Aurelia. Your father will have your head for running. You know that. You'll be on your own now. You need everything you can get. This is the best I can do for you."

The backs of my eyelids burn as I nod and accept the few notes he's holding out.

"Go, Lia. And fast."

Throwing my bag and then myself into my car, I hit reverse and head out to the street, slapping a shield of invisibility over my car. This time of night, it will be fine to drive unseen, but once daytime came and traffic increased, I'd be asking for someone to crash into me. Hopefully, I'll be far, far away by the time the sun clears the horizon.

Xander

I stand with the Slaughter Brothers Inc. behind the smouldering ruin of Halfeather's mansion, wiping the old beak's blood off my face. Tearing Halfeather's skull in half had been both pleasurable and satisfying in every possible way. Burning his mansion to cinders with my own flames was another type of dream come true. I'd have to thank whoever had started the fire, but only dragon fire could turn a building like this to cinders.

We'd let the female staff go except one Scythe had tied up and thrown outside for the police with a message tied around her neck. Of the males, only Beak escaped, who Savage had really wanted to get his claws on for flirting with the snake girl. Before us stands her father, the Serpent King, looking down his nose at us with beady black eyes. Eyeing him with my magical sight, Mace Naga is shrouded in heavy, oily power. Scumbag serpent magic. The filthy, slithering creatures are known for it, and it's one of many reasons everyone hates snakes and the purge had been done, *and* why a dragon would never lower himself to deal with one.

The fact that my mate had come from this evil bastard? I've done many shameful things in my twenty-three years, but I've never been so ashamed in my life.

But as a member of this mating group, I am bound to help these males who had become my brothers. We are just as soul-bound to each other as we are to the snake girl.

We fight like brothers do, and it is just as well that these beasts are one of the few males who can handle my angry blows. Scythe had laughed the last time I'd landed a lucky blow and shattered his nose. The one and only time I *had* seen him laugh, crazy bastard.

So it was with great annoyance that our escape was stopped by a bunch of snake shitheads and their king.

Savage had dragged me along to speak with the father of the regina he was pussy-crazed for. Initially, I thought he'd wanted to kill the man, but something bigger is at play here.

"As loath as I am to admit it," the serpent king says in a dull voice that has me instantly suspicious, "Aurelia organised this fire to kill us all. I believe her mates were in mind when she started it at the dungeons."

I narrow my gaze upon him, trying to detect any falsehood. But the truth is that I have been wondering why the fire started underground. The fact that he knows we are her mates is also surprising.

"She tried to kill us," Savage repeats, not quite believing his hot piece of ass would try and kill him. I've known all along she was capable of something like that, though. She *had* to be powerful to be regina to the Slaughter Brothers and me.

And she'd been lying to us the entire time she'd been down there.

Scythe is seething. I can see the icy cold force fluttering around him like lethal shards. He's livid about many things right now, but knowing that his regina is purposefully hiding herself is going to set him off on a rage, especially considering what had gone on between him and his own parents.

Hell, *I* was seconds away from shifting and launching myself into the sky.

Cracking my neck, I raise the volume on my device and change the song. It shuffles to one of the new songs the snake girl has given me. I rip the USB out of the player and throw it into the grass.

Savage sees me, scowls, and runs to pick it up from the ground, cradling it to his chest as he returns to us. He sniffs it as if he can chase her scent on it. His nostrils flare as he tries to get a whiff of her and fails. He's been sniffing the foil chocolate wrapper every hour for the past two days, but hasn't been able to get a read from it.

"She's been hiding her scent from us." Savage frowns. He holds it up to Scythe, who takes it from him and sniffs it, too. I know already there's nothing to sniff on it, nor on the track pants she gave Scythe.

She's forgotten one thing, though. She let her protections down that night we were all at her house, and Savage was able to scent her properly then.

Whatever her stupidity, these gifts had been cunning ways to manipulate us.

"Yes, that is a complication of her peculiar powers," the serpent king says. "That is why I need you, as her mates, to track her down. She needs to be stopped. She needs to be executed."

Fucking hell, he's outing his own daughter. The whole family is off. I thought mine were bad, but this guy is worse. At least my family keeps their punishments within the court.

"You want us to do it?" Scythe's rasp is raspier than ever from smoke inhalation, but there is no sign of pain as the Great White assesses the snake king.

"She'll be charged for murder and sent to the prison for ferals. It will be a kindness to execute her."

Savage blows out a breath. I can see he's upset about his regina being taken away from him, the sappy bastard. But trying to kill us is a kind of blasphemy that beasts hardly ever see. It's a real sort of mad anima who tries to kill the other pieces of her soul group.

Fuck. I really do think she needs to die, and if she has no scent, Savage is the only one who can track her, having tasted her.

"We'll do it," I say, edging away from him.

Savage glances at me, then at Scythe. Our great leader doesn't make any movement, but that's normal for him. I glance his way and see a green aura of assent around his head.

"You must make a blood binding to the terms," the snake says. "Or she may try to manipulate you. You will recover her. You can do whatever needs to be done to bring her back, but you will *not* mate with her. When she comes back, I'll deal with her the Old Way."

I roll my eyes at Savage, who is so pussy-crazed that he's foaming at the mouth to get back to her. I don't know if he'll agree, but this is personal now.

"Fine," Savage bites out. "We'll do it."

Shrugging, I offer my hand first to get it over and done with. The serpent king brings out a ceremonial serpent dagger and pricks my index finger, muttering the binding over the wound. My entire finger burns like it's been stung by a bee.

The thought of mating with her makes me feel like being sick. She tried to manipulate us, then kill us, now she's run away from us all. It's not natural. It's a heinous crime, and though it's a shame I won't have a regina, I won't stand by such an insult.

"I agree not to mate with my regina," I say. "And I'll deliver her to you." Light flares from the cut and it becomes a coiled black marking.

If I mate with the girl, the thing will curdle my blood and kill me from the inside out. When we return her, the binding will fade away.

Once he's repeated the ritual on the Slaughter Brothers, he says, "There. Now you are bound. Go and find my daughter."

Aurelia

In my many fantasies about running away, I'd given a lot of thought as to exactly how I'd do it, and it is this that saves me now. I need to get as far away from Halfeather's mansion—and my father—as possible, and going north is my best bet. I imagine myself in a sleepy seaside town, going to the beach every day and working in the local coffee shop owned by a quaint family. In order to be completely safe from my father, I will need to move as many states away as possible, and going to the west coast is my best chance. I'll drive, keeping to the highway until I get as close to the border as I can manage, sleep during the day and travel at night when I can hide my car completely. It's a fool proof plan, because while my father can track my scent on foot, by car, it's a whole lot more difficult.

He'll never get the authorities involved. No, this ruse about me causing the fire is just to get the suspicion off him. I have no doubt that he'd married me to Halfeather and caused the fire that killed him. He's probably already received whatever money he was owed and wants me back under his thumb.

The anima inside me wants to admit that my father's plan is brilliant.

But I know I'm not stupid either. I *can* do this. I will no longer cower in fear while men make decisions for me and force me to comply to their whims. I will not be prey. I will become the predator my mother's side of the family were. The ultimate predator of them all. I just need to gather my wits together and *do* it.

The excitement of making a new life for myself bubbles up alongside the adrenaline of running. Do I really think Savage and the men will hurt me if they find me? They are dangerous males, I have no doubt, and not at all that right in the head. I really have no idea what they will do if they catch me like they'd promised.

My best bet is to keep my secret safe and use it against them all.

I drive for four hours until the adrenaline fades and turns into weariness. I stop by a petrol station to fill up, buy three energy drinks, and continue on for another hour and a half. As the morning traffic starts to pile up, I quickly check my phone for a nearby motel.

There's one owned by a lion family, and what a treat because snakes *hate* lions with a passion, so it will be an excellent cover for me.

I drive right to it with my eyes heavy and my limbs aching. It's a small but smart, clean-looking place with a gravel carpark and single storey of suites. I could park, then shield my car and no one passing by would have any idea I was here. Very proud of myself, I park Maisy and head into the office where a young male lion, no more than a pimply teenager with a mop of blonde hair, smiles shyly at me. I pay him in cash and he hands me a shiny black key with a room number on it, as well as papers with a bunch of useless tourist information. I grin at him and go to find my room. I park my car a little way down from my room, so if my shield goes down due to tiredness, I still won't give my exact room away.

As soon as I get inside, I collapse onto the bed and fling up a shield around the perimeter of the hotel so I'll be alerted if a snake enters the premises. Once I'm happy that I'm secure, I immediately fall into a deep sleep.

When I awake, dusk is settling around the motel and I feel a sharp pang on my shield. I sit bolt upright, my heart pounding as I register a serpent animalia entering the motel.

Not one snake, *four*.

My father's lackeys are here. How the hell had they tracked me so quickly with no scent?

I close my eyes to hone in on my shield, but I can't do any remote viewing with my power—I can only feel who's inside. There are four of them, three men and a woman in their human forms. I recognise two of my father's retrieval squad, but not the other two. They head straight for reception, and I know right away they will threaten the young lion. As soon as they tell him they are here at the behest of the Serpent King, the kid will give me up for sure.

I need to get out of here.

Darting around the room, I collect my phone and duffel before throwing the key on the bed and rushing out the door. If I can just get into my car and get a shield around it, I can leave the carpark without being seen or heard.

Cloaking myself in my strongest possible shield, I step out of my door and look down the building to see two of the men standing outside reception like guards.

They notice my door opening immediately—as well as the lack of any visible person coming out of it.

"There!" one of them shouts.

Shit. They will have been briefed about my abilities. Swearing, I leave the door swinging and make a run for my car.

Footsteps thunder on the pavement behind me as I sprint down the carpark for all I'm worth, my duffel bouncing by my side. I reach the bubble of magic my car is in, open the driver's door and throw myself in.

Outside, the two men hesitate, sniffing the air. I turn on the ignition. While they can't see or hear it, they *will* see the way the gravel moves as my tires flee the scene. I've parked rear-in, so I take one deep breath, and put the pedal to the floor.

They shout, pointing directly at me while one of them exclaims into a walkie-talkie. I swear again. *Of course* they've brought back-up. Something heavy lands on my car and in my fright my invisibility shield shatters, and I struggle to gather my wits enough to get it back up.

I head for the road, only to find a black Mercedes screeching to a stop across the driveway, my exit blocked. Another snake gets out of the driver's seat, grinning at his friends.

His smile turns from joyful to horror within seconds, but he's not looking at me. He snarls and bolts past my car.

A high-pitched scream sounds from behind me, and I whirl around in my seat to see a blur of activity. There's another scream followed by a bellowing, then the sound of bodies falling.

I remain in my car, clutching my steering wheel as if it will save me, panting like I've run a marathon. I have no idea what to do now. There's no way for me to drive out.

Everything goes quiet. I look around, but I can't see anyone.

Until a lion wearing a navy three-piece suit casually strolls around my car, wiping bloody hands on a pocket handkerchief. His walk is the swagger of a pure apex predator as he comes to a halt directly in front of my car. His amber-eyed stare is stern and serious.

I know he's a lion by his tanned, angelic features and the mane to match—long, honey-gold hair tied back into a ponytail at the nape of his neck. He has the look of a put together aristocrat, not a hair askew and definitely out of place in this motel. A bounty hunter maybe? No, not dressed like that, and my father would die before he dealt with lions.

When he speaks, his voice is deep and holds the command of someone used to being obeyed. "Get out of the vehicle, Aurelia."

He knows my name. I hide my fear with a scoff. He just pins me with his amber eyes and says, "You and I are going to have a chat."

Somehow, he makes me feel like I'm back at school again and I'm in trouble for doing something stupid. He's freezing me with the most lethal glare. He can only be in his late twenties, and fuck, he's hot. Who the hell is he?

Aurelia

He sighs, as if irritated by me. "I'm not here to hurt you, Aurelia. But if you don't get out of your car, I'm going to tear it to shreds, piece by piece."

Shit.

I have no choice here. I slap my palm to my forehead and swear out loud at my well-laid plans falling apart. Has he heard about the fire? Has it made the news? I haven't yet had the chance to check if it's made it into *Animalia Today*. Halfeather was wealthy enough that his death has every right to be on the news.

I look back at the lion, who is glaring at me as if I'm wasting his time. *Shit, Aurelia, we can do this. Predator, remember? That's what you are. And we can't let him hurt Maisy.*

Slowly, I unlock my car door and push it open. Trying not to tremble, and very aware a six-foot-six tall lion is watching my every move, I step out.

The first thing I do is look behind my car, where I find the bloodied bodies of the four snakes. One has a broken neck, but the other four have been disembowelled with long, bloody slashes. I quickly look back at the lion, who has walked two steps closer to me since my brief look away from him. I jump a little and take a step back, looking down at his hands where, no doubt, claws had been just a minute ago.

He's killed four of my father's hunting snakes in less than a minute.

I meet his eye and say darkly, "My father will kill you for that."

The corner of his lip quirks, but he does not smile. "Oh, quite a few people try regularly. I rather enjoy sending them back corpses."

Something about his arrogant tone angers me, and I narrow my eyes at him. "Who do you think you are? You can't just come in my motel and—"

"*Your* motel?" He raises an elegant male brow.

I cross my arms and he nods to the buildings behind me. "Incidentally, this is one of my motels."

I only just manage to stop my jaw from dropping. "What the fuck?"

"Language, Miss Aquinas," he chides.

I stare at him. He's talking to me like a high school teacher. Who the hell does he think he is?

He must see the crazed look on my face because he says drolly, "My name is Lyle Pardalia. I'm Deputy Headmaster of Animus Academy."

Oh shit. He's come here to retrieve me. They sent the Headmaster *himself*?

"You're not safe here." He looks at my car with a slight curl to the lip, as if he finds it distasteful.

"I know that," I say through gritted teeth, taking great offense. "That's why I was leaving before you interrupted me."

He levels me with a very unimpressed look that has me instantly raging. "You cannot be running around as you are."

Running around?!

"Aurelia." He says my name as if he's reading from a very long, particularly boring shopping list. "Let me help you."

I stare at him and take a deep breath to calm myself. "How did you find me?"

He leans against my car, regarding me like a particularly boring specimen. "Your phone is trackable."

The feeling of pure idiocy that spins through me makes me want to hurt. I can't believe I've been so stupid! Beasts have been hunting each other forever and technology has just helped us be more efficient at it.

"Why are you here?"

He looks at his fingernails where blood has crusted around the edges. "Some problematic beasts are after you and you are no longer safe in the wider world."

I frown at him. I know that already. They are a bunch of psychos. But to hear that they *were* actually hunting me is a bleak confirmation that makes my stomach knot. Did I really think I could out run *them*?

He sighs as if he's explaining something to a stupid person. "You need to come to the Academy where we can keep you safe."

Why does every male around think they own me? I bristle where I stand, meeting him gaze for gaze. I'm not going to *another* place where a man thinks he can control me. "That place is for criminals and feral shifters. I don't belong there."

"I don't care, Aurelia. We need you where we can keep an eye on you while we work to hunt the others. You will be safe there. You can still get your education, we offer a range of healing courses for shifters. That's what you would like to pursue as a career, is it not? Healing?"

He knows a lot more about me than I like. And who's *we*? The Council? Of course they'd have a hand in this now they think I've killed Halfeather. Fuck.

I frown in annoyance at my clenched hands. This male is planning out my life as if I don't have a say in it. But I *do* have some say. On one hand, I'd be safe from my father at the school—students are off bounds to everyone, including court royalty. There'd also be others at the college and means of boosting my power. I also wouldn't have to worry about paying for tuition. Everything at the Academy is Council-funded.

I raise my head and look at this lion—knowing full well they've sent the *Deputy Headmaster* of the Academy for ferals after me because I'm in big bloody trouble. I've never been in trouble for anything before and it's a foreign, gnawing feeling.

But if I go there and they rope up my mates, we'll all be stuck together in one school and I'll be forced to interact with them.

No, there is no way I'm going. I glance at my duffel, still dishevelled in the passenger seat, thinking about how I'm going to make an exit. Lions have a strong instinct to chase, like other predators. If I simply *ran*, he would more than happily chase me down for days. Glancing up at the sky, I see that it's a clear day, practically cloudless. I can do this.

I set my jaw and uncross my arms as if I've given in. "Fine."

"Good." He straightens so smoothly he might have been made from water and turns on his heel, heading to my passenger door to grab my bags, I guess.

"My car is waiting around the corner," he says, pulling a phone out of his pocket. "I'll let the driver know."

I glower at him, darting back into my car through the driver's side and snatch up my bags before he can open the door.

He frowns at me through the windscreen and I shake my head, yanking my bag up and thinking rapidly about what I can carry. Cash. That's all I can manage. The phone is a big loss, but that can't be helped. I shove the wad into my mouth, tearing up as I look around at my beautiful Maisy.

Goodbye for now, old girl.

Lyle is striding down the driveway towards the road, expecting me to follow like an obedient student under his control. Joke's on him because I run in the opposite direction, my wad of cash in my mouth. Lyle lets out a shout as my sneakers pound on the gravel. I take one jump, shifting into my eagle form, my clothes and shoes falling off around me. I frantically beat my wings and Lyle gives a fairly distinct, "Fuck!" That just proves what an asshole he is for telling *me* not to cuss. I ascend into the sky, Lyle's dress shoes rapidly crunching on the gravel after me.

I've guessed right, he's not the type of beast to fully shift in public, not that it matters—I'm in line with the roof of the motel now and I've found a solid beat with my wings. I've also overestimated the size of my beak and the cash slips sideways. I scramble to catch it, trying hard not to lose my wing balance.

It's no use. The cash tumbles out of my beak and I watch it fall straight towards the motel carpark, where Lyle Pardalia catches it in one broad, tanned hand. He looks back up and there's a truly terrifying expression on his handsome face as he scowls up at me.

Swearing in five different ways, I leave it all behind me and concentrate on beating my wings to get my freedom.

Aurelia

My eagle form is not a cure-all to my issue. Lyle will have access to the recovery team, which tracks down feral and rabid beasts and takes them to prison, or if they are under twenty-five, to Animus Academy for rehabilitation and education. That recovery team will include winged animalia trained in hunting.

Not knowing how he'd come to find me in the first place, I'm still not safe and I don't know how quickly Lyle is going to get a team together—or how long it'll take him, as a lion, to hunt me down again. It will be embarrassing for him to return without me, and lions have big egos, second only to dragons. He won't stop until he finds me, I just know it.

That just means I have to be cleverer than anyone else.

I focus on gaining as much height as I can and head north, as I'd initially intended. So I don't have my car. This might be a blessing in disguise because travel for me now has no boundaries, and with my eagle sight, I will be able to see anyone coming from land or sky from miles away. If I can find a tall tree to roost in for the night, I can even sleep as a bird for one or two nights. Any more than that and I will likely turn feral myself, letting my anima take over in its animalistic mindset. And all my anima wants to do right now is find my mates. No, my human brain needs to be in control at all times.

I can't believe my awful luck. In the span of a week, I've managed to find three of my mates and the other two know what I look like from my little siren call that one night. And now them, this lion and the Council are hunting me. Savage likely has my scent from that one night of disaster, and if he's following his instincts, he will scent me out in no time on foot.

The image of him standing over me, sucking on his fingers, fills my stomach with tumbling emotions. I want to cry, but I just can't afford to lose focus.

Flying is one of my greatest joys; as an eagle—or hawk or raven, it's all brilliant. I felt closest to my mother when I was an eagle because, apparently, it was her preferred form. The feeling of the currents shifting below my wings is at once comforting and exhilarating. It feels like true freedom to be up here as an actual bird of prey, capable of simply *seeing* the world in the highest definition. Mice scurried in the fields below me, tiny sparrows flitted through the trees and I even saw to rabbits going at it under a bush. At least someone was getting some action.

If I'm not careful, it's easy to get lost in the sensation of flying. When I think of this, understanding why animalia become feral or even rabid is not surprising.

But alas, my anima knows that I am not an eagle by nature.

I'm getting a little tired because my wing stamina isn't the best as I don't fly very often, so I push myself to get as much distance as possible between myself and what feels like the entire world pursuing me.

Before long, I'm weakening in the dark of night, and though my eagle eyes are brilliant in the dark, I need food and a place to rest for a bit while I recover for the next long stretch of travel. I make a slow, controlled descent, following the twinkling lights of a shopping district and heading to the outskirts of that, spotting a small group of half constructed houses.

There has to be a warm, vacant spot there for me to sleep in, undisturbed and hidden. I wheel down, choosing a house that looks like it has only just gotten its bricks set today. Heading in straight to the open entrance, I sigh happily through my beak. I dare not shift back to human form tonight, though. I have no clothes after all, and I imagine a tableau where human builders arrive early in the morning for work and find a naked girl in their construction site.

Huffing, I settle down in a corner, pulling my wings about me to snuggle in for a nap. But even as tiredness pulls me down like a heavy blanket, my heart pounds like I'm still in danger.

Adrenaline spikes through me like a wild wind and I'm on high alert immediately, blinking through the dark. Crickets chirp outside. The wind whistles through the empty house, stirring my feathers just slightly. I smell concrete and drying cement.

It should be peaceful. But instead, the world around me is buzzing with raw, dangerous energy. Something is nearby. Something powerful.

And then a voice like shadows and dark places effortlessly pierces my seven shields. *"I've been inside you, princess. You can't hide from us."*

Savage is here.

This is the beginning of *Her Vicious Beasts*, a spicy reverse harem fated mates contemporary fantasy series.

The story *really* gets going in Book 1, coming in September 2023. Pre-orders are open now.

About EP Bali

Ektaa E.P. Bali was born in Fiji and spent most of her life in Melbourne Australia. She is a dreamer of the fantastical and faraway places and loves to write complex, morally grey characters and stories wrought with spice, darkness, humour and romance.

Her favourite tropes to write are: enemies to lovers, fated mates, villain gets the girl and bada$$ boss main characters

Website: www.ektaabali.com
Facebook Page: Facebook.com/ektaabaliauthor
Instagram: @ektaabaliauthor
Tiktok: @ektaabaliauthor
Twitter: @ektaabaliauthor

The Devil You Seek

ISABELLE OLMO

About the Book

A vampire killed my family. Years later, I travel across Texas to hunt down the killer. Until a man saves me from a burning building. Dressed in black and mysterious as the night, he says his name is Leon. He hunts the same man as me. Forming a shaky alliance, we embark on our journey across the wild west to find our monster. A journey filled with hungry coyotes, maniacal preachers, and a bond I never sought.

My name is Dania Gonzalez.

This is my bloody tale of revenge.

Chapter One

PECOS COUNTY, TEXAS, 1868

The man across from me has nothing more than a pair of fives, but daddy always said that a man could win a country with a set of deuces in the right game on the right night.

Too bad this is not that game because as I slide my last card, an ace of spades appears. Now it's my pair of aces against his pair of fives. You see, the trick is to allow them to underestimate you. The world becomes compliant when they don't consider you as a worthy adversary. Their jowls slacken, their drink comes quicker, and the small flittering smiles tell me everything I need to know.

He believes he can win, but he doesn't understand that I work on two things in life: my poker playing ability and hunting one man.

"You're gonna display me your cards, pretty lady?" He slicks a shriveled cigar into his yellowed teeth and looks at me the way I look at roast pork. *Hungry.*

I smile and set my cards face down on the table, then lean back and watch him.

"I raise you five," I say in a demure tone.

Men like demure tones. They're familiar with them. It unearths something deep that aggrandizes their belief in their subpar abilities. Most often used in fucking, but also applicable to poker.

He laughs, spit lands on the wood. He casts looks to his fellow men who have folded already and allowed him the center stage. His companions cackle with him. I give a little shrug of my left shoulder. A lash is strategically bated.

"Girly, do you even have five dollars?" He asks with a chuckle.

"I reckon I do," I reply, still smiling, still enticing him. Men are fools for smiles. Then I set down the five-dollar bill. His eyes follow my movement.

He glances down at his cards one last time and pulls out the cigar from his clenched teeth. "Tell you what I'm going to do. I'm gonna win this game, take your five dollars, and buy you a drink. But you gonna drink on my lap, you see."

I lean forward and place my chin on my palm. "First win the game, Mr. Stows, *then* buy me a whiskey."

He chuckles, and keeping his eyes on me, he tosses a five to the center pile. "*Now,* show me your cards. I'm thirsty."

I'm about to reveal my cards when the door to the saloon bursts open and the child's voice that calls my name silences the saloon.

"Dania!" A small girl in a nightgown, no more than eight, comes running to me. Her face is ashen gray, and her braids are coming undone. "Dania, come quick! Mamma said the man returned, and he's awful drunk and trashing the place, broke a window and granny's urn!"

I hold the groan back at my unmasking. Mr. Stows' sharp eyes are on me and before he can say a word, I slap down my pair of aces and watch the realization overrun his face. His lips pull back in a snarl and suddenly he can see through my carefully crafted façade.

He's already pushing his chair backwards and standing, his hands going for his gun. But I'm faster. I grasp the handle of my ivory colt Paterson revolver. Before his fingers can arm him, I fire once into his face. It splits it in half as the force slams him back, dead on the ground, the pair of fives man.

The only one who screams is the young girl next to me when I pushed her behind me.

I was already standing as the men drew their weapons. I don't put mine away. My eyes scan the crowd. On the table are his pair of fives for all to see. Most folk mind their business. They turn away, chewing their tobacco and nursing their whiskey. Stow's friends snarl at me.

"Good game, gentleman," I drawl. "Now, I reckon none of you need to die for your friend. I won this game fairly, so I'm going to take my winnings and follow this young lady out with none of you sniffing after me."

They lick their lips in consideration, taking in my average frame, and the newly displayed talent with the colt. I've got four shots left and I could land them dead if I wished. But I'm not a killer. I'm not my enemy. My humanity might be threaded in fragile gossamer, but I won't be a monster.

"I'll have no gunslinging and murdering in my town," a deep voice comes from the entrance of the saloon. I feel a little of the tension unclasp itself from between my shoulder blades.

Sheriff June stands six-foot three, taking up all available space, his Winchester slung casually over his shoulder. His white beard showing nothing of his quickness with his gun. His glassy eyes are sharp on the men at my table. I let the annoyance of his interfering roll over me. This is the reason I avoid Pecos County.

When no one responds to his threat, he casts a look at me. It speaks of disappointment and frustration. I've never cared for his looks, not even when daddy was alive.

"Get on out of here, Dania. Take your winnings," June says in a low tone.

I make a great show of sliding my coins and bills into my brown leather satchel and wink at one man who stares at me as if he'll hunt and murder me. I'd love to see him try. I would hear him in the dark by his heavy footfalls and open-mouthed breathing.

"Good night, gentlemen," I say and turn to the young girl whose face had paled. "Show me the way."

I push past my audience until I was face to face with Sheriff June. He's focusing on the men behind me, but I know he'd like a word later. He'll have to wait. I've a woman to save.

I walk into the cool night. My satchel is laden with money that will last me a few more weeks before I must procure another game of brag to refuel.

Posa, my sorrel quarter mare, neighs when I grab her reins and the two of us follow the girl.

Her ponytail bounces as she cuts through buildings and turns sharply on corners. I had an inkling the man would return. Men who've been told to go away often revisit on the belief of property. He thinks because he's entered a woman, she now belongs to him even when she's told him to go away too many times.

The small house is nestled against other downtrodden wooden homes in the decrepit town. Sinking under the despair of the summer draught. The ground is arid, a dust so dry it floats into your nose and settles, pressed against the concave corners of your nostrils.

I hate the desert; it makes me long for lush valleys and cool rivers. Those natural amenities that others take for granted.

The sound of harsh knocks and angry words reverberates before we turn into her street. I instantly pull out my colt when the small two-room house comes into view. I hold the girl back as her hands shake and her eyes widen in the deep night.

"Where's mama at?" I ask in a whisper.

The girl's brown eyes flicker to the home. Tear tracks run down her cheeks. "In the back room, with the baby. She won't come out. He got madder, but there's something not right with the house it feels…"

"Dead," I finish for her.

She clutches her small chest, which reminds me of myself as a child. I was twelve when a man with no blood in his veins killed my family. After shooting him twice, no blood came. All he did was laugh.

Slowly, I turn to the house. My colt will be no use here. That's for humans who can be just as dangerous as the monsters. In this situation, I'll need my amber. A slim sharp blade blessed by a padre out in San Antonio. I made the blade to kill one man. But that's not the man terrorizing a mother and her children tonight.

"Stay out here and watch my horse," I say slowly as I turn to Posa. The animal breathes out, sensing the shadows that we hunt. I run my fingers over her neck to soothe her. I pull out a small vial of holy water and douse myself with it. The girl watches me, almost bouncing from one foot to the other. From the saddle, I pull out the amber blade.

"If I die, get Sheriff June, tell him what happened," I say quickly and hand her Posa's reins. "But don't go in after me, you hear?"

The girl nods as she tightly clutches the leather reins. I turn back to the home and follow the glow of the moon into the home. The thumping against the wood intensifies.

"Let me in, Annie! Don't be a bitch! Open Up!"

My jaw twitches. The entrance is wide open, and light floods the entrance to the small home. Glass peppers the ground from the broken window. I carefully step foot inside and instantly find the man with his face pressing against the bedroom door.

The home was modest, with handmade sparse furniture, a small burning stove with a boiling pot, and a table with two overturned chairs. There's a basket of blankets and knitting, and a cool iron on top of a pile of well-read books. A doll, with black button eyes, stares at me from her discarded place on the floor.

Yes. Something lingers in this house. I can sense it. It's a strong sense of claustrophobia that invades my skin and presses against my throat.

"There's a reason the door is locked," I say as I position my blade behind the man.

I've startled him, and he looks at me with a hazy expression. Nothing about him seems out of the ordinary. Just a drunken fool in search of entertainment. Yet I still feel the presence. I'm intimately acquainted with that presence. It danced over my family's dead bodies.

"You ain't Annie," the man states as he leans forward to prevent himself from toppling over. His words are slurred. Drool dribbles down his lips into the dusty boots on his feet.

"And you've got to leave," I say as I brandish my blade.

He stares at the sword, then back at me, confusion still clear on his incredibly mundane face. He laughs slightly; a bubbling amusement mingling with dubiety. He scratches his cheek, then takes another swing of the liquor he carries in his other. It sloshes down his chin.

My skin tingles when he does this.

The dead cannot drink.

He's not the devil I hunt.

A fool and a drunkard, and an abuser, but not the monster that is tainting the home. My eyes turn sharply to the locked door.

"You need to leave, fool," I whisper.

"I ain't leaving until I got Annie." He burps.

I take a step towards the door. The pressure gets stronger, it's a filth in the air.

"Annie's dead," I say.

He's further thrown into amazement. "*My* Annie?"

"Get out of here," I say and meet his eyes, glassy as they were. "*Now.*"

It must be in my tone or the darkness that lives in me, a fetid residue that comes after great pain. The loss of genuine laughter and the wonderment of life.

Whatever lurks, I can face it. I've faced worse foes and survived.

The man stumbles on a chair, falls on the floor, and crawls out. My eyes did not leave the door.

"Dania?" A small voice comes from inside the locked room. "Miss Dania, is that you? Is he gone?"

The tremble in Annie's voice is authentic enough. The slight vulnerability. I clutch my blade tighter. There is one rule I have. I don't converse with monsters. I draw another step. I had to break my rule.

"He's gone, Annie-girl. Come on out," I say, and my spine tightens as I crouch down.

A breathy sob. "I can't, Dania. I'm trapped."

I lick my lips to save the parching skin. "*How* are you trapped?"

"Please help me." The cries would turn the heart of any simpering fool. The cries are a brilliant theater for me. It didn't want the drunk. It wanted *me*.

"Can't help you unless you let me in," I say as I take another step. I'm a foot away from the door. The holy water in my coat is cool.

It cries, the soft vulnerable sobs of a helpless woman. "I'm hurt, Dania, I'm hurt, please help me."

Then a small whimper and a wail, but the wail didn't belong to a woman. It belongs to a babe. The baby was alive. Inside of a room. With a monster.

Without thinking twice, I pound my boot into the wood and kick open the door.

The moment the door swings open, a woman in a white nightgown launches herself at me. Like a tarantula, she crawls on all fours, hands out, mouth agape with sharpened teeth. I swing my blade and slice through her, but she screeches and backs away. I can see her eyes between her ratty hair, bright crimson eyes of the dead.

"Dania!" It hisses.

It looks like Annie. It animates her dead body. But it's certainly not Annie. She launches at me once more and bypasses my blade, latching on to my neck as I try to shove her off. Her hands meet my wet clothes and smoke scalds her skin. It howls as I gather my composure. It jumps on the ceiling, crawling like an angry spider over me, mouth wide and menacing. The child screams in its basin. The child matters, nothing else. Not even me and my little thirst for vengeance matters.

"You bitch! You hurt me!" The ghoul cries as its feet patter around the ceiling.

I cast a glance at the oil lamp on the dinner table. The first lesson I learned when I realized bullets did not kill the monsters was fire. Fire kills them nicely.

I launch for the lamp, but the creature jumps on me, and we fumble to the ground. It catches my legs as I kick and try to dislodge it. It opens its mouth, fangs elongating, ready to chomp on my calf. Then I stab it in the shoulder. It moves so quickly I can't decapitate it. It howls and lets me go. I run to the table and the ghoul grabs my back and pins my shoulders with its extraordinary strength. Its fingers painfully dig into me as I scream. It tries to bite my neck, but the holy water sends it screaming with a furious roar of frustration.

I elbow it in the face, and it stumbles back. It gives me enough time to grasp the lamp and turn to it. Its fangs are bare as it crouches on the ground to launch at me when I threw the light at its face. Annie's hair catches fire. Burning like dried firewood.

I've no time to linger until it dies.

I bolt to the room and find the cradle. The baby is red in the face, screaming. I take off my leather coat, wrap its wiggling limbs into it, and hold it tight to my chest. The home erupts in flames as I turn to leave.

I close the door to block the fumes and I see it. Annie had nailed her crucifix on the back of the door. That's why it was trapped. It's made of solid silver. Inadvertently, she'd saved her oldest daughter.

I yank it off, then look out the window. The smoke enters the small room under the cracks of the slanted door, making me cough violently. I hoist the screaming babe under my arm and grab a lonely, lumpy pillow Annie once used to sleep. I press it against the aperture and then punch as hard as I can. The glass shatters and I dust off the glass with the pillow. Flames eat at the door. I have seconds. The window is too high. I can't make it with the child. I'll have to toss it out and hope it doesn't die.

But then a shadow flickers at the window and a man stands there.

"Give me the child!" He yells when he sees the fire. "Come now! You want to die in there?"

I didn't have time to hesitate. I hand him the child and he left to take it to safety. When I grasp the frame of the window, I slice my palms on the glass shards. Groaning, I pull myself out.

I land outside with a thud. I stumble forward as the house explodes behind me, sending me flying. The heat is so intense I think I've burned.

My stomach is on fire. But someone is dragging me over the ground. I've no strength to shove them off or tell them I was well. Because honestly, I'm not sure if I am well at all.

Chapter Two

The next time I wake, I can already tell it is late afternoon. Sun filters through ratty curtains and I shift on the bed. Immediately, the dull throb of pain coming from my hands fully wakes me. I sit up and find the palms of my hands bandaged and I'm dressed in a cotton nightgown. My stomach is not burned. My hair is wild around me, and my mouth hasn't been washed in a few days. It's completely dry. I cough, desperate for a drink. "You gonna state your name, stranger?" I ask.

A woman comes to my side. She presses a cup of water to my lips and helps me drink back the delicious fresh water. I question nothing other than the sweet feeling of a soothing throat. When I've drunk the entire cup, I blink up at her as I lay back on the bed.

Dimly, I recognize her. It's Nalin, Sheriff June's lady. A quarter-Apache woman in her late 40s that owned a ranch ten miles out of town, deep in Pecos County. Her face is sunburnt and heavy with age and her lips withered. It didn't take away her natural beauty. Her hair is a solid black color that goes down her waist, speckled with white.

"How long I've been asleep?" I ask, voice murky and phantom-like.

"Three days," she says and leans over me, inspecting my hands. She unwinds the gauze. I hardly dare move and try not to wince in anticipation. She makes a pleased noise deep in her throat. "They're healing nice. A sight better than when they brought you."

I watch her methodically work as she wraps my hands in fresh bandages. The cuts didn't look too bad. Better than a bullet which would've needed to be extracted. I have a scar under my right rib to attest to that.

"Who are they?" I ask.

Her deep hazel eyes cusp a serene wisdom I could never accomplish. "June and the man in black."

I feel my throat tighten; it had nothing to do with my thirst. "What man in black?"

She raises her brow and examines my face. A tactic I recognize with sour remembrance. My mother used to do it when she would attempt to determine if my sister or I were lying.

"We were going to ask you the same question," she says.

She sets a small bowl next to my bed and helps me sit up. I gratefully take the meal because the smell of potato soup makes my stomach grumble.

"He seems to have found you and the girls outside the burning house." Nalin leans back to work on some knitting.

I slurp the thick soup despite the bandages covering my palms. I'm so hungry I don't care if I spill it all over the nightgown. I dimly recall the man's face, but I'd been so preoccupied with saving the baby and my hide I couldn't identify anything of the man who came to my aid.

"Where are the children?" I ask, swallowing a piece of soft potato.

It tastes amazing, like nothing I've had these many years. Home cooking. I'd missed this. I missed Mami's beans and the feel of tortillas when rolled and dipped in *caldo de pollo*. I recall Mami fearlessly decapitating a shrieking chicken as she prayed to the old Aztec gods in gratitude for our meal. She would hang the animal by its feet and allow the blood to drip down to a bucket. She did all this methodically. Then she would pluck the chicken and season it with coriander, oregano, cumin, salt, and pepper. The taste of Mami's food was so tangible I recalled it as sweet as the smell of her hair. As bitter as the sight of her neck twisted in death.

I wish I'd been more curious about everything to do with being Mexican, but I was young and silly and now I'm truncated from my roots. Belonging in the in-between.

"The baby, Anabella, is asleep in the cot June set for her on the cool porch. She likes it there, likes to fall asleep to the sway of the afternoon breeze." Nalin points her chin out the window. "The girl, Mary, is a good girl. She's been helping me around the house without much complaint. I suspect she's used to honest work."

I finish the soup and sigh against the thin pillows. "I suppose it's much to ask to take them in? It's two mouths to feed in this drought."

Nalin keeps her eyes on the cloth she sews, one of June's old shirts. Her lips wrinkle slightly as she threads the needle through the hole she's mended. "Had a little boy once. Copper, that's what his daddy named him. Died of yellow fever when he was only five. Had no more children. My man died not long after."

I swallow thickly and study the bandages covering my hand.

"I know what you hunt," Nalin murmurs.

I freeze and blink at her. Her gaze is hard and unrepentant. She takes a sharp breath and looks back to the sewing.

"My grandmother's people, the Apache, believe in spirits that roam the vast land," she says in a grim tone. "No one ever believed me, but I think Copper's daddy was killed by one of them. He and I didn't speak much after our boy died. But he'd come each evening and make sure I had plenty of wood and hay for the horse and cow."

The way she enunciates her words tells me there's a hidden pain, like she'd loved him. Like he'd meant something to her.

"It was a cold November; the night was hallowed. As if the earth sucked all the living creatures from it. I watched that great big man walk out my door to chop some wood, had an ax on him half my size. It was a sound like a fox, quick, sharp, brutal. I called and called his name, but he didn't answer. Then I saw *him*. A man with eyes like rotting apples dripped in poison. I closed the door, and he knocked and knocked, then he pounded and pounded and demanded I open the door. I never did. The door wasn't locked. He *couldn't* enter."

Her words land a rock of foreboding in my stomach. It tightens my insides and prickles my skin.

"I sat in bed all night, rifle in my hand, Bible between my thighs. Cried the entire night thru. When the sun come up, he was gone. Found Copper's daddy dead. Cold. Throat ripped open." She meets my eyes dotted with a tormented fury that didn't understand the passing of time. "No blood anywhere."

Her last words are ominous. They frighten me deep in my core, though I knew exactly what she meant. My family had no blood left either.

"Does June know about them?" I breathe.

"Not that we've ever spoken about. I rather he didn't know. Once you know the world changes, don't it?"

She wasn't wrong.

When I could stand and explore the small house, I dress in my trousers, vest, and strap my guns to their usual place. Low on my hips. I find June on the porch, rocking back and forth on a rocker. Slowly, he brings a pipe to his mouth; his eyes fork the horizon. The children are inside with Nalin. The babe feeds on goat's milk, and the girl aids Nalin, peeling the potatoes for supper.

"You see something out there?" I study the land, the arid earth speckled with dried bush. The orange colors canvased the sky in the most beautiful end of day rendition.

"Strange things happen at dusk," June says in that low raspy voice of his. Too many years smoking and drinking and living a life with little expectancy of seeing old age. Yet old age came when it was not asked for. "Got to look out for something now that I'm no longer sheriff."

His words surprise me to such a degree that I've to appraise his seriousness. His cool eyes cut to me, then back to the setting sun.

"Don't look at me that way. Got a dead young mother in my hands, two orphaned girls and you all cut up and dragged like a bag of flour to my door. Thought you were dead," he says as he brings his pipe to his mouth.

"Well, I'm not," I snip.

A smile flitters his face. "You're hard to kill, aren't you?"

His words wound me deeper than anything because he knew—could read it in the cut of my brow—how much I wished daily the monster killed me along with my family. The dead were always the lucky ones. The living always remembers.

I turn to the horizon. "I'll die when I'm ready."

"You sure behave like your daddy, though he wasn't your blood," June says with a chuckle.

I curl my hands over the porch railing. I'd always known the man who raised me wasn't my blood-father. He had pale hair and blue eyes and me and my sister were brown, like our mother, with thick brown hair and a squat nose. But he'd been a father, regardless. He worked all day and came home at sunset to tend to the farm and help my mother. He put us to bed and told us stories of his adventures, though I know now they were just stories.

"Well, he raised me. What do you expect, old man?" I push my hair back. It's slightly singed, and it smells like toasted bread left too long on a hot plate.

He didn't answer, he simply sat on his rocker — like the old gunslinger he was and smokes his pipe. His rifle sits across his lap with a finger on the trigger.

"Tell me about the man in black," I finally say when he allows the silence to linger. I hate silences. You hear all manner of things in the silence. Twigs snapping, critters digging, wind howling. I've no use for silence.

"Tall fella," June says with a sigh. "Black hat, black boots, black coat... clouded spectacles."

I try to envision such a man; he seems to have fallen from the pages of a dime novel. Mysterious and gallant. Saving women and babies from burning buildings. I hold my scoff deep in my mouth, clenching it between my teeth. I have little regard for heroes, they never held my interest. Humans are selfish by nature and to meet one that wasn't makes me question their motives.

"Quite a fella," I whisper, and June makes a noise of agreement, as if he too held little regard for such tall tales.

The sun touches the ground in the distance, the daily kiss to complete the day. The wide sky turns a burned orange, and the trees become silhouettes against the rays. A dappled landscape that belongs to no one and would end our lives if we allow it. That's how we live. In perpetual mercy.

June groans as he stands, his joints creaking. I remember him being taller. Either I grew or he was shrinking. He stares down at me, past the brim of his hat.

"Keep your wits about you, girly. The night is no saloon, and your pretty face can't save you in the shadows," he says and stuffs his pipe back in his mouth. He turns and enters the ranch.

I stand watch for a long time, June's old dog—a wheat colored mutt snoozing close by as he sleeps off the scraps he's received for dinner. Inside, I can hear the small makeshift family speaking in hushed tones, as Nalin tells the young girl tales of coyotes and shifters. Spook tales to get the child to behave.

Then I hear *it*.

The slow trotting of a horse and its rider. The dog raises its head, ears alert as he makes a low growling noise. I slink into the shadows, my eyes on the night. The rider comes closer and closer. A burning fury erupts in my stomach, like a strong indigestion. The pressing silence almost muted the sound, but I could still hear it in the whispers of the dark.

Then it stops. My breath hitches, my hand already on my gun. Even bandaged up, I can grasp it and shoot it faster than them.

"Is it wise?" A voice comes from the emptiness.

My throat tightens. My fingers slip into the trigger.

"Who's the wiser one? The one who watches for danger or the one who comes uninvited?" I ask. It feels silly to say such words out loud, not when I can't even see an outline of a person.

Another step from the horse. I slide the gun out of the holster and point it exactly where I hear the hooves.

"I won't hesitate," I warn. My finger was itchy. I wouldn't miss. The dog presses against me with bared teeth as his fur bristles in warning.

"Good," the man says in a husky tone. "You'll live longer."

He steps into the light. I'd not heard him dismount from his horse. Yet he stands proudly not four feet from me. The dog growls. My gun doesn't move from its aim of his chest. Slowly, he raises his head and stares at me.

True as June described him, he's dressed in head to toe black. A good built on a muscular frame and a sharp face with sunken cheekbones and a smirking mouth. I can't see his eyes because he wears small, round shadow spectacles as if he strutted into the noon sun.

Chapter Three

His smirk deepens. "Leon."

"*Leon*," I repeat in a near scoff.

"And you're Dania." He cocks his head as he takes me in. "At least that's what the good Sheriff called you."

He has a slight accent I couldn't place. It was a tinge, as if softened like a pounded river rock. Smoothed to perfection. He has two black colts low on his hips with a leather cartridge belt. He comes well-armed to a small farm.

His eyes flicker to my gun, which never wavered. "Hardly a polite way to greet someone who saved you."

I couldn't clasp the sneer from my lips. "You came for gratitude, *Leon*?"

He seems even more amused, and I watch as he slowly brings a rolled cigarette from behind his ear. He pulls out a match and shows it to me. I nod. He strikes it against his belt, then lights the cigarette in slow, precise movements. His fingers are long and pale. His eyes never leave mine.

"Now, I might not know much," he says as he blows out smoke. "But a woman like you doesn't say thank you."

"Then why are you here?" I ask as he pulls his cigarette from his lips.

Slowly, he removes his spectacles and tucks them into his jacket. He has pale blue eyes. They seem unearthly, stark against his black hair.

"I have a few questions," he says and dusts the ash from his cigarette.

I study the tilt of his head, how it bends to the night as if he were part of it, as if he lives in it. I should be afraid of this man, but I wasn't. I didn't get that morbid sense of foreboding around him. Still, he holds himself like a fist, much the way I do.

"You a marshal?" I ask.

This makes him smile. I'm surprised at the whiteness of his teeth. I've never seen teeth that white before. Like they were polished and new. Most men of my acquaintance are missing most of theirs and what was left was yellowed wedged between inflamed gums.

"Of sorts," Leon said. "I'm hunting the man who killed Annie Williams."

My throat tightens and my grip slightly slacks on my gun. "That was no man," I said, in a spiteful tone.

His face loses all mirth, his eyes harden, and I feel like he shows me his true face. It's filled with lingering anger. This I could understand.

His fingers pull out the cigarette from his lips. "Perhaps we should talk, Miss..."

It was an invitation, and I am weary of invitations. I lower my gun and slide it into my holster. My palm throbs against the gauze. Surely, I've reopened the wound Nalin took great care to heal. My stomach is twisting, pulling away from my body and towards this strange man.

"Dania Gonzalez," I say and point to one of the rocking chairs.

His eyes linger on me. "Are you from around here?"

"Of sorts," I said and turn to sit, waiting for him.

Leon takes his time going up the two steps of the porch. To my surprise, he pauses and pets the dog, whose tail now happily wags. He whistles into the darkness and his horse comes into view. A black beast with pebble onyx eyes. The man sits next to me in the rocking chair. He pauses when it rocks back, as if he's never been on a rocking chair before. He seems out of place with his fine clothes and shiny spurs. He settles back and turns to me; those crystal eyes don't blink. His proximity makes my body fill with warmth. I attribute it to the swiftly changing weather.

"Now, Miss Gonzalez—"

"Dania. Just call me Dania," I said.

Ms. Gonzalez had been my mother, and I didn't need more reminders of her. Today, they already drenched me with her memories. Leon smiles, an amused look on his serious face.

"*Dania*," he repeats, as if testing the word. "Do you know what your name means?"

I sigh and stare at him with no amusement. He speaks in riddles, and I hate riddles.

"God is my judge," he informs me without stimulation. "*À propos*, don't you think?"

I've no interest in knowing things like this. It painted clearer pictures of my mother, naming me when I was born, and then being taken before I could appreciate her.

"And *Leon* means lion. Now that we're well acquainted, are we going to speak about the monsters?" I snarl.

He seems unconcerned as he smokes more of his cigarette, cutting a fine figure against the low glow of the lamp that hangs from the porch.

"Do you believe in God, Dania Gonzalez?" he asks as he studies the cigarette in his hands.

I shove the sentiment of annoyance down as I masticate his question.

"Sure," I said with little meaning. I have no use for specters who claim to protect us but were starkly absent when needed.

He chuckles, diverted by my obvious sentiment. "In Europe, we call them vampires. Heard of *them*?"

In an instant, my skin feels clammy, as if I'm developing a swift fever that rode in with the wind. To name the dead feels like a validation. I'd killed now fourteen of them, except the one which matters. The one whose face was painted on the inside of my eyelids. The one who haunts me while I hunt *it*.

"You're from Europe?" It was the only thing my tongue could formulate. The rest of his words hold a plethora of questions I can't wrap my mind around.

"Yes. France, to be exact," Leon smiles. "But that was a long time ago."

I nod. "So, you hunt the vampires too?"

He takes a deep breath and tosses the bud of his cigarette over the railing into the night. "Only the bad ones."

I scoff. "They're *all* bad."

He chuckles once more, then crosses his legs elegantly. His spurs glint in a sort of wink in my direction.

"When was the last time you saw Annie Williams before that night?" He asks in a soft tone, his eyes glaze on the darkness.

The old mutt whines and lays his head next to Leon's boot.

"That morning," I said. "Met her in the general store. Tried to buy flour to make dinner for her and the girls, but she didn't have enough coin. I bought her a large sack, though it emptied my funds. A game filled up my pockets later that night."

He smiles and glances at me. "I know. I was there. You had a fair hand. And you used your pretty face to distract the dim-witted fool."

I scan my memories for a flash of his face, a sense of his presence, but I hadn't felt him. "You were *watching* me."

This time, he laughs unabashedly. "I watched for the one who carried the silver saber and a satchel full of holy water. That person just happened to be you. You know a lot for one that knows nothing."

I feel my face flush and hope the shadows obscure it. It is that dormant, constant anger that lingers in the tips of my fingers and in the corners of my eyes. Born the day I lost everything and upon its birth; it had simply grown into adulthood.

"I've been killing these things for years. I never asked you to come take a tally and rank my technique." I point a finger at my chest in a harsh, stabbing motion.

He is unmoved by my words. His long hand slides up his leg, an oddly soothing motion. "Dania," once more my name sounds foreign in his tone. "Please understand. I'm simply tracking."

"Tracking *who*?" I ask. I tire of polished words with hidden meanings practiced in parlors in Europe. This was Texas. We had no time for pretty words.

He glances at me. "I've followed a linear line of patterns across Texas. This area seems to be the cluster of attacks. They're close by. At first, the attacks were sporadic but methodical and... careful. Now they've become emboldended and, frankly, messy."

I study his profile, the sharp cut of his chin and the elegant nose that seems bred for drinking champagne in France.

"That's why you were there. You were there for Annie, not me. You just happened to spot my saber and went through my belongings. You're hunting the vampire who killed Annie," I said in realization.

He meets my eyes steadily. He holds no apologies for his pursuit or actions. He's beholden to none. That makes me flinch, though it was a long time since anyone made me uncomfortable.

"Yes. He's the same one you also hunt. The one who killed your family, Dania Gonzalez. The monster called Ryle McAdams."

Chapter Four

I stand up and look down at him, all poised and elegant with the dark aura of mystery he enjoys so much.

"You're not from around here, so let me make one thing clear. We don't take to liars in Texas." I clench my teeth and my body coils like a pouncing panther.

He lifts his clear lapis eyes. They shine in the night like crystals stolen from the bowels of the earth, sitting against his pale skin, encased in curled lashes.

"Yet you continue to elect them," he says with a hint of amusement.

I look away and pace the porch. The problem with only knowing the face of your family's killer is the constant frustration of not knowing his name. While visiting towns, I always see him from the corner of my eye. But he was never there. What did I know about him? A man of average height with a scar across his cheek and a satanic laugh. If I questioned people about him, folks would think I was crazy.

"You didn't know his name," Leon said in realization.

I pause and hold out my hand. "Cigarette."

He raises a finely shaped brow but doesn't question me further. Instead, I impatiently watch as he pulls out a leather satchel of tobacco and rolling paper. He packs it well, tight, with expert fingers. When he finishes, he surprises me by bringing it to his lips and lighting it. Then he offers it to me.

I feel the moistness of his saliva against my lips. In another time and another place, the sensation would disgust me. But this moment was now. It lives on its own terms. Today I know who my target is, I didn't care whose spit I had in my mouth. The smoke fills my lungs, trembling against the caves within. I sigh and stare out into the night. With a name, I can find him. He would finally be within my reach. A debt long owed.

"You intend to go after him," Leon said as he stands, his long body stretching like a spring twig.

I turn to him and hold out my bandaged hand. "I rarely say this but thank you. For giving me the name."

He gazes quickly at my fingers, then back at me as he takes a step closer. His eyes hold a sincere darkness I can't place. "The Ryle McAdams of your memories is not the Ryle McAdams that exists today. He killed his maker."

We all come from God, so the thought of him chasing down God himself makes little sense to me.

Leon sees the confusion on my face. "His maker. The vampire that made him. It's called a sire. There's nothing like sire-blood. Only once is a vampire allowed to drink it; when they are turned. Any time after that, it is forbidden. It can alter mental balance. Their acts become more violent and they, by extension, become physically stronger."

He looks away and studies the night, but it seems like a different sort of perusal. One where he can make out the shape of the trees against the murkiness of the land.

"It explains Annie and the others I've found. You said you saw her not hours before and in a matter of half a day, she's turned, coherent, moving... was she speaking?" He looks at me, a genuine question, as if he's uncovering a hidden treasure.

I nod. "Yes. Full sentences, but she was feral. Wild. She..." I gulp as my arms shiver, though the night was mild. "Walked on the ceiling."

He raises his brow, then pulls more tobacco from his jacket and rolls it. We silently smoke together, digesting the implications. I can ascertain that Annie's behavior was not normal. I dimly wonder how many of the fiends I've battled were tainted by Ryle. Perhaps I had been killing bits of him all along.

"You seem to know a lot about vampires," I said.

It's a leading statement. He is no fool, and his response is a severe poker face. Unreadable bastard. I take a drag from the cigarette; it's down to the bud, and I toss it to the dirt.

"I'm coming with you," I say with an intensity I didn't expect. It feels right, like he was meant to find me that night and provide me with the information I've needed.

My words don't surprise him. His eyes are unmoved, marking the night.

"You may know a lot about these creatures, but I know Texas. I know the towns, the terrain, and the people. If you want to find Ryle McAdams as much as I do, then you'll need an expert hand." I speak quickly, formulating a plan even as the words filter through my teeth.

"I can't let you do that. The dangers are—"

"Don't paint yourself in nobility, marshal," I snap. "I've been knocking on death's door for a long time. You lose your fear when you watch your family butchered and must live next to their stiff bodies for two days before Sheriff June arrived at my home. I don't need your pity, so don't soften your eyes. I need revenge. I want to kill that bastard, and I want to make sure he begs for death before the end."

I hold my hand out once more. Steady and sharp, like my constantly troubled thoughts. A desperate line. I have a feeling that if he refuses to let me come, I will lose him to the mountain terrain, even if I follow him. I can't let that happen.

He surprises me by turning to me and studying my face. A chill goes through my bones at his proximity. I can see the grain of his skin and imagine the texture of it beneath the pads of my fingers. There is a strangeness to his presence. As if I'm being pulled with a string from my belly. I yank myself away from it because I have no time for attractions.

As if sensing my inner discord, he smiles. "We leave tomorrow night. I'll come get you."

He shakes my hand. The moment our skin touches, it floods me with unexpected electricity, a living vibration I've never felt. As if his soul lives in his fingertips and I can intimately feel it. His long fingers wrap themselves around my hand, encasing a part of me within him.

I swallow a gasp and brick my face to show nothing. Desperate to distract myself, I mull over his words. Leaving tomorrow when we could leave now? I wish to leave right at this moment and travel through midday tomorrow. We could be in Halston by noon.

"Why not leave now? Or early tomorrow morning?"

He flicks off his cigarette and smiles, a disarming smile. It makes his right eye wink. That strange sensation floods me once more, and I hate how easily it sways my sentiments. I didn't like to lose control; it was one of the few things I still have left in this damn miserable life.

"Miss Gonzalez, let this be your first lesson. You want to catch vampires? You only travel at night." He jumps down the two steps and stands by his horse. The beast nuzzles against his chest and Leon pats its cheek. "Sleep as much as you can. It's a long ride to Alto Pass."

He lifts himself up to his horse, and the animal neighs.

"Alto Pass?" I ask, aghast. "Why are we traveling north?"

Leon smirks and bites his lower lip. His white teeth glimmer in the night. "Good night." He tips his hat and turns the horse. The darkness swallows each inch of him down to the trotting of his horse.

Chapter Five

I sleep until the sun is halfway up the morning sky, exhaustion depleting all my strength until I'm nothing more than a corpse on the floor. I woke up because I sensed I'm being watched. That startles the heck out of me, and I scramble back. The years of uneasy rest and constant danger carved said response into my bones. What I find is not a threat.

It's children.

Specifically, Mary, the oldest. Her dirty blond hair is no longer unkept and tossed. It was washed and braided. Her face scrubbed and her cheeks rosy. She still holds that sorrow only children can display. A haunting of the eyes. Next to her is the small babe, which, at closer inspection, is not as young as I thought. Likely a year old. She's skinny for her age with a tuff of red hair and a pair of bright green eyes with long ruby lashes. She sits next to her sister with an unsteady posture as she stuffs a quilted lump into her mouth. It seems to serve as her toy.

"You sleep with your mouth open," Mary said in a matter-of-fact tone.

As I rub the sleep from my eyes, I sigh and sit up. I didn't know how to converse casually with children. I'd been the youngest child in my home, my sister was older by four years, and we lived isolated enough that I seldom met other children. These children are also bathed in the aftermath of their demise. I am more like them than I care to contemplate. But, if I hunt their mother's killer, they won't have to live with the thirst I've held deep in my throat.

"Papa June says that you're leaving tonight," Mary said. She flicks a string from the frayed edge of her homespun dress.

Papa June. He must love that. I groan as I slowly stand. The girl's eyes follow my movements, deliberating me as I slip into my boots.

"Are you taking us with you?" Mary asks, her face hesitant.

I look around the small home. It's cozy, filled with warm things such as a wood stove with a pot of coffee and a plate piled high with biscuits. A handcrafted rocking chair. A bed hiding behind a curtain made of bits of cloth sewed together to form a patchwork, and a cot for the children to share dressed in warm banquets by the stove.

"No," I say and amble to the pot of coffee. The kettle is still warm, and I find a chipped mug, pouring myself a hearty cup. The liquid goes down easily.

I turn back to the girls. They hadn't moved. Still watching me with wide eyes.

"Are they going to send us to the orphanage?" Mary asks in a small voice.

My stomach sours because that had been my fear at age twelve, when the same thing happened to me. I lick my lips and take a biscuit. It's still soft and my mouth waters. I eat quietly as I lean against the warm stove and watch the girls.

"No," I said finally. "Old June never sent me. I doubt he'll do the same to you."

Mary looks doubtful, her nose scrunching. "Your mama died too?"

The biscuit feels hard as it coasts down my throat. I wash it back with coffee.

"Yes," I said. A subject I don't wish to blather on about with children, especially ones whose situation starkly resembles mine. My skin feels tight around them, and I felt younger than my twenty-six years. As if I'd not maimed and killed many creatures and men who've crossed my path.

Mary, deceptively wise, is not discouraged. "Are you going to kill the man who took mama?"

This I can answer. This I can chat about. This is my purpose.

"Yes," I say.

Mary slowly rises and picks up her sister, hefting her up on her slim hip. The child is half as long as she was, but Mary seems used to carrying her sister. I dimly wonder if that was how my sister once carried me, in that time before memory began.

"With the man in black? The one that saved you and Anabella? The one who brought us to Papa June?" Mary walks to me, the babe dangling down.

"Yes. Now, enough questions." I'm sitting at my wit's edge. Being around them makes me feel something I'm not prepared to feel. A *softness*. I need no softness for what I'm about to face.

"Here," Mary said as she digs into the pocket of her ratty dress. In it is the crucifix I saved from her home. The only trace left of her mother. "It'll protect you."

I can't tell her I don't believe in God while I douse myself in holy water to fight vampires.

Still, I'd long lost my use for God. If God had abandoned us, then we must turn to the devil, for his deeds were constantly on display.

"It's all you have left of your mama," I say and make no move towards the cross.

The silver of the item glints in the late morning sun, as if it beckons me to grasp it. Mary shrugs: her hand still outstretched.

"You're just borrowing it," she said. "Bring it back once you kill him."

She says it with a confidence I can never have. An assuredness that the woman before her was an avenger of the night. I take the cross and slide it into the pocket of my pants. It's still warm from Mary's touch and the irony of a Mary gifting me a cross is not lost on me.

Nalin roasted a chicken with stewed carrots, plucked right from her small garden that somehow survived the drought. The chicken is thin and stringy, but it's a home-cooked meal. I lick every morsel from my fingers and enjoy that magic contentment of a full belly. It's a strange sensation to sit at a table with smiling faces and soft chatter. Nalin is patient with the youngest girl, feeding her a small bowl of mashed carrots and pieces of chicken. Old June is quiet until Mary asks him about his hometown and the old man leans back with his pipe and recants the stories of his youth. He paints a picturesque story, which I knew to be purely fictional.

As night begins its slow arrival, I am packed and ready. June comes to stand by me, young Anabella on his hip as the child snoozes against his warm chest. He looks at me with those hooded eyes that know too much and seldom divulge information I thirst for. He's the one who buried my family down by the broken hill on the outskirts of our farm. Plain wooden crosses with their names neatly carved.

"And you leave again," he said.

I tie my bag tightly and heft it over Posa. The horse neighs and grunts in that annoying way she does whenever I saddled her with too much. But I didn't know how long this hunt would take… and if I would even make it back.

"Thank you for taking the girls," I say with a glance in his direction.

I didn't wish to meet his eyes. Not tonight. He held a tinge of judgement. As if he wishes I would be at peace with my desire for revenge. As if he saw it bringing my premature death. I have no time for such judgement when I'm about to become a judge and executioner.

"From the moment you could take care of yourself, it seems I only see you two ways; your back as you're leaving and your pretend innocence when you're playing cards," June said as he pulls at his pipe.

I stare at the agrarian pattern in the horse's mane. "I don't pretend innocence," I said between clenching molars.

June chuckles and the baby stirs. "Girly, you forget I've known you for longer than anyone alive."

The words bite my throat, and I finally look at him. "I have a *real* chance this time. This time I know his name. I won't come back until he's dead."

His eyes harden and he sighs, that look of eternal disapproval crosses his face. "And what then?"

I don't need such questions. Those are killing blows and I've no intention of dying just yet. I turn from him and fix the saddle of the horse, concentrating on the methodical work. Behind me, June grunts and walks closer.

"If you finish your quest..." he allows the 'if' to bite my back and make me bleed. "Will you come back?"

I glance at the house, where Nalin teaches Mary sewing in a quiet voice. A part of me hates he cares. It takes away from my pity-story.

"Why do you want me around, old man?" I ask.

We look at one another. I watch the twitch in his eye and I feel like a spoiled girl at that moment. I had no one when he took me in, gave me shelter, taught me to shoot, and how to survive in the harsh Texas sun. Yet I'd treated him like an acquaintance. Always had. It's because if I cherish him the way he secretly cherishes me, I'd admit I had *someone*. I had people. Having people took away the fire of revenge and I won't give that up for anyone.

"You be careful out there. Here comes your man in black." He points his chin to the man bathed in shadows that rides his silent horse up to the house.

I feel a strange shiver when I see him, cloaking with the darkness, as if he himself dragged the night through the great Texas sky. That same belly-pull, a current like a wave from the sea, yanking me to him.

I lift myself up on my horse and stare down at old June. His skin is pockmarked, it hides behind a bristly white beard.

"If I make it... I'll come back," I said, and it surprises me to find that I meant it.

Leon reaches us, his hat low over his face, cigarette dangling from his lips, a statue in black. He hides each part of himself, even his eyes shelter behind his circular spectacles.

"Good evening, Sheriff," he said as he tips his hat. All grace and manners.

"Mr. June will serve me fine," June said, and he takes a long pull of his pipe. He studies Leon carefully; it was a neutral expression, but I knew better. He was sizing him up because he didn't trust strangers.

"Mr. June," Leon said slowly, that strange European twang to his words. He looked at me and nodded. "Best get started. Long ride ahead."

After turning my horse, I follow him into the night. I cast one last look back at June standing on the porch lit by a single lantern with a sleeping dog at his feet, and a sleeping child in his arms. He might have watched me leave each time I took off. I didn't know. Of all the times I left him, it's the first time I look back. He smiles and raises his hand in a last goodbye.

A strange sensation came over me as I move away. For the first time, I dare to imagine a life where anger wasn't my ruling planet. A life where I simply lived.

Leon speaks little. Though I'm used to solitary quiet rides, the haunting night and the task at hand make my thoughts wander to places I never allow them to wander before. An hour passes before I finally glance at him. His eyes scan the horizon through his spectacles. His gait is relaxed, a body languid with the movement of the horse. Even his chest seems still, as if he didn't need to breathe.

"How long have you been in America?" I ask, casting him a look of inspection.

He doesn't bother turning to me. "A long time."

I resist the urge not to roll my eyes at the vagueness of his entire persona. "Where were you born?"

He smiles a little and lights a cigarette. "In a house."

I bristle and look away, scowling at the vagueness he enjoys. And why should I ask questions about a man who's said so little? His business is his own and I'm no one to demand details that are not mine to peruse. Still, I hunger for them. An unquenched thirst dampening the back of my throat. To ease the burn, I drink a little water. That should do it.

Another hour passes before we speak once more. We ride over a small hill, bypassing a farm fence in the middle of nowhere. The moon hangs low, and I can see the path ahead, over bramble bushes. We keep a steady pace, which should have us in Alto Pass by dawn. Leon's sharp eyes turn to our left and he takes off his spectacles, tucking them neatly into his coat.

"Animals," he hisses.

"Coyotes?" I try to see what he means, but I can't hear anything. They usually announce their presence with their howls.

"Yes. Smaller wolves." Leon hums. "Hungry."

I raise a brow as I take out my colt. Leon holds his rifle over his thighs. The moon shows nothing. The world is silent except for the tiny insects that survive in this terrain.

"I don't hear them," I whisper.

Leon rides on, his eyes still forked in the distance. "They're inching closer. Accessing us."

The land is empty, and I'm tempted to call him a fool, a skittery European that knew nothing of Texas and our harsh world. I shake my head and put away my colt.

"Coyotes howl." I huff in annoyance. "It's likely something else."

Then, as if the world wishes to prove me wrong, the howling begins. Leon smiles and I scowl as I scan the horizon. Nothing. My eyes rake over the land as the howls expand to more animals. Then I see them, small flecks at the base of the mountain. They are still far away but I knew how fast they move, how they can round a prey and take it down.

More howls came from our right. An opposing pack? Did we walk into the middle of a turf war? Leon halts his horse and lifts his rifle, aiming at the animals. They're too far away. No rifle can reach them. But it can scare them. It might scatter them. Depending on how hungry they are.

He fires the rifle, and the animals yelp and scramble. Leon drops his aim, judging if it'd worked. It has, but only for a few minutes. We move on, but our eyes are on the pack, who is slowly creeping its way closer. The horses grow restless, sensing the coyotes. They huff in warning.

"What does your expert Texas mind suggest?" Leon asks.

"Noise," I said as I scan their desperate approach.

I pull out my colt and fire my gun in their direction. Still too far to hit any of them, but the blast deterred them for a moment. Then they work together, encircling us, their yelps and howls encasing us in a warning chorus. When I was a child, coyotes kept stealing our chickens. Daddy went into the night and handled them, killing a few because he made a coat for my sister to wear in winter.

Leon and I both shot again, but it doesn't deter them. I can see the glint of their teeth, speckles of white and yellow with bold promises of dismemberment. Being eaten by wild animals was not something I wanted to do. I rather have a bullet to the head than to see that sort of end. I could sense the Texas landscape wishing to take us down. Refusing us rain, refusing us water, promising us death at each corner of the Texan canvas. It cares little for people, that parasitic creature that lingers on its terrain.

"They're too close," I say, my voice a clenched warning. "There's too many of them."

His body bristles with tension. I have a strange notion that he wishes to dismount his horse and fight them by hand.

Texas threw its last finishing touch when the clouds, which refuse rain, cover the moon, and encase us in darkness.

I become nervous. The drought rendered these animals desperate; they are hungry enough for their emboldening pursuit.

"Ride!" Leon says with suddenness.

He spurs his horse, and his beast leaps forward. I follow as we dash through the field. The moment we move, the coyotes bolt after us. All I can do is follow the trail of his horse. The night is pitch black, as if my lids were closed and I ride at the mercy of the terrain. We gallop for miles; the coyotes attempt to follow but soon give up as the horses outrun them and we are in the clear. The clouds move away from the moon, and we have a clear path before us. Leon slows his horse to a trot, and I follow suit. Soon we are simply walking as he thoroughly scours the area.

I'm out of breath, and I press my water jug to my lips. When I've got my fill, I offer it to Leon. He didn't seem at all perturbed by the chase. He shakes his head.

"Do they often attack like this?" he asks instead.

I look through the mountains. "No. The draught has been bad. They're starving."

At least animals have cause for attack. It is instinctual; it is the desperation of survival. They have no ill intention other than living. I halt my horse and look around at a nicely sized dry bush to my left.

"What?" Leon stiffens.

"Bathroom," I mumble.

He considers my statement, then turns his horse away. He pretends to peruse the area while allowing me privacy. I jump down and meander to the bush. I've only travelled once with a group of men and those were long days and nights spent with my hand on my colt and one eye open. Too many things happen out in the wild.

I cast one last look at Leon to ensure he's adverting his gaze. He sat like a black shadow in the night, eyes firmly etched away from my general direction. I sigh and squat down and do my business as best I could. Just as I am tying my trousers, something grabs my leg. I fall face forward on the ground.

I take a good two seconds to realize it's a coyote. Larger than any I've ever seen. His mouth is firm on my leather boot as he growls and drags me. I fumble for my gun, point it when another comes from my right and clamps down on my arm. I try to hit and kick as another runs at me, his eyes intent on my throat.

That's when the most ferocious growl I ever heard comes from behind me.

In a flash, the coyote on my arm is yanked off and lifted into the air.

Leon is there, his face transforms into wild anger. His eyes are blots of fire red, his mouth agape with elongated fangs as he roars at the animal. Then his hands tear the animal in two. Blood gushes down around me. The other animals yelp and scatter, but Leon dashes after them into the night. All I can hear are vicious growls, yells, yelps, and the squelching of more blood.

Then the night is silent.

Chapter Six

I lay on that dirt like death. The realization that I'm alone, in the middle of nowhere, with a man who is one of the monsters I hunt freezes me. Was this his plan all along? To gain my confidence, take me out where I was alone to devour and drain me? Turn me into a vampire? He notices my inspection. "Ask what you will."

I scramble for my gun. My hands are slick with coyote blood, and I push myself away from the mutilated body of the one he killed. My eyes desperately scan the night. I could get back on my horse. Outrun him. Ride straight north to Alto Pass and seek help. Seek help from *what*? Tell what to folks? A vampire hunts me? A vampire tricked me?

I'm hours away from June and, like he said, this was no saloon.

I slowly stand with my gun still pointed as I walk back to the horses, who are just as spooked as me. My hands tremble and my feet are unsteady. The yelps and cries stop. Which means Leon is returning.

Travel by night, he suggested. It wasn't to find Ryle McAdams. He likely didn't know Ryle McAdams. A tall tale to get me to leave with him. I rifle in my satchel and speak to Posa in soothing words. I take one vial of Holy Water and douse myself with it. My breath comes short, my eyes wild as I try to make out the outline of Leon.

I can't see him. I can't hear him. All I can discern is the distant howls of warning that coat the plains. The animals can sense Leon out there. Had they been able to sense him the entire time? Animals are smart, they can tell when something is afoot. When something is unnatural. I was the damn fool who fell into the trap.

A movement to my right startles me. I swing my gun and shoot. I miss as he slowly emerges from the shadows.

"You said you wouldn't hesitate," he drawls. "Good."

He looks very much like he always did. Missing his hat, the moonlight illuminating his pale face. His eyes are wild red dots of malice, his body is speckled with blood. Still, he stands calmly as he regards me. That unnerves me more than anything. His calm. He calculates while I scramble to survive. I pressed my finger against the trigger. I won't miss this time.

"If I wanted to hurt you, I would've hurt you already, Dania," he said.

I cock my gun, aim still sure. Not that it would do much good. When I'd shot Ryle McAdams, he'd laughed. Will Leon laugh too? I'll have to relieve the worst day of my life, die in the dirt with my tongue still thirsty for a revenge that would never come.

"*You're* a vampire," I state the fact bouncing in my mind.

Leon nods and takes a small step towards me. I tense and my mouth thins.

"Regular bullets won't do much to save you," Leon says. "Let that be your second lesson. But I think you know that. I think you know you need *silver*. You need your blade, but you've not taken it yet. I assume it's shock."

I swallow. Yes. I'm shaken to my core. I'm angry at myself and *afraid*. Afraid I'll die this night without accomplishing much.

"I'm gonna get on my horse and I'm going to ride out of here," I say as neutrally as I can.

He studies me in the moonlight. "Are you hurt?" He sniffs the air around, like dogs do when seeking a hare. "You're not. Your leather saved you."

I didn't feel pain from any bites, just the ghostly sensation of teeth clamping down on me.

"You're also doused in holy water. Smart, but I knew you were smart. Which is why I sought you out," he says and takes another step.

I raise my gun higher. "Get back! A bullet may not do much, but a bullet in your forehead will give you pause enough for me to grab my blade."

He laughs; it's a dark laugh that splinters my spine into tremors.

"I wielded swords before America became a country. I fought alongside your founding fathers," he says darkly. "Your skill is like one of a child."

"Quiet! I don't want to hear your lies," I say as I move closer to Posa, spotting the hilt of my blade from the corner of my eye.

He sighs and shakes his head. "You wish for the truth. Here it is. *Yes*, I am a vampire, but I am not a vampire in the manner Ryle McAdams is. My name is Leon Laurent. I was born in a house, a common country house in Provence, France. The year was 1648. I had a wife and a child, but they are long dead now. They turned me when I was twenty-seven, which means I'll look twenty-seven for the rest of time. Or until you run me through with your saber."

I shake my head and step closer to the hilt of the blade which is within reach. I lounge for it, swiftly sliding it out. Leon was still fifteen feet away, but the moment the sword was in my hand, he's before me. He grasps my fist and pulls me tightly to him. He leans in on me with those violent red eyes, fangs protruding from his mouth.

"If I wished you were dead, I would've let you burn in that house," he says harshly.

I pull back, but his hand is wrought iron, as if I've been encased in mortar and left to dry. My heart gallops erratically, my eyes zoom in on his teeth. All I can hear are my breathy gasps of air. I smell burning when I realize his hands are sizzling against the holy water. The only sign he gives of pain is the twitching of his jaw.

"You were right when you accessed me. I *am* a marshal. I'm the deputy commander of the Vampire Legion. My assignment is to hunt down and dispose of Ryle McAdams. I tracked him to you," he speaks as if he were attempting to calm an animal.

I shake my head even as his proximity explodes; the pull connecting to my stomach. There was something about being encased in his arms that vaults my thoughts. I lose control of my body, and I wrangle it to dominance by sheer will.

He leans forward, and I gasp. "I only feed on *willing* humans—yes, there's always humans who are willing. I just fed on a couple of coyotes. Vampires don't need to eat every day. We can comfortably go three days without a meal and seven before we go feral. You're safe. Now stop this, think rationally and not about your fear. We can speak and you can ask the questions dancing on your tongue."

His voice is so calm, as if we're speakingb over dinner, between goblets of wine.

Slowly, he lets go of me. His palms are bright red and burned. The indentation of the hilt of my blade scores his right hand. He finally grimaces, shaking them out.

I can hardly move. I'd sworn that I was dead. That he would tear my throat out and drink me, toss me back like whiskey. I'm even more startled to find that I'd yearned for it. A thrall, that's what he has. It's the only explanation. These are not my feelings. These are not my thoughts. I wish them gone. I wish he was gone. He dulls the thirst for revenge, and I can't have that. Not tonight. Not ever.

I'm petrified of moving, but I'm also trying to push past my fright and into the rational part of my mind. We've had plenty of alone time. He could've killed me *and* the girls. Instead, he took us to June. I swallow and finally nod.

I lower the blade, though my hands still tremble.

"You're a vampire." This time it's not a question. "Who hunts other vampires."

He glances at me. His eyes are losing the red tint and soothing themselves into their usual blue. "I told you last night, only the bad ones. The ones who go astray. The ones who break our laws. Whose behavior threatens to expose us. If the world found out about us, we would be hunted down and strategically killed."

"Because you're demons," I say matter-of-factly.

A small look of offense crosses his face. "We're folk, just like other folks."

I almost laugh at his explanation. He would live forever. He can kill with one hand. He can drain a human of life for his survival or amusement. He can seduce me and *that* was a crime I wasn't willing to forgive.

Still, I suppose he is not vastly different from many other humans I've encountered.

"You can't be in sunlight," I said.

He looks up at the moon. "No, I can't. Which is why we need to make it to Alto Pass before sunrise. We've lingered enough. You can ask more questions as we ride."

The thought of riding through the night with him next to me tensed my entire back. No, he wouldn't kill me, but now I'm consorting with a demon. A creature I seek to kill.

"I can't," I say and sheathe the blade. "What if you're not able to feed? Am I the little snack you carry just in case?"

At this, Leon laughs. He shakes his head and goes to his horse. He reaches into his saddle and pulls out a hefty black bag, then tosses it to me. I catch it and look at him questioningly. It's incredibly heavy.

"In that case, you'll strap me with this to a tree or a rock. Let nature take its course." He points to the bag.

I open it to reveal a chain made of pure silver. It's long enough to wrap around him and a rock if I needed to. I stare back at him. "You don't want to live."

He couldn't. Not when he has his death planned so meticulously. Not when he carries something like this that would guarantee his end. I've met people who sought death but never one I'd shared midnight conversations with.

"I've lived already. I've died already. All these years have simply been extra," he says with a twirl of his hand.

It seems to me a sad existence. But who was I to pass judgement on sad existences considering how I live my life? Considering the perpetual sallowness of my thoughts. I swallow and close the bag, then hand it back to him.

He slips it back in his saddle and casts me a glance. "You're covered in blood."

My stomach turns as I realize this. I step back and study him. "Will that be a problem?"

He smiles once more, his fangs bright in the moonlight. "No, Ms. Gonzalez. The drying blood of animals is off-putting."

"How about drying human blood?" I ask.

He laughs. "That's a different story."

Flushing, I mount Posa.

I notice trivial things I never saw before; the fine shape of his throat. Curved and long, shaved clean and smooth. His shoulders are wide under his coat, strong and well formed. That pull in my belly chants his name and I subdue it.

Chapter Seven

I study his profile. I had thought he looked different and now I see it. He belongs to a different time. With his high cheekbones, his elegant nose, and the long pallor of his fingers. They plucked him from history books.

"Why did you come to America?" I ask.

He shrugs and examines the horizon like he's done since we left. "It seemed a good place to come. Fewer people. A better chance to remain hidden. My bloodline died with my grandson. His only child passed, and he died without more children. Everyone I knew was dead."

It sounds like an awfully lonesome existence. One which I understand well, and it bothers me that I have something in common with him. I don't aspire to have anything in common with a vampire.

"The Vampire Legion wanted to establish a presence in the Americas, so I volunteered. Came with two other vampires. The journey across was the worst one I ever undertook. I've not been back since." He cast me a look. "Humans don't take well to transport of corpses, so we had to hide in boxes for weeks. Our caretaker would feed us rats or pig's blood. Chicken blood sometimes. It's my least favorite, but it kept the hunger at bay."

I grimace, disgusted by the entire notion.

"I didn't like it much either," he says when he spots my horrified stare.

He becomes quiet as we ride under the moon high in the sky, illuminating our way. We urged the horses, keenly aware dawn was but hours away. It feels as if I've already died. As if my life is a patchwork of incredible but terrible things. I deeply envy other folk who didn't have to live through what I had to. How peaceful they rest when their heads touch their pillows. They don't have haunting recollections.

"How did you die?" I finally ask.

I felt, more than saw, the stiffness of his body. A feeling I keenly understand. I didn't like to discuss the day they killed my family, either. I too was a hallow, animated creature of the night.

His shoulders slump, a defeat. "I was a fool. I always had a proclivity for *les belles femmes*. The beautiful women. Though I was married to a good woman, I searched for more. Whenever I had extra coins, I would seek another and another. One day, I found the wrong one. Madame Giselle was her name. A grand vampiress."

I allow him to compose his story from long ago and I picture it so clearly. I can almost see the gilded facades of France and the tinkling laugher of an elegant vampire luring him.

"She enchanted me. She grew fond of me and one day she turned me. When you're first turned, you're much like a human babe. It takes months for coherent thought to come. A fledging. By the time my thoughts settled, my wife thought me dead and had moved in with another man who raised my son."

He looks at me, and I understand the hollow sadness on his face. He keeps it concealed, and I've asked him to expose it. And he obliged. I didn't know what to make of such a show of trust because I feel I didn't earn it. It makes it hard to only perceive a monster instead of simply a man.

"Which is why your description of Annie Williams is so strange. One freshly turned is hardly capable of thought. Which means something rotten turned them," he says ominously.

I lick my lips and drink from my water. Sinister stories told in wretched darkness do nothing for my nerves. Not when I ride with the devil at my side.

"You said Ryle McAdams killed his maker. His sire," I said.

Leon peers back at the horizon. "Mr. McAdams has always been volatile. I studied his problematic case for a long time. I read about your family and what he did. The Vampire League forbids such attacks. They deposed him three times, and he ignored it. We needed someone who could take him back to Boston, where our headquarters are. We sent the one who could wrangle him. His maker. He never came back. Mr. McAdams sent us his ashes in the post."

I swallow thickly and look ahead, trying to wrap my head around such a creature. "What do you mean ashes? He burnt him?" I feel a shiver slide up my arm.

"No," Leon says carefully, as if trying to gather his words to mingle properly with his thoughts. "Vampires decompose quickly. In a matter of hours. We turn to ash."

I watch him for a moment as I wrap my head around so much new information. I envision his body disappearing in a moment, snatched from the earth after wandering it for so long.

"The damage he's been doing up and down this area... tells me he's likely formed a lair," Leon admits.

"A lair? Like a group?"

"Yes. Lairs are usually volatile, and most vampires prefer a solitary life. Raw power can only control lairs. Those are my suspicions," he whispers.

The reins feel heavy in my hand. "So we should prepare for many of them."

He nods.

"We should ride faster. If this is as you say... I may need help," I admit, though I hate to admit it. But I have no intention of being turned into a vampire. I would not die before I got my vengeance. The creature or... man next to me is the only one who can properly help me.

Leon tips his hat. "Glad to be of service, ma'am."

As we rode, the night cooled. An hour before sunrise, we realize that to make it Alto Pass without turning Leon into a pile of ashes, we're going to need to rush. Leon slid on his shaded spectacles and closed his coat around him when the first rays of sunlight flickered on the horizon. At that moment, Alto Pass came into view.

We galloped the last leg of the journey. Leon seems to know his way around the town. He went straight to the saloon without preamble. He jumps off his horse and rushed into the place as the first streak of sun lands on the road.

I'm shaking by the time he's slid into the doors and into safety. Why? Why did I care? Was it the belly-pull? What is that I see him as a person and not a monster? I feared witnessing him combusting into ash next to me. I didn't like those visions, but I hate even more that dislike them to begin with.

I take the horses to a local stable, disturbing the proprietor, who claimed it was no time to wake up good folks. I pay him an extra five dollars for his trouble and lug both saddles to the saloon.

Once I was inside, I realize a few things. I'm drained, my lids are heavy with exhaustion, and I'm hungry. I stumble to the bartender, who looks at me with interest.

"A man in black just came in for a room," I say and point with my chin to Leon's saddle. "This here is his. I'll need another room for myself."

His mouth remains unmoved under his bristly mustache. "I only had one room, but Mrs. Channing runs a boarding house up the street for *ladies*."

The way he says it almost makes me snarl. A combination of the weakness in my knees and the strain of carrying Leon's heavy saddle. I have no interest in boarding houses run by *respectable* ladies. I'd known quite a few in my time. Strangers have to sit for meals together and they made idle chatter and inquiries. Lips were turned at the sight of my trousers and lack of corsage. I rather sleep in the open. The other option was sharing a room with a vampire.

I won't sleep a wink.

Chapter Eight

I sigh and lean against the bar. The place is mostly empty, with a few patrons asleep, slumping on tables from their late-night frivolities. I felt dirty with the animal blood over me. My attire is not lost on the bartender, who inspects me.

"Got attacked by coyotes a ways back," I explain. "I'm not hurt, but I desperately need a bath."

The man comes closer with a knowing face. "Mr. Laurent paid for his room and explained you would join him. He's requested breakfast and a bath to be brought up. You'll find I don't ask many questions, miss. I mind my own business. That's how I stay alive. Second door up the stairs. Bath will be up shortly."

I fight bravely to keep the snarl from my mouth, so I nod and stiffly amble up the stairs, dragging the saddles with me. I find the door with little trouble; it opens the moment I step before it and Leon stands there without his coat. His black shirt is still crisp, but his hat and spectacles are gone. The tug in my belly flourishes and brightens my neck and ears. He looks so human and tangible, as if I could run my fingers down his shirt and explore the concavities of his chest.

He quickly takes both saddles from me, making it seem as if they weighed no more than a couple of pounds. Leon turns into the room, and I follow. It's a small, dingy place with a single downtrodden bed, a table, and a chair. On top of the table is a plate of stewed beef, a boiled egg, and overcooked beans.

"I apologize. They only had one room." Leon sets the saddles carefully on the floor, then turns to me.

I'm so tired I almost sway. Despite the unappetizing nature of the food, my stomach growls with need. I nod at the vampire and go for the plate, pushing around the beans with the metal spoon.

"How does sleep work for vampire?" I ask idly as I eat a spoonful of beans. They are bland and mushy, nothing to the refried beans Mami had cooked for me and my sister.

Leon sits on the bed, and it creaks under his weight. I'd not realized his height. He is a large man, taller than June with long limbs that would be uncomfortable in most beds. I relax on the chair as we faced one another.

"Much the same as humans, though we do not need as much of it," he explains. "I don't get tired until around noon and I sleep from noon until around four o'clock."

I sense what he means in between well poised words. He's suggesting I sleep first while he stays awake doing *what*? Watching me? No matter how tired I am, I won't be able to rest under those conditions. Also, the thought of sleeping while he watches me unsettles my stomach. I figure I'm starving, so I crack the egg and take a bite. It's the best part of the meal.

"Try sleeping now," I insist between mouthfuls of yolk.

"I'm not tired, Ms. Gonzalez," he says with a tinge of a smile as he watches my eating process with great interest. As if he recalls the taste of eggs and yearns for them.

His insistence on my formal name bothers me. It reminds me of my mother and what a superior meal she would prepare than the one I'm being subjected to. Also, it feels as if we didn't spend a harrowing night together, as if we're still strangers. Perhaps I delude myself into believing I know this man. This creature.

"I told you, just Dania. Ms. Gonzalez was my mother," I say and finish the egg.

He studies me, head tilted to the side, as if he inspects a book. "You're weary of sleeping in a room with a vampire."

Obviously. But also, an image dances in my mind of him naked in the bed. I wonder at the hard planes of his muscled body, the one he pressed against mine. I flush and look away. If he can sense my body temperature change, then I'll appreciate if he didn't mention it.

He presses his lips together. "I understand your hesitation, but I fed a few hours ago. I'm not hungry and I won't be for a day or two. You can rest easy."

I almost laugh, but a knock interrupts us. Leon is instantly on his feet, taking long strides across the room. He pauses before the door, as if he can sense or hear what is beyond it. He goes for the handle.

"Your bath. You'll feel much better after it," he says and tugs the door open.

An older woman and a young boy struggle to carry a copper tub into the room. Leon instantly helps them, making a slight work of the heavy task. They stare at him in confusion as he sets the tub down in the middle of the room. He hands them a few dollars each and thanks them for the service.

He's so normal that, for a moment, I think I've hallucinated his vampiric state. For a moment, he was nothing but gentlemanly.

My eyes linger on the curve of his back as he bends over. His trousers taunt on the fine line of the back of his thighs. It confirms his muscled frame. Solid, like a steady rock that doesn't yield to a roaring river. I swallow and look away.

"I'll..." he hesitates. "I'll enjoy a drink downstairs and return once you're dressed."

He didn't allow me to agree. He simply left, guns still slung low on his hips and leaving the room empty of his presence. I wait a few minutes, assuring myself I was truly alone, then I undress. Once I'm naked, I sink into the warm water and sigh contently as it covers me. I didn't have a proper bath at June's. Water is too scarce, and I idly wonder how much Leon paid for a bath.

I scrub the lye soap over my arms and in between my legs, then wash my hair, working the suds into the strands until it's clean. I glance at the door. Still closed. My soapy fingers travel to my breast and my thoughts linger on Leon's bent form. I stifle a moan as I rub the pad of my thumb over my nipple. In the warm water, I rub myself without explanation. How can a creature that tore coyotes in half arouse me so? With clenching teeth and shut eyes, I bring myself to pleasure. I imagine Leon unclothed, hovering over me, and lapping his tongue over my sex.

I'm so exhausted by the time I finish I slide down, deep in the tub, and contently rest in the warm water. I did not intend to fall asleep, but I did.

When I next woke, I am tucked in the bed naked under the white cotton sheets. The room is dark except for a small lamp that flickers low. I didn't know the time. I quickly sit up and scan the area, my eyes wide as I breathe sharply and try to understand what happened.

The tub is gone. My vampire companion sits on the floor with his back against the wall, legs stretched out, and head rolled on a pillow pinned to his shoulders. He is completely asleep. His chest doesn't even rise.

"Leon!" I shout.

He doesn't respond.

"Mr. Laurent!"

Nothing.

I look around the room. Nothing seems amiss. My clothes are folded over the desk, and I spot a note left on top of my shirt. With my eyes on the vampire, I carefully rise, wrapping myself in the sheet as I lumber for the note. I can hardly make out the words in the room's dimness.

I limp to the lamp.

Ms. Gonzalez,

Sleeping in water is dangerous for humans. Do not worry, I did not look. I need my rest for the night ahead. Do not bother attempting to wake me. It is impossible once we get to our state of rest. Eat well today and I will speak to you in a few hours.

L.L.

I blush deeply at the thought that he found me naked and asleep in the tub. Fleshly self-pleasured. I'd not even woken when he entered. He had to heft me out of the water and lay me on the bed, then thrown a sheet over my bare breasts. Was he able to smell what I'd done while he was gone?

I want to kick him while he sleeps. Especially if he won't wake up. How *dare* he? To think that I'd brought myself to pleasure imaging him naked. Serves me right for lusting over an ungodly creature.

My shirt is a little moist. My fingers linger on the cloth; he'd cleaned my shirt removing the blood stains. I shake my head and continue dressing. Once I have my guns on me, I feel secure. I stand before Leon and kick his foot. His body is stiff, unmoving. Chills run down my arm; all it did was jostle his hardened body. It would be easy to kill a vampire in this state. One just has to get to them while they sleep. He is... vulnerable like this. I can't stray far; anyone can enter and harm him.

I kneel and study his face. He is very handsome in that untouchable manner that lacks faults, and anything that lacks faults is decidedly inhuman.

I stand and meander downstairs to find the saloon livelier than I saw it before. There is a different bartender, one with soiled blond hair and a frizzy beard that goes down his neck. Patrons press themselves against the bar and order drinks—some even have meals. My stomach growls. It looks to be mid to late afternoon, and I don't think Leon will be in his vegetative state for much longer. I might as well grab food to prepare for another long ride with a vampire.

Chapter Nine

When I make it back upstairs, Leon is awake, and I flush scarlet. I did not expect his serene eyes raking over me the moment I enter. It is my intention to remain unaffected by his closeness and the reality of what happened while I'd been asleep. Or more importantly, what sent me to sleep to begin with.

"I can smell your embarrassment from here," he says quietly as dusts his hat. He pulls out his tobacco and packs the paper.

Apparently, being a vampire allots him unique abilities. Which means he *knows* what I did. Lord help me, I want to hide. I'm too damn old to be embarrassed by such things, but here I am.

"A good man would've stepped out of the room and allowed me to wake on my own," I say between clenching molars. I'm fighting the battle of my life to keep my skin from flushing red.

Leon raises a brow and peers at me over his spectacles. His blue eyes hold a tint of amusement. "By the time I found you, only your nose was above water. A few minutes later and you would've failed at your grand revenge plan."

I lose the battle to prevent the flush. I brighten down to my neck. It's so intense it stings my back teeth. "A good man would've at least tried to wake me."

He finishes his cigarette and dangles it from his lip. He smirks. "You assume I am a good man when I am indeed not a man at all. But you need not worry about my lingering eyes, *Dania*. Despite the monster in me, I was quite careful to preserve your modesty."

My nostrils flare as he lights his cigarette and stares at me from the smoke. I have a feeling his *lingering eyes* had perused me at length.

"In the next town, we get separate rooms. Or I'll tie you to the city flagpole with your silver chain and let, what was it you said? Nature take its course?" I drop my tone. My words harden into pitted hallows.

His cheek twitches, and I can tell he's struggling not to smile. I didn't think it was humorous. The way I'm feeling right now, I would like to see him blow up in flames. My mouth is dry and I'm desperate for something I can't name or cup into words.

"Humans are funny about their naked bodies," Leon says in an almost open conversation. "At the end of the day, we're all naked. We just happen to strap clothing over our flesh."

I clench my teeth when Leon unbuckles his cartridge belt and slings it over the chair. Then he unstraps his guns and takes off his glasses. To my horror, he undresses.

"Stop this," I demand, moving away. "I don't want to see you naked."

I don't. I do.

"I insist," Leon says as he opens his shirt to reveal a muscled torso of pale, firm flesh. Just as I envisioned it. My sex contracts. He looks up at me, opening his arms. "See, here is my chest."

I scoff and look away, intent on leaving him alone and naked. But he slid his pants down to stand nonchalantly naked before me. I quickly advert my eyes from his penis and pointedly stare at the window.

"Come now," he seems to laugh at me. "Take a look. I've seen you naked and now you've seen *me* naked and we're even."

I'm ever so grateful for the darkened room to cover up my scarlet flush. The entire thing is ridiculous, and it didn't make me feel better at all. On the contrary, the pull he has on my belly harshly yanks my head to stare at him. I keep my eyes on his face and didn't dare glance down.

"There, I've seen you. Now dress, the hour is late, and I'd like to sleep in a nice bed tonight," I snip and look away. The only thing my eye catches is the trail of dark hair that travels from his stomach down to his...

"Dania, you're still angry," he says with a tsk.

His deep voice courses through my spine and arches it. I pace away from him, my hands on my guns, ready to shoot him to end this torment. I'm... unfocused. He's... distracted me. Made something other than anger and hate fill my brain and I don't know who I am or why I do the things I do. He's providing alternative thoughts, and I'm not ready to let go of my hate or my task.

"Because this is foolery! We must hunt a killer and you've undressed," I growl.

To my horror, he steps closer. "You were angry even before I undressed."

This makes me swirl on him with a snarl. He serenely looks at me, content with goading me. My theatrics simply brought me physically closer to him. It's a mistake. All I have to do is reach out and feel the skin of his chest.

"It's just flesh," he says, but his voice is warm. As if he's offering a simple explanation that provides comfort. He shrugs.

Emboldened by his nonchalance, I do what I imagined doing. I place my hand on his chest. The silken skin startles me, and I push him back. I almost double over at the sensation brushing his skin causes in my stomach. A fiery hell that spreads through me.

"Fine. Step back, let me take a proper look at you since you're an *exhibitionist*."

At this, he smiles and takes a few steps back. He opens his arms wide to display himself properly. I rake my eyes down to his body and then back to his face. His penis is nestled in a bed of soft brown hair, and his body is finely muscled. My sex contracts when I meet his eyes.

He raises a brow. "To your liking?"

All solid thoughts exit my head. The ghostly feel of his skin under my fingers is still palpable. Yes, very much to my liking. Exactly to my liking, to be honest, but I have no intention of providing him with these compliments he's not earned.

"Get dressed. We have a task," I say in a stony tone.

A smile lingers on him, then he shrugs and pulls up his pants. My eyes remain on him as he dusts off his shirt and buttons it. The air is thick around us as I drown in a sliver of disappointment. Without preamble, I leave the room.

I wrangle my thoughts back to Ryle McAdams, chanting the killer's name like a plea to God to give me back that fiery hate I carry. Because at this moment, it's simmered so low it's scarcely warm.

Sundown is forty minutes away. I walk about the small town, gather supplies, and get the horses. They look refreshed and ready for the journey ahead. By the time I escort them to the saloon, Leon stands on the porch, casually holding both saddles. The sun and its poisonous rays are gone, and the town was getting rowdy as their thirst makes itself known.

"Where to next?" I ask as I strap the saddle on Posa.

Leon provides his horse with an apple, which the animal chomps on quickly with a happy neigh. "Liventown, much closer, and we should be there a little past midnight. I think that's where our next clue will be. I spoke to the owner of the saloon and there are rumors of children missing from Liventown."

I heft myself up the horse and stare down at him. "*Children?*"

Leon's face is a hard line. "Yes. It's not unheard of."

My stomach coils in disgust at the implication. Either Ryle is taking the children as meals or he's turning them, cursing them to remain looking like children for the rest of their existence. This spurs anger in me. Thank goodness. I needed that. I needed that focus. It's my purpose.

Not to peruse the naked body of my companion.

"Then let us go," I say and turned Posa, not waiting for him to lead the way.

Chapter Ten

I knew the way to Liventown. It's on the banks of a small but steady river, which helps many local farmers that lived there. It's one of those towns I didn't frequent because of the overzealous religious hacks who lived there. A small church started led by a charismatic young preacher and it's grown exponentially in the past years. Each time I've gone, the feeling of being watched grows.

I hope our stop will be a few quiet hours. I don't wish to converse with the strange vampire or linger on the implications of my own unexplained desire.

About twenty minutes outside of Alto Pass, as the moon peeks over the horizon, Leon hums. It's low and steady and a glance over his face tells me he's relaxed in his saddle and enjoying the ride.

"Do you like being a vampire?" I ask.

Naturally, I wondered. He seems so different from the creatures I hunt, the ones who attack me with bared fangs and mutilated mouths. He looks like any other human with the pesky ability to hunt in the dark and tear out a throat with his bare teeth. Or perhaps I'm attempting to justify my attraction, a way of defining the phenomena.

He ponders my question, savoring or juggling answers that will satisfy me.

"At times," he says and lights the cigarette he's rolling. "It's been interesting to watch the passing of time, how humanity changes and advances. They find cleverer ways of killing each other."

His words are dipped in honesty. I'd not expected it. He looks at the world from the sideline instead of living in it. I don't expect I would like everlasting life if that's all I have to look forward to. A life on the sidelines.

"I would imagine it's lonely," I say with little thought.

He goes reticent, his eyes intent on the horizon and the only noise around us is the critters of the night and the soft hooved steps of our horses. The arid dry ground is dusty under us, desperate for a drink of the sky's water, pleading for a respite.

"Yes," he says after a lengthy pause. The bud of his cigarette is nothing but a stub and he tosses it on the ground. "Time passes differently, I suppose. We avoid mingling with humans because..." he casts me a look. "Eventually you die."

Emotion unexpectedly seizes my throat. I've never understood a sentiment more than I did at this moment. Much the way my own life had disintegrated, those I loved were long gone, and here I am... a carcass. My interactions with humans are over a table of cards, a passing chat with a saloon bartender, a momentary lover to appease the body's needs. Watching others live their lives filled with smiles, happiness, dreams, and aspirations, while I meander from place to place.

Such lives are worthy of envy. He is, much like me, a specter.

"You envy humans," I say.

"Just like you." Leon provides me a genuine smile, one I've never seen before. "I can see why. You lost everything at an early age and from then on, you've lived clutching on to your anger and your need for retribution. I think I would do the same in your shoes. But it's lonely. After a while, we all need someone."

He sees me so clearly and presented his assessment with such care and lack of judgement that it stirs something in me. Something I didn't expect. An unspoken closeness.

"I have June," I admit and focus my eyes on the distance, on the winding road.

The breeze carries the scent of June's aftershave. I sense the feel of his callused fingers over my knuckles, like when he taught me to shoot.

"But you didn't want June. He's not your father and how dare he come into your life and play at being one," he says with a perceiving glance.

I swallow and tighten my hold on the reins. "You speak a lot, Mr. Laurent."

He chuckles, delighted in the discomfort he landed on my shoulders. "And I thought I was being quiet."

"Best we focus on our task instead of the past," I say testily.

"Aren't you the least bit curious?" Leon asks.

I chew my lip, wrestling with that warmth sensation that continuously assaults my senses when around him.

"About what?"

He raises a brow. "About me."

I sigh and look off into the distance. "Fine, tell me about you."

He chuckles and allows a few moments to pass in silence. I think he simply teased me and I'll not be privy to any of his past. Then I realize he's gathering his words. He's careful with words; he doesn't cast them frivolously.

"I don't think I've lived much for the past one hundred years," he breathes.

In the distance, an owl hoots as it hunts its mice. Confessions can also hunt down pains long left to slumber.

"But you've been alive," I say.

"To be alive and to live are two different things," he says in a matter-of-fact tone. "You wake, you exist, you eat—or drink—"

He chuckles to himself, amused. I simply stare at him, repulsed. He doesn't mind my looks. My looks lengthen his smiles.

"Sounds like a bore," I say.

"Most days are," he says, then points to the distance. "The mountains cease to be impressive; humanity ceases to be interesting, and all one has to look forward to is the varying taste of blood."

Sure, I didn't drink blood, but I understand his explanation. How many years have I traveled through this landscape only to grow bored with the same mountains that should impress me and leave me in awe? Perhaps I too am simply existing. Perhaps I too have forgotten to live.

I have no other words, and I don't wish to hear more from him. In my mind, I wish he would be quiet and allow me to linger with my thoughts.

To my surprise, he does.

Liventown began as a small settlement of cattle wrangles and gamblers who scoured the area for the best place to raise cattle. It's a town much like many others I frequent as I roam from place to place, fiercely seeking prey. In the past few years, it changed. There is a small white church built at the edge of town, with a vaulted nave and a bronze bell generously provided by one of its upstanding citizens.

It's hard to appreciate the majesty of the church as we arrive when the moon is high. Much of the church, God-fearing the residents of Liventown are nestled in their beds. The town is quiet except for the center, where the town's saloons are. The first thing I notice is how dry the river is. It's a trickle from what it used to be. The drought has certainly impacted the place. It looks... abandoned. The moment we ride next to the church, a deep darkness pitted with gravity takes over my senses. I stop and Leon looks at me with a raised brow.

"You sense it. How interesting," he says, studying me.

I look around, attempting to find the source. "Why do I feel it?"

His hat shadows his face, casting a near unreal look to his features. "I'm uncertain."

I ponder his words as we wander past closed shops and quiet homes, stray dogs and cats that stroll from establishment to establishment.

"Why don't I have that same reaction to you?" I finally ask.

I've speculated about this; I should get the same sickly bitter sense I got when I entered Annie's house. Yet around him there is that... *draw*. I can't explain it and I have no intention of contemplating what it means, though perhaps I should.

He looks straight ahead, his eyes dark as he scans the area and takes in our situation. "I'm uncertain of that, too."

We advance past the closed post office when we spot the Sheriff's office. A tall man with a badge leans against a railing with two colts on his waist while he smokes his cigar. Next to him is a young preacher. A man I've seen before, though a handful of years older. There is something about him that chills my spine and curls the toes in my boots.

"Evening, strangers. Arriving in town rather late, aren't you?" The Sheriff asks with a stone face behind a bristly mustache.

"Evening, sheriff," Leon says amicably.

The preacher moves forward, hands demurely folded before him, a bland smile and steely blue eyes that open too wide and stare at you like they will soak the sin from your soul. A juxtaposition to Leon's warm ones.

"I'm Thomas Rein; the lord has placed me as shepherd to the flock here in Liventown. Forgive our curiosity, as your business is your own, but we've had a trail of peculiarities lately. Do you mind sharing what your business is in Liventown and how long you plan to stay?" The preacher hardly moves, as if he's cemented his body and only his mouth animates.

I can sense Leon glaring down at the young preacher whose eyes were intent on me.

"A few days," I say and toss back my coat to allow them to see my guns. "We're hunting vampires."

A silence descends over the small group as all three men stare at me. I tip my hat and smile at the preacher.

"In the name of the lord, of course." I nod and turn my horse as I stroll further into town.

There's a distinct sense of drowning though water was scarce. A thickness in the air, as if I can touch it and watch it ripple.

I stop Posa in front of the saloon as Leon comes up next to me. He seems unsure if he wishes to chastise me or laugh at my bluntness. I have no intention of apologizing for my words; I don't like men who intimidate others in the name of God.

I dismount the horse and wait for Leon to do the same. I hand him my reins and our ungloved fingers brush against one another; our eyes instantly meet. The closeness of his body flushes me once more, and I step away. My stomach continues its flaring burst each time he's near. I can hardly stand it.

"Something's wrong with this town," I mumble. Something is also wrong with me, but I won't share that.

He nods. His gaze lingers on my lips. "Be alert. Stay armed."

"You too," I agree and enter the saloon.

Chapter Eleven

I'm greeted with the smell of smoke and sweat coming from the sinning men of Liventown. For a town this size on a Friday night, the place is relatively empty. Instead of the loud chatter I'm accustomed to in saloons, it is hushed words as if whispered during a Sunday sermon. I have a feeling the good preacher and his obedient sheriff have something to do with this. That or the drought has folks moving to places with better prospects. Still, they attempt to enjoy the evening festivities of card games and clasping saloon girls on their laps. Leon turns and stares at me; his eyes are still red-tinted but his face is slack. "No, my dear. You have it all wrong. It is now *I* who belongs to you."

The amiable bartender greets me with a pleasant smile, eager to pour me a whiskey. I desperately need whiskey. I motion for one and gulp it back in a swing. The liquid burns down my throat, coating it in that familiar pleasant feeling.

"I'll need two rooms if you have them," I say as I motion for another. He obliges me and leans forward, relaxed. He's a large man with a red face and a pleasant disposition.

"What do you need two rooms for?"

"Do you have them?" I ask with a raised brow before I toss back the liquid.

"Only one." He stuffs a pipe in his mouth, smoking it as he studies me.

Damn. More nights in a room with a vampire I'm distinctly attracted to.

"I'll take it then. For a few days," I say as I set down the glass on the counter. The contents seep into my empty stomach. "A man in black is my travel companion. He should come shortly."

The bartender sighs as he rummages for the keys. "You won't stay here for long," he says under his breath. "Whole town's drying up unless you count the pious and the righteous."

I observe his dejected shoulders. The small number of patrons gives him plenty of time to ponder and... gossip.

"Yeah? Met your preacher out there, the sheriff answers to him?" I ask as he studies the keys. My words make him pause and he looks at me, as if attempting to determine if I'm a friend or foe.

"Our old sheriff just died," he admits. "This new one is from... California. There's no trusting city folk."

He tsks and hands me my key.

"They sure ain't," I say in comradery. "We don't get many city folks out in Pecos County."

He abuts himself against the bar as he appraises me in approval. "First the river dries up, now this business with the kids." He angrily shakes his head. "Good folk are leaving nothing but the righteous, who are eager to point fingers at anyone who touches whiskey. They say the devil takes the children."

My stomach freezes. "The devil?"

"Aye. There's a ranch out five miles north of here, past the horned tree. They say it's haunted. Bull crap, if you ask me," he bristles, and runs a finger through his wiry mustache as he sniffs.

I feel the flicker of hope ignite in my stomach as I thank the man for his help. I wonder if we could make it out there tonight, but I know Leon would caution us to analyze the situation before rushing blindly. And he would be right.

The room is a better sight than the one in Alto Pass. Welcoming sheets and a wide window that highlights plains beyond painted like an artistic illustration. I throw my satchel on the bed and toss my hat, letting my hair cascade down my back. I want to formulate a plan, but the liquor has gone straight into my head.

By the time Leon enters, I've unbuttoned the top of my shirt, trying to free myself from the confines. He glances at me, then sets down the saddles in the room's corner.

"We seem to have very little luck with rooms," he says as he straightens and takes off his hat.

I sit up and scoot to one side of the bed to allow him access to his own. Though I have a feeling, he'll decline to sleep. He doesn't look tired. I suppose this is the equation of the middle of the day for him while my internal clock is inverted with the night hours.

He looks at the empty side of the bed, then back at me. His movements are slow as he sets down his hat on the small table. "You are tired."

I press my hand to my cheek. It feels heated. I drank the whiskey too fast on an empty stomach. "Whiskey."

He nods and sits down, his hands going for his tobacco as he packs it carefully. I'm transfixed by the movement of his fingers.

"Is it a vampire's side effect?" I ask suddenly, hardly able to stand the constant pull my belly has towards him. To watch him, and memorize the way his fingers roll the paper, the way he turns his head in contemplation.

He looks at me with a raised brow, those blue eyes questioning my meaning.

"The feeling I get," I say and press my stomach to show where I feel the tug.

His movements pause. Still as a statue, his eyes focus on my stomach. "What do you mean?"

I sigh and lean back on the pillows, frustrated with the dizziness my mind constantly feels around him. The lack of focus for my lifelong task. It's diminishing my thirst and makes me think of things I've long discarded on the side of the road to revenge.

"Like a bellyache," I whisper, and close my eyes. "A pull. It follows you. Jumbles my thoughts."

I feel him stand and move closer. When I open my eyes, I find him staring at me. He studies my face, taking in the details I didn't like and those I appreciate. There's a slight flash of his fangs hiding under his upper lip.

"How long have you felt this?"

I shrug. "Since I met you. Is it normal?"

Perhaps it is. Perhaps when someone spends enough amicable time around a vampire, this happens. A thrall. Leon moves closer, his steps almost hesitant as he stands over me, covering me with his shadow. He seems larger than life, a specter of the night. The closer he moves, the stronger the pull feels within my stomach, yanking at my organs. It's warm and nearly tinged with discomfort.

"I imprinted on you. I didn't mean to," he admits with a sigh.

Seconds tick by as I wrap my head around the ominous words. The implication hunches my shoulders, as if a mist settled on them.

I sit up and stare at him, eyes wide as I try to digest the meaning. "What does that mean? Can you undo it?"

To my surprise, he sits at the edge of the bed, his hip presses against mine. The burning intensifies, and I almost gasp. His hand slowly moves over my stomach and his face contorts with worry.

"It is forbidden," he whispers and meets my eyes. "And it cannot be undone."

We stare at one another. I feel myself growing frustrated with his truncated words, his small reveals that always hold something back. Something beyond my comprehension. And now I'm imprinted, I didn't even know what that meant!

"When did you do this to me?" I ask.

He looks genuinely sorry; his fingers linger over my arm, but he drops his hand. "It must have been the night of the fire. It *can* happen. It's not unheard of. In an intense moment, a vampire can imprint a human they wish to save. To keep alive. Usually it's done under duress."

I try to understand his words, try to recall that fateful night, our interactions had been but momentarily. How could this happen? We'd not even spoken!

"Why? You didn't know me; you knew nothing of me!" I grasp his jacket and shake him, feeling anger nipping at my front teeth.

He meets my gaze. He seems calm, but maybe he's as devastated as I am. The decades on this earth have allowed him to shadow his emotions deep within his human skin. What if he feels inside but never shows it? Keeps it for himself. Well, I want it now. I want his emotions and his thoughts. I demanded it of him.

"Stop it," he snaps, his face twists in pain, wincing.

I let go of his jacket as he runs his hand over his face; he takes deep breaths t control himself. "What? Stop what?"

"Don't *demand* things from me." His voice is low, a carnal growl, his eyes tint red. He's bathed in fear. It's corded in his skin.

"Did you... can you hear my thoughts?" I ask, a flush covering my cheeks.

"We can feel intense demands through an imprint," he says between clenching teeth. "And yes. I do feel. I feel *plenty*. Just because I don't often share feelings doesn't mean I don't have them."

He looks away, as if he can't stomach my eyes on him, the way I study him. But we are so close that I can sense each particle of his body, like it belongs to *me*. I gasp and slide back on the bed.

"Do I..." I swallow, a fiery pit of anger boiling in me. "Do I *belong* to you? Is this what it is? Is that what an imprint means?"

He stands abruptly but pauses. I observe him, dreading the words he will say, dreading the implications and the consequences. Was I damned too? Had I sought for too long for what I shouldn't have and now I am lost?

Chapter Twelve

I try to process his words as I stare at his defeated form. As if he's finally been captured. I stand and face him. At no point did I wish for anyone to belong to me. Naturally, I don't want to belong to anyone myself.

"We can undo it," I say, sure of a task I've no concept to execute.

He shakes his head, his eyes soft as he stares at me. I don't want him to behold me in such a manner. I reject all of this. Then I wonder if this imprinting is the reason for my attraction. Would this cause my need to pleasure myself at the thought of him? Now I don't know where my genuine emotions end and where the imprint begins.

"Dania." He places his hands over my shoulders.

I step away from him. "No! I have a task! I must avenge my family! He took them, he destroyed everything. He laughed when I shot him. Laughed! I can't be distracted. You must undo this! Imprint someone else! Someone who wishes it, someone who wants it."

He comes closer and that awful pull delights in his proximity, yanking me to him, but I wrestle with it. My determination twists and battles against the curse.

"I am sorry," he says.

"I demand you undo it," I blurt. He said he needed to comply with my demands, well here was my demand.

His face twists and I realize I'm hurting him. Somehow, I've hurt him with my words.

"If you wish it," he says tightly. "Come sunup, I'll walk out into it."

I stare at him for a moment as I comprehend his words. The only way to undo it is for him to die. To end his life. And I can be free. I shake my head and look away, unable to allow such a thing to happen.

"No," I say dejectedly, feeling my body's energies zap, feeling a crumbling coming. I lean against the chair, grasping the back of it to steady myself.

He comes closer, his hands encircling my waist and pulling me up. The moment he presses me against him, I sigh. I rest my forehead against his chest. His hands slowly hold me soft and tenderly.

The second we embrace, the ache in my belly magically subsides. It thrills me with delight, warming me with pleasure. I'm limp against him, like I've taken a sleeping tonic. He chuckles and I feel the rumble under my cheek.

"This explains why you slept so deeply after I took you out of the tub," he says against my hair.

I turn to stare at him. My eyelids are languid as his proximity provides me with relaxation. His face feels warm, though I know he isn't warm.

"Admit that you looked," I say.

He smiles and pushes my hair back. "I looked. Did *you*?"

"I looked." I return his smile.

He draws me to bed. "You're exhausted. We can speak more tomorrow. I'm afraid you'll have questions I'll have no answers to."

I don't know what that means. There's not been a question which he didn't possess the answer to. He helps me lie on the bed, but before he pulls away; I grasp his hand and make him sit next to me. It soothes my stomach.

"What else makes sense now?" I ask.

He takes a deep breath and his hand lingers on my arm, softly caressing me. I lean into his touch.

"My reaction to the coyotes." He casts me a look. "I did not intend to go feral. I startled myself that night, though I didn't share that with you. If you're ever in trouble, I'd know it. I'd react to it. Wouldn't be able to control myself if I'm honest with you."

His hand traces my arm and I twist my hand to touch his fingers. My stomach sings in delight at the contact.

"Why do I feel it and you don't? The stomach pull?"

His gaze lingers on our intertwined fingers. Slowly, he tentatively grasps my hand, as if he's never done this before.

"Vampires are used to feeling nothing but anger, hunger, pleasure, and pain," he says quietly. "However,... I suspected it."

"How so?" I study his bottom lip, soft and curved as it is.

"The feeling when you are away from me," he whispers. "It was different. Like desperation. I kept wondering where you are, what you are doing, are you well? Fills my mind, I can't think straight. And then when we touch—like this."

He plays with my fingers and the stomach fluttering delights. I hide a smile.

"It's the loveliest feeling. Like I'm warm," he says.

Tiredness drenches me. I sigh against the pillows and my eyelids feel heavy. "Wake me in a few hours."

I hear him agree and, as I drift to sleep, his hand never leaves mine.

When I wake, I'm curled into a body, my legs hooked into a knee, and my head pressed against the crook of an arm. I look up to find Leon observing me. The light of the morning wisps through the curtain. However, encased in this bed, we were away from any harmful sunlight. I push myself off him, confused by how I ended up splayed over him. But his arm tightens around me and keeps me in place. He furrows his brows, and his blue eyes are steady yet dance with confusion.

"I'm sorry," I say as my mind desperately gathers an excuse for my body's reaction to his proximity. As if it can't stand not being entrenched in him.

"Don't be." Leon's hand gently traces circles on my shoulder.

Unsure of what this sudden need to hold me is about, I allow myself to lean into his body. It pacifies my stomach to such heights it almost feels pleasurable. As if I can feel it directly into my sex.

"What happens when I die? To you, since you are mine," I ask.

He meets my stare, then sighs and looks up at the ceiling. "I die."

I study his profile, something I do often, because it's beautiful. It belongs to something found in the afterlife. When death has stamped its mark on us, when things are vibrant, forged away from the decease humanity can be.

"I've lived so long I never expected the coming end," he swallows. "I saw an extensive field of endless years, a catalogue of never-ending days. I scoffed at imprints all my life and now... now, it seems welcoming."

I shake my head, not wishing to tie him down to my mortality. I could die today, hunting Ryle McAdams. That would be *my* journey, *my* task, *my* vengeance. No one needs to die for my exigency for closure. Especially a mystical creature of night who's wandered the earth before America became America. It doesn't seem fair.

"Maybe the Vampire Legion can help. Maybe they have a solution," I urge him. "You can't just give up. What if I die tomorrow? In a year? Life is fickle."

To my surprise, he smiles as he looks down at me, as if he finds it endearing that I seek options to save his life.

"I can't go back to the Vampire Legion," he says, and pulls me closer. "I'm afraid an unauthorized imprint condemns me to execution."

My mouth drops open at the implications. I've ruined his life. I push myself off him and glare down.

"*Why* did you follow me? *Why* did you save me? I could've handled myself, I had for years." I fist my hand on his shirt. "You knew nothing about me!"

He maintains that affectionate study of my behavior. "No, I didn't know you were the Dania in the newspaper clippings I studied of Ryle McAdams' destruction. But I saw you playing your hand of poker. I saw your move and your coquettish ways, the way you smiled at the man while you kept your loaded gun nearby. It was admirable, and it intrigued me. Then you killed him and followed the girl out. I couldn't rush after you fast enough. I made my decision."

He pulls me over him, closing our distance, and pushes back my hair.

"And I don't regret it," he says and then he kisses me.

It's so unexpected that I'm startled for a moment, but then the pull from my stomach erupts into pure pleasure and desire. I gasp against his mouth, and he does the same. We wrench apart as we stare at one another, eyes wide. I can question the reaction our bodies have, but the feeling is so acute, I need it immediately.

I clutch his mouth once more, devouring it as the pleasure uncoils all the way to my sex. It flutters, making me convulse against him. He twists our bodies so that he pushes me into the mattress. His hands dig into my hair as he kisses me with such fervent passion, I think I'll faint.

My thoughts are a scattered desolate plain that cares only for Leon, his body, his mouth, his cock. Immediately, I need his body. I wrap my legs around him and vault up to meet him. We gasp against each other's faces. Then he buries his head in my neck and for a mad moment, I think he'll bite me. Kill me. It makes sense and a maniacal part of me wishes it. Wishes to feel his fangs enter my body in the same manner his cock will.

But all he does is kiss and lick me, suckling against the artery that dances underneath my skin.

"Dania," he whispers in a harsh tone. "Let me have you. Bid me welcome, I beg you."

I cup his head, burying my fingers into his hair and nuzzling his forehead. My body is alight with pure desire. Rational thought doesn't exist within this space. In that moment,

I would've let him have me entirely. Fangs and all. But he doesn't seek that, he seeks to enter me. To be encased in the warmth of my human body.

We shove clothing off, a scattering of fabric that cascades around us until our flesh is pressing against one another. The connection makes me tremble at impact. I shake so hard that he has to cusp me in his arms and soothe me.

"I'm on fire," I say between shattering teeth.

That's what it feels like, a burning inferno that originates in my sex and spreads over my skin like a raging forest fire. He kisses and cups my face into his. The coolness of his hands soothes the intense heat. I desperately clutch at him, seeking abatement to my suffering. He slides in me with a fell stroke and my nails bite into the skin of his back, casting half-moon circles on the planes of his shoulders. His fangs glint over me, his eyes pit red. A monster, a demon, a death shadow. And I want him because he's *mine*. Mine to command, mine to protect. I'd asked for a devil and God, in his infinite wisdom, gifted me one. A companion, a partner. A weapon cast in alabaster skin.

He thrusts harder into me because I commanded him to. His eagerness to meet my demands leaves me breathless. A flitting thought from me spurs him to action. I can sense his emotions as if I were reading them on a page. He's lonely, desperately lonely. Year after year he'd meandered the earth. Was he searching, or was he waiting and bidding for his time? Perhaps this is why it's forbidden to imprint. If all vampires imprinted, then few would live long languorous empty lives at the bidding of a Vampire League.

Well, they wouldn't touch *my* Leon.

For years now I've lived in hate and now that something tender has stepped foot through the cracked opening of my heart, I desperately cling to it.

I might not have been able to save my family, but I would damn well save him. I clutch his hair and flip us over so that I ride him as he watches me. He's hypnotized by the bouncing of my breasts.

He's so deep in me he can feel the beating of my heart through the walls that contract around his cock. I sense all of this through that link that coats us, that imprint made of human souls meshed with his animated body.

Leon makes wild animal noises, and I capture them with my teeth, biting into his neck as if I too have fangs. Each time I nip his skin he groans and howls, a desperation of violent need we can never sate even if we fuck for one hundred years.

The tug in my stomach rises to a crescendo as I ride him without mercy, without allowing him a moment to control himself. I want him to lose control. I wish for the entire world to lose control.

I feel the pleasure explode from within and course through my body like volcanic ash. He thrusts up and up until I feel I'm floating, needing no feet to walk the earth.

Afterwards, I lay encased in his arms for the longest time, living in that space where the outside world doesn't exist. Each part of my body touches each part of his, pressing together like a flower left to wilt amongst the pages of a book.

"I hope every time it's like that," I whisper against his throat.

His hand traces an indecipherable pattern between the bones of my spine. His cool fingers soothing that heat I feel around him.

"It's never been like that before," he says with a chuckle.

I turn and stare at him. His eyes are back to crystalline blue. He's soft and tender at this moment. Open, like he's willing to share of himself. He's dropped the constant awareness of his surroundings and in this light, he looks young and hopeful.

"Never?" I tease him, even surprising myself.

He smiles a little and the fangs I once equated to heathens bring soft affection to my heart. He caresses my face, studying each line.

"Your desperation to avenge your family is strong. I felt your hate, your sadness, your determination."

Despite not wishing to think about Ryle McAdams, it's the first time someone feels what I've felt for twelve years. I've been alone in such sentiments for so long that it was like walking into a world apart. A lived alone in that world with my hate and my resentment.

"We'll find him, and we shall make him pay," he says in a deep tone of seriousness. And I believe him.

"I don't want to own you," I confess. "Don't feel right to own anyone."

"It's not ownership." He twirls a strand of my brown hair on his finger. "Belonging is different. Like a... marriage."

My stomach twists at the thought.

"You can leave a marriage," I point out.

"*You* can leave," he counters.

But I didn't want to. It feels a little like abandonment. Perhaps he felt the same thing. Compelled to stay together the way a nail fuses to the skin. The nail was not owned by the finger, it simply existed together.

It's near noon, and he tires. The day pulls him into his impending sleep. We quickly dress, ready to investigate the town the moment he wakes in the afternoon. Perhaps we can decipher clues for our coming task. I never thought I would have someone at my side as passionate about my revenge, but here he is and despite my hate for my family's killer, I am no longer alone. Even if he's a vampire, too.

Once dressed, he lures me to him and kisses me once more. That singing warmth delights at his touch. I sense the impending separation of the four hours when I can't have him.

As our bodies are lax to sleep, the door bursts open.

Leon jumps up with extended fangs; ready to attack. But they threw a silver net over him. I scramble for my gun, but someone grabs me and hoists me back. I watch helplessly as Leon collapses on the floor in a twist of anger and pain.

"Let him go!" I snarl, but then I'm hit on the head with such force that I black out.

The last thing I see is Leon's hand reaching for me between the silver mesh.

Chapter Thirteen

I find it hard to move when I wake. As if I'm trapped, bound tight into something I can't name or describe. It takes a few minutes before my mind clears and my thoughts center. It takes even longer to open my eyes. Good. That's exactly what I want.

My lids finally slide open and all I see is darkness. My mouth is dried to the bone, as if I've spent days asleep and fevered. I blink as I try to sit up, only to realize my hands are restrained. Not even screaming helps, as someone tightly roped something around my head, and they trapped a moldy cloth in my mouth.

Leon! They took Leon. They tossed over him a silver mesh and he cannot help me. *I can't help him.* My mind races with the endless possibilities they can do to hurt him. Set him on fire, throw him into the sun, brand him. I yank harder at my bounds, desperate to sense him, to feel that tug, but I feel *nothing*. He isn't nearby.

A small sliver of light filters into the room. It comes from the circular window to my right. I attempt to calm myself, to think rationally, and I study the area. It's a space with boxes and crates, but I hear noises. Small sniffles. I shift and lean forward, trying to call out behind my muffle.

"Shhh..." a small voice hushes me. It's a child's voice.

Fear drenches my body as my heart leaps to my throat.

"He'll hear you and come back," the child whispers.

Through the messiness of the room, I see a slight figure huddling in the far corner. A tiny face peers at me, soot covered cheeks, sunken and hallow, and dressed in meager rags. The child looks ghostly, as if life has already abandoned them.

Panic grips my heart. Leon mentioned they could turn children into vampires and perhaps I'm the offered meal. Even trapped within a childish body, they are fast and strong, and I'm bound and dizzy. There is little I can do to defend myself.

I've no gun or saber.

The only thing left on me is the hidden crucifix Mary had charged me with. It's my only defense against a vampiric attack, but I can't reach it. It's twisted into the pocket of my shirt and impossible to grasp.

But the child doesn't move. Doesn't lounge for its offered dinner.

On the contrary, the child looks as petrified as I am.

"Preacher will hear you and come back," the child whispers in a tone dripping with consternation.

A mixture of rabid anger and fear coated each bone in my spine. That bastard. If there's one thing certain in life is that monsters hide within human visages.

My hands are bound to my legs, and it takes a concentrated effort to twist myself and pull back my gag. I must find Leon before they hurt him, or worse—kill him. I can't extricate the bind, so I push my face against the corner of a crate, scrapping my face until I'm able to shove the gag down and take a deep breath.

"No, no," the child tearfully whispers.

I lean my head with a sigh against the crate and look back at the boy. He's young, about nine years old and most importantly, he'd not bound. He simply huddles in the corner, presses himself against the walls. I can only imagine what he's seen to cause such distress. To be kept in such a place, under the threat of pain and abuse. My ire bubbles to the surface, and I have to remind myself my anger has no place here. Anger breeds clumsiness and I need to be smart and strategic if I wish to save myself, the boy, and my vampire.

"Come here," I whisper to him. "Come untie me." My voice is deceptively sweet, honey.

He shakes his head and crams his face against the wall corner. He's nothing but skin and bones, a poor boy taken from a family of farmers. I lean forward, making sure he sees my face, trying to smile and comfort him even when I'm trembling myself.

I need any information I can use before Thomas Rein wanders in to see if I've woken.

No one will come to save me; I'm on my own. June is days away and I have a sinking feeling the preacher knows exactly who and what resides in the ranch the bartender had indicated. He'd come armed with a silver mesh for Leon. He knows vampires, and he knows them well.

"What's your name?" I ask the boy, hoping to have him speak to me.

"Wayne," the boy whispers, his face still faces the wall, his entire body quivers like a winter leaf.

"Hello Wayne," I say, twisting my bound hands. "I'm Dania."

He peers at me sideways with gaping eyes.

"How long have you been here?" I ask in a hushed tone.

Wayne is silent for a long moment before he shifts and looks at me. He still doesn't move forward, but at least he's open to conversation, truncated as it is. He licks his lips and twitches.

"A few days," his voice is so low I can scarcely make it out.

My stomach twists, thinking how long they've scared him and how desperate his family must be to find him.

"Did they hurt you, Wayne?"

I don't wish to hear the answer but knowing is imperative to understand how much he can help me. Without information, I can't get him out of here. I can't get myself out. I can't find Leon and I can't put a bullet into Thomas Rein's head.

Wayne's face turns even paler, and he presses his hands against his eyes. My wrath blooms deeper, a bright flame that eats my insides. For the first time in days, the pull in my stomach is not the dominating sensation. There's a special place in hell for people who harm children. I desperately want to ensure the preacher sees that hell as soon as possible.

"They took Lisa," he says. "They took her yesterday."

I do not know who Lisa was, but I have a sense Lisa was a fellow child. Where Lisa went is unknown, but I understand the dynamic.

Thomas Rein has an agreement with Ryle McAdams — if that is who lives on the ranch. In exchange for leaving the people of Liventown alone, he provides Ryle with his choice of victim. It works well for Rein, as he's seen as the savior of the town. They likely desperately clung to him when the draught arrived.

"Took her where, Wayne? Do you know?" I ask as I attempt to slacken my binds. I don't think we have much time.

The boy shakes his head, clasps his hands, and looks haunted in his expression. "No. But I think I'm next."

No. That won't happen. I won't let it. This won't be how I die, not at the mouth of my lifelong revenge. Not when I'm so close. I won't die at the whim of a maniacal preacher. This won't be how Leon goes, not after last night, not after what happened. I will live. I will release myself from this bondage and pull the trigger for the preacher man.

I yank harder at my binds, but all it does is scrape the skin from my wrists.

"Wayne, listen to me. I can fight. I can get you out of here. Don't you want to go back home? Don't you want to see your ma?" I ask, aware that I sound like I'm begging.

The boy sniffs as he cries, with a small face contorted in pain.

"Walk to me, as quietly as you can. Help me out of these binds. I'll take you to your ma. Wayne, I swear it. I'll help you."

I hold my hands out at him. A prayer, an anguished prayer. He stares at me with wide eyes, his lids softening as he studies my frame.

"You've no gun," he points out. I take that as a win. It isn't a no.

"No," I admit. "But... I can throw a mean left hook."

He looks doubtful.

I sigh and plant an enticing story. "I have a friend... he's a monster. A *good* monster. Once I find him, no one stands a chance."

Wayne's eyes widen. "A good monster?"

"Yes." I nod fervently. "Preacher don't stand a chance."

The boy licks his lips, a consideration.

"He saves children. He saved two little girls not a few nights before. I swear it on my parent's grave," I say. "Dragged me from a house fire. He's the fiercest warrior. Tore a coyote in half with his bare hands to save me."

I'm acutely aware my words paint Leon like a hero from a dime novel, but I don't care. The boy needs a savior and children understand heroes far better than adults ever could. We lose our innocence when reality drenches our lives and soils hope. The hope of being saved becomes a distant dream cast in childhood beds.

He truly considers my words as he openly appraises me. His eyes remain clouded. He must've seen terrible things.

To my surprise, he slowly stands on shaky, pale ankles. His bare feet silently walk closer to me, swinging his eyes at the door.

"It's ok, preacher won't hurt you," I say hoping to assure him. "Get me out of these and we can escape."

Wayne kneels before me; his eyes are a pale green, and his lashes are wet with tears. He smells rancid, as if he's been made to sit in his own waste. Before he can touch my binds, I reach with the tips of my fingers and grasp his hand.

"It's alright, Wayne. It's alright," I whisper. "Quickly, get me loose."

He nods and his small fingers work the knots of the rope. I feel it loosen slightly and we disentangle my hands from my legs. He knows his way around knots, that's for certain. I try to help him as best as I can, feeling the freedom within my reach.

But the door is thrown open. Wayne screams and hides behind me as I turn to Thomas Rein, who takes in the situation with a growing angry face. Behind me, Wayne whimpers and clutches to the back of my jacket. I try to shield him as best I can, focusing my eyes on Rein. Malice paints his lips as he realizes I've been aided by the same poor boy he's likely scared to death.

"Wayne," Rein's voice is deep disappointment, and I feel the boy shiver behind me. "What happened last time you disobeyed?"

"Don't you dare touch him, you bastard," I snarl.

Though my eyes are on him, my fingers continue to work on the loosening knots. My hands tremble with the need to choke the man to death as he gasps for his final breath.

Rein's eyes slide to me, a dark pit of hate. "You think you're able to help him? You dirty bitch who *fucks* devils."

My stomach tightens, coiling into itself as I try to figure out a way out of this predicament. I can't fathom the notion of Leon living through so much, for so many centuries, to die at the hands of this ice-hearted monster.

I set my face in hard stone.

"You feed *children* to these devils, you hypocritical bastard," I sneer, and Wayne snivels pitifully behind me.

Slowly, Rein smiles as he kneels before me, studying me carefully. "Not just children. They're just easier to catch and store. He'll have a banquet with *you*. I don't think I'll have to feed them for a few nights. It'll be a relief. Honestly, I need some days off."

All the while I've hunted a devil, the devil was flesh and blood and donning preacher's clothing. I shake my head, inching my fingers out of my binds, desperate to grab and bash his head in. Desperate to feed *him* to the monsters.

"But first... I have a service to lead. It's a shame you can't enjoy it. It's going to be spectacular," he says with a malevolent smile, a canine grin that split his face in half. "God is good to us despite his denial of rain. How long did I assure them that the lord would provide? They wished to remove me from the pulpit. Nothing works as well as fear. So, the devil took the children, and they were back at my door, desperate for my help. My tales kept them sated for a while, but just as my congregation trembled... the lord sends me an answer. Just as my desperation grew... you ride into town and bring him to me."

Leon. The answer to why the children are disappearing. He would kill Leon before his congregation. I feel my skin turn clammy at the thought of his plans. His ploy poised as God-sent is evil and murderous. I'm running out of time and options. I need to do something drastic because only in chaos will I have a chance.

Rein smiles and reaches out to push a hair out of my face. I wheel back and headbutt him. The moment of impact makes me dizzy, but it's satisfying enough to watch him stumble back and land on his ass, clutching his nose.

"You bitch!" He hollers.

Rein growls as he crawls up and shakily gets to his feet. Blood dribbles down his nostrils and to his lips. He gingerly touches his nose, and his fingers come back wet with blood. He glares at them, then at me. Then Rein kicks me in the stomach. I double over, pain lacing its way through my center. The hours of pleasure with Leon forgotten as I feel split in half. Somewhere in the distance, through the lines etched in our threaded bond, I knew Leon felt my pain. His anger is so intense I feel it like electric shocks spiked in the tips of my fingers. I have no way of reassuring him I am well.

"You know what? I think I *do* want you to watch. I want to make sure you see him *burn*," Rein says with delighted malice.

Chapter Fourteen

The nave is narrow and tall, painted stark white, with rustic pews handcrafted by locals. However, the pulpit is fine oak, waxed and polished until it shined. A large gold cross sits in the center where Thomas Rein will announce his findings. The people scream, confirming the words Rein declared.

The good sheriff drags me to a small storage room behind the altar. My luck strikes when they don't check my bindings. They're still loose from my tinkering. No one can see me, but I can certainly 'enjoy' the planned spectacle. The sheriff's face is entirely too close as he smirks at me, displaying yellowed gangrenous teeth.

"Maybe a pretty lady like you forgot what it's like to be with a real man," he says as he rubs my upper arm, his mouth thick with saliva.

I fight the urge not to squirm away because seeming docile is vital. I lower my eyes and ensure my bottom lip trembles. A scared woman. That's what I need to be at this moment. Because the fool has his gun slung low on his hip and I must finish freeing myself. They've already unbound my feet, and that is all I need to save Leon and put a bullet in Rein.

Upstairs, in the storage room, is a petrified Wayne. He doesn't realize how vital he is to me. These town folk might not believe an outsider, but they will certainly believe a scared boy they knew to be missing. Rein wants a miracle? I will gladly provide him with one.

From my vantage point, I can see a large box covered by a black tarp. It's placed by a window flooding the nave with sunlight. I'm certain Rein's intention is to burn Leon in the sunlight on this fine Sunday morning. The pull in my stomach erupts, and I know Leon can sense me. I wonder what I will find under the tarp. The man who held me or the monster who killed the coyotes. Despite my genuine tremors of anxiety, I work the knots as discreetly as I can.

The church fills with folk dressed in raggedy shoes and hats that have seen better days. They scrubbed themselves clean for their Sunday's best. Little girl cling to their mothers; their hair finagled into fine braids that fall down their backs. Underneath it all is the sense of sorrow, a deep pitted sentiment that cannot be ignored.

Amongst their copious loss, they worship at the altar of the man who caused the suffering. In the crowd, I recognize the bartender who served me. His beard and hair is combed, and he greets folks warmly, inquiring after them and reassure them as best he can.

People take their seats and I feel the distinct sick presence as it slides up behind me. It's Rein. He dons his pressed guard, starch black with a white collar. He stares at me, grasping my chin, and smiling that angelic, demonic smile.

"Don't fret, my lamb. Tonight, I'll save your soul but first to kill a devil," he says.

I can't help but yank my chin away. His nose is bruised, and I'm glad for it, glad that I got one hit in case my plan fails. In case I'm forced to watch my lover burn. In case I fail at my revenge. A few days ago, I would've never thought I would be desperate to save the creature I hunted. Even though we'd only known one another for a few days, the comradery of our journey feels much like a pit encased in a peach. To yank it out would leave a devastating craterous ruination.

Reine slithers his way through the church, piously greeting folks, a few times offhandedly explaining that he'd clumsily smacked his nose on a door frame. The good people of Liventown nod, freely accepting the poison words that flow from his forked tongue.

"Brethren!" Rein stands behind the pulpit with his hands open, cupping their attention with his tone.

Folks quiet, staring up at him adoringly. A desperate thread of hope, an answer to their calamities. People wish for simple explanations, but explanations for murder were seldom simple.

"We've had a trying few weeks. *Sin* has covered our small pious town," he says.

I desperately twist the bonds, biting down my grunts. There's a small piece of rope that I can't get through the loop. The more I tug, the tighter the bindings become. I must look. I have to see what I'm working with, but I can't alert the sheriff.

"We've run off most of the sinners and the heathens," Rein continues. "The adulterers, the *loose* women!"

Folks clap and shout 'Amen' in accordance. I feign a cry of despair and look down, faking a breathy sob as the sheriff chuckles behind me.

"Still, we must remember the lord answers the prayers of the pious, the true believers. Last night I went down on my knees, and I cried out to him—God!" Rein casts his hands to the sky.

More claps and agreements.

I see the small bit of rope that I need to loop through the knot and push it between my fingers. My hands are slick with sweat, my skin rubbed raw. The tug in my stomach deepens. My frantic sentiments overwhelm me, and Leon can sense it. I almost feel his growl of anger, as if it will burst forth from the container which encases him.

"I said God! Help us! They also take our young Wayne!" Rein, in his theatrical element, laments.

A young woman wails in the front pew, her face ashen, her straw-colored hair limp and disheveled.

"What fiend infests our community? What malice has Satan brought down upon his people?" Rein works himself up to a fury, his face crimson, his mouth a lake of frothing saliva. "Then, in God's pure mercy, I saw the *devil*. Flesh and blood come right into this town, ride a horse, and speak to me like he was a *godly* man. A *worthy* man. But the lord—"

He walks around the pulpit, his black bible fat in his fingers as he waves it around.

"Spoke to me clear as day, like a friend," he whispers and the congregation leans forward, masticating his words. "And said to me. *This* is the devil. This is the devil that has taken the children and *killed* them."

The people gasp, some clutch their chests and mothers weep as they beg for mercy from a God who's never entered this church. A psychotic display of manipulation. I flood with anger at his antics, at the way he masters their emotions like a puppeteer. Because he loves the power, he loves the strings attached to his fingers laced with biblical words.

My efforts grow into agony as Rein moves to the large crate and places his hands on the black tarp. My stomach erupts in pain. *No!* I don't know how long it takes for vampires to burn, but I must make my move *now*. Feeling the ropes to be loose, I yank one last time and slide my hands free.

In a sharp turn, I elbow the sheriff, who stumbles back in surprise. I go for his gun, but his hands are on me, and we grunt and struggle, our noise disguised as the congregation chants for the death of the man in the box. I dig my nails into his face and scratch down, leaving a marked journey of my hate.

"You fucking—"

And then I punch him full in the face. He blinks twice before I slip his gun out of his holster and knock him on the side of the head with the colt. I'm sweating and panting as I shove myself off him.

"And if he ignites in fire, then we shall know that he is a soulless killer!"

I stumble forward, gun out and ready to shoot just as Rein yanks the tarp back to reveal a large cage. Leon crouches angrily inside, his fangs bare and his eyes blood red.

Chapter Fifteen

The good people of Liventown scream at the sight of Leon snarling as the sunrays sizzle through his skin. I feel his pain deep in my bones and, without further thought of consequence, I run out. I poise my gun at Rein's back, my finger on the trigger. The years of practicing culminate in this moment. The thrill of the kill sings in my veins as Rein turns and stares at me. He has a stunned expression, the same as those who constantly underestimate others because they're so preoccupied with themselves.

I pull the trigger. He moves, the shot catches his shoulder, and sends him flying across the room. He lands in a heap on the floor. I've no time to ensure myself of his death because Leon is screaming and burning.

Grasping the black tarp, I throw it over the cage. I hear his shuddering breaths of pain and rage underneath. I press myself against the cage, as did Leon. We feel our bodies through the gaps as I try to soothe him. He's safe, wounded, but safe. I'm still clutching the gun in my hand, and I turn to the congregation.

Everyone watches me in horror as the preacher pushes himself up, agonizing by the wound. It spurts dark red blood, which I'm certain Leon can smell because he growls under the tarp, his body pushing against the bars.

"You cunt! You bitch!" Rein snarls, and I cock my gun as I hold it with a steady hand.

"I would bite back sermons, preacher. I'm not your target audience," I sneer.

The tension within the nave is palpable. I'm not the savior in their eyes. I'm a wild 'loose' woman who saved a demon and shot their good preacher.

"Devil!" Wayne's mother screams at me with wild eyes.

I face them, a sense of desperation filling my throat, cupping my words, and shaking my hands. "You want a devil? I'll show you one." I point at Rein, whose face is pallid with pain.

"Don't listen to her! She's bedded this devil! She's sold her soul to Satan!" He screams.

This is all true, but at least I don't stand before people and pretend to be something I'm not. I know I kill and hunt; I know I bed devils. I know I'm a lonely, desperate soul in a great big world, but at least I own it.

I scoff. "You want proof of his deceit? I'll give you proof."

Rein's face shifts to one of pure malice. I glance at the bartender, who watches me open-mouthed.

"You." I point to him. "Go upstairs and bring down the boy you find there. Let *him* be the witness to the debauchery of this... *man of God*."

The bartender hesitates for a moment, but I know where his thoughts are because he'd revealed them to me over a shot of whiskey. He didn't like the preacher; he didn't like the madness. I watch as he slowly makes his way to the back of the church. When he stops and looks at the sheriff's body, I can hear him gasp. I face the crowd alone with my gun pointing at Rein, wishing he would attempt something. A shot to the shoulder is not enough for me.

We didn't have to wait long. The bartender returns and, in his arms, was Wayne, half limp but awake. His mother lets out a scream of relief as she rushes to him. The boy laments for his mama and I feel the child in me understand his alleviation. How many years had I wished I would find *mami* and daddy alive? To feel their arms around me and assure me it was all a bad dream. But the years passed, and I never felt that relief. The disillusionment of it settled like a seeded pit in my stomach, flourishing its hate.

The townsfolk shift with conflicting emotions. They gawk from the mother and son to me, to the preacher. They murmur amongst themselves as the veil of deceit cascades down and displays the backstage of their religious production. I must strike in the depth of their confusion.

"He's been taking your children and killing them. He took Lisa," I say with a resolute voice. My heart tightens when a mother screams, collapsing into the aisle as others help her. "And the many before her. We rode into town a day or so ago. We heard about the missing children and came to help. This man—" I point the gun at Rein's face. "Is the devil you seek."

For a moment, I think they won't believe me, that they would tear me apart once I run out of bullets. That they'll tear my body piece by piece as Leon watches, defenseless, within his silver cage. It's a terrifying moment of keen apprehension. I feel Leon's desperation, his wish to kill them all and take me out of here. But no. I would not suffer innocents to devils.

My salvation comes when Wayne's mother kneels before her son, her face sincere and comforting.

"Tell mama who did this to you, tell me the truth," she urges him as she fervently kisses his forehead.

The boy, ashen and swaying, slowly points a small, dirty finger right at Preacher Thomas Rein. I almost collapse against the wall. The hostility I've felt since we entered the town is bubbling up in frantic waves.

The congregation cries out in disbelief, a sonata of incredulity and realization. A few men stand and demand Reine's execution, but others thirst to do the deed in the very bowels of the church. My body coils tightly as a mob mentality rises and I feel their bodies closing in on me, ready to charge past me and dismember the preacher.

For a moment, I think of stopping them, of assuming the preacher was *my* kill, *my* hunt, *my* revenge. But what have I lost compared to them? Their children taken. Their old sheriff killed while Rein led them in an orchestra of frenzy religiosity. He masqueraded their pain behind the true evil he perpetuated. It's not my place to lead them, and I will not rise as replacement preacher to caution them against depravity.

I'm saved from any sort of denouncement by Wayne's mother, who stands next to me and raises her hands. Wayne clutches her skirts. For a moment, I think she will advise them against it. Heed them in the ideal direction.

"Brothers and sisters!" She says and they hush, waiting for the judgement of a mother. "Will we stain our souls with revenge?"

I feel her words like a knife in my heart. *Revenge.* I painted it in my veins, a tattooed ink that will never disappear. I'll gladly damn my soul for revenge. Not everyone walks the same path. Some paths are covered in Spring flowers, and others are a desolate and rocky terrain. The realization that Ryle McAdams might've taken my family, but I'd been the one to take my own life, covers me. I made a choice because I couldn't handle the grief of their loss and I live my life to the tune of hate. I've no happiness because I've denied it to myself.

Then the mother turns to me, a wise slash across her weathered face. "This monster in the cage. Is he a danger to *us*?"

"He's a good monster," Wayne says as he pulls at her skirts, then turned his quiet eyes to Rein. "Preacher don't stand a chance."

And I realize what he means. I'd made him a promise upstairs, a promise to destroy Rein with my monster. I'd painted Leon gallantly and now I'm expected to deliver on my promise. My fingers slide over the black tarp and Leon vaults within.

"Let me have him," Leon hisses.

So... he wishes to be the executioner. I won't deny my lover his request.

Wayne's mama watches me with pitiless eyes.

I nod. "Tie the preacher up, then everyone gets out."

Their angry hands grasp him as they wrestle him down. He cries and pleads, provides excuses, then cast blame on the wind, to the devils nestled in the stars, but their ears are sealed. He'd sealed them himself.

The church empties, a slow lumbering exodus of pained bodies with too much grief to articulate. There's no returning their children, and it's a grief I can't help them with.

They take the sheriff as he struggles and tries to place his blame on Thomas Rein. His words fall on hardened hearts. The men make plans to ship him to El Paso where he'll stand trial for the kidnapping and murdering of Lisa, the only child killed during his tenure.

The bartender is the last to leave. He lingers by the door and looks at me. His eyes flitter between the crying preacher and my black cage. "Do you need anything?"

I walk to the center aisle as I look around the open windows, which I'll have to close. "Our horses. Food. And information about the haunted ranch."

And strength. I need plenty of that.

He raises a brow and glances at the covered cage. Wisely, he doesn't comment, and I give him credit for his discretion. I'm certain he doesn't wish to cause more panic amongst the people of his small town.

Behind me, the preacher screams into his gag, begging not to be left behind. But the good pious people of Liventown have tied him up good.

The bartender closes the door to the church amongst Rein's muffled screams. I stand there for a moment, processing what I'll do. What I will allow to happen. Rein's eyes are pits of desperate wildness, a refusal to allot space for his own demise.

I suppose humans don't understand death very well. It always seems like something that happens to other people because it does. It always happens to someone else. Not to us. Until it does and by then, acceptance is too late.

I circle the nave, closing the windows.

"You know, preacher," I breathe, my voice echoes inside of the empty church, and I can see the appeal of an oratory incantation within these walls. "A vampire killed my family. Drained dry in the middle of the night out in Pasco County."

I allow those haunted faces to invade my mind. All these years, the strongest memories I had of them were of their last moments. But those won't be the memories I'll allow to visit me now. I want happy ones. They deserve it. Daddy sitting at the table as he explained the rules of poker. Mami teaching me how to properly roast tomatillos. My sister, Anita, is wearing her white dress and twirling it before me.

I close the last window with the scent of Anita's hair still in my nostrils. I turn to Rein. He's exactly where he needs to be. I could imagine where he went wrong in life, but the fact was that many people go wrong in life. Life has a way of scraping you raw and leaving you bleeding. That doesn't mean you orchestrate the atrocities Thomas Rein did.

"I've spent the rest of my life hunting down the monster who killed them." I pulled back the tarp of Leon's cage.

He grasps the bars of the cage, and I kneel before him.

"Leon," I whisper and bid him closer. I need to make sure this is what he wants.

He struggles to focus on me as he hungers for Rein. His fangs elongated as a hiss slithers from his mouth. "I'm in a dark place, Dania Gonzalez."

I nod. "I'll do it then—"

"Don't you dare," he growls. "He's mine."

And his eyes flicker bright red right on Rein. The preacher vaults against his binds, his moves frantic.

With trembling fingers, I reach inside of the cage and encase my fingers into Leon's fine dark hair. A lover's caress. The pull in my stomach warms, cooing at the feel of Leon. My lover is hungry for vengeance. Starved. A feeling I know well. The man who laid with me on cotton sheets is dormant and the monster dominates all his actions. The monster wished for blood, and I will oblige.

In a quick motion, I shoot the chain that binds the cage's door. It clanks to the ground and the moment it does, Leon bursts through the cage like a shooting bullet. I force myself to watch.

Leon pulls up Rein above his head and the preacher's feet dangle in the air as he desperately shakes. His blood-curdling screams fill the church when Leon yanks off his binding.

"MERCY!"

Leon's snarl twists into an awful laugh. "Not from me, preacher."

In a sudden movement that I can' hardly comprehend, Leon's mouth latches to Rein's throat and he sinks his fangs into his taunt, pale neck.

Chapter Sixteen

Leon slumps to the floor the moment Rein's heart stops beating. I scramble forward and pull him off the preacher's body, turning him on his back. He's breathing deeply with closed eyes. His skin is flushed pink down to his chest.

"Leon," I urge, helping him sit but end up sliding on the floor. His head falls on my shoulder, and I cradle it. He's shaking, his fingers trembling as I kiss his forehead.

Perhaps I should be afraid of him; I should run away. I don't know the intricacies of a feeding. How long will he be feral? Am I damning myself?

I don't care because I'm so tired and drained. As if he'd fed from me. I've nothing left to give after the few horrible hours we've lived through.

His hands slowly slide up my back and he pulls me to him, sighing into my shoulder. All I smell is blood. It covers his face and chin, dripping onto his neck. He is death and I am at death's door, gladly knocking.

He raises his head and looks at me. His eyes are a wild red tint. A few days ago, I was afraid of him. Of his eyes. Of what he was. But now my hand trails down his chin and he leans into my touch as I run the pad of my thumb over his protruding fang. The warmth inside of me dances in delight at the intimacy.

"You should be afraid of me," he says with a slight lisp as he carefully studies my face.

Yes, I should. I should hate him and what he is. But to hate him, for what he is, equates to hating myself and I am tired of hate. I am tired of anger and vengeance. I've exhausted myself in my years of frenzied hunting, seeking a resolution that will never provide me with the satisfaction I crave.

"I'm not," I mumble.

"I couldn't smell you. I tried, but you were far away," he whispers.

I can't help but smile. He blinks, confused. "My *smell*? What do I smell like?"

He nuzzles my face; I dig my fingers into his hair. "Like hope."

To be the hope of someone when I've meandered the world lacking hope is incredible to me. Or perhaps I don't know what hope is or how to identify it. But, for the first time since they killed my family, I feel something above hate and revenge.

I feel relief.

He chuckles against my shoulder. "I haven't slept in two days. I need a nap."

I pull him with me, dragging us both away from the stench of Rein's body. "Good, let's nap. We *hunt* tonight."

As he sleeps, I find raw scars crossing his back and a quickly healing welt where iron had branded him. Rein had tortured Leon. Any sympathy I might've had for the corpse next to us dissipates. I'm glad he's dead. Even if I never find Ryle McAdams, I've seen *someone* get their justifiable end.

Exhausted, I lower myself next to Leon and, in the crook of his arm, I fall asleep.

At dusk, he wakes and pulls me up with him. The church smells like perdition, a tangled web of blood and rot. We speak little, but it feels as if we didn't have to. As if he knows where we need to go and how our journey will end.

We mount our horses and ride north. We leave the preacher spread out and bloodless on the steps in his fine, white church.

Based on the directions the bartender provided, we follow the dead shrubs to the edge of town, past the dilapidated farm, keeping our eye out for the horned tree. The night is cold and dry, and a swift wind tosses tumbleweed across the plains like specter ghouls that haunt our path.

I'm finally on my way to kill Ryle McAdams.

That hardened hate has somehow softened to a dull pain. I don't know when it happened. All these years I was under the notion that there was nothing worse than Ryle McAdams. But these days I've realized evil lives in the details. Evil lives in the hearts of men, entangling itself between the God-given soul and the selfish hate. I can see how I too, can become evil. I too, can be self-serving and cruel. I too, can release a monster to dismember a man. And when I accomplish my revenge, when I slash my sword across Ryle's throat, what then? What is there for me?

I look at the man who rides next to me, whose body I've warmed with my own, whose kisses sunk into the jagged heart left closed for so long. Whose fingers lingered at the base of my spine and traced momentary patterns.

He belongs to a world of wilderness and monsters, night skies and desolation. He flitters in and out of time like a needle that mends an old shirt. We aren't real, not really.

The trees were real. Their roots burrow deep into the earth and change with the seasons. We are wanderers and wanderers move about because the realization that our life is as fleeting as a tumbleweed on a plain is too painful to bear.

I want to belong somewhere and feel that sense of contentment that others scoff at. I want to be at peace. It's been so long since I've known peace.

We come upon the horned tree, a jagged monolith of a time before people. Its body twisted and spiked, a shadow against the night sky. The bark dried long ago and left the skeleton as a stark reminder that even eternal beings perish.

The ranch is a sprawling place that once housed prosperous owners. But time and the draught made them abandon their home and the surrounding land.

Something peculiar happens as we approach it. Darkness. Ryle McAdams is here. Leon loads his guns with silver and gives me silver bullets should I need them. I wish to use my sword; I have all my hate welded into it. I still take the bullets. You never know.

But the place is quiet.

And serene. A slumbering haunt.

Leon meets my eyes, the iced blue sparkles in the moonlight. I nod at him, dismount my horse, and slide my saber out of Posa. The horse neighs and I place a hand against her neck to soothe her much the same way I did when I confronted Annie's monster.

My walk to the ranch is the longest of my life. I question everything. My ability, my strength, my determination. To kill without anger is a strange thing indeed. However, it allows for strategy. I won't foolishly amble into a place where Ryle can easily kill me.

The next best thing is to lure him out. Without overthinking it, I shoot the window and the glass flings shards across the porch. I can hear him distinctly cursing and yelling, then someone ambling through the dark house.

"Ryle McAdams!" I shout, and just as I do, a loud thunder crashed over the skies. Within a second, the heavens open, and the rain pours over the withered land. Long sheets of water long held hostage by stubborn clouds of the gods that dance in the heavens.

I stare at the rain in awe as it drenches me, covering me with its cool relief. The pellets land on my face, and I blink through the stinging water as a figure appears at the door of the ranch.

Through the storm, I see him. The same as before. Tall, wide, and sloppy. A mess of a monster who'd once been a man.

"You shot my window, girly!" He snarls, leaning against the door frame. Confused by my presence, confused by the rain.

"I'm Dania Gonzalez," I shout through the sound of the storm.

He rubs his face, stubbled with beard, as he studies me. "Don't know no Dania Gonzalez."

Naturally, his kill twelve years ago is a memory that means nothing to him. Another kill. Another feed. A meaningless death. That is the crux of revenge. The avenger lives perpetually drowning in the pain while the pursuant lives free of guilt. No matter how painful I make his death, he'll never understand what he stole.

"Twelve years ago, you went to a small farm out in Pecos County. You killed a man and his wife and their daughter," my voice shakes. My tears mingle with the rain. "You left me alive. I shot you twice. You laughed. You remember *that*, old man?"

Ryle McAdams scratches his head, trying to piece together my story. "I kill many people, girl. I ain't had dinner yet and you look mighty tasty."

My hand tightens on my blade. "Your preacher ain't coming, McAdams. Drained dry in his own temple of lies."

His eyes flicker to where Leon sits on his horse, calmly watching, saying nothing, leaning forward on his saddle as if he's here to enjoy a show.

"If it ain't Marshal Laurent," Ryle says with a chuckle. "You bring some girlie here to do your dirty work, marshal? Vampire Legion must be getting desperate."

Leon stares at him without moving. He looks like a shadowy ghost with cool blue eyes. Ryle slides me a look, and that same toothless smile covers his face. He points at my saber with his chin.

"You know how to wield that little knife?" he asks.

"Come and find out," I say.

That's when I sense movement to my left, and I inhale a sharp breath when I realize we are circled.

From the cavernous depths of the house, a dozen sets of eyes stare at us, and I recognize this was a lair, a feast of vampires against just Leon and I.

Leon's hand move before mine. He shoots into the house as one vampire launches at me. I lose my saber in my race to roll on the ground and avoid the one who attacked.

My gun is in my hand, and I shoot blindly.

Chaos descends in the rain as I scramble to hide behind the watershed.

In the storm, Ryle McAdams laughs.

Leon runs across the yard, his hands moving swiftly as he fires off his weapon. I hear the scream of another vampire as Leon fires off his shotgun.

Leon lands with a thump next to me, our backs pressing to the slates. The vamps shoot at the structure before Ryle orders them to stop.

I breathe deeply and press the barrel of my gun against my forehead.

"You don't know *why* the Vampire League wants me dead, do you, girly?" Ryle's voice booms in the rain. "Well, I'll tell you. I was once a marshal too. Bet your vampire didn't tell you that."

My throat constricts, and my insides twist. Leon stiffens next to me and his shoulder pushes against mine. I don't wish to hear lies, but I'm desperately thirsty for truth.

"I didn't go to your house to kill your ma; I went to your house because they imprinted her. Imprinted by Ray Holmes, the man you called your daddy."

I feel my insides burn; a gasp evaporates from my lips.

Ryle chuckles and I notice vampires moving across the property, surrounding us. I aimed and shot at one. He lands dead with a squeal.

"I was sent there by the exceptionally *fine* organization that hunts me now. The same organization that will hunt the two of you once they find out you've imprinted—yeah, I can smell it."

I shake my head; the rain drowns all my thoughts and cascades them to the ground.

Leon shoots past the shed, three quick rounds and a snarl from Ryle which tells me Leon got a few more of his men.

In revenge, his words aim at the heart.

"Your mama came out with a shotgun loaded with silver bullets, had to defend myself. Didn't go out there to die. I *was* a little violent, I admit. She got me angry, that one," Ryle says with something akin to fondness.

"Shut your mouth!" I snap and twist to shoot at the house. I can't see anything. It's dark, wet, and murky. A shadow moves and I fire but miss.

I jump back to my hiding spot, pressing against Leon. His breath is steady, while mine is erratic.

"Hurts, don't it?" Ryle laughs. "Your pa died with her, couldn't even help her. Then your sister, she was feisty, picked up the same shotgun. Didn't mean to kill her, but I had a thing for her. She was ripe, you *know*. Sweet sort of blood, licked her dry."

I feel my brain drain through my ears.

The festering wound I carry in my heart burns, and, with a yell, I turn and shot at Ryle. But he'd moved, and I shoot instead one of his henchmen. He flails with a snarl and a thud.

A shower of bullets drenches the shed, and a bullet skids past my ear, but Leon grabs me and pulls me to him. He saved me. We stare at one another through the rain; the water plasters his hair against his pale face.

"You can do this," he whispers, and I tighten my hand into his.

I nod, not knowing what I can and can't do. Leon points to the small stable. We would have to run through the open and hope to God a bullet doesn't catch us. Leon grasps me under my arms, tightening my waist against his.

"Just hold on," he says, and I'm being yanked at unnatural speed through the night.

Gunshots fire at us and as he slides into the stables, my legs collapse when a bullet attacks the fleshy fat of my arm. I cry out and I can hear Leon growling in anger.

"I'm fine!" I hiss, pressing my hand against my arm.

My lover frantically studies the wound, his fangs elongate as he does. My arm throbs painfully and I grimace at the burning sensation of the laceration.

They shoot into the stables.

"I smell your blood, girly!" Ryle mocks. "My boys are hungry now!"

Leon's entire body ripples. He crouches and snarls. I grasp his shirt and draw him to me. Our eyes meet, and I feel I can do this for a lifetime. Hunt the devils together. Needing the courage, needing the fire, I pull his lips to mine, his fangs cut into my lip and the burning pull in my stomach erupts in a dance. I can't feel the pain in my arm. All I can feel is Leon.

When we pull back, Leon stares at me with red eyes. He licks the droplets of my blood that linger in his mouth. He smiles slightly. I can sense that my blood tastes like fresh honey in his tongue. A reawakening of his abilities and senses.

"I'll be right back, darling," he whispers.

I gasp as he speeds out, faster than I've ever seen him. All I hear is shots firing faster than I can process. Monsters yelling and running for their lives.

I step out of the shed, gun in hand, shooting at anything that moves. I pause at the sight before me.

Leon has six dead vampires at his feet, his eyes feral, his shirt torn. That same creature in the church is unleashed.

Ryle stands, gun in hand, pointing it at him. He doesn't hurt Leon because I shoot Ryle McAdams. I shoot his hand because I want him alive.

He doubles over with a scream, clutching the hand that dropped the gun. He twists to me with a furious look.

"You finally righted yourself. You didn't die that day because you picked up the other gun. Regular bullets. Saved yourself with your mistake." Spit slips from his mouth.

"Not today," I sneer.

The remaining vampires dash out. I shoot them as Ryle runs for cover and Leon goes after them. I shoot one and duck behind a bush as a bullet flies at me. Leon's violent moves drench my ears in the rain. I cast my eyes to the ground, where I had dropped my saber. Without overthinking it, I launch for it, rolling on the ground, painting the soil with my blood. The hilt slides into my palm, and I turn to point it at Ryle.

His eyes are red in the night, his men dead at Leon's feet.

"They didn't have to die! My mother and sister were *innocent!*"

Ryle slices me a look of disdain. "There's no such thing as innocence."

"Dania!" Leon howls and I can see him running at us as Ryle pulls a gun from behind his back and shoots me.

I see the path the bullet makes, a traveling inferno of death.

"*A man could win a country with a set of deuces in the right game on the right night,*" daddy said one night.

I close my eyes and wait for the end. The force of the bullet hits me with unexpected force. I land feet away, eyes wide on the cloudy sky. Pellets of rain drown my eyes. Breath leaves my lungs as I gasp, trying to feel the pain, but there is no pain.

I pat down my chest, searching for a wound, but there is none, just a sharp poke of *something*. I tear into my shirt and there's Annie's cross. The cross a girl named Mary gave me. In the center is the bullet, bending the crucifix.

As if I've ignored it for years, I see people care for me. I'm not alone.

A snarl and a crash sound, and I scramble up.

Leon tackles Ryle and the two, fangs elongated, grapple one another, twisting in the dirt, noises like battling lions resounding in the night.

I stand and rush at the battling vampires as Ryle tosses Leon against the house. His body cracks the porch beam, and the structure partially collapses over him.

With a swing, I raise my arm and slice Ryle across his back. He cries out and pushes me off. I fly, once more, across the mud, out of breath.

Ryle launches towards me, body so quick I barely see him move. And I'm a young girl. A monster is in my house. I become encased in memories of my father, of his death, or any sign I could've had through the years that he too was a devil.

But there hadn't been.

He'd been a good man. He cared for *mami* and my sister and me. He'd always provided food and shelter. He'd taken care of us. His love for *mami* and us had been his end. With their memories etched in my eyelids, I swing my sword and slash at Ryle McAdams's belly. My sword clatters on the ground.

He howls and ambles backwards. We stare at one another, not four feet apart. The rain drenches us in the truth. He is a twisted bastard, an unforgivable force of nature.

It didn't matter daddy was a vampire. What mattered was that he loved us. He tried to save us. I'd survived. I picked up the wrong gun.

I meet Ryle's eye and in a second, I raise my gun, loaded with silver bullets, and fire twice into his chest. He clutches himself, mouth agape in horror.

"Well shit," he murmurs as he meets my eyes. Drool seeps from his mouth. "I must've pissed you off."

And then he slumps dead on the ground. Eyes wide as the deluge drowns him with her tears.

I fall to my knees and heave; my vomit speckles the land. When I finish, I realize I'm crying. June's face comes so clear to my thoughts that it splits my belly in half for longing. How he'd bent down, picked me up, and carried me away from the gruesome scene. How I was no longer afraid. And I recall how he'd waited for me to say a last goodbye as he stood on the porch holding Anabella. Under the light, wishing to get one last look at me. Thinking I was a goner, thinking I wouldn't return.

I've spent so long chasing the shadow that stole my happiness that I never allowed myself to see that I was given a second chance. For years, I've discarded it and tossed it to the wind. I didn't want it. I'd been a child, a stubborn, focused child.

Had June known about vampires? Had he sensed Leon was one? I doubted it. He wouldn't have let me leave with him. I'll have to tell him and try to explain to him the reality he might've suspected for years.

Dimly I feel when Leon sits next to me. He presses his body against mine and the warmth that we share covers my skin. Reminding me I have people. I have someone.

I look at him through my tears and the rain. His sharp cheekbones are downturned in sadness.

"You knew about my family," I whisper.

"I did," he says.

I sob and clutch my lower lip against my teeth. Then his hands are on my hair, and he presses his mouth against my temple.

In the night, amongst the dead bodies and the blood, we kiss. Our moves become frantic, and I shove his clothing — or what's left—off him.

His flesh is cool against mine as we fuck, a coupling of wild need and fresh sorrow. His tongue laps vigorously against my wound until it aches no more, sealed by his desire. When we are spent, his cock still encased within me, softening within, I nuzzle his face.

"Will they come for you and me? Will they hunt us down?"

His jaw tightens, and his eyes darken. "They might."

A resolution casts my heart in iron. I pull him to me, and he holds his forehead against mine. Let them come. I've faced monsters before. I've lost my fears. They won't catch me off guard the way they did my mother. If they wish to find me, they will find a lioness.

We discover the bodies of the children, and the old sheriff piled up in a backroom. The smell is so intense I heave. A fleeting thought swims through my mind. Had I been able to save them? Had I been faster in my pursuit, would they be alive? They remind me of my family's bodies, and I'm suddenly a young girl waiting amongst the debris of my happiness before June found me.

The inside of the ranch is still dry, so we set the place on fire.

We stand in the rain and watch the inside burn before the water puts out the flames. It's as best a cremation as we can manage. The vampires and Ryle's body are already decomposing, swiftly seized by the night.

Leon holds me in the rain, my head tucked under his chin. I feel a strange sensation coursing through me, something I've not felt in a long time. Fullness. Like I consumed an enormous meal, and my stomach sits happy and sated. *For now.* It won't last and I'll feel the itch again. The itch to hunt and I know Leon will happily go with me when the time comes.

He kisses the side of my head. I've had no one belong so wholly to me before.

"Let's go home," I say.

About Isabelle Olmo

Isabelle Olmo was born in San Juan, Puerto Rico and was raised on a diet of 1980s fantasy films and Sweet Valley High. She graduated from the University of Central Florida with a degree in English Literature. She has a passion for storytelling, blending genres, and travel. Queen & Conqueror was her debut novel.

https://isabelleolmo.com

Feathers of Truth

BRITTON BRINKLEY

About the Book

Here's what I can tell you about me:
  1. I'm a homicide detective.
2. I'm a hitwoman.
3. I'm that last Phoenix in existence.
Or so I thought...

My life was simple. Solve crime as a Chicago homicide detective. Murder the targets my boss gives me. Simple. I lived a life of solitude and loneliness being the only creature of my kind. I grew up with an adoptive family never knowing my parents. Never understanding how it is that I came to exist. Years and years of searching put me no closer to the answers I so desperately want.

That was until my newest murder case brought me face-to-face with a woman whose eyes match my own and my newest target led me to the answers I've sought my entire life. My simple life will become a tangled weave that threatens to strangle me. For once I'll be forced to pick a side — the enemy or my family. My real family. My only question is, will I survive the raging battle between the two?

Advisory

The following are themes and tropes to be aware of when reading this work.

Explicit sexual content
Murder
Attempted Murder
Violence
Guns

Chapter One

That saying "you only live once" applies to the creatures and people that walk this earth, but not to me. Never me.

A wicked grin pulls at the corners of my full lips. The tiniest gesture that would terrify any normal human, but not the burly one in front of me, with his gut lolling over the waistband of his slacks. Dirt and grime clinging to his fingernails and cheeks. Rivulets of sweat break free of the streaks of gray at his temples down his mottled skin.

On the surface, he looks unimposing. Non-threatening. No one would ever fear this glutinous piece of shit casually walking past them on the street. More likely pity him for the extra weight around his middle and neck, and the sheen that always seems present on his forehead.

They don't know that he runs one of the world's largest drug organizations. His cocaine quality irresistible to druggies of all types. A hit of heaven they'll never get elsewhere. Mario Silarno is one of the most dangerous men to grace our streets, but the man I work for wants him dead. I don't care or know why. All I know is Mr. Silarno made a grave mistake when he pressed the muzzle of his gun against the pristine skin of my forehead.

I can sense the uptick in the rhythm of his pulse. Not from fear. No, this man fears nothing but losing his high-paying clients. It's from the extra exertion of his heart. The adrenaline making the weakened organ work too hard when he found me clad in my favorite leather jacket and skinny jeans, nestled into the armchair in the corner of his study. The gloom of the night slithered through the opening between thick curtains, covering me in shadows while I waited. My hits never know I'm coming... until I'm here.

"What the fuck are you doing in my house?" Spittle flies past his thin lips, streaking my face in the stench of steak and cigars. Dude could use a serious breath mint but never mind that now.

"Oh, Mario. I think you know." The flirtatious lilt to my words a pseudo-security blanket, confusing him. His mind whirring at warp speed, attempting to determine who I work for. Just who has come to take what he built?

I came to take from him, but not what he thinks. He protects his drug empire. I protect the interests of the man behind the curtain. The one who has paid me millions over the years to dispatch the scum — and sometimes good people — he no longer wants to inhabit the Earth. I've never asked questions. I don't care. In the end, the answers won't change anything for me. They won't make me any less alone than I already am.

"Get the fuck out of my house, you bitch."

My smile widens as his face reddens. The anger and irritation surfacing in a torrent of emotion. Many men are like him, living as cavemen, expressing a minimal range of authentic emotions.

We've been alone in this compact room long enough for our eyes to adjust. For him to take in the features of my face. The scrunch of his brow revealing his concentration. Memorization he won't need in the next five minutes.

The high cheekbones. Sultry mouth like Angelina Jolie. Slanted dark eyes and bridged straight nose. On the outside, the appearance of a supermodel, an asset I've used to my advantage my entire life. It's easier to get what you want when you have a gorgeous face and cunning wit to get by in life. Thankfully, my looks serve as a glamor for what I am. A revelation that nearly crippled me with excitement at ten years old.

"What are you going to do with that, Mario?"

My forehead presses into the gun. His arm only recoiling slightly. A slip in his guise of pretending he has complete control over this situation. As if convincing himself he's not experiencing the dread finger-walk its way up his spine, he pushes back. The metal no longer cool against my warm skin. The rim heating to match my rising temperature.

"I. Will. Shoot. You." The punctuation of each word meant to frighten me into submission. Little does this twat of a man know I bow to no one. Not even the one who pays me for the unspeakable deeds I do.

"Pull the trigger. By the time I leave here tonight, you'll be dead and this place will be up in flames."

Mario's Adam's apple bobs in his throat, his audible gulp echoing throughout the enclosed space. *Good.* I Like him shaking in his boots and wondering if my threat is real. It is. He could shoot me countless times, but in the end, he'll be the only one no longer amongst the living.

Slowly, I rise to my feet, the gun firmly still pressed against my skull. To his credit, he doesn't flinch as I move toward him, torturous step by step, his elbow finally forced to bend to accommodate for me closing the distance between us. His breath leaves his parted lips in unsteady pants. No longer able to hide how uncomfortable he is. As if possessed by my intent, his steps mimic my own. The click of my heels forwards the beacon for the draw of his thudding steps back until his thighs meet the side of his mammoth mahogany desk.

"Let's make this easy, shall we? I'm starving and you've wasted too much of my time here."

Boredom bleeds into my words. A clear sign that I've already spent more time here than I'd intended to. The last thing I need is for him to shoot. An even bigger zap on time, requiring my return, and then chasing after his lard ass as he tries to escape from his self-proclaimed palace here.

"You'll put down the gun. Do as I say. Then I'll be out of your hair in no time." My nonchalance punctuated by a careless shrug.

Thick brows knit together. A dead giveaway that he's contemplating doing as I ask.

"What do you want?" Hesitation guiding his question versus the anger at finding me here. Confidence wanes as I continue to stare him down with the muzzle of his gun still against my head.

"Only what my boss wants. So, will you cooperate or will you make this hard for me?"

Another swallow, as the gun shifts in the slightest. Just enough for me to swoop in and trap his wrist under my armpit, twisting and grabbing the gun with my left hand. Yet another way I am unusual. He's panting now, his flabby chest heaving under the white button-down shirt, perspiration soaking through the fabric.

It's my turn to point the gun at his head. He doesn't beg, just stares me down as I pull the trigger. The quiet thunk of the bullet hitting bone before his body slumps against the desk to its resting place — music to my ears.

There's no point in cleaning off my fingerprints. They won't find ones like mine. A smile graces my face as I stroll from the study.

No looking back. Never look back.

With a single ring, my cell connects me to my boss. "It's done." Just as quick a click ends the call. There's nothing else to say.

By all means, murdering Mario Silarno should have been a greater challenge. I was convinced he would pull the trigger. No matter. He could have a million times. Lucky me, nothing kills what I am.

There's no death for the last Phoenix in existence.

Me.

Chapter Two

Violent wind whips at my shoulder-length hair, the waves loosening as they swirl and flip through the air. There's no such thing as Fall in Chicago. We go from warm weather to a slight chill, barreling into winds that threaten to carry you away, then dumped into blistering cold. We're teetering on the edge. The threat of snow is right around the corner. It's a quiet night out here in the suburbs of Winnetka. All the wealthy families long since tucked into their beds in their silk pajamas.

The click of my heels and the crash of the waves of Lake Michigan — not far to my right — serve as my soundtrack as I make my way back to my 4Runner. What I like to call my upgraded mommy-and-me van I use when coming into the burbs. It allows me to be inconspicuous. Blend in with all the other moms toting around their toddlers and teens when I come to places like this.

The engine roars as I start the car. Nothing but waving trees around me, as I pull out onto the road and head for downtown. The roads are nearly empty at eleven p.m. on a Thursday night. As they should be. The traffic-free trek, not giving me adequate time to fixate on my Phoenix. At its displeasure of remaining caged tonight. There are only ever two occasions when it emerges. With death and when I call, reaching down into the belly of my being where it sleeps, dormant until needed.

I was ten years old when I realized what I was. Back then, I lived in the mountains of Montana with my adoptive family. The loving couple that found me abandoned on the side of the road.

There was a cliff with a deadly drop-off that served as our extended backyard. The very one I was explicitly told to never play near. I've never been one to listen, even from a young age. I went there most days, peering over the edge at the burnt sienna rock leading to the rolling river below. Even then, I knew I could fly. I felt it within me. So one day, I jumped.

I remember the rush of air on my face as my eyes shut. Just a tiny moment of being transported back in time. The pale blue dress I was wearing billowed around me. The cool air sent goosebumps across my exposed flesh. As quick as they came they faded, my skin heating, the sensation so much more intense than any fever I'd ever had. As if a record on repeat, I told myself I could fly. Over and over and over. Waiting for magical wings or fairy dust or something to keep me from becoming the new decor for the rocks and water below.

The fall seemed to be in slow motion as feathers the color of the sun spread across my arms, and writhing flames enveloped them. I cried out, thinking my flesh would burn, but it didn't. Only seconds for my entire body to change, from the tall, lanky girl to a creature that only existed in the magical worlds of my books. With a snap, what had been my pouty mouth was a beak. My vision, which was near perfect, enhanced, allowing me to see for miles. My first taste of what power feels like. I loved it.

I was no longer falling, but... floating. My wings — each longer than my five-foot-two frame — stretched to the sides, catching the wind, so I soared over the flowing water instead of crashing into it. I flew there for hours that day, watching my reflection, seeing the creature I became. As a child, I should have been scared, but inside, I was elated. I strove to be different, but this proved I really was. It was a secret only for me.

Over the years, that secret faded from a happy one to one of loneliness and seclusion. By the time I was twenty and making my way through college, I'd become so recluse I doubt anyone would have noticed if I disappeared. That was the year I took up shooting lessons and self-defense. I may have been magic, but I was still a woman, walking around my college campus late at night, attempting to find places to let my Phoenix soar.

It wasn't until I turned twenty-five and moved here to Chicago, becoming a CPD cop that Salvatore Danarius, my boss, found me. Even now, as I slide onto my favorite bar stool, all the way at the end, tucked into the corner, I can feel his essence next to me. An invisible presence reminiscent of the night he found me. I was in this very seat, nursing the same Basil Hayden. Taking small sips to feel the burn on my insides. The only inconspicuous way to feel the way my Firebird made me feel.

After my kills, I come here. Often enough that Mike, the bartender, doesn't even need verbal communication from me to have my glass waiting directly in front of the only stool I ever sit on. Seven years of routine will do that. Me dispatching of men and women that never see me coming. Most know that someday someone will come to take their thrones. I am that someone that arrives in the night. I'm the last set of eyes they look into before they die.

To this day, I don't know why Sal approached me. What he saw in the dark depths of my oddly colored eyes that made him pick me. The number of times I've been told I've never seen a black woman with navy blue eyes is exhausting. I assume it has something to do with my lineage. With what I am. I never knew my biological parents, so there's no way for me to know. Sometimes I wonder if that's why they gave me away. Their soul-crushing reason for not wanting me. I wish I knew if they were dead or alive. I would yank the answers from them before burning them to the ground for leaving me alone in this big, wicked world.

But I've done my research over the years. I am supposed to be a myth. I'm not supposed to exist. Years of countless nights of me rummaging through old texts for someone like me. Another Phoenix to be a kindred spirit with, and I've never found one. Not a single one. Only legends of what I am.

Twirling the glass between my fingers, eyes focused on the glistening amber liquid, I ignore the male body that slides onto the stool next to me until his gravelly voice drags me out of the depths of my thoughts.

"Why does a gorgeous woman like you look so lonely?" The stranger asks, his own glass, full of light beer visible in my peripheral vision.

"Gorgeous people can be lonely too," I scoff, downing the remaining two fingers of my drink. Mike hands me another glass before the original touches the wood of the bar. I down that one too. Three large gulps as the burn glides over the delicate tissues of my throat and belly.

Not bothering to fix the bored expression on my face, I glance at the man next to me. Powerful jaw. Pronounced nose. Doe-brown eyes that sparkle. Complexion battling Casper for the pasty award. Freckles dot majority of his face, neck, and exposed forearms. Thick forearms, corded with muscle. He'll do. Anything to curb the loneliness. Even just for a while.

"My place or yours?" My last words before downing my last bourbon of the night.

His brows raise in surprise. Fumbling hands clasping around his own glass before chugging his beer and wiping his lips with the back of his hand. His heavy footfalls follow me out into the whipping wind of the Chicago night, thick fingers pressing into my lower back.

Time for a little fun.

Chapter Three

No surprise he lives just like most single men my age in this city. Minimalistic furniture with just enough class to convince people he's more sophisticated than he actually is. The one small mercy is the lack of nasty gym shorts and crumpled boxers strewn about as I follow him into the cramped corner kitchen. Refusing to turn on the lights, only the soft glow from the open refrigerator door aids me in gawking at the man before me.

He has a stronger frame than I realized on that bar stool. His height towering over mine. A challenge sometimes when you're a woman that's five-ten and wears almost exclusively six-inch heels everywhere you go. He's already removed his coat, the thin shirt straining as it's stretched across the bulging muscles of his back. He's quite the specimen. I hope his dick matches the rest of him or it'll be another night of me faking an orgasm and doing my best to disappear as quickly as possible.

"Hope Sam Adams is okay." He shrugs, handing me the newly opened bottle. I drink deeply, letting the carbonation fizzle down my throat and bloat my belly. Not as good as the fire of the bourbon, but it will do.

Just to be clear, this has nothing to do with liquid courage to screw this guy. No, I have no shame in my sexual promiscuity. I like to fuck. A lot. Doesn't matter who he is. Yet another perk of being what I am, is disease never claims my insides. So, I've never been concerned with contracting anything from my various partners. But still, I abide by the "no glove, no love" rule, mostly.

I don't date. Relationships are something too personal. A bond I'm not willing to engage in; lacking the luxury of giving that person all of me. I can see it now, "Hey handsome. Glad we're getting along so well. Just so we're clear, I'm a Firebird that's reborn if I die. You cool with that?"

"This works." I tip the half-empty bottle in his direction, leaning against the unforgiving edge of the counter. He's staring at me as he takes repeated swigs from his bottle. Nerves. This isn't something he does.

"Show me your room," I smirk. Turning my back to him and sauntering down the narrow hallway to the right. Destination bedroom. Hand outreached, I push the door wide as I enter.

The comforter and pillows draped across the bed are crisp and clean. Everything in its place. The blue light of the television shining bright against the dark. I stare at it, captivated by the color. Since I realized what I am, I've dreamt many nights of a Phoenix, just like me, but with feathers of cobalt, bright and vibrant, just like the light glaring at me.

Giant hands snake around my waist as he sidles up behind me, his hard length already pressing into my lower back. Tender lips trail up the side of my neck, heating me in an entirely new way. Spinning in his arms, I tug his head down to me. My fingers tangling in the hair at the nape of his neck. The man can kiss. Let's pray he can fuck, too. Because I need one. A way to bang my sins out of my system. To forget that I just murdered someone else without even blinking.

Clothes shed from our bodies, thrown into various corners of the room, leaving him naked, his rigid cock pressed between our bodies, and me in nothing but my lace bra with the extra lines of fabric cutting across my cleavage. Bending at the waist, he shoves the cup aside, biting my nipple between his teeth, drawing a groan out of me. I like it when it hurts. When they're rough. When they don't question if they could actually damage my not-so-fragile body.

Our feet and legs tangle as I force us to the wall, shifting at the last minute so my back slams into the hard surface. He's surprised by the laugh that escapes me but doesn't hesitate to thrust his tongue back into my mouth and his fingers into my pulsing core. *Fuck.* Those damn sausages he has for fingers fill me more than I would think possible. His stroking and probing against my walls, pulling at the storm brewing in my lower belly.

"Quit dicking around and get to work," I growl, pulling his face back from mine by fisting his hair.

So many women want to be wooed and worshiped. Not this one. I want to be fucked stupid. Ravaged until I forget my name. Forget my past. Forget that I am completely alone in this world. That there's no one like me.

My giant does as he's asked, large hands gripping under my round ass and hauling me into the air without a bit of effort. Before I can pull him close, the telltale ruffle of foil fills the space. His hand sliding between us to sheath himself. Instinctually, my aching thighs wrap around him tighter as he draws back his hand, dragging him close. Hand braced between us, I edge him into my entrance. Thanks to the no sickness thing, I prefer to go bareback when men are willing, but most humans do their part. No babies wanted here.

The one thing I'm unsure of is pregnancy. I've been on birth control since I was a teenager because one thing Phoenixes still have is a menstrual cycle. Once a quarter, so I figured I could still become pregnant just like anyone else. I wasn't having sex back then. Choosing to guard my virginity until after I graduated college. Still, a baby was not something I wanted at all in those days.

Age has softened me, though. The need for me to find that blue Phoenix of my dreams lingering in the back of my consciousness. What it would be like to actually share my life with someone? Like my co-workers and their families.

With no concern for my comfort, he thrusts in with a single flex of his hips. Punishing my core for squeezing him tight. The first orgasm rages through me. The fire that lives within roaring beneath my skin with enough ferocity, focused concentration is the only way to keep it locked down. I wouldn't want to fry the guy while we're having such a good time. With steady breaths, my bird relaxes again, riding out the orgasm as our hips grind together, my fingers jamming against my clit to draw it out.

"Fuck. You feel so good, baby."

"Mmm hmmm," I hum in response. Nothing I haven't heard before. A line most men use. They love a tight cunt and a willing woman to fall into bed with them. Or in this case, the floor as he trips over some article of our clothing, my back crashing into the carpet.

His rhythm doesn't slow, the pumping of his hips and his wide girth threatening to tear me apart. I need every bit, as my teeth sink into his freckled shoulder, his growl only makes my muscles squeeze him tighter, keeping him from retreating from my slick heat. In an instant, he's thickening inside me, his balls drawing up.

With as much strength as I can muster, I throw him from me. His large body landing in the spot just next to me.

"What the hell?" he groans.

"I'm not done with you yet." My tone, flirtatious.

Let them come, it'll be the only one.

It's too soon. I need at least another three orgasms before I'll be satisfied.

Laying back on the edge of the bed, I spread my legs wide, running my lithe fingers through the arousal now dripping down my inner thighs. "Come clean up this mess."

Like a dog eager for a treat, he crawls to me, eyes never leaving mine. The darkness of the room makes them appear as black as demons. Gripping under my thighs, his thick arms hold me in place, the tip of his tongue driving up through my sensitive flesh.

Not only can the man screw, but he eats me like a starving man. Licking, sucking, and biting in the right places. His pace intensifies the pleasure, curling my toes. It's not long before my second release ricochets through me, my abdominal muscles convulsing from the force of it.

The giant gives me four more orgasms before I finally sit up on the edge of his bed, slipping back into my lace panties.

"What the hell is that?" he croaks from behind me. His colossal frame laid out on the opposite side, the thin sheet doing nothing to hide the outline of his thick length.

I know what he's referring to. The tattoo on my back that trails down the underside of both my arms. He wouldn't have seen it because I never had my back to him. The answer is always the same. I give no explanations when they ask.

Refusing to answer just yet, I finish shimmying into my jeans, boots, and t-shirt.

"Well?" he questions.

"It's me," I whisper before disappearing out of the bedroom and quietly shutting the apartment door behind me.

Chapter Four

The choice to become a cop had nothing to do with being noble. Not driven by stopping criminals or being outraged because a family member was murdered, the case now cold. An endless collection of evidence accumulating dust in the basement of a police station. It was about the thrill. The danger. Surges of adrenaline to pump through my veins. It was hard to find time and places to let my Phoenix fly free. A constant emptiness inside me being deprived of that high.

I had a friend obsessed with true crime. Her favorite pastime, reciting the ever-changing murder rates across the country. Chicago's had skyrocketed.

That was my sign. Become a cop. Get my thrills from dangerous situations. Per the legends I'd studied for hours as an undergrad, it's near impossible to kill a Phoenix. No matter what, I should be reborn. I was banking on that when I became a rookie cop. A fearless woman in a sea of arrogant men, with a compulsion to live on the edge.

Being a street cop was enough for a while, but I wanted to be on murder cases. Making detective was the only natural progression. The position I've been in for the past two years. Working my ass off to be the only female homicide detective in my precinct. It works for me. The guys are crass, but that just means I can be too. But being one of the guys means getting teased like one.

"Hey, Luxe. Rough night?"

No doubt I look as ragged as I feel. I got a good romp in, but it only took the edge off temporarily. I'd sat awake on my balcony all night, sipping more bourbon than I should have. Legally, I'm likely still considered drunk at the moment, but my magical blood also means I recoup quickly. Internally, that is.

Externally, my eyes are likely bloodshot. My waves not coiffed into submission, but my natural pattern now wind-tossed. I didn't bother putting on makeup this morning. We're lucky my dress slacks and blouse even happened instead of a hoodie and leggings. Mornings like this the mirror is not my friend.

"I could ask you the same, Gomez," I snort back at my partner. His taunts saved just for me. A straight-shooter with more sarcasm than a Brit. It's why we get along.

Other than our complexions and dry humor, there's nothing remotely similar about us. Where I stand tall, he's just over five feet. His small stature and trim frame in opposition to mine. I grew up a thin girl. Adulthood gifted me a new body with curves and a butt. Still waiting on the boobs, though.

The guys all *ooh* in unison, rocking into their seats with laughter.

It was interesting joining homicide. I'd already been under Sal's wing for years at that point. The fear that one of my kills would end up on one of our desks made me the first to jump at any murder case. Funny, no fear of death, only being trapped behind metal bars for life. Cops that end up in prison don't last long.

I may be immortal, but rebirth is a painful ordeal. As I took a new breath, the bones and tissues broke apart. The individual molecules separating only to resettle anew. For weeks, my body remembered its reformation. Learning its improved form.

"Anything good, fellas?" I chuckle as I collapse into my seat, Gomez already handing me a piping cup of coffee. I should chug some water, but the near-black stimulant steaming in this mug wins.

"Nothing new yet, but those weird cases always seem to find their way to you," Garrett Booth, one of the younger homicide detectives, scoffs.

He's the type I would take home. Almost considered it once when he asked me on a date. He's tall, dark, and handsome. The complexion of an Egyptian god, chiseled bone structure, and deep-set hazel eyes. As fun as it would be, I keep business separate from *my* pleasure. The last thing I need is for him to know any of my secrets.

My shoulders tighten just the slightest at his joke. He's referring to the tall stack of unsolved murders. A large chunk of them are my own handy work. The hours spent trying to link them together, a waste. The search for a signature, pointless.

I am the serial killer they're looking for. My kills were all carried out with opportunity weapons. The less messy, the better. Getting blood out of clothing fucking sucks.

"Weirdo magnet, I am."

A forced laugh escapes as I power on my computer, knowing there will be a mountain of emails waiting for me. There always are. Random tips or the Medical Examiner's office or Forensics sending along information for the many cases Gomez and I still have open. For every case we haven't solved yet — most being mine — we've closed three others.

Our solve rate trumps the rest of the department. The sole reason our captain lets us get away with the shit we pull most of the time.

The morning passes in a whirlwind before Captain Barlow comes in, dropping a folder on my desk. "Luxembohrg. Gomez. Hot one for you." He's the only one that uses my full last name. Everyone else opting for the shorter version, Luxe.

"What's the rundown?" I ask, my brows knitting together, reading through the thin file.

A small sigh of relief leaves me as I realize it's not one of mine. No, this one was a murder in a residential home in Lincoln Park, where the houses cost millions and the soccer moms take mid-morning walks with their strollers.

"Middle-aged couple found stabbed repeatedly in their home. Neighbor found them. When she called through the front door, no one answered. Let herself in and found them both in the living room. No signs of forced entry. Only thing we know for sure is homicide."

Grabbing my coat from the back of my chair, I'm nearly running to the elevators. Gomez understands I love the thrill of solving a crime. There's no time to waste. The longer it takes for us to get to the crime scene, the more it will be altered. CSI will take what they need, swabbing and photos and bagging, preserving what they can. Likely EMS dirtied up the place, too.

It takes a solid thirty minutes for us to reach the crime scene; the area taped off in the bright yellow streamers blocking the public from getting closer. An officer meets us at the edge, spewing off everything Captain Barlow already told us. I wave him off. His lack of pertinent information not helpful. These rookie cops can be the worst. I should be able to sympathize with them. I was one once, but I don't. They just get in my way and piss me off. I learned how to be helpful early in my career. It would be best if they learned to do the same.

Turning into the living room, blood spatter coats nearly every surface. The *drip, drip, drip,* of it from the coffee table onto the cream carpet, louder than it should be amongst the voices and shuffle of bodies.

Deep breath. Close your eyes. Listen. Feel it.

My mantra before I take in every crime scene. When my eyes open again, everyone fades away. The noise and live bodies. The nuances of what happened here coming into view with vivid clarity. As if the scene rewinds and replays itself for me. The husband was incapacitated first. He's on his back now, but I would bet my life there's a stab wound along his spine. The first wound for him. Once down, he'd rolled over, attempting to protect himself, only to take the knife to the gut, shoulder, throat, thigh, and cheek. The face had been just before his heart stopped. Only a trickle of blood slipped free.

His wife heard the commotion running in after him. The angling of her body tells the story. She found the culprit still crouched over her husband. It was then she tried to run. The assailant slammed her head into the molding, the small chip of paint stark in contrast to the gory laceration and her skin tone. She'd fought back. Her arms and hands mutilated with defensive marks.

My heart breaks for these people. Faces similar enough to mine to pass for my parents. The man's eye shape. The woman's nose and hair color. It's the sliver of her irises that makes me stumble, colliding with a CSI behind me. The narrow strip of navy blue, so much like my own.

No, Ari. You're just seeing what you want to see. It's not her.

Chapter Five

A chill trickles down my spine — one I can't shake — as the images of that couple flash through my mind. Their faces seared into my brain. This isn't the first time I've looked into the faces of strangers and wondered if they were my parents. If I looked into the eyes of the people who brought me into this world and left me alone.

"What's the deal, Luxe?" Gomez asks as he idles in the traffic along Lake Shore Drive, exactly where we'll be sitting for at least another hour.

"That woman's eyes..." My voice trails off, locked on the luxury condos just outside my window.

With a heavy sigh, Gomez drops a hand to my thigh. The most paternal touch a man could give. Gomez is a touchy-feely person, but there's never been anything uncomfortable about it. He has four young kids and a wife he's been married to since he was eighteen. He's always been a comfort though, someone I would call a friend if I let anyone actually be one. "It's not them, Ari."

Using my first name pivots the conversation from business to personal. One of companions that share secrets and provide reassurances even if they're making promises they can't keep.

"But... I've never seen eyes my color on another person."

Gomez laughs. The sort you give your child when they tell you something outrageous, but you just might go along with it. "Ari, there are millions of people who might have navy blue eyes and you've never met them."

I know he's right, but I still push, unable to shake the feeling creeping up inside me.

"Yeah, but are any of them a black woman with my nose?"

He says nothing more, as we inch through traffic, blaring horns filling the pregnant silence between us.

I don't stick around once we get back to the office. Heading home to become one with my balcony and bourbon once more. I can't shake their faces. Can't stop thinking about them or staring at the photos from the crime scene in the file as I sip my drink. The burn is so good. Its heat provides me with the focus it should strip away.

I'm blanketed in the dark of my balcony when I come to. The folder still clutched in my hand and my glass empty. It's not unusual for me to fall asleep outdoors when on a fresh case. The sounds of the city and the brush of the wind against my cheeks help me think. Clarity I can only find here or at the lakefront.

Buzzing deep beneath the pillow pulls me from my thoughts, my fingers probing for where my phone is wedged under me. The caller ID tells me everything I need to know as I press the green button.

"My house. Ten p.m." *Click.* Sal's voice already faded into the night. I'm only called to his residence when he has a mark considered a VIP.

I still have two hours. His condo building being only three blocks away from my own is enough of a comfort for me to sink back into the cushions. Coincidence? I don't know, but it sure is convenient when he calls his dog to heel.

Flipping open the file folder again, I skip past the crime scene photos and go straight to the one depicting the happy family. The woman, Syriah James, flanked by her son, Tucker James, and husband, Lanham James. They were a beautiful family, bright smiles flashing. The file revealing they were in their sixties, the features of their pleasant faces telling a different story. One of youth like my own.

They could be my parents.

They're old enough.

Shaking my head as if it will clear the thoughts, I flip through the pages again.

The son, Tucker, lives in the city too. An area where quaint homes line the streets. He's only three years younger than me. The light waves on his scalp and curve of his brow, reminding me of my own.

Slamming the folder closed, hands running through my wind-blown hair, I exhale a loud breath. I've spent so long looking for my family. It's no wonder I see it in every face. Willing similar features and skin tones and smiles to be a match for my DNA. I'm not alone then.

Gomez is right. I'm seeing what I want to see.

I need to focus on the facts. Solve this case just like all the others.

A hot shower, large pizza, and two cups of coffee later, I'm riding the private elevator up to Sal's penthouse. He lives in a place most only dream of. It's not that I couldn't afford it. But what would I do with a two-story penthouse? It's just me. No one to share it with. He at least has a wife, unconditionally devoted to him, and three grown children of his own.

"Drink?" he asks as I step into the foyer.

I don't miss him eyeing my attire. Skinny jeans may be my go-to, but Salvatore has a dress code for entering his home. My trendy suit, with the off-center zipper and wide-leg slacks topped with black Louboutins, seems to appease him.

"I'm good." I raise a hand to wave him off. "Who is it?"

There's no point beating around the bush. Sal prefers my simplicity. My forward nature to get straight to the point. No time to waste. With a smirk — a glass of red in one hand — he grabs his iPad with the other, lowering it into my palms like priceless crystal.

The face of my next target greets me. The man with eyes like emeralds is gorgeous in contrast to the overweight grimy drug lord that was my last assignment. A jaw so chiseled it might be carved from stone. Thick sandy brown waves wild atop his head. His only soft feature, the copper freckles speckled across his proud nose. His stature tells me he's strong, not only physically but in his mind, too. The scowl he wears indicates just how much bullshit he's willing to put up with. None.

"Any information?"

"Already sent."

With a nod, I hand him back the iPad. Long bony fingers curl around the edge of the device before dropping it onto the sofa next to him.

"Time?"

Sal always has a deadline. There are no open ends to his requests. He wants what he wants when he wants it. A guarantee I can make him, while he carries out his dark plans for world domination.

"Three weeks."

There's no hiding the widening of my eyes. That's one of the shortest time frames he's given, but it's no never mind. I like a challenge.

Chapter Six

Nearly two weeks have passed. The dueling halves of my life warring with one another. My search for another murderer that isn't me and the next hit on my list for Salvatore. Dark circles pool in the puffiness under my eyes. My hair — normally tamed into submission — becomes frizzy, tucked into a tiny ponytail. One that barely contains the short stray hairs that like to fly free at my temples. The worst is my temper. Flaring at even the most minuscule of things, all while enduring the looks of pity from Gomez every time he catches me staring at the photos of the James family.

It's a feeling I can't shake. A force taking hold inside me. Telling me I'm connected to these people somehow. Maybe they aren't my parents, but there are unexplainable ties that bind us. There's a familiarity in their features and the way they hold their posture in the family photo. More than once, as I prep myself for the minimal hours of restless sleep, I stand in the mirror analyzing the way I hold my shoulders or the curve of my nose or jaw. It's not just the hue of the blue, but even every sliver of silver matches the now-dead woman.

Tonight is the first Gomez and I haven't pounded the pavement until well past nine, giving me time to trail my next target, Adrian Alexander. The type of name that accompanies models and movie stars, not accountants. Those that crunch numbers for fun — and a living — come with names like Bob and Joe. Just my luck, Adrian's gorgeous features match his sexy name. Even memorizing his squeaky-clean background makes my libido hum. A sensation I can't say I've felt before hunting any of my targets.

Much like me, he leaves the office late at night, checking his surroundings discreetly before he leisurely makes his trek home. His office is in the heart of downtown, a tall onyx building of glass along Wacker Drive. The streets are busy enough this time of night, making it easier for me to blend and weave through the throng of bodies as I follow him.

I'd yet to track him home, as he often visits other places before finally tucking in for the night, but tonight it seems luck is on my side. He heads for the L Train, his satchel slapping against his thigh, as he looks left to right once more — this time more obvious as if he wants people to notice. *Interesting.*

For a boring accountant that seems to live a clean life, he checks his surroundings an awful lot. Some dark secret hidden beneath his polished image. Good enough reason for me to be even more careful as I trail him. Hunt him, like the prey he is. No matter the outcome, I have my trusty dusty detective badge I can always rely on. Though, without finding a single indiscretion on the man, I can't imagine what sort of lie I would tell to go with it.

He boards the train; me following just close enough that he's long since seated himself at the far end, his back to where I now stand by the doors. He may be my target, but I'm in no way disillusioned that Salvatore doesn't have his own enemies. One gunning for his hitwoman before she can come for them. You hear the whispers loud and clear through the dark underworld I often ingratiate myself into. As far as I know, no one definitively knows my identity, but I can't put trust in assumptions.

We weave through the quieter streets of Lakeview. That familiar churn of Lake Michigan waves in the distance soothing me. As counterproductive as it is for a Firebird to love the water, I do. The sounds and smells and spray always being what I crave most in my human and bird forms.

I'm lost in my own thoughts, my focus frayed — an unusual occurrence for me — when I nearly expose myself to Adrian as he unlocks the front door to an unassuming brick home on the corner of West Wellington Avenue. Darkness stands firm behind the sheer-curtained windows as endless minutes stretch by. Using the shadows of a large oak on the corner, I wait. Expecting lights to surface on the main level first, I'm surprised when a front room on the upper level becomes illuminated. The shadow of the man should be dancing across the curtains, giving me a peep show. There are no shadows.

I've learned to be a patient woman, keeping my shoulder pressed against the flaking tree trunk. For the second time tonight my mind wanders, eyes latched onto the lone lit room in the house. It's enough that I don't hear the nearly silent footsteps behind me, or have time to react as a large hand snakes across my nose and mouth or the arm that wraps around my waist.

Heat roars through my body, my Phoenix itching to break free and rescue me. Tonight it won't be necessary. I can defend myself, except his grip is unyielding as he drags me through the gate at the back of the house and inside. I expect him to attack or subdue me. But he releases me the moment we're through the door, locking the several latches and a bolt. Panting, my hands stay braced against the granite countertops, my back still to the man that just dragged me inside.

"Care to tell me why you've been following me, Detective Luxembohrg?"

My eyes shut tight, my lips pressed together so as not to curse audibly — my cover now blown. In all my years doing what I do, not once has anyone ever figured it out until it was too late. A gun to their temple or knife at their throat. Not once was I ever made before I chose to reveal myself. Their own personal grim reaper already on their doorstep.

Slowly turning, hands still gripping the counter, I stare down the Adonis before me. He looks like a fucking Greek god in a cheap suit and I know what he makes annually, so there's no need for him to wear something so ill-fitting.

"How long?"

His eyes squint. He knows what I'm asking. How long he's known I've been following. The urge to ask what gave me away is like an itch that can't be scratched. My refusal to show any weakness the only thing keeping me from clawing at my forearms. If I play my cards right, I can likely end this asshole tonight. Salvatore has always rewarded early delivery with a couple extra hundred thousand and a longer break between kills. I could use one about now.

"Since day one. I could sense you."

I have no idea what he means. *Sense me?* Like he's some sort of trained dog that could sniff me out. It's becoming clearer there's more than meets the eye with this one. Something dangerous hidden there beneath the surface. A threat to Salvatore. *Not my problem.* I just need to get my job done. Clean kill. No sign of me being here. Simple.

"That's great. Look, Mr. Alexander." The use of his last name the only respect I'll show him. "If you know who I am and that I've been following you, then you know why I'm here. I would suggest you make it easy for me."

In an instant he's in my space, that brick-hard body pressing mine into the countertop, long strong fingers wrapped around my slender neck. His nose less than an inch from my own as trembling breaths escape into the space between us. There's no fear. Only an attempt to restrain the temper he's clearly fighting to hold on to. His fingers tighten, ever so slightly, just a shred of my air supply inhibited.

"Ms. Luxembohrg, I would suggest you get out of my house before you regret coming here in the first place."

His hand releases in an instant, the force throwing my head back. He shares no further words or even a look as he casually strides from the kitchen, up the stairs, and out of sight. The quiver in my hands is enough to stop me from following him.

Exiting the way he carried me in, I stay in the shadows. I'm near the gate when a vibrant blue flash of color catches my eye. A single feather fluttering in the grass near the fence. It's not the feather of just any common bird. I know it. It's the same as mine. A single. Phoenix. Feather.

Chapter Seven

"I need more time."

I swallow loudly, waiting for Salvatore's answer. I've never asked for an extension, but it feels necessary now, as I twirl the blue feather between my fingers. It took me three days to buck up the courage to call him. Three days to decide if trying to pursue someone who might be like me or know where I can find others like me was worth pissing Sal off enough that he may no longer see me fit to be amongst the living. Little does he know he can't kill me. I would just rather not be hunted for life.

"Reason?"

I'd practiced this in my mind. Over and over. What I would say. How I would justify the need for extra weeks — not days. "There's a reason you want him dead. I don't need to know it. But in the weeks I've been hunting him, there's clearly more we don't know. Let me get you additional intel. Then I'll sweeten the deal and dispose of anyone else in his group you want gone, too. Free of charge."

Silence greets me on the other end of the line. No background noise. Not even Salvatore's breathing as he ponders what I've asked of him. I have every intention of dispatching Adrian once I've got the answers I need. The chance of finding even just one more creature like me is too good to pass up. It's like the cure to my loneliness has been presented to me on a silver platter and I would be a fool to say "no, thank you".

"How long?" he finally asks, his words punctuated by a dramatic sigh.

"Another three weeks."

"Fine." The line goes dead, but at least I've bought myself more time.

*****

Today was one from hell. Gomez and I called it quits early, so that gives me plenty of time to wander back to Adrian's house. It's just past dusk as I slip in through the back door, my memory recalling what types of locks held it shut. It's odd that he would have so many, but again I need to remind myself he has more to hide than he lets on.

Once I've snuck into his home, breath held deep in my lungs, listening for any sign of other inhabitants, I wait. Minutes tick by, remaining statue-still until I'm satisfied I'm here alone. Despite the house looking narrow from the front, it's quite large on the inside, sporting seven bedrooms, four bathrooms, and even a basement. The house is decorated in a sophisticated fashion, all white and shades of gray. It's quite dull actually but fits that of an accountant. Despite the sculptures and paintings on the walls adding to the elegance, there's no personality here. Nothing that tells me more than I already know.

Taking up my favorite position while waiting for one of my victims to come home, I settle into an armchair in the living area, darkness creeping over me. Hours must pass before the telltale click of the front door unlocking pulls me from my haze of thought. I expect only Adrian to enter, but he's not alone, as Tucker James and another female the size of a large child walk in behind him.

There's no conversation as they enter the house, casually shoving the door shut. "You could have turned on the light," Adrian sighs in my direction before the fluorescent glow of energy-efficient light nearly blinds me.

"I wanted to surprise you," I snicker, hands resting on the arms of the chair.

Eyes of cerulean blue stare at me. Tucker's eyes, his lips pressed into a thin line. If I thought my eyes were unusual for a black person, he definitely has me beat. They're brighter than the photo lets on. His features more masculine and strong with time since the picture was taken.

"And you are?" the female asks me.

Not bothering to even pay her any mind, my focus turns to Adrian. His face devoid of any sign of what he might actually be thinking.

"My new stalker, apparently," he sighs before dropping his bag to the floor.

The girl's eyes go wide as she takes in Adrian's words. Her small stature and blonde waist-length hair making her appear unimposing.

"We need to talk," I say, pulling the conversation back in the direction I need it to go. "They need to leave."

Neither Tucker nor the girl move. Adrian makes no attempt to dismiss them, simply settling into the middle of the sectional couch in front of me. His elbows rest on his knees, fingers steepled beneath his chin as he continues to stare me down. Discomfort flares under his scrutinous stare, not only because he seems so unfazed finding me here, but because all I want to do is mount the man right here and now. I clearly need to go find another rando in a bar tonight.

"How did you find me? I've been looking for you for years."

It's my turn for my eyes to gouge themselves from my head. Tucker's words dancing through the space around us. *Find me. Why?* How is he connected to all of this with Salvatore? Not to mention his parents were just murdered with no sign of who the perpetrator was.

"Like I said, I need to talk to Adrian. Leave."

"If you recall, this is my house. They stay. You speak." Glaring at him once more, he continues. "You don't like it. You can go, but this is your one chance to ask whatever stupid questions you have. I won't let you back in again."

Let me back in. This motherfucker. How dare he talk to me like I am some simple child. I broke in. *Me.* I shouldn't be proud of that being a homicide detective and all, but I am. It took time to learn the art of being discreet and getting into the sacred spaces of peoples' lives. The places where I shouldn't have been.

Pulling the feather from the inner pocket of my leather jacket, I twirl it between my fingers. Much like I've done for the past three days. Watching the slight iridescence glimmer in the light like flecks of tiny glitter. All three of their faces stay stoic as they watch my fascination with the single feather. Only when I pull out a second, one of fire engine red and copper, does Tucker suck in a gasp of air.

"So, since we're all staying. Care to explain to me who this feather belongs to and where I can find them?"

Silence. Soul-crushing, deafening silence.

Chapter Eight

Silence surrounds us. My rapid breathing and the steady pace of the three of them staring back at me the only sound to break it. My impatience grows as I wait, only Tucker showing any outward signs that he's on the cusp of breaking. Of letting the floodgates open to either put me in my place or spill all his secrets. I'm wagering on the latter by the uneasy shift of his eyes and the brief twitch of his long fingers against his thin thighs.

It's easy to see what type of frame Tucker has. Strong, lean, almost stretched as he towers over the girl. His clothes fit him perfectly as if designed for someone with his build. Yet his shoulders remain as broad as his chest. The angle of his jaw would make him look like a vicious villain if his anxiety wasn't peeking through.

"Well?" I question, waiting for someone to give me some sort of response to my inquiry.

Tucker takes a breath, ready to speak, stopped only by Adrian holding his hand out. A signal for him to keep his mouth shut. Tucker obliges, making no effort to fight against Adrian's request.

"Ari, we owe you no explanation."

"But —" Tucker tries again, taking a single step in Adrian's direction. Another hand halts him mid-step, his enormous foot suspended mid-air.

"What are you?" Adrian asks me.

His question unsettles me for a moment. The unexpected, thrown back at me. A question I couldn't have prepared for. My arrogance blinding me once more when it comes to Adrian Alexander.

Narrowing my eyes at Adrian, I toss the question back. "What are you?"

A wide grin spreads across his face as he leans back into the cushions, his legs spreading wide in his charcoal slacks. "You're holding my feather, so you already know." Long arms spread across the back of the couch, my mouth hanging open at the obvious answer he just gave me.

"You're like me?" The words whisper past my lips before I can stop them.

All these years, I've been so alone. Thinking I was the only one. That there were no others like me, only to learn that a mere twenty minutes away, there was another of my kind.

"Did you know?" I breathe.

"Not at first. Not for sure until I found you lurking outside my house." The nonchalance in his response makes my blood boil. Those flames licking beneath the surface.

"And you weren't going to say anything?"

"No."

The single word makes me want to throttle him. Tear at his perfectly quaffed hair and wrap my fingers around his throat as he did to me only days ago. Thank goodness I heal quickly and it's cold out, otherwise, I wouldn't have been able to hide the bruises he left behind.

"Well. That's it then." Planting my hands on the arms of the chair, I move to stand. Ready to get away from this asshole as fast as I can. He may be like me, but I'd rather be lonely than have to spend extra time with him.

Yet I still owe Salvatore his death and he's the only one who may be able to give me answers. Locking eyes with Tucker and the girl, I suddenly remember their presence and I know at that moment they are like me, too.

"If you're a Phoenix..." my eyes locked on Tucker. "How were your parents murdered?" He doesn't answer right away. His eyes filling with unshed tears.

On a deep breath, he gives me yet another dose of honesty I wasn't ready for when I came here tonight. "*Our* father wasn't a Phoenix. Mythical being, yes, but not like us. *Our* mother still lives."

Our. That word implies more than one. Surely not Adrian or this girl. They look nothing like Tucker, but maybe for non-humans genetics don't work the same. The phenotype inconsequential — yes, I studied genetics too, another attempt at trying to make sense of what I am.

"Who is *ours*?" I ask, already sure I know the answer.

Tucker takes several sure steps toward me, extending his hands as if he wants me to take them. I don't.

"Ari, you're my sister. I've been looking for you for years. I'm your younger brother."

The world drops out from beneath me. My knees buckle as I tumble back into the chair I'd just been in.

"Great, now that we've had our family reunion. We have business to tend to. You might be one of us, *Ari*..." My name spews off Adrian's lips like a curse. "But anyone who breaks into my home with the intent to murder me for Salvatore Danarius isn't welcome in my home, so kindly get the fuck out."

Shock at tonight's revelations and the hope blossoming in my chest make it so I barely register Adrian's words. Only when he stomps over grabs me by the biceps and marches me towards the front door — Tucker on his heels pleading — do I slither out of my stupor, tearing from his grasp.

"I'll enjoy killing you when the time comes, especially if you ever forcefully put your hands on me again. I don't care who you think you are." Turning so I'm as close to being chest-to-chest with Adrian's giant body, I press in close. "If you ever manhandle me again, I will be sure it's the last thing you do."

I'm met with nothing but a smirk as the front door opens and I'm shoved out, nearly colliding face-first with the pavement under my feet.

Fuck. Him. And his poor attitude too!

An unfamiliar feeling tugs at my insides as I stand at the curb. It's been years since I felt it. Years since I was unsure of my purpose or what to do. How to move forward in the way that would benefit me best. What would put me in a position of protecting myself while still trying to get answers to who my family is; why I am what I am?

Standing in the cold with only the soft glow of the streetlamp above, I'm lost. Time passes quickly. Slowly. I'm unsure. Only the numbing of my fingers tucked tightly into my pockets brings me out of my meaningless thoughts. There's no haste in my steps as I make my way to the train station, retreating the same way I came.

I've gained only a few feet of distance before I hear slapping footsteps behind me. Then a hand on my shoulder. In any other circumstance, I would have broken someone's hand, wrist, or arm for even thinking of touching me unwarranted. There's no fight left in me tonight, as the owner turns me to face him. *Tucker.*

"Ari, I'm so sorry. I tried to talk sense into Adrian." I have no response, as she stares at me, studying the features that so closely resemble his. My brother. I have a brother. And a mother still living. "Let me take you home."

A nod is my only response as Tucker leads me to a sleek black sedan. Don't ask me the make and model. I wouldn't know. Cars aren't my thing. Why do I need a fancy fast set of wheels when my wings can carry me so much further, so much faster? When they offer me freedom, no other mode of transportation can.

Chapter Nine

Tucker's quick to speak as we slip into his car, the purr of the engine softer, quieter than that of my 4Runner or my Mustang. "Our parents are something like royalty in the paranormal domain. They hold a lot of power. Power men like Salvatore Danarius want to control."

At the mention of Sal's name, my head whips around, an audible gasp escaping me before I can stop it.

"What does Sal have to do with all of this?"

Tucker's brow quirks in confusion, his true focus never leaving the densely packed city streets of Chicago. I should ask him if he needs directions, but I don't. The opportunity to hear the secrets this stranger seems willing to spill, overshadows the need to return to my lonely apartment unharmed. An internal pull inside me tells me I'm safe with this man that claims to be my brother. That same part of me knows it's the undeniable truth. No proof needed.

Settled deeper into my seat, my gut begins to uncoil. Thirsty for the information Tucker has for me. Secrets that I feel entitled to as his sister. As another phoenix.

"You're serious?" Disbelief wrapped tightly around his words.

"No, I'm asking because it's fun."

A chuckle comes from Tucker, his long fingers curling around the steering wheel before loosening again. Braced at ten and two like a new driver. It's astonishing how young he appears, almost like a teenager, but with the carriage of a full-grown man. I know he's twenty-nine, three years younger than me. A time difference that barely qualifies as a gap, yet the chasm of time seems vast. Impossible to bridge having spent our lives apart.

The weight of my current life status threatens to crush me. My target is a phoenix, too. Finding my brother. Learning my mother is my case — just like I thought—and not actually dead. Let's not forget there's a whole supernatural world I never knew existed, but should have because what I am is real. *Twilight* and *Underworld* — my favorite movie franchise of all time—immediately comes to mind, hordes of werewolves and vampires fighting one another. I know better. The term paranormal crafted to define those that resemble humankind, but come equipped with other magical gifts, expands far beyond the Twihards.

"You're so much like mom. Equipped with a viper's venom and sharp bite."

My brow scrunches at his analogy. Comparing us to a snake. My mind takes the comment as a show of disrespect. The need to slap him stupid, making me tuck my hands beneath my thighs. He knows her and I need to remember that. I don't. I know the Luxembohrgs who raised me. Then let me fly free — figuratively and literally — when I left for college at eighteen and never came back.

"Salvatore?" My teeth grind painfully as I attempt to piece together what my boss has to do with any of this.

"He's a warlock. There is a balance that should be maintained, but some are greedy. Some want more and they do what they can to take just that. Salvatore is one of them. Each species has a ruling family, for lack of better terms, in each country. Our father was also a warlock, a creature easily killed, but not our mother, despite Salvatore's efforts."

I sit quietly, listening. Thinking back to the endless murders I've committed for him. How many were "different" like me? How many were just humans whose lives I stole to further whatever agenda that greedy asshole has been running for who knows how long? How many lives have I destroyed for him?

Tucker continues, "With our parents gone, as well as many other high-ranking paranormals in the world, Salvatore can ease himself into power using force."

He doesn't have to add *easily*. The implication clear in tone and word choice. Something other than indifference settles in my gut for the first time.

"How, if he's only a warlock? Can't he only be the ruling body for them, from what you just said?"

"Not if everyone fears death by his cronies, which I understand you are."

The muscles of Tucker's jaw tick repeatedly. His words like a knife to the throat. A blunt exclamation of what I do... what I've done, not sitting well with him. Why would it? I've been executing for some sadistic pig. I knew Salvatore had big ambitions. Why else would he have me kill the ones I have? Sadly, I always knew I wasn't his only, just the one reserved for higher priority targets.

"Yes, I've been on Salvatore's... payroll for seven years now." A hard swallow follows, fear forcing hesitation at asking the next bit of information I want to know. "Do you know the ones I've killed?"

He shakes his head, those fingers tightening once more before pulling to a stop at the curb. He'd brought me straight home. How he knew where I lived, I don't know. As if he can read my mind — maybe he can — he answers, "Adrian knew your address. Just like you've been following him, he was doing some digging into you, as well. He suspected you were... different, but couldn't tell what, uh, kind until he got close to you."

It's suddenly clear why he dragged me into his house that night. A chance to analyze me the way I have been with him. An opportunity to get close. To learn what I am. I'd read that creatures like us can sense the same in another, or just "other".

"And no, I don't know who you've killed." Sadness settles into Tucker's eyes and his hands drop to his lap. "But Adrian will need to know. You'll meet him tomorrow at seven p.m. to review each one." I nod, reaching for the door handle. There's no protest left in me.

"Tucker, one more question." The swivel of his head back in my direction, quick. One of my booted feet already planted outside the car. "If Adrian is a phoenix and we can't die..." My words fizzle out before I can continue. "How did Salvatore think I was going to kill him?"

"Did he ever give you a special weapon? Gun? Knife? Told you to always carry it with you on kills and use it if someone is difficult?"

My heart seizes in my chest. The words from my brother's lips nearly matched the ones Sal delivered to me so many years ago. The custom Glock and bullets cradled into my eager hands. He said he usually hands out knives, but I seemed like a gun girl. He'd placed the weapon in my hands and given me those exact instructions Tucker just recited. Now, the dense plastic just seems to burn as it digs into the soft skin of my lower back. The location I often keep it.

With a nod, I exit the car, hearing Tucker's last words before I shut the door. "He'll be here tomorrow at seven." Then he's gone, pulling away from the curb and disappearing around a corner. Feet rooted to the sidewalk beneath them, the wind whipping my dark waves against my cheeks, my eyes remain trained on the city before me. A city I thought I knew.

I'm getting so much more than I bargained for.

Chapter Ten

Gomez has been regurgitating information at me all morning. His words in one ear and out the other. With a deep breath, I do my best to refocus. Today's trip to the morgue will hopefully provide us with some answers. The Chief Medical Examiner requesting we trek out to the office specifically to review her findings.

Assistant ME, Dr. Sharon Maurin, had already signed off on the release of Syriah's body to the family to be cremated. There was nothing of note other than various stab wounds and a head laceration. Exactly what we saw at the scene. Cause of death exsanguination. Manner, homicide. Simple. Clean. Only I know there was no cremation. At least not one she didn't rise from when no one was looking.

It's not Syriah we're here for. It's Lanham. Chief Medical Examiner, Natalia Ridolochan, called us in this morning, the quiver in her voice enough to make us move. "Dr. R, what do you have for us?"

Both Gomez and I shake her hand as we follow her down the white hallway, cast in shadows and scented with bleach and formaldehyde. Oddly enough, it's one of my favorite smells. The number one reason I loved so many of my science classes in college. I was the only double major in Biology and Ancient History and Mythology. An odd combination, as reported by my advisor. Her making it crystal clear she believed the history portion to be a waste of time when I was going to be a doctor. She didn't understand. No one did and I couldn't tell them. Being a phoenix has always been my secret. Alone. Until last night.

"Well, it's odd. With the number of stab wounds Mr. James incurred, he should have bled out. He didn't. He may have appeared dead at the scene, but his heart was still beating, so slowly, I presume, no one would have ever picked it up. No machine could have picked it up. It's almost as if he's suspended in time. Like his body is frozen in a state of pre-death. I can't explain it. Nor have I ever seen something like it. But see for yourself."

Shoving open the double metal doors of the examination suite, Lanham's body lies on the silver metal table in the center of the room. His chest and abdomen flayed open like a fish. Majority of his organs are still in place, but it's his heart that Dr. Ridolochan points to.

"Watch. Closely. Don't blink or you'll miss it."

Gomez looks like he's ready to vomit. He's never been great with dead bodies or the smells of the morgue. For me, it feels like home. Somewhere I always should have been. Yet, I believe I'm meant to be a detective, too. It seems we are meant to be many things in this life. Or maybe that's just me.

The silence blankets us, barely blinking, eyes drying by the second as we watch. As we wait. Then Lanham's heart beats. Just a single tiny flex. My dad's heart beats. Tears burn behind my eyes. Tucker was wrong. Our dad is alive, but I have no idea how.

Gomez drives us back to the station. I don't stay, stating I have a few things I need to look into. I really just want to be alone. The need to release the shuddering breath that escapes me the moment the lock to my apartment clicks shut, near crippling. Back pressed to the door, I sink to the floor. How the fuck had my life completely shifted on its axis overnight? Everything has changed and I don't know how to process any of it.

I know I'm not alone. The only truth I can latch onto with confidence. I have a family. There are others like me. *I am not alone.* My final thought, as my eyes close, hands tucked under my cheek, cuddling into my microfiber couch.

Darkness surrounds me when I wake again, the insistent knocking on my door making me bolt upright. Wiping the string of drool from the corner of my mouth, I stumble through the dark toward the noise.

Adrian stands there, a bag of Chinese in one hand, dressed casually in a hoodie and dark-wash jeans. *Fuck my life.* How is this man even sexier in his casual clothes?

"Are you going to let me in?"

Nearly tumbling backward, my socks slipping on the hardwood, I move out of the way, the door creaking as I pull it wider.

"Did you not pay your electric bill, or are you a wannabe vampire?"

The warmth that had been pooling between my legs at the sight of him quickly chills to ice. He's such an ass. Like he intentionally just wants to irk my nerves because he can. Flicking on the light, I guide him to the kitchen, pulling dishes from the cabinets and silverware from the drawers.

"Definitely wannabe vampire," I scoff, dropping everything in front of him.

I don't wait for his response as I head back to the couch, sprawling out while he plates his food. My forearm drapes across my eyes, the light an unwelcome intrusion after the four-hour nap I took.

The clash of a plate against my coffee table draws my eyes back open. "Try not to break my shit —" My words stop short when I see he made me a plate too. A mix of beef and broccoli, shrimp fried rice, egg rolls, and chicken lo mein smothering every surface of the oversized dishes.

"Didn't know what you like, but I'm starving and it's going to be a long night."

The fog clearing I remember the real reason for Adrian gracing me with his presence. I leave for the second bedroom I use as an office. He doesn't pause slurping down noodles and chugging his glass of water, as I drop the stack of kills on the table between us. The weight enough, my table does a little wobble as they hit. The silverware jingling to drown out his chewing.

"Thanks."

My only response as I scarf down my food as if I've never eaten before. Truth be told, I forgot to eat today. Even on the days when I remember, I devour calories like a linebacker. Men are always either disgusted or shocked that I don't order a salad to keep my fit cop bod and instead prefer greasy and fried. I'm not thin by any means, but I keep. So far the poor food choices haven't caught up with me, so I just keep doing what I do.

This is the first time I've been self-conscious about a man watching me chew with my mouth open or inhaling my entire plate in five minutes. Adrian's gaze bores into me, mouth open and fork poised as he was just about to take a bite.

"What? Salvatore doesn't pay you enough to eat?"

The raging boil of my blood surges through my veins again as I drop my fork and plate back to the table. "What the fuck is your problem?" Perched on the edge of the couch, I'm ready to throttle Adrian once again. He raises my temper and gets me hot and bothered in more ways than one. It's insufferable and infuriating.

"Other than the fact that you're still planning to kill me for Salvatore, none at all, Princess."

"Well, I'm not thrilled to be in your company, either. So, let's get this over with so we can be done with one another."

Adrian looks like he is going to respond, before he glugs the rest of his water, heading to the kitchen to refill it. He returns only moments later, the condensation already beading against the clear glass, before grabbing both our plates and filling those again, too. Gently placing mine back on the table with a grunt. "Eat first. Then we work. I'm not dealing with your hangry attitude if I don't have to."

"Dick," I whisper under my breath as I clear my second full plate of greasy deliciousness.

"I heard you."

"Good."

There are no more words shared between us as we both finish our meals. Only stolen glances of me glaring at him under my thick lashes. No response from him, though. Not once do I catch him looking anywhere but at the plate of food cradled in his hands. Where I eat like a caveman, he's all controlled poise, wiping his mouth more times than I'd care to count.

Once we've finished, he pulls the first sheet off the stack. I'd prepared for this after Tucker dropped me off last night. Printing the summary sheet for every kill, one by one. Looking into the eyes of everyone I've murdered the past seven years tightens the knot at the base of my belly. Kills for a mission I didn't even bother to understand. I did as I was told. A loyal soldier. The only way to feel alive while my bird stayed trapped inside.

He asks about each one. Details and whereabouts. I hadn't even noticed the laptop case he walked in with until he pulled his Mac free, diving into databases. Getting through the first twenty took us well past midnight, attempting to piece together Salvatore's plan. Tying together what each — paranormal and human alike — could potentially give Sal with their deaths.

"I'll be back tomorrow night to go through the next bunch." Adrian shoves his laptop into his bag.

"Can't wait." Sarcasm thick in my tone.

"Lock up that petulant attitude. I'm not going to put up with it."

Fuck. Him. Fuck. Him.

No one. No man talks to me like that. "Let me be clear about something, Adrian. I'm not killing you… yet—" My eyes trail up and down his body, attempting to look like a menace, but more than likely only achieving lovesick teenager. "I am helping you, but you're not going to be an asshole to me. I don't care how you talk to other people, who the fuck you think you are, but I'm not the one."

His face nears mine, our noses nearly touching. "Let me be clear, Ari. You answer to me. Want to know who sits below your parents? I do. So get in line and stop pushing my motherfucking buttons."

He's already got the door open. His foot across the threshold. The temptation to let the door slam into him is strong, but I don't give in to the impulse.

"Text me what you want for dinner." His version of goodbye as he saunters down the hall, leaving me to watch him go.

Chapter Eleven

A week of Adrian showing up at my place promptly at seven, a bag of takeout in hand, becomes my norm. I forget that I have a deadline. He's still my target. His constant attitude making me want to murder him most days.

Baby Got Back blares through the car. My phone coming to life in my pocket. Gomez eyes me but doesn't ask as I answer it.

"You're late." His growl sounds through the speaker.

Gomez's brows nearly touch his hairline as he hears Adrian's voice. I keep my personal life pretty private. Keeping my sex life away from the guys' eager ears. My life is simple. Sex. Murder. Solve cases. There will be questions when a man's voice comes through the Bluetooth oozing bitterness.

My night routine, once he leaves, has become finding randos in the bar to fuck the aggression out of my system. No one raises my blood pressure the way Adrian does. Lucky me, the guy from a few weeks ago was there Friday night. David — I think that's his name — so I haven't had to find someone new for a days. The downside is that the guy wants to take me on an actual date. No, thank you.

"I'll be home soon. Let yourself in."

Gomez is still staring at me when I hang up. "Who was that?"

"My brother." An immediate response. A stupid one, because I've never talked about my adopted family. Not in detail. I was their only child, that much I'm sure I've said before.

"Brother?" Gomez throws me a knowing look. Lips pursing and eyebrow raising again. "Look, I don't need to know, but he needs to watch how he speaks to you."

One of the many reasons I love Gomez. Always defending my honor. The unofficial brother I've gained since being partnered with him.

"I've got it. Promise."

I throw him a wink before peeling out of the car and waving him off. Most days I don't drive to the office. I would rather walk. Feel that Chicago breeze on my face. It gives me time to think. Time to forget the horrible things I see and the equally unforgiving things I do. I find perspective and healing and clarity. Not tonight, though. Tonight, all I can think about is sitting side by side with Adrian for the eighth day in a row. His pine scent filling my nostrils while I try to focus on doing what I can to help.

Our dynamic remains tumultuous. He's a bigger dick than ever. Our tempers flare at the tiniest details. I've seen Tucker a few times for lunch this week, his plea to stop testing Adrian falling on deaf ears. It's not my fault. He's the one with the snotty remarks and underhanded comments. No hesitation in revealing everything he disapproves of when it comes to me. His repeated jabs that the Phoenixes are lucky Tucker exists because I would never be fit to lead them. That one hurts the most.

Not because I want to lead. I barely understand this "other" world. Only because all I've ever wanted is to belong. To have a family and be wanted and loved. Sure, the Luxembohrgs did that. They've always given me nothing but love even as I've stayed away all these years, but it's not quite the same. They aren't like me.

Adrian's stretched out on the couch when I enter, a chill making me shiver as I close the door behind me. "Steak's in the oven."

"Thanks," I call, stripping off my coat as I make my way to the bedroom.

I've been in these clothes all day. All I want are fuzzy socks, sweatpants, and a baggy sweatshirt.

It never occurs to me to close the bedroom door. Adrian has no reason to come this way. Yet, the sound of his voice behind me has butterflies coming to life in the depths of my belly. My heart erratically pumping in my chest.

"Hurry up," he grunts.

Spinning around to face him, completely ignoring the fact that I'm in a lacy bralette and panties to match. Electric blue ones at that. That same knowing smirk pulls at the corner of his mouth, his thick arm resting against the doorframe as his eyes scan my body. The heat of a flush creeps over my skin. Heat that belongs to my libido when it should be from my anger.

This ass barged into my private space without my permission.

"Get the hell out of my bedroom, you creep."

"Or what?"

A taunt. A dare. Well, two can play that game. I'm so sick and tired of Adrian Alexander. Marching straight to him, chin angled up to make up for the height difference, my eyes narrow to slits.

The distance provided by being on the other side of the room solidified my plan. Ready to tell him off for coming into my private space. I was ready to put him in his place, but as I stand in front of him, our chests nearly brushing, my nipples pebbling beneath the lace fabric, his jaw ticking in time to my pulse, I don't have words. His head tilts to the side, lowering closer to mine. Nearly nose-to-nose. Our daily face-off.

"Or. What?" he drawls, his warm breath spreading across my lips.

An audible gulp is my only response as he knots his fingers in my hair, lips crashing into mine. I'm still for a moment, unsure of what's happening, as he breathes me in. Only when his lips move do mine follow, my hands snaking around his waist and pressing flat against his back, pulling him flush against me. The bulge behind the fly of his jeans tells me just how much he's attracted to me. Is this like when you're in elementary school and boys tormenting you equates to a crush?

His lips sculpt around mine, drawing a moan out of me. One hand drifts under my barely covered butt cheek as he hoists me into the air, my legs wrapping around his waist. Even as my back slams into the doorframe, our mouths stay glued together. Our tongues warring as we do with our words. His torso flexes as my hips roll against the planes of muscle.

My skin is on fire. So hot, I need to open my eyes to be sure I haven't actually caught flame. I've ruined several cute tops that way.

His lips leave mine, tongue tracing along my jaw before he whispers my name in my ear. The heat already pooling between my legs becoming molten lava. My name being called by a familiar male voice as my front door slams shut pulls me back to earth.

The spell is broken. Hatred fills my eyes once more as I glare at Adrian, pounding at his chest to release me.

"Ari, where are you?" Tuck calls from down the hall.

"Just — Just a minute," I stutter, shoving Adrian out of my way, as I slip into the clothes I pulled out. Nearly running from the room, I leave him standing there, finger-combing my hair as I hustle down the hallway. For once, I am thanking the gods above for lips so full, collagen injections could have created them. Hopeful that Tuck won't notice they're swollen from my momentary lapse in judgment.

As I skid into the living room, I find Tucker and Talia waiting. Just like the night I first met her, her pin-straight blonde hair hangs loose, shimmering in the light. His girlfriend of three years. Now equipped with that knowledge, it was so clear. How they angled their bodies just enough to protect one another. He told me she's a phoenix too, but where our birds resemble fire, and Adrian's the hues of the ocean, hers has the greens of a garden. Each bloodline comes with gifts. The feather color eludes to what elements they originate from. She even brought me a feather so I could see for myself. A show of faith.

Just as I pull up the sleeves of my sweatshirt, I feel Adrian behind me. Tuck's face shifting to disbelief.

"Come on, man, that's my sister."

Kill me now.

Chapter Twelve

Talia's eyes dart between mine and Adrian's, then back to mine, skipping to Tuck's as she takes a loud slurp of her green smoothie. It's rare to see the girl without one in her hand. Rather, it's amusing how much she values only ingesting healthy meals and clean fruits and veggies — certified organic — when sickness can't touch her. Still, she never wavers. Sweets rarely cross her radar and she eats nothing fried.

"So..." That single word drawn out so long I wonder if she'll have to catch her breath after she lets go of the note. A mischievous gleam sparkles behind her eyes, self-restraint wrapping her slips around the straw before she says anything more.

"Nothing happened," I snarl, marching toward the kitchen. The container with my dinner slaps onto the counter, the aroma of the medium-well meat making me salivate. I'm careful to keep my back to the group. I can't bear to see the look on Tucker's face. Whether it be anger or excitement or disappointment. I've always wanted a family. He's my brother and I only want him to love me. Real-life to match the fantasy in my head.

Talia's opinion matters much less, but I know she's important in our community. Her actual role is unclear to me, other than knowing she is a genius when it comes to hacking and all things IT. She is the sole brain behind the database Adrian and I have been sifting through that harbors the information on every known paranormal in existence.

Hushed words are shared between Tuck and Adrian as Talia joins me in the kitchen. She says nothing as I shovel tender filet mignon and red-skinned mashed potatoes into my mouth. Her sipping her smoothie. "You know he's our leader until your mother can come out of hiding, right?"

Glancing her way, mid-chew, I pause. I do know. Deep down, but hearing her put into words — Adrian's real importance — makes my pulse race. The time he has spent sequestered in my apartment instead of stepping up to lead. It almost makes me forgive what an ass he is, but stubbornness wins. I refuse to accept his newfound responsibilities as an excuse for his behavior.

"I'm aware."

I wince at the bite in my tone. I've got no qualms with Talia. She's been insanely helpful introducing me to a world I thought I alone lived in. The small O of her mouth revealed her shock at what I did and didn't know. There wasn't much that surprised me. Only the nuances of the creatures that roam in the shadows. Hidden from the humans that fail to realize there's truth to the movies. The myths and legends that shouldn't exist. But for me since age ten — maybe even before that — I already knew did.

"Then you should know, it's best that you steer clear. He needs to focus. We have too many enemies against us right now. To be honest, none of us have really decided if you are one of them or not."

With a quick quirk of her doll-like mouth, she hops from the counter, sauntering back into the living room. Her soft lilt drifting from the room beyond. "Enough boys. We have work to do."

Taking advantage of my last few minutes alone, I remain rooted in place. The food I'd been consuming only moments before turning unappetizing. A flavor akin to dirt, not a red wine reduction. Pushing the lid closed, I join the crew in the living room.

Tucker's seated in one armchair, his glare pointed solely at Adrian. Talia sits on the arm of his chair, rubbing soothing circles into his back. It's clear they aren't working as Tuck shuffles through the remaining stack of my targets.

"You messed up the order." I race over, pulling the sheets from his hands. Hoping none of them tear, even though it would only take me moments to reprint them. The protectiveness of my indiscretions driving my outburst.

"Sorry," he mumbles, slouching into the pillows.

There are only two options for seating. The floor or the couch near Adrian. Neither is appealing.

"Learn to wipe your face," he growls, as I do my best to reorder the papers.

"Screw. *You*!"

Talia and Tuck groan in unison, her unsure words whispered into the quiet tension. "Are you sure you guys aren't sleeping together...?"

"No!" we both bark in unison.

Clearing her throat, and pulling her own laptop from a bag, she mumbles, "Maybe you should."

It's my turn to grimace in her direction. That... What happened between Adrian and me tonight was a hormone-driven mistake. My libido is just a greedy little whore and latched onto the first breathing male in sight. These stress-filled days might be the death of me. His excuse, I was the only option present. Sure, I can admit I am wildly attracted to his handsome looks, but his attitude is worse than dog shit. Let's not forget Talia just warned me away.

"Do you know who this is?"

Tuck holds up a photo of my last kill. Mario Silarno. I can still picture what a filthy mess he'd been that night. One of the few drug lords I've never had the pleasure of investigating as a detective. One not afraid to get his hands dirty as he beat his carrier to within an inch of his life in the alley before coming home that night. I'd watched from the shadows. His fists. The slick metal bar that had been lying near them repeatedly thumped against the bone and tissue of a guy no older than twenty.

Watching that scene play out, I'd been more than happy to end Silarno's life. To erase him from this planet. I see something different now. Those electric amber eyes stare back at me from the page. I know without a shadow of a doubt he was like me. Like us. A Phoenix.

"How did you kill him?" Adrian asks his body angling towards me, knee brushing against my thigh, sending a tingle down my spine.

My eyes close, a deep inhale filling my burning lungs. I should have known. The gun was different. Its weight heavier than it should have been. The catch with the pull of the trigger. A millisecond delay that isn't there with a normal gun. I was so eager to end the poor fool's life; I ignored all the details. The specific scent that I've always associated with my Firebird, filled the space of that room. The one true giveaway.

"His own gun. One similar to mine," I mutter. The words draining the life from me. "He was the last hit ordered by Salvatore before you."

"How many others have been Phoenixes?" Talia asks.

"Twenty-four out of the seventy-two we've sorted through so far," Adrian answers, his fingers pushing against tired eyes.

"And others?"

"Ten werewolves, two vampires, fourteen witches and warlocks, three other animal shifters, one siren, and the rest humans."

A curse escapes Tuck as Talia pulls him into a hug. Her fingers swirling through the short waves atop his head.

"What do we do?" Exhaustion infused my words.

"You will do your part and help walk through each one of these you've murdered, then I don't give a fuck what you do. Just stay out of my way."

The shove at Adrian's chest barely moves him, my temper flaring once more. "You can get out of my house."

"Apartment," he corrects, moving on to the next victim.

"Get. Out." I point at the door, my torso arched over him. He remains unaffected by another of my outbursts. His attention stays trained on his computer screen, completely ignoring my raging disposition. I'm over the disrespect.

"Let's call it a night," Talia coos, pulling Tuck to his feet.

"We've barely gotten anything done. We need to figure this out sooner rather than later," Tuck retorts.

"Now," Talia gives an unnatural grin. Tuck finally follows her to the door with a groan.

"I'll see you tomorrow. Lunch?"

"Please." I smile.

I truly have loved Tuck's company. Getting to know him and our parents. We're not the siblings who hug yet. Our relationship barely beyond that of strangers, so an awkward wave is all we share.

Adrian is still typing away on his laptop when I turn back to him. "I told *you* to get out."

"Doesn't seem like you want me to leave at all," he drones, eyes still focused on whatever holds his focus.

"Well, I do." The fight to maintain my anger versus frustration is a losing battle.

"Your panties say otherwise," he grins.

Chapter Thirteen

Another week slips by. Tuck and Talia playing chaperon for Adrian and me. That's exactly what it is, no matter which way they try to cut it. The excuses of "we just want to help" and "we *all* need to figure this out together" are weak. Their best attempt at keeping us from physically clawing at one another's throats.

Tuck is always here to serve as the guaranteed buffer, picking me up most nights. I tried to bring up what he thinks he witnessed, but I'm cut off at every turn. His warning is the same as Talia's *stay away from Adrian*. Although our bickering has lessened with the passing days, I don't like Adrian anymore than I did the day Sal sent me to kill him.

The weight of the clock ticking down hovers over me. That dark cloud ever-present. Trapping me in a cage I can't find my way out of. Salvatore wants his head, no exceptions. No excuses. I'm not sure how I'll get out of it. How I'll pull the coup of all time. I may not be a fan of Adrian, but I won't kill him. I refuse to murder any other paranormals. Let Salvatore come for me. His life is much easier to take.

"Where's your head at?" Tuck asks me, turning onto a residential street in the suburbs we've never been on.

"Nowhere. Everywhere."

"Penny for those thoughts."

I throw him a small smile, my skull pressed into the cushy headrest. I'd been so lost trying to find a solution to my Sal problem, I hadn't noticed that we weren't going to Adrian's house. A small prize when I announced I wouldn't kill him under any circumstances two nights ago. He'd stared into my eyes, testing me. Searching for the truth. He found it. His only show of kindness, allowing be back in to his home.

"Where are we going?"

Tuck lets out a chuckle. His smile wide, displaying large white teeth, whereas mine was small, reserved, nearly nonexistent. "There's someone you should meet."

He pulls up outside a large home in the cul-de-sac of the long residential street. Where the other homes are large, and many newly remodeled, this one is massive. Its appearance more similar to that of a castle than anything modern.

Leading me to the front door, he doesn't knock before putting in a code, followed by his thumbprint. The clicks and brushes of metals seem loud in the early evening, the mechanism within whirring with life. A final thunk sounds, the door shifting open a breath before Tuck pushes it wide.

The space is brimming with immaculate pieces. The decor akin to something out of the Palace of Versailles. It is impossible to not fall into the attraction of the place. Fingers tracing over every surface. Like walking into a private museum. For a history geek like myself, it's nearly orgasmic. My mind already tracing the origin of the side tables, paintings, and vases welcoming me.

"Like it?" Tuck bends to whisper in my ear.

I need no words as a huge smile spreads across my face, a nod shaking my waves wild.

A woman rounds the corner. Her navy blue eyes well with tears the moment she sees me. Syriah James. My mother. *My. Mother.* Without thinking, we run for each other, like in the movies where the family gets reunited after what seems like a lifetime apart. Her powerful arms wrapping around me as pulls me close. Her scent one that seems so familiar, like the waves of the ocean. But I couldn't remember her. I was barely four months old when the Luxembohrgs found and adopted me.

Holding me at arm's length, she finally pulls away. The tears left unshed now streaming down her face. A gorgeous face. One so similar to mine.

"I'd hoped I would find you someday," she sniffles, hugging me close once more. I hold her back, intent on never letting go. She leads me by the hand, down a hallway with paintings of beautiful nature settings dancing with life. "You must be hungry. Adrian tells me you never stop eating."

Rolling my eyes at her back, I keep my lips pressed tight. Focused on making a decent first impression, I choke down my hateful words reserved solely for Adrian Alexander. Just my luck. He's seated just ahead — at the kitchen island — his phone in hand, back to me as I enter.

"Hello, Adrian," I coo at his side.

"Sweet boy, Ari has finally arrived." My mom streaks a hand across Adrian's cheek. Sweet is not a word I would ever use to describe this asshole. For the second time, I keep my mouth shut. She clearly has a soft spot for him. "Thank you so much for looking after my little girl."

The groan from Tuck pulls all of our attention, but my mother's smile never breaks. "Boys, go set the table. Ari and I will plate everything and bring it into the dining room."

They do as she says, while I assist my mom around the kitchen. She quickly learns that my domestic skills are lacking, but she never stops talking to me. Asking me questions about my life, keeping it strictly to work. Not once does she mention her case. Or what I've been working on with Adrian. She asks me if I have a boyfriend and what he's like. Her cheeks glowing with excitement. That's the only time a pang of hurt squeezes my chest, as sadness springs to her eyes. "Oh sweetheart, you shouldn't be so alone."

If only she knew how alone I've been all this time. How it nearly consumed me and ruined me as the years flew by. How I carelessly sleep with too many men to cure it and drink too much bourbon to drown it out. The way I've searched my entire life for them, for anyone like me. How the kiss with Adrian a week ago was the first time I felt anything remotely good. Like, I fit with someone.

Dinner passes slowly, the laughter never dying down. My mother and the other elder phoenixes, seated with us, do their best to make Tuck and Adrian blush the entire time. My brother is the youngest at the table, something I wasn't expecting. I was sure Talia was younger than him based on looks alone but came to find she's almost ten years older. I was convinced Adrian only had a few years on me, too. Although he refused to divulge his actual age, it's made clear he's seen several centuries. *Mind blown.*

It's been decided that we'll all stay at the house tonight. A safe haven for any in need. There are several of them across the state sanctioned by my parents and the ruling families. It's where my mother has been hiding out all this time. Only those on a short list knew.

"Here's your room." She ushers me into an ostentatious room of midnight splashed with gold.

"Um... Mrs. James —"

Her eyes narrow, hands wrapped around my biceps in a vise grip. "I may not have been there to raise you. It should never have taken us so long to find one another. I won't force you to call me mom, but you can if you'd like." There's hope in her eyes. An eagerness to hear the simple word slip past my lips.

I nod. Daring myself to test the word. "Mom..." Pause. "Mom," I breathe, less shake to my voice. "Mom." A third try. "Can we talk in the morning? Just you and me?"

I feel like a little girl asking for permission to play with my toys. A vulnerability on display I haven't allowed for years.

"Of course. We'll go walk along the beach." She kisses my forehead before hugging me once more and disappearing down the hall.

Skulking into the room, I kick my boots off on the way to the bed, removing my blouse and unbuttoning my slacks as I go. There are silk pajamas laid out for me and toiletries waiting in the bathroom. Clad in nothing but my undergarments, I head for the en suite bathroom.

A pale gray high wing-backed chair sits in the corner. The lights are not lit, so I initially missed the hulking form lounging in it.

The flick of the switch reveals my visitor. My heart in my throat as Adrian stares back at me. His posture so regal all he needs is a crown of jewels.

"Are you kidding me? You nearly gave me another heart attack. What is it with you and being in people's bedrooms without permission?"

I'm racing for the bed, attempting to slip the nightshirt over my head and hide my body from him. One he's already seen plenty of.

"Just yours."

An audible sigh escapes me, my head falling back in exhaustion and frustration. "Adrian, I am in no mood to fight with you tonight. Can you please go?"

"Who said anything about a fight?" A wicked grin pulls at those lips. Lips I wouldn't mind kissing again. "I just want to... talk."

Immediate dampness seeps into my panties and I know I'm in trouble. If I don't put distance between us, I will not be able to keep my hands to myself, so grabbing the bottoms from the bed, I run. Down the hall. Down the stairs. As far away from Adrian Alexander as I can get.

Chapter Fourteen

The cold bites at my exposed skin. Frost already collecting on the individual strands of grass tickling the bare soles of my feet. The silk pajama set does little to stave off the chill, forcing me to call on the flames that live beneath the surface. The warmth slowly replacing the severe frigid air.

Deep breaths fill my lungs. It's not that I'm out of shape, but unless I am chasing criminals, I don't run. If you see me running, run too — far away. It's the one activity that can control my temper. Saved for when I've traveled to a land so far past rage, even a good fuck can't wind me down. Times my bird threatens to free itself so I can escape everything holding me down.

"We're going to need to work on your speed."

My eyes shut, blocking out the sexiest voice I've ever heard.

"I'll add it to the list of reasons you think I suck," I murmur, the sarcasm drenching every word like viscous honey.

I'm usually so sure of myself. Confident in who I am and my abilities. So sure of what I do and don't want. Until Adrian is near me. Then I question everything. Not because of my sexual attraction to him. That fucker being the first to foresee me coming, threw me so far off balance I can't right myself again.

Those feelings of inadequacy bubble to the surface. Their origins reach all the way back to growing up an orphan — thankfully, adopted by lovely people — but believing my family didn't want me.

It's been a treacherous fight, overcoming those feelings. Stomping them to a pulp so deep inside me, they would never surface again. Adrian destroyed it all in one night. His long fingers wrapped around my neck. Demolishing any notions that I'm stealthy in following my targets. In his presence, I am the prey. Him the deadly predator.

"Can you just disappear?"

His low chuckle fills the space beside me. Still clad in the same casual wear he wore at dinner, hands tucked into his jeans pockets, shoulders hunched against his powerful jaw. As much as he infuriates me, he also makes me feel alive. So much less alone. I hate it.

"You know, I just came to tell you I think I know what Salvatore is up to."

With a huff, I turn to him, arms crossed against my chest. Partially a show of defiance and partially to stave off the winds whipping at my back. "And knocking on my door after I was dressed was such a stretch?"

"It's more fun to see you frazzled," he croons. That gorgeous face dipping close to mine. Our noses nearly touch, just before he pulls back again, turning away from me. Eyes focused on the trees beyond, the waves of Lake Michigan rolling in the distance.

"Well, out with it. It's freezing out here."

"You're the one who ran out here nearly naked. Not my fault you lack the common sense of a child."

My blood is boiling. The flames that I usually keep at bay threaten to break free across my flesh. *Not the time.* Regardless of the fact that my current attire does little to keep me warm, I would prefer not to walk back into the house in nothing more than my birthday suit. *Deep breaths.* The fresh air filters in through my nostrils and out past my now chapping lips.

Without prompting, Adrian removes his thick sweater. It's impossible not to watch out of the corner of my eye, attempting to keep my cool. Keep my distance. Why the hell is he undressing out here? He orders me to lift my arms, his tone that of how you would order a child to obey. The desire to pout is overwhelming, but I refuse to give him that kind of satisfaction. I refuse to let him hold that kind of power over me.

As if aiming to touch me as much of me as he can, he lowers the sweater over my head, freeing my hair from the hole before sliding his hands down my arms and sides as he lets the thick warmth surround me. Wanting to throw my arms around him for the bit of kindness, I instead clench my fists at my sides. This asshole deserves nothing from me. A nod of thanks is all I'm willing to give as the words start flowing from him.

"There's a balance that has to be kept amongst the paranormals. Each region has a 'ruling' body, per se." His fingers form air quotes. "Then each country has its own council of regional leaders. Every three decades a new member from those councils is a representative of the world council. It's a delicate political puzzle. Your parents are the regional leaders for both the warlocks, witches, and phoenix species. Many thought it was a power play on their part when they first announced their engagement. Two species coming together with the bloodlines and power they possess unheard of."

"Is that what it was?" The words fly from my mouth before I can catch them. All I've wanted is to know my family my entire life. Now, without prompting, Adrian is offering a piece of them willingly to me.

"No. Not at all. "

A shiver wracks my body, teeth chattering. Even my internal flames do nothing to combat the fierce winds. Taking my hand in his, Adrian leads us back into the house. Directly upstairs and into the warmth of my bedroom. He's silent as he moves us to the small sofa against the far wall, pulling a blanket from a closet I hadn't even seen and draping it over me.

"So, like I was saying. It wasn't a power play. Has Tucker told you anything about how our species find their life partners?"

I shake my head. Our conversations were charged with funny stories about him growing up and boundless curiosity about me. Sprinkled with the years of him searching for his sister. Assuring himself that I was still alive. That I was still here.

"For our kind, it's the Pairing." With a quirk of the corner of his mouth, he gazes at me. "Original, I know. Anyhow, it's very common among creatures such as us and vampires, warlocks, etc. Rarely does it happen between different species, but that's exactly what happened to your parents. Once that bond is formed, it's unbreakable."

"How do you know you've Paired with someone?"

"Your magic calls to them. It's like an invisible rope tethering you together. It's impossible to stay away. To see anyone else. It'll always be there even if you choose someone else. There's only one way to lock it into place."

Idly, I wonder what that one thing is. What could possibly further anchor you to someone that your soul already belongs to? If that's what it really is. All the crazy mating stuff I'd read in books is real. I'm suddenly curious if Adrian has gone through this. If there's someone that holds the very core of who he is? Whether or not he chose her.

"Have you gone through... it?" I'm unable to find the right words. Too nervous to ask if there's someone in the background. Someone who had been waiting for him when he kissed me that night.

He pauses. His eyes unsure for the first time since I met him. His Adam's apple bobbing with his swallow. "I have a Pair, but have not locked in the bond."

He says nothing more for long moments. Sitting beside me in silence before continuing his story.

"Your parents were one of Salvatore's targets. I assume you know you're not his only hitwoman?" A nod of acknowledgment. "Looking at the list of targets you've had, the paranormals he's specifically targeting were higher-ranking individuals with unique gifts, but your parents are the only leaders so far. However, then looking at his human picks, it became clearer."

"Well, don't leave me in suspense." I'm not sure I want to hear what he has to say. Yet, I need to. The urge to understand what I am going against by not killing Adrian as planned.

"Simply put, a takeover of the paranormals. With the right ones on your side, it's possible to access the powers or magic within other paranormals, especially as a warlock. If he can acquire the magic someone like your parents have coupled with the other enterprises, such as the drug and gun trade he has been taking over, there will be no choice but to bow to him."

"What's the point, though? This sounds like a bad X-Men movie."

"Wish I knew." His teeth audibly grinding.

There it is. The root of Adrian's frustration. The core of mine. We can't prepare for what we don't know. What we don't understand.

Chapter Fifteen

Shimmering morning light drifts through the parted curtains rousing me from sleep. I'm still snuggled under the plush comforter, wrapped in Adrian's sweater. The soft material still smells like him. My resolve to hate him faded a bit with his honesty last night. An openness he's always been reluctant to share with me. He's still an absolute ass, but if he's willing to give me the information I need, I can deal with that. Make this whole "partnership" work for me.

A soft knock at the door sounds before my mother enters, a small smile playing on her lips. Her eyes drift to the sweater my body drowns in, a knowing smirk follows.

"I'm glad you're up." Her steps are sure but feather-light as she saunters to the bed, balancing herself on the edge. "Why don't you get dressed? There's so much we should talk about."

With a nod, I scoot out past her, aiming straight for the en suite bathroom. I don't bother showering, simply tying my loose waves back from my face, before conducting my ridiculous skincare routine — the products I normally use all lined up on the countertop as if I was expected to stay all along. Aiming for casual, I slip into skinny jeans, knee-high boots, and a wine-colored knit sweater.

My mother is right where I left her. Eyes focused on nothing in particular. I studied her face last night. My face, someday. Even though the woman before me barely looks five years older, I know from Tuck she's nearly eighty. A difficult concept for me to wrap my mind around. How slow we age. Our time on this earth monumentally longer than our human cousins.

Without a word, she guides me through the house. Past the same back doors, I ran through the night before. Our steps taking us across the wide field of grass and directly into the trees. I don't question where she leads us, but I'm careful to look for markers. Bread crumbs to guide me back should something go wrong. A hidden attack or this woman who has shown me nothing but kindness turns into my enemy.

She finally stops in a wide clearing encircled by trees that seem taller than average. A spot that can only be manmade, the perimeter perfectly curved. The dense woods shelter its location from easily being seen. The treetops so high, the sky seems further away than usual. Taking my hands in hers, my mother looks into my eyes.

"I never thought I'd see you again. See the woman you've become. Tucker knew, though. He always believed he'd find you."

Tears well in my eyes, matching hers. The same navy blue eyes with silver flecks I've looked into my entire life. An endless search to find the one with a pair to match.

"I knew when I saw your eyes at the crime scene... I knew who you were then. Even when my partner said I was imagining it."

She gives a soft smile, her hands rubbing over my own. "We do have a unique coloring, courtesy of your grandfather." My heart beats a little faster. Hope building in my chest that I'll meet him soon. As if knowing the direction of my thoughts, she answers. "He passed some years back, my sweet girl."

I do my best to hide the sadness. The opportunity to meet my entire family torn from me before I had the chance.

"Uh, Mo-" The word stalls in my throat. *Mom.* All I've ever wanted was to know my mother, to call her mom. "Mrs. James," I try again. "What happened when I was a baby?"

With a sigh, she settles onto the chilled ground, legs folded beneath her. "It was a tumultuous time between the werewolves and our kind. They attacked our safe house in the middle of the night. Shifters of any type have always had a hard time seeing eye to eye. We all made it out alive, but the one who was responsible for getting you to the next safe house never showed. We never saw him again. No inkling of what became of you. We searched for years before..."

Her words trail off. *Before giving up.* She doesn't have to tell me how that sentence ended. Before determining, I was nothing more than a lost cause. Dead or taken. No longer worth coming after.

I am not an emotional person. The tears fall just the same. All those feelings of not being enough to hunt for — not being wanted — come rushing back. Full force. The tidal wave drowning me along with the chill in the air.

"Oh, sweetheart. We never gave up on you. Not even for a second. There were other issues to deal with. Assassinations against our kind and other paranormals, dwindling our numbers, our families, *our* people. As council members, your father and I had to maintain those duties, too. So when we found you —" Her fingers brush under my chin, lifting my gaze to hers. Those matching eyes stare back at me. "You had a world worth living in to come back to."

I hug her then, arms draped around her slender neck. Her small hands rubbing my back through the sweater. We stay latched to one another for more time than I would have imagined.

"Now." Her hands pat my thighs. "We have some catching up to do. Today and tomorrow you'll learn from me. Then Oliver Borneo, our Training Officer, will spend time with you as much as your work schedule allows. We all grew up among the phoenixes, but you didn't. I want you to know how to protect yourself." Her fingers graze my cheek. My shoulders tensed for the icy touch. Instead, I'm greeted with eternal warmth.

Moments later, my mother's shift begins. A marvelous sight I've never actually seen. Only read in books or seen animated depictions of. Her fingers elongate transitioning into the feathers of her Phoenix. The same shades of radiant flames as mine. Where I thought my wingspan broad, hers is nearly double the length. It only takes minutes for her bird to stand before me, those piercing blue eyes brighter now. Her expectant stare the nudge for me to do the same.

I can't remember the last time I'd let my phoenix soar. The last time, I let it free. It takes longer than it used to for me to channel it, to call it forward. Feeling the heat simmer and my pulse slow, it makes its way to the surface. The anatomy of my human skeleton stretching to become expansive wings, my lips turning into my beak and my small child-like teeth becoming sharp daggers inside my enlarged mouth.

With a nod, my mother ascends toward the cloudless skies. That's when it hits me. What this place is. There is a reason the treetops sit so close to the heavens. Why the clearing spreads so wide. Not wasting another second, I charge into the air after her. Happiness flooding my chest for once.

Chapter Sixteen

Turns out Phoenix training is so much harder than regular workouts. There's a soreness that lingers. My bones and tissues unfamiliar with the constant changing I'd done over the past week. My mother and Oliver — one of the funniest men I've ever met — assure me in time I'll get used to it. That my body will fully understand what I am.

As it is, I did myself a huge disservice treating my bird the way I have. Keeping her cooped up and letting her only fly when my human side deemed it appropriate. To become the real me, I need to accept that my Phoenix knows what's best for the both of us. This human shell of a body a disguise, but the Phoenix is the true heart of who I am. A heart of fire and feathers. My truth. It's the very essence of everything I am.

My free time is filled with Oliver's grueling regimen. A welcome reprieve from Adrian's sour attitude. A small mercy. Seeing him at all is a reminder that I'm past my deadline, delivering his death to Sal's doorstep. I've done my best to play this as carefully as I can. It's still a secret to most that my parents aren't really dead. Well, my mother, at least. None of us really understand what my father did to himself to keep him frozen between the land of the living and the dead.

As if on cue, my phone rings. "Luxembohrg," I answer, knowing full well it's Salvatore on the other end of the line. My heart rate races, but I call to my bird to slow it. To take control. Just as Oliver taught me.

"You're late."

"I've got more cases than usual. Complicated ones. I need more time."

Silence greets me, but I hear the grinding of his teeth. See the scowl on his face while he makes me sweat out his response.

"I like you, Ari. This time I will let it slide. My place tomorrow night. I would like a full update on everything you've found. *All* of it."

The line clicks dead. Sweat dripping down my scalp, snaking through the hair at the nape of my neck. The room is suddenly stifling. The air too thick to draw into my lungs.

I do the only thing that might help. I text Tuck.

Me: *Salvatore knows.*

His response is immediate. The ellipses dance at the bottom of the screen. His messages appearing in rapid succession.

Tucker: *How do you know?*

Tucker: *What did he say?*

Tucker: *Adrian will pick you up after work.*

Tucker: *Meet at the safe house.*

Tucker: *Why aren't you answering?*

Tucker: *Ari*

Tucker: *Ari?*

Tucker: *ARI! Answer. Me!*

Me: *Well if you gave me a chance to respond I would.*

Tucker: *I'll see you tonight.*

There should be no room for laughter. No place for amusement, but despite Tuck being younger than me, he's become a fierce protector. Just two days ago, he caught Oliver and me, huddled together in laughter, his rangy arm stretched across my shoulders. His brotherly speech only made our laughter roar louder. Oliver is almost a hundred years old. Yet Tuck and his twenty-nine years thought he could put him in his place.

He'd been spot on, though. Oliver and I bonded quickly. His cool and charming demeanor won me over. A drastic difference between the desperate men who fuck anything with a hole from the bar and Adrian's broody ass. Our conversation comes easily, and he's done amazing teaching me how to master my skills. Even honing some of the magic I didn't even know I had, thanks to my dad's bloodline.

That same night, he'd ask me to grab a bite with him. I'm always starving, so the natural answer was yes. It was nice to have a friend that I could joke with. An ally who knew the real me. Who knows what I am and looks at me with pride. I'm not sure I should be making nice with the Training Officer, but it's been lonely, with only Tuck and Talia welcoming me into the fray. Many of the others look at me with distrust. The hatred and skepticism swirling in the scrutinous glares.

That night, walking out of the training facility, an old warehouse on Division Street, Adrian caught sight of us. Anger flared his nostrils and etched his normally beautiful features into something deadly. A lesser woman would have feared what was clearly his way of showing jealousy. I just pulled Oliver closer, arm tucked around his waist, my wave dismissive of Adrian's attitude.

The day passes in a blur. Gomez is out due to his youngest having some sort of stomach virus. I love kids but when they get sick, *gag*. I hadn't lied to Salvatore when I said our caseload had grown. More and more murders, some similar to the ones I'd done myself, others similar to the James'. There's no reduction in the basic ones either. Gang, drug, and domestic violence crimes continue to multiply. Either way, my desk is littered with folders and cases that all need my attention.

It's after eight when my phone buzzes, pulling me away from the deep dive I'd been lost in. The endless lines of digital communications never-ending.

Adrian: *You have 2 minutes to get out here before I drag you out.*

Fuck him. Just to spite him, I stay put. Reading through lines and lines of messages between the suspect and his victim, a middle-aged woman clearly starved for attention. There's nothing but pity in my heart for her. The world tells us as women we are useless if we're over the age of thirty, not married, and without kids. Deemed undesirable if not in the workforce, maintaining the home, and raising demon children. Such bullshit.

My heart jumps into my throat as Adrian's voice sounds behind me. "I said let's go. I have better things to do than be your chauffeur."

Turning in my chair, a smirk pulls at my lips. "Then go. I do have my *own* cars. I can get myself to the house."

"Get up, Ari. I'm not in the mood for your games. Or would you prefer to slaughter me here?"

Something like hurt blossoms in my chest. I may not be nice to him, but how could he think I was still willing to kill him? I made it very clear I would do no such thing. That I would protect him and make sure I kept him safe the best I could. Yet this fucker throws it back in my face every chance he gets. I told Tucker because I thought he could help. That he could make this better.

"Fuck you, Adrian. Get out of my precinct."

He charges me before I can react, his body bowed over mine as my rolling chair presses back into the desk. My body follows suit to create as much space as I can between our faces. Adrian's warm breath coats my skin. My heart is racing in anticipation. A part of me hopes those firm lips brush mine. That he touches me at all. The muscles between my thighs pulsing with want.

His nose skims my neck, lips brushing my earlobe as he gives me orders. "I don't answer to *you*. I don't care who your parents are or if you're fucking an officer. Get out of this damn chair and let's go."

How dare he presume I'm sleeping with Oliver. Not that I wouldn't, but still. My hand draws back. The crack of my palm landing with enough force to snap his head to the side. Pink blossoming.

"Talk to me like that again Alexander, and I will have your balls next."

Pushing him aside, I grab my purse and stalk outside, right past his car. Straight to my apartment.

I'll drive my damn self.

Chapter Seventeen

Entering the safe house is like walking into the circus. Bodies everywhere. Many faces I don't recognize, but many that I do.

"Everyone downstairs," a voice calls. The masses stomp down to the basement, across the expansive room, and then down another flight of stairs hidden behind the wall.

I had no idea this was down here. Logically, I knew a house like this included a massive basement. There was just no reason to come down here yet.

Grave faces line the front of the room, Syriah James at the forefront. The leaders of the vampires, werewolves, warlocks, and witches, sirens, and animal shifters a feather's width behind her. The varying faces are only a small group of representatives. So many others exist in the world, gathered in the countries where their lore originated from. Oliver throws a small smile my way, earning a scowl from Adrian, as he catches me grinning back.

"Salvatore Danarius has been after us for a long time. We will take greater precautions moving forward. Luckily, with the holidays lingering close, we will be able to remove the young and those unable to defend themselves discreetly. Our human counterparts won't notice. In the meantime, we've come into some knowledge of Salvatore's current kill list. We already knew Adrian Alexander is one due to him being Ari, my daughter's target, but we've gathered other names now."

My mother's voice arches across the room. Commanding her audience, pulling them all in with curiosity. Their gazes shifting my way for mere seconds at the mention of my name.

A man with dark eyes and darker hair steps out of a group, gray peppering his beard and thick locks. "And how did you come upon this list?" His accent pronounced. The skepticism clear in his voice. Distrust a thick fog filling the room. We hold our breath, the illusion of oxygen being sucked from the room keeping us still.

"Bronson, bring him in." A warlock specialized in binding spells comes into view, with another man walking straight-legged in front of him. There are no cuffs, no visible bindings at all. The warlock's hands relaxed at his sides. Eyes focused on the back of the head of the pale-faced man in front of him. Clearly, it's his powers holding him in submission. The type of chains that are impossible to break.

"Mr. Pillnick, please tell us who you work for."

His neck twists as he grimaces. His only way of combating the order. He fights long and hard, sweat coating his brow and underarms, spreading as he continues to keep the words trapped behind his dry lips.

"If you will not talk, then we shall siphon your secrets from you."

With a wave of her hand, my mother calls for the man who questioned her. As he passes me, those black pupils widen, taking over the whites of his eyes, before shifting to a crystal blue so clear and vibrant they resemble sheets of ice. His fangs elongate, stabbing into the flesh along the column of the prisoner's neck, his scream vibrating through the room.

The slurp of blood being drunk from the prisoner quiets the room. The sharp metal tang — one I know so well from years of crime scenes and my own kills — permeates the space. A scent that never churned my stomach before, but does now. As his fangs slip free of their puncture wounds, the man's eyes roll back into his head, before his body crumbles to the ground, Bronson's binding magic no longer holding him upright.

"I have the answers we need," he announces, flicking his tongue to the corner of his mouth to clear the spot of blood smeared there.

"Council, please follow me to our meeting room." My mother orders her fellow leaders, followed by hushed words filtering through the room.

Like school children, a line follows Syriah single file, the vampire locking eyes with me as he passes. Those creepy orbs still glow brightly as if he's still hungry for more, sending a chill down my spine.

I'm startled by Oliver's hand on my shoulder. His gaze apologetic. He leads me out of the room and into another sequestered behind yet another wall. It's clearly a walkthrough with a door directly across from us leading to somewhere deep within the house. *How big is this place?*

"Why didn't you speak up?"

"About?" I'm confused about what I was supposed to say. What exactly was I going to contribute when everyone in the room oozed with the desire to rip me apart limb from limb? My mother made it clear I was a hitwoman, Adrian as my mark. Was that not enough? Did that not draw enough unwanted attention my way?

"The list. You had to have known."

I shouldn't be offended. Although Oliver has treated me with kindness and never with disdain, he harbors the same feelings as our kind. For the first time, it's clear in his eyes.

"Sal gives me one name at a time. I don't get a list. I've never had one." My words are a low growl. A warning. I shouldn't feel betrayed, but I do. To have Oliver look at me the way he did gut me.

"I'm sorry. I just... this is a lot. We have kept the phoenixes safe for a long time and then the attempt on your parents. Add you to the mix with Adrian." He shrugs, eyes downcast. "I had to ask."

I understand. I would be cautious of Ari Luxembohrg — no, James — too.

"It's fine." I brush it off.

I've got one foot toward the door when Oliver pulls me back. His large hand clasped at the back of my head. Our eyes lock, breathing ragged but synchronized just before his lips brush mine. A question. My answer is pulling him closer, consuming the taste of him like a starving woman. I wait for the butterflies to come. My insides to heat, but nothing happens as our lips dance against one another. That's not true for him, though, as his length hardens between us. Logically, I want nothing more than to want him.

The slam of the door against the wall draws us apart. Adrian's venomous stare and heaving chest to greet us.

"What the fuck are you doing?" His words directed solely at Oliver. As if I'm not even in the room.

In an instant Oliver's eyes go wide, pushing me away as if my touch burned him.

"What the hell?"

"I'm — I'm sorry," he stammers, making his way to the door at his back. "I didn't know." He throws a few more apologies before closing the door behind him. Leaving me alone with dark and stormy.

"What was that?" My hand gestures for the door before slapping against my thigh. "Are you that pathetic that you have to ruin everything for me? Why can't you leave me alone?"

I'm so frustrated I want to scream. Want to tear at my hair. All Adrian does is make my life miserable. Yet the burn in my belly I wanted with Oliver comes when I look at him. I stamp it down. I'll never want this pretentious asshole. He can burn in hell for all he puts me through. For the way he talks to me.

"It's law not to put your hands on another's Pair unless it's announced a Pairing won't happen."

I pause. *Shit. Shit. Shit.* I knew it was too good to be true. Things were too easy for me to catch a break with Oliver. Of course he has a Pair. Someone he should love instead of me. Continue the bloodlines and all that. Shame fills me. I may be reckless with my sexual activity, but I'm not a homewrecker. I'll apologize the first chance I get.

"I didn't know he..." I can't finish the sentence.

"Not him. *You*," Adrian growls before leaving the room the door slamming behind him.

Me?

Chapter Eighteen

The snow falls in thick flakes as I make my way into the lobby of Salvatore's building. My heart pounds in my chest. I don't want to do this.

The prep needed was grueling. After the council met I was called in. A rare occurrence. Even Adrian stated he's only been called into a council meeting a few times throughout his stint as Second.

They shared the list with me. The names were no surprise. Many have been on my radar for years. The mix of humans and paranormals nearly even. The council members filled me with information to feed to Salvatore.

I'll have to be convincing. No room for hesitation. Knowing now that Salvatore is a warlock, with power nearly rivaling my father's, the stakes are higher. The room to slip up, greater.

I'm escorted to the elevator, a customary procedure for Sal's visitors. The immaculate modern finishes scream of the wealth that lives in this building. Sal pays me well, but whereas those that live here pay cash, I'd be paying a mortgage. Just the same, the level of extravagance here is of no interest to me.

The elevator makes its quick, quiet climb to the penthouse suite atop the building. Floor ninety. Why would someone want to be this high up? There are only two escape options: the elevator and a hidden stairwell on the main level. Knowing Sal's truth, maybe he's not worried because he has flight abilities or some other random magic I know nothing about.

Mundane thoughts swirl through my consciousness. The insignificant things that cross my mind, but never deserve analysis. I only allow it now as a distraction from what I'm about to do. From the lies I am about to tell. Close enough to the truth that only a microscope could prove them irrefutably false.

As the doors slide open, I'm greeted by two security guards. Ones I usually see around, but not in his home. Everything about tonight feels off. Wrong. If it's a trap, I may make it out. My chances higher with Adrian, Tuck, Talia, Bronson, and a wolf-shifter named Lucas all crouched on the roof, waiting for any sign of distress from me.

Passing the guards, their scents permeate the air. Recognition of the twin werewolves now at my back. Guard dogs primed for attack.

"Ahhh, Ari. You've arrived."

Sal comes traipsing from the back of the condo with a goblet of wine in hand. He shimmers in the recessed lighting clad in a silk, gold suit with matching slippers. Usually, he's less ostentatious. One more detail that's not right. I will my breathing to slow. A silent prayer on repeat for the contents of my stomach not to make a sudden reappearance.

Keep it together, Ari.

"Drink?" he asks, swishing his hips to music only he can hear in his head. His pupils are pinpoints. He's taken something, but who knows what. Sal has never been secretive about the wild array of drugs he drowns his body in.

"Of course." If he's changing the course of our normal meetings, I will do the same. I don't take drinks at Sal's home. Business and pleasure don't mix. It's not a good look. "A bottle of beer if you have it."

He pauses, his rear facing me, slowly turning to smirk my way. "If I was going to poison you, it wouldn't matter what the drink comes in."

With that, he continues towards the kitchen area just around the corner and returns with a tumbler more than half full of dark amber liquid. "It's your favorite."

He hands it to me, followed by my tentative sip. Flagging me to sit, I do as he asks. Planted in the decorative chair across from where he sprawls on the table, one leg crossed overtop the other, I breathe even to keep my calm.

"Now, why don't you tell me how long you've been on to me?"

I pause my drink mid-air, ready to take another sip in hopes it steadies my nerves. *Fuck, this is bad. So, so bad.*

"I found out right after you assigned Adrian Alexander to me."

A knowing smirk. "It sure took you long enough to figure it out."

"So, can I assume you've known what I am since we met?"

"You're a smart one. That's why I picked you. It also helped that you're an orphan and had no ties to our world. That much easier to make you kill your own kind."

Flames flare beneath the barrier of my skin, my blood boiling. I'm pissed that Salvatore thought he could use me as an unknowing pawn in his game. I'm even angrier at myself for having to be told I was nothing more than that. That I couldn't see the signs for myself. Sal will pay. For the heartache and the attempt on my parents.

"I guess you still are, with your parents out of the picture." He takes a long gulp of his wine. "I am sorry about that." A smug note to his words.

I'm not an orphan. I never was.

"I didn't know them. It means nothing to me." My chin lifts a little higher. A show of nonchalance, even though my insides shatter at speaking that lie. Yet another pain point I will make him and his followers pay for.

"You have information for me, then?"

"I do."

I tell him everything. A word-for-word recount of the script I was handed. Only pausing when he asks questions. The dull tap of a finger on a tablet screen stills for a moment, the dog behind me grunting at my responses. I assume the conversation is being recorded as well, both audio and visual.

Fine by me. Let them search. Let them try to come for us. We're ready this time.

It takes me nearly an hour to get through it all, taking one last gulp of my bourbon, sporting my shit-eating grin.

"That's everything."

"Yes, well, thank you. Quite informative." The twitch of his brow makes me cross my legs to hide the shifting in my seat. *Is he doubting me?*

Eager to remove myself from Sal's sanctuary, I turn for the exit.

"One more thing," he calls after me, stopping me in my tracks. "Since Adrian is clearly out of the question for you now, I guess I'll need to hire someone else to dispatch of him." Not a question, but a statement.

A chill steals down my spine, mixing with the sweat pooling at my lower back. He knows I won't kill Adrian. Yet, there's one last card to play. "Salvatore, I am still in your employ. You choose what needs to be done."

A full smile spreads on his face. A sight so rare, bile rises up my throat. "Yes, I'll have someone else take care of him. Wouldn't want to break your little *bird* heart."

Falling for the bait, I bite. "Why would killing Adrian Alexander break my heart?"

A terrifying cackle escapes Sal before he slaps his thigh, heading into the heart of the condo. "You should ask him. Come back to me if his answer doesn't align with what I said."

The guards shuffle me to the elevator, the doors closing to the sound of Salvatore's boisterous laughter.

Chapter Nineteen

The knotting of my intestines steals my attention as I slide into the nondescript SUV beside Adrian. The weight of their stares nearly makes me look up. Sal's words crawling over one another in my head. I'm incensed by his insinuation that I couldn't do what needs to be done. There's nothing about Adrian that would make me change my mind about killing him if that was what I was still resigned to do. Not even being of my bloodline could stop me.

"Are you going to fill us in?" Tuck calls from the front passenger seat.

I hesitate, deciding what to tell them. It seemed as though Sal consumed what I fed him. That hunger in his eyes and that telling smirk pulling at the corner of his mouth as I relayed the truth I wanted him to hear.

What he said about me murdering Adrian doesn't add up, though. I have no deep-set feelings for him, only loyalty to my family. To my kind. If he disappeared, I would go about my life, not being taunted by him. Not wanting to crawl out of my skin because once again he gained the upper hand.

I can tell myself that story. Feed it to the pit of darkness deep inside me, but a small part of me knows it's not the truth. Knows that on some level I would miss Adrian and his broody stare. Or his ability to ruin any bit of fun or happiness for me. The way his eyebrow quirks, nearly touching that one tendril of hair that sometimes breaks free while we argue. What I would miss most, the way he looked at me when he caught Oliver and me tangled in the dim lights of that room. The way he sent him away and confessed what a betrayal it was to kiss someone else's Pair. Almost as if he was happy and angry, all at once there's someone out there just for me.

I tell the only truth my friends need to hear with a deep exhale. "Salvatore knows I won't kill Adrian. He's sending someone else."

If he could slide any further away from me, he would. Curling his enormous frame into the door. I've never seen Adrian show genuine fear. Never coiling into himself at the prospect of him being the next paranormal to meet their maker. No, Adrian Alexander, stands tall against it. Ignores it.

The rest of the drive back to the safe house was quiet. The residents of the upscale suburb had long since returned home and sequestered themselves indoors.

Hand poised on the handle of the door, Adrian's fingers wrap around my opposite wrist. "Walk with me." I give him a nod before hopping down to the curb.

Tuck remains, glare snapping between the two of us. That brotherly protectiveness radiating off him in waves. Before Adrian pulls me behind him, Tuck stops him, hand on his shoulder. "Tell. Her."

The words a whispered command. Not meant for me to hear. A warning from my brother to our Second. A tone only Tuck or my parents could get away with. I don't miss the shifting of Adrian's eyes from Tuck's face to mine. Or the way his muscles tense and shoulders rise to nearly touch the lobe of his ear. The press of his lips into a straight line. Resignation. A fight for defiance, but acceptance, too.

Tuck releases him, quick strides carrying him to the front door, where Talia waits. Adrian's grip on my hand doesn't loosen as we huddle through the cold and wind. He leads me around the side of the house, through the yard, and down to the beachfront at the very edge of the property.

"Are you going to tell me what Sal actually said to you about me?"

I ponder this for a long time. Knowing any rendition of bringing the words to life will sound ridiculous. "He said it would break my heart to kill you. That I should ask you why." His grip on my fingers tightens, but his focus remains on the crash of dark waves ahead. Lake Michigan becomes quite brutal with the wind, but it's my favorite scent, sound, and sight of all.

He's quiet next to me. Long enough that I'm convinced no answer will come, my mouth opening to speak, just as his lips collide with mine.

His warmth envelopes me, powerful arms pulling me close. His very presence consumes me, like the flames that I often let soar over my body when too much has bottled up inside. As his tongue slips across the seam of my lips, I let him in. The taste of him is one I don't think I could ever get enough of. Ever replace.

Oliver's kiss comes unbidden to my mind. His and every other man before. They've never felt like this. Their bodies never fit with mine the way Adrian does. His very presence like the air I need to breathe. The skies I need to soar through.

Just as suddenly as his lips found mine, he pulls away but keeps me close. Our foreheads pressed firmly together. I have more questions. I need more answers, but I can't breathe. The air won't flow into my lungs and back out as it should. That is what Adrian does to me. I've tried so hard to ignore it. To pretend I feel nothing for him other than disdain. But it's a lie. I knew that when Sal looked me in the eye, vowing to send someone else to take this man's life. To take him from me. Someone who isn't mine to have.

"Are you going to tell me?" I whisper. His fingers knotted in the wool of my overcoat just below my waist.

"Do you remember when I told you that you had a Pair?"

I nod. Our foreheads still pressed firmly together. Those bright eyes of his now wide-open focused on me. They've always been vivid, piercing orbs of green. Vibrant. But tonight it's almost as if they are glowing. As if a neon light shines behind them.

"It's okay, Adrian. I know we never see eye to eye. I know we hate —" He cuts off my words, his mouth molding to mine, before quickly pulling away.

"I could never hate you, Ari James. Not even if I tried. Not even if I wanted to. You're my Pair."

His words drift into the space surrounding us, a warm blanket making my heart stop.

My Pair.

Chapter Twenty

I do my best to avoid the safe house and Adrian for the next week. I may have admitted I want him — to myself. His truth about us being paired was a surprise, though now obvious. A small truth cradled in my hands with a question mark, so much heavier than the feathers I keep tucked in my worn leather jacket. I don't know how to handle it or accept it or deny it. Trying to fathom what I might actually want — to claim it for myself, absurd.

"Yo, Luxe," one of the burly cops next in line to make detective calls to me as I hustle down the hall, lost in my own thoughts. "That case you solved earlier this week. Seemed like a long shot. If you, uh, have some time..." He absentmindedly adjusts his gun belt. A nervous tic. "I would love to talk about what you saw. You know what the rest of us missed."

There's a genuine interest driving the upturn of his mouth. Many of the men pretend that I just get lucky. That I don't have actual skill as a homicide detective. That all I have to offer is my pretty face and the sway of my hips to get people to talk to me. Few take me as seriously as Chief Barlow and Gomez. This guy, Johnny — I think that's his name — definitely does. This is the first time he has asked me to review a dicier case, though.

"I'll meet you at the bar at seven. Have my drink ready." He flashes another wide smile before disappearing in the opposite direction. The decent ones like him make my love of what I do that much more important. Their acknowledgments make it that much more worth it.

"Ari, you ready to head out?" Gomez is perched on the side of my desk, his thick hair disheveled and damp.

"You look like a wet dog." Laughter bubbles around us. The guys making a show of me picking on Gomez. Typical. Truth is, I don't think I would survive this job without having him as my partner.

"Let's go." I grab my coat, balancing my coffee in one hand, wallet in the other, and keys between my teeth.

We're back on the James case today. No matter how many of our leads run cold, we're thrown back in with a new one. Our resolve to solve the case never wavers. Deep down, I know we won't get anywhere. I doubt we'll find who actually did this. Not for lack of trying or wanting that justice. Sal had someone try to murder my family and I want them dead.

Just two days ago, I was allowed to see my dad again. His body long ago sewn closed. The stitches faded and his skin healed. Oliver left me alone with him for hours, while I kept my ear to his cotton-covered chest, my eyes pressing shut with each heartbeat. He's still alive, suspended in time.

Bronson explained the magic that he had to have in his system. A custom potion to suspend life. Unfortunately, the magic needed to pull him back out is rare, and Bronson doesn't know it.

So I stayed there, ear-to-chest, and listened to his heartbeat so sedate I convinced myself I wouldn't hear it again. Fear that I wouldn't be able to help and I'd be powerless overwhelmed me. My only chance to meet the man I've been longing to know my entire life vaporized.

The lead we're following today is a former informant for the PD. His life of varied crimes and substance abuse, the anvil that we can dangle over his head to make him cooperate. A laundry list of charges we could still arrest him for should he go against us. Lamont Wills looks all of his forty years and then some. The graying strands through his thick dark beard, the ashen gray of his skin that should still be taught, sagging from the years of drugs polluting his system, coupled with the stints in prison and rehab.

"Lamont," I call his name as we pull into the alley where we know he loiters most afternoons.

"Gorgeous," he coos, a smile creasing my face. He may not be the type of company I would normally keep, but his jolly spirit still always lifts mine.

"Language," Gomez chides as he slams the car door behind him. Lamont's hands lift in a placating gesture before throwing me a wink.

"Tell me what you've got for me."

I slump onto the hood of the car, focusing solely on Lamont's face. Knowing Gomez won't take his focus off his hands. Lamont's always behaved, knowing his place in the world now. If they're not careful, the eyes will give them away. His hard years have worn on him; every emotion, every thought broadcasted on a big screen for my viewing pleasure. Perfect for me.

"There's a guy, Rolan. I don't know no last name. Dresses real suave-like. Shiny shoes. He was fucking with the ladies around here, bragging about all the people he been killing."

My teeth grind. Sal is getting sloppy. If this was one of his guys, he would be quite unhappy to hear he's running his mouth around town, even if they were just prostitutes. "He's a regular?"

"The last few months, yeah. Comes like clockwork. Every Friday night."

I nod in thanks, throw Lamont a hundred-dollar bill, and get back behind the wheel. Peeling out of the alley, I'm seething. The heat radiating from my body, making the air flowing through the vents nearly suffocate me.

"I know what you're thinking, and the answer is no."

Gomez knows me better than I wish he did. His intuition regarding my thoughts, irritating at best. A partnership that allows him to see right through me. No, never mind. He can't stop someone like me. Never could. Not a chance.

Chapter Twenty-One

Johnny's seated at the bar, his stool guarding the one in the corner I claimed as my own. It's embarrassing how predictable I've become over the years. The realization slapping me in the face with Adrian upending my life.

My phone was a non-stop vibration in my pocket on my walk here. Adrian clearly thought if he kept calling it would make me answer. I'm not ready to face *him* or *us* or *this*. You would think my avoidance tactics would have sent the message. Not for Adrian. A man who always gets what he wants. The question is, does he actually want me or is it just this pair thing keeping him attached?

"Hey Johnny," I pat his back as I round behind him, my other hand grabbing for my drink.

I've barely taken my first gulp before he dives right in. His analysis of the case rolls off his tongue as if practiced. The evidence he thought crucial and the pieces he knew I called out that everyone else didn't. I don't have to say much as he rifles through it all from memory, only referencing notes on his phone a few times when he's trying to remember specific dates or numbers. I'm thoroughly impressed by his preparation, nodding along with his assessment.

Once I've given him mine, the conversation drifts from work to funny stories about him growing up. How different he and his brothers are. His poor mother birthed six of them, each wildly distinct from the last.

It's nice to just sit and talk to someone. To not have the weight of two worlds on my shoulders for just a little while. Then I see him. His looming form filling the doorway, nostrils flared like a raging bull's.

Quick, long strides carry him toward me, all the light-hearted energy that had been billowing through me dissipates. Johnny doesn't notice, regaling about the time his brothers decided they were going to make water slides off the roof of their house.

"Is your phone suddenly not working?" Adrian breathes, the calm coating his words hiding the searing rage beneath. The bulging of his veins at his throat and across the backs of his hands gave it away. It's only as his fingers grip my biceps, pulling me to my feet, that Johnny steps in, attempting to block Adrian from me.

"My phone is fine." I jerk away from him, only causing myself more pain as his grip tightens.

"When I call, you answer. When I text, you better fucking answer." His words growled into my face. His jaw tight, lips pressed firmly together, but it's his eyes that hold his truth. The same anger doesn't live there; fear does. That glow that I swore I saw the other night, flashing.

"Adrian." My voice is soft. My touch even softer. "Tell me what's going on?"

"Ari?" Johnny questions, clearly not understanding what's happening here.

"It's fine, Johnny." My brain freezes, searching for a way to explain this man's hands on me. To explain his temper and his frustration directed only at me. "My." Gulp. "... boyfriend."

His glare darkens. His gaze drifting from Adrian's hand wrapped around my arm to his face.

"I don't care who he is." He squares up with Adrian as he says his peace. "You don't put your hands on a woman like that! Especially a cop."

Glowing emeralds never leave mine as he responds, "With all due respect, *kid*. You have no place telling me a damn thing. Ari, let's go."

With a small smile in Johnny's direction, I follow Adrian from the bar, down the block, and around the corner to his parked car. The moment the doors close, I'm in his face. The release of my anger and embarrassment a roaring assault. He takes it all. Something like shame shadowing his features.

"I was scared something happened to you."

"Scared?" The shock clear in my tone. "Of what?"

He tells me everything. The attack on the safe house. The message filtered out through the paranormal phone tree. Ten more bodies, various species sprawled out for anyone to find in the park. My fury cools as he pulls out onto the Chicago streets, navigating to an even more distant suburb I've never been to.

The sprawling land surrounding this house compliments the grandeur of the estate. The gap between residences so vast, a car is the only practical way to reach your neighbor's driveway. A couple of dozen cars line the street and triple that along the mile-long drive. Adrian leads the car through the wood line to the garage. The door well-placed at the side of the monstrosity.

There are bodies everywhere. Not just my kind, but all. I don't think I can sense emotions, but every bit of space is crowded with a mixture of them. Tumbling over each other, overwhelming my own ability to keep calm. Adrian pulls me close, shoving us through the throng until we find my mother in what must be a family room. Relief seeps into her features as she sees me, pulling me away from Adrian and into her embrace.

"What's going on... mom?"

I'd started using the term shortly after we met but still hesitate from time to time. It has never been a question of loving her. She's my mother. It's openly stating who she is that's hard. Voicing that single word still gives me pause.

"We'll explain everything soon." Her finger brushes my cheek before Adrian's arm is around me once more. "Give him a chance." She gives a small smile before being approached by a squat man, his nose pinched and angled like a goblin. I'm wondering if those exist, too.

"Luxe," a familiar voice bellows over the chorus of chatter. I turn to find Gomez coming towards me, his wife and children in tow. "Shit, I'm glad he found you."

Found me. What the hell is going on? Why is my partner here?

"Care to tell me why you're here?"

He smiles like he always does. That knowing look he gives me. "I thought for sure you'd have figured it out by now."

Searching my mind, I try to find the answers when it hits me.

"All this time... You're a werewolf."

His grin widens, showcasing canines I always thought were unnaturally large. "Wolf-shifter, actually." He shrugs. "Someone had to keep an eye on you."

"Have you known this whole time? Everything?"

He shakes his head, taking his baby girl from his wife. "The Salvatore part was news to me. I knew what you were when we met. Why do you think I requested to be your partner?"

Adrian grabs the little girl, her stubby arms reaching for him. Her tiny body even smaller against his. A lopsided, toothy grin spreads and her small chubby hands pull at his cheeks. "Thank you for always keeping her safe," he mumbles, his words garbled as those same little fingers pinch his lips together.

Gomez nods before pulling the little girl back to his hip.

"Everyone, I need your attention."

My mother may be a small woman, but nothing but quiet breaths fill the room as we all heed her command. A longing pulls at my chest. A need to make her proud. To learn from her. To be just like her someday.

Chapter Twenty-Two

The leaders gather behind my mother. Just as they had the last time we'd brought our different species together. Just as before, Syriah James stands just a hair's breadth ahead of them. I would expect the way we've gathered here, they would all stand in line together. But the formation says something more. My mother is the one they stand behind.

Pride and dread mix in my chest. It's an inspiring display. The way they look to the woman who birthed me for guidance, protection, and direction. Yet not understanding this small power move reminds me just how much I don't know and understand about our world. I'm in the dark despite being thrown in head-first months ago.

"Salvatore Danarius has declared war on all those who stand against him. He has matching numbers in his shadow, for those we have on our side. They have no boundaries, no cares for breaking the laws that govern our kind. We'll need to be prepared to loosen the reins we've confined ourselves to. It's the only way to ensure those of you in this room survive and support of our leadership remains in the end. Anyone who walks out of this room in opposition or betrays us in any way will be executed with prejudice."

There's no hesitation in my mother's words. The meaning permeates through the pores in our skin. Captivating us. Binding us to her without a second thought. Young, old, male, female, every eye stays focused only on her. No flinches, no outward signs of rebellion.

I flinch, though. Recoiling at her words. I shouldn't. For all the lives I've taken without remorse, without caring what it meant to anyone but Salvatore. I should be comfortable with the brutality, but I'm not. Somewhere along the way — finding my people — killing them became the one thing I'm not willing to do.

Listening to my mother continue her rallying speech, I know I will have to find the Ari I'd been before. It's clear some of us will die. Some of us will get cold feet and run to whoever is winning the war. Just as the thought clutches at my consciousness, my mother's navy blue eyes find mine. The same glow I've seen in Adrian's shines in hers. The flecks of silver a near clone to my own, bright and glaring.

Her piercing stare tells me everything. *It's time to stand tall, Ari.* It will be me fighting at her side. Leaving the mercy I've only recently found behind me once more.

"Tell us, where will we send those that can't fight?" A high-pitched male voice from the rear of the room calls. The quiver in his words revealing his fear to the entire room.

A man I've not seen before steps forward, a mesmerizing appeal to him. The lilt of his words draws me in, the comprehension of what he's saying not computing. Many of the others in the room lean into his enchantment as our bodies angle toward him. I can't explain it. Can't resist the pull to go to him.

A hand on my wrist holds me where I am. Adrian's grip keeping me at his side as if he knows, but can resist whatever it is drawing me forward. I don't fight it, as he laces his fingers through mine, my focus solely on the magical voice drifting over us all.

His plan is simple. Those needing to remain out of harm's way will be safe. Gomez's daughter whimpers behind me. So young and innocent. I assume they don't have control of their wolves yet. Their lack of being one with their wolves doing nothing to give them the protection they might need. Yet, behind their eyes lies the truth. They understand war.

Fear-driven questions are thrown at my mother and her counterpart. Fractions of the crowd listen intently, others begin conversations amongst themselves. Leaning in close to Adrian, inhaling his scent as I do, I ask what's been plaguing me. "Why is my mother speaking for everyone?"

His jaw twitches. Those muscles flaring to life the way they often do when I've asked him a question that wears on his nerves. He doesn't answer me as he grabs me by my arm, threatening to leave bruises along with the ones from earlier tonight. He throws a nod to someone to my right, our movement just quick enough that I don't see who it is.

Anxiety and anger roar from the crowd around us as we shove through. A door appears, seemingly out of nowhere. Adrian pulling it wide and shoving me down the stairs with a yelp. Heavy steps follow me. Two sets of them.

Adrian guides me through the dark before a light flickers to life. The fluorescent glow stings my eyes, despite only being in the dark for mere minutes. My frustration grows as I lock eyes with the three men in the room alongside me. Adrian is beyond pissed, his arms crossed at his chest and legs spread shoulder-width apart at my side. Tuck looks like he's about to shit himself and Oliver just flat-out confused.

"Someone better start talking. I'm tired of always being in the dark about something between you three."

"Well, Tucker," Adrian snarls. His glare pointed solely at my brother.

"Care to tell me why Ari is asking me why *her* mother is speaking for everyone?"

Tuck shuffles from foot to foot. His eyes stay trained on the floor, the uncomfortable shifting of his feet adding to the tension in the room. More truths kept from me.

"And you, t*raining officer*," Oliver's title thrown at him as a mockery. A clear lack of respect for how he's performed his duties. "You never mentioned how the hierarchy of our world works during those training sessions? Just didn't come up?" A shrug of his heavy shoulders.

Oliver's Adam's apple bobs before Tuck finally opens his mouth to speak. "Ari, well we are, um." Stuttering hesitance is a look I've never seen on my brother, one I am not accustomed to dealing with. Although we've gotten to know each other well, he's still practically a stranger. I recall my mom's fierce look, so I dig deep for old Ari and demand answers the way I always would have.

Charging forward, my hand pushes into Tuck's chest, backing him against the nearest pillar. "Talk," I grit through my teeth, baring them. The flames flicker beneath the surface, threatening to break free, but I hold them at bay.

"There's a hierarchy," Tuck begins. He goes through the structure. Regional, state, country, worldwide. The endless grappling for the balance of power that goes into creating each council. Constant scrutiny of the laws that bind us all, always at the forefront. Then he drops the bomb on me, the one I should have known. Something I should have understood long ago.

"Since before, many of us can remember, there's one true ruler. Head, leader, whatever term you want to use for all paranormals. A Phoenix. Always a Phoenix."

I can't breathe. The pieces come together in surprising clarity. Why it was such a problem for my parents to pair and wed. Why we have the protections we do. The wide birth everyone gives me. The respect my mother has from just breathing. How they all follow her blindly without a second thought, regardless of species.

"Our parents preside over every paranormal..." It's not a question as my eyes close, the weight of the truth sinking in. I'm not an anxious person. Not easily overwhelmed. I rarely give in to my emotions like others do. I'm rational. Detached. A bit of a daredevil. But I'm done.

I wanted to be part of it. This is just too much, too fast.

Pushing Tuck aside, I'm trudging up the stairs. Even my name on Adrian's lips doesn't make me look back. Not this time.

I pause at the top step. Hand poised on the doorknob. My last words drifting down into the space below me. "I can't do this. I can't continue to be kept in the dark and live amongst you like it's all fine."

They don't stop me as I leave the house. I have no car here. No way to get back to *my* home. I'm not even entirely sure where we are, so I just start walking. Letting the click of my heeled boots scrape against the concrete. When they finally ache, my feet swelling within my leather footwear, I finally call for an Uber, standing on the side of the road, alone.

The need to keep space from them is my only concern. My apartment isn't an option. The beach is my only place of solace. Ass planted in the freezing cold sand, with the wind whipping across Lake Michigan stinging my skin, I stare out into the darkness. Tears I haven't shed in over a decade finally fall. I'm not alone anymore, but I'm just as lonely as I've always been.

Chapter Twenty-Three

I don't rise until the sun does, finally making my way back to my apartment. My feet throb and my heart hurts, but I make it back in record time. Exhaustion pulls at my limbs, slowing my thoughts and movements, as I remove my clothes, piece by piece. A sudden cough stops me as I unbutton my slacks, fingers frozen mid-maneuver.

The frantic racing of my heart nearly knocks me into the far wall, my body instantly alight with flames. Even as a child, I could always control them. When I wanted to see how long it would take for my skin to burn, I called for the blazing inferno. I never had to master that control. Yet, my intruder destroyed that leash I never had to hold tight to.

Only when my mother rounds the corner into the entryway the threat diminished, do the flames stop arching for my ceiling, keeping close to my now exposed skin. My clothing burnt to gray ash at my feet.

Surprise raises her brows toward her perfectly straight bangs. Her petite mouth caught in an O. Likely, not from my nakedness, but the raging flames that nearly burnt the place to the ground.

It takes nearly twenty minutes of concentration for them to fade completely. Deep breaths and closed eyes. All the shit they teach you in meditation to center yourself. Something Gomez insisted I needed for my raging temper actually coming in handy for the first time. As my lids peel open, ready to face the woman who birthed me once more, a final stuttering breath escapes me.

"Have you always been able to do that?" she asks, her inflection skeptical. Questioning, as if it's not common to spontaneously ignite on a Tuesday. Like every phoenix doesn't crackle with licking flames of chaos.

"Since I first called on my phoenix," I admit.

She nods but makes no move to come toward me. Taking that as my one chance to escape, I slip down the hall into the comfort of my bedroom.

Sunlight beams brightly through the floor-to-ceiling windows. Its warmth staunching the chill that sunk into my bones from my night by the water. Once dressed, I join her again, nestling into the couch across from her.

The little girl in me curls in on herself. Legs crisscrossed, despite my knees begging me to choose any other position, a pillow nestled in my lap, so I have something to hold on to. A shield I'd never need with Syriah, but comforts me just the same.

"Why are you staring at me like that?"

"Curiosity." Her soothing voice drifts over me as it often does when we have these moments alone. I wish I had more of them. If our time together is short-lived, I want to keep the little pieces of her. When you've lost everything, you learn to grasp onto the little bits that are most precious when you can.

Pulling the oversize sleeves of my sweatshirt over my hands — mostly to hide the tremble — I wait for her to say more. The silence stretching between us seemingly endless.

"Why?" I whisper.

"Fire magic isn't common."

Without thinking, my head tilts to the side, taking in her statement. *Fire magic.* It never occurred to me the flames weren't part of being a Phoenix. The commissioned art in the texts always shows the birds in flames. Although, they're referenced at times of rebirth. Why would I think we could summon that gift anytime like we could our inner birds?

"Can you?"

She shakes her head, a small smile pulling at the corners of her lips. "Your father has fire magic. Rare these days, but it was the dominant element of his bloodline. When we first met, he set himself on fire, thinking it would impress me." A distant chuckle bubbles past her lips as she fiddles with the thin chain of the necklace I'd noticed before, but never asked about. Her eyes drift as she gets lost in the memory of her and him. Love shining bright behind them.

I want that someday.

"I figured we all caught on fire at will." The statement sounds ridiculous as I say it out loud.

She's quick to come sit next to me, pulling me into her side. I let her, needing the physical contact. The desire for someone else's touch usually found in the beds of random men. A pastime no longer existent since diving into my double life. No time. No energy. No interest.

"Mom," the term finally slipping from me with ease. Her hum in response, chin pressed to the top of my head, is reassuring, encouraging me to go on. "Did you know Adrian was my Pair?"

"I did. Likely before he did."

"What if I'm not sure I want him?"

My voice is small. That little girl staying present. The teenager who wanted her mother there to guide her through those days of liking boys driving the knotting of my hands in my lap. The many questions I would have asked. *What do I do? How do I act? How will I know?* Whitney Houston's lyrics playing on repeat in my head.

A burly laugh vibrates from her chest. A laugh she's never shared with me, but I secretly love. "Oh sweetheart, if you even remotely thought that was the truth, you wouldn't be asking me." Her hand smooths the wild waves from my face. "We have more important things to discuss."

I sit up, looking directly into her matching eyes. The color I've studied for years. Memorizing every nuance, so when I saw their match, I would know it instantly. I would know who my family was.

"I should have been the one to tell you how important our family is. It should never have been something I allowed someone else to do for me. I didn't want to push you. You and Tucker had already formed such a bond. I thought it would be easier coming from him." Her hand brushes my cheek and under my chin.

"Now you know, though. As a Phoenix, they chose us to lead. When a Phoenix dies, a new one must take their place."

"We don't die though." Confusion clear in my tone. I'd studied it. Searched every book, every website. Consulted every expert. I mean, we die — eventually — but not at random.

"We do. Mythology is just that. The tales of our kind are mostly true. We have two ways to die. Choice and penetration with a very specific metal. It nulls our regeneration powers. Instead of being reborn from the ashes, the ashes will be all that remains if the rebirth process begins." Choice is the version printed in the tomes of textbooks lining my shelf.

My eyes close. The gun Salvatore gifted me. Equipped with bullets only he could supply. He'd always told me to use that when in doubt. For the times when "usual" methods for murder didn't do the trick. Now I understand why.

"Is it the same effect on other supernaturals?"

"Absolutely." She gives a small twitch of a smile before frowning. "For most, death comes as easy as it would for a human."

It all makes so much sense. The privilege of having a Phoenix rule our world of make-believe. Why others look to us. We're nearly invincible. The closest thing to true immortality. A way to ensure continuity through centuries. My brain aches with the sheer amount of information I've gathered these past few months. My world being turned upside down.

A knock at the door steals the moment. "Ah, breakfast." My mother laughs, driving her small fists into the cushions to hoist herself from the sofa. She reemerges, balancing several bags with the Yolk logo and multiple drinks. "Now, I know you like to eat the way I do, so let's dig in while I answer any questions you have."

That's what we do. Gobbling down bacon, eggs, potatoes, pancakes, coffee, and orange juice. I'm grateful for picking such loose clothing as my belly distends from my indulgent intake of carbs and meat. I'm not a small woman; my mother is. But we just ate enough for six men.

Head resting in her lap, we laugh and talk, her fingers combing through my tangled strands, the tips brushing against my scalp soothing me.

The loneliness I felt last night abates, a feeling like hope blossoming in my chest. Resolution in my gut. Decidedness in my mind. I may not have known this woman for long, but she is my mother and she loves me.

My counterparts are doing what they can to fight for an undisturbed existence. For happiness. She loves them too. I would do anything she asked of me to protect that. To keep her and Tuck and my dad safe. To protect Adrian.

He's weaseled his way into my heart. I may accept the truth in our bond, but I don't know how to make that commitment to him. I have never made any sort of emotional pledge to anyone but Gomez and me. Gomez, so he makes it home to his beautiful family every night and for me to be the strongest woman alive. How do I give the man that makes me see red another piece of myself?

A tomorrow problem if I ever heard one.

Chapter Twenty-Four

By the time I wake, the living room is draped in darkness. My tired body still curled into a protective ball. At some point my mother left, leaving me in the exact spot I fell asleep in. A sticky note on the coffee table explains it all. Her need to return to one of the safe houses, so she's properly guarded.

I know where she'll go first. Back to my father's side. Like ships passing in the night, we've caught one another coming and going from his room. The sense of longing pulling at her angelic features. I miss him too. A man I've never met.

Stretching with a loud groan, I shuffle to my room in search of my phone. Fortunately, I'd dropped my coat on the floor when I heard my mom cough earlier, so it didn't burn too. Otherwise, I'd be scraping melted metal from my hardwood floors tonight. Not something I want to do again. It is not cheap replacing three random floorboards.

There are a series of text message notifications. Several from Tuck demanding I call him, along with five missed calls from him.

Straight to voicemail. *He'll get back to me.*

There are a few GIFs from Gomez and the guys. A practice that's become common amongst us detectives. We see such horrible things every day. We all need to lighten the mood sometimes. To remember how to laugh and let go of the tension that coils our shoulders and knots our insides.

I'm surprised there's not a peep from Adrian. I expected his overbearing alpha-hole personality to come shining through after he told me the truth about us. Nothing, though. I need to talk to him. Lay down ground rules for us to operate by. I need time to figure it out. I'd be a liar if I said I'm not overwhelmed with everything. Adding in a fated mate or some shit is more than I can manage. I can definitely do without that cherry on top.

Donning a pair of black skinny jeans, a fitted tee, and a leather jacket, I stalk down to the garage. Normally, I would take a walk. Stretch my legs. The only exercise I ever gave my bird. But tonight there's a tension in the air. The unknown lurks in the shadows. A weight hanging over us all waiting to drop. Hopping into my SUV, I've only just started the ignition when Salvatore's name pops up on the caller ID.

"Hello?" The lone word a question for the first time. After our last encounter, I hadn't expected to hear from him again so soon. I knew in time the taunts would come. The attempts on Adrian's life, too. Something I refuse to let happen. I'm not in love with the asshat by any means, just the same, I can't imagine a world without him. Not anymore.

"I have a job for you."

Ice shards fill my gut. It can't be Adrian he's asking me for. He already knew. Knew, I wouldn't kill him for any amount of money. How he knew the man is my Pair, is beyond me, but I can't afford to underestimate Salvatore.

No, the piercing fear that has me clutching the steering wheel so tight I may pull it from the dash is because I don't want to hear the name of the next paranormal he wants me to murder. My kind, a stepping stone for him to have power that was never his.

"Who?" The faintest quake in my voice. One I hope Sal misses thanks to the car speaker and the rush of the wind from the open window. It's entirely too hot in here and if I catch on fire again, it's going to be a bigger problem than showing mom my birthday suit this morning.

"The info's been sent. You have five days."

The line goes dead. The tires rotating against the pavement are the only addition to the soundtrack of my erratic breathing. Two months ago, I wouldn't have blinked at a spontaneous call from Salvatore, asking me to murder some unsuspecting someone. I would have quirked a grin at the dollar amount wired to my bank account. The pep in my step so bouncy you'd think I was a kid on Christmas.

Not tonight, though. As I pull to the curb in front of Adrian's corner lot, my heart hurts. Panic floods me. Sadness beckons to pull me under the waves threatening to drown me. How many more will I take out of this world so I can keep living in it without one of Salvatore's bullets through my chest?

I've never questioned an assignment. Not until Adrian. Not until immersing myself into a world I wasn't sure existed.

Cutting the engine, the neighborhood around me is quiet. It's relatively early in the evening. I would expect soccer moms still strolling the block, walking their golden retrievers, kids running in the park, but there is no one around. Most of the houses have lights on. *The Brady Bunch* families never passing the sheer curtains they insist on for decor. The lack of opacity as if they wanted to expose their entire lives to their neighbors' nosy whims. Not me. Blackout curtains only.

Adrian's doorbell chimes like any other. The silence from behind it sends a chill up my spine. He should be home. There's nothing going on at the safe houses tonight. I checked my emails before I left. I ring again before my fist wraps against the door. A low creak as it drifts open with the second *tap* of my knuckles.

Deep breath.

This is the stuff of movies. The moments we yell at the screen for the actors to run. But I don't run. I've always bolted toward danger. Even when every fiber of my being told me not to. When logic encouraged me to go the other way. Drawing my gun from the holster at my hip, knees bent into a crouch, I push the door open further. My boots make the slightest tap against the hardwood floors. Otherwise silence.

Eyes wide, I take in the space. Hurricane Katrina must have swept through. Every inch of fabric shredded. Every piece of art shorn apart. Table legs splintered as if heavy bodies crashed into them. Floorboards scraped and lunging upward. Boulder-sized holes in the walls, the railing of the stairwell hanging at a precarious angle.

I know better than to call out. To draw attention to someone stumbling upon the scene. I have no idea if I'm here alone. The one thing my phoenix isn't good for. Easing the door closed behind me, the soft click signifying it's in place, I bolt it shut. Yet another dumb move. But if someone else is still here, I want them trapped with me. No easy escape for the criminal I'll steal a last breath from. They won't make it out. I only hope that Adrian wasn't here when this happened. That he is safe.

I don't pray. Not until now. For Adrian. For all of us.

Slowly, I creep my way through the entire main level, only releasing the breath I was holding when I circle back to the entryway. The culprits made a point of destroying as much as possible. No surface or item left untarnished.

Staying along the edge of the stairs closest to the wall, so as not to step on any areas that may creak, I make my way up to the second story.

In movies, cops always keep their guns pointed down. Not me. Mine stays high, left arm extended, and ready to take my shot. I've been in too many situations where those seconds are precious. Moments you won't get back if you lose them. The milliseconds that add up to your death versus theirs.

Much like the downstairs, they left the rooms in complete shambles. I've never been up here, but it's obvious these rooms were decorated similarly to the downstairs. Adrian's delicate balance between modern and historical. There's none of it left now. Only a disaster that will have to be cleaned. Hell, he might have to gut the damn place to get it back to what it once was.

I know I've come to the master bedroom as the scent of him fills my nostrils. What was once a grand king-size bed now topples to its side, as if its legs gave out and couldn't stay standing for another second. Nearly three-quarters up the wall, gashes tear into the paint and drywall. Slashes that could only come from massive claws. Nothing human did that. My throat suddenly goes dry, my gun arm dropping just a fraction for the first time I can remember.

Adrian, where are you?

Just as I back out of the room, confident there's no one left here with me, I'm grabbed from behind. A muscular arm strapped across my stomach, trapping my shooting arm, with the other hand clasped tightly over my mouth. There's no time to scream. No time to react, as I'm dragged backward, disappearing into the wall just outside the bedroom door.

Only once we've slunk so far into the darkness, there's no telling how far we've gone, does the man let me go. My breathing ragged huffs stealing the quiet around us.

A phone flashlight illuminates the empty space between us.

A sob escapes me. Genuine tears break free as I wrap my arms around his neck.

Maybe, just maybe, prayer works.

Chapter Twenty-Five

I swear I'm living in Hollywood tonight. I do my best to step where Adrian steps, to keep my body angled just as his is, as he leads me through winding tunnels and hallways hidden inside his house. Who the fuck has something like this?

People that are like me do. Paranormals that are high-ranking. Ones that have to stay alive to protect our species.

It seems like hours before the cool breeze sweeps across my flushed cheeks, having just climbed out of a hidden window that sits just above the grass. It blends perfectly with the exterior of the house. Camouflaged so there's no proof it's a window from outdoors. From the inside, the view is the same as any other pane of glass. I may be nerding out just a bit about it.

Adrian takes my hand, leading me from his backyard to one of his neighbors through a bundle of bushes that are definitely just for aesthetics. The damn thorns hurt like a bitch, cutting into my thighs, hands, and jacket. Just another set of clothing ruined today. We slink from shadow to shadow, keeping ourselves hidden until he clicks the keyless fob for an unassuming silver Honda, tucked into an alley several blocks away.

Before he can drive off, I throw my arms around him again. Pulling him into me. He holds me back this time, inhaling deeply. A calmness finally starts to settle, knowing he's safe, for now. But this isn't over. It's just the beginning.

Salvatore had sent beasts after my man tonight, intending to kill him, all because I refused to. Sal will keep sending his band of murderers after him. He won't stop until Adrian's heart does.

Unless... A dark seed takes root.

"I'm going to kill Salvatore Danarius."

Adrian lets me go, tucking a wave behind my ear.

"We're going to talk later. We need to go."

Reaching across me, he pulls the seat belt into place, the satisfying *click* his cue to fasten his own. As if there wasn't an assassination attempt on him tonight, he leisurely takes us from the city.

We're well into the suburbs when he finally stops at a Target. He remains mute as we shuffle through the store, tossing food, clothing, toiletries, and a few books in the cart he pushes. No one would suspect a thing. Humans likely only think movie characters go into hiding. Not the average suburban-looking couple idling next to them at checkout.

Nearly five hundred dollars later, Adrian loads everything into the trunk before driving away again. It's another hour before he pulls into another suburban neighborhood. These houses are reminders of historic colonial homes tucked away and forgotten. They've been well maintained, but it's obvious they've aged with time.

The car pulls into the drive of a white-sided home, the worst looking one on the long street of packed houses. The garage door rises and then closes snugly behind us, leaving us in pitch-black darkness.

We're quiet as we move the bags from the trunk. My temper threatening to bubble over. The urge to slam him into the wall and demand answers, all-consuming. I remain calm, for both our sakes.

The inside of the house is nothing like the outside. Decorated a bit more like a bachelor pad with leather couches and an outdated coffee table. Curtains that clearly weren't purchased to match the house, but block out the outside world. It's simple but clean. Clearly looked after, but not lived in.

"Are you going to tell me what's going on?" The question tumbles from my lips before I can stop it. My impatience wearing thin at once again being kept at arm's length.

He's frozen, bent at the waist, arm extended, ready to place the orange juice into the door of the fridge. Moments pass where he stays in that very position before he finally gingerly places the juice in its spot, slowly closing the door. Hands braced against the edges of the unit, his back muscles roll beneath his shirt. Fingers curled around the metal, his breathing deep as if trying to control himself.

When he spins to face me, his eyes are glowing brighter than I've ever seen. The luminescence makes me take a step back as he stalks toward me. *Step. Step. Click. Click. Step.* Until my back collides with the counter.

"Ari," he groans.

I thought it was vampires that moved with grace and speed. Apparently so does Adrian Alexander. He's hoisted me onto the counter, his narrow hips positioned between my spread legs, lips pressed firmly against my own. For the first time, I do nothing to fight my pull toward him. Whether it's the pairing or just my attraction to him growing is unclear. Still, it's the question that weasels its way into my thoughts nearly every second of every day.

My insides heat. A temperature so scorching, I crack an eye to be sure I didn't catch fire. Hands in my hair and braced on my cheek, he devours me. I'm arched into him, hand fisted in his shirt between us, desperate for more. Damn near dying to have every inch of him pressed against me. Just as I shift forward, wrapping my legs around him, I feel him there. Between my thighs. Poised. Ready. Rock solid. I want him to take me. Right here on this old granite countertop.

The streak of his tongue across the seam of my mouth distracts me from his hand traveling beneath my top, lithe fingers yanking down the cups of my bra to expose me to his touch.

A moan escapes as he bites my taut nipple through my t-shirt, nudging me toward his eager mouth.

"Adrian," his name a breathy moan. A plea.

His lips curve across my neck just after letting go of my nipple. "Don't." *Nip.* "Say." *Squeeze.* "My." *Kiss.* "Name." *Pull.* "Like." Another brush of lips before nipping my flesh, eliciting a whimper. "That."

A warning. One I am too frantic and horny to abide by. Fighting against his hold on my hair and teeth at my collarbone, I work his shirt free of him. It's not the first time I've seen Adrian without one. There's a lot of working out that goes on at the safe houses, but to feel him up close is an entirely unique version of sensory overload. To run my fingertips over the taut flesh of his abdomen. The muscles rippling and flexing under my touch.

"Fuck." *Kiss.* "Me."

"No." As if cold water had been splashed on us, he steps away. The connection instantly gone, while the moisture in my panties still lingers behind.

I should be upset about being rejected when he so clearly wanted me only moments ago. But I'm pissed. A raging fire building within.

Deep Breath.

Breathe, Ari.

Breathe, goddammit.

Prying my eyes open once more, my mouth presses into a straight line. He leans against the fridge, his frown deepening as if I'm the one who rejected him. *That's rich.*

"What the hell is wrong with you? You won't talk to me. You kidnap me to wherever this is. Get me all hot and bothered and then won't even man up and screw me."

With a heavy sigh, he runs his hands through this hair before meeting my stare again. His eyes are still glowing. Casting a spray of light across his thick lashes. The piercing vibrancy making me shift in my spot on the counter.

He's slow to come toward me again. Slipping his shirt back into place as he does. Hands gripping each thigh, he spreads my legs once more shifting to stand between them. I do my best to resist his pull, but he's stronger. *Dammit.*

"Ari. Baby." Bright eyes meet mine. "I will give you anything in this world but that. Not until I know you... want... it."

He is completely daft. Of course, I wanted sex with a hot guy. My eye twitches, knowing how out of control my libido is right now. All the stress of the past few months compiling every day.

"Fine." I push him away, hopping from the counter. "At least tell me what the hell happened tonight."

He recounts his evening, never turning to face me as does. He'd been prepared knowing an attack was coming. He knew what it would mean for me to kill him. That knowledge of him being my Pair the secret everyone kept from me for who knows how long.

Even if I chose not to accept him and the bond. Even if I hated him. A small sliver of me would die with him. For the rest of my life, that loss would fester like an infection. It's what my mom described as a bond similar to the mates werewolves and vampires experience.

Sal sent the whole gambit after him tonight. Two wolf-shifters, a hitman, a Witch so dark, even the veins lining her body appear black, and a phoenix — one Adrian thought died hundreds of years ago.

"Wait, how old are you?"

He gives me a wry look, shifting the steaks around in the pan. The sizzle is as intoxicating as the scent. I'm nearly salivating, ready to ingest the filet mignons we purchased and the garlic mashed potatoes. I honestly have no idea how I'm not on my *600-lb Life* with the way I can consume calories.

"Two hundred and seventy-four."

With a giggle, I gain his attention again. His eyebrow cocking at the girlish sound. "Ew, I'm supposed to marry an old man. Gross."

He lunges forward then. Peppering my face in kisses as I squeal to get away from him. Really, I don't want to, though. These are those moments you read about in romantic comedies, the ones you hope for someday. It almost makes me believe I might be happy with him in the distant future. That there's more to his icy demeanor than he lets on. I want to get to know him.

That's new.

Just as quickly as he reached for me, he refocuses on cooking. His story of tonight continues. It's almost too much listening to this detailed recap of the night. Slipping between the walls, to keep watch of what was happening to his home. His possessions. The sound of Salvatore's snarl through speakerphone when they didn't find him there.

Our meal passes with comfortable conversation, our choice topics having nothing to do with the situations we've found ourselves in. I'm surprised by how easy it is with him. Just the two of us tucked away in this little house.

As we prepare for bed, he shows me to a guest room, three doors down from his. It's decorated much the same as the rest of the house. So different from his home. There are no pictures or paintings of any sort on the walls. The shelves and dresser are sprinkled with knickknacks reminiscent of his life. Accumulating here over the years.

An old house like this is bound to creak at night. Its bones straining against the raging elements outside. Determined to make the simplest sounds come across eerie and ominous. It's not long before the anxiety of sleeping alone, in an unfamiliar space, forces me from my bed.

The door groans as I tiptoe into Adrian's room. I planned to sneak in and just slip under the comforter without him knowing, but his voice startles me as I lift the edge.

"What are you doing here?"

On a swallow, I answer, "With everything going on, I just..." My voice trails off, not wanting to admit I was terrified tonight. Scared of losing him. Petrified to let him out of my sight. The spike of adrenaline at every shadow or noise, fear that Sal has found him and his luck won't hold next time.

Without needing to hear the rest, he lifts the blue duvet, cocking his head to signal me to climb in. I do. Lying flat on my back. Stiff as a board. He curls into me, his head on my shoulder, arm wrapped around my waist.

"Sleep. I've got you."

My heart flutters. Just a little.

Chapter Twenty-Six

Brushing grazes trace the feathers inked across my back, pulling me from the most glorious sleep I've had in quite some time. With a heavy sigh, last night comes back into sharp focus: The pile of rubble that now makes up Adrian's home. Crippling fear nearly stopped me in my tracks at the thought of losing him. A loss I can't handle. Our escape to yet another safe house hidden in plain sight. His silent welcome into bed beside him — whether he knew my reasons for coming to it or not. It was too much to bear alone.

I knew the moment we arrived, this house was different. A space personal for Adrian. A private sanctuary.

"It's gorgeous," he breathes behind me. Warmth brushes against my tangled hair and bare shoulder. A shudder running through my body at his inspection.

My muscles tense and shift as he continues to explore the exposed skin. The tank top I'm wearing is by no means risque. It's cut revealing enough of my back and the entirety of the rear side of my arms for him to ogle. Tuck once asked me about the crimson, tiger, and marigold feathers that line the back of my arms. My own representation of my wings. I'd told him the truth. How having the array of feathers etched onto my skin made me feel just a bit less alone in this world.

"Are you going to tell me about it?" Firm lips press against my exposed shoulder, making me wiggle, keeping my head turned away from him.

Problem one: my morning dragon breath. The primary reason, to keep him from catching the tears pooling behind my eyes at his fingering and questioning. That small piece of me that was my curated "family" since I turned eighteen and had it done.

"No."

He shifts behind me, his bare chest pressing against my back. "I want to see the whole thing."

With a shrug, I shuffle to my knees, pulling the tank over my head, balling it into my fist. I don't bother to cover myself, before lying face down, head rotated in the opposite direction. I know the moment he spots the single cobalt and gold feather in the center of my back, nestled below where the neck of my bird's feathers branch out in a brilliant spread of burnt orange and marigolds. He sucks in a breath, stealing all the oxygen in the room for himself.

There's no denying the feather is a near-perfect match to the one of his I found in his damp grass months ago. What I won't tell him is he's the exact phoenix I imagined as a child. The one I would find someday and have little Firebird babies of our own with. The answer to my loneliness. After meeting him and seeing his bird up close, it made me wonder if I'd ever met him — even for the briefest of moments as an infant — before I was torn away from my parents.

Even if I had, newborn me wouldn't have a memory of him. It's more likely the Pairing between us brought images of him to my dreams. A way to tell me I wasn't alone. The surety that my soul matched that of another Phoenix.

Throughout my adolescence and even into adulthood, I dreamt of him. Now he's real. He's here, stroking intentional fingers down my spine tracing the perimeter of the feather that belongs to him.

"Don't ask," I groan, shoving my face into the pillow.

"It's mine." His voice is soft. Quiet. Gentler than I've ever heard. It's enough to make me turn to look at him. His gaze still trained on that single spot. The glow that always seems to happen around me, blinding. Luminescent.

"Adrian, I really don't want to talk about it. Or my tattoo. I want to..."

His eyes snap up to mine. Locking me in place.

I want to be with you.

I want us to be safe. You. Me. My family. All of us.

I want to stay locked in this bubble with you, where you aren't an asshole.

My cowardice keeps me from allowing myself to recite the list out loud. Releasing my tank, I keep my back to him, shifting it back into place. My only guard of protection. From me. Him. Both, maybe.

"I want to find Salvatore. What's our next move?"

There's no point in turning around. I cannot bear to see that icy glare he wears like a coat of armor.

"You think you can just walk up to his front door and shoot him? You're more naïve than you pretend not to be."

"Fuck you, Adrian." The cop in me sits up straight, shooting invisible daggers. The hitwoman roars to life. "I've known Sal a long time —"

"Not longer than I have," he grunts, throwing the comforter aside as if it personally offended him.

"Sorry, I'm not sorry for wanting to protect my family and others like us from being slaughtered." The words a violent hiss as I launch myself from the mattress.

The door handle cracking against the wall should be enough to stop me in my tracks as I stalk away from him. My sure steps taking me back to the room he declared as mine the night before. I need space from... him.

Who does he think he is? How dare he think he can tell me what to do. I'm not naïve. I know how to kill, even if I don't understand this underworld the way he does. It's what Sal groomed me to do for years now. Ruthless assassin. No remorse.

That was true enough, not long ago. Except, now, the guilt has finally found me. My family falling back into my life, changing things. The meaning of Adrian's massive hand around my throat altering my internal compass.

"Have you calmed down now?"

Of course, he followed me. His arms cross his bare chest, shoulder resting against the doorframe, that smug smirk pulling at those firm lips. His legs crossed at the ankle, revealing just how nonplussed he was by my tantrum.

"Adrian," I breathe, running my fingers through my hair. "I can't do this with you."

I hadn't planned on doing this now. Yes, it's the reason I sought him out last night, but all at once my chest is tight. I'm suddenly unsure. But if I don't say everything I'm keeping deadbolted inside, I won't be able to do what I need to do with Sal.

He takes two steps toward me. I take three in retreat. My hands raise in front of me as if they will keep him at a distance. Nothing keeps Adrian Alexander from getting what he wants.

"I can't do this with you," I repeat. "I can't be with you. I can't do this bickering married couple thing we do. I know we're paired and I'm not saying no to that, but I can't be worried about you and do what I need to do. I can't have you on my mind constantly distracting me. I don't know how to commit myself to someone else, but somehow, without my permission, my heart and body have decided for me. My mind though..." I release a breath, as he moves close enough that only a sliver of air can pass between our torsos, lifting my chin to meet his gaze. "My mind is still in control."

The words tumbled free before I settled on what the sentences would be. My unfiltered feelings released into the universe. Stepping out of his hold, I round up clean clothing from the small loveseat.

"Is this because I wouldn't have sex with you?"

His words stop me mid-step. I'd nearly forgotten he rejected me last night. The hurt and embarrassment wash over me anew. Shallow breaths filter past my lips as I pivot to face him.

"No. Contrary to what you might believe, I can live without your dick. This is about protecting the people I love and care about. Sorry, you made the list." More of that honesty, I should have kept locked away.

With a shrug, I make a second attempt to retreat into the adjoining bathroom. His movements stopping mine in the same breath, turning me to face him. A firm grip on the back of my neck. A squeeze. His hold enough to force my face up to his as he captures my mouth in a possessive kiss.

He was supposed to walk away. He was supposed to understand, but instead, he's here, with his body pressed to mine as he ignites my internal flames.

It's only seconds before the clothing gripped in my hands is forgotten, my fingers releasing them to hold on to his warm sides instead.

Milliseconds more before we fall to a heap on the mattress. The bedding the exact way I left it the night before. Barely ruffled.

His lips and hands explore my body. Devouring me, learning my curves as I pant beneath him. The word *hypocrite* ricochets through my head. Only moments ago, I'd told him sex wasn't something I needed from him. Yet, here we are, rolling in a frenzied heap, with our clothes being the only barrier between our heated skin.

His hardened length presses between my legs, the sleep shorts doing nothing to guard me against the nudge of his head. There's no stopping the roll of my hips forward. A need to get impossibly closer. To feel him inside me.

I can't. I won't cave. I just said I wouldn't.

"Adrian."

He hums against the pulse of my neck.

"Adrian." My tone more urgent this time.

He finally pulls back to look at me. "I told you I won't give you that, but there are plenty of other things I can give you."

A wicked gleam morphs his emerald irises into dancing embers of green and gold.

Fingers looped into the waistband of my shorts, he slides them down my thighs, pulling my panties along with them. There are many women who do the whole commando thing, but it always makes me cringe. The sole reason I couldn't do ballet as a kid. They expected no undies under the tights and leotards.

No. Thank you!

The small memory quickly fades as the extended inhale from him at the apex of my thighs pulls me back to the present. *Well, that's a first.* He does it again, before running a finger down my slick folds. The same precision and ease he trailed the feathers on my back this morning carried into this moment.

My body writhes against his touch, minimal as it is. I want to be closer to him. I want more. As if he can read my mind, firm lips pull at my bud, suckling it like a sweet fruit, before dragging his teeth, making my nerves shoot electric bolts into my lower belly.

His exploration continues, slow and torturous. There's no rush as he licks, sucks, and tastes all of me, the torrent of an orgasm building within me.

"Adrian." His name a huffing breath, as my fingers sink into his hair.

"Do it," he challenges. His breath tickles my sensitive flesh before his tongue pierces me.

Sensations I've never felt soar through me. With each passing second, the need to keep my fire at bay increases. With another expert flick of his tongue, my release coats his mouth. His lips. His face glistening with the evidence of what he does to me. It's not my release dripping down his cheek that catches my eye, though. It's the carefree smile. All his pristine white teeth showing, the corners of his eyes crinkling.

Did I just make Adrian Alexander... happy?

Chapter Twenty-Seven

It takes two beers, thirty chicken wings, and five episodes of *Criminal Minds* for Adrian to finally fall asleep on the couch. It's my only chance. He'd have a conniption if he knew what I actually had planned. After hours of him pleasuring me every which way — minus actually having sex with me — the plan came to me. My resolve hardened. My determination locked in.

I may have become an incapable *human* these last few months, but I've always handled life on my own. It was me who forged the badass homicide detective I am today. Much of it was me that became the killing machine Sal needed so badly. With Oliver's and my mom's help, I've learned how to truly accept what I am, becoming a stronger version of Ari in the process. No matter who has been there to guide me along the way, I did the work. That was me. It will be me that ends this.

It's Wednesday night. There's only one place Salvatore ever goes on Wednesdays. The underground club located beneath one of the many Chicago skyscrapers. Hidden away from the general public, so only those with an invitation could find it. Normally, I would only walk in at his request. Show Sal I can hang with the big boys, but not tonight.

For this to work, he can't see me coming. He'll know the moment he looks into my eyes, I'm only there for one reason. To end him. To destroy everything he is and what he stands for. This world will be a much better place without him. I will make it so no one ever has to bow to him again or fall to one of the hands he's hired.

It's a silent night as I slink from Adrian's house, a zip hoodie I found in the closet wrapped around me. I keep it bunched high around my chin, inhaling his scent. Hoping like hell it won't be the last time I get to.

I'm not stupid. My plan to walk in and kill Sal on his own turf is risky. The possibility I don't walk back out is high. If he pulls one of his custom guns on me, my phoenix may not be enough to pull me back from the brink of death, no matter how much I wish, hope, or pray for it. I'm willing to make that sacrifice so no one else will have to.

Those that I've come to love and adore flash unbidden through my mind. Tuck. Talia. Oliver. Gomez. My mom. Every phoenix I've gotten to know these past few months. My dad.

A choked cry escapes me. No matter what we've done, he lies in the same place. Frozen in that stalled state, he put himself in. I hope this won't be my last chance to meet him. I need more time.

Shaking the sadness from my mind, I stalk forward. My peripheral vision serves as my best friend, my only intel to reveal if I'm being followed. I've made it five blocks up and three over, the location my Uber will meet me. He pulls up only moments after I make it to the curb in front of the address I gave him. The inside of the gray-sided house shrouded in darkness. Not even a porch light to cut the dark, signifying it's occupied. But the manicured lawn and his and hers rocking chairs on the front porch tell me it is. A happy couple living their lives together. Not a care in the world.

The drive into the city stretches, my thoughts whirling through my mind. Draped in darkness, I enter my apartment. Tonight the shadows are my only friends as I stare at nothing, letting them circle me. It's hours before I change into attire worthy of entering Prime 79 — one of many exclusive clubs Salvatore owns. His safe zone I'm happy to infiltrate.

The bodycon dress fits me like a glove. Every curve on display for men to gawk at, eye fucking me like the desperate dogs they are. I chose it purposely. There's not much left to the imagination, my back exposed under angled strips of fabric, and the low cut V in the front, giving me the appearance of cleavage I wish I actually had.

For as delectable as I appear, I'm strapped to the nines. Four knives secured to my body in various locations. Sal's gun tucked into the built-in holster on the right and a backup Glock on the left. The pins holding the front of my hair off my forehead in an artistic swoop of waves, really miniature sheathed razors capable of slicing through flesh like any other blade.

Lips coated in a wine lipstick so dark, the color appears nearly black in the shadows, I'm ready.

I take another Uber to the location of the black and chrome skyscraper that hides Prime 79 beneath it. Only those on the exclusive list would even know there's anything two stories below the lobby. The entrance classic, glass double doors where the security scans for facial recognition before allowing entrance to the elevator at the far end, slightly obscured by an abstract marble slab. By day, it elevates you to the penthouse. By night descends to the underground — where debauchery is the way of life.

My heels click loudly across the marble floor as I strut forward, drowning out the loud beating of my heart. The clock is ticking. Dwindling down to the moment Adrian wakes from the spot I left him in. I'd debated leaving a note. Opted against it, knowing he'll eventually figure it out. That there will be no hiding from him once he does. At least this way it buys me time.

I hope he doesn't come for me. I need him to stay safe. That's why I'm doing this.

Adrian, I'm sorry.

My last chance to take a steadying breath is the chime of the elevator. The *whoosh* of the opening doors tosses my ends just enough to break contact with my shoulders. My last chance to back out. To walk away and find a better plan. A safer plan. One that doesn't sacrifice me or potentially innocent people downstairs fucking and drinking without a care in the world.

No. There's no turning back. He has taken enough from us.

Stepping into the elevator, the guard's eyes narrow as I turn to face him before widening. The recognition hit him too late. Who I am. I recognized him immediately. A lower-ranking flunky on Sal's roster, but one that he trusts enough to man this building.

The sixty seconds it takes to descend the two stories seems to stretch on. Sweat beading at the base of my neck, down my back, and between my breasts. It's not fear. It's anticipation.

Sal will be the first kill I've ever actually wanted. Needed.

The heavy bass of the music and flashing neon lights assault me as I step out of the elevator, straight onto the black marble floors of the club. He's spared no expense decorating this place. The plush seating areas and high-top tables, plated in the same ebony marble. Top-shelf liquor only. The servers dressed to the nines, as is expected for all guests.

Nearly every square inch is filled. Bodies moving about, boisterous laughter flitting around me. A man dressed in a custom-fitted suit bumps into me, eyes roving down my body before flashing an apologetic grin. If not for the two women that drag him along a proposition would be the only thought on his mind. He wouldn't be the first. *Bore.*

It's a battle moving through the main floor of the club; the area Sal calls the commons. By normal club standards, these would be your VIPs. The ones that turn up their noses at everyone while they sip their drinks and pretend their shit doesn't stink. Not here, though. At Prime 79, they are the bottom feeders. Scavengers looking to sink their teeth into the first person to get them into the restricted areas. A small chuckle escapes me. How true that statement might be. How many are "other" like me?

Shoving my way through the throng of sweaty bodies, I head for the bowels of the club. Tucked in the coves where the private rooms are and the stairs to a small loft area where only Salvatore lounges can be found. His resolve as to who may enter, not shifting much in all the years I've known him. The frosted glass door emerges as if rising from the floor as I clear the top of the spiral staircase leading to the secluded area. Two guards stand outside of it. One addressing me with a smirk and a nod. Brian — I think — has always been partial to me. Gifting me unwanted winks and not-so-subtle ass grabs.

Without question, he opens the door for me. In unison, both guards slip to the side, allowing me entrance. The space is no larger than my living room, with suede curved couches of onyx lining one wall complemented by low-back armchairs. Several women lay sprawled across the couch beside Sal, one with her lips suctioned to the side of his neck. Two other men are in the room. Their lips cresting their tumblers of liquor.

It takes longer than I expected for Salvatore to notice my presence. His eyes finally peel open as the second woman removes her hand from his crotch, where she'd been rubbing him as if her life depended on it. It's disgusting. Sal has been married for God knows how long, but here he is, letting random women feel him up. It's not like I haven't seen it before, but my time shifting away from being his pawn has taken me from admiring him to realizing what a waste of space he really is.

"Ah, Ari. Join us." He gestures, arms wide, drink sloshing over the rim of the glass.

Cocking a perfectly manicured brow, I'm ready to perform. This night entirely dependent on him believing I'm here for nothing more than a bit of dirty fun.

"Of course." Brian appears behind me, as silent as a cat, passing me a tumbler of what I assume is bourbon. Raising my glass, I take my first sip. The tiniest one I can muster. I need my head clear. I'll only get one chance.

Sal's eyes stay locked on me as he shoos the woman away, draping one arm across the back of the sofa, bringing what's left of his drink to his lips.

"To what do I owe the pleasure?" It's not an actual question. But a confrontation. The number of times I'd declined to come here, the suspicion of my unannounced appearance is clear in the pinch of his brow and minuscule purse of his lips.

"Am I not to join you for fun? Does one missed kill really exclude me from enjoying..." I allow my words to drift off as I purposely eye the man to my immediate right. They are attractive enough. Men I would have slept with in a heartbeat. That was before. Before... Adrian.

"Well, take a seat." He pats the spot next to him. "Or do you need to stand for what you actually came to do?"

My gaze darts back to him. The tiniest tell that he's thrown me off balance. *It's now or never.* With a turn of the glass in my right hand, I pull the gun he gifted me with my left, pointing it directly at where his heart should be.

Adrian

I wake to a silent house, alone on the couch, with a blanket anchored around me. Ari had definitely been beside me. Checking the time, I think nothing of it. It's after midnight. No doubt she likely went to bed. Preferably mine. As much as she drives me up a fucking wall, I loved sleeping next to her last night.

I wasn't looking for a relationship when she came barging into my life. From the very first night she set out to follow me, thinking she was some sort of super spy, I felt the bond. Anyone could have spotted her. Should have. Most aren't trained the way I am, though. Programmed to watch their surroundings with a relentless focus. As Second I don't get the luxury of a fuckup. Everyone depends on me all the time.

I'd have it no other way. It's supposed to be an honor to be of my bloodline. Yet, I'll never be proud of the blood that runs through my veins. Phoenixes in my line are exceedingly rare these days. It's better that way. A smaller pool of enemies.

I'm wandering through the lower level of the house. Every light is out. No sign of Ari. *Upstairs, then.* I check her bedroom first. After fooling around for hours, the bed remains disheveled. The memories assault me. The scent of her arousal still thick in the air. I wanted to sleep with her. Every time she looks at me with those big blue eyes, the desire to drop to my knees and give myself to her is overwhelming.

She'd asked me to fuck her. Repeatedly. I kept my composure, knowing what it would mean if we did. The irreversible position we would be in. The fear that she'll reject me still cripples me some days, so I refuse to seal our bond. Not yet.

Her room was untouched. So is mine. Panic creeps into my chest and then my throat. My hoarse voice calling out for her.

Silence.

No answer.

"Ari," I bark, sounding pissed but really just terrified they took her and my dumbass had been asleep instead of protecting her.

Surely I would have heard something. If someone was here, if they'd taken her, I'd know.

Racing back downstairs, I'm frantic as I search beneath the pillows on the couch for my phone. If she left, there's only one person who might know where.

"Where is she?" I growl.

Tuck's silent on the other end. He's used to my temper. The asshole everyone gets to interact with, an accurate representation of who I've become. It's not just reserved for her, even though I'm sure she believes that. Ari just gets an extra dose, because no one can push my buttons the way she does.

"I don't know..." Those three words riddled with anxiety. He knows something is wrong too. "She's supposed to be there with you. Where the hell did she go?"

Shame drains my energy. "I don't know."

"Get back here. Now."

Not even bothering with shoes, I race out to the garage. The door barely opens before I'm peeling out and down the road. I'm well out of sight of my house when it occurs to me, I may not have even closed the door. I don't care.

I have to find her. Before someone else does.

Sal already knows of our connection. Our Pairing. I have no doubt in my mind he's not above using her to get to me. My unique set of gifts, a prize that would make him nearly invincible if he could siphon them. That much we learned. That's why he wants what flows through my veins. Dead or alive, it doesn't matter. He wants the power I possess.

There are more cars on the road than should be. Their sole purpose: to piss me off. The traffic always funneling into the small pockets of open space I'm darting in and out of. Like me, Tuck lives in a single-family home on the outskirts of the city. Our need for space more important than convenience.

He's outside waiting for me, clearly tracking my location to know when I would arrive.

"How do we find her?"

He waves me inside, down to the basement, where we keep certain prisoners sometimes. The cement walls of their cells laced with the metal alloy that stifles our magical gifts and shifting abilities.

A few weeks back, we captured one of Sals' inner circle. One of the grunts that spent enough time around his operations to give us some answers we needed. It was around that time Tuck stopped bringing Ari here. He didn't want her to know what kind of man he really is. His dark side kept far from her inquisitive nature.

Tucker is one of the nicest guys I know, with a deadly violent streak. We all have our roles to play. When it comes to torture and information, he's our man. A practice his mother often doesn't approve of. He transforms from the caring boy next door to the Joker incarnate, giving no mercy to those that move against paranormal law. He shows no leniency to humans versus our kind. They all get the same treatment.

"Hello, Jared."

A thickset guy, at least four inches taller than me, tied to a basic metal chair, looks up. His head moves so slowly you'd think it weighed an actual ton. His lip busted so wide it appears more like pulverized flesh than a single curve as the bottom of his mouth. One eye is swollen shut, the bruising leaving purple in the dust, and settling on a slate black.

Where he always smirked or laughed at us when he first arrived, now he looks at us with hesitation. The lowering of his brows a telltale sign of his fear of what we might do next. How much more pain we'll inflict. He knows he won't leave here alive. He can't. It's not an option.

"Where would Salvatore be tonight?"

Jared bows his head again like there's no way he can hold it up any longer.

Striding to the corner, Tuck grabs a bat — made of that same metal alloy — matching the chair we strapped this piece of shit to. Angling the bat under Jared's chin, he forces his gaze back to us.

"Now Jared, we've become such good friends. I think you're going to want to answer me," he hums. The tone menacing. Terrifying. I always thought I was a bad fucker until I realized how deranged Tuck's other half is.

"Prime." He coughs. Blood specks coat his dirty jeans and the floor at his feet. A small puddle of dark liquid splashes to the floor as he coughs again. "Prime." A heaving breath. "79."

Tuck drops the bat from beneath his chin only a second after I've already started sprinting for the door, stopping only long enough to slip on a pair of Tuck's sneakers by the main entrance.

Hearing that name out of his mouth, I know Sal didn't take Ari. She went to him. Just like the beaten-down warlock in the basement, Ari also knows Salvatore's movements. His intricacies. His way of life. She left to go after him. She said she'd kill him, and I brushed it off, knowing she was shaken and scared.

It was a problem I thought we'd have time to solve. My girl does things differently. That brilliant firecracker takes matters into her own hands. I've seen it in the way she talks about him now; the puppet no longer willing to be controlled by her puppeteer.

She was strong. Invincible. Unstoppable when she found us, but reuniting with her kind and her family has only heightened that. Maturing her in a way I can't put into actual words.

The Honda swerves through the downtown streets, careening through yellow lights trying to get to her. I need to get to her. My chest tightens, resignation settling in my gut — I may not make it in time. Anything could happen before I get there.

I refuse to waste time finding a legitimate parking spot as I pull up outside the imposing glass structure of a building. It's ominous in the daylight but at night a tower of nightmares. Two guards stop me at the doors to the lobby.

"Sir, you can't enter." One holds out an arm, keeping me from crossing the threshold. Fuck him. I'm walking in there.

"You'll let me in." A grin pulling at the corner of my mouth.

"No, Sir. I won't."

"You will. Tell Salvatore Adrian Alexander is here to see him."

Both sets of eyes go wide, the smaller one taking a few steps to the side to speak into a sleek watch on his wrist. He throws us a nod, both men leading me to an elevator I hadn't even noticed.

The doors slip open immediately, the initial guard pushing a few buttons before stepping back out, eyes focused on me as the doors close. Just as a guard left me in the elevator, another retrieves me as the doors shift open, gripping me lightly behind the arm and guiding me forward.

He doesn't talk to me at all, allowing me to take in the surrounding club. I've heard about this place. Anyone in our world has. It's just as it's been described. Dancing strobe lights, nearly naked women, and hungry men. Endless cocktails and liquor on every surface. The dark blue hue casting the place in shifting shadows.

I'm led up a flight of stairs. That thick hand holding me in place at a door of frosted glass. Clearly, it's meant to lead me to a private room. One I'm sure Ari and Sal are in.

She has to be here. Please let her be here.

The door swings open. Sal seated on the couch, ankle crossed over his knee, wearing a smug grin. Ari with her gun pointed at his chest. There are others in the room. Their positions at the far reaches of the space, inconsequential. Unimportant.

She's here. The tightness in my chest relaxes just a little. *She's here.*

"Ari," I breathe.

It's as if the sound of her name broke whatever trance she was in. Her eyes flicker back in my direction — an almost imperceptible motion. The second enough for Sal to slip the gun from his lower back. The distraction enough for her to lose the focus she needed to take her shot.

The entire scene plays out in slow motion, my legs heavy as if filled with hardened cement as I try to run for her the instant the gunshot rings out. Her chest curved into a C, hair flying forward as she falls, bright blood glistening around the bullet hole just over the edge of the fabric covering her breasts.

I catch her just before she smacks into the marble flooring beneath us. She doesn't move. Limp as she sags into my arms.

About the Author

Britton Brinkley was originally born in New Jersey and now resides in Northern Virginia.

Growing up an avid reader, she was mesmerized by the sciences and ancient civilizations. She has always loved immersing herself in new and different worlds. Britton now enjoys creating her own, as well with her writing buddy Jay Gatsby (the cat).

When she isn't writing she's likely either reading, watching *Criminal Minds*, or some other true crime show on Investigation Discovery.

Tik Tok: Blivingamillionlives
Instagram: Blivingamillionlives
Facebook Group: Britton B's Book World
Email: author.britton.brinkley@gmail.com

Grown from Tainted Seeds

DARTANYAN JOHNSON

About the Book

Oden and his brother, Philip, are Apprentice Elementalists awaiting orders to enter the war that has taken the lives of their friends. But after years of being away from home, they're allowed to attend their sister's wedding. Reunited with their loved ones, the brothers can finally relax and have fun... until the war lands on their doorstep, forcing them to engage in a battle that ends in bloodshed. Will the war take the lives of their family as well, or will Oden and Philip somehow save the people they value the most? And crazier still, who invited the blood-sucking vampire?

Advisory

This story contains depictions of graphic violence. If this material is upsetting to you, please proceed with caution.

Chapter 1

Blood spewed from the soldier's mouth as a fist connected with his cheek. He collapsed to the floor, and the onlookers in the mess hall cheered.

"Come on, Tobias! Finish him already!" Oden's voice boomed over the noise of the crowd. He had a large sum riding on this fight, and the man he'd bet on was about to win. All Tobias had to do was leap atop his opponent and pummel him, but the bonehead stood a few feet away, grinning stupidly and gesturing for the felled man to get up.

Spindly arms shaking and with his left eye nearly swollen shut, Flanagan struggled to his feet. He sneered at Tobias, who circled him with outspread arms then charged with a roar, leading with a looping right hand. Flanagan ducked under the blow and caught Tobias with a punch to the gut, making him wince and backpedal to create space. But Flanagan was on him in an instant, swinging with wild punches. Tobias barely dodged the blows before eventually rushing forward and wrestling his opponent to the floor.

Unfortunately, Flanagan was stronger than his small, wiry frame suggested. He overpowered Tobias and worked his way behind him, wrapping an arm around his neck in a sleeper hold.

"Bite him!" Oden yelled. "Gnaw on his arm, you bastard!"

Tobias flailed his arms to get free, but his eyes were fluttering closed. He wouldn't last much longer. A few breaths later, he was out cold.

Lieutenant Leegos, a bald boulder of a man, forced Flanagan to release the hold and hefted him to his feet, then held up the victor's hand. "We have our winner!"

The onlookers erupted into cheers, and Flanagan beamed, displaying a gap where a tooth had once been.

Someone clapped Oden on the shoulder. He knew who it was without looking.

"What did I tell you? Brains will beat brawns every time," Philip said.

"Whatever." Oden swiped his younger brother's hand from his shoulder. He glowered at the unconscious fighter Leegos was trying to wake.

When Tobias finally stirred, Philip leaned in and said, "Time to collect my winnings." Then he strode off, shaking hands and laughing with a few soldiers who had been watching the fight.

"Time to collect my winnings," Oden mocked in his younger brother's voice. "What a jerk."

Some soldiers made for the exit, but most sat down to finish their meals. Oden sighed heavily as he eyed his table. He still had food on his plate, but his appetite was gone. What he wanted was a smoke—or maybe a stiff drink.

Philip's laughter carried through the mess hall. Was it deliberately loud to piss Oden off or was he imagining intent because he had lost most of his coin? Whatever the case, he needed to get some fresh air before he went mad.

He stepped out of the barracks into scorching heat. It was summer in Elkin, and the weather had been intolerable for the last few days. He wanted to disrobe where he stood, head to his room, and put on something more comfortable to better tolerate the sun's wrath, but that would be against regulations. As an on-call Apprentice Elementalist, he was required to wear his brown robe—enchanted to deflect minor magical attacks—rain or shine.

Wiping sweat from his forehead, Oden scanned the soldiers strolling across the park that stretched from the barracks to the Academy, where magic wielders like himself lived. Master Aysa, the highest-ranking Battle Mage, was approaching him wearing her bright red robe and an unreadable expression. On either side of her were a pair of Elementalists—Master Lisette and Master Kaylor—whose expressions were clearly grim. Oden's insides turned to jelly. Was this it? Was this the day he'd finally play a part in the war that had taken the lives of his friends and mentors?

He forced a smile. "Master Aysa, how can I help you?"

The Battle Mage and her entourage halted before him. "Good evening, Oden," Aysa said with a curt dip of her chin. "Where's your brother?"

Oden swallowed. "He's in the mess hall. Is something the matter?"

Aysa pulled a folded piece of parchment from her robe and handed it to him. "Looks like you two are going on a trip."

He hesitated before taking the parchment. "I see." It was surely a command. He was officially reporting for duty. "Where are we being stationed, if you don't mind me asking?"

A corner of Master Aysa's lips curved upward. "There's a train leaving later this evening," she said, ignoring his question. "Your tickets will be waiting for you at the station. Also, Headmaster Meridel would like to speak to you and Philip."

"Headmaster Meridel?"

Meridel was not only in charge of the Academy, he was also said to be one of the strongest Grand Sorcerers in the world. The only time Oden had ever spoken to the headmaster was right after his brother and he had been recruited to the training program five years ago.

Aysa nodded. "And if I were you, I'd hurry to his office. You wouldn't want to keep him waiting."

"Of course. I'll find my brother and we'll be on our way."

While Aysa and the Elementalists walked toward another group of mages, Oden unfolded the parchment and immediately recognized the handwriting.

"Isabella."

This wasn't an order to attend the war efforts. It was a letter from his little sister. He hadn't received a letter from home in months. Was she well? Had something bad happened to their parents? He skimmed through the page and smiled at the update. Mom and Pop were doing just fine, and business was booming. He read on, then paused at the words, "I'm getting married."

"This can't be right."

He re-read the part of the letter where she invited his brother and him to her wedding. Who was this guy she was supposedly marrying? How could their parents agree to this?

Oden had to remind himself that Isabella wasn't a little girl anymore. At nineteen years old, she was a woman. He sighed at all the years he'd missed. She'd used to run from the neighborhood boys, but he supposed it wasn't possible to outrun your heart. So, who had she fallen in love with? Their village was pretty small, and everyone knew each other.

He read to the end of the letter, noting that the wedding would be held at the village hall, as expected. The paper shook in his hand when he reached her sign-off.

I hope this letter reaches you in time. Rufus and I can't wait to see you again. I love you.

-Isabella.

"Rufus?" Her fiancé's name came out as a growl. "I can't believe it."

"Believe what?" Philip inquired.

Oden spun around, clutching the letter like a weapon. "Isabella"—he could barely get the words out—"is getting married."

"Married?" Philip grinned. "That's great news. Why do you look like someone pissed in your ale?"

Oden shook the letter at him. "Read."

Philip read it aloud. "Hello, Oden. Hello, Philip. My two favorite brothers in the world."

Oden paced.

"I apologize for not having written sooner, but the family's bakery has kept me busy. Though our parents are always tired at the end of the day, they couldn't be any happier. I, on the other hand, could really use a vacation. Speaking of me; guess what? All right, I'll tell you. I'm getting married. The wedding will be held in the village hall on the 15th of this month. I can't imagine walking down the aisle without my wonderful brothers present, so I hope this letter reaches you in time. Rufus and I—" Philip's eyes widened.

"Salamander," they said together.

Rufus Salamon was a scrawny, pimple-faced kid who had followed Oden and Philip everywhere they'd gone. The brothers had tormented him in the hopes he'd get the hint one day that they didn't want him hanging around them, but the annoying kid had never learned.

"Is she serious?" Philip asked, matching Oden's frown."

"Unfortunately. Isabella wouldn't play around with news like this."

"But it's Salamander. D'you think she's gone blind?"

Oden finally stopped pacing. "I have no idea." He took a few calming breaths. Being upset wouldn't help the situation.

"The 15th is in two days," Philip pointed out. "We won't make it unless we leave soon. Tomorrow at the latest."

"Actually, we've been approved to depart tonight by train. Our tickets should be waiting for us at the station."

Philip's brows rose. "Really?"

"According to Master Aysa. She's the one who handed me Isabella's letter. She also said the headmaster wanted to see us."

"See us about what?"

"I guess we're about to find out." Oden snatched the letter from Philip, scanned the text once more, then shook his head in disgust. "Rufus Salamon. Unbelievable."

Fueled by their excitement at leaving the camp, it didn't take long for the two brothers to arrive at the school.

The Academy was a stone palace with dozens of windows, and statues of mythical creatures surrounded the building. It used to be the headmaster's family's place of residence but had been repurposed as a school at the beginning of the war. The gray marble floor usually had hundreds of feet trampling on it, but now it was empty; the students were presumably in class or in the cafeteria on the other side of the palace.

When they arrived at the headmaster's office, the door clicked and swung open before Oden could knock.

"Come in," the headmaster said.

Oden dropped his hand, and the two brothers stepped into the massive room. Near the far left wall was an assortment of enchanted weapons—swords, daggers, maces—locked in an elaborate display case. Shelves filled with tomes and odd trinkets spanned the wall on the right.

In front of the brothers, still sitting at his desk, was Headmaster Meridel. Without looking up from the scroll he was writing on, Meridel waved a hand and the door slammed shut. Finally, he lifted his quill, examined his work, and nodded in satisfaction.

"Well, if it isn't Oden and Philip Rye," he said, meeting their gazes and gesturing for them to sit. They obliged, taking seats across the desk from the headmaster.

"Master Aysa said you wanted to speak with us about something," Oden prompted.

"Indeed." Meridel carefully dipped the quill in an ink jar before writing on the scroll once more. "Before I begin, I'd like to say congratulations on your sister getting married."

"Thank you," Oden said. "And trust me, it has come as a surprise."

Meridel smiled, then sighed. "What I wouldn't give to be young and in love again." He pulled his quill away from the scroll and finally set it down. "On to business. You two are probably wondering why I'm allowing a two-week vacation?"

"Two weeks?" Philip asked with a growing grin.

Oden peeked at the scroll in front of Meridel. It was a map, and upon closer inspection, he recognized the area. "We're going on a scouting mission."

"Smart man you are, Oden." Meridel leaned back in his chair.

"Scouting mission?" Philip echoed. "In Cotsketta?"

"There has been a lot of activity near your hometown. Roaming around the area is a werewolf named Eugene. He used to be our accomplice in this war, but he has decided to part ways and do things how he best sees fit. According to sources, he's been building an army."

"To fight against us?" Oden asked.

"Not sure," Meridel admitted. "I doubt he'll lend aid to our enemy, but he's been ignoring orders from our war council to cease turning innocent people into werewolves. We have no choice but to view him as a threat."

"Wait," Oden interjected, "he's making an army with the people he's turning into werewolves?"

"That's correct. From my understanding, he's been leaving victims scattered across the country."

Oden and Philip shared a look.

"And you think he's been in our hometown?" Philip asked.

"I can't be too sure, but if you see him, you need to report him to the scouts I've sent that way weeks ago. He spends most of his time in between forms. You'll know if you come across him. Trust me." He tested the drying ink with a press of his finger, then rolled the scroll. "Believe it or not, Eugene's the least of our worries. Someone has stolen the Sword of Tumahn."

Oden had read about the Sword of Tumahn; it was an enchanted weapon that gave the wielder the ability to create illusions. If the wielder was powerful enough, they could also bring the illusions to life.

"Didn't Master Calahan have that sword?" Oden asked.

"He did. But now Calahan is dead."

The shock was a blow to Oden's chest. "No way. Master Calahan was one of our strongest Battle Mages."

"He was. According to reports, a vampire by the name of Donovic was seen fleeing from Calahan's dead body. He comes from a well-known family with a lot of influence. I had hoped they'd side with us, but it appears they've chosen their alliance. If this is true, Elize has managed to wiggle her way into my territory."

The country of Telkendor was split into two warring forces. Headmaster and Grand Sorcerer Meridel controlled one side of the country, and Grand Sorceress Elize ran the other.

"This vampire knows how to wield magic?" Oden asked.

"Either he knows magic or he's giving the sword to someone else. Both options are terrible. We do not know where Donovic is at the moment, but if you happen to see him, don't confront him. He's a dangerous man even without the Sword of Tumahn, and I can only imagine how difficult he'd be to defeat if he has it. My daughter will be visiting the nearby towns with a small reconnaissance team, but her base will be in Ulikin. If you spot him, you let her know."

"And what does Donovic look like?" Philip inquired.

"I'm assuming he'll be the one with fangs," Oden said with a smirk.

Philip side-eyed his brother.

"Don't get mad at me after asking a stupid question."

"Does Donovic have any defining qualities other than his fangs?" Philip asked, turning back to the headmaster.

"He has a tattoo on his chest of a bat wearing a crown," Meridel said. "His hair is normally blonde, but if he knows we're looking for him, he's bound to have that altered. As with most vampires, Donovic is nocturnal, meaning he does his meddling at night."

The two brothers nodded.

As if remembering something, Meridel unrolled the scroll, dipped his quill in the ink, and began to scribble. "That's all I have. I wish your sister well. Marriage is a sacred bond, and I'm glad she has found a life mate." With a wave of his hand, the office door swung open. "You two need to hurry and pack," he continued. "Enjoy yourselves."

"Of course. Thank you, Headmaster," Oden said, getting to his feet.

"Thank you, Headmaster," Philip said with a bow.

Meridel grunted his affirmation but didn't look up.

Chapter 2

"I can't wait to see the family," Oden said once they'd entered their dorm room. "Hopefully, I can get Mom to make that lamb stew I can't get enough of."

Philip sighed. "Mom's lamb stew is to die for, but you know what trumps that?"

Oden raised an eyebrow.

"Finding a lady friend," Philip continued, "if you know what I mean."

"And make your right hand jealous? Such a scandal."

"Perhaps you need someone to wrestle with under the sheets—alleviate all that hostility."

"Hostility?" Oden scoffed. "You must have me mistaken. I ooze niceness."

"The fact you said that with a straight face proves my point," Philip said with a chuckle.

Oden rummaged through his dresser, pulling out his meager possessions and tossing them on his bed before stuffing them in his dingy brown rucksack.

"When we see that twerp, Rufus, we'll have to give him the talk."

Philip tied his satchel closed. "The talk?"

"Let him know that if he breaks our little sister's heart, we're going to break his face."

"Ah." Philip nodded. "But I'm certain we won't need to. Izzy's always been able to take care of herself. Besides, our pop's no pushover. He might have let that scoundrel date his daughter, but he'll set fire to anyone who does her harm."

Oden knew his brother was right. As he was tying his own bag shut, an amusing memory surfaced. "Do you remember that day you, Rufus, and I climbed that tree by the river?"

"He was so ecstatic to finally be invited to hang out with us, he ignored his fear of heights."

Oden chuckled. "We left that idiot in the tree crying for help and went home."

"Well, it wasn't like we didn't try to get him down," Philip added. "He was just too frightened to do what we suggested."

Eventually, Rufus's tall, thin father had come to Oden's house looking for his son. After discovering they'd left him in a tree, he'd stormed off to find him. Rufus hadn't come around for weeks after that, and he'd never brought up the tree incident.

A knock on the dorm door interrupted their reminiscing.

"One moment," Oden called. He opened the door and smiled good-naturedly at the short, auburn-haired boy who was shuffling from foot to foot. "How can I help you?"

"I was instructed to tell you the carriage is ready."

"Thank you, young sir," Oden said, and Philip strolled forward with both their bags in hand, grinning.

A small procession of Elementalists had gathered in the courtyard along with their superior, Master Aysa, the headmaster's daughter. It was strange, but in a good way, to see the Battle Mage dressed in casual clothes instead of her usual red robe. In her tan trousers and dark blue blouse, she resembled a regular person.

A carriage driver gestured to Oden and Philip. "You two are with me."

It didn't take long to reach the station and receive their tickets. Soon, the conductor was calling for everyone to board the train.

"Isn't this exciting?" Philip pushed through the crowd and entered the car, which had cherry red walls and a plush, emerald-green carpet. It was much nicer than the standard passenger trains Oden had been on. Philip shoved a man aside and flopped into the oversized window seat. The man gave him a dirty look but continued down the aisle.

Oden sat across from him, shaking his head. The seat was comfortable, soft against his backside. When the parting horn blew into the night sky and the train picked up speed, he propped his bag against the window like a makeshift pillow and let the soothing sounds of the wheels on the track lull him to sleep.

* * *

Someone was shaking Oden. He yawned and opened his eyes, assuming they were about to disembark, but the train was still moving. He dug in his pocket and pulled out his timepiece; the arrival time wasn't for another two hours. Philip was smiling and gesturing toward the window.

"Teshaw Lake," Oden said, sitting up. The familiar lake was one of their father's favorite fishing spots. He put his timepiece back in his pocket.

"It feels like we're already home, doesn't it?"

A sensational smell tugged Oden's attention to the small table between them. In front of Philip was a plate with the remnants of a meal.

"Roast beef and boiled potatoes. It was divine."

Across from the plate was a bowl with a bare plate atop it, which Oden lifted.

"Is this—?"

"A crab salad," Philip finished. "I ordered us something to eat not too long ago, but I didn't want to wake you."

Oden's mouth watered as he grabbed a spoon from the tray. The crisp red onions, savory chunks of crab, and mixture of sauces had him nodding to himself and making pleased noises. "This is sublime."

"It better be for what I paid," Philip said. "Fortunately for me, I'm about to win it all back." Grinning mischievously, he reached up to the overhead rack and retrieved a small wooden box and a folded checkered board.

Oden smirked. "You're going to get yourself hurt messing around with that. Chess is a man's game."

Philip moved his plate aside before opening the box and pouring the contents onto the table. "Two silver coins per game," he said as he unfolded the board.

When Oden was done eating, he placed his bowl atop Philip's plate, then spun the board around so the white pieces were in front of him.

"I'm the oldest; I go first."

It took nearly an hour to complete the game. Oden sat back, his lips curving upward. "Check mate."

Philip scrutinized the board for a long time.

"You can stare at it all you want," Oden teased. "It won't change the outcome."

Philip gathered the pieces. "One more."

"You're on."

A screeching sound, followed by the train's deceleration, made Oden turn in his seat. Half a mile down the track, the train station was visible.

The conductor walked down the aisle and stood at the car's exit, smiling at the patrons who met his gaze. When the train stopped and the door opened, Philip was the first to exit. Checking his brother's abandoned seat, Oden sighed at the forgotten bag.

"I should pretend I never saw it," he mumbled before picking it up. He nodded to the conductor in passing and stepped onto the platform.

Philip was twirling slowly, his arms outstretched. "We're back."

Oden dropped Philip's bag at his side. "Next time, I'm going to leave your stuff on the train."

"Sorry about that. I was just so excited." Philip hefted his bag, then lifted his nose in the air and inhaled deeply. "I think I can already smell Mom's lamb stew. Can you?"

Oden shook his head. There was only smoke from the train and a stale odor from the passengers. "Come on. Let's fetch a ride."

Several carriages waited outside the train station, the drivers waving and opening their doors as people exited the building. Oden eagerly approached an older driver, who was leaning against his carriage with his arms crossed.

"My fair man," Oden greeted. "My brother and I would like a ride to Cotsketta."

The man smiled and stood tall. "No problem. That'll be five silver coins each."

Oden flinched. "Five silvers? Perhaps you're unaware of where Cotsketta is." He pointed to the trail that led to the forest ahead. "You go that way for four miles, and voila."

The driver's face darkened, and he leaned against the carriage once more. "Looks like you two will be walking. Move along so a *paying* customer knows I'm available."

"Fine, we'll fetch a ride with someone else." Oden stormed off, followed by his brother.

"And they'll tell you the same thing," the man called after them.

"Why is that?" Philip asked, turning back.

"Bandits," the man said simply.

Oden smirked. "Bandits? You must be talking about yourself because you're the only thief here."

The man narrowed his eyes. "Look here, pal. My fees are fair. If you ask around, you'll notice I'm the cheapest of the bunch."

Oden surveyed the other carriages. They all had passengers climbing aboard.

"Looks like it's just me left," the old coachman said, smiling. "What'll it be?"

Philip shrugged and looked at his brother. Oden didn't want to walk all the way to Cotsketta, but he wasn't about to pay some crook ten silver coins for such a brief journey. He repositioned the bag on his shoulder. "Sorry, but we'll try our luck with the *bandits* lurking in the forest."

"Suit yourself." The coachman waved toward a potential customer.

When the brothers made it to the forest, Philip glanced over his shoulder, then at Oden.

"D'you think that guy was telling the truth?"

"Of course not. That guy was a conman. I wouldn't be surprised if all the carriage drivers were in on the whole thing."

Philip eyed him skeptically.

Oden sighed. "My poor, naive, idiot brother; you have to be mindful of your surroundings. You need to get your head out of the clouds and come back to the real world. Everything revolves around money. It motivates people to do whatever it takes to make more of it. You ever heard of a thing called greed?"

"Lying about bandits in the forest is a bit much for extra coin."

"Trust me when I tell you that there are no bandits. And even if there were, we have our wands. We'll turn them into firewood."

"We're not supposed to use our magic on civilians."

"Yeah, I know, but our sister's wedding is tomorrow, and I'll be damned if I'm going to wrestle with some hooligans and possibly suffer an injury. Besides, who's going to find out?"

"You've got a point. The last thing I need is someone damaging my pretty mug."

"Pretty mug?" Oden scoffed. "You have the kind of face only a mother would love."

"Yeah: the mother of your children."

Both men stopped walking and stared at each other for a few beats before erupting into laughter.

"What a bastard you are," Oden said. "If that wasn't such a terrible retort, I'd have kicked you in the balls."

"Good luck with that. I have balls of steel. Mess around and break your toes."

It was muggy in the forest. Not as uncomfortably hot as at the base, but enough to make sweat trickle down Oden's back. He chided himself for not putting on something more comfortable when they'd been preparing for the trip, but they'd been short on time.

He dug in his rucksack and pulled out a water container. The cold liquid quenched his parched throat.

"I hope Pop finally installed a heating system for the cistern."

Philip winced. "I forgot all about that. He's been talking about replacing that broken system for years. If he hasn't, we'll be heating the water in the cauldron like savages." His shoulders slumped. "I'm starting to miss the school already. I don't have a problem with bandits, but I draw the line at engaging in slave work to take a hot bath."

"We could always force Salamander to fetch and heat the water for us," Oden suggested. "Make him earn the right to call us his brothers-in-law."

"I like the sound of that." Philip tilted his head up and eyed the canopy. "It'll be like having our own little servant. Knowing Salamander, though, he'll find a way to screw up the job." His sigh quickly turned into a chuckle. "Speaking of screwing up, I wonder if Cousin Tilden was invited."

"That guy has two left feet for certain, but I doubt he'll be there. He's stationed on the other side of Elkin. He would have had to leave his base two days ago to make it in time."

"You're probably right."

"I'm still surprised someone let that clumsy bastard into their academy to study mag—"

A woman's scream split the air. Oden and Philip halted, then scanned the trees.

"Did you hear that?" Philip asked.

"I think every creature in this damn forest heard."

"How far away do you think that was?"

"I don't know." Oden placed his bag on the ground and grabbed his wand from the leg holster hidden underneath his robe. "But if something comes our way, I'm cutting it to shreds."

The two men continued to appraise the forest. Oden shifted from foot to foot at the sound of hurried footsteps.

Philip whipped his head to the right. "Wait, I think I see something."

Suddenly, a woman burst from the trees wearing a torn gown and running in their direction. Charging behind her, with predatory grins, were three men. One of them snatched her by the hair, and she flailed in his grasp.

"That's right," the man said. "Let me know you still got some fight in ya." He tossed her on the ground and fumbled with his trouser belt.

Philip power walked toward the men and cleared his throat. They flinched and whirled on him.

"Mind if I interfere?" Philip asked.

Oden joined his brother and inspected each man for signs of concealed weapons.

"Who the hell are you?" the man with the undone belt asked. He looked to be in his late twenties, with a head full of red hair and a face dotted with freckles.

His two companions—a young, skinny man who also had red hair, and a tall, husky man with a bushy beard—stepped forward, their hands hovering near their waists.

"We're good Samaritans, here to do our duty," Philip said.

"Yeah?" the freckle-faced man asked. "And what's that?"

Philip gestured to the young woman. "Save the lady and report you three to the officials."

"Report us?" Freckles chuckled darkly. "You got to be alive for that."

The other two men joined in on the laughter.

"Look here, this is what we're gonna do," Freckles went on. With the flick of his wrist, a knife appeared in his hand. "You two will keep walking, and me and my boys will pretend you never interrupted our fun."

Philip frowned and shook his head. "I'm afraid we can't just walk away and let you morons defile this poor lady. How about you three leave this forest and turn yourselves in to the local authorities? I heard there have been bandits wandering around, and I think it's safe to assume you're them."

The three men smirked at one another.

"It looks like they're onto us," Freckles said to his companions.

"Seems that way," the husky man rasped. "What d'you wanna do about it, boss?"

Oden muttered a silent spell, and the ground formed an impression around the three men's feet.

"I say we gut these assholes," the skinny man said, retrieving a small knife from a holster around his waist. "And as they bleed out, they can watch us fuck the lass."

Freckles grinned. "Kyle, you wicked shit, I think that's exactly what we'll do."

Oden shouted a command, and the grass surrounding the men formed into tendrils that grabbed each man by the ankle. Their eyes widened, and then they tried to yank their legs free.

"What in the hell is happening?" Freckles asked, his voice rising an octave. "Who are you guys?"

"We're the assholes who tried to warn you," Oden said, "but you were too stupid to listen. Now, you'll have to die."

He poured his fire magic into his wand. An orange flame rose from the tip, illuminating the surrounding darkness, and he mentally formed it into a blade.

All three men fell to the ground, grabbing handfuls of grass as they tried to scurry away. Oden chuckled inwardly. This was the exact response he'd been expecting. Then he noticed that the young woman was curled in a tight ball, more afraid of *him* than she'd been of the bandits.

Way to go, you idiot. He withdrew some magic so the blade wasn't as intimidating.

Philip stalked toward Freckles. "How about we try this again? You three let this lovely lady go, and we all can go our separate ways."

"Separate ways?" Freckles echoed.

"That's right," Oden said. "And don't come back to this forest ever again, if you know what's best for you."

"I'll do anything to get away from you devil-bred bastards." Freckles's voice was shaky, his eyes flitting from Philip to Oden.

Oden raised a hand, and the tendrils shriveled, becoming grass once more. When the men's ankles were released, they shot to their feet and ran off.

"I really wish I could've killed those guys," Oden said as the men faded into the dark trees. He stopped channeling magic into the wand.

The woman had uncurled herself, but she tensed when Philip approached. He crouched five feet from her.

"Hello, Miss," he said kindly. "My name is Philip, and that man over there is my older brother, Oden. We won't do you any harm."

The woman glanced at Oden, and then at his wand.

"It's all right," he said, returning it to its holster. "I fight for the United Army of Telkendor, and that weapon is how I train my magic."

"The United Army?" The woman perked up. "You two are soldiers."

"Sorcerers, to be more exact," Philip corrected. "Very powerful ones at that."

Oden hid his eye roll. Philip offered a helping hand, and the woman took it, dusting herself off once she got to her feet.

"I didn't catch your name," Philip said.

"Oh. I'm"—the woman hesitated—"Tessa. My name is Tessa."

Her breath hitched after stating her name. She had likely lied, but her real name was irrelevant. Philip was trying to make her feel comfortable, and it seemed to be working.

"All right, Tessa," Philip went on, "if you don't mind me asking, where are you headed? My brother and I would gladly escort you."

"No, you don't have to do that. I'll be fine." She surveyed the area, her body still shaking.

Philip nodded. "I believe you. I'm sure those idiots are long gone, but it would make me sleep better if I knew for certain that you'd safely made it to your destination."

"We're on our way to Cotsketta," Oden chimed in when Tessa still appeared reluctant. Her eyes lit up at the name. "You're free to tag along if your destination is anywhere near there."

"What business do you have in Cotsketta?" she asked.

"Our sister is getting married to a salamander," Oden said gloomily.

"You mean a Salamon?"

Both brothers did a double take.

"Wait, you know Rufus?" Philip asked.

Her face reddened. "I don't know him that well, but my family does business with his family. Rufus is the one who invited us, but I was the only one who could make the trip." She frowned. "You said your sister's getting married. Isabella's your sister?"

"She is," Philip confirmed.

Tessa sighed and stared off into the distance. "She's a lucky woman."

"To have bothers like us?" Philip puffed out his chest.

The woman snapped out of her trance and eyed Philip, then Oden. "Why, of course."

It was clear that wasn't what she'd meant at all. She thought Isabella was lucky to be marrying Rufus? The pool of available men must be very shallow.

"Well, since you're going to Cotsketta," Philip said, "then it's settled. We're walking together."

"If you insist." She said it calmly, but there was pep in her step as she walked between them. "You two are really sorcerers for the United Army?"

"We are." Philip slung his rucksack over his shoulder. "That weapon you saw my brother wield is only given to renowned warriors such as ourselves."

It was a blatant lie, obvious to anyone who understood how wands really worked. These were practice tools, used mostly by apprentices to learn how to better control the energy in a power stone. Inside each wand was a small rock, infused with the four magical elements: wind, water, fire, and earth. When Oden had made the fire blade, he'd connected his magic with the magic in the stone, drawn out the desired element, and shaped it into a weapon. Against a regular person, the wand was deadly, but had they been battling an Elementalist or Sorcerer, it would have been useless. Higher mages knew how to draw power from the stone itself and use it at will, even if the stone was in someone else's possession.

"I must admit, that thing terrified me," Tessa said.

Philip chuckled and stepped closer. "We'd never hurt a lady. Especially one as pretty as you."

Oden *did* roll his eyes this time.

Tessa appraised him. "Is that so?" From her tone, she didn't believe him.

"What? I'm being serious."

"I'm sure you'd say that regardless of what I looked like. Even if I were a hideous troll."

"If you were a hideous troll, Philip would've left you in the custody of those nitwits we scared off," Oden said, and Tessa cocked an eyebrow. "His chivalry only travels so far. I would have rescued you, though, troll-face and all."

"He's just messing around with a false assessment of me," Philip said to Tessa. "He's always saying the darndest things to gain people's favor."

Oden shrugged. "He's right. Usually, I over-inflate myself to make it appear I'm more important than I really am."

Philip narrowed his eyes at his brother before turning back to Tessa. "Tell me, are you friends with our sister?"

"Isabella? No. I only heard of her recently. Rufus is the one who told me about her. He kept going on about how *perfect* she was." She released a long sigh.

As the three of them traipsed through the wood, they shared stories of their upbringing. Tessa was from Zelsh, a small town just a few miles east of Oden's village. Two of her closest cousins had moved to Cotsketta a few months ago, and she'd thought it would be a grand idea to pay them a surprise visit before attending the wedding.

Philip regaled her with tales of their adventurous childhoods, leaving out all the parts that included Rufus. An hour later, the torchlights lining the streets of Cotsketta came into view. They exited the forest, and Philip turned to his brother, grinning from ear to ear.

"Do you see that?"

Oden nodded his agreement, knowing the words would come out strained if he opened his mouth. He'd missed his home, but he hadn't been prepared for this kind of emotion. *Mom, Pop, Izzy, Uncle Clementine, Aunt Jen...* He was about to reconnect with all the family he'd missed so much. It took time for him to settle his breathing. Finally, he cleared his throat.

"Yeah, I see it."

"Well, what are we waiting for?" Philip set a hasty pace. "If we make it in time, we can catch supper before Mom puts the food away."

The trio strode by tiny homes and storefronts. Just as Oden was wondering how far Tessa planned on following them, the Clark family's meat market door swung open, and two young women in dark dresses walked out holding paper bags.

Tessa rushed forward a few steps. "Fiona? Ella?"

Both women whirled around, and all three squealed as they held each other in long embraces.

"What are you doing here?" one of the other woman asked Tessa.

"I'm here for—" She glanced over her shoulder as if just now remembering her escorts. "Thank you so much for earlier."

"Don't mention it," Philip answered.

"I wish I could pay you guys back."

"Save me a dance and we'll call it even."

"Deal." Tessa turned back to her cousins, and the ladies strolled down the road.

Philip playfully elbowed his brother. "I think she likes me."

"I beg to differ. How much do you want to bet she already forgot your name?"

Philip held out a hand. "I bet she'll be falling all over me before the end of the wedding."

Oden hadn't meant for the bet to be taken literally, but this was too good to pass up. He grasped his brother's hand and gave it a firm shake. "One week of laundry duty."

"Too easy. You wear the same robe every day."

Chuckling, Oden pushed his brother away. "I do not."

From the corner of his eye, Oden spotted a stocky man with a graying beard approaching, smiling and wagging a finger at them.

"I knew I smelled trouble," the old man said.

Philip guffawed. "Old Man Mitchell."

Mitchell appraised them, then nodded. "It's good to see the war hasn't worn you down. You two still look young and healthy." His pleased expression faded. "Not too many of the soldiers from Cotsketta can say the same. Most have either died or come back missing limbs."

Five years ago, recruiters had arrived in Cotsketta and required every man aged fourteen to twenty-five to perform rigorous physical acts. The ones who had performed the best had been forced into the military. Oden knew now that the recruiters were

Elementalists, and though they needed soldiers for the war, they were really looking for people who displayed magical abilities.

Recruits with no magic were shipped off to training before eventually entering the war, while those with untrained magic were sent to the Academy, where they learned how to draw on and master their underdeveloped powers. Since magic-wielders were so scarce, they only fought in the war when it was necessary, leaving most of the fighting and dying to the common man.

"That's very unfortunate," Oden said.

"Unfortunate indeed. Well"—Mitchell's expression lightened—"I don't want to hold you up. I'm sure Bray and Sheila will be excited to see that their boys are back." He clapped each brother on the shoulder. "We'll catch up another time."

At the end of the road was a large apple tree the brothers used to climb. To the right, there was a small cottage with a wooden sign that read "Rye Bread Bakery" on the front door.

Oden and Philip ran down the walkway and up the porch stairs. Getting to the door first, Philip turned the doorknob and barged inside, and they both halted in the small living room. Everything was exactly how Oden remembered it.

Chapter 3

A family portrait from when Isabella was a toddler hung over the fireplace. Next to the fully stocked liquor cabinet in the corner was an antique leather chair, and in that chair, with his fingers wrapped around a teetering glass, was a snoring man.

Pop. There was some gray in his beard that hadn't been there before, and a pair of glasses hung from a string around his neck. Oden lifted the glass and set it on the nearby end table.

"Hello?" a woman called from the kitchen. "We're in here."

Despite how grown-up she sounded, Oden recognized his little sister's voice. He dropped his rucksack on the living room floor and hurried into the kitchen with Philip behind him.

Two women hovered over the stove, adding herbs to a steaming pot. The shorter and plumper of the two swayed from side to side as she hummed a tune, while the other tilted the lid of the pot open for the seasonings, leaning forward slightly, a stirring spoon in her other hand. The hip swayer turned when the song she'd been humming came to an end, and her eyes glazed over.

"My boys!"

Isabella whipped around and beamed. She placed the lid back on the pot, and the two women approached with faces brimming with emotion. They gave one another a huge group hug.

"We're home, Mom." Oden kissed her on the temple.

"How I've missed you two," she said, pulling away and dabbing at her eyes.

Oden wiped the wetness from his cheek. "Yeah, I've missed you too."

"Your cooking most of all," Philip said.

Frowning, she pinched their cheeks. "You two look so thin. Are they feeding you?"

Oden chuckled. "Yes, Mom. They feed us."

"But not nearly enough," Philip added, peering at the pot of food.

"Let me fatten you up." She made her way to the cabinet, pulling out two bowls.

"Please do," Philip said, following her. "Do you need help with something?"

Isabella hadn't moved since breaking away from the group hug, and tears continued to streak down her face.

"Izzy," Oden drawled in a low voice. He wiped her tears away with his thumb.

"I didn't think you guys were going to make it." She stuffed her face into his chest, and he wrapped his arms around her. "You guys sharing this moment with me means the world."

"When do you have to go back?" Mom asked.

"Two weeks," Philip said, sitting at the table with a bowl of steaming food.

Isabella stepped back, smiling. "Two weeks? That's good, because there's so much to catch up on."

"Speaking of catching up," Oden said as he took a seat in front of another bowl of food, "where's the salamander?"

Isabella chortled. "Salamander. I forgot you guys used to call him that."

"Used to..." Oden said. "That's his name."

"Stop it, you know that's not true." She sat next to him.

"Sheila, whose bags are these in the middle of my floor?" a man's voice boomed from the living room.

Oden winced and got up. "I had better calm the big guy down."

He hurried into the living room, where his father, Bray, had his bag on the couch and was preparing to rummage through it, grumbling under his breath.

"You might not want to do that," Oden said.

A smile replaced his father's frown. "I'll be damned." He rose to his full height. "I thought some homeless bastard had broken into my house and thrown his trash onto the living room floor."

They closed the distance in a few strides and embraced. The familiar smell of tobacco smoke and whiskey on his father almost brought another wave of tears, but Oden held them back.

"Funny you should say that because it was your bag."

His father chuckled. "How have you been, boy?"

"I've been good, Pop."

"Well, you look good." He glanced at the remaining rucksack still on the floor. "Where's your brother?"

"Your favorite son is right here," Philip said as he entered the living room. He gave his father a tight hug. "It's good seeing you, Pop. Now, if you don't mind, I need to get back to this wonderful bowl of stew."

"Dinner's ready?" Pop asked.

"Your bowl is waiting for you, Papa," Isabella called.

"Good because I'm starving."

The three men sat at the kitchen table.

Pop picked up his spoon, rice and broth spilling off the sides. "How long have we got you for?"

"Two weeks," Oden said, stirring the food in his bowl.

"That's perfect." Pop nodded briefly. "There's work out back I need you two to do."

"Are... are you serious?" Oden asked. "We're on vacation."

"You're on vacation from the military," Pop pointed out. "There's no paradise here, only work." He chuckled to himself. "How's the war treating you? Every time a mail carrier steps onto the porch, I always imagine they're bringing grave news."

"We're surviving," Oden said, "but we've been lucky so far."

Pop glanced down at his bowl. "It would be nice to have you two home again. Then maybe I could... finally get a good night's rest." He blinked several times as he concentrated on his spoon.

"Yeah, I hear you, Pop," Oden said. His mother was dabbing at her eyes again; the war seemed to have hit them hard, if only emotionally. Oden had had it rough at the Academy, and he'd missed his family, but he'd adjusted to military life by now.

They ate in silence. When dinner was done, their mother collected the bowls and began to wash the dishes.

Pop patted his full belly. "It's time for me to hit the sack."

"You already slept," Oden reminded him. "When we walked through the door, you were fast asleep."

Groaning as he got to his feet, Pop waved away the words. "That was only a warm-up—a pre-bed nap." He kissed Isabella on the forehead. "Don't let these two keep you up all night. You have an important date tomorrow."

"I won't," Isabella said fondly.

Pop pointed at each of the brothers. "If I hear her giggling in the middle of the night, I'm coming for you."

"You don't have to worry about Oden making anybody laugh," Philip said. "The guy's got the comedic talent of a corpse."

Oden held out his spoon as if it were a dagger. "You're going to be a corpse if you keep on talking."

Isabella stifled a laugh.

Oden stood. "Do you need help with the cleaning, Mom?"

"No, no," she said as she scrubbed a bowl. "You two relax. I know you're probably tired from the trip."

"You got that right." Philip yawned, stretching both hands in the air. "I am beat." He rose to his feet and kissed their mother on the cheek. "Dinner was excellent. Better than I remember."

She chuckled softly and hummed a low tune as Philip left the kitchen.

Before following him out, Oden hugged his sister. "I'll see you tomorrow, Izzy. I'm skeptical about that guy you're marrying, but I'm happy that you're happy."

Isabella batted his arm lightly. "Goodnight, Oden."

"Goodnight."

Two small beds with mattresses but no covers sat across from each other in Oden's old room, and supplies for the family business were stacked against the wall opposite the doorway. Apparently, in their absence, the room was used for storage.

Philip stood in front of his bed, his hands on his hips. "I don't recall our beds being so small."

"I was thinking the same thing." Oden tossed his bag on the mattress, then rummaged through the chest in the room's corner for sheets and blankets. Finding a stash, he lobbed bed coverings to his brother and plucked a pair for himself.

"I can't wait until tomorrow." Philip flattened out the sheet on his bed. "I wonder what Tessa will be wearing."

Oden unfolded a blanket. "You're wasting your time."

"Nope." Philip flopped on his bed and kicked his shoes off. "I think not."

"You know what your problem is?" Oden asked, pulling his robe over his head. "You're delusional."

"It's pronounced, 'optimistic.' Do you know what your problem is? You're a pessimist."

"It's pronounced, 'realist,'" Oden retorted, climbing under the blanket. "You should try it sometime."

"You going to bed already, old man?" Philip asked, sitting on his bed with his back against the wall.

"Yep. We had a long day, and I'd like to be prepared for tomorrow's festivities."

"You mean the dancing?"

"I mean the food and ale. You won't catch me dead on any dancefloor."

Philip stretched and scanned the room. "We've only been gone for five years, but everything in this house seems so much tinier."

"That's because everything in the Academy is enormous by comparison." Oden closed his eyes. "I was pleased by the size of our dorm at first, but as we've gotten older, you've gotten messier. Now, I dread living in such a large space."

"Ha ha," Philip deadpanned, then yawned. "But we both know which of us really is the slob."

"You can't be serious. You've turned our dorm into a retirement home for random trinkets. I bet you don't even remember how to use half of those things. And don't get me started on the tomes about alchemy and dark magic. You'll probably get arrested if Master Meridel ever discovers you've been gathering illegal books. You're just lucky I'm your brother and not some kiss-ass punk hoping to gain favor by turning you—"

A loud snore rippled through the room, cutting him off. Cracking an eye open, he saw that Philip was asleep with his head tilted to one side. Oden watched his brother for a time, then finally closed his eye.

"Goodnight, Philip."

Chapter 4

For breakfast, the Rye family had an assortment of pastries, piles of eggs, bacon, sausages, and fruit.

"If I keep eating like this," Oden said after he'd picked his plate clean, "the army is going to put me back in boot camp when I return."

During important events such as weddings, every business in the village donated their services. Philip and Oden helped their father transport baked goods to the village hall, where the food would be prepped for the reception, and for the rest of the morning Oden tried to stay busy to stave off his bristling nerves. The closer they got to the wedding, the stronger the fluttering in his stomach became.

Too soon, he was dressed and staring at himself in the bathroom mirror as if *he* were the one taking the big leap.

Someone pounded on the door. "Are you all right in there?" Philip asked.

"Of course. Can't a guy take a piss in peace?" Oden washed his hands, though he hadn't really been using the bathroom, and finally stepped out.

"Everybody's waiting on you," Philip said. He was biting at his lips, and Oden realized his brother was just as nervous as he was.

"Well, I'm ready. Lead the way."

Twenty minutes later, they were at the village hall, where there was already a line of villagers at the door waiting to enter. The traffic was expected; events such as weddings didn't happen often in such a small village, so when it was time to celebrate something as sacred as marriage, people showed up in droves.

A red carpet runner separated the main room into two sections. The left side was reserved for the friends and family of both wedding parties, and the right side was for everyone else. A quartet played a soft melody while the villagers found their seats. Oden waved at the family he hadn't yet connected with as he sat next to his parents.

Then two men approached the altar. When they turned to face the waiting crowd, Oden immediately recognized one of them. Rufus's father looked the same as he remembered, his graying, short-cropped hair freshly cut. Next to him was a young, tall, handsome man wearing a white button-up shirt, blue trousers, and a pale green tie. He had a soldier's build, with broad shoulders and sizeable arms—a stonemason, maybe. His features were familiar, but Oden couldn't put a name to the face. He leaned toward his brother.

"Who's that guy standing next to Todd?"

"I was about to ask you the same question."

As if sensing their stare, the man looked in their direction and beamed, displaying a chipped front tooth.

Oden and Philip drew back. They knew that goofy grin.

"Salamander?" they said simultaneously.

"But how?" Oden said. "When did he...?"

"That boy was a gargoyle before we left."

"Quiet, you two," Pop grumbled.

When Pastor Mathias entered, hunched over from old age, the music died down and everyone got to their feet. Still awestruck by Rufus's transformation, the two brothers were the last to rise.

The pastor squeezed Rufus's shoulder affectionately before standing behind the altar. "You may be seated," he said, and everyone obliged. "Rufus Salamon has been an important part of this community, always ready to lend a helping hand to those in need. If anyone deserves to stand here waiting to embrace happiness, he is the perfect candidate."

Philip nudged Oden. "Important part of this community?"

"Right. What in the seven Hells has happened since we've been away?"

Pop cleared his throat, and the brothers fell silent once more.

"And if there's a lady lucky enough to have stolen his heart," the pastor went on, "surely it's the lovely Isabella."

A door in the back of the room opened, and in walked the bride, practically glowing in her soft green dress. Sounds of adoration filled the room.

"Look at our baby, Bray," Oden's mother said, already on the verge of tears.

"I see her, Sheila," he said in a shaky voice. "I see her." Pop wrapped an arm around his wife's shoulder and pulled her closer to him.

Rufus's father met Isabella halfway and held out a hand. She placed her hand in his and everyone quieted.

"It is tradition for the father of the groom to welcome the bride-to-be into the family, but you've been a part of our family since you were a little girl. My wife and I used to sit on the porch and watch you two play, knowing all the while that we were witnessing fate's hand. I am truly honored to officially introduce you as a Salamon. If my son ever breaks your heart, you just tell old Todd, and I'll set him right. I swear it."

Isabella gave him a big hug, and they both pulled away, eyes shining.

Todd guided her to the altar and moved aside so the bride and groom could face each other.

"Marriage is a bonding of souls that might be tried and tested but will never break," Rufus began, his voice deep and steady. "I am your weapon and your shield. I am your true mate. When death parts us, I will find you, Isabella. I will find you, and court you, and stand before you once more, reciting this vow."

Beside Oden, Philip was sniffling.

"Are you crying?" Oden taunted him.

"Of course not. There's something in my eye."

"Yes, I see it. They're called tears."

Rufus pulled a silver ring out of his pocket and slipped it onto Isabella's finger. Then they both turned to the crowd.

The pastor raised his hands, and everyone stood, already clapping. "I welcome you all to Mr. and Mrs. Salamon."

The newlyweds shared a long kiss, and the band started up again. Workers entered and folded the chairs to prepare the other room for the reception. Oden's parents approached their daughter, engulfing her in a hug, then conversed with Rufus's parents.

When the brothers reached the bride and groom, Oden couldn't help surreptitiously appraising Rufus, who was much taller than he remembered.

"I'm glad you could make it." Rufus held out a hand.

"I wouldn't have missed this for the world," Oden said, then frowned at the vicelike, almost painful grip of their handshake.

Rufus smiled, his eyes never leaving Oden's.

Is he challenging me? Oden tried to squeeze harder, but Rufus's pressure never wavered. Finally, Rufus released his grip and shook Philip's hand. When he pulled away, he nodded and turned to join the conversation between their parents.

"I think he just tried to break my damn hand," Philip said in a hushed tone.

"Mine too," Oden said, flexing his fingers. "What a bastard."

"When did he get so strong?"

"I don't know, but if he tries it again, I'm setting his ass on fire."

A beat later, everyone was being ushered into the next room. Tables lined the walls, each one housing platters of food. Everything smelled sensational, but Oden's attention immediately zeroed in on the dozen kegs in the room. He made a beeline to one of them, grabbed a cup from a nearby table, and began to fill it up.

"Step aside," Philip said when the dark golden liquid reached the brim, pushing Oden's cup out of the way with his own.

"You almost made me spill a drop." Oden brought the ale to his lips, and his shoulders relaxed after the first sip.

Philip stood beside him and followed his gaze to their sister, who was now sitting next to her husband at a table. "She looks happy, doesn't she?" He took a large swig, beat his chest, then burped loudly.

"She does."

Philip plucked a pastry from a nearby table, bit into it, and sighed. "Everything at the Academy is gruel compared to this. You're gonna have to drag me back to the train kicking and screaming."

Some of the wedding party stood in line to get their meals while others, including Tessa, danced to the music in the middle of the room. Philip must have noticed her the moment Oden did, because he stuffed the rest of his food in his mouth and downed his drink.

"Get ready to do my laundry," he said, shoulders bouncing as he strode toward the dancing woman.

To Oden's surprise, Tessa smiled at Philip and broke away from her group.

"Damn it." This was another bet Oden was about to lose to his brother. Gulping the rest of his drink, he refilled it while scanning the crowd. A familiar face peered back at him, the skinny man's young features twisted in a snarl.

"This can't be right," Oden muttered. In the far right corner was another man he recognized. Though the husky man blended in well with the crowd in his dark gray suit, his bald head and bushy beard gave him away.

Oden barely registered the cup of ale slipping from his grasp and spilling on the floor. Elsewhere in the room, the red-haired bandit with freckles pointed at Philip. Standing next to him was a clean-shaven stranger with a razor sharp jawline, brown eyes, and long black hair tied in a tight bun. The man closed his eyes for a heartbeat, and when he opened them, they were bright red.

Oden's heart almost leapt from his throat. "Vampire." Was this the vampire Meridel had warned them about, or was this some other bloodsucking bastard?

The vampire was opening a long cello case, but before he could pull free whatever was inside, Oden ran onto the dancefloor.

"Philip!" he boomed, retrieving his wand from his leg holster. "Vampire!"

Philip was slow to respond, but a sudden wave of magic ripped through the room causing him to turn. That's when the lights in the room shut off, and the windows where the sun streamed through went black.

Chapter 5

Oden shouted an incantation that dispelled the illusion, allowing him to see the vampire as he closed in on Philip with Master Calahan's stolen sword. Pouring wind magic into his wand, Oden formed a blade. It clashed against the Sword of Tumahn as Donovic brought it down to slice Philip.

Donovic smirked when their eyes met.

The band had stopped playing, but there was a new song in the air—a symphony of screaming as the three bandits stabbed people at random with wickedly sharp daggers.

Philip shouted the dispel incantation and formed a sword of fire, and nearby guests scrambled away from the flames.

"What's going on?" Philip asked Oden as they defended themselves against Donovic.

"Those three idiots from the forest are here."

In Oden's peripheral vision, a man was stabbed from behind. The lights had never gone out, but everyone else in the room was still blinded by the illusion.

Oden sidestepped a strike at his abdomen, then swung at Donovic's neck, but the vampire was too fast and easily evaded the blow. A spinning heel kick sent Oden to the ground, and when he got to his feet, Philip was knocked down by a fist to the side of his head.

Donovic was preparing to finish him when he suddenly whirled to his left. With unnatural speed, Rufus grabbed Donovic and threw him across the room. The vampire slammed against a wall and fell to the ground, then leapt to his feet, baring his fangs. Oden watched in horrified awe as Rufus charged the vampire with balled fists and began dodging the sword strikes.

Philip caught his brother's attention as he got to his feet, holding his midsection.

"Are you all right?"

"I might have broken ribs," Philip admitted. "How is Rufus—"

Behind them, a woman howled Bray's name.

Kyle, the skinny, redheaded bandit, pulled his blade free from a falling body—and before Oden could pick out whether it was his father or not, he was already running, pushing through the crowd.

Kyle hunched over the body and lifted the dagger once more, but Oden was there in an instant. With one swipe, Kyle's hand tumbled to the floor along with the dagger. The young man brought the bleeding stump to his face and screamed, but he was quickly silenced by the wind blade slicing through his neck and removing his head from his shoulders.

Oden knelt next to the writhing body of his father. Blood stained Pop's upper arm, and Oden winced at the deep wound.

"Pop, are you all right? Pop?"

"Damnit," Pop groaned.

People pushed against them in their attempt to get outside. He had to get his father up before they were both trampled.

"Pop, I'm going to lift you."

Pop's eyes slid to Kyle's head. "Who was that guy?"

How was he supposed to answer that? Should he tell his father about meeting the attackers in the forest—that the reason they were killing the villagers was because of Philip and himself? Heat flushed through Oden's body at the realization that this was his fault. If he had followed his intuition and killed the men, none of this would be happening.

"I don't know, Pop," he finally said. After he'd helped his father to his feet, he turned to see where Philip was and how Rufus was faring against the vampire, but someone slammed into him, knocking him back to the ground.

"Isabella!" Rufus's voice boomed over the chaos. "Get your hands off my wife!"

"Someone stop him!" Pop yelled.

When Rufus got to his feet, Oden spotted Donovic on the run—and in the vampire's grasp was a flailing Isabella. Glass exploded outward as he jumped through the large window. Rufus tossed people aside as if they weighed nothing and leapt out the window after them.

Oden quickly appraised the room. All the bandits were down. Mom and Rufus's parents appeared unharmed. Philip disappeared through the front door, chasing after Donovic.

"Have someone see to that wound," Oden told his father.

Without waiting for a response, he pushed through the lingering villagers as they tried to make sense of what had just happened. Outside, people were still running while peering over their shoulders at the hall. Philip was ascending the hill leading to the vast forest.

Oden darted after his brother, lungs and thighs burning as he pushed himself to catch up. At the top, Rufus was pacing back and forth in front of a giant wall of black smoke that obscured the entrance to the forest.

"What's going on?" Oden asked, gasping for air while Philip slowly brought his hand to the wall.

"Another illusion spell," Philip answered, "but this one is much more powerful than the one he cast in the hall."

"Can you do anything about it?" Rufus asked with a growl. "The longer we're on this side of whatever this is, the more ground we'll have to cover."

"I'm aware." There was a sharp edge to Philip's tone. His hand glowed white, and he stepped forward and touched his hand to the wall. Lightning rippled through the smoke, and then the wall was whisked away with a violent gust of wind. A fog blanketed the land, and the daytime sun that beat at their backs didn't extend into the dark, eerie forest with its trees bare of leaves.

The magic signature from the Sword of Tumahn gave away Donovic's position, but it was fading fast.

"Whoa!" A woman's voice caused Oden and Philip to turn. Tessa was peering dubiously into the trees. "Does it always look like this?"

"Who cares?" Rufus stepped deeper into the forest. "I have to find Isabella."

"We have to move with caution," Oden said, but Rufus showed no sign of hearing. Oden held his weapon at the ready, then told Tessa, "Go back to the village."

"No." She shook her head. "I want to stay with you guys."

"It's not safe here."

"He's right," Philip agreed in a soft voice. "Go back to your cousins' home and wait there."

Tessa's face contorted in anguish. "Both of them are dead," she whispered. A tear streaked down her cheek, and she hastily wiped it away. "I don't want to be there by myself." She opened her mouth to say more, but Philip placed a hand on her shoulder.

"I'm sorry," he said, holding his weapon at the ready.

"I don't want to see their bodies again." She paused, collecting herself. "I'd feel a lot safer with you two."

Oden couldn't spare the time convincing her why accompanying them was a terrible idea. A few steps into the fog, he saw the newlywed sniffing the air, his fingers outstretched at his sides. The way he was standing, Oden expected to see claws protruding from his curved fingers.

"What's wrong?"

Rufus slowly scanned the area. "Do you smell that?"

All Oden discerned was mud and wood rot. "I'm afraid you'll have to tell me what I'm supposed to be sniffing for, because at the moment, I don't..." He trailed off at the sight of glowing red eyes and a familiar grunting and chattering of teeth.

"What is that?" Tessa asked, pointing and backing away.

"Goblins," Oden muttered in disbelief. "I *hate* goblins."

"They're an illusion, right?" Philip asked. "They can't hurt us."

Oden retrieved his wand as the goblins exited the fog. There were at least a dozen, but more were charging forward. "I don't think they were made from a simple illusion spell. They are the real thing."

"How are we going to fight them off and get to my wife?" Rufus asked, baring his teeth at the incoming force.

Oden glanced at his brother. "One of us has to stay and hold them off."

Philip spun. "You'd better not be thinking what I think you are thinking."

"You sense the faint trace of magic from the sword, don't you?" Oden asked. "It's only a matter of time before we lose track of it."

"I'm the better fighter," Philip retorted. "I should stay."

"And I'm the better caster."

"They're closing in!" Rufus announced.

"Go, Philip," Oden said, pushing his brother away. "I got this."

"You can't fight all of them off by yourself." Philip's voice was strained.

"We don't have time for bickering. Do what the hell I tell you for once," Oden said, but the anger he tried to summon wouldn't come. Philip was right. There was no way an Apprentice Elementalist could successfully kill a horde of goblins. This was a suicide mission, and they both knew it. His throat tightened the longer he held Philip's gaze, and he forced himself to look away.

"Damn it, Oden," Philip said so only they could hear. "You'd better not get yourself killed."

"You should know me better than that." Oden poured his earth magic into the ground. "I'm too stubborn to die."

Philip turned to the others and said, "Let's go." Darting toward the clear path to the left of the goblins, he summoned a wind blade. Tessa was right behind him, but Rufus hesitated, looking from the goblins to Oden before trailing after Philip.

Several goblins moved toward the trio, and Oden recited an incantation, transforming the nearby rocks into gleaming jewels. Goblins had many flaws, one being their obsession with shiny objects. Immediately, they were transfixed.

"That's right, you ugly bastards. Come to me."

The gawking goblins closed in cautiously. The illusion itself didn't require too much energy to sustain, but Oden couldn't maintain it while on the run, or else he'd be on his brother's heels.

A goblin plucked a jewel from the ground, and the jewel reverted to a mundane stone. The goblin tossed it aside and picked up another. It, too, transformed into a rock. Slowly, the goblin turned its sneer on Oden.

Recanting the illusion, Oden pushed wind magic into his wand and went on the offensive. With a spin move, he cut the heads off three goblins, then sliced another in half. All four poofed into black smoke, which was whisked away by a breeze.

The number of goblins had multiplied. There were at least a hundred now. Oden turned his wind blade into a wind whip, then swung, taking out four more. He lifted his weapon for another strike, then screamed in pain as a goblin bit into his leg, tearing off a chunk of trouser and thigh meat.

Oden cut the supply of wind, replaced it with fire, and rammed the flaming blade into the culprit's chest.

"Come on!" he shouted, shifting his weight the best he could with his damaged leg.

Two goblins rushed him. He stabbed both of them through the chest with a single blow. Whipping around, he decapitated another and another—and then something heavy landed on his back, knocking him to the ground. A goblin bit into his shoulder. As he tried desperately to get to his feet, more teeth clamped onto his left forearm. He wailed in agony but managed to kill three more goblins before they piled atop him.

The blade of fire vanished. Tears burned his eyes. This was supposed to be a joyous night. He was supposed to be celebrating the happiest day in his sister's life. Instead, he was about to be eaten alive by fucking goblins. He roared as he tried to summon the strength to rise to his feet and run, but an even louder howl echoed through the night sky. The goblins stilled, then turned toward a fast approaching figure running on all fours. Oden couldn't believe his eyes.

A werewolf.

Snarling and peeling away from Oden, the goblins faced the new threat. The werewolf tore through the horde, teeth and claws converting the goblins into puffs of smoke. It bit one on the neck and ripped its head from its body, then spun and did the same to another. Some of the goblins retreated from the fight and fled into the fog, while the others continued their fruitless assault.

The werewolf ripped the last of the goblins apart, then turned around looking for more. When its eyes landed on Oden, it halted, and his heart sank to the bottom of his stomach. Patting the ground, his gaze still on the werewolf, his fingers brushed his wand as the beast stalked toward him and stepped into the moonlight. Oden took in the werewolf's broad shoulders, its massive maw, and the eyes that seemed to burn into him. Then it stood to its full height, and he gasped.

White dress shirt, green tie, blue trousers.

"Rufus?"

Chapter 6

The werewolf closed the distance and carefully lifted him off the ground.

"What's going on?"

Cradling Oden close to his chest, Rufus bounded off.

Clashing weapons drew Oden's attention, and he angled his head. Philip was blocking the vampire's strikes with a stone blade. Earth was the easiest element to control and required the least amount of energy to sustain. That meant his reserves were running low.

Tessa was watching the battle from the cover of a large tree. One hundred feet beyond her, pressed against a large boulder by something that looked like a spiderweb, was Isabella. She, too, was watching the fight between their brother and Donovic. Relief washed over Oden at the sight of his sister squirming to get free. She was still alive.

Rufus carefully placed Oden on the ground next to Tessa, who leaned away from the werewolf. She didn't appear frightened, though. She must have seen Rufus shift.

"I thought I smelled a mutt," Donovic announced as he dodged an attack from Rufus, who had bared his teeth and joined the fray. Philip backed away from the fight and fell to one knee. He heaved in air, then staggered to his feet.

Tessa examined Oden and gasped. "Are those bite marks?"

"Trust me, it looks worse than it feels."

"I doubt that."

His vision swam like he was on the verge of passing out, but he couldn't afford to rest. Philip was struggling, and Oden didn't know how long Rufus could keep the vampire at bay.

"Help me up," he said with a groan.

Tessa frowned. "What for?"

"I need to help. Maybe I can get to my sister and free her."

"But you can't," she said vehemently. "If you get too close, the giant spider will get you."

"Giant spider?"

She pointed. "It's atop that large rock. You can't see it now because... it's invisible."

"An Invisible Spider," he muttered.

"I know; it sounds crazy."

"No, that's not it. Invisible Spiders are a magical species of arachnid. They're not too difficult to kill."

"Are you certain?"

Something about her tone made him pause. "Fairly. Why?"

Tessa shuddered. "It was just so... enormous."

"It'll be all right. With your help, that spider won't stand a chance."

"My help?" She drew back. "Help you how?"

"When I attract the spider's attention, I need you to stab it from behind."

Tessa's breathing quickened. "I can't go near that thing."

Oden rested a hand on her shoulder. "Control your breathing. You'll be fine. The Invisible Spider isn't too smart. Once I get it to focus on me, it won't notice you creeping toward it for the killing blow."

Tears shined in Tessa's eyes. "You don't understand; I'm afraid of spiders. Really, really, really afraid. I either scream or freeze up every time I see one."

Oden's hand slid from her shoulder.

"I'm so sorry," she said.

He restrained his sigh. "Don't worry about it." He'd have to do it by himself. If he could cut Isabella loose before the spider attacked, he was sure he could hold it off long enough for her to run the short distance to Tessa. Whether he lived or died fighting the spider was irrelevant so long as his sister was safe.

A pained howl filled the air. Rufus was on the ground, blood dripping from a wound on his stomach. Philip and Donovic circled one another as they contemplated their next moves. The vampire's face and chest were shredded, and his left shoulder hung as if broken. Philip didn't have any visible wounds, but Oden hadn't forgotten about the possibly fractured ribs.

"Wait here," he said to Tessa. "I'm going to free Isabella and tell her to run to you."

"By yourself?" she asked in a panic. "You can barely move."

He made it to a kneeling position. If the trio failed to kill the vampire, he could at least get the word out to Master Aysa. She needed to know that they'd found Donovic and that he knew how to use the magic in the Sword of Tumahn.

"When Isabella makes it to you, I need you two to run as fast as you can to my parents' house. Inside my bedroom is a brown rucksack, and in that sack is a piece of paper with a woman's name and address on it. That man fighting my brother and Rufus is a vampire. His name is Donovic. Head to that address as soon as you can and tell Master Aysa everything that transpired since our meeting in the forest."

"What if she doesn't want to come with me?"

"Drag her away."

The clash of weapons resumed.

Oden loosed a long breath as he considered his next words. "I won't lie to you, Tessa; we might die here. Just in case, I want you to tell my parents—"

"No," she cried out, the color draining from her face. "I won't."

"This is important, Tessa. Please." His throat constricted. "Tell them Philip and I lived with no regrets... and that we were satisfied." He had to force out that last part. Turning away so she wouldn't see the tears building in his eyes, he channeled wind magic into his wand. It wasn't a lot, but it should get the job done.

Grunting as he got to his feet, he limped toward Isabella. His sister noticed his approach and her eyes widened. She shook her head frantically and a muffled yell escaped her. She was trying to warn him about the spider. He picked up the pace until he was sprinting. Thirty feet, then twenty, and then... the spider revealed itself and quickly descended the boulder. Oden froze.

Tessa had informed him that the arachnid was a giant, but it was now clear they had different interpretations of the word. A spider the size of a dog was "giant." A spider as large as a grown man was "giant." What stalked toward him was a monstrosity—a carriage on stilts. Oden's head tilted upward. It was damn near twice his height.

"You've got to be fucking kidding me."

He held his weapon in front of him and swiped at the spider, and it backed away and crouched. Then the spider's rear end vibrated. It was about to lunge. A blink later, Oden leapt and rolled on the ground as the spider blew past him. His thigh burned from the sudden movement, but he jumped to his feet and ran to Isabella.

Ten feet, then five feet... Something thin yet powerful slapped against his shoulder, knocking him to the ground. The spider loomed over him with a wide-legged stance, its fangs rubbing against each other. A drop of liquid fell from its mouth, and the ground near Oden's head sizzled.

Oden prepared for an attack, clutching his... his... Where the hell was his wand? He sensed the magic from his weapon, then let his eyes flit to his right; one of the spider's claws was pressing it into the ground.

You idiot!

This was his second time dropping his weapon. The spider lowered its mouth, and Oden squeezed his fingers into a fist.

Then something pelted against the spider's body and thumped to the ground. It was a large rock. The spider shifted, and another rock hit it, this time on the head.

To Oden's surprise, Tessa was hurling stones at the beast. Like before, its abdomen shook. It lifted its leg from the wand as it maneuvered for a lunge, and he rolled to his weapon, shot to his feet, and rammed the wind blade into the spider's abdomen, slicing the arachnid all to way to its mouth. Limbs buckling, it squealed, then vanished in a puff of black smoke.

A pair of arms wrapped around him from behind, and he turned to see Isabella hugging him, fresh tears falling down her face. Apparently, the web restraining her had disappeared along with the spider.

"I wish we had more time to talk," he began, "but do you see that woman?" He pointed to Tessa. "She has something to tell you. Hurry."

She glanced at the fight, then back at Oden. "What are you about to do?"

"My fist is about to get better acquainted with that asshole's face."

The concern in Isabella's eyes was palpable, but she said nothing. She hugged him once more, lingering for several seconds before running to Tessa.

The two ladies shared a brief conversation. Isabella seemed hesitant to leave, but they eventually sprinted away. Hopefully, any remaining goblins would be confined to the parts of the forest where the sword's illusion reached, and Oden was certain the women could outrun them.

He hobbled toward the fight.

Chapter 7

"If it isn't Donovic," Oden said.

"I see you're well informed." Donovic dodged a swipe from Rufus's claws.

"Your men killed a lot of people in that hall. Good people."

"I told those morons to stop robbing carriages near the train station—that one day the officials would get involved. Did they listen to me? Of course not. But their ignorance paid off. It brought me to you two—soldiers from Meridel's army. I can tell by those weapons you wield."

"Just to let you know, they're all dead. Unfortunately, you'll be paying for their crimes. But because you come from a prestigious family, I'm sure if you turn yourself in now, you'll get a fair trial."

Donovic laughed. "Is that right?"

"It is. So, drop that stolen sword on the ground, take ten steps back, and kneel with your hands behind your back."

"Stolen weapon? This sword was a gift."

A kick to the stomach sent Philip flying backwards. He got to his feet to continue his assault, but Oden held out a hand, palm forward, to halt him.

Rufus backed away, taking a breather, and Donovic did the same.

"Gift from who?" Oden asked.

"From the previous owner." He laughed again.

"Who helped you?" Oden asked. "I don't mean to insult you, but Master Calahan was a Battle Mage, and while your skills with that sword are impressive, there's no way you could have killed him on your own."

Donovic smirked. "I'd tell you my secret, but I don't see how it matters. You three won't make it out of here alive to tell the tale."

"I beg to differ."

Donovic looked from Oden to Philip. "Well, why not? I'll indulge you. Considering you know the traitors, seeing the shock on your faces should be worth it."

"What makes you think we know them?"

"How did my name come up?" Donovic quirked an eyebrow. "Who mentioned me?"

"What does that have to do with anything?" Philip asked.

"Everything. Think about it; two Elementalists find the body of a Battle Mage and somehow knew it was me who did the killing?"

"They saw you fleeing," Oden pointed out.

A lopsided smile exposed one of the vampire's fangs. "Or they're the ones who killed him." His smile widened at the surprise that must have shown on Oden's face. "Do the names Kaylor Trebekia and Lisette McAllister sound familiar?"

A shiver ran down Oden's spine at the names of Master Aysa's confidants. Could Donovic be telling the truth? Grand Sorcerer Meridel had never disclosed who had reported the Battle Mage's body, but those two Elementalists did routinely leave the compound.

"You're lying," Philip said, stepping forward.

"Why would I? What do I gain by lying to lackeys?" Donovic twirled his sword. "No matter. Believe me or don't. You'll be taking that information to the grave." He attacked Rufus with a side slash, barely missing his stomach.

Philip and Oden went on the offensive, but the vampire evaded each strike, countering with attacks of his own. Oden pivoted to escape a lunging blow, but he didn't move fast enough and the sharp blade slid along his side. He collapsed, holding the deep wound. His hand faintly glowed as he channeled what little healing magic he knew to stop the bleeding.

Donovic kicked Philip in the face, leaving him writhing on the forest floor, then executed a spinning move with his sword that almost severed Rufus's arm. Rufus howled as he cradled the damaged limb. Slowly, the vampire appraised the battlefield, then stalked toward Oden.

"Looks like this is the end for you three. I'm actually quite disappointed." He shook his head. "I expected so much more."

Oden tried to scurry away, but all his strength was gone. He didn't even have any energy to pour into his wand.

Donovic lifted the sword over his head—and the tip of a stone blade protruded from his chest. He looked down at it, confused. Philip's weapon withdrew from the vampire's back and he stumbled. Isabella moved in front of him and stabbed him again, this time in the heart, and his eyes rolled into the back of his head as he swayed. Then, just like the spider, Donovic and the sword poofed into black smoke.

"What in the world?" Oden said hoarsely. Had Donovic also been an illusion? Even the sword's magic signature was gone.

Suddenly the fog lifted, revealing thick, healthy tree trunks and a green canopy above. Streams of sunlight illuminated the forest floor.

Hiding his smile, Oden said, "You two aren't supposed to be here." He turned to Tessa. "I thought I told you to drag her if you had to."

"I tried," Tessa said with a shrug, "but she's stronger than she looks."

"Don't you get mad at her," Isabella said, kneeling at his side. "Once she told me your last words to our parents, I knew I couldn't leave you two to die."

"Thank you, Izzy, but if there's ever a next time, I'd feel a lot better if you'd just do what I say. I'm serious. You could have gotten yourself killed."

She examined his wounds, pressing his sore flesh.

"You should probably check on your husband. He's in awful shape."

She glanced at Rufus, who was shifting back into his human form. "He's a lot tougher than you think. He'll be fine. You, on the other hand, desperately need a medic."

"What I *need* is to contact Master Aysa," Oden said, sitting up. "If Donovic was telling the truth about the spies, then she's in grave danger. She has a competent force supporting her, but if there are indeed traitors among her team, she might not see the threat until it's too late. And if something bad were to happen to her, there's no telling what the Grand Sorcerer would do."

"Isabella," Rufus called. She turned and stood, and Rufus crashed into her with an embrace.

"I'm fine, Rufus."

With his hands on either cheek, he pulled her in for several kisses. "I don't know what I would've done if I'd lost you."

"All right," Oden said as he got to his feet. "I hate to disrupt your moment, but you two have some explaining to do. How and when did you become a werewolf?"

Rufus scrunched his face at the memory. "About a year ago, Isabella and I spotted some old guy in the forest. He was mumbling to himself. We thought he was delirious. When we asked if he needed help, he got a crazed look in his eyes and said something about a war and needing more soldiers to fend against the impending evil."

"What the hell does that mean?"

"I don't know. He turned into a werewolf after that," Rufus said, "but not like my transformation. He was still in human form but with sharp fangs, long claws, and yellow eyes like a wolf. We tried to escape, but he pinned me down."

"I punched and kicked the man," Isabella said, "but the blows did nothing."

Oden pinched the bridge of his nose. "You tried to fight a werewolf with your bare hands? Do you have a death wish?" When his sister didn't answer, he went on, "And then what happened?"

"The werewolf ran off after it bit me, and we never saw him again."

Wincing at the pain in his leg, Oden held out a hand and helped Philip to his feet before turning back to Rufus. "I'm assuming no one else in the village knows you're a werewolf?"

"No. Only Isabella."

"Good. If that vampire returns, though—"

"What do you mean?" Isabella asked, falling into step beside him. "I killed him. He *is* dead, right?"

"Honestly, I'm not sure. That the sword disappeared as well gives me the impression we were battling another illusion." He sighed. "If anyone knows what that sword is capable of, Master Aysa should. We need to see her as soon as possible."

"You need to rest up and heal, Oden," Isabella said.

"Nonsense. I already stopped most of the bleeding. I'll sleep in the carriage."

"How far do you have to travel?" Rufus asked. "Maybe we can accompany you. If you think that vampire is out there somewhere, we stand a better chance fighting him together."

"Don't think you're leaving me behind," Isabella said, meeting Oden's gaze defiantly. "I'm coming too."

"I was afraid you'd say that, and frankly, I don't have the patience to tell you otherwise. Besides, I'd feel a lot better if I could keep an eye on you—make sure you're safe." He turned to Rufus. "We're going to Ulikin. We should be there by morning."

"What about me?" Tessa asked. "Can I come with you guys? I don't want to stay here, and I'm really not looking forward to walking home by myself."

Oden considered saying no, but her sorrow persuaded him otherwise. She'd been through a lot in such a short time. He was surprised she hadn't already broken down in tears. She was much tougher than her timidness suggested.

"Why not? You saved my ass against that monster of a spider. Thank you for that."

Tessa shrugged as if it was no big deal, but her face reddened and a smile tugged at her lips.

"I need to see Mom and Pop first," Oden went on. "See how they're faring. Then, we leave."

* * *

Dark Mage Kortel disenchanted the sound amplification spell he'd used to listen in on the group's conversation. His hands tingled, and not from the use of magic. He'd suspected Meridel would assemble a team to investigate the death of one of his high-ranked Battle Mages, but he'd had no idea he'd send his own daughter.

"So, how'd it go?" Donovic asked, kneeling next to him. Sweat drenched the vampire's face and upper torso from using the Sword of Tumahn for an elongated period.

"Better than expected." Kortel held out a hand, and a bird formed in his palm, then immediately took flight. It would follow the group as they made their way to wherever Aysa was stationed, then scout the area. "You were right to fetch me after discovering there were magic wielders nearby. If we play our hand right, Meridel might never emotionally recover and this war will be as good as ours."

Donovic stood and sheathed his sword. "Would you like me to inform my father? His army is ready when you are."

"Not yet. I still have a job for you."

"Oh?"

"Tomorrow morning, I want you to head back to the village and burn it to the ground."

To be continued...

Note from the Author

My stories tend to end in a way that suggests there will be more. Therefore, I'm always forcing myself to remain in a world I was only supposed to visit. As usual, I fell in love with these characters, and with that love came the need to continue their journey. I don't know what's in store for Oden, Philip, Rufus, Isabella, and Tessa, but I'm ready to see how it all pans out. If you want updates regarding these characters and more, sign up to my newsletter or follow me on TikTok (@author3djohnson).

Thank you for taking the time to read Grown from Tainted Seeds. I hope you enjoyed it.

Also By Dartanyan Johnson

Space Opera

Book 1 in The Crystal of Life Series

A kingdom cast in shadows, a family's dark history, and the crystal shard that brings them together. Crestahn Kingdom has always prospered under the Sovereign's dominion, so imagine Sha'ella's surprise when she discovers her father is part of a coup to take him down. What's worse, he wants her to aid in his betrayal. But turning on the ruler of the galaxy might get her killed, and refusing to do her father's bidding will draw the rebels' ire. Can Sha'ella find a way to please both sides, or will she be forced to make a decision that will put a huge target on her back?

TW: Death of a Loved One Graphic Violence

Dark Fantasy

Empress Elmira: A Prequel to A Heart Stained Blue

In this series of short stories, you'll discover what molded the daughters of an outcasted witch and a renegade soldier, into becoming the most feared trio in the Majestic Forest. *Story One:* Amid a war between two elven kingdoms, two young witches save a wolf-shifter boy from a life of servitude. *Story Two:* On a hunting trip gone awry, Vance has a run-in with a golem constructed by dark magic. Now he must fight to save his mentor's life, even if that means sacrificing his own. *Story Three:* Awakened by a horrifying dream, Miliandra notices her mother hasn't returned from her trip to the market. *Story Four:* The fairy queen has sat back and allowed the elven soldiers to hunt the magical beasts in the Majestic Forest for far too long. Tired of the forest dwellers not getting the proper protection, Elmira challenges the fairy queen's reign. *Story Five:* Elmira senses a disturbance. A demon lord has infiltrated the magical barrier surrounding the forest.

TW:

Death of a Loved One

Graphic Violence

About Dartanyan Johnson

I wrote my first script during my 6th period class as a senior in high school. I was so bored (sorry Mrs. Noonan) that I decided to pull out my folder and start writing. I finished my first draft in a couple of months. It had to be one of the greatest stories ever told! Almost 20 years later, I ran across that very screenplay and almost cried from embarrassment. It was trash. But that sparked the desire for writing my first book.

The ability to express one's self through various genres is probably one of the greatest self-healing practices in creative writing. It lets me speak about serious issues and work them in an elaborate storyline, while allowing others to confront a difficult past.

Being the introvert that I am (as most authors seem to be), there are entire worlds in my head with characters that feel a lot like family. My job is to pull you into these worlds, introduce you to these characters, and let them live rent free in your head as they've lived in mine.

Beautiful Untamed Things

NIKITA ROGERS

Advisory

The trigger warnings for Beautiful Untamed Things are pretty light. It is a story of friends, family, social commentary, but with that, there are a few things you may wish to be aware of. This includes:

Domestic Terrorism

Violence

Bombings

Murder

Death

Ritual Magic

Cutting of hands for the use of spells

Blood

About the Book

There are three rules that a witch must abide by in the modern world.
1. Never perform spellcraft in public. If a normie catches you, it's curtains.
2. Always keep your mark hidden.
3. Craft with care. Whatever you cast will come back times three. Always.

Unfortunately for Margot Fawn, magic at its purest form can never be completely tamed. Living in a city where the witch population are persecuted, arrested and executed by a tyrannical government, Margot has lived her 19 years of life pretending to be human and living a normal life. Living as a normie, however, is proving harder and harder by the day, and the battle to keep the magic contained inside her veins is a war she cannot win.

When her magic inevitably slips, resulting in the murder of a man, Margot finds herself pushed into the world of witchcraft for the first time, teaming up with a group of misfit orphaned witches to try and locate a necromancer to undo her misdeeds, before the government finds *her*. However, the battle between human and witch, normal life and the craft, is a war only magic can win.

Beautiful Untamed Things is a story about finding family in the most unlikely places, of magic, political unrest and underground rebellion.

Gubbins

There are three rules that a witch must abide by in the modern world.
1. Never perform spellcraft in public. If a normie catches you, its curtains.
2. Always keep your mark hidden.
3. Craft with care. Whatever you cast will come back times three. Always.

At least, that's what her book of shadows told her. Generally, witches kept their company limited to their own. It kept them safe, away from those who would do them harm and strengthen the bond within their coven. A coven, however, was something Margot did not have. A coven would suggest you had a family, or siblings, or... anything really. All she had that tied her to her family was the dusty book of shadows that lay on her lap, complete with frayed edges and dog eared corners from the many times she had read it. The magic that ran through her veins seemed to scream at her to let it out when she touched the pages, but she never dared. Living as a human was much easier, and much safer. She hoped if she swallowed the magic down long enough, it would eventually disappear.

Magic, however, had a nasty habit of making itself heard, no matter the place, and no matter the consequence.

Margot trailed her finger down the first browned page of the book, stopping half-way where a beautifully scrawled 'Heather. A. Fawn' was scripted in red ink. Her mother, she assumed, considering they shared the same surname.

She didn't know what she looked like, or what her voice sounded like, but from reading her mothers' innermost thoughts scribed in the pages of her book, it almost felt like she *knew* her. She didn't, though. Her mother had been taken by the suits when Margot was just a baby, leaving her under the caring wing of a normie woman named Jane with nothing to know her by except *this book*.

Being raised as a human wasn't easy, however. Jane had her own set of rules that she governed with a kind smile and a stiff shoulder, but the older Margot became, the harder they were to follow.

1. Be careful of new friends, not everyone is a witch sympathiser. Even if they were, they would never admit to it, lest they be captured too and executed.

2. Be wary of your emotions. Don't get too excited, or too scared, or too drunk. Even the smallest flash of magic will get you taken by the suits.

3. Don't go looking for other witches. The only way to keep yourself safe is to hide in plain sight, living as a normie.

4. If you let anyone see your mark, don't bother coming home. They will follow you and take away everyone you love.

That was what happened to her mother. Jane had told her that the makeup that was covering the mark on her shoulder had smudged, revealing the glowing outlined star that every witch was born with somewhere on their body. Luckily, Jane had swooped in and taken her, skipping towns and cities until they were far enough away not to be followed. She was safe, living as a normie. *Incredibly bored*, but safe.

Still, no matter how secure it was living this way, she always longed to feel the pulse of magic inside her chest run free. She only wished she had the nerve.

Margot let out a deep sigh, closing over the heavy cover of the book of shadows and pushing it back under the bed. It wasn't the best hiding place, but it wasn't as if anyone was going to come and steal it. Everyone in the house knew what she was, and frankly, they didn't care. That was the beauty of being under Jane's care. So long as you accepted her rules, she accepted *you*, no matter your quirks.

She stood from the floor, scooping up her phone from the bed to check the time. It was just after 10 P.M, and there was a slew of messages that had gone unanswered while she had been reading.

Text: Tiffany Williams

"When are you leaving?"

"Hello?"

"Margot! Answer your fucking phone!"

"I'm leaving to go to The Cloaked Cat, you better be there!"

"*DAMN IT MARGOT!*"

Margot smirked, running a hand through her dark-red hair to fix it back into place. Tiffany was nothing if not impatient. She was spoiled and used to getting her own way, which usually consisted of alcohol, bad boys, and watching whoever was playing at *The Cloaked Cat*. Tonight, that was a local band called 'The Junkyard Dogs', and *she* was going to be late.

Knocking drew her attention away from the screen of her phone to the heavy wooden door of her bedroom. It opened just as she was tucking it away into her pocket and fixing the hem of her dark blue jeans. Liam's head of blonde hair poked through the crack in the door hesitantly until she gave him indication to come inside. He pushed the door open with his foot and leaned on the door frame with his arms folded and a serious expression knitting his eyebrows. Liam was Jane's biological son. They shared the same-coloured hair and deeply suspicious outlook on life, and he was the oldest of them all. Something he liked to remind her of on a daily basis.

"We made popcorn, with sugar and cinnamon, and those stupid chocolate covered mini pretzels you like," he said, jutting his thumb over his shoulder towards the hallway. "Lydia is waiting for you, and you know what she is like when it comes to snacks. If you don't come now, they will all be gone. The movie is about to start."

Margot hissed through her teeth and grimaced, clenching her hands into fists at her sides as the familiar sense of guilt washed over her body. "Shit."

"You forgot?" Liam asked, studying her and frowning deeper. When he realised from her expression that she had, he breathed out a sigh and pushed off the door frame. "Of course you did. Well, I'm not explaining to her why you are bailing, you can deal with that yourself."

"Liam, I'm sorry!" Margot called to him, but he was already stalking back into the hallway, leaving the door open and allowing the room to fill with a chilled breeze.

She stood for a moment, watching the emptiness in the doorway while her fist-tight fingers at her sides relaxed. The third Friday of the month was *always* movie night. It was a tradition Jane had enforced since she was young to keep the family she had created together and *talking*. Talking wasn't Margot's strong point, and the movie nights always ended with Jane having fallen asleep, Liam scrolling on his phone and Lydia becoming over-hyped from the numerous snacks she had stuffed into her mouth, while Margot half listened over the pages of one of her novels. It was sweet, really, and as much as she enjoyed those nights with her adoptive family, she knew there would be more of them to come. It wasn't every night that 'The Junkyard Dogs' played in *The Cloaked Cat*, though.

The sound of Lydia's happy giggling moved Margot's feet towards the doorway, where she grabbed her handbag and closed the door over quickly with a heavy *thud*. Lydia was hanging from Liam's back while he spun in the middle of the living room, her little legs kicking backwards so far they almost hit Margot in the chest.

"Wow! Looks like someone is already halfway into a sugar-high, huh?" She laughed as she came up to their side and reached to tickle Lydia's ribs.

Her skin-tingling six-year-old shrieks filled the air, and her arms instantly unhooked from Liam's neck so she could fall to the floor and wrap them around Margot's legs instead.

"Yes! We made's your favourite! And mommie is makin' us all hotty chocolate n' marshmallows, and the princesses on TV are gonna go to the castle!" Lydia squealed.

Guilt pulsed in her chest at the sound of her excited voice, and after sharing an uncomfortable look with Liam, she took Lydia's arms and crouched down in front of her. Her face was covered in the remnants of chocolate, and her eyes were wild with childhood joy.

"Kiddo, I know you are excited for the movie, and I wish I could stay with you, but I really need to go out with my friend tonight."

Lydia's happy expression fell from her face. Her hazel eyes grew sad, and she looked up from under her mess of blonde hair to look at her brother for confirmation while she hugged her arms around her little body. Liam placed his hands on his hips and shrugged.

"She isn't staying?" she asked, her voice smaller than before. She turned to look back at Margot, her brows knitting together. "You aren't staying? B-but it's movie night's, and we made your favourite. . ."

When Lydia's voice cracked in the threat of tears, Margot reached forward and pulled her into a tight hug, rubbing circles on her back and kissing the side of her head. "I know. I'm so sorry, but I am going to make it up to you, okay? Tomorrow we will snuggle up in my room, and we can pull out all my make up and play make-over, and I'll do your hair in those curls you like. We will have a girl's day, okay?"

Small sticky fingers snaked their way into Margot's hair as she held her. She could feel Lydia's chest shudder, but she hadn't started crying yet. "You promise?"

"I promise. Tomorrow. You and me," she replied, pulling back from the hug to look into her eyes.

Margot stood again and watched as Lydia shuffled off to slump on the couch with her blanket and bowl of popcorn, just as a montage of dancing princesses and knights on horses graced the television screen. She smiled warmly, then turned to look at Liam.

"Mom wants to talk to you in the kitchen before you go. Probably the usual lecture," he said, brushing past her to sit beside his sister and dig his hand into the bowl.

She watched them for a little longer, then turned on her heel and quietly made her way to the small kitchen. Jane was standing by the kettle, her shoulder-length dirty blonde hair falling around her face as she stared down into her cup. She was already in her pyjamas and fluffy slippers, with a dressing gown wrapped snugly around her tense shoulders.

"Hey. Liam said you wanted to speak with me before I head out," she said as she walked to her side and leaned in for a sideways hug.

Jane sighed deeply when she faced her. Her hand reached out to lace her fingers in one of Margot's deep red locks beside her ear, teasing it back into place. "Where are you going?"

"The Cloaked Cat. Tiffany got us tickets to see a band we like, and I promised I would go with her. I'll be careful."

"Hmm. . ." she puffed out a sigh and pulled back her hand. "And your mark, it is covered?"

"As well as a mark on your hand could be, I guess." Margot shrugged, pulling her hand up to her face to show her the makeup she had blended over it as best she could. "Waterproof."

"But *not* bulletproof," Jane said, her head tilted as she took her hand and stroked the back of it fondly, then lowered her voice to a whisper. "It is simply bad luck that yours is on your hand. Your mothers' was on her shoulder. Most other witches have theirs in a place that can be hidden, but not yours. It's dangerous."

"It could be worse. It could be on my forehead." Margot laughed, but when Jane didn't return the gesture, she took her hand back and placed both of them on her shoulders. "I'm going to be fine. It's just a bar with a friend. I'm not going to get myself into any trouble. I'm good at this *human* thing, I've had a lot of practice."

"The fact you believe that matters, scares me," Jane replied, then pushed Margot's hands from her shoulders so she could pull her into a hug. "Be safe. I love you. And if you get your cover blown—"

"Don't bother coming home. I know the rules," she said, pulling back from the hug with a roll of her eyes. "Go to the locker at the train station, grab the money and run as far as I can."

"I know it's harsh, Margot, but if you get caught and you come home, we will all be arrested. They could kill us, including Lydia and Liam. I can't let that happen. If they catch you, you k—"

"Keep my mouth shut. God, Jane, I *know*. Okay? I got it. Can I go now? Please, I am going to be late."

Jane sighed deeply, her eyebrows frowning in that concerned expression she always wore. She nodded once, then reached to hold Margot's face and leaned in to kiss her cheek. "Go. Have *fun*, or whatever it is you kids do these days."

Margot wrinkled her nose and pulled a face, making Jane scoff a laugh and let her go. "For the record, I love you too, Jane."

She turned, walking quickly to the back door and opening it wide, the chill of winter air hitting her in the face and forcing her to pull her leather jacket close to her skin. Just as she stepped out onto the porch, Jane's voice drew her head back inside.

"Oh, Margot?"

"Mmmhmm?"

Jane smiled at her around the doorframe, her hands wrapped around her cup of steaming coffee as she brought it up to her lips. "You look just like your mother tonight. She would be very proud of you."

Margot bit down on her lip, but she smiled through the tingle that Jane's words left on her heart. Her face was turning red in a blush, and for a second, she thought she could see it mirrored on Janes. Words didn't seem to form a reply in her throat, so instead she nodded once and gave her a small wave, then closed the door and made her way down the steps and onto the snow-covered footpath.

The Cloaked Cat wasn't exactly the most modern of bars, but it did have character. *'Character'*, Margot had come to learn, was a simple synonym for *'completely run down'*. Still, there was no place she would rather be on a Friday night than in the front row, watching the band play and screaming along to the lyrics with her best friend. The reasonably priced, yet incredibly strong vodka-soda's would, at the very least, warm her body from the cold that had settled in her bones from the walk across town.

It was snowing again. Cold white flakes were collecting in her dark-red hair as she stood opposite the bar, her hands shoved in her pockets and her shoulders hunched up to her ears to save them from the chill. Tiffany was standing outside the red paint-chipped double doors, waving frantically and bouncing in her hot-pink miniskirt and gigantic black fur coat. Margot waved back, waiting for the last car to drive past before she took off across the road in a half-walk, half-run that made her slip when she reached the icy pavement. Her arms shot out either side of her body, flailing to keep herself steady.

"Woah! Jesus, you think they would salt the pavement," she said, righting herself and coming to Tiffany's side. She was frowning deeply at her through narrowed eyes. "What's that look for?"

Tiffany puffed out an angry sigh. "I have been waiting here for you for forty-five minutes!"

With a roll of her eyes, Margot hooked her arm through her friends and pulled her into her side before she tugged her towards the back of the queue of people waiting to get inside. "It's not my fault you are criminally early *every damn time.* The door's aren't even open yet, Tiff."

"I am aware, but the earlier you are, the closer to the stage you get, and I wanted to be here in case the boys got here early, too," she said, stopping at the back of the line and poking her head around the person in front to get a better look.

Margot let Tiffany's arm go from her hold, shoving her hands back into her pockets and frowning at the back of her friend's blonde head. "What boys?"

"Nothing."

"Tiff!" she snapped, grabbing her arm to turn her around again from her snooping. When she finally looked at her, she set her face into a grimace and shook her head, "What boys?"

Tiffany squirmed on her feet, reaching her hands towards Margot with splayed fingers to try and calm her down. "Promise you won't get mad!"

"I swear, if you don't start talki—"

"I invited Jake and Will," she interrupted, grabbing Margot's shoulders when she started to groan. "I know you don't like them, but I *really* like Will, and he said he would only come if Jake could come with *you*, so I said yes! He likes you, you just need to give him a chance."

"I gave him a chance, Tiff! Remember? When you blindsided me when we were supposed to be bowling, and they were there, and suddenly I'm on a double date I *didn't* want to be on! You promised me you wouldn't do this again. . ."

"I know! *I know*, I'm sorry." Tiffany hissed through her teeth, her nose scrunching as she rubbed Margot's arms to warm her. "I promise, I won't blindside you ever again, but please, just do this for me tonight? This will be my third date with Will, and tonight could be *the night*, ya know? Be my wing-woman! Please!"

She pulled her hands away and replaced them against her chin with her palms together, silently praying with her eyes shut tightly and her mouth pulled in a wide smile.

"Tiff. . ."

"Pleasssseeee?" Tiffany cracked an eye open and laughed when she saw Margot's quickly dissolving expression. "I'll love you forever?"

"Jesus, fuck. Fine."

A happy scream erupted from Tiffany. She threw her arms open and enveloped her in a tight, jumping hug, spinning them on the frosted pavement while her head of blonde hair fanned around them in the wind. "Thank you!"

"Yeah, alright, but you owe me."

Tiffany let her go, a wide grin on her face as she held Margot's hands and pulled her forward. The line was beginning to move, and within a few moments they found themselves near the double red doors. The heavy humming of music was filtering through them as they neared, the tell-tale signs that the support group was getting ready to play. She could feel the low bass notes vibrating all the way through her chest, quickening her heart and making her grip Tiffany's hand back tightly.

"Girls."

The sound of Will's voice cut through the music like acid. She tried to hide the roll of her eyes as she stared at Tiffany, who gave her a flash of a warning look before she spun to face him.

"Will! You came!" She chirped, jumping on him in a chest crushing hug. He wrapped his arms around her and leaned his face into her neck, eliciting happy giggles from her friend.

"Of course we came. I wouldn't miss this little pink skirt for the world," Will mumbled into her neck, his hands already snaking under her huge fur coat.

Margot tried to ignore them, until she felt the heavy weight of an arm wrapping around her shoulders. Jake stared down at her with a crooked grin. He smelled like whiskey and cigarettes, masked with overtones of mint-flavoured chewing-gum and obnoxiously too much aftershave. His dirty blonde hair was combed and gelled within an inch of its life, and his eyes were hooded from obvious intoxication.

"Hey." he grinned.

"Hey," she managed to say back, her smile thin and her body tense.

"I've been looking forward to this all day," Jake said, leaning heavier on her shoulders as he moved in closer.

"Yeah, I bet," Margot said flatly, moving her head away from him and pushing him off her shoulders so she could walk forward quickly. "Line's moving, we need to get inside."

She walked in front of Will and Tiffany, who were feverishly kissing and ignoring the world, to the front of the line where she flashed the bouncer the ticket on her phone. He glanced at it lazily, then waved his hand to usher her inside. After thanking him, she walked through the dark corridor as quickly as she could to get out of the cold and away from Jake's arm. She figured if she could get to the stage quickly, it would be so loud that there would be no need for small-talk. Perhaps, *she hoped*, he would get the hint.

The room inside was dark and filled with people. Loud laughing and the clinking of glasses from the bar filled the air among the fog from the machines at either side of the stage. Electricity littered the atmosphere and hit her in the face as she walked closer to the stage, weaving her way through the sea of warm, moving bodies until she found the perfect spot in front of the stage. A support band she didn't recognise was already playing music on strangely shaped guitars, their faces adorned with white and red masks and their lyrics screamed so loudly she couldn't make out what they were saying. Still, the atmosphere was enough to lull her into a daze until the music stopped and the house lights went down.

"I think 'The Junkyard Dogs' are about to start!"

Margot turned to face Tiffany when she appeared behind her. She wasn't sure how long the support band had been playing, but it had obviously been long enough considering Tiffany had managed to weave her way to the bar to get the drinks. She had two plastic cups filled with what looked like vodka and cola in her hands, and she pushed one out towards her. Will was standing right behind her, chugging a beer with his other arm looped around Tiffany's body. She had discarded her black fur coat and was now able to show off the tight white shirt and pink mini skirt she wore. She looked beautiful, and happy to be pulled into his chest. As much as Margot found him completely irritating, he did make Tiffany smile, and that was all that mattered. Jake, on the other hand, was the kind of irritating she *couldn't* run with. He was rude, and pretentious, and demanding, and every time he leered at her he made her feel like she needed a shower. Not that he seemed to care.

"What are your plans after the show?" Jake asked as he pushed in front of Tiffany to stand at Margot's side. He leaned in close to her ear just as the house lights went back up again, and loud riffing guitar notes thrummed in the air.

"I can't hear you!" she lied, tapping her ear and then pointing to the stage, ignoring him by taking a large gulp of her drink and watching as the singer sprung onto the stage and instantly started screaming into the microphone.

The crowd *erupted*. Bouncing bodies jerked into her from all sides, leaving her with no other choice than to down her drink, discard the plastic cup to the floor and start to jump with them, her hands in the air and her hair whipping around her face. There really was nowhere else she would rather be than lost in a sea of people, losing her mind to the music she loved and becoming *part of something*. It was like experiencing what it was like to be a cell in a living, breathing musical organism, *every single body* an essential piece of a complex system that made the experience truly special. And she was part of it, part of *something*. Finally.

It wasn't until the music died down again and the sea of bodies finally relaxed after an hour of moving that she was able to stop vibrating and take a deep breath of stale, warm air. She was sweating, her hair sticking to her forehead and her smile wider than it had been in a long while. The crowd was still in the throes of their musical high, and when the DJ started after the band left the stage, they all started jumping again, bouncing into her sides and forcing her off her feet and straight into Jake's waiting arms.

"Woah! Lets go get another drink!" he shouted, taking her by the arm to drag her away from the middle of the crowd.

As much as she didn't like Jake, and she didn't want to leave the happy surroundings of the dancefloor, she was absolutely exhausted and in dire need of ice water. She nodded, gasping a breath and allowing him to take her by the shoulders and guide her towards the bar. She scanned the area for a glimpse of Tiffany and Will, but they were nowhere to be found. Come to think of it, she hadn't seen them since the music started. Though, to be fair, she hadn't witnessed much except 'The Junkyard Dogs' in all their glory.

"That, was amazing." Margot panted, leaning heavily on the bar and tilting her head back to gasp at the air. It was clearer over here, with the door that led to the alleyway opening and closing as the barmaid took crates of empty bottles outside.

"Yeah, you looked like you had fun," Jake said, reaching forward to loop his arm around her waist and swipe some hair from her face.

He leaned in close, and Margot had to turn her head at the last second and squeeze past him to go further down the bar to try and catch the eye of the barmaid. She wasn't paying attention, spending her time cleaning the taps with a cloth and looking bored. She had a shaved head, dark skin with shimmery gold powder dusted on her chest and arms, making her look like she was glowing. Bright blue eyeliner lined her brown eyes, and her ears were pierced all the way down the curve of both her ears with gold hoops and studs.

"Hey!" Margot called.

The barmaid ignored her again, continuing her cleaning.

"Hello?!" she asked, rolling her eyes and turning to look at Jake when he snaked up behind her, pressed his chest to her back and rested his chin on her shoulder. She frowned, then turned her head to look at him. "Where did Tiff and Will go?"

"Why?" he asked, his hands holding her hips and his lips dangerously close to her neck.

She flinched, placing a hand on his chest and pushing him back so she could disconnect herself from him. He was drunk, she could see it all over his lazy expression. "You need to drink some water, and I need to find my friend."

Jake sighed and rolled his eyes, waving his hand sluggishly in the direction of the door that led to the alleyway. "I think I saw them go that way."

"Thank you."

Margot gave a thin-lipped smile, then moved around him so she could make her way down the corridor to the door. She pushed her hands down on the lock release and pushed it open, then stumbled out into the cold night air of the alleyway. The air outside was so fresh and cold compared to the hot, stale air of the dance floor, that breathing it almost *hurt*. Still, she took several deep lungful's of it into herself, closing her eyes and enjoying the sting.

When she opened her eyes again, she inspected the alleyway. There were large recycling bins, trashcans, barrels and empty crates, but there were no people. It was barren of voices, and the only tell-tale signs that anyone had been out here recently, were the footprints that littered the ground in the snow. The door closed behind her, and she turned in time to see Jake walking towards her.

"They aren't here, are you sure they came this way?" She asked, already taking her phone out of her pocket.

Before she could unlock it, Jake's hands enveloped her and pushed her back into the wall of the building. She blinked in surprise, her hands gripping her phone and her head tilted.

"What are you doing, Jake?"

"You need to loosen up. You are so tense all the time, what's your deal?" he asked, his hand cupping her face and his face moving into her neck again. He kissed her there, and she flinched, pushing her hand against his chest to create space, but he didn't budge.

"You need to get off me, stop it."

She pushed again, but he tightened his grip on her jacket and pressed her further into the wall. Panic settled in her chest, and she could feel her skin start to shiver from the cold as her breath began to build. Chilled flustered breaths vented from her mouth as she pushed at his chest, her body wriggling and her hands in fists. Finally, she drew back her hands far enough so she could shove him, and he took a staggering step backwards.

"What is your problem?!" she shouted, shoving him again.

"*My* problem? Are you serious? This is our third date and you haven't even *kissed* me yet, Margot! What the fuck is *your* problem?"

Margot's eyebrows raised, unable to stop the smirk that pulled the corners of her lips. "Are you dense? This isn't our third date, this isn't even our *first* date, Jake. You are drunk, and I am not interested, I don't know how much clearer I can make it for you to understand."

Jake frowned deeply, his hand moving to slick through his hair. "Will said you liked me."

"Will was lying to get into Tiffany's pants," Margot said, then frowned and looked at the door just as it opened. The barmaid stumbled out into the alleyway, a crate in her arms and her eyes cast away from them, but she left the door open wide. "Now, if you will excuse me, I need to find my friend."

She moved past him, heading for the door just as Jake reached out and grabbed her hand. He held it tightly and tugged her, trying to pull her back into him. "Margot, come on, just give it a chance! I'll take you on a real date, just stay here with me. I'll make it worth your while. . ."

"Jesus Christ, Jake!" she shouted, tugging her hand but he held firm, pulling her and trying to get her to stay. "Let me go!"

She pulled hard, and her hand came free from his grip so she could point a finger in his face. "Touch me again, Jake, I fucking dare you."

Jake's pleading expression seemed to change from frustration, to sheer panic in an instant. He tripped backwards on unsteady feet, his eyes turning wide and his face blanching as he stared at her. His hands raised defensively against his sides, his breathing coming in pants and his body completely tense.

"Uh, I'm sorry, I didn't mean to shout at you, but you really sh-"

"Witch. . ." Jake gasped, his hand trained on her hand and his feet taking him a few more steps backwards. "Witch!"

"What?" she mumbled.

Margot's heart started to race in her chest, and a buzzing sort of panic filled her ears so loudly she almost couldn't hear him as he shouted. She jolted, looking down at the place where her mark was hidden on her hand, but when she found it, she realised it was no longer hidden. It was right there, the small star glowing in the dim light of the alleyway. She had been sweating and dancing so frantically that it must have disturbed the makeup, and Jake's pulling of her hand had smeared it so much that it was completely wiped clean. Her hand started to shake from where she was still pointing her angry finger at him, mid-air.

"Witch!"

"No! No, shh! It's okay! I-I won't hurt you!" she gasped, taking a step towards him, "Please keep your voice down, I can explain everything!"

Jake stumbled back on the snow, his hands turning to fists and his shocked expression switching to anger. "Stay the fuck away from me!"

"No, Jake, *please*!"

The magic in her stomach and chest rumbled in warning as pure, unfiltered fear pulsed through her body. She couldn't let him tell anyone, she needed to keep him quiet, but he was already taking more cautious steps backwards. Then, he turned, keeping his head down as he started to jog down the alleyway and away from her. Before she knew what she was doing, Margot's feet raced after him.

"Jake! Stop! Just wait, I can explain!"

He didn't. His jog turned into a run, and Margot sprinted after him just as he neared the end of the alleyway. When she reached him, she grabbed his arm, spinning him around and staring him in the face.

"Don't touch me!"

"Please, Jake! Just stop!" she shouted, tugging him hard and trying to ignore the magic as it screamed in her ears. She had never felt it this strongly before, but it was flowing in a rage she felt wholly uneducated in taming. He struggled again, and she reached out to grab his shoulders. "Just STOP!"

A flash of white light burst from her palms against his shoulders, and she screamed. Jake's eyes went wide, his body jolted, then his eyes rolled into the back of his head and he collapsed at her feet in the snow. He was utterly silent, and Margot's hands shot up to her face. They looked normal, but they felt ice cold and were tingly all over as they shook in front of her. Tear's pooled in her eyes, and she started to breathe terrified gasps of air.

"N-no no no. . ." she whimpered, sinking to her knees in the snow and rolling him over onto his back so she could check his pulse. "No, no, please wake up!"

He didn't. She couldn't find a pulse under her fingers against his skin, and she found when she reached for whatever medical knowledge she had in the crevices of her memory, they were fogged by panic and fear.

"CPR, CPR, CPR," she repeated to herself, trying to force her body to move and help him. She couldn't though, her body was frozen solid.

"Are you fucking *crazy?*"

Margot turned her head, blinking her tears away enough to see the barmaid as she jogged towards them. She crouched down beside Jake's body and pressed her fingers to his neck, confirming what Margot already knew in her heart.

"He's dead. You fucking idiot! Didn't anyone teach you how to control that shit!?" she hissed angrily. She moved to Jake's head and reached down to slip her hands under his arms and pull his body up. "Don't just stand there, grab his legs!"

"W-what?" Margot sniffled, wiping her cheeks dry.

"I won't ask you again, grab his damn legs!" she snapped, beginning to drag him in the snow.

Margot moved quickly. She grabbed onto Jake's ankles and lifted him as best as she could, but he was heavy, and they had to resort to a half-lifting, half-dragging motion while the barmaid guided them back down the alleyway and towards a wooden door right at the back.

"W-where are we taking him? Is there someone who can help?" she asked when they reached the door.

The barmaid shot her an angry look and dropped Jake so roughly he smacked his head against the ground with a sickening *thud*. "For your sake, you better fucking hope so."

Margot watched with wide eyes as she hammered the door with her fist, her other hand on her hip and her foot tapping against the ground in irritation. There was a sound on the other side, like the scraping of a panel and the squeaking of a hinge.

"Password?" the small voice on the other side said.

The barmaid shook her head and glanced at Margot briefly before she replied.

"Gubbins."

Untamed, stupid magic

Jake's head smacked against every step on the way down into the basement of *The Cloaked Cat*.

Smack. Thud. Smack.

If he wasn't dead before, he was definitely dead now.

The stairs led into a large, stone walled room that looked like a mixture between a clubhouse, and a bedroom. There were bunk beds in the far corner, pull out cots on the floor, three ripped and worn brown leather sofas, and what looked like a barely functional kitchen. Dishes were piled high in the metal sink, and pizza boxes littered the top of the long dining table that sat in the middle of the room. Sitting on the chairs at the table was a girl who looked around twelve years old. She had long, straight black hair that she hid her face behind, and she was wearing an oversized pastel purple cardigan and black leggings. Opposite her was a boy, aged around seventeen. His hair was dusty brown in colour, and was taut against his head in tiny curls. He looked up at them when they emerged from the stairs, setting down his hand of cards and leaning back in his chair.

"You know, this place isn't going to stay secret for long if you keep bringing people here," he said, his eyebrow raised as his eyes met Jake's head. "What's wrong with him?"

"He's dead, that's what's wrong with him," the barmaid snapped. "Don't just sit there, help me get him on the table!"

The boy sighed deeply and stood, walking towards them and grabbing Jake's jacket so he could heft him onto the table. His body flopped down hard, his dead weight solid and his head tilted to the side.

"Are you sure he's dead?"

The barmaid shot him an angry glance as she rested her hands on her hips.

"Alright, okay, yeesh," he mumbled, looking between the body and his friend, "How did he die?"

"Magic. Untamed, *stupid* magic," she said, turning to face Margot. "What the hell were you thinking? You let a human see your mark and kill him right outside our bar! Who the *fuck* are you?"

Margot stood deathly still from her space near the stairs. She had her arms wrapped tightly around her body, the leather of her jacket feeling cold against her skin as she stared with wide, watery eyes. Her body was freezing, and she was shivering so badly that her teeth were chattering. "I didn't mean to."

"That's not what I asked you. What is your name?" she asked, taking a step forward that made Margot flinch.

"Margot." She sniffled, "I didn't mean to hurt him, you've got to believe me. He just. . . he—"

"Saw your mark, I know." The barmaid rolled her eyes, turning away again so she could walk to Jake and take his chin in her hand. She turned his face upwards to look at him, studying his features.

"Wait, this witch got made, and you brought her *here*?"

The voice came from the sofa. She hadn't noticed before, but when her eyes darted in the voice's direction, she saw a man with shoulder length dark hair laying back on it. He was wearing dark jeans, black boots and a tight black t-shirt that had a rip in the middle of the neckline. He sat up, his blue eyes staring a hole through Margot's skull.

"I didn't get made. W-well, I did, but it's not like he can tell anyone about it now," Margot replied, rubbing her wet cheeks with the heel of her hand.

He smirked, standing from the sofa and pulling a cigarette from behind his ear. "I thought you said you *didn't* mean to hurt him. . ."

"I didn't! I—" she breathed out a frustrated sigh and gripped at her hair, "I just grabbed him, I panicked. Who are you all anyway? Are you witches?"

"Guilty," The man with the cigarette said, placing it between his lips and speaking around it. "I'm Felix. That's Theo." He pointed to the boy with the curly hair, then pointed to the barmaid who was now rifling through Jake's pockets. "That is Naomi, and the one who barely speaks is Juliet."

Juliet looked up when her name was spoken to look around the room. Her face bore no expression, but her eyes seemed scared. She looked away again without speaking.

"Witches. All of you?" Margot asked. She had never met another witch in her life, never mind a group of them. If she hadn't been so scared, she would be excited about that fact. Felix nodded, pulling a lighter from his pocket. "Why are you helping me?"

"I never said we were helping you." Naomi looked up from Jake, taking his phone with her. She turned it off, taking the battery out and the sim card before she broke it in half and threw the pieces on the table beside his body. Then, she looked at Felix. "If you light that thing in here, you will be as dead as him."

"Whatever." Felix rolled his eyes and put the cigarette behind his ear again, then walked to the table and leaned on it at Jake's feet. "So, he's a dead human. What exactly are we supposed to do with him? Does he have tracings?"

"That's not for me to find out. I have work to finish," she said, rubbing her palms against her sides to wipe away the invisible signs of death from her skin. She walked around the table, stopping to look between them all. "I will be back after closing. Find a way to make sure this doesn't get traced back to this building. I'm not losing everything I built here over a sexually frustrated man with too much hair gel."

"Well, you should have thought about that before you brought him into the heart of our place, Naomi," Theo finally piped up, looking at her as she stopped dead at the base of the stairs.

"He dropped dead right outside our doors! The cops would have come for him, and the second they figured out it was magic that killed him, the suits would have swarmed this place, and we would all be taken. Is that what you want?!" She snapped, raising her finger to point at them when no one spoke again. "Then. Fucking. Fix. It."

Naomi turned on her heel and stomped up the stairs without waiting for a reply from anyone. The heavy door to the basement opened, letting a gust of wind and snow to flow in before the doorway slammed closed again. The only other sound to break the awkward silence was the lighter Felix had in his hand. He was flicking the silver lid open and closed with his thumb as he stared at the wood of the table.

"What happens now?" Margot asked, looking between them all and wringing her hands in front of herself.

"We need to check him for tracings," Theo said, finally looking up again and moving around the table. "How did you kill him?"

"I don't know. I've never really done any magic before, I always tried to hold it in. But when I grabbed him—"

"Where?"

"His shoulders, I think," Margot said, watching him as he nodded solemnly and started to undress Jake from his jacket.

Felix snapped his lighter closed and placed it back into his pocket, then turned to look at her as he ran his hand through his long dark hair. "Hold on a minute. How old are you?"

"Nineteen. Why?"

He smiled again, then shook his head and sat down on the edge of the table at Jake's feet, folding his arms across his chest. "You mean to tell me you have been alive for *nineteen years*, and have never used your magic?"

She shook her head, then took a small tentative step towards the table to get a better look at Theo as he stripped Jake of his shirt. "No. My mother was a witch, but she died when I was a baby. I have been living with her best friend, as a human, so magic has always been off-limits in our house."

"Well, that's stupid," he replied, then shrugged when Margot shot him a glance. "You can't simply decide *not* to be what you are. The older you get, and the less you use it, the more wild it will become. Especially if you have never been taught how to wield it safely. That's how people like this poor son-of-a-bitch end up dead."

"Will you both shut up for a second?" Theo snapped, looking up at them.

The top half of Jake's body was stripped, and he lay there on the table under the bright light that hung from the ceiling. He looked so pale, and his lips were turning blue. The whole scene reminded her of a medical examination table in a cheesy cop TV show, but it wasn't. No, this was real, and Margot did this to him.

"You shocked him. The magic escaped through your palms, entered him here, and here—" he said, pointing to each shoulder. There were large white marks on his skin that spanned over his arms and chest. They looked like lightning tattooed on skin, and they sparkled like frost. "These are called tracings. Magic will always leave its mark. Some are small, and some are wild like this one, probably because you didn't know to reign it in."

Margot walked to his side and reached a curious hand towards the marks on Jake's left shoulder. She couldn't bring herself to actually touch his skin, but her fingers hovered mere millimetres above, and she followed them all the way down to where they ended near his elbow.

"And this is what will give it away that a witch was the one to kill him?" she asked.

"Exactly. There is no denying it. That is why Naomi is so freaked out. If he is found here, the suits will swarm in and search every inch of this place. They will look at the CCTV, find you with him, track you down and take you away. Not to mention, they will test every person associated with *The Cloaked Cat*, meaning we will be on the chopping block too. We live here, we have nowhere else to go." Theo frowned, looking up at each of them. "Naomi is right, we need to make sure this doesn't come back to this building."

"Before that, we need to put him in the freezer," Felix said as he pushed off the table and wiggled an eyebrow. He seemed to be enjoying it all a little too much for Margot's liking.

"The *freezer*?" Margot asked with a surprised blink, moving to press her hand against her forehead to try and calm the headache that was looming behind her eyes.

"It's not like he's going to stay fresh, and if we plan on fixing this he needs to be in perfect condition. Besides, if we leave him any longer, he will start shitting himself," he replied, helping Theo to replace the shirt and jacket onto Jake's body.

Juliet looked up from her seat, her palms rubbing the top of her thighs anxiously. She hadn't moved her eyes the whole time, but now she seemed on edge. "No," she said in almost a whisper, chewing on her lip. "I just put my favourite ice cream in there."

Theo reached to ruffle the hair on the top of her head. "We will get you new ice cream."

They both hefted the body off the table and moved him towards a door near the back of the room, disappearing behind it for a few long moments. Margot could hear them talking in hushed voices, then the sound of a heavy door and the moving of ice. When they emerged again, Felix was placing his cigarette back into his mouth and lighting it with the silver lighter from his pocket.

"You do realise that when the medical examiner does an autopsy, they will know he was frozen," Margot said, walking unsteadily to the table and pulling out a chair so she could slump down before her legs went from under her.

"That won't matter. There won't be an autopsy," Felix grinned, taking a large draw from his cigarette and blowing the smoke out as he stood at the top of the table.

Theo returned to his seat opposite Juliet, lifting the hand of cards he had been looking at when they were interrupted. "Why?" he asked, rearranging the cards and throwing down a six of diamonds onto the pile that had been under Jake's thigh.

Juliet lifted her own pile, flicking through them and throwing down a card on top of his.

"Because, they aren't going to find his body at all. Like you said, if they find his body, they will trace his last movements, which will lead them straight back here," he replied, looking between them with a smug grin from around his cigarette.

"Jack changes to spades," Theo mumbled, throwing the card down and looking up at Felix. "Then what is the plan, exactly?"

"We. . ." he said, puffing out another puff of smoke and leaning heavily on the table with his hands, "are going to find a necromancer."

Rise and Shine, Motherfuckers

Margot rolled onto her side from her place on one of the torn brown leather sofas in the middle of the room. By the time she had calmed down enough to ask what exactly a necromancer *was*, Juliet had already hefted herself into one of the bunkbeds, and Felix had disappeared out the main door to 'deal with something'. Whatever it was, he hadn't yet returned. Naomi, on the other hand, had arrived around 3am, looking exhausted and irritated as someone who had just finished work and carried a dead body down stone steps would. When she saw that Jake had been dealt with, she ordered Margot to sleep on the sofa while everyone got some sleep, so they could deal with Jake in the morning with fresh minds.

Sleep, however, was something Margot's body couldn't reach.

She grabbed her phone from her pocket and watched the screen illuminate. The time read 08:13, and she had no messages aside from the morning notification from her news app. After unlocking it, she pressed on Jane's name. If she didn't check in, she would worry, and a worried Jane was the last thing she needed right now.

Hey. I'm fine. I slept over at a friends. I'll be home a little later. Love you Xx

After sending the message, Margot looked over the top of her phone to look around the room. It was quiet, save for the slow breathing of sleeping people who seemed wholly unbothered by the night's events, as if the murder of a man was a casual, *normal* experience for a Friday night in the dead of winter. She chewed anxiously on her lip, then looked back down at her phone and opened the web browser.

The first images that appeared on the screen when she typed in the word 'necromancy', was pictures of men with their hands at their sides, glowing green magic radiating from their palms while their long black cloaks fanned behind them in the wind. Rolling dark clouds framed them, and below them were bodies in various stages of decomposition.

She wrinkled her nose, then clicked on the definition.

'Commonly referred to as 'death magic', Necromancy is the practice of black magic, involving communication with the dead. This includes, but is not limited to: the summoning of spirits as apparitions or visions, resurrection for the purpose of divination and foretelling the future, to return the dead to life, or to use the body as a weapon.'

To return the dead to life.

That was *exactly* what she needed.

The main door at the top of the stairs swung open, the cold dim blue light of early morning filtering through. When she sat up, she glanced towards the stairs to see Felix jogging down them. He had a large brown paper bag in one hand, and a cardboard drinks carrier in the other with four tall cups slipped inside.

"Rise and shine, motherfuckers," he announced, switching on the light above the main table and setting the bag and cups down on its surface. "Breakfast's up."

Margot sat upright, pushing her phone back into the pocket of her jacket and swinging her legs so her feet rested on the concrete floor. She could hear Naomi groan loudly and stretch from where she was lying in the bottom bunk under Juliet. Theo was first to get up. He got out of bed and ran a hand through his tight brown curls to loosen them, then dragged his feet all the way to the table.

"Coffee?" he asked, slumping down with a wide yawn.

"Yep, and bagels," Felix replied, grabbing his cup and sitting on the edge of the table.

Juliet was the next to rise. She climbed down the ladder of the bunk bed and walked across the room, her slippers slapping on the concrete with every step. She paused when she reached the table, her hands wringing the front of her pink pyjamas. Her eyes were darting from the paper bag, to Felix, then back again.

"Yes, I got you your usual. Pancakes, maple syrup, and hot chocolate," Felix said with a smile. He passed her one of the tall cups, then reached into the bag and pulled out a plastic container and set it on the table. "Dig in."

Juliet instantly sat down, opening the container and ripping off pieces of pancake to dunk into the maple syrup. She moaned around it, her legs swinging under the table happily.

"Newbie, you're up," Felix said, pushing a paper-wrapped bagel over the table top while Theo helped himself to his own.

Margot subtly sniffed the air. The coffee scents were amazing, and her stomach rumbled audibly when she saw the cream cheese and bacon on Theo's bagel, but she didn't move.

"If I was going to poison you, I wouldn't do it with a bagel. I'm much more creative than that," he said, slipping into a chair beside Juliet.

Finally, Margot relented. She made her way to the table and sat down, reaching for the bagel and coffee that was waiting on her. She brought the coffee cup to her lips, taking a long sip and trying not to moan as loudly as Juliet was.

"Thank you," she said, pinching the corner of the paper wrapping of her bagel. "Why are you being so nice to me?"

Theo and Felix shared a glance. Felix shrugged and took a messy bite of his food while Theo wiped his mouth with a napkin and turned to her. "Because we all know what it's like when we mess up with magic. It happens."

"And witches stick together," Juliet whispered, sinking in her chair while she held her hot chocolate. She gave a small half-smile, then downcast her eyes again.

Margot smiled back weakly, then opened her bagel and took a bite. It wasn't warm anymore, but it tasted good, and she chewed while covering her mouth. "Are you guys a coven?" she asked after swallowing.

Everyone at the table started to laugh. Even Juliet's small chuckles echoed around the room, and her maple covered lips were pulled into a grin. Theo dusted the crumbs of his food, then grabbed his coffee again and leaned back in his chair.

"Kind of. Having a coven would suggest we actually *cast* our magic together, but we don't. Mostly we just hide together."

"And how did you find each other?"

"Fate, I guess. When the suits come and take your parents and family members away for crimes of witchcraft, it doesn't exactly leave a kid with many options. This is Naomi's place. Her boss gave her this basement in return for working. He isn't a witch, but he doesn't ask questions either. Naomi knew Felix from when they were young, and they found *me* two years ago when I was living on the streets after my parents were killed. Then I found Juliet six months ago, when the same thing happened to her," he said, taking another sip.

Margot nodded in understanding. Juliet was silent again, her legs now drawn up against her chest and her fingers picking at the lid of her cup. "It's good that you have each other. I couldn't imagine losing my family like that."

There was an agitated groan from the bunk beds, and Naomi finally sat up. She rubbed her eyes and stood, and when she stretched her arms above her head, Margot spotted her witch mark. It was blue-silver in colour, shaped like a star just like hers, but

Naomi's was pinned on her hip and shining against her brown skin. She caught her looking at it, and pulled her arms back down again so she could tug her shirt over it again.

"As touching as this history lesson is, we need to figure out what to do with the guy in the freezer," Naomi said, walking to them and grabbing her coffee. She kissed the top of Juliet's head, then found a seat at the head of the table and leaned back so she could put her feet up on the wood and lounge back.

"Already figured it out," Felix said, lacing his fingers on the table and leaning on his elbows.

"You?" she asked, her eyebrow raised and her face a picture of scepticism. When he nodded, she pinched the bridge of her nose and breathed out a sigh. "That's worrying. Your plans always suck."

"You only say that because you were born without the ability to have any fun."

"No, I say that because I know the difference between fun, and perpetual stupidity," Naomi said, dropping her hand to look at him again, "but sure, continue. . ."

Felix sat up straighter, excitement in his eyes and a wide grin on his face. "We are going to defrost him, and find a necromancer."

Naomi instantly started laughing. She threw her head back and almost toppled her chair as she dropped her legs back down from the surface of the table and looked in his direction. "You are fucking crazy. A necromancer? Do you know how rare they are? Shit, have you even ever *met* one? Where the hell are you going to find a necromancer?"

"I heard there is one in the coven in the west of the city. I know some of the members, I can get us in to speak with him."

"And you think they are just going to let us walk in and use his services, for *free*? Were you dropped on your head as a child? They are going to need payment," Naomi said, her laughing slowing and her head shaking in disbelief as she sipped at her coffee again.

Margot chewed on her lip in thought. "If necromancy is just another form of magic, why can't we do it ourselves?"

"You can't just *dabble* in necromancy. It's a skill you need to practise as an apprentice for *years* to obtain the power and knowledge required to do it. It's not as simple as compulsion magic, or elemental magic. It's deep, dark shit," she replied, lifting her own bagel and taking a large bite from it. She swallowed, then pointed in Margot's direction. "Besides, as you yourself admitted, you don't know shit about magic, nor witches. You need to brush up on the history of your kind before you start contributing ideas that don't make any sense."

She stood and walked to a bookcase near the back wall where she pulled out a large black scrapbook. She walked lazily to Margot and dropped it in front of her on the table with a heavy *slam*.

"Study material. There are terminologies in there you need to learn, and some history on witches in this country, and our collective persecution," she said, returning to her own seat.

"I told you, I don't live as a witch. I don't *do* magic, and after this whole thing with Jake is fixed, I am going back to my normal human life," Margot said as she looked down at the big black book.

"Bullshit," Felix said. "You can't just go back to being normal, not after feeling what it's like to *do* magic. It will live in your brain, and if you don't start to understand it and respect it, shit like that—" he said, jutting his thumb over his shoulder in the direction of the room with the freezer, "is just going to keep happening."

Margot frowned. Deep down, she knew he was right. Since the magic that shocked and killed Jake the night before, there had been a shift somewhere inside her body. She couldn't quite place exactly where it was, or *what* it was, but something was different. There was a new piece of something burrowing its way inside her, rooting itself into the fibres of her body and cementing itself to her being. No, she was never going to be able to forget what using magic felt like.

Her fingers were already tingling at the idea of casting it again.

To stop herself from fidgeting, Margot let the others talk between themselves about the logistics of contacting the necromancer while she opened the cover of the scrap book. As she flicked through the pages, she found the section on terminology.

Compulsion – Magic that when used will compel the person to do or say anything the witch asks of them.

Telekinesis – Magic used to levitate, move or compel objects towards the witch.

Luck magic – Magic used to bend the hand of fate and infuse the witch with luck on the intended subject for a limited time.

Memory magic – Magic that when cast may wipe memories, or change details of memories the person wishes to keep.

The list went on for *pages*. Terminologies and definitions that made her head spin with possibilities and wonder. Really, she couldn't imagine how half of these types of magic even worked, or how one could study them to the degree needed to be able to use them. Though, she supposed, now she would have all the time in the world.

She passed the section on terminologies, flicking the pages until she came to cut out articles from newspapers. They were dated twenty years previous, when witches were simply ostracised, not arrested. Back then, witches kept to themselves, but didn't need to be hidden. That was when the propaganda started. According to the articles, witches were the sole reason the whole country was in ruins. It was witches who tipped the scales of what was natural, and unnatural. They were murderers, and dangerous to humans and their way of life because they could change fate on a whim. It scared the government to have no control over what happened in their cities. So much so, they made being a witch a punishable offence, and rounded up every witch they could find to be experimented on, and ultimately executed.

There were pictures at the top of each article, showing witches as they were pulled from their homes and rounded up into vans by men in suits, guns in their hands and scowls on their faces. The next article showed a protest outside one of the government buildings. The headline read:

'*W.A.P.M protesters storm government building.*'

"What is the W.A.P.M?" Margot asked, looking up at the faces around the table as they were mid-sentence, talking about something Margot hadn't been listening to.

Naomi stood and walked around the table to come to her side again. She leaned on the table and pointed to the headline with her finger, a wide smile on her face. "Witches Against the Persecution of Magic. They were a resistance group who stormed government buildings and fought for witches' rights. They were mostly witches themselves, but some humans were in the group too. They were amazing, but they have all been captured and killed by now."

"They were terrorists, technically," Theo said, looking over to the page.

Naomi rolled her eyes. "Okay, so technically they bombed a few places, but when the government won't listen, you need to make your voice *louder*. That's what these women did, they *screamed*. And their leader, she went down in a blaze of fire. When the government started taking people from their homes and imprisoning them, the W.A.P.M and their leader went into the government building and planted the bombs. Something went wrong and they went off early, taking out both the leader and some of her members."

Naomi flipped the page to the next article and pointed to the picture in the newspaper. It was of two women, one had her arm over the shoulder of the second woman, and her other hand was in the air, her hand clenched into a fist and her mouth open in an yell. The other woman was looking up at the first woman, her hair falling around her face in a bob and her eyes looking at the woman in awe. She studied her face, and Margot's eyes began to water. She recognised her face. She was younger, and hadn't yet learned her serious expression, but it was her.

"Jane. . ." Margot gasped, pulling the paper closer to get a better look.

"What? No. This—" Naomi said, pointing to the leader with her fist in the air, "Is Heather Fawn, leader of the W.A.P.M, and this. . ." she pointed to the woman beside her, "is Amelia Hawthorn, her human lover."

"No." Margot spluttered, pushing her chair back and standing upright. Her heart was beating loud and fast in her ears, and she was starting to feel lightheaded. "No, that's not right. That's Jane Parke."

"No, it's Amelia Hawthorn, what is wrong with you?" Naomi asked, her voice and expression genuinely concerned.

Margot calmed her breathing and wiped her eyes, then shook her head and pointed at the paper. "Tell me again what happened."

Naomi tilted her head and folded her arms cautiously. "Heather Fawn and her girlfriend Amelia planted the bombs in the government buildings. Amelia left first and the bombs went off before Heather could get out. She died in the building, taking half of the building out with her. Why?"

"Where did this happen?"

"In the capital city out east, where the main government buildings are. This happened like, eighteen years ago, Margot," she said, shaking her head. "Are you okay?"

"No. I need to go, can I borrow this?" Margot said as she grabbed up the article and stuffed it into her pocket. "I need to go home, but I'll be back later to deal with Jake."

"Ooooooo-kay. . ." Naomi said, her eyes wide and her eyebrows raised.

Margot pulled what money she had left out of the pocket of her jacket and set it on the table, noting each of their confused and concerned expressions. "For the breakfast. I'll come back."

She turned on her heel and walked across the room, then darted up the steps. She struggled with the lock on the large metal door, and she had to push hard on the sliding lock to open it. She could hear Felix calling her name from downstairs, but she ignored him, opening the door and stepping outside into the freezing air. The sun was bright against the white of the snow, and it stung her eyes like acid, making her throw her hand up and shield her eyes.

"Margot!"

She ignored him again, starting her walk down the alleyway until she heard Felix run up behind her and take her by the elbow. When she turned, he looked down at her. His brows were knitted together and his shoulder length hair was falling in front of his face.

"What's going on?"

Margot sniffled. She could feel her face getting red from frustration and anger, but she knew she couldn't take it out on him. They had been nothing but kind to her. "I. . ."

"The truth. I don't deal well with lies." He raised his brow and let her elbow go.

She chewed on her lip and shifted on her feet. "I think the woman in the photo is my mother. Heather Fawn. That's the name in my mother's book of shadows that I have at home. We share a surname. I'm Margot Fawn. A-and the woman beside her is not called Amelia, she is called Jane, and she is the woman who I live with. I need to go home and find out the truth, but I promise I will come back. I won't leave you guys to deal with Jake alone."

In all honesty, they seemed to know exactly what they were doing without her, but she couldn't just leave them with a dead body.

Felix's eyebrows raised and he took a shocked step back from her, "What? Shit." He breathed out a sigh and shoved his hands in his pockets uncomfortably. "Well, if you get kicked out you know where we are. You remember what the password is, right?"

"Gubbins?" she asked, giving him a small smile.

Felix nodded once, then started his walk back towards the door that led to the basement. She watched him, then tilted her head and called out to him again.

"Felix?"

He turned.

"What does gubbins mean?"

Felix gave a laugh, then shrugged and opened the metal door as he replied.

"A person or object with little or no value. Like us."

Beautiful, Untamed Thing

It was snowing heavily again. Margot was standing outside the rear door of the house, her back leaning against the fence that separated the garden from the other houses. So far, she couldn't bring herself to take the last few steps into the building. Instead, she just stood there, her hands stuffed in her pockets and her fingers on her right-hand toying with the edges of the newspaper clipping. Her heart raced inside her chest, and her lungs felt tight and cold. There had to be some kind of reasonable explanation, some *reason* that Jane's face was in that photo with another woman's name under it. She hadn't pulled the clipping out of her pocket to look at it again since she placed it there, too fearful to look upon her mother's face.

A murderer's face.

Finally, when the snow was collecting thick in her dark-red hair, Margot pushed off the fence, trudged up the steps and walked into the house. No one was in the kitchen, which was surprising considering it was after 10:00.

"Hello?" she called, closing the door a little too heavily and making her way into the living room.

Jane emerged from the hallway. She was dressed in her usual blue jeans, white t-shirt and checked red shirt that hung down to her knees. Her hair was up in her signature '*I haven't brushed my hair today*' bun, and she had a basket of laundry rested against her hip.

"You stayed out late. Are you okay?" she asked, setting the basket down and frowning at her face. "You are pale, what happened?"

Margot couldn't reply straight away. She studied Jane's face, trailed her eyes over every feature she had come to know and adore. She was her *mom*. She wouldn't have lied to her. Right?

Her heart tightened in her chest in a dull pang, and she pulled her hands from her pockets to wipe her cold cheeks and fix her unruly hair behind her ears. "Where are Liam and Lydia?"

"Liam took her out to get snacks for lunch," Jane said wearily, her head tilted and her eyes narrowing. "Margot, you better start talking to me. What is going o—"

"What is your name?" Jane's voice sounded so demanding and harsh that Margot blurted her reply before she had even finished her sentence.

"What?" Jane asked, closing the space between them. She took Margot's face in her hands forcefully and pulled it into the light to look at her eyes. "Are you on drugs? What did you take?"

"Don't fucking touch me!" she snapped back, waving Jane's hand's away and moving away from her back towards the kitchen. "What is your name?!"

Jane followed with her hands out in front of her defensively, her fingers splayed in a gentle plea for Margot to calm down. "I genuinely have no idea what you are talking about, Margot. Did you hit your head? Please, I'm very worried, tell me what happened."

"You're worried, huh?" She sniffled back tears. They felt hot on her snow-frozen cheeks and left trails down her skin. She reached into her pocket angrily, pulling out the newspaper clipping. "Worried about what, hm? That I did something bad? That I hurt people? That I'm a *terrorist*, like my mother?"

Margot slammed the article down on the counter in the kitchen, resting a shaky finger on the photo of the two women, "that I'm a murderer like you, *Amelia*?"

Jane's body stayed eerily still. Her breaths came slow and even, and her hands lowered from where they were out in front of her so she could rest them on the surface of the counter. She was staring at the photo, her eyes holding something Margot couldn't quite place behind them. "Where did you find this?"

Margot's lips parted in disbelief, and she shook her head. "Is that all you have to say? You need to explain this to me! Why are you standing in this picture, with another woman's name under it? Is that my mother you are standing with? Tell me, please! I am losing my mind!"

Jane reached for the clipping, taking it in her hands like it was made of something truly precious. Her eyes were watering, and the closer she looked, the more her body relaxed and her shoulders slouched.

"Yes. That is your mother," she said, sniffling thickly as she trailed her finger over their black and white printed faces.

Before Margot could open her mouth and ask her anything else, the sound of a dying engine and opening car doors filtered in from the front of the house. Jane's eyes went wide, and she turned to pass the clipping back to her.

"Go to your room. I will settle Lydia and ask Liam to watch her, then I will be in to see you." She took Margot by the arms and pushed her towards the hallway, "I will explain everything, I promise."

Margot shrugged Jane's hands from her arms. When she turned to look at her, she saw a kind of pain in Jane's eyes that she hadn't expected to see. It made her heart pang in her chest in sympathy, but she wouldn't show it, not until she knew her sympathy was warranted. She stared at her a moment longer, trying to shake the images in her head of bombs and protests and murder, before she shook her head and made her way down the hall towards her bedroom.

When she closed the door after herself, she ripped her leather jacket from her shoulders and threw it to the corner of the room. She couldn't even bring herself to sit down on the bed. Instead, she paced the floor of her room, as she always did when she was so angry she wanted to scream. The clipping was still in her hand, and she had to remind herself not to clench it too tightly, less she damage it. She could hear Liam and Lydia enter the house, then the sound of the television in the living room turning on, with happy music from the kid's cartoon screaming from the speakers.

Jane walked into the room moments later, halting Margot's pacing. She closed the door behind her quietly and turned to face her, her hands nervously flexing at her sides.

"Please sit down," she begged, a sad frown clouding her features.

Margot relented. She kicked off her shoes and climbed onto her bed, where she sat with her legs crossed underneath her, and her back propped up against her pillows.

"I know you want answers, and I will do my best to explain, but you need to promise me that you will keep your voice down. If Lydia knows you are home she will rush straight in here," she said, sitting down at the end of the bed, purposely leaving space between them.

When Margot nodded, Jane reached out a hand to take the newspaper clipping again, and looked down at it with an expression that was flowing between the fondness of warm memories, and pain.

"God, we were so young then," she sniffled.

Margot clenched her fists in her lap. "Jane, cut the shit. Why is your name different on that paper? And I was told that my mother died in a bombing *she* created, not by being taken by the suits, like *you* said. What happened? Who was my mother? Did she hurt people?"

"No." Jane looked up at her quickly, shaking her head. "No, your mother didn't hurt anyone. At least, not on purpose."

Margot stayed silent. The raise of her eyebrow was the only movement she gave, giving Jan indication to go on.

"Your mother and I met in college. We weren't friends, exactly, but we knew each other in passing. I would see her every day, out on the lawns studying, or during student protests fighting climate change, or animal cruelty, that kind of thing. Always the activist, your mother. It was one of the things that pulled me so close to her. She was this beautiful, untamed thing that stopped at nothing to fight for what she believed in.

Years passed, and we graduated. The next I saw her it was when the government started to come down harder on the witch community. She was at a protest in the middle of the city, flying a flag and shouting her chants. I didn't plan to, but I ended up lifting a sign and standing with her. I'm not touched by magic, so I didn't really know much about her cause then. I just wanted to stand close to her. We became good friends after that, and we shared coffee and she told me all about the group of witches she was spearheading. The W.A.P.M, she called it. Witches against the persecution of magic. God, she was so excited.

By that time, Liam was born. He was just a baby, and his father and I separated. He didn't agree with my friendship with witches, and told me to choose. I told him to beat it."

Jane laughed, but there was a wateriness to it that wobbled her voice. She sniffled and wiped her cheek, then looked up at Margot.

"One night, your mother came to me, crying and shaking. She found out she was pregnant with you, and your father didn't want anything to do with either of you and bailed. She had nowhere to go, so I invited her to stay with me and Liam. She moved in and. . ."

"You both fell in love?" Margot asked, her voice soft and quiet.

Jane hiccupped a sob and nodded. "We didn't mean to. It just happened. Neither of us had ever been with a woman before, it was foreign, and exciting, and she took my breath away. We became a little family all of our own. Me, Heather, and Liam. You were growing so well, and she was *so* excited to meet you.

But by this time, the lives of the witch community were getting very hard. No one touched by magic could get jobs, they were kicked out of their homes by prejudiced landlords, the witch homeless population tripled. It was a mess, and your mother was *angry*. More people joined the W.A.P.M, and some of those people were more extreme than we predicted. They started causing riots in the city, burning things and causing a general ruckus, but Heather thought it was warranted. They weren't being listened to, and she said they needed to be louder. So she started learning how to make bombs, with the help from some of the other members of the movement."

"So, she did kill those people in the blast at the government buildings." Margot frowned, shaking her head, "how could she do something like that?"

"It didn't happen like you think it did. She had just given birth to you when the plans for the first few bombings arrived at her desk at headquarters. The deal was, they would go inside the targeted building at night, and set everything up, then everyone would get out safely and they would detonate from the outside. They did it at night, when they knew no one would be inside, so there would be no casualties. They didn't want to hurt *anyone*, they just wanted the buildings down so it would be harder for the government to recover. If the lists of known witches were burned in a blast, those witches would be *safe*. They just wanted to cause some damage, no loss of life. Night-time blasts *only*."

"So, what went wrong?"

Jane started to cry, looking down at the picture and stroking her finger over it again. She took a long moment to compose herself, then closed her eyes like she was reaching for the memory to retell it.

"You were six months old, and the climate was getting even worse. The government was pushing back by arresting witches for crafting, and the members of the group were starting to get tired of the gentle bombings they had been doing. They called a meeting, and your mother took you with her, wrapped up in one of those blankets she knitted you. It was rare to see her without you glued to her hip, but the members didn't mind. Anyway, the meeting didn't go well. They told Heather their frustrations and said they were going to bomb the government buildings again. This time, they wanted to do it in the middle of the day, when the most people would be inside so they could *really* send a message. Heather dismissed it the second the words left that man's mouth. She *explicitly* forbade it, and she excommunicated him. We thought the matter was over with, we never thought they would go behind her back and do it anyway.

The next morning, your mother and I, and you and Liam, were in the city for lunch. That was when she got the tip off that the plan was still on. Men were heading into the buildings to plant the bombs. We ran all the way to the steps of the building and she pushed you into my arms and kissed me, telling me that she had to go inside to warn everyone.

I *screamed* at her to stop her. I grabbed her hands and tried to get her to stay, but she wouldn't listen. She said she would never forgive herself if she didn't at least try. So, she kissed your head, and ran into the building."

Margot's heart shattered in her chest as she listened to Jane. They were both openly crying, but Jane was shaking in a way she had never seen before. She had always been so strong, and unmoving, but right now she looked. . . broken.

"Nothing happened for a few minutes. You were screaming, so I carried you tight against my chest, and held Liam's hand as he stood on his little legs beside me. I thought she did it, I thought it must have worked, because there was such a long pause, and then. . . the building just *exploded*. I'll never forget how loud it was, and how much dust came out of that doorway. I waited, and I cried, and I waited longer, but she never came out again. God, Margot, I loved her *so* much. I loved her so much it *hurt*, and she just. . ."

Margot shifted from where she was sitting so she could reach out and take her hand. She clenched it, pulling it closer to her so she could comfort her. "I'm sorry," she whimpered.

Jane simply nodded and set the newspaper clipping aside so she could wipe her wet cheek again. "When I saw that no one was coming out, I knew I had to take you both home. When I got back to the house, the blast was all over the news. They had pulled her body out, and because she was the leader of the W.A.M.P, and her body was found near one of the bombs, they assumed she did it. I knew they would swarm the house, so I took some bottles and milk and clothes for you and Liam and I ran. I ran as far as I could go, and as much as I fucking *hated* them, I let the W.A.M.P find us somewhere safe. They got me, Liam and you a new identity. I was no longer Amelia Hawthorne. I was Jane Parke, and you became Margot Parke. My sweet girl, and the last thing I had of Heather."

She reached out and placed a gentle hand against Margot's cheek, stroking her wet cheeks with her thumb.

"But why not tell me? Why keep this from me? You must have known I would find out eventually, that I would search my mothers name and find all this out?" Margot asked, curling her face into Jane's hand.

"In my defence, I only told you her *first* name. I didn't know your mother had written her full name in that book of hers, not until you told me when you first found it there. I thought I was keeping you safe by keeping you away from the legacy that was forced upon her. I am so sorry for keeping her from you, I thought I was doing the right thing," Jane said, bursting into tears.

The second she started crying again, Margot closed the space between them and pulled her into a tight hug. She buried her face into her hair and curled into her side, allowing Jane to hold her like she used to when she was young. "You did. You kept me safe, and happy. It's okay. I'm sorry."

They held each other for a long time, just allowing themselves to feel each other in their shared grief. When they had both calmed their tears and their breathing for long enough, Jane pulled back to look into her face again, stroking Margot's dark red hair out of her face.

"You remind me of her every day. You share the same fire for life, and the same passion for the things you believe in. That is your mother, she still lives with you. As much as some of her methods were harsh, she did what she believed was right for the people she represented. She never meant for this to happen, and I *know* she never meant to leave you."

Margot nodded and sat up straighter again, rolling out her shoulders from the tension that had settled there and trying not to let her mind spin from all the new information that was swirling inside it. Her heart hurt, and her neck felt sore from the stress of the last day, but she tried to push it away. "Does Liam know? Does he remember any of it?"

"No, and I would like to keep it that way for now, if you don't mind?" Jane asked, chewing on her lip awkwardly. "Listen, Margot, I know I'm not the best mom, bu—"

"You *are* the best mom, Jane. I am alive because of you, don't think I don't know that."

Jane smiled weakly, then continued, "thank you. But, I have been raising you all your life, and I know when something fishy is going on. You didn't come home last night, and when you do, you come home with all of this information from seemingly nowhere. What is going on? Are you in trouble?"

Margot shifted where she sat, trying not to look as guilty as she felt. She hoped it didn't show on her face. "I met a group of other witches," she said, then spluttered when Jane instantly sighed. "But it's safe! They are hidden, and they are very, very careful. I promise."

"You better hope so, Margot, because I can't lose you, too. I wouldn't survive it. Not you."

Margot blushed, then leaned in to kiss Jane's cheek. "You won't ever lose me. I promise, but you do need to trust me."

"Hmm. . ." Jane said, passing the newspaper clipping to Margot and standing from where she was sitting on the bed. "That's exactly what your mother used to say, too."

When Margot didn't say anything, Jane walked to the door of the room and opened it, looking back in at her. "I am going to fix some lunch for Lydia. I'll be in the kitchen if you need me, but you should sleep. I don't know what you got up to last night, but you look like hell."

"Well, damn, thanks." She laughed, reaching to scratch the back of her neck awkwardly. "I'll sleep, thank you."

Jane nodded once, then started to close the door.

"Oh, mom?" Margot called, smiling at Jane's face when she peeked back in again. "I love you. . ."

Jane's smile renewed, and she blew her a kiss.

"I love you, too."

Melting Memories

Margot pulled the sleeves of her olive-green woollen cardigan down over her hands as she stood waiting to cross the road opposite *The Cloaked Cat*. The snow had stopped at least, but the wind still held a bitterness to it that bore into the marrow of her bones. She had spent the morning curled up under the duvet in her bed, getting some much-needed sleep. Granted, the sleep had been fitful and full of anxious dreams of her mother.

And the guy in the freezer.

The oncoming car finally passed, its wheels rolling slowly through slush that was once snow. Margot took her chance and crossed the salted tarmac road. The metal shutters of *The Cloaked Cat* were pulled down, graffiti sprawled all over the front in bright red and blue spray paints of tags and symbols she didn't recognise. She had never seen *The Cloaked Cat* closed before, having only been near it when there were crowds of people awaiting entry to the various concerts it held. It seemed strange to see it so barren of people. It was silent.

Dead.

She bypassed the metal shutters, continuing down the path until she came to the alleyway. The melting snow still had footprints stamped into them, all huddled together and guiding her all the way to the door that led to the basement. They looked like melting memories that held a story she could never decipher. Memories of lost people with big hearts that relied on each other like family. A family of misfits. A family of *gubbins*.

The only pair she could identify was Juliet's, considering hers were significantly smaller than the others. They stayed very tight to a pair of larger ones, which she assumed were Theo's, since they seemed so close.

When she got to the heavy metal door, she pulled her sleeve away from her hand and knocked hard, her head leaning in to try and listen for movement. It took a while, but finally the sound of footsteps ascending the steps came from the other side. There was a pause, then Felix's voice filtered through.

"Password," he said. She could practically hear his grin dripping off the word.

"Gubbins."

"Ah," he said, then gave a tutting sound, "sorry, Red, but we changed the password. Give it another go."

Margot rolled her eyes and stepped back from the door. "Is it, open the door or I'll punch you?"

The lock on the other side scraped open, and Felix pushed open the door with his foot. He was leaning against the wall with his arms crossed. "Alright, alright. Don't shock me," he said, his face cracking into a grin. He pushed off the wall and uncrossed his arms so he could wag a mocking finger at her. "Always with the violence, hm?"

Margot watched as he turned and sauntered back down the steps to the basement, leaving the door open so she could follow him.

Juliet was sitting at the table beside Theo, a large slice of pepperoni pizza hanging limply from her hand as they both peered over the pages of a book. Naomi was lounging back on the brown leather sofa, her head tilted back and a wet flannel draped over her forehead. None of them acknowledged her arrival until she got closer to the table and trailed her eyes over its surface. It was littered with greasy pizza boxes, newspapers and old books.

"What are you guys doing?"

"You should have told us your mom was Heather Fawn," Naomi snapped, not moving nor opening her eyes from under the flannel. She raised her hand, pointing an accusing finger in Margot's direction. "You lied to us."

"How did I lie, exactly?"

"You sat there while I explained all that shit to you about the W.A.P.M, like you had no idea what the hell I was talking about. Why?" she asked, finally sitting up and pulling the wet cloth away. "What is your game?"

Margot's jaw tensed. Under normal circumstances, she would have told her to go fuck herself by now, but these were no *normal* circumstances. These were serious, *life and death* kind of circumstances, and she needed them. "I am playing no game, Naomi. I promise. I didn't know anything about my mother. That photo in your paper was the first time I've ever seen her face. My foster mom lied to me. I had *no idea* who she was."

Naomi stood from where she was sitting and pointed her finger again. "If I find out that you are lying to me, Margot, I swear—"

"Cut her some slack, Naomi. She said she didn't know, and it's not exactly the biggest problem we have right now, is it?" Felix asked. He was sitting on the edge of the table while tucking a new cigarette behind his ear.

"It's okay. I get it. I am a stranger who brought trouble to your door, but this information is as new to me as it is to you," Margot said, taking a few steps towards her. "I wouldn't lie to you, not when you have all extended your help to me."

Naomi chewed on the inside of her lip, seemingly mulling over what she said while she looked Margot over. She nodded once, then closed the space between them and eyed the bag hanging from Margot's shoulder. "Fine. Do you have any painkillers in that thing? I've a migraine."

Margot cracked a smile and tilted her head, "Of course, how many do you need?"

"All of them." She walked around her and slumped down into one of the chairs at the table, holding her head in her hands while she rested on her elbows.

Pulling the strip of painkillers out of her bag, Margot peeled two of them free from the foil and handed them to her gently. "Two. Any more and you will make yourself sick," she said, sitting down beside her. "Isn't there some kind of healing spell you could do to make it go away?"

"I'm not the best at healing magic. I always end up making it worse," she said, popping the pills into her mouth and chasing them with a sip from the can of soda in front of her. "Besides, we don't have time to play *happy coven families*, not when we have a dead guy to resurrect and a necromancer to find."

"On that note, I think I got us an invitation to meet with the West City Coven," Felix said with a crooked grin and a wiggle of his eyebrow.

Naomi narrowed her eyes. "You *think*, or you did?"

"I did."

Theo finally looked up from the book he was reading to Juliet. He sighed deeply and closed the cover, keeping his index finger between the pages so he wouldn't lose his place. "We can't go for a meeting with them without some protection. The West City Coven are a different breed. They aren't like us, they are dangerous."

Felix rolled his eyes and reached for a slice of greasy pepperoni pizza, shoving it into his mouth and speaking around it. "You think I don't know that? I wouldn't walk in there without a little protection, I'm not stupid."

"Debatable." Naomi sighed, pressing her fingers to the sides of her head at the temples and looking over each of their faces.

Margot didn't know what not '*like us*' meant. The '*us*' clearly meant '*them*', excluding herself considering she wasn't actually a part of this group. Dangerous, however, was a word she was becoming increasingly familiar with.

"How are they dangerous?" she asked, lacing her hands on the table.

Juliet sank back in her seat, drawing her knees up to her chest and hugging them tightly, while Theo rested a hand on her shoulder for comfort.

"They have a nasty habit of being involved in the underworld of magical dealings. They sell heavy duty curses, irreversible hexes, and if you end up on their bad side or even *slightly piss them off*," Theo said, darting his narrowed eyes to Felix, "you will probably be found with a missing limb or two. Or worse."

"The last person to fuck with them ended up hanging from the bridge overlooking the river. Well, most of him, anyway. I'm not sure where his arms went," Naomi frowned.

Felix cracked a smile. "Or his eyelids."

"I forgot about that bit."

"Wait." Margot gulped, unlacing her hands so she could splay her fingers and brace her hands against the table. Her blood had started to run cold, and her arms under her olive-green cardigan had goosebumps all over. "You are telling me this coven are a bunch of unhinged murderers, and you want to ask them for *help*? Are you high?"

"A little, but that's hardly the point," Felix said as he threw the crust of his pizza onto the cardboard box and dusted the crumbs from his hands. "I don't *want* to ask them for anything, but the fact remains; we need a necromancer. The only known necromancer in the city is a member of that coven, so the way I see it, it's either the West City Coven, or the suits. I don't know about you guys, but I'll take my chances with the unhinged murderous witches over the government any day. Besides, at least we have something in common with them."

"Murder? Or magic?" Theo asked, sitting back heavily in his chair.

Felix shrugged and folded his arms, a flash of excitement glinting in his eyes. "It's dealers' choice at this stage, no?"

The room fell silent, all save for the dull creak of the table as Felix swung his leg back and forth. As much as she didn't want to admit it, Felix was right. The only thing she knew for certain, was that she couldn't let the suits find Jake dead and covered in a magical mark. If they found him, they would find her, and if they found *her*, everyone she loved was dead.

Margot took a steadying breath and looked up to Felix again, trying to set her face to look more confident than she truly felt. "When do we meet them?"

"Tonight," he said, standing and flashing her a smile before he headed towards the stairs, "but first, we need to get that protection. Let's go."

Glancing around the table and noticing that no one else was moving, Margot realised Felix was talking only to her. She gave each of them a thin-lipped smile and stood, throwing her bag over her arm and following him quickly. "Where are we going?"

Felix looked down at her over his shoulder, taking the cigarette from behind his ear and placing it into his mouth as he crested the stairs. "Field trip."

The city was quiet for a Saturday. The train Felix led her to took them straight into the middle of a district Margot had never been to before. Not because she didn't know about the area, but instead because the place was a derelict *mess*. The crumbling walls of buildings loomed over streets and alleyways, cutting off what little sunlight was able to filter through the thick clouds. Apartment buildings with boarded windows and rusted broken gates littered the sidewalks, all balanced on top of each other like broken toy blocks. There was the odd house that didn't look like it was completely neglected, but aside from the sounds of loud televisions from inside, and the occasional stray dog, the whole place screamed *blatant abandon*.

"Where the hell are you taking me?"

Felix shrugged. He didn't have the same swagger in his walk, or as confident a grin on his face while out in the open as he would have back in the basement of *The Cloaked Cat*. No snarky remark or sharp witted joke came from his mouth. Aside from gentle jingling coming from the chain that hung from his jeans pocket, he didn't make a sound.

"Seriously, Felix. You haven't said one word to me since we left the train," Margot said, reaching out to take his arm to slow him in his fast walk. "Where are we going?"

"We are almost there. Just keep your head down. This is suit territory, and the last thing we need is to be pulled over by the government because we look suspicious," he said, his eyes staying forward. He didn't pull his arm away from her, but he did tug them forward faster.

Looking around at the buildings again, Margot couldn't understand how the suits would be anywhere near this place. The buildings didn't look like they housed many people, and the pavements were barren of footsteps. There were no witches here to capture. Still, she didn't push the conversation. The look on Felix's face was all she needed to keep her mouth shut tightly.

Finally, they arrived at another dingy alleyway. Felix gripped her hand and pulled her into the dark shadows and along the slush covered pavement until they came to a large red door. It was wooden, and the paint was chipped quite badly, but it had no handle or knob to open it. Without saying a word, Felix let her hand go and pressed his palm on the surface of the wood. With a glance over his shoulder towards the entryway, he made sure no one was watching before he mumbled something in a low breath. A small sliver of light pulsed from under his palm against the wood, and the door creaked and groaned in response before it cracked open. The glint of a smile came upon Felix's face as he opened the door with the tip of his shoe and walked inside.

He led her down wooden steps to a very narrow and dimly lit corridor. At the end stood a doorway, and although this one had no wooden door, it did have a crushed velvet curtain that hung completely over it. Chittering voices, soft classical music and the clinking of glass bottles filtered in from the other side, forcing Margot's brow to pull into a confused furrow.

"Will you *please* tell me what is going on?"

"Welcome to the apothecary," Felix grinned, dropping her hand so he could pull back the curtain and dramatically bow beside her.

Margot took small tentative steps inside. The room was large, with stone walls and tall bookcases lining every inch of them. They were packed with bottles filled with unidentified liquids, jars stuffed with various dead insects and overflowing bowls of animal bones. Tables littered the floor, each seemingly used for different purposes. The one closest to her was filled with baskets of different dried flowers and herbs. The middle table was cluttered with stacks of human bones, their skulls staring back at her with vacant eye sockets that seemed to still somehow watch her every move. The furthest table was the only one that seemed somewhat normal. It had a cauldron on top of a camping stove, and a pair of scales that an old woman with long silver hair was hunched over, meticulously measuring the weight of translucent flakes from the jar in her hand labelled '*Dragonfly wings*'.

"You brought me to a healing room? I think Jake is well beyond healing at this point, Felix," she said, trying to keep her voice down so as not to disturb the woman in her measuring, or grab the attention of the two tall men who stood beside her.

"Hey, Bonnie doesn't just make healing tinctures and balms here, this is a one stop shop for anything witchcraft related. Curses, hexes, death potions, stun bombs that make you bleed through your eyes," he said with a dismissive wave of his hand, "Ya know, all the cool stuff."

He guided her around the table of flowers and herbs and down the aisle towards the old woman, who was filling a jar with the dragonfly wings mixed with some bright green glittering liquid. She pushed a cork into the top of the jar and dipped the top of it into a pot of melted wax, then blew on it. It dried instantly, and she held it out to one of the men who stood watching her.

"No more than three droplets a day," she warned, holding onto it tightly while the man tried to take it from her.

"We know, you told us that yesterday," the man replied with a roll of his eyes.

"I mean it," she hissed, finally letting go of the jar. "Any more than that and you will grow fingers where fingers aren't supposed to grow. It's a nasty business getting rid of them again, and it'll cost you double."

"We know," he said again, then stuffed the jar into his pocket and pulled his friend along the aisle and out through the curtain.

Bonnie watched them leave through her pale blue eyes, tugging her charcoal-grey cardigan close to her body and chewing on the inside of her lip like she didn't quite believe them. "Stupid bastards," she mumbled under her breath, then turned to look at Felix.

Her expression turned from a staid and unamused frown, to absolute disdain when her eyes took him in. She raised her hand beside her head and closed her eyes. "I swear to the Gods, if I am not hallucinating from my afternoon tea and you *are* indeed standing in front of me, Felix, I will shave the skin from your face."

"Now now, Bonnie, you know you love me," he said, reaching forward to take her hand and give it a squeeze.

Bonnie snapped her eyes open and pulled her hand free so she could slap him hard across the side of his head. "Love, indeed. Did I, or did I not warn you that if I ever saw your face again, I would lay a curse on you so thick your ancestors would feel it? Get out of my home, before I make good on my promise!"

Felix sighed, rubbing the sore spot against his head and flashing Margot a sheepish look. He turned back to Bonnie and held his hands up defensively. "Bonnie, my favourite little kitchen witch, I promise I haven't brought any trouble to your door this time."

"That would be a first." Bonnie huffed, walking away from him and waving a hand in his direction. A flash of light burst from her hand and Felix's knees went from under him. He fell hard onto the stone floor, making him wince and gasp from the pain. "Get. Out."

Felix dropped his cocky demeanour and twisted his face into something Margot could only akin to shame. "I'm sorry I caused you trouble. You know I meant no harm, but I wouldn't be here if it wasn't super important. Please just hear me out. . ."

Bonnie stopped walking, hovering her hand over another jar. She didn't quite touch it with her fingers, but she let them gently stroke the area above the cork as she hummed in contemplation. She spun to face them again quickly, her silver hair fanning out around her body and her arms folding in front of her chest as her eyes fell on Margot. "Who is your little friend?"

Margot gulped thickly and shifted on her feet, "My name is Mar —"

"It doesn't matter," Felix interjected, placing his hand on the nearest table so he could heft himself back onto his feet. "We are in a bit of trouble, and we need some of your potions. I swear, if you help me this time, I will never darken your door again."

"Don't try to sell me shit and tell me it's sugar, Felix. I am not dense," she sighed, uncrossing her arms so she could place them on her hips and tap her foot anxiously. "What do you want?"

"Stun bombs, a couple of death potions, bottled pain elixirs, you know the drill. Some of those beautiful little protection bags you have, maybe one of those potions that turn your bones to jelly, that kind of thing," he said with a wriggle of his brow.

"Sounds like you are going to war," she said, studying him and tilting her head. "Who are you using them on?"

"Hopefully no one, but we have a meeting with the West Side Coven and we can't go in unprepared."

Bonnie deflated in a deep, belly shaking sigh, then turned and grabbed a cardboard box from the nearest shelf. "You still have a death wish, I see."

"Something like that," Felix said, rubbing his hands together now that it seemed Bonnie was complying.

She only hummed in response and started to walk along the many tables and shelves, collecting small vials, little jars and bags and setting them into the box. By the time she returned, the box was packed tightly, and she shoved it into his arms.

"How are you planning on paying me today, exactly?"

"She's paying," he said, jutting his thumb in Margot's direction while he rummaged through the items.

Margot looked between them, her eyebrows raised and a gape on her face. "Wait, what?"

"This is your problem, and I am broke," he shrugged, "Ergo, you pay. Wait, which one of these is the one that makes you bleed through your eyes?"

"The yellow one," Bonnie said with a roll of her eyes. She walked to Margot and looked her over from the tip of her head to her toes and back again, and her scowl changed to a wicked grin. "You are a pretty little bird. Whatever trouble you are in, you can do better than seeking help from the likes of him. For a price, I could—"

"She's desperate, but she isn't *that* desperate, Bonnie." Felix looked up from the contents of the box and closed the lid, placing it under his arm. "How much?"

A grimace that deepened the lines in her face came upon Bonnie, and she tutted disapprovingly before she relented. "One hundred, and a lock of that pretty red hair."

Margot blinked with wide eyes, "One hundred? I don't hav—"

"It's this or nothing. You either got it, or we are screwed," Felix sighed, sitting on the edge of the table as he waited.

Margot rolled her eyes and dug her hand into the bag on her shoulder to pull out her purse. She fished inside for all of the notes and coins she could find before counting it out on top of Bonnie's waiting open palm. She had ninety total, and when she finished counting it, she looked up at her sheepishly. "New customer discount?" she asked hopefully.

Bonnie closed her fingers around the money in a tight fist, looking at her through narrowed eyes. "Fine, but I want that lock of hair."

Margot ran her hand through her hair anxiously. She liked her hair. It was a connection to her mother that she always kept a sense of pride in, and the idea of cutting it unevenly made her stomach flip. She knew it was silly, but the concept of cutting her hair stung more than paying the money did. She nodded though, and when Bonnie pocketed the money and handed her a pair of decorative golden scissors, she pulled a strand from the nape of her neck and raised the scissors to it.

"A bit bigger than that, love. I need to make it last me a while," Bonnie said.

Margot sighed pushing the scissors up higher and snipping them closed. The piece of hair fell into her waiting hand, and she pinched it together between her fingertips so it didn't fall apart. "What are you going to do with it?" she asked, handing it over to Bonnie.

"Does it matter? Would my usage of it change your mind?"

"No, I suppose it wouldn't," she mumbled, setting the scissors aside.

"Well. . ." Felix trilled, pushing off from where he was sitting against the table, "As interesting as all this is, we gotta go. Thanks for the help, Bonnie."

He grabbed Margot's hand and pulled her along the aisle and away from the old woman, heading towards the red curtain that acted as the door.

"Oh Felix?" Bonnie called. When he turned to look at her, she pointed another stern finger at him. "If you come back through these doors again, I'll make you shit out your organs, am I clear?"

His face pulled into a wide grin, "I love you too, Bonnie!" he called, then pulled her back out of the room and up the steps before she could chase after them.

Felix pulled her back out into the cold city air, the door slamming closed behind them as they tumbled and slipped on the icy pavement. Small gentle flakes of snow were blowing in the wind again, and they settled in her hair and on top of Felix's beanie. He jiggled the box in his arms and wriggled his eyebrows.

"Well, we got what we came f—"

Loud shouting and screams coming from the main road stifled the words in his throat. The sound of slamming metal doors and a gunshot rang through the air, making Margot's body flinch and her hands grip into fists.

"We need to go." Felix tucked the box under his arm and started to walk further down into the alleyway.

"No, wait, we need to see what's going on!" she hissed, breaking from him and edging closer to the entrance.

"No! Marg— Ugh!"

Felix ran after her, grabbing her bicep in a crushing grip and pulling her back just as she stepped out into the pavement. He tucked them close into the wall so they could poke their heads around it and watch the scene.

Three black vans were parked down the edge of the road outside the apartments. Men wearing police armour and helmets stood in low stances with guns in their hands aimed towards the doors while other armed police pulled a screaming family down the steps. The doors to the vans opened, and two men in black suits walked out of them, one with a phone to his ear and the other keeping watch as the family were ripped from each other. The man was resisting, trying to cling to his wife's shoulders before the butt of a gun came crashing into his temple and he was sent to the ground, only to be grabbed and a white metal collar to be clipped around his neck.

The wife screamed again, holding the crying baby in her arms closer to her and trying to grip onto her toddler with the other hand, but the men were upon her quickly. They backhanded her across the face and pulled the baby from her arms, clipping a collar around her neck too before the toddler was lifted and they were pushed towards the open van doors.

"Margot we really gotta go!" Felix hissed.

"We can't just let them do this, Felix! They are going to kill them!" she said, trying to keep her voice down, but anger was fuelling her blood and her body was shaking.

He squeezed her arm tighter and pulled her back from the entrance, pushing her hard against the brick wall and shaking her.

"Are you dense?! There is nothing we can do for them right now. If you go out there, you die too, is that what you want?" he snapped, letting her go roughly.

"N-no, but—"

She paused, gritting her teeth as tears filled her eyes. The images of her mother at the protests and rally's, her fist pushed high in the air and the look of conviction on her face was filling her mind. Her heart was beating so fast in her chest that it felt like it might just break. She had never seen the suits take a witch before. Now she knew exactly why her mother had fought so hard to end this.

"My mom, she wouldn't let this just *happen*, Felix." She sniffled, her body flinching as she heard another loud shout from the main road.

"Your mother is dead, and if we don't leave *right fucking now*, we will be too. There are other ways Margot," he said, grabbing her shoulder again and pushing her down the alleyway.

Margot relented, allowing him to guide her while she looked over her shoulder towards the road. Her feet were slow, but her heartbeat was fast, and it filled her ears with the sound of rushing blood. Once the screams stopped, she managed to calm her breathing, and she looked ahead at him again.

"What were those things they put around their necks?" she asked.

"Collars. A new little invention the suits created after all the experiments they did on witches. It somehow stops you being able to access your magic, leaving you defenceless."

He didn't look back at her, instead keeping his eyes on the end of the alleyway where a tall metal fence gate blocked their way. He placed his hand on it and tried to jerk it open, but it didn't budge, and he let out an irritated growl, spinning to look at her.

"Are you mad at me?" Margot asked, looking up at the top of the fence. It was high.

"Yes," Felix replied honestly, "but we don't have time to be pissed, you need to get your ass up that fence."

Bleed

"Are you sure this is where they told you to meet them?" Theo looked sceptical as he looked around the junkyard.

The moon was full and high in the sky, making the stars hard to see clearly, and there wasn't a cloud in sight. It was still bitterly cold though, and the breath left each of their mouths in plumes while their body's shivered. They had opted to leave Juliet in the basement in case something went wrong while they met with the West Side Coven. She was too young, and too meek, and too scared to come with them, and they hadn't wanted to force her to lose sleep for the rest of her life if one of them ended up dead.

"Yep. The junkyard has always been West Side territory, so it makes sense," Felix said, looking over each of them while his hands fiddled on the inside of his jacket pockets. "Everyone has their insurance, right?"

"If you call a deadly breakable jar of liquid death *insurance*, then yes," Naomi mumbled.

Her eyes were trained and focused on every car and piece of metal as if waiting for someone to jump out from behind them. She looked calm. Her breath was even, and her shoulders were relaxed. Margot had a nagging feeling that it was all for show though. One couldn't be too careful with this Coven, if Theo's stories were anything to go by.

"How do you know these guys, anyway?" Margot asked Felix as she looked around the junkyard. So far, nothing had moved. "How did you set up the meeting?"

Felix shifted awkwardly and reached to scratch his head under his beanie. A wince clouded his face, and he looked sideways to her while trying not to look at the others. "I may or may have not been sleeping with the daughter of the Coven leader."

Guttural groans came from the throats of Naomi and Theo, and Felix threw his hands up defensively. "It was a while ago! I know you guys warned me about sleeping with the enemy, but in my defence, she is super fucking hot."

Margot couldn't help but roll her eyes while the group bickered between themselves. That was when she noticed it. Dark green smoke was starting to fill the air at the bottom of the junkyard. It was lingering between two rows of broken and rusted cars, making the fences and wall at the end harder to see.

"Guys."

They ignored her, continuing to mock each other while the green smoke billowed larger and thicker. She could see movement in it, the light of the lamps behind it revealing shadows of bodies, and silhouettes of large dogs that waited patiently either side of them.

"Guys!"

When they disregarded her again, Margot snapped her eyes away from the smoke and stalked towards Felix, whipping her hand over the back of his head to get his attention.

"What the fuck was that for?!"

Margot grabbed his head in both of her hands and turned it towards the row of cars, and when his eyes fell upon the greenness of the air and the shadows that loomed there, they went wide and his face paled. "Get ready, I'm not sure this is going to be a warm welcome."

The shadows pushed through the fog, revealing bodies of at least fifteen men and women with a pack of dobermans at their heels. They all wore similar dark clothing, looking somehow uniformed without actually needing to wear one. The closer they got, the clearer she could see their faces. Most of them seemed to be in their forties or fifties, except for the few to the left who were in their teens. A girl with long black hair that was tipped at the ends in bright pink, moved away from the group to lean heavily on the top of a silver trash can with her elbows. She gave Felix a wave and an amused grin, then looked towards the man in the middle.

He was their leader. She could tell that simply because of the respect he seemed to command from the rest of them. They gave him space, not coming too close and allowing him to take up the area right at the front while they made sure to stay a few steps back. They had baseball bats in their hands and guns in holsters on their hips.

The man was tall, with broad shoulders and large arms that were barely contained inside his leather jacket. He had greying brown hair that was slicked back with too much hair gel, and a large beard that reached the middle of his chest. There was a scar on his face that reached from the missing earlobe on his left ear, all the way across his cheekbone and down to his chin, and he was staring at them through one squinted eye, the other hidden behind an eyepatch.

He didn't speak for a long time. He simply looked each of them over while he puffed plumes of smoke from the cigar in his mouth. When he finally pulled it from his mouth, he looked between Felix and Theo with a deadly frown.

"Which one of you is Felix?" His voice was gruff, and deep, and it felt like it shook the very air around them.

Margot didn't move, forcing her body to stay deathly still and not give Felix away. The others didn't seem to have the same thought process though, and they turned to look directly at Felix, who gave an anxious half-laugh, half-groan and raised his hand.

"That'd be me."

The man placed the cigar back in his mouth and took a long draw of it, rolling the smoke in his mouth and tilting his head back so he could blow it back out again. "Hm. You have balls, kid." He flicked the cigar, and the ash fluttered to the ground by his boot. "My daughter tells me she was quite fond of you, until you disappeared one-night last year. Dead, or captured, she figured, but *no*. Here you stand, requesting an audience like I won't simply snap your neck. You are either brave or incredibly stupid. Which is it?"

"Stupid, probably," he said almost too quickly. He gulped, then pulled his hands out of his pocket and took a few steps forward, but the man held up his baseball bat and pointed the end at him to halt his steps.

"Far enough. I am only here because my daughter seems to think you are somehow still worth her attention, which makes you a problem. That makes you *my* problem, Felix, and I don't like problems."

Naomi frowned, breaking her stiff posture to walk to Felix's side and take his arm to pull him back. "You are Meraki Blackthorne, right? Leader of the West Side Coven?"

"Aye," he huffed, "Who are you, and what do you want?"

"Naomi." She folded her arms across her chest and set her face in a stern frown. "We didn't come for trouble, and we didn't come here to piss you off with Felix's bad decisions. He's a walking, talking, bad decision, and he knows it. He's sorry."

Felix gave a sheepish squirm and held his hands up, shrugging. "She ain't wrong."

Meraki studied them, then dropped his bat from where it was still hanging in the air in front of his face. "Then why did you call me here? I don't take kindly to people wasting my time." As if to prove his point, the doberman at his heel growled and sunk low like he might just rush at them.

"We ran into a bit of trouble. Witch trouble. Our friend accidentally killed a human guy, and there are magic tracings all over him. If the suits find him, they will trace him back to us, and we like being alive. We need help," Naomi said. Her body was relaxed, but her hands were gripping her arms tightly.

Meraki's eyebrows raised in surprise, and his mouth cracked an amused grin. He looked between his Coven, each of them starting to smile and laugh lowly before he looked back to them. "Which one of you killed the kid?" he asked.

When no one answered, he took a slow walk towards them. He stopped in front of Naomi, and he looked into her face while studying her eyes. "Not you. You are too smart," he mumbled. He glanced at Felix and rolled his eyes. "Not you either, you are too *stupid*."

Meraki tucked his arms behind his back, holding the bat there and walking down the line to Theo, where he stopped and grinned at him. "Not you. Too meek. You haven't looked me in the eye *once* since I arrived."

Margot's heart picked up its thundering pace the closer the man got to her. When he stopped right in front of her, it was beating so hard she figured he might just hear it. He stood closely to her, his height making him have to hunch over to look her in the face. He was so close that she had to bend backwards to try and keep her eyes on his.

"You," he said, taking his hand from where it was linked behind his back so he could pinch her chin and tilt her face, his cigar still lit between his fingers. "You look like someone I used to know."

Before she knew what she was doing or had the time to consider the dire consequences of it, Margot's hand flew. She slapped him hard across his bearded face and pulled her chin from his grip. "Don't touch me."

The rest of the West Side Coven raised their weapons. Their hands ignited in angry magic ready to strike, and the dogs started barking loudly and pulled on their chains, begging to be let loose. Meraki held his hand up, stopping them in their movements while he took a step back from Margot and laughed deeply in his chest.

"Yes, definitely you. You have an anger problem, little lady. I assume that is what got you into this trouble in the first place?"

"And you have a problem with touching women when they didn't invite you to, huh?" she snapped.

She wasn't sure where her newfound confidence had come from, but she knew if this man looked upon her face like prey, she would never get him to help them. *Granted, a slap to the face would perhaps make him want to help them less.*

Meraki placed his cigar into his mouth once more, puffing it and glaring as if contemplating what to do with her. He took so long to move again, and his stare was so cold that Margot's skin had blanketed itself in ice cold sweat by the time he opened his mouth. "How did you kill him?"

"I don't know." Margot sighed. She ran a stressed hand through her hair and glared back at him. "He saw my mark, so I ran after him and grabbed him, and I guess I was so freaked out that my magic slipped, and I shocked him. I've never used my magic before, but it bubbled over before I had a chance to stop it."

He leaned heavily on his baseball bat that was pointed into the gravel at his feet while flashing her a toothy grin. To her surprise, none of them were missing, but he did have the odd gold one that glinted back at her. "First time killing someone huh? How does it feel?"

Her brows furrowed. "Awful."

"Liar."

He turned back to look at his Coven and discarded his cigar onto the pavement at his feet. His eyebrow under his eye patch raised as he gestured to the girl with an open palm. He didn't say anything, but she must have known exactly what he was asking for, because she pushed off from where she was leaning against the trashcan and walked to him. She placed a silver dagger with metal skulls acting as the hilt onto his waiting palm, then took her place again.

Meraki grinned, then turned back to look at Margot. He wagged the end of the blade mockingly at her while he tutted. "You never told me your name."

"Margot," she said through bared, gritted teeth as she crossed her arms over her chest.

"Margot," he repeated. "What exactly do you expect me to do to help you with this little situation?"

"We heard you have a necromancer in your Coven. We figured we could come to some sort of arrangement?" Felix interjected.

Without looking at him Meraki moved his arm from pointing the dagger at Margot, to pointing it straight at him. "I didn't ask you to speak. I will deal with you later." He pointed it back to Margot. "If it is a necromancer you came for, then I can't help you. I don't do that shit anymore."

"You are the necromancer?" she asked, ignoring the blade in his hand to instead study his face. There was something in his expression that had changed. Where there was amusement and cruelty in his features before, now there was only concern. Or fear, perhaps. When he nodded once, she gulped thickly and uncrossed her arms. "I need your help. I need this douchebag brought back from the dead. *Please*. I will pay you anything."

"Anything, hm?"

Meraki frowned and turned back to look at his coven. He studied each of their faces, then rolled his tongue over one of his gold teeth in irritation. He seemed to be mentally struggling with something. Perhaps weighing the cost against the gains in his head. It didn't take long for him to turn back to look at her.

"I did some due diligence on your little group before this meeting. My daughter tells me you have a translator in your ranks, is that true?" he asked, casting his eyes over the rest of the group.

Margot didn't know what that meant, but the only one to shift on their feet nervously was Theo. He kept his hands shoved so deeply into his pockets that his shoulders were hunched up near his ears. His skin was a pale white that almost looked green, and his eyes stayed cast down.

"You," Meraki said, walking down the line again and stopping right in front of him. He leaned his face close to Theo's, making him shrink back. "You can translate the old language, right?"

"C-certain scriptures, yes. I am good with the old language, but sometimes depending on the codes certain ancient Coven's used, it can get a bit hazy," Theo said, looking up at him finally. "Why?"

"We recently got our hands on some ancient dark magic incantations. It took us a long time and a shit tonne of money to get, but we got it. Trouble is, we can't read the damned thing. We have been looking for a translator for a while. It seems your luck may be in, kid."

Meraki looked back to Margot, then stepped away from Theo, who gave a shuddering, relieved sigh. He took his place back in front of her and turned the knife in his hand, his other still holding the baseball bat as it dragged behind him on the gravel.

"I'll bring your guy back to life, but I need that incantation translated."

Theo gulped thickly. "I'll do it."

"Good," he said, then grinned at Margot, "and I want two years of your life."

Confusion must have blanketed her face, because he grinned his gold-toothed smile and chuckled deep in his chest. She fought the urge to roll her eyes and instead stared at him unblinking. "How exactly do you take two years of my life?"

"Simple blood magic, really. I'll take a cup of your blood and do the ritual myself, and I'll gain two years of your lifespan." He shrugged, then beckoned her closer with the knife.

"How do I know you won't just take *all* of my years? I don't trust you," she said honestly.

"I am many things, Margot, but a liar and a cheat are not among them. I keep my word. Two years." Meraki dropped the baseball bat at his feet and opened his hand. With a click of his fingers, a jar appeared in the centre of his palm. It was empty, with a corked lid that he pulled open with his teeth. "Let's do this, I don't have all night."

Clenching her hands into fists, Margot mulled over the idea of losing two years of her life. She wasn't even sure how something like *life* could be measured. It was an uncertain, incalculable force that refused to be recognized or argued with. It came and left with no regard for emotion or reason, and it *definitely* didn't adhere to the human concept of time. She wasn't sure how many years she had left, but she was certain that whenever her end came, she wouldn't be around to regret missing two of them.

She nodded, probably more to herself than anyone else, then took a few steps towards him. "How does this work?"

"Just stand still and don't scream."

Meraki moved fast, and before she knew what was happening, he had reached out and grabbed her arm. He pushed the sleeve of her dark-green cardigan up to her elbow and placed the knife against the inside of her forearm. The blade sliced deep, leaving a long angry red trail across her skin. She fought the scream in her throat, but the pain burst through her body like fire, forcing the sound to collect in her throat. She hummed out the pain, tears springing to her eyes so thickly she had to blink wildly to clear them. They dripped down her cheeks anyway.

He pushed the jar under her arm while holding her wrist in a firm, leather gloved hand. The blood poured out of her arm, dripping into the bottle and filling it. When Meraki was satisfied, he let go of her wrist to cork it again, and Margot pulled her arm back to her chest. She pressed her hand down on the wound hard, trying to stem the bleeding, but it slipped between her fingers and dripped onto the gravel at her feet.

"Meet me at the entrance to the crypt in the graveyard. Three A.M. Bring the body. If you are late, the deal is off, and I will still use your years. I will call on your translator when I need him." Meraki pocketed the jar, then flashed her a grin as he turned his back on her and started to walk away. "Heal yourself."

Margot bit back the pain from her arm by clenching her teeth and begging the tears to stop leaking from her eyes. "I can't. I don't know how."

"Then bleed." He shrugged, scooping the baseball bat up from the ground and resting it on his shoulder as he walked away. "Now get out of my fucking yard."

This Won't Be Pretty

Walking in the snow through a graveyard while pushing a dead body in a wheelchair with a wonky wheel, was the last thing Margot expected to be doing at 3am on a Sunday morning. The air was cold, and the grass that wasn't covered with snow and slush, was thick with frost that made the wheels stick.

"Are we close?" She panted, pushing the handle of the wheelchair while Naomi shoved the other. "We are going to be late!"

Between leaving the junkyard and making it back to the basement of *The Cloaked Cat*, the time had seemed to slip away from the group. Hefting a frozen body from a freezer and finding a heating spell that they could actually *use* was more of a taxing task than any of them had anticipated. Felix had been the one to find the broken wheelchair, but none of them had the will, nor the enthusiasm to ask him *how*. He didn't offer any explanation either, and instead had shoved Jake's body in a large coat and placed his beanie on his head to cover his dead eyes. He was currently running his hand through his shoulder length black hair to fix it back into place while looking longingly at his beanie atop Jake's head.

"It's just up ahead," he said, shoving his hands into his pockets and looking ahead. "I'm never going to be able to wear that in the same way again."

"Wait, you are planning on wearing that shit again?" Theo asked. He had walked ahead and was now walking backwards so he could look at them while he talked. His brows were raised, and his mouth was pulled into a slanted grimace.

Felix shrugged. "When have I ever been one to waste a perfectly good beanie?"

No one answered, and instead they fell silent while they rounded the frosted pathway and came to face a large stone crypt. It was bigger than she had expected it to be. The walls were tall and old, with ivy sprawled over the pillars and roof, with uneven stone steps that led to the open iron door. Engravings above the door looked back at her, but they were old and fading to time so badly that she couldn't decipher them.

Movement tore her eyes away from trying to read them. Bodies shifted from the sides of the crypt, coming out of the shadows and into view. Margot recognised them as members of the West Side Coven they had met earlier in the night, and they stood with their baseball bats while watching them with feline-like grins. Meraki's daughter was among them. She had a doberman on a leash and was walking with a saunter towards Felix. When she reached him, she raised her hand to run her fingers through his long dark hair.

"I don't think I've ever seen you without a hat on," she said, her head tilted so the pinks on the ends of her hair would frame her face. "Not even when we—"

Felix coughed to end her sentence, and he flashed her a handsome smile while he reached for her hand to pull it away from his head. He clasped it anyway, but his body seemed more tense than usual. "Yeah, well. Needs must. Where is your dad?"

"Downstairs. He is set up and ready for you, if you wanna head down," she said, taking her hand back from his and sauntering back towards the open iron door.

Theo and Felix followed her, leaving Margot and Naomi to fight with the chair all the way up the steps. Margot had to turn and walk backwards while pulling the handles of the wheelchair as Naomi held on to Jake's body so he wouldn't topple out of it. She tried to ignore the eyes of the men that flanked the steps, who were watching in half-amused, half-dumbfounded expressions. She connected eyes with one of them anyway and flashed him a thin-lipped, embarrassed smile as they crested the top and wheeled Jake backwards into the crypt.

When she turned, another set of steep stone stairs stared back at her from the middle of the room, only this time, they were descending deep into the ground. She could see Felix and Theo already walking down them, their bodies a silhouette against the light of the flaming torches at the bottom.

The shock of the sight of the stairs must have shown on her face, because Meraki's daughter started laughing. She tipped her head over the side, looking down them with an amused smile. "Better get cracking."

Naomi cursed under her breath and moved to grab the front of the chair so they could heft it down the stairs, making the girl with the pink tipped hair roll her eyes almost audibly.

"You know you could just hover him down there, right? It's a simple telekinesis incantation. It would save you the stress of trying to *carry* his ass," she said. At the clouded look of confusion on Margot's face, she uncrossed her arms and waved her hands. "I'll do it. I'll send him down after you."

Naomi didn't say another word. She dropped the front wheels of the chair and turned, jogging down the steps like she was glad to be rid of it. By the time Margot had thanked the girl, Naomi was already gone.

She descended the steps a lot slower than the others did. When she reached the bottom, the room she was met with left her feeling colder than she had when she was walking above. It was huge, spanning out further than the building above it. Pillars that held up the ceiling ran in two rows all the way to the end, with carved gargoyles and stone bats hugged against them where they met at the top. The floor was wet, with puddles dotted around the many dented cavities in the stone floor, while rectangle body-sized holes in the walls looked back at her like a morbid kind of honeycomb. Each of them held a coffin in various states of rot, and some of them had disintegrated so badly she could see the odd skull poking through the wood as if they were watching right back.

"Take your time."

The voice sounded bored, and strained, and the words were spoken in a way that suggested she better *not* take her time. Just as she looked at the back of the room to see Meraki standing at the long stone table, she felt something nudge the back of her legs at her knees. She turned, finding Jake's body and his chair waiting behind her, small wisps of pink energy filtering away from behind him.

She took a deep breath of the damp, stale air and rushed to grab the handles of the wheelchair, pushing it over the rocky cobbles and down the pillared aisles towards the group. They were standing around the ends of the stone table, while Meraki was leaning with heavy hands in the middle.

Margot gave Meraki a sheepish half-smile when the wheels stopped. "Thank you, for helpi—"

"This is a business transaction. Nothing more." Meraki pushed off the table and straightened his back. "Put him on the table and strip him down to his underwear."

The boys moved quickly. Felix looped his arms under Jake's and lifted, while Theo grabbed him under his knees. They hefted him onto the surface of the table, his arms at his sides and his head tilted to the left. When he was settled, Margot reached forward and started to unbuckle the belt that was around his waist, a smirk tempting her face before she realised it was there.

"What's so funny?" Meraki asked, watching as the group made short work of Jake's shirt and shoes.

Margot shrugged and tugged the jeans down over Jake's hips. "I don't know. I guess this was all the poor guy was looking for. Me unbuckling his jeans. He would be *so* pissed if he knew the only way that was happening was because he was dead."

"And stiff in all the wrong ways," Felix said, snatching the beanie from Jake's head and placing it back on his own.

They discarded the clothes, draping them over the back of the wheelchair along with his shoes, then looked upon the body. He was very pale, almost blue. The white lightning shaped markings were still tattooed there, spanning from each shoulder, over his chest and down his arms. They still sparkled as if made from frost. Margot flicked her eyes from them to look at Meraki, who was standing with his large arms crossed over his chest. He was staring down at the tracings with furrowed brows.

"You did this by *accident*?" he asked, looking up at her with one eye from under his peppered eyebrow. He looked wholly unconvinced, and it showed all over his face.

"Yes," Margot said. She stared right back, and although she could tell he didn't believe her, she felt no need to elaborate further. "Does it matter? We have a contract."

Meraki ran his tongue across his teeth and slipped his frown into a smile, "No, I suppose it doesn't matter. Still, if it was by *accident*, this is a lot of magic. If you really are as uneducated in the craft as you suggest you are, then you need to learn. If you don't, this shit is just going to keep happening, and you don't have enough years to trade to fix your mistakes."

"Frankly, I didn't come here for advice," she said, backing up from the table so he could work. "If you could get on with the job I paid you for, that would be great."

He watched her for a long moment with one eye, his eyepatch on the other raising from his lifted brow. "You should watch that pretty little mouth of yours. Perhaps during all of these pleasantries, you have forgotten who I am."

No. She knew exactly who he was. A necromancer. The president of the West Side Coven. A murderer. The kind of man who fed on weakness. If she planned on leaving this place without being completely screwed over, he needed to know she was not going to cower. No matter how much her knees felt like they might buckle and betray her, she knew she couldn't show it on her face.

"I thought you were the kind of person who didn't appreciate pleasantries, and I know you want to get out of this shit hole as quickly as we do," she said, slipping her hands into the pocket of her black leather jacket. She could feel the little potion bottle there against her fingertips, and she grabbed onto it in case she needed to have it ready. "Please just do the magic."

"Oh I like it when you say please," he grinned, wagging a finger at her. "Fine. Step back, this won't be pretty."

Felix moved away from the table completely, stepping to one of the pillars so he could lean against it with his hands in his pockets. Theo stayed closer than everyone else, watching in interest at the book that Meraki lifted and laid on Jake's chest. He didn't seem as nervous as he had the first time he met him, and instead was silently watching the pages flick open with genuine anticipation. He liked books more than he was aware of his nerves, it seemed.

Naomi made sure they were settled before she nodded once, more to herself than anyone else, and walked to Margot's side. "Well, here goes nothing. If this doesn't work, we a—"

"Silence."

Meraki didn't look up at them when he spoke. He was studying the pages and flicking between them until he found the correct section. He reached a hand to his eyepatch and pulled it off his head, revealing a completely white eye. It had no pupil, or at least not one she could see. He set the eyepatch aside and cleared his throat, then pushed his jacket sleeves up to his elbows and readied his hands by splaying his fingers and hovering them over the tracings on Jake's chest. He mumbled words she didn't understand, while his hands moved in small slow circles. After a tense moment of nothing happening, the centre of both his palms began to glow in a gentle blue haze. The light shone downward out of his skin and rested upon the tracings, and after a while of chanting the incantations and massaging the air above them, they started to fade. They lost their frosty sparkle, then shrunk from the ends and receded all the way back to their sources at his shoulders where they swirled smaller and smaller until they were gone from his skin.

When Meraki was satisfied they were done with, he stopped chanting and pulled his hands away, the light from his palms ceasing the second his words did.

"The magic you left on him is gone. We don't have to do this next bit. We could just leave his body somewhere and save us all the hassle of retrieving his soul."

"That wasn't the deal. If they find his body, they will be able to trace his last movements, and that leads the suits straight to me, magic tracings or not," Margot said, her eyes not leaving Jake's chest. It was as if the white sparkling scars were never there. It was impressive, really.

Meraki groaned and closed the book. He grabbed the spine and threw it onto the floor before he leaned heavily on the top of the stone table. His brow was furrowed and he was staring down at the body with an expression that she could only describe as *fear*.

"Wait." Margot grinned. She took a few steps towards him again and stopped when she was at the table, opposite him. She leaned on the surface the same way he did and looked up into his face amusingly. "Are you *scared?*"

He flashed her a warning glance and his hands where he was leaning changed into fists. "If you even *slightly* understood what it cost to do this kind of magic, you would be apprehensive too. There is a reason necromancy is rarely used. The land of the dead does not like their patrons taken from them, and the source of that theft *always* pays a price. Namely, me."

That made Margot pause. She straightened up and wiped the smirk off her face. "Then why did you agree to this?"

"Because I like knowing I have many years under my belt, no matter how many scars my body gains," he said, then puffed out a sigh and looked back down to Jake's body. "When I start this process, there is no stopping it. I will send for his soul, and it will return here, but while that gateway is open, the dead *will* come. They will come in *droves*, and you better be ready to hold them back, because every single one of them will come to reclaim that soul, and I will be no use to you. My members will be here to help you, but you need to take that magic you have in each of your pockets and use it wisely."

He pointed to the wall where there was a stack of baseball bats waiting for them. "Take one. There is enough to go around and they have been enchanted, so they will work against the dead. Once the incantation is over and the soul is back inside this body, I will close the gate."

Margot glanced over the faces of their group. Naomi's face was pulled into a pissed-off kind of frown. Theo looked so nervous that his body was practically shaking. Felix, in contrast, was grinning widely. His hands rubbed together like he was excited, and he took off in a walk towards the wall to lift one of the bats. To test it, he aimed at the wall and swung, and where the wood connected with the stone, a bright blue blast burst from the end, sending him back onto his rump.

He groaned, scrambling to his feet, but he was grinning widely. "*This* is fucking awesome. Can I keep this?" he asked, turning the bat over in his hands and studying it.

"I couldn't care less. Just get ready." Meraki rubbed his hands as if to warm them and looked down the row of pillars to the staircase.

He whistled, prolonged and slow, and before long the bodies of the men and women in his Coven were walking down the stairs. They each had their own baseball bats or chains in their hands, and where their amused and smirking smiles were once on their faces, now they only looked upon the scene with serious expressions.

Margot was pulled away from watching them by Naomi, who was tugging on her sleeve and guiding her towards the pile of baseball bats. She lifted one, then passed one to Margot. "When this is all over, you owe us *big time*."

"I know. I appreciate everything you have done for me, Naomi. I'll make this up to you," she said, gripping to the bat with her bandaged covered hand and leaned to give Naomi a hug. She stiffened under her arms, but she tapped her back with one hand anyway.

"Not a hugger, but thanks," Naomi said, walking back towards Felix.

Theo lifted his bat with tentative fingers. He looked Margot in the eyes and shifted on his feet. "I've never been a fighter, Margot. I don't know what to do."

"It's okay," she said, reaching to rest her free hand on his shoulder. "You are stronger than you realise, Theo, and you have us. Stay behind me, whack anything that moves."

He gave an unconvinced half-smile and let her guide him back to the group. Meraki was holding his hands out in front of himself again, and everyone had placed themselves at opposite sides of the aisle, leaving the front of the table free of bodies.

"Here goes nothing," Margot mumbled.

Meraki started his incantations. His voice was a few octaves deeper, like the sound was coming from deep within his chest instead of his throat. It seemed like the noise of it was vibrating the atoms in the air so dramatically that she could feel it press against the skin of her face. The stale air in the room picked up in a breeze that came from nowhere, and when she looked around at the other faces in the room, she could see their hair beginning to whip around their faces. Though, it was nothing compared to the sight of Meraki.

His coat was fanning out behind him, like the wind in the crypt was aiming directly at him, and his face was tilted up towards the ceiling. His eyes were shining in bright neon greens, and his working one had lost its pupil. He seemed completely *gone*, not reacting to any of the sounds in the room nor paying attention to the rest of them.

A rumble on the floor tore her eyes away from him. From the centre of the crypt, a swirling portal of green fog and wind opened in the floor. Cracks formed in the stone and worked its way like a jagged snake across the floor towards their feet, making Margot step back from it. That was when she heard them.

Screams came before she saw anything. They were screeching in a metallic chorus, forcing a ringing sound to burrow into her ears and rattle her brain. It made her skin tingle and her blood run cold, but her feet held firm. Theo gave a nervous whimper from behind her, and she turned to look at him with a comforting smile.

"It's gonna be okay!" she called over the wind.

He didn't look convinced, so she turned to look back at the open portal to save him from having to reply. Ghostly boned hands were beginning to climb out of the hole, and when the bodies pulled themselves free, she was faced with the crumbling apparitions of *dozens* of skeletons. Their bones were covered in a dripping yellow-green liquid she didn't want to know the origins of, and a foggy mist was clinging to them, somehow seeming to solidify the spaces between their bones so they could move.

The skeleton at the front climbed to its feet and screamed its metallic scream in their direction while its comrades flanked either side. They joined in with the screaming, then bolted, bony fingers stretched out in front of them like claws.

Surprisingly, Felix was the first to meet them. He raised his baseball bat up behind his head and swung hard into the chest of the first one, sending bright blue magic blasting where it connected. The magic blew the bones apart, sending shards against the walls while Felix grinned happily. He seemed in his element.

The animated skeleton bodies seemed quite easy to deal with. The problem was how *many* of them there were. More and more of them were crawling out of the hole, and Margot knew if Meraki didn't finish the incantation fast enough, they would have a swarm on their hands that they would have no hope of overcoming.

Margot swung hard, her baseball bat connecting with the head of one of the oncoming bodies. It blasted into shards, the bones turning to dust and shards that stuck in her long red hair. By the time the green dust settled enough for her to see, another was right behind it, and she had to whip the bat upwards quickly to connect with its chin. It burst, and she stumbled back against Theo's chest, who was wide eyed and frozen.

"There are too many of them! Theo, you need to help us!" she shouted.

Theo took more steps back, shaking his head.

"Shit," Margot panted, looking back to the room.

In the few seconds she had spent trying to convince Theo to help, the swarm was too close. Skeletal hands grabbed her by her hair and forced her down to her knees. Its mouth was wide open and the closer it got to her face, the more she could feel the breath beginning to leave her body. Angry, *hungry* green magic was seeping into her skin. It felt like every drip of moisture was leaving her body, leaving her dry and exhausted while her skin became thin and paler. The figure wasn't necessarily *hurting* her, but the magic it was wielding was draining, and she found herself unable to move from her knees. She couldn't even scream.

A blast of blue light burst from somewhere to her left, and the skeletal figure disintegrated in front of her. The second its hand's let her go, breath returned to her chest and her skin returned to normal, albeit still cold. Theo stood with his bat raised, cold sweat dotting his brow and a look of clarity on his face. He lowered his arm from his swing, then helped Margot to her feet.

"I'm good. I'm sorry," he said with a determined nod. "Let's go."

Together they pushed forward, swinging frantically and trying to force the hoard backwards. Among the plumes of green mist, Felix was blissfully blasting everything in his path. He was so enthralled that he had pushed further into them than anyone else. He had a wide smile on his face and his eyes were big, like he had been waiting all his life to beat the shit out of something and *this* was his moment.

A scream to the right pulled Margot's eyes away from him. Naomi was on the floor, a set of skeletal bodies descending upon her. Theo must have heard her too, because he bolted in her direction and started to beat at the bodies to free her. There were just too many.

Margot took a few steps back so she could breathe and think. The baseball bats were good, but they were slow, and the enchanted skeletons were too fast. *They weren't fast enough for hellfire though.*

She dug into her pocket for Felix's liquid insurance and pulled out the bottles. They were small, but she figured after meeting Bonnie, that the old kitchen witch knew how to pack a punch. She looked up at the hoard and pulled back her arm, throwing the bottle hard into the middle of them. It slipped through the bodies and smashed on the floor, instant red flames engulfing anything around it. The screams got louder as more and more of the skeleton bodies were reduced to dust. From between the flames and the green mist, she noticed a ball of white light beginning to emerge from the centre of the portal. It floated into the air above their heads and floated calmly in the roaring wind while it travelled towards Meraki and Jake's body.

Margot took a few precious moments to watch as it made its way directly to the table. It lowered, and Meraki turned one of his shining palms so it was facing upwards. The ball of white light settled into his palm, and he finally lowered his gaze from the ceiling to look at it. A smirk grazed his lips, and for a moment Margot thought he glanced at her, but his eyes were still white and she couldn't decipher the direction in which he was looking. He tipped his head down anyway.

Meraki closed his fingers around the ball and placed it to the centre of Jake's chest, then slammed the heel of his hand against it. The second the ball of energy disappeared into Jake's chest, his eyes snapped open, and his body jolted violently. He rolled onto his side, coughing and shivering while his body got used to his renewed life and regenerated pumping blood.

While he was recovering, Meraki shouted the final incantation, and the wind stopped. The whole crypt fell eerily silent, nothing but the sound of Jake gasping new air into his lungs to break it. Then, the boom of wind burst again, only this time, it was sucking back into the portal.

Every skeletal body that was left standing screamed in their eerie metallic unison, the wind forcing them back into the hole while they scrambled to stay. It didn't take long for the last body to be pulled back into the portal, and the moment its hand let go of from digging into the cobblestones of the floor, the hole disappeared.

Silence returned to the crypt. Everyone was exhausted, their hair in various states of disarray and sweat beaded on all of their brows, but they had smiles on their faces. None wider than Felix's.

"*That* was awesome!" he panted, his hands in the air and his baseball bat still fused in his fist.

"Yeah, let's not make a habit out of it, eh?" Margot panted, wiping her brow and dropping her bat so she could move towards the table.

Meraki was slumped back against the wall, his head in his hands and his body shaking. Whatever magic he had to do to perform the ritual had taken its toll on him, and it was showing. Badly.

"Are you okay?"

He looked up, his face strained in pain. His mouth pulled with a grimace as the scar on his face that ended at his chin began to grow, trailing down his throat and leaking bright red blood. "Get your friend and get out of my crypt," he panted.

Jake was still panting and clutching his chest, but Margot ignored him to watch as the new scar on Meraki's neck bled. "What is happening to you?"

"Nothing you can change. Occupational hazard," he said through gritted teeth. "Now leave."

Margot didn't want to simply leave him there bleeding, but he wasn't giving her much of a choice. She tipped her chin up and turned to look at Jake. He was sitting up and looking around the room with wide eyes.

"W-where t-the f-fuck a-am I?" he stammered.

"Ah shit." Naomi walked to him quickly, and with a swift hand she placed her fingertips to Jake's forehead. "Sleep."

His eyes rolled back into his head and he flopped over again, completely still, but breathing.

Margot worked as if on autopilot. She grabbed his shirt and threw it to Felix, then took his jeans and began to dress him again. "Dress him. We need to carry him out of here and get him home."

Felix, seeming unwilling to part with his baseball bat long enough to help, passed the shirt to Theo, who rolled his eyes and grabbed it. He slipped it down over Jake's head, then carefully pushed his arms through the holes and tugged it down his chest. Once he was dressed again, they lifted his body back into the wheelchair, and Margot let Naomi take the handles. She adjusted the backpack that was still hanging on the back of it, making sure it was secure before she pushed him back down the aisle without looking back.

Theo and Felix followed quickly, leaving Margot hovering near the now empty stone table. She played with her hands anxiously, then looked over her shoulder to Meraki. "Are you going to be okay?"

"Do you care? You got what you came for," Meraki said, swiping the blood from his neck with his hand and flicking it off his fingers.

"Of course I *care*." Margot sighed, crossing her arms over her chest and tilting her head. "I guess I'll see you around."

Meraki gave a single nod, then turned his back on her so he could scoop down and lift the book where he had discarded it on the floor. Margot gave him one last glance, then turned on her heel and rushed after her group. Luckily, by the time she reached them, Jake and his wheelchair were already hefted back up to the main room, and when she ascended the steps, she found her friends already waiting outside the iron door.

"What now?" Theo asked.

The second Margot stepped out onto the frosted grass, the iron door behind her slammed closed. There were no West City Coven members in the area, since they had opted to stay inside with their leader, so they were finally alone again.

"I guess I will take him to his house, but I'm not sure how I am going to explain this. How long will your sleeping spell last?" she asked, looking at Naomi.

"A few hours at most, but you are not taking him home," she said, taking the backpack off the back of the chair and slipping it onto her shoulder. "If you take him home, they are going to ask him where he's been."

She took the handles of the wheelchair and pushed, guiding him all the way down the pathway, over the frozen grass and towards a row of old gravestones. They stuck out of the ground like loose broken teeth, leaving uneven edges that made the ground hard to walk on.

"Where are you going?" Margot asked, racing after her, but Naomi's feet were fast and her convictions strong. Naomi ignored her until they came to a large tree in the centre of the stones. It was bare of leaves, but with the shelter of the branches, the ground seemed to be less frozen than other areas.

"We are going to leave him here."

Naomi hefted the handles of the wheelchair and tipped Jake out of it. He landed hard on the frosted grass near the base, and she pushed the chair out of the way so she could lift him under the arms and prop him up against the trunk.

Margot blinked, watching Naomi as she hunched down and took the backpack from her shoulders so she could rummage through the contents. "We can't just leave him here, Naomi! He will freeze!"

"He's not gonna *freeze*. It's practically morning, he will be awake in a few hours, and he has a jacket," she said, pulling out the jacket that was stuffed into the backpack.

Naomi pulled it over his arms and zipped it up at the front to keep him warm, then dug her hands back into the bag. When she pulled her hand out, she produced a large bottle of whiskey. Opening the bottle, she took a large gulping sip of the liquid inside, screwing up her nose before she tipped some of the contents all over the front of Jake's shirt.

"What are you doing?! Don't waste it!" Felix shouted, trying to snatch the bottle from her, but she pulled it away from him.

"We are going to make it look like he spent the last two days getting wasted. He is going to have no memory of anything other than the gig at *The Cloaked Cat*, and waking up here, so we need to give him a reasonable explanation for that. Being black out drunk is the best excuse I've got, and he doesn't exactly look like it would be out of the realms of possibility anyway."

"I suppose that is kind of genius," Theo mumbled, kicking the toe of his shoe against one of the stones near the tree while Naomi poured some of the whiskey into Jake's mouth. He didn't need to be drunk, or hungover, but his mouth and clothes did need to *smell* like he had been.

"Can we all at least have a celebratory sip before it all goes to waste?" Felix asked, looking longingly at the bottle.

Naomi grinned, taking another sip of it herself before she passed it to him. He grabbed it, tipping his head back and taking a few long sips of the liquor. He coughed when he pulled it away and offered it to Theo, who shook his head.

"Nah. I'm good, thanks."

"You are telling me we just spent the night pushing a dead body around the city, making bargains with the deadliest Coven gang we know, and fought an army of the undead, but you are scared of a little sip of whiskey?" Felix asked. His eyebrow lifted and he shook the bottle at him, the liquid swirling inside.

Theo looked unconvinced, but at Felix's wiggling eyebrow, he snatched the bottle from his friend's hand and tipped his head back. "Fuck it."

Margot laughed at the instant disgusted face Theo pulled at the taste of it. He pushed the bottle into her hand while coughing and spitting the excess from his tongue onto the grass. She shook her head amusingly, then took her own small swig and handed the bottle back to Naomi, who rested the neck of the bottle in Jake's hand and left it on his lap. To her credit, he really did look like he had been drinking and passed out. *More importantly, he didn't look like someone who had been dead for two days and was just brought back to life.*

Naomi stood, and Margot quickly grabbed the handles of the wheelchair, nodding down into it. "Get in."

Her eyebrow lifted. "What?"

"Get in! You deserve some rest."

Naomi eyed the chair, and although she tipped her head back like she was going to stubbornly ignore Margot's request, the tiredness in her eyes defeated her resolve and she cracked a smile. "Fine," she said, slumping down into it.

"Felix, take it away." Margot winked.

Felix gave a devilish grin and took the handles, pushing her back to the smoother path where he started to run, pushing Naomi as fast as he could towards the gates of the graveyard. Naomi threw her arms in the air, waving her hands and kicking out her legs, while Margot looped her arm around Theo's shoulders and pulled him along.

"Come on, let's get some sleep."

We Will Not Be Silenced. Not Anymore

It had been six weeks since Jake had been brought back from the dead. The snow had finally stopped falling, but the air still held the threat of it. Since the night they gathered at the graveyard, Margot had spent nearly every afternoon with Theo, Juliet, Naomi and Felix in the basement of *The Cloaked Cat*. They had introduced her to the basics of spellcraft and she was starting to get the hang of compulsion, fire magic, and levitation, but healing was still proving hard to learn.

The weeks had gone fast with her newfound friends. Between covering shifts for Naomi at the bar and her studies with Theo, the group of gubbins had become more like a *family* than friends. She had never felt more like she belonged somewhere than when she was sitting at that big table with them.

Still, the time she spent with Jane, Liam and Lydia were as important as ever. She had made up her missed movie nights and makeover days, and Lydia had seemed to forgive her. Liam was as quiet and withdrawn as usual, and Jane was finally beginning to relax with the idea that she had *witches* for friends.

As much as her life seemed to be back on track, if not better than before, there was a gnawing kind of need that had settled into her heart that she couldn't shake. It was a hunger that never seemed to be satisfied, no matter how many wonderful things she filled her life with. This was why she was sitting on the rug in her bedroom, the floor covered with large sheets of card, paint trays with various coloured acrylics and magazines cut into small pieces.

Lydia looked up at her from where she was sticking the last few glittery hearts on the edges of the poster they were working on. She had a triumphant grin on her face, and her fingers were covered in paint when she reached forward to slip onto Margot's lap. She clapped her hands and rested back happily.

"It's finished!" Lydia bounced, looking down at their work. "Does you think your friends will like it?"

Margot smiled warmly at her childish phrasing and wrapped her arms around Lydia's middle so she could snuggle into her. "Yes, I think they will like it very much. Thank you for your help, kiddo. Now, you should go and eat your lunch while I pack this up. Do you remember what I told you?"

The little girl jumped up from Margot's knee and turned to place her glitter covered hands on Margot's cheeks. "Don't tell mommy."

"That's exactly right." She laughed, leaning in to kiss her nose. She patted her behind and gently pushed her towards the door. "Now scoot. Eat your veggies!"

Lydia groaned dramatically as she bounded out the bedroom door, leaving Margot to fold the card poster into quarters. She added it to the pile of others, then put them into a bag and stood from the floor.

She was woman enough to know when she was nervous, and right now her stomach was doing flips. She knew that her half-baked idea could be received by her friends like a brick to the face, but she couldn't let something like *fear* stop her from doing what she felt was right. Margot *knew* that this was right. Dangerous and stupid, maybe, but right.

The newspaper clipping of her mother and Jane that Naomi had given her was sitting atop her vanity. She glanced at it in its new silver frame, a small smile gracing her face as she walked to it and lifted it in one hand. Her mother looked so young in it. So happy. So *wild*. The passion in her eyes leaped off the paper so violently she could almost taste the ink.

"Wish me luck, mom," Margot said softly, laying a quick kiss on the glass before she set it down and walked out of the room.

"Where are you rushing off to?"

Jane stood in the hallway, a suspicious smile on her face and her hands clutching a basket of clean laundry. She set it on the floor and moved to take Margot's hand, checking the back of it to make sure the makeup was sufficiently covered.

"To see my friends," she said, clenching Jane's hand in return. "You don't need to be worried about me."

"I will always worry about you." Jane shrugged, letting her hand go so she could cup Margot's face with her fingers, much like Lydia had. "You should let me meet these new friends of yours, if you are planning on spending so much time with them."

"You will, soon. They are just a little jumpy when it comes to newcomers. I am surprised they have taken to me so quickly."

"Understandable. Smart, even, considering the circumstances," Jane said, leaning in to kiss her cheek. "Off you go then. Be home for dinner tonight, please. I am making your favourite."

"Oh, of course. Thank you, mom." Margot didn't have the heart to tell her that *sausage pasta* hadn't been her favourite since she was a child. Instead, she kissed her cheek and made her way down the hallway. "I love you!"

"Gubbins."

The metal door of the basement opened quickly, and Juliet stood waiting on the other side. She instantly hugged her arms around Margot's legs, not saying a word as she shuffled inside and closed the door behind her. When she let her go, Juliet took her hand and guided her down the steps into the room below. Felix and Theo were in their usual seats, and Naomi was standing beside the rundown stove, stirring a pot of boiling ramen.

"S'up?" she asked, not looking up from her wooden spoon. "I'm making food, do you want some?"

"No, I'm good, thank you." Margot smiled, letting Juliet's hand go so she could wander back to her seat beside Theo. "I actually have something I would like to show you guys."

"Is it drugs? Tell me it's drugs," Felix said, not looking up from the playing cards in his hands.

She knew he wasn't being serious, but it made her roll her eyes anyway. "No, obviously, but it is pretty serious, and I need you to pay attention."

Margot reached forward and took the cards from Felix's hand, setting them face down on the surface of the table.

Felix frowned and sat straighter in his chair. "Hey! I was winning."

"Like shit you were." Theo looked up at him with a grin, then set his own cards down so he could rest his elbows on the table and lace his hands. He moved his eyes to Margot and nodded to the bag she was carrying. "I guess what you have to show us is in the bag?"

"Wait," Naomi mumbled, throwing the contents of the flavour packet into her ramen and stirring it frantically.

When she was satisfied it was mixed, she threw the spoon aside and lifted a set of chopsticks from the drawer before she took the whole pot back to the table. She sat down on the edge of it, the handle of the pot in one hand and the chopsticks stabbing the ramen in the other. She shoved a large ball of it into her mouth, then spoke around it.

"Okay, shoot."

Margot shifted nervously, then pulled the bag open and set it on the table. She pulled the folded posters out, but kept them closed while she held them with tight fingers. They were all watching her with confused and attentive eyes, except for Juliet, who was more concerned with the tub of ice cream on her lap.

"I haven't been able to stop thinking about my mother. The things she did, the people she knew, the places she would have gone if she had the chance to. She was an advocate for change, and yes, I didn't know her, but I *know* she was making a difference. When Felix and I went to get those insurances, we saw the suits rip apart a young family, and every time I close my eyes, I see their faces. I hear their cries when I try to sleep, and it is haunting me knowing they will probably never see each other again. You guys know how that feels, right? Everyone at this table has had their families ripped apart by the suits and the government and their draconian regime, and I can't sit by anymore and watch it happen."

Theo had his head tipped down, his brows were furrowed and his eyes held so much grief in them that Margot felt instantly bad about bringing up their families. Juliet had stopped eating her ice cream, her little hands holding onto the tub tightly, while Felix sat back in his chair with his arms folded, just staring at her. Naomi was the only one still moving. She was still eating hungrily at her ramen when she looked up.

"Family emotional trauma aside, what do you expect us to do about it?" She shrugged. "We are five people in a basement, we can't change anything."

That made Margot crack a smile. "That's the thing, though! Even the biggest wildfires start with the smallest of sparks. We could be that renewed spark. *We* could be that wildfire. We need to show them that we will not be silenced. Not anymore."

Juliet looked up at Margot finally, and she was surprised to see a small smile on the girl's face. Theo looked up too, but only long enough to wipe under his eye with his thumb.

"So, what? We storm the government like your mom did? Die in the process?" Naomi asked, setting the pot aside and folding her arms, looking wholly unconvinced.

"I know it is dangerous, and I know it might sound crazy—"

"I like crazy." Felix smirked.

She flashed him a thankful smile, then unfolded the first poster to show them. Right in the middle was the old W.A.P.M logo, then the government crest with a large red line over it, and slogans she found from old articles. They read '*we will not be silenced!*' and '*Witches against persecution!*'.

"I know it won't happen overnight. I know that we need allies and a good plan and more members, but it's a start. We can't sit here living like scared mice anymore, waiting for the day that door gets kicked in and we get dragged away *screaming*," Margot said, holding the ends of the poster in tight fists. "Please. Make a wildfire with me."

No one moved. Not even Naomi. It took so long for anyone to even breathe that Margot thought for sure she had done the wrong thing. They could think she was crazy. They could kick her out and never let her back in. She was holding her breath for so long that she felt lightheaded until the sound of Juliet pushing out her chair allowed her the bravery to let it out.

The small girl set her tub of ice cream on the table and stood, looking over everyone's faces before her eyes fell on Margot's. A grin spread on her face, and she moved around the table until she was face to face with the poster. Her eyes scanned the words and the pictures, the little gemstones and messily painted logos. She reached out her hand and took the poster, then returned to her set and watched the group expectantly.

Margot opened the next one, and Felix was the next to move. He didn't get up from his chair, but he did reach his hand far out over the table to take it. "I'm in."

Theo gulped thickly and ran his hands through the tight curls on his head. He was clearly arguing with himself, but he finally relented and nodded with conviction. "I'm in too."

Grinning, Margot handed a poster to Felix so he could pass it down the line to Theo, who took it and opened it, flattening it out on the table with gentle fingers. She had one left, and she opened it and wriggled the card at Naomi so she could see the words on it.

"I can't do this without the fiercest woman I know," she said hopefully. "That's you."

"Well obviously." Naomi rolled her eyes and unfolded her arms. She stood and walked so she was face to face with Margot, her eyes studying hers as if looking for something unhinged. "You are insane, do you know that?"

"Obviously."

"well. . ." she trailed, extending her hand to touch the ends of the poster. Her mouth curled into a smile at the edges, and her eyes flicked down to the words on it that read '*Witch persecution ends here!*'. She gripped it, pulling it away from Margot and into her own arms. "Who am I to stand in the way of a wildfire?"

About Nikita Rogers

Nikita Rogers lives in a little rustic village in Northern Ireland. She lives with her husband, Lee Rogers, an insanely talented musician, her wonderful step-kids, and their cats, chickens and pygmy goat.

She has been writing for 18 years (as of 2023). During the day, Nikita spends her time working in her tattoo studio where she has etched designs on her customers since 2008. At night, you will find her curled up on her sofa with a good book, creating sketches and designs, or writing in her pyjamas with a good cup of coffee.

She is currently working on book three of the Whisper of Witches series, a spin off series, and a completely different untitled Fae series that will be released sometime 2025. Come say hi on her socials, she promises she doesn't bite.

Instagram: @Nevermoreink

Tiktok: @nikitarogersauthor

Email: nikitarogersauthor@hotmail.com

Find her husband's music also:

Instagram: @leerogersmusic

Facebook: Lee Rogers Music

Twitter: leerogerstweets

Spellbound

JL CASTEN

About the Book

A drop of blood changed Melisandre's world in ways she could never have anticipated.

After finding her soul's mate and discovering the truth of her identity, Melisandre must now naviagte the politics of her world to retake her throne.

In order to protect a valuable ally, she must call upon Zaleria's former lover, and tear open wounds best left to scar.

Amalia will cast a spell that could cost her everything, but can it be broken in time to save their world?

Advisory

Some aspects of this story may be upsetting to some readers. Some elements include:

Violence

Abuse

Death

Prejudice

Starfall

The halls of Starfall Citadel teemed with activity as servants scurried from one place to the next. Draven, the Regent King of Elythallas, was expected within the hour, half his Court in tow. Ysildea stalked through the glistening halls toward her chambers in disgust. She'd been locked away in the Citadel for as long as she could remember. Her mother had been directly descended from Melisandre, with flowing silver hair and deep brown skin, brown eyes ringed with amber. She'd been a beauty in her youth that was unparalleled. It had been her downfall. That, and the blood that flowed through her veins.

Draven had claimed her when she was barely twenty, and Ysildea was the result of that unholy union. She hated him. Her father, if one could even call him that. He'd killed her mother in a political ruse to eliminate more of the True Queen's bloodline and used Ysildea to strengthen his claims to her throne. So long as she lived, he would use her to legitimize himself.

"Lady, please come to the baths. His Lordship will be mightily cross if you are not present when he arrives," Tilda pleaded with her.

Ysildea ignored her vapid requests, rolling her eyes and continuing on her way. She was no fool. The whispers among the servants and handmaids the past few weeks had shifted, become more frantic. It had piqued Ysildea's curiosity so that she had hidden away in a wardrobe to discover their secrets. What she had heard chilled her to the bone.

Draven was not merely coming to meet with his allies in the Northern Kingdoms, he was coming to marry her off to the worst of them. Even as she seethed with the rage of it, Idrovas was closing in on her. The secretive and deceptive alliance between her father and the North was about to become widely known. It would stir unrest within the continent that had been rumbling for centuries.

A hand closed around her wrist and Ysildea stopped, her muscles tense and her jaw clenched. She breathed in deeply before she spoke.

"Take your hands from me before I remove them from your body," she hissed through teeth ground together so tightly she knew she must look sinister indeed.

A whimper echoed behind her as the culprit quickly pried their fingers from her flesh as though burned.

"Mistress, I apologize. You must come quickly. Please, hurry," a sheepish voice replied.

Something in the tone made her pause and consider. She had no desire to abide by whatever protocols her father had laid out for the servants. No will to please him or consent to such lunacy as being wed to the Warlock who controlled the Northern Kingdoms. She turned, a brow raised, and gazed down at the slight framed boy who'd been brave enough to grab at her.

He was too thin, as so many were in this place. His stringy brown hair was stuck to his head and matted in several places, and he trembled as he bowed low before her, not daring to raise his eyes to hers. The poor boy was what she called an in-betweener. A servant shoved into the Citadel whom no one would care about should he go missing. It was likely his family had been killed or had starved to death, or had been pressed into servitude themselves in the Court. Many orphans were indentured here, and there was never enough food to go around.

Ysildea sighed heavily. She felt badly for the young man. Surely there was something important or he'd have never approached her.

"Very well then, what is it?" she huffed at him.

He straightened, relief flooded his features and he nearly grinned in appreciation at her. "This way, quickly, please. We have to hurry..."

He bit his lip and shrugged at her when she cocked her head to one side and furrowed her brow. Apparently it was the only explanation he would give. He hesitated, then turned and rushed in the opposite direction. Only glancing back once to wait for her decision.

She groaned, but squared her shoulders and followed him. He raced through the tower, home to herself and her 'staff', which was truly mostly comprised of orphaned younglings with a smattering of noble maidens in attendance of her. In reality, they were hostages. Living certainty that their families would remain loyal to the Usurper. Her father.

When they reached the long glass corridor that connected her domain to the rest of the Citadel she straightened her spine and set her face into a mask of indifference. They moved quickly through scholars, magic users, and warriors in training. Ysildea took note of the shocked faces, the scowls, and those who bowed low to her. She had no friends. Supporters of Melisandre's line hated her for the blood of the Usurper in her veins, and her father's supporters saw her only as a pawn in an elaborate game. To be used and moved as they saw fit.

Finally, they entered the levels of the Citadel that housed the kitchens, store rooms, and holding cells. She relaxed slightly, relieved at the lack of eyes on her once more. The boy skidded to a halt before a long arched walkway. She knew where it led. The coach houses. Dread pooled in her belly and she ground her toes into her slippers as she stopped, her eyes wide as she stared at him once more, certain he'd betrayed her.

"I promise it isn't your father, Mistress," the boy sputtered as though reading her mind. "You must come. We have to work quickly." His eyes softened and he stood straight for the first time.

She inhaled a harsh breath and clamped a hand over her shock. He was no boy at all, but a man grown. Too thin, to be sure, and in dire need of bathing, but not one of her household. Her father would never allow a man unattended in her retinue.

"Mistress, *please*," he begged, urgency lacing his voice teetering close to panic.

Ysildrea hesitated, her lower lip tugged between her teeth as she contemplated her options. She could try to ignore him and hope she could race quickly enough to the kitchens he would be unable to force her. A glance down the hall behind her and she knew it was impossible. He would catch her before she came near them. Stars above, why had she allowed him to trick her so?

"Who are you?" she commanded with an air of certainty she did not feel.

"I am Suvok, at your service, my lady," he said with a hurried bow. "I will gladly explain, but if you wish to escape your father's machinations I must insist we do it elsewhere."

As foolhardy as she knew it was, he said the words she most wanted to hear, and she rushed forward into the dusk. She yearned for freedom, and this stranger seemed a gift from Melisandre herself. She would not squander it.

Flee

Suvok had warded the carriage as best he could and hoped it would prove enough. The stars were hidden as they moved swiftly through the night, the horses bolstered by his magic as well. They raced from the Northern border in silence, and he shifted uncomfortably under Ysildea's gaze. She'd been staring at him since she'd climbed in the carriage. After him, of course. He was certain she thought he meant to kill her. He found it hard to blame her. If his father were Draven he likely wouldn't trust anyone either. It didn't mean he liked it.

"I am not one of Draven's henchmen, lady," he finally mumbled with an eye roll and a sigh.

She met him with a steely gaze and narrowed eyes, crossing her arms and raising one arched brow.

"It makes little sense to kill you, Princess. You are much more valuable alive. Frankly, he was an absolute fool for leaving you unprotected. You're lucky, really, that I found you before someone with less well meaning intentions did."

Her jaw unhinged and her mouth hung open slightly in shock. It was enough encouragement for him to keep going.

"Surely you didn't think he was the only one who could find use for you? Ysildea, you are Draven's offspring, but you are also descended from Melisandre herself. Either side could use you in half a dozen different ways."

Ysildea barked out a cynical laugh and her face hardened before she spoke. "They could damned well try."

Suvok sighed heavily and shook his head. He felt for the woman. She had no idea what the desperate were capable of.

"They would not need your permission, lady."

"Then I doubt they would be very successful at all. What good is Melisandre's blood if I refuse to align with their will? If I back my father's claim? Or better yet — what good is it if I denounce my father and scream his treachery to the masses?"

"You would never be allowed near the masses, lady," he answered simply.

Ysildea's eyes went wide with fear and he could see the moisture she fought to contain in the corners of her eyes. He held up his hands in a show of surrender. "I have no desire to lock you away. Neither does the Queen I answer to. But it would serve you well to know she is your best and safest ally. Do not squander the blessings because you cannot understand their worth."

Ysildea was very still, her light brown hands clamped together in her lap so tightly he could see each tendon as it strained. Her jaw was tight and he could see how forcefully she clenched her teeth together, her arms tight to her sides and her spine painfully straight. She was a picture in control, but her fear shone through despite her best efforts.

"And what is it you want with me, Warlock? Are you meant to deliver me to Idrovas? We all know the puppet queen in Velyra is little more than a shell for his own rule. I'll not take her place at his side willingly, and damn you to the netherrealm for suggesting it a blessing."

Her words were clipped, harsh, the malice behind each syllable nearly intimidating. If she'd had any power at all, he would likely be afraid. "Idrovas is dead, lady. Killed by a Queen you will, hopefully, find more appealing than the puppet Queen of Velyra."

Ysildea gasped, and the tears she had been so staunchly keeping back flowed down her cheeks with her relief. He didn't blame her for thinking he was sent as a ruse, but it did chafe. To be lumped in with the like of Idrovas was irksome and foul. He bit back the rage that threatened to consume him. The evil bastard was dead, he could harm no one further.

"I may be a warlock, as you so crassly pointed out, but I do not align with those in the Northern Kingdoms. I have never, and will not, compel another being. Especially not Vampires, can you imagine when they wake from their enthrallments?" he guffawed in disbelief and mock terror. "They'll tear the heads from their Warlock captors quickly enough. No, my dear, I'd rather not be caught in the bloodbath the North will be when that comes to pass."

She heard him, certainly, but she gave no response. It was just as well. They neared Asema Pass, where the warlord Idrovas had been slain. Suvok would need to focus on repelling the dark forces that would linger there for far too long. When Idrovas had traversed the Pass on his way to Starfall from the port city of Minirath he'd cloaked his contingent in dark magic.

It had not dissipated as Suvok would have hoped. Instead, it lingered, pulling in dangerous and deadly creatures to the area. Night was the most active, but they'd had little choice on when they could travel. Draven was likely learning as they moved that Ysildea was gone, and soon the whole of Starfall would be on their trail.

As though the thought called them, he heard the guttural chittering of manticore. He cursed under his breath and pulled aside the velvet drape to peer out the window. There was little light to see by, but he could make out two of the beasts galloping alongside them, long sharp teeth dripping with poisonous saliva.

"Shit," he muttered, pulling the velvet back to hide them as quickly as he could. "I don't suppose anyone taught you to fight?" he asked mockingly.

"Fight?" she repeated, now attuned to the danger and shaken from whatever inner thoughts she'd been mulling.

"Whatever you do," he demanded as he wrenched ope the door and clung to the frame. "Keep this door shut until daylight. If something should happen to me, the horses will not stop until you've reached Vorus. Seek out the vampire Zaleria, she will help you from there."

He didn't wait for her reply. He flung himself out the door and flipped his body to land atop the moving coach. Calling upon his magic, he began tossing fireballs toward the shadowy figures all around them. If he survived this, he told himself, he was going to find a willing woman and stay in bed for a week.

Night Ride

Ysildea shook with fear as she listened tensely to the fighting outside. The carriage jostled and bumped precariously as they sped through the Pass, and she found herself once again cursing her damnable father. She was as useless as moldy bread, forced to sit here cowering, hoping to Glory that Suvok would be able to beat back the beasts without getting himself killed.

She was shamed that her reasons for wanting him to live were more for her own benefit than his. After all, she had no coin, no experience, and no idea who she was meant to find. A particularly violent bump propelled her into the opposite seat, and she cracked her head against the wooden frame as she went.

"Do not open that door, Princess!" Suvok screamed from above her.

Above her? Stars, the madman was riding atop a death trap moving at far greater speeds than was safe under the best of circumstances. She was certain they would both die, and wouldn't that just be a shame now that she'd finally got free?

The sound of wood splintering accosted her ears as the door Suvok had been so adamant she not touch was ripped from the space it occupied by a massive, clawed paw. Ysildea screamed and scurried into the far corner, making herself as small as she could. She stared in horror as Suvok tumbled from above and landed on the back of a creature she couldn't have imagined in her worst night terrors. It was the last thing she saw before another jostle sent her flying, this time enough she lost her grip on wakefulness, and slipped into inky black.

"Suvok, she's cold as ice!" a feminine voice pinged around inside her head as she stirred, warm hands grabbing her and lifting her into equally warm arms.

She tried to open her eyes, opened her mouth to protest but only a weak moan escaped her lips.

"Sh, sh. You're alright now," the voice said warmly. An odd growling sound followed that sent shivers up Ysildea's spine.

"Zaleria!" the voice warned. "She's practically my descendant, stop your nonsense and get out of my way."

A whiff of jasmine and vanilla assaulted her senses as a strong breeze rushed past her face. She felt herself moved, and was shortly being settled onto a plush surface and covered in decadently warm fabrics. She sank into them, her addled senses thankful. After a few moments she was able to crack her eyelids, and fuzzy images floated before her. She could almost make out features, but it was more shadow and light than anything. Two obviously female bodies moved about her, one standing stiffly behind the other with long bright hair, only shifting when she was in the way. The one closest to her moved rapidly, throwing more warmth atop her.

"Suvok, what in hells happened?" the brooding one spat.

"Manticore in Asema Pass, mistress. I managed to hold them off, but...Ysildea was banged up a bit inside the coach," he responded sullenly.

"She was *inside* that jumbled heap?" came the terse reply.

"Zaleria," warned the woman moving about. She stopped and stood, her back to Ysildea as she stared down the one called Zaleria.

Ysildea watched as Zaleria's face pinched and she stared down the woman, and Ysildea wondered if this would come to blows. Instead, she was surprised when Zaleria nodded curtly and averted her eyes. The woman turned back to Ysildea and it made her breath catch.

She was tall, slender, with flowing silver waves and dark brown skin, her eyes a brilliant amber. Ysildea thought could have been her mother's twin, so similar in appearance were they.

"Hello there, Ysildea," the woman cooed softly, a warm smile on her face. "My name is Melisandre."

The name ricocheted through Ysildea. She felt her eyes widen and she struggled to sit up.

"No, no," Melsiandre cautioned as she pushed gently against Ysildea's shoulders. "Stay there, please. You need rest. There will be time enough later for explanations."

"Amalia could—" Suvok said.

"No," Zaleria interrupted, suddenly pinning him against the wall and scowling.

She'd been so fast, Ysildea had not seen her move.

"Zaleria!" Melisandre scolded again as she huffed and stormed over to the pair. She laid a gentle hand on Zaleria's arm and pulled her close.

Zaleria folded into her. Long blonde hair tumbled over Melisandre's back as Zaleria lay her forehead against Melisandre's shoulder with a heavy breath.

"I'm sorry, my love," Ysildea heard Zaleria whisper. "This has me all out of sorts."

"I know, my heart," Melisandre replied as she stroked a hand over Zaleria's head. "While I appreciate your protectiveness, it is a bit overboard today. Amalia could help heal her much faster, and we are running out of time."

"Meli," Zaleria whispered, a pleading tone to her voice.

"She's the only Witch in Vorus," Melisandre replied firmly. "We have little other choice."

Ysildea stiffened. Witches outside the Northern Kingdoms were exiled, and dangerous. Many demanded payment in ways she was not prepared to accept. The one in Vorus, was the most heinous of them all.

"No," she managed to force out weakly.

The pair turned their eyes to her, each with a furrowed brow and confusion on their faces.

"No...Witch," Ysildea insisted.

Melisandre bit her lip and studied her before nodding slowly. "Alright, little Princess. We'll try it your way. For now," she agreed.

Ysildea sagged in relief and allowed sleep to claim her.

Distractions

"Zaleria," Melisandre warned as she pulled her mate into their room after shooting a command at Suvok to keep watch over Ysildea. "You can't scare our allies, my love. I will not hold that girl against her will, and if she leaves Draven *will* find her and use her as a stopgap against war in the North."

A low, rumbling growl sounded in Zaleria's chest but she said nothing. Her eyes were rimmed in bright red, and Melisandre knew Zaleria was struggling against the need to shelter and protect her. There was so much that would not be within their control. So, Melisandre did the only thing she knew to do and grabbed Zaleria by the neck, taking secret delight in the way her pale flesh blushed, pushed her against the wall, and captured her mouth roughly. Zaleria responded immediately, grabbing her ass and lifting, Melisandre's legs wrapping around Zaleria's hips as they collapsed onto their bed.

They rolled in a tangle of limbs, teeth, and nails; each ripped through fabric to press skin upon skin. Melisandre gave over control as Zaleria pinned her to the bed and straddled her. Zaleria's fangs were long and prominent, preventing her from fully closing her lips. Liquid heat rose between Melisandre's legs and she palmed her breasts, offering them up to her lover. Zaleria's eyes went dark and she leaned forward, licked a trail along Melisandre's collarbone, and dove for her breast. Zaleria sucked hard on her nipple, making the flesh pucker and yearn for more before she opened her mouth wide, pulled in more nipple, and sank her fangs into the delicate, sensitive bundle of nerves.

Pleasure shot through Melisandre, and she moaned loudly as Zaleria drank in deep, sensuous pulls of blood. It brought Melisandre to the brink of completion before Zaleria quickly licked the wound closed and pulled away with a wicked grin. Melisandre whimpered in protest and wriggled her hips beneath Zaleria.

"Oh no, not yet you wicked thing," Zaleria said in a breathy, deep tone that pebbled Melisandre's skin. "Tell me what you want, love."

Melisandre fought through the fog of pleasure to arch her back and widen her knees, hoping it would be enough.

"Words, Majesty, use your words," Zaleria teased as she reached back and ran a finger across the sensitive lips between Melisandre's legs softly. Once, and with the barest of touches. Just enough to drive Melisandre mad.

"Zaleria," Melisandre moaned. "Please, touch me."

"Well, since you said please," Zaleria responded before moving between Melisandre's legs and pressing her thighs apart with her own.

Zaleria sat on her heels, Melisandre's legs draped over her own, and pressed her hands into the supple flesh of Melisandre's hips to pull her ass off the bed and rest it against her. Zaleria spread Melisandre's lips with one hand, exposing her. A lust filled smile took residence on Zaleria's face and she stroked one ice cold finger along Melisandre's folds, taking time to gather moisture without inserting it, despite Melisandre's whimpers and wiggles that begged her to do so.

Melisandre knew Zaleria would take her time, would wrench every last drop of pleasure from her before finally finding her own. Zaleria leaned down and pressed a kiss to her inner thigh, scarping her fangs along the hyper sensitive skin there as she slowly, decadently, pressed a finger into her opening. Melisandre felt ever inch, her pleasure heightened when Zaleria moved a thumb across her clit in soft, smooth circles.

Melisandre's hips arched up to meet Zaleria's hand, thrusting her pelvis to maximize the sensations. Soft, increasingly loud moans of pleasure left her lips as she climbed higher and higher.

"That's it, gorgeous," Zaleria encouraged. "Come on baby, let go for me."

Melisandre screamed as Zaleria picked up the pace, one hand wrapping beneath her before Zaleria leaned down to capture her in her mouth. Zaleria's tongue danced over Melisandre's bud with painfully delicate strokes, coaxing her pleasure to its highest peaks. Just as Melisandre crested a particularly intense wave, Zaleria snaked her hand from her ass to her breast, squeezing it and pinching the nipple. It undid her. Melisandre spiraled into the sensation as her body trembled its release, her back arched and her head flung back as a scream ripped from her throat with Zaleria's name on her lips.

Zaleria would not be so easily sated, though. She pulled wave after wave of pleasure from Melisandre, lapping at her folds with ravenous hunger, her hands now pressing into Melisandre's thighs to keep them spread for her. Melisandre's hands fisted in Zaleria's hair, half puling her closer and half shoving her back so delirious was she. Melisandre's body thrashed beneath Zaleria's mouth and she quivered and quaked uncontrollably.

"Good girl," Zaleria praised as she finally raised her head from between Melisandre's legs with a wicked grin before sucking on her fingers, eyes locked onto Melisandre's. "My stars your taste is addictive. I'd gladly live between your thighs."

Melisandre, her body still quaking from Zaleria's attentions, felt herself heat when Zaleria rubbed one nectar laced finger across Melisandre's lips, coating them with her own desire. She grabbed the pale wrist in her hand and sucked the digit between her lips, running her tongue along it as she watched Zaleria's pupils widen.

"Ride me," she commanded, one brow arched as she released Zaleria's wrist and pulled on her, coaxing her up her body. Zaleria settled her knees on either side of Melisandre's head and gripped the newly replaced headboard as Melisandre stroked her languidly with her tongue. Melisandre kept her eyes focused on Zaleria's, their gazes locked as she licked her, then speared Zaleria with her tongue as she rocked her hips against her mouth. Zaleria's head rolled back on her shoulders and Melisandre smacked her thigh, causing it to ripple and Zaleria to cry out and grind against her.

Melisandre pushed her back, enjoying the cry it pulled from her vampire lover. She shoved Zaleria backward and circled her neck with a hand. "Keep your eyes on me, or I stop. Understand?" Melisandre demanded.

Zaleria nodded, her eyes wide and her hips rolling beneath Melisandre's body. Keeping one hand around Zaleria's throat, Melisandre crawled between her knees and stretched them wide, then pushed two fingers inside her. Zaleria called out, her lids fluttering, but managed to keep them open enough to look at Melisandre.

"That's right," Melisandre cooed. "Show me how good it feels. Tell me," she growled and gripped Zaleria's throat tighter. "Tell me what you want."

"Harder," Zaleria moaned.

Melisandre slammed her fingers in, and Zaleria bucked against her with a cry.

"Yes," Zaleria yelled.

Melisandre released her throat and pressed her thumb and finger against Zaleria's clit, rolling it between them.

"Fuucc—" Zaleria groaned and closed her eyes.

Melisandre pulled back immediately, removing her hands from Zaleria's body. Zaleria cried out, her eyes opened wide and she whimpered, "Please."

Melisandre grabbed her hips and flipped her onto her belly, raising Zaleria's hips in the air and spreading her legs. She smacked Zaleria's ass, causing the woman to whimper and squirm.

"Oh, yes," Zaleria mumbled, her face pressed against the bed covers.

Melisandre knew what she wanted, and leaned across the bed to grab a thick, rectangular paddle. She ran it along the backs of Zaleria's thighs, which pulled a sigh of anticipation from her as she raised her hips, giving Melisandre better access. Melisandre pressed a kiss to her upper thigh, then nipped at her before she sat back on her legs and gently struck Zaleria with the paddle.

Zaleria moaned with pleasure, moisture leaking from her folds. Melisandre grinned, and landed another light blow that connected against her pussy, and up her ass. Zaleria leaned in, and Melisandre picked up her pace. She struck a steady rhythm of soft blows until Zaleria's skin pinkened, and she was writhing against the paddle. Melisandre quickly shot across the bed and grabbed a ridged phallus made of stone before teasing it against Zaleria's opening.

"Oh, yes, please, fuck, Melisandre, yes," Zaleria pleaded, wiggling against it and pushing herself onto it. Melisandre watched as it sunk into her, moisture dripping from Zaleria as it did. She darted forward and captured her lips once the toy was fully seated and sucked the moisture from them, ensuring to nip at her clit. Zaleria called out and bucked, her body shaking a little.

Melisandre knew she was close, so she flipped onto her back and leaned up to lap at Zaleria's nub.

"Mmmhmmm," Zaleria moaned and pressed into Melisandre's hand that held the phallus inside her. Her legs trembled and Melisandre sucked her clit into her mouth as she began moving her hand, pulling the toy out and slamming it back against Zaleria's rocking hips. They met in violent slaps that caused liquid gold to gush from Zaleria as she screamed with pleasure.

"Don't stop, oh, Glory, Meli, harder," she cried out, her slim fingers gripping the sheets beside her head as she slammed her hips back.

Melisandre obliged, lapping at her with quick, firm strokes as she pounded into Zaleria. A loud, guttural scream wrenched from Zaleria's throat as she came, and Melisandre's mouth chased her as her hips drove back, pushing hard against Melisandre's hand. Zaleria landed in a seated position with her legs wrapped around Melisandre's head and she threaded her fingers through Melisandre's hair, holding her to her clit as she quaked and trembled. Melisandre lapped at her greedily and wrenched the toy from her to lick at the honey that had gathered.

"Ahhh," Zaleria protested, but widened her legs for Melisandre. Zaleria's fingers went limp as she whimpered and trembled, but she did not push Melisandre away. Melisandre licked at her before placing a kiss to her mound and pulling back as Zaleria collapsed against the bed, spent.

Melisandre grinned with a sigh and collapsed against Zaleria's belly, sated and happy.

"You could have just asked me to go for a walk if you needed me to behave," Zaleria teased, her voice languid and sleepy.

"Oh, but what would be the fun in that?" Melisandre shot back, a hand tweaking one of Zaleria's nipples. "I much prefer bending you to my will."

"Mmm," Zaleria agreed. "I have to admit, I prefer it as well. You're also terrifyingly good at it," she murmured as she drifted off.

"Rest now, my little Vampire," Melisandre said sweetly. She raised up on her elbows and gazed at the peaceful face of her Soul's Mate. Planting a kiss on her forehead, Melisandre gently rose from the bed and grabbed a warm, thick gown to drape over herself.

She worried about Zaleria as they moved froward. The woman was zealously protective, and Melisandre was about to place herself in the most dangerous situation she'd ever knowingly been in. She was still unsure how she would tell Zaleria she would have to stay behind.

Shaky Ground

"My Queen, we have to wake her. You can't wait much longer, or the element of surprise will be lost. The longer we wait, the larger the chance Draven finds out Idrovas is dead, and that we have Ysildea—" Suvok rambled.

"Suvok!" Melisandre interrupted with a stern look. "Quiet, or I'll have to finish what I started and end you."

"You have to beat Draven to Umbra Vale and ensure the support of the Shadowblades. If they fall to Draven this war will be nearly unwinnable," he warned quietly, his head ducked as he refused to meet her eyes.

Melisandre sighed heavily and raked a hand down her face. Damn the warlock, he was right. She knew he was right, but it was so much more complicated than he knew. The Shadowblades were insular, untrusting, and would balk at outsiders. Even if one of their own brought them in, and Melisandre was one of the best among their rank.

Zaleria would not be allowed to accompany her into Umbra Vale. If she did, the mission would end before it began. The scouts would see her and there would be a patrol on them before they could inhale, it would be a bloodbath — and Melisandre would be forced to harm her people to defend her mate. No. She couldn't risk it. Mistbriar, the forest boundary of the Fae lands, would have to be where they parted.

"Alright, warlock. Wake the Usurper's daughter and let's see if we can convince her to join us."

Suvok visibly relaxed, and Melisandre wondered if he'd thought she would truly end him. The thought amused her and she suppressed a snicker as she settled herself into a plump, overstuffed chair across from the couch they'd laid Ysildea on. Vaekietha had said the woman would be easily convinced to ally with them, but Melisandre was not quick to trust anyone with Draven's blood coursing through their veins. Gruesome images of him standing over her cradle with her mother's blood on his hands whipped across her mind.

"Mistress," Suvok said softly, his hands moving in a rhythm Melisandre had difficulty identifying above Ysildea's sleeping form. "It is time to wake, lady."

Magic crackled in the air and made it taste of copper and rain. Melisandre shivered as it brushed against her skin, and she knew her eyes likely glowed amber in response. She had magic enough of her own, though she rarely used it. She had been trained to fight, and most of the spells she'd known were for healing and battle. Of course, bits and pieces of her previous knowledge was slowly trickling back into her mind, but she still felt odd when she thought of using magic in other ways.

Ysildea stirred beneath Suvok's ministrations, iridescent waves of light enveloping her and dissipating just as quickly. She was beautiful, though very young. Melisandre had only met a handful of the surviving royal line. All had silver hair and amber ringed eyes, to varying degrees, but she now saw why Draven had been meticulous about sending her far from home when the nobility was called upon to gather.

The resemblance between Melisandre and Ysildea was unmistakable, and impossible. Melisandre had been born into this life outside her previous bloodline. Her mother had been a maid in the Winter Lord's Court — of good standing but no blood claims. Melisandre should not look as she did, and she wondered that Draven had not simply killed her in her swaddling.

Ysildea stretched and sat up, interrupting Melisandre's thoughts as she focused her attention on the young woman. Ysildea would be vital in convincing some of the Lords and Ladies to join with Melisandre. It had been too long, and many of Melisandre's Court had given up hope of her return.

"My Queen," Ysildea whispered reverently and bowed her head.

Melisandre startled and her eyes went wide. She had not expected this to be so easy.

"How do you...that is...Ysildea, you know who I am?" Melisandre asked in a stuttering, uncertain way. She kicked herself for it, but it couldn't be helped.

"Why would she not, dearest?" Zaleria's voice echoed softly behind her shoulder. Melisandre leaned into the touch when her mate placed an icy hand on her neck.

"I would know you anywhere, Majesty," Ysildea said, conviction clear in her voice. "I have seen you in my dreams since I was a small child. I have always known you."

The simple proclamation stole the words from Melisandre's lips and she stared in shock as Ysildea lifted her head slowly and smiled sweetly at her. Zaleria cleared her throat and ran her fingernails along the base of Melisandre's skull in a soothing motion.

Suvok beamed at Ysildea as though she were showing off a particularly difficult spell meant to impress.

"I'm sorry," Melisandre nearly choked. "Your dreams?"

"Yes, Majesty," Ysildea nodded emphatically. "For as long as I can remember I have seen you every night. Riding on a massive blood stallion, covered in shining armor with your hair streaming behind you, a sword raised in the air, and my father's forces lined against you."

Melisandre was speechless. Her eyes were wide as they took in the woman's face and searched for any hint of deception. Ysildea sat and stared back with a face that could have marked them sisters for its similarity, save the deep brown of Ysildea's eyes was rimmed in a luminous purple instead of her own amber. Ysildea wore a serene expression and sat relaxed and trusting across from her. No hint of treachery surrounded her.

"Ysildea," Melisandre began carefully. "Are you…do you see future events?"

"Oh yes," she admitted with a smile. "They aren't always as clear as the one of you, and sometimes not as straightforward as they seem, but yes."

"Do you know why you are here, then?" Zaleria asked, and Melisandre didn't need to turn around to know she was finding this turn of events highly amusing.

"I would guess it has to do with the Court Nobility needing to justify support of your cause, My Lady," Ysildea preened, her wide eyes focused on Zaleria.

"Do you know me then, too?" Zaleria asked.

"How do you think my father knew who to send her Majesty to kill?"

The question landed in the room and seemed to suck the air from it. Melisandre inhaled harshly and stiffened, unsure how to react to the news.

"How long has he known that bit of information, lady?" Suvok asked, and Melisandre felt the answer to that question would alter her past in ways she had yet to reconcile.

"Since I was about three, sir. Though he knew Her Highness would return before I was born, from my mother," Ysildea admitted sadly. "I didn't know the name of her mate, only a description, and that she would be a vampire. It was enough for him to discern the rest, and set the bounty."

"You're from the Dawn Court," Melisandre whispered, horrified.

"Yes," Ysildea admitted. "My mother was."

Melisandre fought to contain her rage. She'd heard how Ysildea had been conceived, knew her mother had been captured and forced into a disgusting sham of a marriage with the Usurper. She had not known he had selected from the purest, most divine of their courts. The court that birthed their holy women, their ambassadors, their exceedingly rare Seers— the court that housed their children.

"That bastard," Melisandre muttered under her breath, her body heating uncomfortably as it always did now when she got too angry.

"Meli," Zaleria's soft voice drifted as she felt an icy hand on the back of her neck. "Calm, my love."

Melisandre leaned into the touch, her eyes fluttering closed as she relaxed against Zaleria's body. The effects of Vaekietha's blood were becoming less easy to handle.

"I did manage to find some Tardum Root in the Citadel's stores, Majesty," Suvok admitted sheepishly.

Melisandre propped one eye open and rolled her head toward him with a menacing stare of disbelief. She could tell by how he cowered Zaleria was likely showing fang. She reached up a hand to pat her mate's and sighed heavily. It would have been helpful for Suvok to have given her the plant when he'd arrived, but even she had to admit it had been a bit hectic. Suvok didn't wait for anyone to speak, instead jumping to his feet and running for his pack, which he dragged to her feet and rummaged through until he yanked a large silver tin from inside to hand to her.

Zaleria was faster than Melisandre, snatching it from Suvok and rushing away. Melisandre grinned. Zaleria was undoubtedly making the tea she'd need to hold her symptoms at bay.

"Highness?" came the whisper of uncertainty from Ysildea.

Melisandre turned and saw raw concern in her eyes, and fear. "No need to fear, Ysildea. It is medicinal, not recreational," she quipped with a raised brow.

She wondered how the young woman would handle the news. She'd been exceedingly fearful of witches, something almost certainly ingrained in her by the Citadel. It was how they kept the secret of Melisandre's return from her people. Melisandre knew it was also why Draven had chosen Ysildea's mother. She had been a Seer, one he had carefully hidden, and the only one born since Melisandre's demise. Until Ysildea, that was, who's gifts he had also hidden.

It was why he villainized the Witches and Warlocks, why dragons were feared and had gone into hiding. It was much simpler to allow the world to think them extinct than to have an entire continent hunting your children.

"Yes, of course," Ysildea reluctantly agreed, but Melisandre coud sense her disapproval.

Tardum Root was often used by many as a way to drug themselves. The effects were well known to be pleasure enhancing and there were entire establishments dedicated to its use. Often well staffed with nicely paid companions, willing to share a bed for a fee. Melisandre studied Ysildea intently and frowned. If she was bogged down by her father's fabricated perceptions this would be more difficult, and they didn't have a lot of time.

Zaleria glided back, piping teacup in her hands, and knelt before Melisandre. "Here, love. Suvok brought back enough to last quite some time, if we're careful."

Melisandre smiled and took the cup, sipping it slowly and allowing the sweet, floral beverage to coat her throat. It worked almost instantly. She felt her cheeks cool, her limbs relax as the fire eased back, the pain receded and she knew Ysildea was taking in the obvious change in her demeanor by her own wary gaze. Zaleria smiled softly up at her as she rubbed one cool hand along the top of Melisandre's thigh in a reassuring manner.

"Now then," Melisandre announced between sips. "I suppose it's time we discuss why you're here, Ysildea."

Plots and Plans

Ysildea straightened and tried to push down her concerns. She knew leaving the confines of Starfall would challenge her beliefs. Her father was a horrid being, and though she had tried to seek knowledge from outside the Citadel, it had been nearly impossible. Melisandre didn't seem as though she was altered. Perhaps what she knew of the root was wrong.

"I had intended to go directly to the Shadowblades, and hoped you would lend support and stand with me," Melisandre began. "However, now I wonder if pursuing the Dawn Court first would be more prudent."

"They are the least affected by the curse, Majesty," Suvok agreed quietly.

"You know entirely too much about my people, Warlock," Melisandre grumbled. Suvok was an ally, she knew that, but he was still a Warlock, and she had trouble trusting him sometimes. Especially when it was obvious he knew all there was to know about the current political climate everywhere, including her people.

As a Shadowblade, Melisandre had known only what she needed to know for each job. That was the way the entire realm operated under Draven. No one knowing so much that they may begin to piece together what had happened, what the Usurper planned. That Draven had orchestrated the High Queen's death, the seclusion of the North, and the isolation of the Fae. Five hundred years with Draven in power had done little to bring the truth to light.

"It has been my duty to know all I can gather, Highness, so I might be of use to you," Suvok said with his chin tucked into his chest.

A pang of guilt struck Melisandre and she wanted to groan. "Of course, I am simply unused to others knowing more than I do. Shadowblades are trained to gather secrets, and it seems I was unable to gather those right under my very nose."

She wondered how many of her counterparts would feel the same, or if they'd been more attentive. Or if they would rather ignore it all and keep to what they knew. After all, they wanted for little, most enjoyed their work, and those who didn't certainly enjoyed the wealth it brought.

"Your desire to know these things was likely dampened by Idrovas' spell, my sweet. You were not meant to care about the state of the Fae, only to obediently carry out his orders," Zaleria reminded her as she rubbed a hand along her shoulders.

"I'm certain he found great amusement in that," Melisandre growled.

"More than amusement," Ysildea muttered with a shiver.

Melisandre's eyes cut to Ysildea, studying her more closely. How much did this sheltered Princess know? She seemed both naive and well versed, a contradiction Melisandre was unsure how to approach. Ysildea was a Seer, which gave her knowledge others did not have. A rarity among Fae so uncommon they were often placed in regard nearly equal to the High Queen herself — but she was also a sheltered, naive woman who's head was filled with Draven's lies.

"Ysildea," Melisandre spoke cautiously. "What can you tell me?"

The woman's eyes lit up and she straightened her spine, lifted her chin, and smiled. "Anything you wish to know, Majesty. My mother saw your mate, not myself. She did her best not to reveal herself, but..." Ysildea trailed off and bit her lower lip.

Melisandre could see the emotions rioting within Ysildea. Her eyes filled with unshed tears and she sucked in deep, uneven breaths.

"She was tortured," Zaleria said what the young woman seemed unable to. "It is what killed her, eventually. What kills anyone unfortunate enough to be caught in Draven's web, and seek a way to escape it."

Melisandre looked up at Zaleria and saw, for the first time, the High Priestess. The leader of a sect of Ancient Vampires — the Covenant — Melisandre believed hated Fae, and wanted to eliminate her people. She'd been made to believe the Covenant had been responsible for the High Queen's — *her* — death. It couldn't have been further from the truth. The Covenant wanted to destroy Draven. They had likely been the first to recognize his duplicity. If Melisandre had listened to their ambassador as High Queen she may very well have prevented her own death.

Melisandre sighed heavily and shook off her thoughts. There was little point in wishing to change the past. "So, why wait this long? I'm more than a hundred years old. Why not send me after Zaleria decades ago?"

"I was only discovered to be Covenant twenty years ago. Until then I hid in plain sight within the Northern Kingdoms. There was no danger in us finding one another until I ran," Zaleria answered.

"He was furious," Ysildea informed them. "You fled while the Nobility were in attendance at the Citadel. My father's hands were tied. He couldn't call on the warlocks for half a moon cycle, not with the Fae nobility in residence. It took another moon for them to answer the call. By the time he was able to take action you had disappeared."

"I received the job ten years ago," Melisandre admitted on a sigh. "The binding was a condition of the contract, and I thought it odd at the time but…"

"The spell Idrovas placed over you as an infant helped them maneuver you into it," Zaleria said, her lip curling in distaste.

"Yes," Melisandre bit out.

"He raved for ages about wanting to witness you kill your own mate. He was nearly out of his mind with it. When you hadn't completed the job within the first few years he became…sullen, moody," Ysildea mused, looking off into the distance as though watching a scene the other couldn't see. "He became violent last year, when whispers of Zaleria's whereabouts began to circulate. He worried the spells weren't working, that you would remember and overthrow him. He almost had you killed…"

The silence was charged and Melisandre didn't need to look up to know Zaleria's eyes were bright red and her fangs were prominent. She nodded and squeezed her mate's hand in what she hoped was a calming way. She had suspected Draven was upset with her. He'd made a visit to Umbra Vale himself to chastise her for shaming the Shadowblades and himself by taking so long to fulfill a contract.

"It wouldn't have served him to kill me," Melisandre muttered. "He would have to wait and watch for my next rebirth, and there was little promise he would be able to control it again."

"Yes," Ysildea agreed solemnly.

Melisandre noticed the woman's eyes were heavy, and she listed a little to one side as she sat. She needed a healer. "Ysildea, you really should be tended to—"

"No!" Ysildea demanded, her eyes going wide as she swayed in her efforts to stand. Suvok quickly wrapped an arm around her waist and pulled her back to sit. "No witches. They cannot be trusted. You did not see…"

"Not all witches are monsters, little Princess," Zaleria mumbled and rolled her eyes in exasperation.

"You have not seen what they do in Starfall..." Ysildea murmured as her eyes drifted closed. "The exiled ones are so despicable even the wretched souls in the North cannot abide them."

Suvok frowned and laid her across the couch once more before turning to look at Melisandre and Zaleria. "Amalia could—"

"Not Amalia," Zaleria interrupted. "There is another witch just north of the city. I can go—"

"Amalia is closer and more adept," Melisandre argued. She stood and scrubbed a hand over her face. "Despite your history with her, Ysildea is fading. There has to be internal damage we do not see."

Melisandre pulled a stiff and anxious Zaleria into her arms and placed a soft kiss upon her brow. "You do not have to be present, my love," she whispered against Zaleria's tousled blonde waves.

Zaleria's arms tightened around Melisandre's waist and she exhaled roughly. A subtle, almost imperceptible nod was all Melisandre needed to give the order.

"Suvok, go to Amalia's home and request her help. Take this," Melisandre pulled a purse from her belt full of coin and held it out to the warlock without releasing her mate. "Tell her I will pay whatever price for her help. If she agrees I will discuss an alliance once Ysildea is stable."

Zaleria stiffened and growled low in her chest at Melisandre's declaration but said nothing. It tore at Melisandre and she wished there were another way to gather the help she would need to reclaim her throne.

"I must have magical beings I can trust beside me," Melisandre said, pulling Zaleria closer and resting her cheek on her shoulder. "We will face an army of Warlocks and Witches. Amalia will know the best way to proceed. It cannot be helped."

Suvok bowed low and left in a hurry. Zaleria waited several heartbeats before she pulled from Melisandre's embrace with a stricken look on her beautiful features. "It is cruel to call her to your side, Meli. Why can we not leave her in peace?"

"There will be no peace, dear heart. Amalia is invested in the peoples of Vorus. She will understand the need to join us. Despite her feelings toward you and I."

"It will tear her heart out, love."

"We will ensure she knows she is respected and well compensated. We will give her a chance to right an ancient wrong that harmed all the peoples of this realm. It will have to be enough, for I can do nothing about her heart."

"Stars above, that is brutal."

"The High Queen cannot always be kind," Melisandre replied sadly, her chin high but her eyes filled with unshed tears.

She did not enjoy what she must do, but she would do what she must.

Homage

Amalia sighed heavily, her wards tinkling softly inside her head. The Warlock had finally come. She'd considered setting a trap for him, barring him from this part of the city, cloaking her house so he couldn't find her. Ultimately she abandoned them all, afraid it would hinder the people of Vorus from seeking her help. It would have only bought her time, anyway. She'd seen what was to come. She knew she would stand beside Melisandre on a field of battle. One day.

It had been a shock to her senses to see the Fae standing in the Dragon's Keep, to recognize Melisandre for what and who she truly was. Amalia had wondered how long it would take for the realization to come to Melisandre. Not long enough, she mused. It had been only days since she'd had to endure watching the woman she had once built a life with fall into the arms of her Soul's Mate.

Amalia had done her best to bury herself in her work, her magic. The Elite had been quiet the past few weeks, though, and it meant little work for her. Aside from the kitchens she ran for those who could not find food, and the spells she produced to help them gain a foothold in this world, there was almost no magic to be done.

She sighed heavily and strode to her door, pulling it open as she whispered under her breath a spell that made her levitate and her hair billow around her. She knew her eyes would be a glowing purple, and her skin would shimmer slightly in the sunlight. It didn't hurt to meet power with power. The Warlock stumbled as he approached, his eyes going wide and his mouth agape as she raised her palms to the sky in a show of cautious welcome.

"I am the power in Vorus, Warlock, and you are late to present yourself to me," she announced, her voice both melodic and menacing. "Your mistress does not exempt you from seeking my blessing to reside within my territory as a practicing Warlock."

"My sincerest apologies, madam," Suvok said as he bowed so low that his knees bent and his forehead brushed the packed dirt that passed for a street in this part of town.

His robes brushed the ground behind him, damp from questionable puddles on the streets just beyond her property. Amalia sighed heavily, rolling her eyes as she waved a hand and cleaned the hems for him. No matter how she tried, it seemed impossible to keep the streets clean here. Too many souls left with nothing, addicted to intoxicants to numb the pain of their existence, to forget their lot in life and the way the Elites used them. She could help, but she could not overcome the caste systems that had developed over the past half a millennia.

"Oh, come in," she groaned, beckoning him forward as she turned back to her home.

She knew very well why he was here. She flicked her wrist toward the stairs and a satchel floated toward her from upstairs. She looked around her sanctuary with bittersweet longing and her shoulders slumped ever so slightly. She had no idea when she would see it again.

"I meant no offense, lady," Suvok pled quietly. "I only just arrived and—"

"And you had a crisis to contend with. Yes, I know," Amalia cut him off and turned to face him.

She raised a brow and allowed her gaze to take in his face now that he was close enough to study in detail. He was handsome enough, blessed with a strong jaw, wide shoulders, lush curling locks and dark skin. His deep brown eyes shone at her, the purple ring faint and almost invisible, and he clasped his hands in front of him. He was tall, nearly four heads above her, and she crinkled her nose at having to gaze up at him. It rankled. She was more powerful than him by far, even this far south of home.

"M'lady, the High Queen Melisandre requests your expertise," he announced in a lilting, gentle tone as he bowed his head. "We have assisted her ladyship, Princess Ysildea, in escaping from Starfall and she was injured along the route."

"Asema Pass, I presume?" Amalia raised one arched brow and pursed her lips when Suvok gave a stiff nod. "What manner of beast, then? Natural or not?"

"Manticore, lady," Suvok whispered, flinching as she cursed loudly.

Amalia rushed around, grabbing vials and herbs as quickly as she could and shoving them into the satchel she clasped in her hands. "How long?" she asked absently as she moved.

"I do not believe she was directly harmed by the beast, madam, but in the fray she was tossed around a bit—"

"If she was unattended I can assure you she was poisoned by those damned creatures. Their claws seep death. It would have taken the smallest of nicks," She muttered, triumphantly raising her arm above her head as she spied what she searched for, before kneeling on the floor to retrieve an herb she hadn't used in a century, at least.

"She has been awake since—"

"I will ask only once more, Warlock. How. Long?"

"Almost a day since," he responded, his brow furrowed and confusion on his face.

"When did you leave the North?" she spat at him menacingly.

"Five years," he replied.

She scoffed and a dark chuckle escaped her lips as she narrowed her gaze at him. "How many abominations have you come across since?" Her eyes pinned him still, and his went wide as he sucked his teeth and averted his gaze.

"This was the first," she said. It was not a question, and he did not feel the need to affirm the statement. "We may already be too late, you foolish man."

Amalia tightened her grip on the bag and strode past him. He would follow, she knew, and she didn't need directions to where they were going. She'd known the moment Zaleria had entered the city, and knew precisely where she was lodged. She felt him breech the door as she rushed up the alley and raised her hand in the air, before clutching her fist and wrenching it to her chest, sealing her home until she would return. She hoped all the spells she had prepared for this held, inlucding the one around her heart.

Fever Dreams

The room was cold, Ysildea's body ached, her eyelids heavy and difficult to prop open. She fought to clear the cobwebs from her mind, but her head throbbed with each labored breath she drug into her lungs. She seemed much worse off than she'd been before, and she cursed herself for denying help, even if that help was in the form of a Witch. Surely Melisandre would be able to keep her safe, even from the powerful Vorus Witch a maiden had told her terrifying stories of.

Her mind wandered, fever dreams wild within her head as she fought to slough off the fatigue. Ysildea had been sick only once, the result of the Covenant infiltrating the Citadel and lacing all the family's foods with a potent poison. Thankfully, it had been so diluted she had survived. Her father had not even been in residence, and she knew he had been their true target. She understood why. The man was vile, evil, and dangerous. It had still been an experience she'd have liked to never again repeat.

This illness felt similar, in some ways, and much, much worse in others. Before, she had been able to open her eyes, speak, even move with help. Now she was so weak her eyelids refused to cooperate, and the voices of those around her seemed distorted — as though she heard them from beneath a thick blanket of water.

In a particularly potent dream, a beautiful woman with dark hair that cascaded around her face like a veil sang sweetly to her. The woman's voice was soft, tinkling, and almost seductive. She had big, wide purple eyes that shone down at Ysildea and her plump lips beckoned to be kissed. Every inch of Ysildea's skin yearned to reach out to the mysterious vision, to place her fingertips against the pale skin and run her thumb against the pouty lower lip. Ysildea wanted to devour the woman in her dreams.

It was a startling thing, the dream. She had been little attracted to anyone in her life, choosing instead to quickly attend to her own sexual needs and move on. A necessary diversion from her life she rather resented. She hadn't thought herself someone who would ever feel such a pull in her belly, such a rush of moisture between her legs as her nipples tightened almost painfully.

It was a damned shame it had only been a dream. Ysildea rather thought she might enjoy an encounter, with that woman as her partner.

Sometime through the night a thick, foul smelling sludge was coaxed down her throat and she gagged against it. Ysildea could hear Melisandre cooing at her as a nimble hand rubbed her throat to encourage swallowing, while another held her nostrils together and her mouth closed. Her stomach revolted and she began to heave, cold hard hands rolling her to one side as the contents of her belly emptied violently.

She felt them move her, a stiff tufted surface was now beneath her and she felt a frigid gust of wind hit her face every now and then. They were in motion, and she drifted in and out of consciousness as they traveled. Bits and pieces of conversation told her they were moving toward the Dawn Court.

It motivated her. She had never been to the Court, the birthplace of her mother. The place she *should* have been raised within. She fought, her will renewed, to rouse herself from this plague. She would not be taken into the Dawn Court in such a state if she could help matters.

Musings

"We must stop for the night," Amalia yelled over the beating wind, her fingers gripping the litter Ysildea lay within, lashed to the back of a massive dragon.

She wore layers of furs and several pair of thick, woolen socks, and still her teeth chattered from the icy chill. She'd placed her enchanted cloak across Ysildea in an effort to keep her warm. The sun was nearly set, and with it any semblance of warmth. Ysildea would not last until morning if they did not find someplace suitable for her to rest. Amalia would have rather put off this journey until the woman awoke, but Draven had discovered her absence too quickly.

It shouldn't have surprised any of them. He arrived at Starfall to find no one waiting. Idrovas should have arrived long before he had, and the Warlock had vanished. It was only a matter of time before Draven found Idrovas had been dealt with, and wasn't the culprit who whisked away his most valuable possession. His daughter. A brave soy within Starfall had sent word within moments of Draven's arrival.

Ysildea was lovely enough, though she bore too striking a resemblance to Melisandre for Amalia's comfort. Amalia tended to her as quickly as she could, limiting contact as much as possible. She would endure what she must to help ensure a safer, more equitable future. The simple fact the woman could evoke any reaction from her at all only spoke to how broken Amalia still was.

She'd left the Dragon's Keep in a haze the day she'd lifted the oath from Melisandre and freed her for Zaleria. She'd saved Zaleria's life, but left a gaping, open wound within her own. She'd stumbled through the streets of Vorus, sobs racking her body as she moved in agony toward a destination she wasn't certain of. Her own home had seemed tainted by the events of the day, and she needed to remove herself from anything that would make her think of *them*.

It had turned out not to matter where she went. She couldn't seem to understand how her heart still beat within her chest when it felt as though it had been wrenched out, her ribcage caved in on the space it had once held. She'd collapsed in a urine soaked alley not far from her house. As she sat there, her tears spent even as she still choked on her pain, she had cared little how filthy it was, how ill it could make her. Some small part of her, hidden away in places so dark she didn't look at them too closely, had hoped she would die there.

Exhaustion had overtaken her and she'd slumped against the frigid, dirty stone of the building and slept fitfully. The next morning a child had woken her and pulled her along until she was within her own warm walls again, ensconced in her home and surrounded by her own magics. One of the orphans that often ran the streets, one who she'd tried to help before, had come to her rescue. The frail girl had led her into the washroom and dumped basin after basin of cold water over her, lathered her hair and body with fragrant soaps, apologizing profusely as Amalia stood there stiffly, silent and shivering.

The rest was still blurry in Amalia's mind. The girl had likely drugged her from within her own cabinets, dumped a sedative in the lukewarm tea she'd forced Amalia to ingest. When she'd woken wrapped tightly in her bedsheets, Amalia had been numb, and the urchin had vanished. She'd done a working so dangerous then, she still tensed when she thought of it. Amalia had walled her heart. Used magic ancient and powerful to close it from her mind so she might function.

Her stomach dropped and wrenched her thoughts back to the present as the great beast dove toward the ground. A questionable inn's lights glinted below them, and Amalia sighed in relief. A distraction from her thoughts was exactly what she needed.

Waylaid

The chill night air stung Melisandre's cheeks as Oksenna barreled toward the ground. She was irritable at having to stop, and knew Oksenna would have to flee quickly the moment they disembarked from her back. Even though this place was obscure and far removed from any large group of people, it was still a risk. She would have rather pushed through to the edge of Mistbriar and settled in there before pushing on toward the Dawn Court, but Ysildea's condition was more pressing.

Oksenna landed with surprising agility and silence, and Melisandre leapt to the ground, her supple boots making no sound as they hit the moss, her knees bending as she crouched and scanned the area for threats. Seeing none, she reached a hand back for Zaleria, who raised one perfectly arched brow in amusement before placing her frigid hand in Melisandre's and gliding down toward her.

Zaleria's body slid along Melisandre's, heat quickly flushing through her body as she gazed into Zaleria's eyes. She cleared her throat and blinked rapidly as she pulled back slightly enough that she could see around her mate. Amalia glared down at them, her face scrunched in displeasure, but Melisandre saw none of the abject torture or heartbreak she'd seen on the witch's face the last time they'd met. Zaleria jumped away from Melisandre as though she'd been burnt, spinning around to face her ex-lover, her face a mask of shame and guilt.

Amalia rolled her eyes and groaned before turning to release the bindings that had held Ysildea in place during flight. Zaleria leapt up to help, ensuring she stayed out of arm's reach and never came remotely close to touching the Witch. Melisandre stood watching for the span of several breaths, debating how she should react to the tension between them, or if she should at all.

Torn between protecting her mate and keeping an ally of Amalia, she sighed heavily and strode to Oksenna's head, leaving the two of them to the task of tending to Ysildea. In truth, Zaleria could have easily and quickly handled lowering the unconscious Fae

Princess alone. Melisandre knew she was too afraid to speak up and suggest it to Amalia, though.

"You're mighty calm for a Fae warrior who's mate is engaging with an ex lover," Oksenna purred at her as Melisandre strolled into the dragon's line of sight.

Melisandre scoffed and rolled her eyes. "I am also the Fae High Queen," she said in a tone that was deadly, one brow arched high as she narrowed her eyes.

"Of course," Oksenna agreed as her head dipped in deference. "I meant no offense, Majesty. All of dragonkind are in your debt."

"Psh," Melisandre dismissed the claim with a wave of a hand. "I did nothing more than what benefitted my people."

Oksenna's nostrils flared as a gust of indignant, disbelieving air escaped her. Melisandre felt the ground under her feet rumble with Oksenna's displeasure. The dragon could be as annoyed as she liked. Melisandre would not accept loyalty born of obligation. She'd saved Vaekietha's life and ensured the continuation of her species, yes, but she had also gained much from the act. It was best for all if they believed her motives purely self indulgent, even if they had not been in truth.

"We'll rest through the night and travel to the Mistbriar half a day from here. There is a field no one dares disturb, which means meeting you there in daylight will be safe. If it pleases you to carry us the distance from there, it would cut days from our journey," Melisandre said, changing the subject entirely.

"As you wish," Oksenna muttered.

Melisandre nodded sharply and backed away as the two women came into sight, Ysildea carried between them. Oksenna's legs flexed and her wings spread wide before she soundlessly took to the air, quickly vanishing into the night sky.

"Amalia, it may be prudent for you to wait with Ysildea while I secure rooms," Melisandre suggested. "Unless you would rather make the arrangements? Zaleria and I are capable of standing watch over your charge while you do if that is preferable?"

It grated on Melisandre to defer to the witch in this when it would be so much simpler to just carry out the task. She needed to somehow gain Amalia's trust, though, and demanding things of her seemed the least likely path to that goal.

"I have no preferences, High Queen," Amalia said smoothly, though her voice held the faintest enmity when she used Melisandre's title.

"Very well," Melisandre said cheerily, ignoring the underlying tone. "Would you care for Zaleria's assistance?"

"No," Amalia snapped curtly, her mouth pressed into a thin line as she shook her head. "I am perfectly safe here while you attend to matters."

Zaleria stood stiffly beside Melisandre and clasped her hands tightly in front of her. It was difficult, but Melisandre managed to nod curtly to Amalia before she took Zaleria's hand gently in her own and led her toward the warmly lit door of the inn.

The inn was warm and welcoming, a stout but kindly man with a weathered face grinned widely at them as they entered.

"Welcome to The White Hart, last stop before the Fae lands," he said jovially, his arms extended wide. "Good you've found us before the storm comes. You'd have frozen out there."

"Yes," Melisandre agreed with a forced smile. "We have another two outdoors, one is ill so it is best we come in another entrance. Avoid the patrons and all that."

"Oh," the man stammered, his brow furrowing and his eyes darting around the room. "Well, I—"

"I assure you, her illness is not contractable. We would just prefer to get her inside and resting for the night. I can pay handsomely," Melisandre said. She pushed power into her voice, warmth and comfort seemed to wrap around the space, visibly relaxing the innkeeper.

"Well, uh, we have...we have two rooms on the top floor. They have their own entrance and—"

"Yes, that would do very well, thank you," Zaleria chimed in, her lips turned up into a coquettish way as she blinked up at him with her chin tilted down.

Melisandre stiffened but kept the smile plastered on her face. She would argue about her mate's obvious flirtation later. For now, they simply needed to get themselves inside and settled.

The man flushed and nodded vigorously, his eyes darting to Zaleria's cleavage as he licked his lips. Suddenly his kindly appearance seemed more sinister. He passed them two heavy iron keys and Melisandre tossed an overfilled purse across the counter as she snatched them. Finally at her limit, she grabbed Zaleria's wrist and dragged her toward the door.

"I'll have my girl bring up a tub!" the man yelled after them.

"Thank you, mead and stew would be appreciated as well," Melisandre snapped back.

She pushed through the door and let it slam back onto the wooden frame, her breath coming quicker as she tried to settle her ire. She would need to address Zaleria's flirtations later, or work out how to endure them without it causing Melisandre to want to maim the target of it. Now she needed to focus on Amalia and Ysildea.

"There are two rooms with a separate entrance around back," Melisandre announced as she approached Amalia. "I am more than happy to bring Ysildea into our quarters if—"

"No," Amalia cut her off. "She can stay with me. If she wakes or her condition degrades in the night it is best I be close at hand."

"Understood," Melisandre acquiesced, bowing her head.

With no further conversation, Melisandre bent and lifted the litter holding Ysildea, Amalia having already hoisted the other end off the ground. She allowed Melisandre to lead them around the building, Zaleria trailing behind silently.

A large wooden door stood beckoning, cracked open and warm light spilling onto the hard packed dirt as they approached. Zaleria rushed forward and pulled the door wide to allow them to pass easily. A set of stairs led to a small landing with two doors and they paused for Zaleria to race ahead and check them.

"This one has a large copper tub and a couch, it should go to Amalia," Zaleria announced from the landing.

The room was large, comfortable, and simply decorated. A large bed stood in the center of the room and a low couch sat beneath a large window beside the tub already filled with steaming water. Melisandre could smell the oils they'd added, a rich floral scent that was soothing.

Amalia lowered Ysildea to the ground once they'd cleared the threshold and glanced around, nodding her appreciation. "This will do," she said softly.

"Is there anything else you need?" Zaleria asked, her voice so soft and cautious Melisandre almost didn't hear it.

It tore at Melisande's heart. Amalia was a vital ally, one she desperately needed on her side. She knew that, she had said herself — the High Queen could not always be kind. It did not mean she was unmoved by the reality.

Amalia looked across at Zaleria, her violet eyes steady, but annoyed. "She should be moved to the bed."

"Where will you—"

"I'd have slept in my own home, but you insisted we leave today. Ysildea shouldn't have been moved at all, the least we can do is ensure she is as comfortable as possible since she was." Amalia's voice was curt and icy, but Melisandre detected none of the agony she had seen in the Witch's face before.

Melisandre reached out and squeezed Zaleria's hand as she shifted to move forward, halting her in her tracks. She inhaled deeply and sought to project a calm, neutral presence before she spoke.

"Ria, my love, why don't you go and see if there is any food to be had, hm?" Melisandre purred, a sweet smile on her face, her head turned just enough that she could meet Zaleria's gaze without losing sight of Amalia. "I'll be along in a moment, I'll just see to this and we can all get some rest."

Zaleria's chest puffed as she inhaled, as though she might protest, before she deflated with a nod, a facsimile of a smile on her lips. Melisandre watched her walk from the room before she spoke again.

"I know very well who and what you were, once, to my soul's mate," Melisandre began slowly, concisely, her gaze boring into Amalia's. "I understand your reluctance to help us, to poke at wounds best left untouched. I would not ask you if there was another choice. It hurts her as well, not just you, to be in such close proximity. Her guilt eats away at her, and even I can't seem to give her solace from it."

"There is no pain, Majesty," Amalia announced with a dismissive wave of her hand. "A mere annoyance, perhaps. A fleeting sadness that is now long past. I am here because you need me, and I see no better way to set right the continent."

The two women stared at one another for a long moment, each assessing the other. There would be no progress here this night, no resolution to their untenable situation. Melisandre sighed and did her best to shove it aside. After all, there were much more important things to focus on, and if Ysildea did not recover she feared the Dawn Court would falter.

Melisandre needed the Dawn Court. She needed their support, and more than that — she needed their loyalty. The future of Elythallas was housed in the Dawn Court, and what good was retaking her throne if she could not protect her people's future?

Unending Night

Amalia slid down into the steaming water, her hair piled atop her head loosely and secured with pins she'd found on a low table by the bed. Her muscles ached, and the warmth was like a balm to them, each fiber slowly untangling and relaxing as she sank back against the copper rim. Her arms hung loosely on either side, elbows crooked against the edges of the basin for support as her eyes fluttered closed.

Ysildea was safely ensconced in several warm blankets, unconscious and likely to remain so for another day at least. They should have called her as soon as the woman had arrived. Suvok was a damned fool. The manticore was a dreadful, toxic beast. Even her impressive abilities were finding it difficult to fend off the poisonous magic coursing through the Fae Princesses body.

A knock at the door caused Amalia to stiffen and sit up swiftly, water sloshing around her and onto the wooden floors. Quickly, she waved a hand and pulled the screen toward her, positioning it between the bath and door.

"Yes?" she called out, trying to disguise the apathy in her voice.

"I've stew and bread, miss. Mead as well, if you'll have it," a voice rang out.

"Yes, come in please," she said, another wave of her hand flicked the key in the door and the bolt slid away.

The door opened and she could hear light footsteps moving across the planks.

"Just there, on the table," Amalia called out. "And take the coin, please. In thanks."

"Oh, miss!" the young voice wavered. "Thank you!"

Amalia waited until the girl had retreated, several more thanks and praise having been lobbed at Amalia as she left. Once finally alone, Amalia turned the key, locking herself in once more. She hauled herself from the water reluctantly and wrapped a linen robe around her as she strolled toward the flimsy wooden door. She placed one pale hand against it and whispered an incantation, setting her wards for the night.

The room was silent, save Ysildea's breath as she slept. Amalia scooped up the bread and tore a large chunk off, dropping it into a bowl of soup before she carried it toward the bed and her sleeping ward. Gingerly, she settled onto the edge of the mattress and sighed.

Though her heartache was closed off to her, being in the presence of the mated pair was still difficult. Her logical mind was just as annoyed with the situation as her heart had been. It didn't matter that her chest no longer felt as though it would cave in upon her any moment, that she no longer felt it a struggle to capture a single breath in their company. The simple facts of her situation were unfathomable. Allied with a woman she had once envisioned a life with, watching as she loved another, unable to tear away from them no matter how she wanted to. Witnessing two souls intertwining with one another while she sat alone, forever, achingly, solitary.

She shook her head to clear the riotous thoughts and pulled the sopping bread from the bowl. Ysildea would be able to do little more than swallow drops of broth, but still she needed sustenance. Amalia patiently pressed the bread to the sleeping Fae's mouth, pulling her lower lip down with a thumb as she watched a droplet trickle between the plush, soft pillows.

Amalia was struck by her beauty. Much as Ysildea resembled Melisandre, her nose was slightly different, her lips fuller and a deeper shade, her lashes thicker and longer as they rested atop high cheekbones. She shook herself, the odd fascination unnerving her, and focused on Ysildea's throat, watching for the telltale swallow. The broth dribbled out one side of Ysildea's mouth, and Amalia huffed in irritation. If she couldn't get food in her, there was a good chance she never woke, and that would play havoc on Melisandre's plans for a Dawn Court backing.

Amalia sat the bowl on the low table next to the bed and shimmied an arm beneath Ysildea's shoulders before lifting her limp, unresponsive form toward her. She slung one leg behind Ysildea and pulled the sleeping woman to her body, pressing her back against her own chest and tilting her head. Ysildea's head lolled against Amalia's arm, but her mouth hung open and Amalia was certain the broth would trickle down her throat instead of out her mouth in this position.

Amalia gently squeezed a few drops into Ysildea's open mouth and then quickly began rubbing her throat, encouraging her to swallow. It was painstakingly slow, but Amalia finally got what she felt was a good amount of the liquid into her unconscious charge.

Amalia's arms ached and her eyelids drooped, the stressors of the day finally catching up to her.

Desire spread through Amalia as she woke, a gentle weight atop her, a hand cupping her puckered breast. She moaned without thought, arching her back into the touch as sleep drifted from her fuzzy brain. In response, she felt a leg press against her thighs. Amalia gasped and flung her eyes open, her heart racing as her confused mind tried to focus on her surroundings.

The room came into view, dim light peeking from underneath the wooden door, the lantern long since sputtered into nothingness. She tensed, remembering where she was, and glanced down to Ysildea. The Fae was still asleep, in the throes of some dream that caused her to writhe against Amalia in a way she hadn't experienced in far too long.

Cursing under her breath, Amalia shifted aside, allowing Ysildea to slide away, replacing her own body with a pillow as she jumped from the bed. Amalia's heart pounded and a hot, potent warmth unfurled in her belly. She felt the moisture coating her lower lips and whimpered as she pressed her thighs together. Obviously, her spell did nothing for desire. She'd need to calm herself before she would get any more rest.

Amalia rushed behind the privacy screen and hoisted her skirts over her hips, sinking onto a stool beside the large copper tub. She flung one pale leg over the side of the tub, exposing her sex to the air and moaning softly when she pressed a hand to her bud, circling slowly. She threw her head back and languished in the feeling, teasing herself as she dipped lower, filling herself the barest inch before snaking her hand away once more to finger her clit. Her other hand she used to yank her top down, gripping her breast roughly. Her hips rocked toward her fingers, anxious and yearning for release. Her slick fingers danced along her slit, the pressure increasing as she picked up speed.

She moaned and shifted her knees further apart, aching to be touched. She was rarely able to bring herself to completion anymore, her mind balking at her own hands. This morning was different, though, Ysildea's touch too fresh on her skin. She pushed away the guilt of fantasizing about someone she'd not even spoken to, instead imaging those warm lips pulling at her clit, that hot tongue flicking over her, diving into her. Release came quickly, her body bucking against her hand as she bit her lip, her scream lodged in her throat. Fluid covered her fingers and she pushed herself further, enjoying the too sensitive flesh as she brought herself to orgasm again, until she slumped against the screen, her legs splayed, her breasts heaving, nipples puckered.

A cough from the bed caused her to freeze, her eyes widening at the thought Ysildea may have woken and heard her. She hadn't said her name, had she? No, surely not. She hurriedly arranged her clothes back into place and squared her shoulders. Plastering a neutral look on her face, she lifted her chin and strode from behind the cover of the screen.

Found

Ysildea lay prone, snoring softly. Relief rushed through Amalia and she swore to herself she would show better restraint. It was unlike her to have such a visceral reaction, but she rationalized it. She'd been so long without a partner, hadn't even taken solace in a lover's arms for a single night in years. She'd found herself taking pleasure wherever she'd been able to find it after Zaleria, but had too quickly realized it would do nothing to fill the void she'd left.

Amalia walked to the small basin and poured water over her hands, scrubbing them with a fragrant bar of soap. Zaleria would smell her easily if she didn't, she might still, but Amalia hoped not.

"Please," a soft cry came from Ysildea.

Amalia ran to her, checking her for fever and prying her eyes open to measure responsiveness. Ysildea was fighting. It was a good sign. The first Amalia had seen from her. The broth had been fortifying, and Amalia thought more might help get the next round of tinctures down. She pulled her bag from beneath the bedframe, rifled through until she found the combination of herbs she needed next. Satisfied, she set them on a table and went to the door, in search of soup, snagging a heavy overcoat on the way out.

The air was too still. The birds silent. Amalia's hair stood on end as she backed away from the door slowly, her eyes scanning the foggy morning woods for movement. She closed the door before chancing a glance toward Zaleria's door.

"Zaleria," she said in a loud whisper, knowing full well the vampire could hear her.

Before she could take her next breath Zaleria appeared on the landing, fully dressed, hair pinned back from her face, eyes red and fangs visible. Melisandre was just behind her, supple armor from neck to ankle clung to her curves, boots laced to her knee, armed to the teeth.

"Go stay with Ysildea," Melisandre hissed, her brow drawn together in disapproval. "We can handle them."

Amalia scoffed and flung one hand haphazardly toward her room, sealing it in an impenetrable ward.

"She is safe enough. No one will get through the wards, and I can already sense another witch out there. You'll need my help," Amalia growled.

Melisandre opened her mouth to speak but Zaleria reached back without looking and stalled her with a hand on her arm. Amalia both resented and appreciated the help. Some ghost of her heartache pulsed for a fraction of a second, and she knew if she could have truly felt it, the moment would have nearly crippled her. She shook it off and inhaled deeply before raising her arms violently, a shimmering translucent blue shield forming around each of them.

"If it fails, run. Whatever Witch they have, she's strong. She will sense it and attack before you know she's there. I'll draw her out, but it may take time," Amalia instructed.

She didn't linger to see if they agreed, instead flinging the door open and striding outside. Amalia's arms moved in a rhythmic dance she had long ago perfected, in her other life as a battle mage for the North. Zaleria streaked past her, long blonde locks flowing behind her. Melisandre stalked next to Amalia, magic of her own sparking from brown fingertips, her eyes bright with it.

Amalia flung a curse toward the soldier nearest her, hitting him square in the chest. Zaleria caught him as he fell, tearing open the flesh at his neck as she drank deeply. It was an old ritual, one they hadn't danced in ages, in which Amalia would target an enemy with her magic, and Zaleria would finish them off. A dance, it seemed, Zaleria easily fell back into.

Melisandre burst forward, daggers in each hand, her face set in a grimace that nearly struck Amalia with fear. The High Queen was ferocious, sliding across dew damp grass on her booted feet only to skid to a stop inches from her victim, her daggers hitting their mark in tender flesh. Spinning, Melisandre pulled her blades from the soldier, her arms making great arcs in which she drug the sharp edge through three different adversaries.

Amalia watched them fall, impressed by the Fae's skill. Melisandre was a Shadowblade, and that came with a certain degree of expectation for deadliness. She surpassed them all. She was brutal, fatal, like she were doing no more than walking through a field of wildflowers instead of slicing down foes like so many grains of wheat.

A stinging shiver arced its way along Amalia's forearms and she pulled her gaze from Melisandre, scanning the treeline for the Witch she knew was there. The warning was an indicator the other woman had begun to untangle Amalia's shields. It wasn't a welcome revelation. It was fast. Too fast for a novice. Whoever Draven had sent after them, she was strong. Amalia was in a weakened state after caring for Ysildea, not conserving her own power out of an obviously misplaced belief they had yet to be found out. Amalia raised her arms and threw her head back to the morning sky, screaming an invocation to the wind, beseeching a Goddess too fearsome to name.

She felt the breath in which her plea was answered, the surge of power filling her lungs, her heart racing with it, her lips curling into a feral grin as she leveled her eyes with a small copse of trees a hundred yards from where she stood. There. She raised one finger, crooking it toward the hiding Witch and beckoning her forward. Bright red hair appeared as the woman was propelled into the open against her will. Amalia sneered as she watched the woman being pulled closer, arms stiff at her sides, body tight, chin tilted up in defiance and fury in her eyes.

Pahaephnie. Amalia did not wait for the traitor to come to her, instead racing forward, her hand already poised to rip the Witch's throat out. Amalia's nails drove into pale skin as the two collided, Pahaephnie helpless to defend herself from Amalia's rage. Blood seeped from beneath Amalia's fingers and she felt Pahaephnie's heartbeat stutter.

"You have ended your own life," Amalia hissed, yanking Pahaephnie forward, Amalia's lips pressing against her ear to ensure she heard every word. "Idrovas is gone, and there is no one to hide behind here. Your betrayal has finally caught up to you."

Pahaephenie's eyes widened, and Amalia felt a surge of righteous fury as she whispered an incantation, her fingernails lengthening, and ripped her betrayer's throat out. Her focus was entirely on the Witch, reveling in the justice she had met out. She was unaware of her surroundings, only shaking off the trance when Melisandre shoved her away, warm liquid splashing across her face as Melisandre drew a blade from the man in front of her.

Not Pahaephenie at all, but an illusion. Amalia glanced at her hands, not a drop of death on them. "Damn it!" she screamed, a grimace overtaking her features as she whipped her head around to search for her nemesis.

"Get up," Melisandre ground out, crouched in a defensive stance in front of Amalia, ichor coating her to the elbows, magic humming from her as she shot off spell after spell in an attempt to give Amalia a chance to get on her feet again.

Amalia felt a wave of shame push at the edges of her consciousness, and pushed herself off the mud and grass. "Thank you," she acknowledged curtly.

Melisandre inclined her head sharply and gave her a hard sidelong glance, her glowing amber eyes skimming Amalia's body before coming to the apparent conclusion she was no longer needed and bounding back into the heart of the fray. Amalia's body was tense as she searched for Pahaephenie, certain she was hiding nearby. The group of men they fought were supernaturally stronger, no more than fodder for the trio in an attempt to tire them enough that the true power behind the attack could easily overtake them.

"What is it?" Zaleria hollered as she leapt toward Amalia and grabbed her elbow, forcing her to look her in the eye.

Amalia frowned, uncomfortable with the contact and the emotion pushing at her consciousness she'd blocked from her awareness. Zaleria's red eyes were blindingly bright, her pale white skin nearly translucent under the light of the sun she had never seen her in before.

"Amalia!" Zaleria screamed, shaking her gently with a concerned look on her face.

"Pahaephenie," Amalia whispered, eyes glassy as she tried to focus on the fight. Too many feelings and thoughts were pressing at her. Something wasn't right, her attention had never before faltered in battle this way. Amalia was uncertain if this was an effect of her own spell, or if Pahaephenie was behind it. She only knew she needed to overcome it. Quickly.

Misdirection

Zaleria scrunched her brow as she stared at Amalia. There was something off about the Witch, more than the detached coolness she'd been displaying since coming to Ysildea's aid. Pahaephenie was the woman who'd betrayed Amalia before she'd fled the North. A former lover who'd allowed the lure of power and status to coax her into turning Amalia in as one in league with the Covenant.

Zaleria gripped Amalia's elbow as she studied their surroundings. If Pahaephenie was indeed here, discovering her would end the attack. A northern soldier ran at them, and Zaleria huffed in annoyance as she reached out and twisted his head with one hand, the loud pop of bone shattering echoed in the air as he crumpled by her feet.

Melisandre was holding the bulk of the attackers at bay while Zaleria attempted to set Amalia to rights. She didn't think it would be so easy as shaking her and demanding she focus. This was larger than Amalia herself, Zaleria could smell the foreign magic around her former lover. Somewhere near, a Witch with power enough to hinder Amalia was weaving spells that could endanger them all.

Zaleria scooped Amalia in her arms and ran toward the inn. Surprisingly, Amalia's shields were still holding, but Zaleria worried they would fail before she could seek out the leader of this group. Flinging the wooden door open, Zaleria placed Amalia inside and closed it behind her. She hoped it would hold.

Zaleria moved quickly, so fast she knew the mortal footsoldiers would be unable to track her movements. Once under the cover of trees she saw what had been hidden from her before. The meadow was empty, save a dozen slain mortals they'd vanquished moments after the fight began. Melisandre slashed at phantoms. It made Zaleria's stomach churn.

A telltale hint of burnt wood and singed air came from the other side of the field, and Zaleria's supernatural eyes picked up the subtle shimmer between the green leaves. There. She wasted no time, scrambling up the tree nearest her before leaping from it. The distance was great, but easy for a vampire. She landed nearly atop the Witch, wrapping her hands in long tresses of bright red hair and yanking the woman's head back. She was careful not to end her life. That was for Amalia.

Instead she sunk her fangs into the tender flesh at her shoulder, ensuring her magic faltered. Zaleria held the Witch close to her chest, running into the field even as she drank deeply. Pahaepehnie's feet dragged beneath them, mud caking the toes of her threadbare shoes as they dug rivets into the soft morning ground.

Melisandre stood bathed in red under the morning sun, her chest heaving from effort and her blades dripping. Zaleria saw the realization dawn in her mate's eyes as she took in the number of bodies on the ground around her, watched as her amber eyes became stormy and her face hardened. Melisandre would not take well to being made a fool of, for expending energy she could have saved.

"What an ingenious little trick," Melisandre cooed menacingly.

"Let her go," Amalia's voice rang out across the eerie silence. "She won't deceive us again."

Zaleria let Pahaephenie fall to the ground at her feet, wiping a sleeve across her mouth that came away tinged crimson. It was just as well, she was fairly certain she'd make herself sick if she drank a single drop more. Amalia stalked toward them, her arms lifted and her attention solely on Pahaephenie. The traitor lay in a pathetic ball on the upturned ground, clutching her shoulder as blood oozed between her fingers, moaning and rocking.

Amalia stopped, her sneer as she looked down at the woman she'd once loved was nearly feral. The hurt Zaleria had caused Amalia ricocheted through her once more as she watched Amalia bear down upon someone else who had broken her heart, guilt and shame that Zaleria had to swallow down, push away. Amalia did not falter, there were no tears in her eyes, as she crouched down beside Pahaephenie, brushed hair from her face, and leaned down to whisper in her ear.

"You will never find a safe place. Your very bones will betray you when you seek to find rest. Your mind will never quiet, and your fears will be ever present. Not one second's peace will find you until you take your last breath in this existence," Amalia hissed so quietly even Zaleria struggled to catch every word.

A cold chill raced up Zaleria's spine as Amalia's curse took hold. Clouds rushed across the sky, blotting out the sun as a fierce wind cut through their clothing, its icy fingers tearing at their flesh. Amalia stood, her face a mask of perfect serenity. It was unnatural, and unlike Amalia. She was not this cruel, unfeeling thing.

"Go," Amalia commanded, then turned on her heel and strode toward the inn.

Zaleria locked eyes with Melisandre, each of them holding a measured fear of and for Amalia as Pahaephenie scrambled across the dirt toward the shelter of the trees. Melisandre's silver waves whipped around her like a cape, slashing across her face. Zaleria closed the distance between them, slipping a hand around Melisandre's waist and pulling her roughly against her.

A heat Zaleria knew came from their bond bloomed, yearning for Melisandre overtaking her rational mind. She needed to hold her mate, to ensure there was no wound she had not seen, to soothe and console her after battle.

Despite the punishing gale, Zaleria felt the warmth in her belly unfurl as she captured her mate's mouth with her own. Her fangs burst forth once more, and she grazed the supple skin of Melisandre's neck as Melisandre flung a leg around Zaleria's hips, gyrating against her leg as she surrendered to Zaleria, her head cradled in Zaleria's hand, her throat fully exposed.

Zaleria gasped when Melisandre yanked her blouse down and exposed her breasts to the harsh wind, her nipples puckered and tight, aching for her lover's touch. Melisandre's hand snaked along Zaleria's waist and gripped her breast, rolling her sensitive nipple between her fingers. Zaleria pulled at the strings that held Melisandre's armor together at the side, hastily pulling at the lacing until she could slide a hand between Melisandre's legs.

Melisandre moaned loudly as Zaleria stroked the knub between her legs, moisture coating her fingers as she slowly circled the bud, Melisandre rocking her hips against Zaleria's hand.

"Yes, please," Melisandre groaned when Zaleria dipped a finger into her entrance. A whimper of protest escaped when Zaleria pulled back, teasing her.

"I want to taste you," Zaleria whispered against Melisandre's ear before lifting her from her feet and setting her on a low branch of the tree nearest them. It gave them some cover from prying eyes, though Zaleria knew Melisandre cared little about who could see them.

Melisandre's eyes watched her hungrily when Zaleria yanked her armor down her body, exposing her completely before placing a cold hand on each of her thighs and sliding them apart. Melisandre's sex glistened with her arousal, her chin lifted, proud to be seen by the woman she adored. It was the headiest sight.

Zaleria shivered in excitement and grinned, sinking to her knees before Melisandre, keeping her eyes locked on her mate's as she flicked her tongue across Melisandre's slit. Melisandre bucked against her and her eyelids flickered, but she kept eye contact.

"More?" Zaleria teased, her tongue flicking delicately and tantalizingly slowly over Melisandre's clit.

"Devour me," Melisandre commanded, widening her legs so that each knee rested against the branch she sat upon. She reached above her and grabbed another limb, steadying herself.

Zaleria needed no further instruction. She bent her head and lapped at Melisandre, long, slow strokes that pulled sensations into Melisandre's core until she felt she may explode. Melisandre's hips rocked against Zaleria's mouth, seeking. Zaleria trailed one hand along Melisandre's thigh until it met her mouth and she pulled back, stroking Melisandre's lower lips, gingerly tracing around her most sensitive parts until Melisandre whimpered.

Grinning, Zaleria slid a finger inside Melisandre, so slowly Melisandre's hips lurched up to meet her, her ass coming off the branch she sat upon. Zaleria gripped Melisandre's waist with her free hand and shoved her back into place. She toyed with her mate, slowly inserting and withdrawing her finger until her hand dripped with Melisandre's arousal. Melisandre whimpered and wiggled, bucking against her arm in an attempt to chase her climax.

Zaleria finally bent her head once more, flicking Melisandre's clit with her tongue and moving more quickly inside her. Melisandre sighed with appreciation, her breaths coming quickly and her moans growing louder. Zaleria plundered her, Melisandre's hands tangling in her hair as Zaleria shifted Melisandre's weight from the branch onto her, an arm now supporting Melisandre's back as she balanced her in the air.

Melisandre's climax was powerful, her screams so loud Zaleria grinned as she buried her face further into her, refusing to release her until Melisandre went limp in her arms, her body bucking uncontrollably against her mouth. Finally Zaleria allowed Melisandre to slide down her body, gently laying her on the moss covered ground.

Melisandre's eyes opened and a wicked grin spread across her lips as she Zaleria sat back on her heels. Zaleria's skin rippled with anticipation when Melisandre crooked one finger, beckoning her close.

"On your knees," Melisandre said as she hefted Zaleria's skirt away from her thighs.

Melisandre wasted no time, fisting the fabric out of her way as she began sliding two fingers into Zaleria, her thumb circling her swollen clit. Zaleria rolled against her, meeting her frantic pace even as she got to her knees beside her and captured her mouth greedily. Whimpers escaped Zaleria's throat as the world narrowed, Melisandre's tongue dancing with her own, Zaleria's body slamming down on Melisandre's hand.

Melisandre gripped Zaleria's throat as she grew more frantic, pulling her mouth forward. Zaleria felt the wave cresting as Melisandre pressed her face into her breast.

"Bite me, love," she whispered against Zaleria's hair.

It sent Zaleria over the edge, her fangs sinking into the supple tissue as copper danced over her tongue.

Aftermath

Amalia stalked across the room, her clothes thrown into the tub, her bare feet slapping against the wooden floors as she moved. She was restless, emotions battering at the spell she'd worked to keep them at bay. Her body vibrated with unspent energy, the aftermath of her curse still bitter on her tongue.

"Who—" a gentle voice echoed in the silent room.

Amalia stiffened, her feet rooted in place as she turned and looked toward the bed. Ysildea had shifted to one side, her head resting on a pillow as her wide amber eyes studied Amalia. They were silent, taking one another in. Amalia was painfully aware of her nakedness, but somehow unable to pry her feet from their place and move to cover herself. Ysildea seemed mesmerized, openly raking her gaze across Amalia's body.

Finally, Amalia cleared her throat and sauntered toward the bed, hiding a smirk as Yisldea's eyes widened in surprise and her heartbeat pounded so hard it could be seen in the hollow of her throat. Amalia took her time pulling the small throw from the foot of the bed and wrapping it around herself. She appreciated the hunger she sensed in Ysildea. It was the same she felt in her own body, the desire, the need that pooled in her stomach and ached in her chest. The purely physical response without the complication of feelings.

"You're awake," Amalia said in an even tone. "That's good news. We'll have to move soon. Your father discovered Idrovas' demise sooner than we'd have liked."

"What? Is he—" Ysildea bolted up, swaying and reaching out to steady herself on the bed.

"Easy," Amalia chided, rushing over and piling pillows behind Ysildea before gently pushing her back to lean against them. "It will be some time yet before the effects of the poison are completely flushed from your body."

"Poison?" Ysildea balked, her eyes narrowing with distrust.

"Manticore, Princess," Amalia snapped, the implication in Ysildea's eyes like ice water over the heat of her previous desires.

Ysildea frowned, looking off into the distance as though looking for something.

"Oh. Yes, that's right," she murmured, a hand reaching gingerly to the back of her head.

When Ysildea found no evidence of her injury her brow pinched further and she looked questioningly to Amalia. With little grace, Amalia yanked the blanket from Ysildea's grasp and lifted the hem of her sleeping gown to expose the angry thin scratch on her side, ignoring the swell of breast it exposed. Ysildea gasped, indignant as she shoved the fabric down over Amalia's hands.

Amalia lifted a brow before leaning back, "The head wound was dealt with swiftly. It was the manticore's scratch you've been struggling against."

Amalia stepped back and wandered behind the screen, snatching her bag from the floor and rummaging through it for a change of clothes. The ones she'd worn during the fighting would be destroyed, too much of the traitor's magic lingered on them. She snatched them up and flung them into the fireplace, flicking her wrist to enhance the flames. Ysildea gasped as they sputtered a sickly green, a cloying sulfuric scent wafting through the room as the magic dissipated.

"That was…Idrovas smelled like…I thought he was dead?" Ysildea screeched from the other side of the screen as Amalia pulled on a set of billowing skirts.

"He is," Amalia sighed. She pulled a flowing cream blouse around her and secured the ties in front of her chest to secure it. "That smell is common among those loyal to Draven, their magic is…twisted. Tainted. Powerful, but…wrong."

Amalia shook her head and plastered a smile on her lips, "Don't you worry, though. She's been dealt with. We have a bit of time before he sends the next group."

"Draven, you mean," Ysildea grumbled, a mix of fear and disgust marring her beautiful features.

A protective urge rose within Amalia she was unnerved by. She cleared her throat and shifted on her feet, turning away from the beautiful Fae who looked too much like Melisandre.

"Yes, Draven," Amalia responded. "I'll be a moment. You need food, I'll…" her voice trailed off as another scent hit her the instant she opened the door.

Fucking mates.

Amalia shut the door swiftly, one palm resting on the door frame as she closed her eyes and took several deep, annoyed breaths.

"It seems our companions are a bit busy out there, instead of in their own damned room, which was a step away from a literal field of battle," Amalia growled out between teeth grit in an unnatural smile as she turned to face Ysildea. "But, apparently, they'd rather fuck where they stand. So,"

Ysildea's eyes went wider than Amalia would have thought possible and her mouth dropped open in shock. Amalia noted how Ysildea clutched at the bedsheets and her skin grew just so slightly darker with heat, her pupils dilated and she ran her gaze down Amalia's body seemingly despite her best efforts. Some primal urge pulled at Amalia's gut, a tether that sprang taut as they looked at one another.

Amalia frowned and took a step closer to the bed, intrigued and concerned about this attraction. She had lusted for others before, but this was...different. Stronger, more urgent.

Ysildea stiffened as Amalia moved, "You're the Witch," she accused, the fear lacing her tone not lost on Amalia.

"I am *a* Witch, yes," she replied, her brow knitting together as her head tilted to one side, her feet planting firmly on the floor.

"You're the one from Vorus," Ysildea nearly squealed, pressing against the headboard in an attempt to increase the distance between them. "The Witch exiled from the North for heresy and heinous practices."

Amalia scoffed, a laugh bubbling up from her reflexively. She shook her head and rubbed the bridge of her nose, in an attempt to provide a response that wouldn't be flippant.

"Princess, you have no idea of what you speak," Amalia began, her voice low and threatening. "So best keep it to yourself. I am, after all, the woman who saved you from the grave."

Amalia rolled her eyes and huffed angrily with a disgusted shake of her head, growing ever more frustrated the more thought she gave Ysildea's words.

"You'd think with all the swooping in to save you that I do, you'd respect me a bit more. Must be a flaw in your line. Entitled idiocy," Amalia muttered.

Ysildea gasped, obviously amazed anyone would dare speak to her in this manner. Amalia couldn't be bothered. She would rather walk past her ex in the thralls of passion than spend one more second in this sheltered fool's presence.

Amalia stalked out of the room, slamming the door behind her so hard it shook the walls.

Misinformed

Ysildea's mouth opened and closed in shock and frustration. The Witch hadn't defended herself, hadn't denied her actions. Ysildea was no fool, she knew not everything her father told her was truthful, that sometimes he and his minions would spin stories that fit their narrative. The tales of the Witch exiled for practices so abhorrent even Idrovas condemned them were whispered even among the servants.

One maiden placed in her retinue had compelling stories of how the Witch had desecrated her brother's corpse, used dark and forbidden death magic to fortify the Covenant. Ysildea held no love lost for those loyal to her usurper father, but there were limits. Even in war. There must be. The dead must be left to rest.

Ysildea stretched and tried to push thoughts of the woman away, but traitorous images invaded her mind. The pale skin at her throat, the soft curving lines of her hips and the way her thick, dark hair swayed as she moved. Her violet eyes as they flashed in anger, and perhaps something more. The delicate hands that had brushed against the swell of Ysildea's breast as she uncovered the manticore's scratch and stolen the breath from her lungs.

Ysildea groaned and flung herself sideways, burying her face into a pillow. It smelled of moss, amber, and sunshine. Heat surged through her, the junction between her thighs aching for release. She screamed, threw the offending pillow across the room, and rolled away to face the fireplace.

Ysildea stared at the bright flames dancing in the hearth and traced her fingers over the skin Amalia had touched, the thin raised scar of the manticore scratch overly sensitive. A need to get up and move around battered at her, but when she tried to sit up once more a wave of dizziness forced her to abandon all movement. Her head, though the wound had closed, was still untrustworthy. Nausea rose in her throat and she squeezed her eyes shut until it passed.

Once the room settled, and her head stopped spinning, she exhaled and rolled slowly onto her back. The wooden beams in the ceiling were dark, a rich brown that reminded her of the Witch's hair. Ysildea balked at the comparison, annoyed at how much the woman consumed her idle machinations.

"Ysildea?" a voice echoed as a knock sounded against the door.

"Yes, come in," she replied, recognizing Melisandre's voice.

The door swung open and the High Queen entered, her vampire close behind. The pair made an awkward picture, Ysildea was so unused to seeing anyone other than the Fae. Her father would use this pairing against Melisandre, and it would work as a detractor for some. How could the High Queen be mated to someone not of the Fae?

"We've brought broth," Zaleria informed her, a genuine smile on her lovely face as she lifted a bowl in the air for Ysildea to see.

"Thank you," Ysildea replied, guilt washing over her at her own treacherous thoughts.

"I am so pleased to see you awake," Melisandre cooed, watching from the end of the bed as Zaleria sank down to sit next to Ysildea, tipping a vial into the broth. "We'd planned to stay another night but..."

"I know," Ysildea said, shifting enough that sipping at the bowl would be possible. "The Witch told me he'd found us."

Zaleria and Melisandre shared a cautious look, and Ysildea sighed. Her dislike of the woman they'd brought to help her was too obvious.

"My apologies, I just—"

"You do know she is not what they say of her?" Zaleria spoke over her, a harsh and defensive look on her face. "That she did none of the things they accuse her of?"

"I—" Ysildea began, but faltered when she could find no answer that would suit. She didn't know it, in fact she knew just the opposite. But was it her place to correct the mate of her Queen?

"Zaleria," Melisandre chided in a cautious tone. "There will be time enough."

"No," Zaleria rebuked, her mouth in a thin, determined line and her eyes narrowed. "Idrovas ravaged the dead of his own people, created horrific, mindless phantoms for his own uses, and used her escape as a ruse to shift the blame to her!"

"Zaleria, love—" Melisandre began.

"Meli," Zaleria pleaded, her eyes going wide and soft, a sadness overtaking the vampire that hurt Ysildea to witness.

There was more here than Ysildea was aware of, of that she was certain.

"I'm sorry, I didn't mean to...that is, I appreciate the help she has given me." Ysildea pursed her lips and crinkled her nose, looking down at the bowl in Zaleria's hands.

Melisandre rushed forward and kissed Zaleria's hair, taking the bowl and settling beside her with a smile.

"There is time enough for this, for now, you need to eat, and take another dose of the tincture. We will be leaving within the hour," Melisandre said as she tilted the bowl up to Ysildea's lips.

Ysildea sipped at the warm liquid, allowing it to coat her throat and relaxing against the pillows. She would worry about the mystery of the Witch later. It was more important they move on. If her father had found them already, he would likely find them again. That would be more difficult if they were traveling.

Tales and Wonders

Ysildea wished she were still asleep. She'd never felt quite so useless in her life as she did laying on a litter, being carried by the High Queen and her lover. Amalia walked several paces behind them, her expression a mask of cool indifference. She hadn't even come back into the room until Ysildea had been taken out of it, and had kept her distance since.

If Ysildea hadn't heard the maiden's stories with her own ears she would think she'd hurt the Witch. Ysildea *had* heard them, though. She'd listened as Alyxia had sobbed, as she had struggled to get the words out. Alyxia had been silent when she arrived at Starfall, jumping at every noise, her eyes always rimmed in red from her many bouts of crying. Then, two moons after she'd appeared, in the dead of night, Alyxia woke from a terrible dream and screamed for help.

Ysildea had rushed to her, held the girl as she had rocked and whimpered for hours before she finally, finally spoke. Alyxia's brother had been one of Draven's personal guard. A promising soldier who'd been promoted quickly, a man who supported his sisters and widowed mother with his pay. A man who'd slept wherever he could make a pallet rather than pay for a room so his sisters might never feel the loss of their father. So his mother could be spared the toil of manual labor she would have otherwise endured.

A man who'd fallen under the spell of a Witch who cared little for the people of the North, in league with the Covenant, experimenting in magic so black it turned one's soul. As a part of Draven's personal guard, Alyxia's brother was in spaces he'd never have seen otherwise, engaging with people so high within Draven's court he was easily enamored by them. Easily deceived. So when the Witch murdered him and used his corpse for her own ends, when she re-animated dead flesh for the Covenant to attack Draven's retinue, he put up no fight. He hadn't known he needed to, until it was too late.

Alyxia received only ashes. Her brother's body was little more than battered mash before Idrovas had been able to subdue the soulless forces sent to kill the Usurper. Kill her father. Ysildea could excuse a great many thing in order to achieve that end. She had no love for the man who had helped create her. Abuse of the dead, of the innocent, was not one of them. Certainly, Alyxia's brother was a soldier for Ysildea's father, and that posed problems of its own, but he did not deserve the death he met. His mother and sisters the poverty they were forced into with his demise.

No, Ysildea would not forget what the Witch had done. No matter how her body betrayed her, longing for touches that should revile her. Or how her mind played tricks when she was not diligent, and visions of raven haired beauty flitted across her mind's eye. She would not align herself with this monster, and somehow Ysildea would reveal the truth to Melisandre.

They walked for what seemed like ages, guilt eating away at Ysildea. She knew they could move more quickly without having to carry her, and she cursed her body's inability to recover any faster. She was still exhausted, requiring too much sleep for her liking. The sun was beginning to dip below the tops of the trees that surrounded them when the sound of great gusts of wind rushed the sleep from her eyes.

Ysildea pushed herself up on her elbows, eyes wide and curious. She knew they were headed toward a dragon, and that she had already ridden on the back of one — much to her chagrin she had been unconscious during the experience — but she had yet to *see* one with her own eyes. Excited anticipation danced across her skin, her cheeks ached with the grin that stretched across her face, the joy she was unable to contain.

Stories of dragons and their deeds had filled her young life, told to her by maidens and servant boys she had corralled into stealing a few moments from. Stories told by mothers to eager children, ones Ysildea yearned for and pulled forth from memories long faded of those around her. She'd grown an odd obsession with the creatures, in her wildest daydream imaginings she conjured a great orange beast, breathing fire and rescuing her from a tower in the Citadel.

It was foolish, of course. The dragons had long since disappeared, save the two left in Vorus. The two her father was unable to reach. The mated pair that allowed the born riders to train upon their backs but never took them into battle. Not since the Great War had a dragon been seen in the skies any real distance from their Keep. Vaekietha had vanished during the battle that killed Melisandre and made Draven a King. What dragons were not killed on that battlefield had not been seen since, and many believed them dead.

Not Ysildea, though. She had always had faith that the dragons would return. When Melisandre was found, that the High Queen's greatest allies would appear as though they hadn't left. The trees thinned and suddenly they stood in a large field, a massive dragon on the ground before them. Ysildea's heart pounded, her eyes becoming glassy with tears she struggled to withhold.

"Oksenna!" Melisandre called out, true joy in her voice.

"Majesty!" the dragon replied, her voice shaking the ground they walked on as the air vibrated with the musical tones of it. "What happened?"

The great beast twisted toward them, her body curling into itself as she turned her upper half to fold into her tail, massive eyes blinking down at them as she studied them intently. The dragon's nostrils flared as she inhaled sharply, her long snout so close Ysildea could make out the shimmering, shifting colors of her flesh.

"You have been in battle," the creature cried out, her concern causing the skin of Ysildea's arms to pebble.

"Oksenna," Zaleria cooed as the dragon's nose nudged the litter in her distress. "Oksenna," Zaleria raised a hand and pressed it gently against the underside of the shimmering snout. "We are fine. A minor scuffle, and one we put down quickly."

A low grumble erupted, the air blowing hair from their faces, but Oksenna did not argue further.

"Come, if you have been found so soon I am certain the menace is not far behind," the rumbling voice commanded as Oksenna lowered herself to the ground gently, making certain to leave them space enough to maneuver. "Quickly, now."

Melisandre wasted no time, nodding briefly to Zaleria before they both leapt forward, causing a gasp and a soft squeal from Ysildea as she was jostled, gripping the edges of her litter. Before they'd had the chance to settle Ysildea onto the dragon's back, Amalia was there, a feral look on her face, her eyes a bright and glowing purple as she pushed both the High Queen and her vampire mate aside.

"Easy!" Amalia screamed, checking over Ysildea as though they had somehow harmed her, lifting arms and pressing her pale hands against every inch of Ysildea's body.

Ysildea stiffened, fury rising even as her belly twisted, her thighs pressed together to relieve the ache that built there, and her breaths came in short, panting gasps. She would not allow some betrayal of her flesh to overtake the hatred she was nurturing for this

Witch. Melisandre and Zaleria both grabbed at Amalia, rage evident on their faces. A loud booming halted them all, save Ysildea, who had recoiled and let fly a hard slap. It connected with Amalia's cheek as Oksenna chastised them without words, and the silence as the world settled was deafening.

Denial

"My, my, little Princess," Oksenna said, the interest and amusement causing Amalia's feet to feel unsteady beneath her. "A bit of an overreaction, wouldn't you say?"

Ysildea's face crumpled in abject horror as Oksenna spoke. She clutched her hand to her chest and tears filled her eyes. Any hint of anger that Amalia had previously seen was washed away, and something buried deep within Amalia's chest shuddered.

"I..." Ysildea stammered and tried to rise from her litter.

Amalia reached out to help but caught herself and jumped away, looking to Zaleria with pleading eyes. Amalia wasn't certain why she felt so strongly that Ysildea needed help, but it was so pressing a need it almost ached. Zaleria furrowed her brow and studied Amalia and Ysildea, her eyes flitting between the two before her mouth formed a small 'o' and her eyes widened. It happened in the span of a breath, and then Zaleria was in motion so fast Amalia's eyes couldn't track her.

Zaleria stood on the ground, supporting Ysildea so she might stand before Oksenna. Ysildea was crying, great fat tears sliding down her light brown cheeks, her amber eyes with their pale purple ring dulled and her thick, long lashes clumped together with moisture. Amalia's gut jerked toward them, and she had to fist her hands to keep herself rooted in place. Melisandre came to stand beside Amalia and gently slid her hand into Amalia's, rubbing slow circles on the tender skin where half moons stood red and angry on her palm.

"Please..." Ysildea sobbed, hiccuping between her words as her chest heaved and her shoulders caved in toward one another, her chin hanging down. "I meant no...offense, I...I would not.."

"Oh, dear sweetling," Oksenna cooed, her massive head lowering to the ground so her eyes would gaze into Ysildea's face. "Chin up. You've done no wrong."

Ysildea sniffled, great body convulsions shaking her frame. Amalia lurched toward her, but Melisandre's grasp on her hand kept her in place. The warmth of Melisandre's hand was a tether to her good sense, and another fissure in the spell around her heart opened up. Riotous emotions whirled just beneath the surface, fighting for dominance, for release.

Oksenna's body shuddered and the dragon huffed, tilting her head to gaze up at the pair still on her back. Amalia stiffened when the large, unblinking eyes fixated on her.

"Oh, little Witch, what have you done to yourself?" Oksenna whispered, in so much as a dragon could whisper.

Zaleria's face hardened at the question, obvious questions dancing across her icy features, though her body stayed soft and supportive for Ysildea. Melisandre's hand slackened on Amalia's and Amalia groaned loudly in frustration, noting that Ysildea still would not so much as look in her direction.

"Nothing of consequence," Amalia spewed, anxiety and confusion rising to the forefront of her mind. "Now, if we could get the Princess on her litter. We've already been found once. It does no one any good to linger here like this."

Oksenna grumbled, the earth shaking under her feet, but she returned her gaze to Ysildea.

"She is right, we need to go. Please, all is well, dry your eyes," Oksenna cooed at a breathless Ysildea. "You are among family now. Not the one you were born to, as it was truly no family at all, but the one that was meant for you all along. Find your peace, little Princess."

Amalia noted the sparkle in Ysildea's eyes when the dragon spoke to her, how her face lightened and her body relaxed, even around the sorrow. It was as though some great bond held the two, easing Ysildea's pain and weariness. She came alive in Oksenna's presence. Amalia shoved at the sliver of jealousy that tried to poke its way through her defenses.

"There will be time to know one another. For now, we must fly," Zaleria reassured Ysildea as she moved to place her back in the litter, now strapped to the massive spines along Oksenna's spine. Melisandre had made quick work of it while Amalia stood gaping like a fool.

Amalia crouched at the foot of Ysildea's makeshift bed, her back to the woman who so obviously hated her. Zaleria and Melisandre sat at Ysildea's side, each holding on to one another as they settled in for another chilly ride. Oksenna's wings spread out beside her as she crouched, then pushed off the ground as though by magic. It took no time before they were above the clouds, Melisandre wrapping magic around them to ensure they would not be seen from below.

Amalia dared a peek from beneath her lashes at the Fae princess, laying on her sickbed atop a great beast. Ysildea looked serene, in awe of their situation. She wore a wide smile, happy tears streaked down her plump cheeks, and her hands clutched the blankets at her chest. She shivered from cold but seemed utterly unaware of anything more than the fact that she was riding a dragon. She was achingly beautiful.

It tugged at Amalia in a way she was unprepared for. Without thought, she pulled her enchanted cloak from her shoulders and wrapped it around Ysildea. Aside from being spelled for warmth, it served the purpose Amalia's linens had at home. The cloak lent itself to helping its wearer feel safe, at peace, calm. A mobile sanctuary. It wasn't as necessary for Amalia since she'd walled off her heart, aside from keeping her warm while on the back of a dragon.

Ysildea was stable, growing stronger by the minute, and needed less care. Amalia was thankful wrapping Ysildea in her cloak hadn't resulted in another outburst of vehemence directed at her, but had kept her distance since, giving medicines to Melisandre and Zaleria to administer, heating bone broth with her magic to hand over for Ysildea's consumption.

It rankled, being unable to supply the care herself, but Amalia was more concerned with Ysildea's well being than anything else. She was also preoccupied with the flashes of emotions that kept leaping to the surface of her awareness. A stutter of her heart when Zaleria reached over and brushed a strand from Melisandre's face lovingly, tears that pricked at her eyes when Melisandre leaned against her ex-lover and allowed herself to relax into the embrace Amalia had once enjoyed as they gazed out among the clouds. The barrier Amalia had erected around her heart was cracking. It was a state of affairs she was unwilling to resign herself to. As soon as they arrived she would seek out the materials she needed to reinforce the spell.

Mistbriar, the boundary to Fae lands, came into view as they slowly and languidly drifted toward the ground and the sun shifted from a bright yellow, hot source of light to a more subdued orange hued warmth. The journey was half as long as the day before, and Amalia was exceedingly thankful. She would not allow her broken heart to cause chaos here. She would find the necessary tools and repair the vulnerabilities. That thought settled her as Oksenna gingerly kissed the ground with her great taloned feet. Amalia's heart could wait.

Mistbriar

Amalia forced herself to keep her distance as Zaleria and Melisandre untied the litter and carefully lowered Ysildea to the ground. She made a show of repacking her bag, organizing its contents and refolding articles of clothing. Her cheeks heated when Oksenna took extra time to reassure Ysildea, inviting her to call upon her at any time and assuring the young princess of their friendship.

A tall, dark skinned man strode from the forest to meet them, dressed in lavish garments that marked him as an ambassador of the Dawn Court. Just beyond him, in the shadows of the forest, stood several Shadowblades. Amalia slid from Oksenna's back as the male Fae dipped so low to the ground in a bow his head brushed the lush moss at thier feet. Amalia could not overhear what was said, but noticed the visible relief in both Melisandre and Zaleria as he addressed them. Motioning forward, he stood aside for them to pass into the safety of Mistbriar, and into the lands of the Fae.

"Amalia?" Zaleria called out, turning to beckon her toward them.

"Go ahead, I have something I need to tend to," she replied, noting Ysildea's hard eyes and pursed lips as soon as they acknowledged Amalia.

"I will send one of my brethren to escort you, lady. Please do not enter the wood alone, the trees are mightily protective," the tall man said loudly enough to reach her ears.

Amalia inclined her head in agreement and understanding before watching them walk away carrying Ysildea. The Shadowblades became nothing more than shadow themselves, though Amalia knew they were still there. Watching. Melisandre cast her one last glance as the forest swallowed them up, but Amalia simply smiled tautly.

"I have words for you, little Witch," Oksenna huffed, sneakily wrapping her tail loosely around Amalia's legs. "You have done foolish magic, sister."

Amalia squared her shoulders and raised her chin indignantly, locking her eyes upon the dragon's. "I have not," she argued haughtily.

"Ha!" Oksenna scoffed. "You have, and it will cost you dearly if you do not undo it."

Amalia frowned and shimmied her elbows into the thick flesh of the dragon's tail in a half hearted attempt to wriggle free.

"What would you know of it?" Amalia asked discourteously.

"More than you, obviously," the great beast replied, her face contorting to the picture of tolerance and disapproval at once. It was an odd expression on a dragon's face. "I count you precious to me, and have done for so long maybe you have forgotten I am also wise and far beyond your years."

"It has nothing to do with you, Oksenna. Now let me pass," Amalia demanded.

"How long have we been family, little Witch?" Oksenna asked, her voice soft and a little sad. "Why would you not trust me now?"

"It doesn't matter," Amalia hollered, her fists balled at her sides as she looked up at the dragon defiantly. "I did what I needed to do. I did what must be done."

"Oh, dear heart," Oksenna tutted. "You've done no more than deny yourself that which was made for you."

"I have matters to attend, let me go now, Oksenna. I don't have time for this nonsense."

"How long have you mourned for her, Lia? How long have you yearned for what Zaleria now has?"

Amalia froze, her muscles rigid and her mouth in a thin, tight line as she ground her teeth together. Tendrils of that pain wafted toward her from deep within, the gut wrenching inability to find love that she was cursed to endure. The absolute desolation of watching the woman she had loved find her true soul's mate. It was unthinkable. Unbearable.

"You have no right to chastize me, dragon," Amalia sneered. "You found your mate so long ago I find it hard to believe you can remember a time you were without him. And you never had to endure knowing you would *never* find him."

"Oh, stop it," Oksenna huffed. "Your own self importance convinced you that you would have no mate. The Mages of the North do not find them because they do not *leave the North*. Not because they are cursed somehow."

Amalia scoffed, "How would you know?"

Oksenna growled low and deep, tendrils of flame licking the air from her nostrils before she finally spoke.

"I am older than you can imagine, and remember the world before the North went dark. Listen to what I am saying you foolish child and rid yourself of this ridiculous spell. Before it is too late," Oksenna bit out before launching herself unceremoniously intro the air and disappearing in the fading light of dusk.

Bitter Truths

Melisandre stalked through the halls of the Palace, on edge and anxious. She'd had a long discussion with the Ambassador who'd welcomed them. A newly appointed Fae called Gerlof from the Dawn Court. It was a rare appointment, and Melisandre was grateful for it. All the courts of Light were Seelie, and therefore loyal to the High Queen, which meant Gerlof took little convincing to win him to their cause.

Amalia had joined them as the conversation was ending and demanded she be taken to the Court's Mage. There was something off about the Witch that Melisandre could not quite identify, but it worried her. Gerlof had sworn he would report back any disturbing behaviors after sending Amalia with a young attendee, and disappeared to follow after them.

Melisandre needed to find Zaleria and then check in on Ysildea. One of the Court's most prestigious healers had been sent to her chambers, and Melisandre could only hope it would accelerate Ysildea's healing. They could not present her to the Dawn Court on a litter. No, she needed to be strong and clear headed when that audience came.

Melisandre rounded a corner and nearly collided with Suvok. "Oh stars above! Warlock, you nearly ran me down," she accused in a teasing tone.

She smiled at him, thankful for his presence. Ysildea was vehemently against being in Amalia's company, but she had so far seemed to take kindly to Suvok. Whether it was because of his participation in her escape from Starfall or something else was anyone's guess. Melisandre knew having someone versed in something other than battle magic would be helpful.

She was herself able to access magic most others could not, but she was wary of tapping into that power. She may be Melisandre, High Queen of the Fae, but she was also Melisande— Shadowblade. It would be some time before she felt comfortable with the memories she now had, the power and authority of the Queen she once was. It was odd, housing the two identities inside herself. She both was and was not — neither of them fitting her properly anymore.

"Majesty," Suvok smiled broadly and bowed low to the floor.

"Oh, get up you fool," Melisandre huffed. "Come on, we are going to see Ysildea."

She didn't wait to see if he followed, knowing he would.

Zaleria sat on a chair by a great crystal hearth, watching Ysildea as she walked slowly across the room when Melisandre and Suvok arrived. The sight of her mate sent Melisandre's pulse skyrocketing, her body heating immediately. Since Vaekietha's blood was warring with her own it made for a painful experience. She was grateful when Zaleria leapt from her seat and rushed over to envelop Melisandre in her arms.

It was all that kept Melisandre standing when the bond's effects became too much for her. The skin on her arms had flushed a darker brown as the heat radiated from her, Zaleria's icy touch soothing the fire of Vaekietha's blood coursing through her. The tardum root lasted only so long, and battle had wasted away most of its effects. Melisandre strove to conserve it for more formal needs. The upcoming audience with the Dawn Court was too important for her to jeopardize with her affliction, so for now she would suffer.

"Ysildea!" Melisandre said brightly as she laid her arms atop Zaleria's at her waist. "It is so good to see you up and about."

"Yes, thank you," Ysildea smiled softly. "It seems Fae healers were all I truly needed."

Zaleria stiffened at Melisandre's back. Thoughts rushed through Melisandre, a cacophony of trouble echoing through her before she spoke. She knew Zaleria was offended on Amalia's behalf. Their past would be an ever present factor so long as they were near, and Melisandre needed to find a way to manage that. The High Queen could not afford for her soul's mate to be seen favoring a former lover, even if Melisandre understood Zaleria's heart.

The Fae nobility, their Courts, would not be as forgiving. They would balk at a vampire mate as it was. The Shadowblades that had been present when they arrived were now a ticking time bomb. Melisandre should not have brought Zaleria, but after being found so quickly she knew there was no way her mate would leave her side.

They could give them no further reasons to be distrustful — and a mate who defended a Witch from the North would be further suspect to any who might bow to Melisandre. It was just as likely one of the many Fae in Mistbriar was already enroute to tell Draven she was here, and accompanied by a vampire suspiciously like the mark she was sent to end.

"Amalia saved your life, Ysildea. Without her you would be gone," Melisandre began, holding a hand to silence Ysildea when she opened her mouth to protest. "Our healers are renowned, and they are especially skilled, but without Amalia's magic, without her help, they would have been able to do nothing for you."

Ysildea opened and closed her mouth repeatedly, her brow furrowed and her nose scrunched in distaste. Suvok stepped forward and took the young Fae's hands in his own gently before leading her to sit in the chair Zaleria had vacated.

"Ysildea, what is the reason you dislike Amalia so? Even before you met her you refused her help," Suvok asked quietly, his head tilted to one side as he focused all his attention on Ysildea. "Is it any Witch? Or Amalia in particular you hold grudge against?"

The princess shook her head and pursed her lips, her eyes darting around the room as she studied them each in turn.

"You don't know what she's done!" Ysildea finally admitted.

Melisandre gripped Zaleria's fingers firmly before rubbing a hand along her arm and pulling her to sit across from Ysildea. Melisandre hoped her mate got the message — they needed to be careful here.

"Why don't you tell us?" Melisandre asked softly as she fixed her gaze on Ysildea, making certain to keep one hand on Zaleria.

Ysildea looked unsure, biting her lip and wringing her hands in her lap as she glanced sideways to Suvok.

"It's alright," he assured, encouraging Ysildea to reveal her concerns to them. "I promise you we will listen without rushing to judgement or dismissing you."

Ysildea nodded slowly, her body curling in on itself ever so slightly as she spoke. The room was eerily quiet as she told them of Alyxia, the maiden who had come to her household grief stricken at the loss of her brother. They made no outward sign of their thoughts as she described to them the horrific ways in which Amalia had abused her magic, and the trust of a young man whose family relied solely upon him.

Melisandre felt Zaleria grow more rigid and agitated with each word that passed Ysildea's lips, and knew her mate's eyes would give her away. To prevent Zaleria from intimidating the poor, misguided Ysildea, Melisandre shifted in her seat and pulled Zaleria's head down onto her shoulder. To Ysildea, Melisandre was certain it looked like no more than a mated pair unable to keep their distance any longer.

Once the story was told in its entirety, no one spoke for several seconds. Suvok knelt beside Ysildea, her hand in his, with his mouth hanging open in shock. Melisandre sat quietly, contemplating how best to proceed, while Zaleria nearly vibrated with the need to speak.

"Ysildea," Suvok began finally, taking the burden from the High Queen. "Did Alyxia tell you the name of the young soldier, of his father?"

Ysildea frowned and shook her head, confused by the question.

"I need you to understand, I have not been in the North in many years," he began cautiously. "When I fled, Idrovas had my family under his control. My only son was forced into service, and he did indeed rise within the ranks quickly, but not for the reasons you were given."

Ysildea recoiled, her eyes wide as she leaned as far away from Suvok as she could.

"Alyxia is my eldest daughter. She is also the one who forced me to flee. Tell me, Princess, how long after she spun this tale for you did Alyxia vanish?"

"I—" Ysildea sputtered, blinking rapidly as she attempted to process what was being said. "She—"

"A week? Perhaps two?" Suvok asked bitterly, rubbing a hand down his face. "I am much older than I appear, I know. Alyxia betrayed her family for a chance at power, she informed Idrovas of my ties to the Covenant, and it was her brother who warned me she had."

"No," Ysildea gasped, standing so quickly she swayed on her feet and her chair rocked off its balance and tumbled into the hearth.

Zaleria broke from Melisandre's grasp and caught Ysildea as she careened toward the floor. Ysildea went limp in Zaleria's arms, staring in disbelief at Suvok.

"Idrovas stormed my home in the dead of night and stole my son from his bed, forced him into service by Draven's side, but not as a soldier. He was a tool, made to do whatever menial tasks they could find for him. They beat him, they starved him, and they ultimately killed him. It was Idrovas, not Amalia, who betrayed him. Idrovas who abused his body once my boy shed this life for the next."

Suvok slumped forward, wiping his eyes before he stood fully and looked unseeing at the far wall. Melisandre's heart ached for him. She had heard this story, of course, when he had begged her forgiveness for nearly killing her. She knew how heavily his son's death weighed upon him, and how he blamed himself for not seeing the treachery in his own child sooner.

"My wife…" his voice broke as he tried to continue his story. "They did not let her live to see the morning. Idrovas used her body and then slit her throat, before barricading my house and burning my youngest child to death."

A sob cut off his words, and he crammed a fist into his mouth. His face was a mask of sheer pain, agony the likes of which Melisandre had seen too much of. Without further explanation, Suvok rushed from the room.

"Ysildea, I will give you the night to accept what you have been told," Melisandre began, drawing her chin high as she looked down her nose at the Usurper's daughter. Despite herself, she saw little more in that moment than the progeny of the betrayer who had caused so much pain.

"In the morning, you will either apologize to Amalia, or I will consider you no friend of mine. I will allow your father's tyranny no further purchase here, and believe me when I tell you, this story was given to you for this express purpose. So you would fear, so you would hate, and so you would divide. Even Draven prepared for the possibility of your escape. I cannot allow those things to continue."

Zaleria inhaled sharply when Melisandre pulled her by the hand from the room, leaving a stricken Ysildea behind. Regret ate away at Melisandre as they left the young princess alone, but she had drawn her boundary. If Ysildea wasn't a force to unite, she would divide, and Melisandre would not tolerate it. She hoped morning would bring clarity. She was not ready to become the Princess' jailer, but she would if she must.

"She does not leave this room. Post a guard until I say otherwise," She said as she passed Gerlof.

She strode past without explanation, but her chest lightened when he bowed. Her authority was tenuous at best, and she had been unsure if her orders would be followed here. It was a good omen, and Melisandre hoped it spoke of things to come. The High Queen was home, and she would destroy those who exploited her people.

Destiny

Ysildea collapsed against the bed, her mind swirling. She was uncertain what to believe. Could Suvok be Alyxia's father? He had been right about the maiden's disappearance, though Ysildea had believed she'd been silenced. Could the entire encounter have been manipulated to convince Ysildea those who fled the North were dangerous?

She buried her head in her hands in disgust. Of course it was possible. More than that, it was likely — and she had taken the bait like a fool. Her chest felt tight, the air in the room too thin. She wavered, the room spinning around her in a sickening way.

As she listed to the side she felt a pair of strong hands grab her shoulders and lay her gently back on her pillows. A muffled command, barked in earnest, pierced her awareness before the world went dark.

Ysildea warily opened her eyes, the light a bit too bright and the voices too loud for her pounding head. A man, the ambassador who'd met them, stood next to her bed arguing with someone. The woman was facing away from her, long black waves cascading around her shoulders. Amalia. Gerlof was in a vehement discussion with Amalia.

Ysildea's gut twisted, guilt and shame and anxiety warring with one another for purchase within her. The heat that rose within her at Amalia's presence less troublesome now, she cautiously explored it as the world came into focus. She'd never really felt any desire for another before, but she imagined this is what it must be. Her belly felt as though a thousand winged insects took flight, her breasts tight and the junction between her thighs warm and pulsing. She longed to reach out, to wrap her hands in the thick curtain of luscious hair and press her body against Amalia's. She yearned for Amalia's hands to brush her skin, to lose herself within those wide violet eyes.

Amalia straightened suddenly, waving a hand toward Gerlof to silence him as she turned and noticed Ysildea, awake and staring intently. She must have assumed Ysildea wished her ill because the color drained from her cheeks and her eyes went wide and sad as she pressed her lips together. She took a few steps back and clasped her hands before her, tilting her chin to her chest and dropping her gaze before she spoke again.

"You have overdone it, Princess," Amalia muttered, half reprimand, half apology. "The healers here have done wonderful work, but recovery from manitcore poi—"

"I am so sorry," Ysildea interrupted, the words leaving her in a rushed yell.

Amalia's head whipped up and she stared disbelieving at Ysildea, blinking several times. The shock and uncertainty on her face hurt, though Ysildea knew they were reasonable given how she had been treated.

"I was...misinformed," Ysildea hedged. "It is no excuse, and I make none, aside from being a foolish, naive idiot. I do not expect your forgiveness, just that I...I will torment you no more. I swear it."

Amalia leaned back as though struck, her brow drawn together. She opened her mouth to respond before shutting it again. Ysildea knew she deserved none of Amalia's good will, no matter how she wished for it. Ysildea swallowed hard and looked down in shame when Amalia turned to Gerlof as though he held some answer she could not find.

"May I... please give us a moment Ambassador," Amalia finally said, the essence of control and authority.

Ysildea's stomach lurched, a sudden terror washing over her. Not in fear of what Amalia may do, but what she might say. Ysildea deserved a thorough chastisement, but she was uncertain she could bear it dry eyed, and she wanted to put no more burden on the Witch.

The door to her chambers shut quietly, and Amalia flicked her wrist sharply, latching it closed. Ysildea's heart dropped, but she bit the inside of her cheek. She would fill her mouth with blood before she succumbed to her emotions. She would accept Amalia's scorn with grace.

"Well, go on then. Say what you need to so I can do my job," Amalia said. Her voice was calm, calculated, her face a mask of indifference.

"Uh," Ysildea stammered, suddenly very aware she was lying in a bed with Amalia looking down at her like she was wasting her time. It was a more painful revelation than she expected. "I just. I mean, I know...you didn't do those things, the stories I was told..."

Ysildea fought to find the words, unable to get her brain to reconcile that she was not being hurled insult after insult, that Amalia was so unmoved by her maltreatment that she couldn't care less for the apology.

"Let me stop you," Amalia inserted gracefully. "I neither need nor want an apology. You believed something you were told. I trust it was a source you felt no need to question?"

Ysildea frowned but managed to nod vaguely in affirmation. She had trusted Alyxia. The little traitor had been very good at portraying a grieving sister. To find that she had been the cause of the ruination she so skillfully mourned…it was slightly terrifying.

"Fine. Then you did what you felt you must. You owe me nothing, and you owed me nothing before you met me. Should I be now offended that you did not defend me? A faceless, evil Witch you had no idea you'd ever meet, much less learn was not so wicked after all?"

"But you are *not* evil—"

"That makes little difference, don't you think?" Amalia cut her off with a dismissive wave. "Now, since you no longer revile my very existence I think I can safely come near enough to examine you without fear of the sting of your palm once more?"

Ysildea could do no more than nod. Her head was swimming with a hundred threads of thoughts at once. Of all the possible outcomes, this is not the one she had anticipated. Somehow Amalia's acceptance stung worse than any rebuke could have.

Amalia didn't linger, striding forward and reaching out to cup Ysildea's chin, turning her head to examine her eyes. Ysildea felt the touch as though it were the most important moment of her life. Amalia's hand was small, but firm, her nails carefully resting against Ysildea's jaw without digging into her skin. The touch of her sent shockwaves through Ysildea that she struggled to conceal.

Amalia's eyes were a torture of their own as she squinted, searching Ysildea's for any signs of illness. As determined as she had been to maintain her composure, Ysildea found herself leaning in, staring into Amalia's eyes with a lust she did not recognize.

Without thought, Ysildea was in motion, surging forward and pressing her lips sloppily against Amalia's. The witch stiffened, Ysildea's chin still in her grasp. It felt like an eternity, the lapse between when their lips met and the moment Amalia slid her hand around the back of Ysildea's head and swept her tongue across the seam of Ysildea's mouth.

Meant

Amalia's heart shuddered within her, as though coming to life again. A surge of feeling overwhelmed her as Ysildea's mouth crashed into her own, and she froze. A moment. Two. Her mind a kaleidoscope, a messy tangle she struggled to grab onto. And then, clarity. Her body relaxed, a sigh of relief as she threaded her fingers through Ysildea's hair and pulled her close, ran her tongue along the seam of her lips and devoured her.

A whimper echoed from Ysildea and Amalia dropped her hand from her chin to wrap around Ysildea's waist and draw her close even as Amalia slid her knee onto the bed and positioned her own body to hover above Ysildea. The kiss deepened, bursts of color erupting behind Amalia's closed eyelids as she lost herself to it. Ysildea felt like home, in a way no other person had.

Amalia pulled back, heart pounding and breathless, and searched Ysildea's face. Ysildea looked up at her, expression open and expectant, lips slightly swollen and chest heaving in such a way that Amalia struggled not to let her eyes drift down. The last remnants of the spell Amalia had done shattered, her heart so achingly full as she looked at Ysildea that she felt she would burst with it.

"It can't be..." Amalia muttered, a hand caressing Ysildea's cheek in wonder.

Ysildea smiled sweetly and her lashes drifted against her cheek as she leaned into Amalia's palm. It was bliss, and Amalia felt as though she were in a dream. Ysildea sighed in rapture before opening her eyes. The deep brown was ringed by bright, luminous purple, her skin held a soft glow, and she smiled.

"Will you stay with me?" Ysildea asked.

The question rocked Amalia, and tears pricked at the corners of her eyes. Ysildea had no idea what was happening. An ache bloomed around Amalia's heart as she rocked back, clasping her hands in her lap and fixing Ysildea with a stare.

"I don't know if I should," Amalia began, and nearly threw caution to the wind at the stricken look that took up residence on Ysildea's face. She was fighting against an ancient magic so powerful she trembled with the effort to keep from reaching out for Ysildea.

"Do you...uh..." Amalia cleared her throat and squared her shoulders, gathering all the courage she could muster. "Do you understand what is happening?"

Ysildea frowned, a seductive smile on her face.

"I thought I was kissing you?" she cooed, running a thumb across the back of Amalia's hand.

The touch sent shivers through Amalia and she couldn't help closing her eyes and relishing the contact.

"Well, yes, but. No, no, I mean. Do you understand why we are so drawn to one another?" Amalia asked, her fists clenched tightly to keep from pulling Ysildea to her.

Ysildea frowned and tilted her head to one side, but the amusement and desire were still there, clear on her face. Amalia could tell she was confused. Much like herself, though, she was certain Ysildea was struggling to focus on much more than the need to touch. To connect. To solidify their connection.

Amalia wondered if some shadow of her spell kept a sliver of her rational mind working. It was certainly impressive that she was able to think clearly at all. The Soul's Mate bond was ancient, powerful, and undeniable. Frankly, Amalia was amazed her spell had held out against it as long as it had. A flittering thought rushed across her mind, how had Ysildea managed to keep this at bay? Had she hated her so? Or was it because of the poison she'd fought for her life against?

"Mates," Amalia blurted out with a shake of her head, trying desperately to clear it of the fog of lust so she could rationalize it all. "We are Fated. Soul's Mates."

Ysildea's eyes went wide and a grin stretched across her lips so wide Amalia wondered if it ached. The wonder in Ysildea's gaze was the most endearing thing Amalia had ever witnessed, and she did not fight when Ysildea cupped her face within her hands.

"Mated?" Ysildea asked in awe. "How lucky for me."

They was the last words spoken between them. Amalia could resist no longer, and a sound of yearning wrenched from her throat as she surged forward and kissed Ysildea as though she were the very air that filled her lungs. Ysildea responded in kind, her hands frantic as they explored as much of Amalia's body as they could reach. Amalia reveled in her touch, the way her fingers snaked under her shirt and cupped her breast, how her leg wedged itself between her thighs and how she rocked her hips against Amalia.

Ysildea pulled at Amalia's clothes until they broke apart only long enough to tear them off, Ysildea's joining Amalia's on the floor beside them. Amalia sat back and admired her mate. Warm, brown skin against crisp white linens, silver curls that haloed around her beautiful face as she lay back against the pillows, panting to catch her breath. The moment was quickly gone as Ysildea grabbed Amalia's hips and pulled her close, one hand instinctively searching for the junction between her thighs.

Amalia cried out when Ysildea grabbed the back of her head and claimed her mouth as she slid her fingers down, around her bud and lower until she had two inside her. Amalia cried out and ricked her hips forward, riding Ysildea's fingers slowly. Ysildea grinned against Amalia's mouth and nipped at her lower lip with her teeth before tilting her head and nipping at Amalia's nipple. The sensation overwhelmed Amalia and she moaned loudly.

Ysildea swirled her tongue around the tight, pebbled nipple as she pumped her fingers against Amalia's thrusts, urgent and frantic. Amalia's head rolled back and she bucked faster, cresting a wave of pleasure and completion. Ysildea's free hand slithered around Amalia's waist, fingertips gripping skin in a desperate way. As Amalia came down, she pressed her forehead against Ysildea's and caught her breath for a moment before pressing a kiss to Ysildea's lips and grinning wickedly.

"My turn," Amalia whispered, scooting back on her knees and grabbing Ysildea by the hips, dragging her down the bed to lie flat on her back.

Amalia ran a hand languidly up Ysildea's thighs, enjoying the shiver it created. Ysildea smiled contentedly up at her, a hand brushing Amalia's hair behind her shoulder. Ysildea's eyes closed and her back arched up as Amalia ran her thumb along the seam of her pussy, pressing against Ysildea's clit, moving up and down slowly, drawing her pleasure out in sure motions until she came apart.

Ysildea's eyes flashed, purple light spilling around them taking Amalia's breath away in its beauty. Their magic mingled, intertwining and dancing as they explored one another. Hands, teeth, and tongues searched over flesh for every gasp and moan, slowly, lovingly, as though time had no meaning and they had no concerns beyond each other. And for that night, they didn't. It was the most precious gift Amalia had ever been given, one she had never dreamed she would recieve, and she would do anything to protect it.

About JL Casten

JL Casten was an Army brat, who then married a soldier, only to become one herself. She has lived a nomadic existence and attended 7 schools before she was 10. She loves the rich and nuanced world she was exposed to traveling and living around the globe. She is now a disabled Army Veteran who loves to write stories and release them for the world to escape into. She is a married mother of 4 and lives in the foothills of the Blue Ridge Mountains.

website: www.jlcasten.com

You can find her on all Social Media platforms as JL Casten.

Acknowledgments

Thank you to each of the authors who put so much time, effort, and heart into this project.

To our readers: You are why we do this, thank you for coming along on our journeys with us.

To the BookTok Community: We hope you enjoy this collection of stories, without you these authors would have never met. We are forever in your debt.

Printed in Great Britain
by Amazon